D1048699

Chung Kuo. The words mean "Middle Kingdom," and since 221 B.C., when the first emperor, Ch'in Shih Huang Ti, unified the seven Warring States, it is what the "black-haired people," the Han, or Chinese, have called their great country. The Middle Kingdom—for them it was the whole world; a world bounded by great mountain chains to the north and west, by the sea to east and south. Beyond was only desert and barbarism. So it was for two thousand years and through sixteen great dynasties. Chung Kuo *was* the Middle Kingdom, the very center of the human world, and its emperor the "Son of Heaven," the "One Man." But in the eighteenth century that world was invaded by the young and aggressive Western powers with their superior weaponry and their unshakable belief in progress. It was, to the surprise of the Han, an unequal contest, and China's myth of supreme strength and self-sufficiency was shattered. By the early twentieth century China—Chung Kuo—was the sick old man of the East: "a carefully preserved mummy in a hermetically sealed coffin," as Karl Marx called it. But from the disastrous ravages of that century grew a giant of a nation, capable of competing with the West and with its own Eastern rivals, Japan and Korea, from a position of incomparable strength. The twenty-first century, "the Pacific Century," as it was known even before it began, saw China become once more a world unto itself, but this time its only boundary was space.

CHUNG KUO books by David Wingrove

Book I: THE MIDDLE KINGDOM
Book II: THE BROKEN WHEEL
Book III: THE WHITE MOUNTAIN

CHUNG | KUO

BY | DAVID WINGROVE

BOOK 4:

THE STONE WITHIN

A DELL TRADE PAPERBACK

A DELL TRADE PAPERBACK

Published by
Dell Publishing
a division of
Bantam Doubleday Dell Publishing Group, Inc.
1540 Broadway
New York, New York 10036

Canadian Cataloguing in Publication Data

Wingrove, David
The stone within

(Chung kuo ; bk. 4)
ISBN 0-385-29876-5

I. Title.   II. Series: Wingrove, David.   Chung kuo ; bk. 4.

PR6073.I53558 1993   823'.914   C93-094218-3

ISBN: 0-440-50569-0

Printed in the United States of America

Published simultaneously in Canada

September 1993

10 9 8 7 6 5 4 3 2

BVG

Whose love of things Chinese and of the
vast worlds of the imagination set me upon
this path. With much love.

"For every one of us it is the same.
Worlds end or open as we go."

Wasps and ants have a mean fate:
how could their power be enduring?

—*Tian Wen* ("Heavenly Questions") by
Ch'u Yuan, from the *Ch'u Tz'u* ("Songs
of the South"), *second century* B.C.

Can't teach a true peach being a prisoner
Skin all round and stone within

—Jukka Tolonen, *Last Quarters, 1972*

Acknowledgments

AS THE BEAST GROWS longer and the shape of it clearer, the list of people I ought to thank grows with it. Let's begin with my editors, Carolyn Caughey, Brian DeFiore, and John Pearce, for sheer niceness and for maintaining enthusiasm, and to Alyssa Diamond ("Hi, David!") for always being cheerful and on the ball. To Nick Sayers, departing editor, huge thanks for all you did (especially for arranging that football match!), and good luck with the new job. We'll meet again, and all that . . .

In the long, lonely business of writing, a man needs a break and a beer now and then, so here's to my brother Ian Wingrove, John "Mad Dog" Hindes, Andrew Muir, Tom Jones, Rob Holdstock, Ritchie Smith, Tony Richards, Robert Allen, Simon (and Julie) Bergin, and Keith ("Teech") Carabine for getting me away from the word processor.

To Mike "the Shark" Cobley ("Hi, Dave!"), fraternal greetings. Get the book done, Mike! And to Andrew Sawyer, first-line critic, thanks once again for the thoughtful read.

To friends new—Ronan, Mike, Niall, Tom, Paul, Laura and Sean, Vikki Lee and Steve, Storm, Sue and Michelle, Mary Gentle, Geoff Ryman, Iain Banks, Bob Shaw, Gill and John Alderman, and Roger ("Dave")—thanks hugely for the wondrous times in Dublin. When shall we three hundred meet again . . . ?

To my old friend Robert Carter, thanks once more for the input on

Part Two and for keeping the science tight. Likewise, to Alex "The Weatherman" Hill, *kan pei* for checking my meteorology homework!

Special thanks, as ever, must go to Brian Griffin, to whom I owe the usual massive debt, for reading the beast at its crudest state and—as ever—understanding it far better than me. May *The Awakening* find the cult audience it deserves.

Music this time around was provided by the late, great Miles Davis, the Cardiacs, Nirvana, Frank Zappa, and the boys from IQ. Bless you lads.

To Gerry Francis and the boys from the Bush, a big thank you for that New Year's Day performance. See you on Saturday.

To Susan and the girls (Jessica, Amy, and Georgia) go the usual thanks for keeping my priorities right and providing a healthy balance to my life. What more could a megalomaniac need?

And, finally, to my biggest fan over there in North America, John Patrick Kavanagh, cowriter of the Chung Kuo screenplay, *Empire of Ice*, fraternal greetings! Here's another to take down to the Keys . . .

CONTENTS

BOOK 4
The Stone Within

The War of the Two Directions

IT HAD BEGUN with the assassination of the T'ang's Minister, Lwo K'ang, some thirteen years earlier, the poor man blown into the next world along with his Junior Ministers while basking in the imperial solarium. The Seven—the great Lords and rulers of Chung Kuo— had hit back at once, arresting one of the leading figures of the Dispersionist faction responsible for the Minister's death. But it was not to end there. Within days of the public execution, their opponents had struck another deadly blow, killing Li Han Ch'in, son of the T'ang, Li Shai Tung, and heir to City Europe, on the day of his wedding to the beautiful Fei Yen.

It might have ended there, with the decision of the Seven to take no action in reprisal for Prince Han's death—to adopt a policy of peaceful nonaction, *wuwei*—but for one man such a course could not be borne. Taking matters into his own hands, Li Shai Tung's General, Knut Tolonen, had marched into the House of Representatives in Weimar and killed the leader of the Dispersionists, Under-Secretary Lehmann. It was an act almost guaranteed to tumble Chung Kuo into a bloody civil war unless the anger of the Dispersionists could be assuaged and concessions made.

Concessions were made, an uneasy peace maintained, but the divisions between rulers and ruled remained, their conflicting desires—the Seven for Stasis, the Dispersionists for Change—

unresolved. Among those concessions, the Seven had permitted the Dispersionists to build a starship, *The New Hope*. As the ship approached readiness, the Dispersionists pushed things even further at Weimar, impeaching the *tai*—the Representatives of the Seven in the House—and effectively declaring their independence. In response the Seven destroyed *The New Hope*. War was declared.

The five-year War-that-wasn't-a-War left the Dispersionists broken, their leaders killed, their Companies confiscated. The great push for Change had been crushed and peace returned to Chung Kuo. Or so it briefly seemed, for the War had woken older, far stronger currents of dissent. In the depths of the City new movements began to arise, seeking not merely to change the system, but to revolutionize it altogether. One of these factions, the *Ping Tiao*, or "Levelers," wanted to pull down the great City of three hundred levels and destroy the Empire of the Han.

For a while the status quo had been maintained, but three of the most senior T'ang had died in the War, leaving the Council of the Seven weaker and more inexperienced than they had been in all the long years of their rule. When Wang Sau-leyan, the youngest son of Wang Hsien, ruler of City Africa, became T'ang after his father's death, things looked ominous, the young man seeking to create disharmony among the Seven. But Li Yuan, inheriting from his father, formed effective alliances with his fellow T'ang, Tsu Ma, Wu Shih, and Wei Feng, to block Wang in Council, outvoting him four to three.

But now, looking beyond the immediate political situation, Li Yuan wants permanent solutions to the problems of overpopulation and civil unrest. To achieve the former, he is willing to make deals with his enemies in the Above—to relax the Edict of Technological Control that has kept Change at bay for so long, and to reopen the House at Weimar, in return for population controls. As for civil unrest, he has devised a somewhat darker scheme: to "wire up" the whole population of Chung Kuo, so that they can be traced and rigidly controlled.

For the first time in years, then, there is real hope that peace and stability might be achieved and chaos staved off. But time is running out. Chung Kuo is a society badly out of balance and close—very close—to total breakdown.

In Wu Shih's great City of North America, the first signs of social unrest have already manifested themselves in movements like the "Sons of Benjamin Franklin," and in a growing desire among the *Hung Mao*—the Europeans—for a new nationalism. But the problems are not merely between the rulers and the ruled. Among the ruled there are also divisions. Divisions that run deeper than race . . .

MAJOR CHARACTERS

Ascher, Emily—Trained as an economist, she was once a member of the *Ping Tiao* revolutionary party. After its demise, she fled to North America where, under the alias of Mary Jennings, she got a job with the giant ImmVac Corporation, working for Old Man Lever and his son, Michael. Ultimately, however, what she wants is change, and the downfall of the corrupt social institutions that rule Chung Kuo.

Lehmann, Stefan—Albino son of the former Dispersionist leader, Pietr Lehmann, he was briefly a lieutenant to DeVore. A cold, unnaturally dispassionate man, he seems the very archetype of nihilism, his only aim to bring down the Seven and their great earth-encompassing City. His move "down level" into the "underground" world of *tong* and Triad marks a new stage of his campaign.

Lever, Charles—Head of the massive ImmVac pharmaceuticals corporation, "Old Man Lever" is a passionate "American" and one of the instigators of the Cutler Institute's Immortality project. A bull-necked, stubborn old man, he will let nothing get between him and what he wants. And what he wants is to live forever.

Lever, Michael—Son of Charles Lever, he was incarcerated by Wu Shih for his involvement with the "Sons of Benjamin Franklin," a semirevolutionary group formed by the sons of wealthy North American businessmen. Cast from childhood in his father's mold, he has yet to break from his upbringing and find his own direction.

Li Yuan—T'ang of Europe and one of the Seven, as second son of Li Shai Tung, he inherited after the deaths of his brother and father. Considered old before his time, he nonetheless has a passionate side to his nature, as demonstrated in his brief marriage to his brother's wife, the beautiful Fei Yen. Having remarried, he is determined to find balance, both in his private life and in his role as T'ang.

Shepherd, Ben—Son of Hal Shepherd, and great-great-grandson of City Earth's architect, Ben was brought up in the Domain, an idyllic valley in the southwest of England where, deciding not to follow in his father's footsteps and become advisor to Li Yuan, he pursues instead his calling as an artist, developing a new art form, the Shell, which will one day transform Chung Kuo's society.

Tolonen, Jelka—Daughter of Marshal Tolonen, Jelka has been brought up in a very masculine environment, lacking a mother's love and influence. Despite a genuine interest in martial arts and weaponry, she feels a strong need to discover and express the more feminine side of her nature; a need matched by a determination not to succumb to the gender demands of her world.

Tolonen, Knut—Former Marshal of the Council of Generals and onetime General to Li Yuan's father, Tolonen is a rocklike supporter of the Seven and their values, even in an age of increasing uncertainty. In his role as father, however, this inflexibility in his nature brings him into repeated conflict with his daughter, Jelka.

Tsu Ma—T'ang of West Asia and one of the Seven, the ruling Council of Chung Kuo, Tsu Ma has thrown off a dissolute past to become Li Yuan's staunchest supporter in Council. A strong, handsome man in his late thirties, he has yet to marry, though his secret affair with Li Yuan's former wife, Fei Yen, revealed a side of him that has not been fully harnessed.

Wang Sau-leyan—T'ang of Africa. Since inheriting—after the suspicious deaths of his father and elder brothers—Wang Sau-leyan has dedicated every moment to bringing down Li Yuan and his allies in Council. A sharp and cunning adversary with an abrasive, calculating manner, he is the harbinger of Change within the Council of Seven.

Ward, Kim—Born in the Clay, that dark wasteland beneath the great City's foundations, Kim has a quick and unusual bent of mind that has marked him as potentially the greatest scientist on Chung Kuo. His vision of a giant star-spanning web, formulated down in the darkness, drove him up into the light of the Above. But, despite the patronage of Li Yuan and the friendship of powerful men, life has proven to be far from easy for Ward, either in business or in love.

Wong Yi-sun—Big Boss of the United Bamboo Triad, "Fat Wong"—a tiny, birdlike man—has won the favor of Li Yuan. Yet his ambitions reach beyond more patronage. He wants to unite the lower levels of City Europe under his rule.

Wu Shih—Middle-aged T'ang of North America, he is one of the few remaining members of the old generation. A staunch traditionalist, he nevertheless has found himself allied in Council with Li Yuan and Tsu Ma against the odious Wang Sau-leyan. Yet with the resurgence of American nationalism he finds himself confronted by a problem none of his fellow T'ang have to face; a problem he must find an urgent and lasting solution to.

LIST OF CHARACTERS

THE SEVEN AND THE FAMILIES

Chi Hsing—T'ang of the Australias.
Fu Ti Chang—third wife of Li Yuan.
Hou Tung-po—T'ang of South America.
Lai Shi—second wife of Li Yuan.
Li Kuei Jen—son of Li Yuan and heir to City Europe.
Li Yuan—T'ang of Europe.
Mien Shan—first wife of Li Yuan.
Tsu Ma—T'ang of West Asia.
Wang Sau-leyan—T'ang of Africa.
Wei Chan Yin—first son of Wei Feng and heir to City East Asia.
Wei Feng—T'ang of East Asia.
Wei Hsi Wang—second son of Wei Feng and Colonel in Security.
Wei Tseng-li—third son of Wei Feng.
Wu Shih—T'ang of North America.
Yin Fei Yen—"Flying Swallow"; Minor-Family Princess and divorced wife of Li Yuan.
Yin Han Ch'in—son of Yin Fei Yen.
Yin Tsu—head of the Yin Family (one of the "Twenty-Nine" Minor Families) and father of Fei Yen.
Yin Wu Tsai—Minor-Family Princess and cousin of Fei Yen.

FRIENDS AND RETAINERS OF THE SEVEN

Bachman, Lothar—Lieutenant in Security.
Bright Moon—maid to Li Yuan.
Brock—security guard in the Domain.
Chan Teng—Master of the Inner Chambers at Tongjiang.
Chang Shih-sen—personal secretary to Li Yuan.
Ch'in Tao Fan—Chancellor of East Asia.
Chu Shih-ch'e—*Pi-shu chien*, or Inspector of the Imperial Library at Tongjiang.
Coates—security guard in the Domain.
Cook—duty guard in the Domain.

Fen Cho-hsien—Chancellor of North America.

Fragrant Lotus—maid to Li Yuan.

Franke, Otto—*Wei*, or Captain of Security, for Zwickau *Hsien*.

Gerhardt, Paul—Major; Head of Tracking, Northern Hemisphere.

Gustavsson, Per—Captain of Chi Hsing's personal guard.

Gustavsson, Ute—wife of Captain Gustavsson.

Hauser, Eva—wife of Major Sven Hauser.

Hauser, Gustav—private secretary/equerry to Marshal Tolonen; son of Major Sven Hauser.

Hauser, Sven—Major; ex-Colonial Governor; father of Gustav Hauser.

Henssa, Eero—Captain of the Guard aboard the floating palace Yang-jing.

Ho Chang—valet to Wu Shih.

Hung Yan—"Wiring" surgeon to Li Yuan.

Hung Mien-lo—Chancellor of Africa.

Karr, Gregor—Major in Security.

K'ung Feng—Third Official in the *Ta Ssu Nung*, the Superintendency of Agriculture, for City Europe.

Lofgren, Bertil—Lieutenant and aide to Marshal Tolonen.

Mo Yu—Security Lieutenant in the Domain.

Nan Ho—Chancellor of Europe.

Read, Helmut—Governor of the Saturn system.

Rheinhardt, Helmut—General of Security for Li Yuan.

Shepherd, Ben—son of the late Hal Shepherd; "Shell" artist.

Shepherd, Beth—widow of Hal Shepherd; mother of Ben and Meg Shepherd.

Shepherd, Meg—sister of Ben Shepherd.

Tolonen, Jelka—daughter of Marshal Tolonen.

Tolonen, Knut—ex-Marshal of Security; Head of the GenSyn Hearings committee.

Tu Mai—security guard in the Domain.

Virtanen, Per—Major in Li Yuan's Security forces.

Zdenek—bodyguard to Jelka Tolonen.

THE TRIADS

Chao—runner for K'ang A-yin.

Feng Shang-pao—"General Feng"; Big Boss of the 14K.

Feng Wo—lieutenant to K'ang A-yin.

Ho Chin—"Three-Finger Ho"; Big Boss of the Yellow Banners.

Hua Shang—lieutenant to Wong Yi-sun.

Huang Jen—lieutenant to Po Lao.

Hui Tsin—Red Pole (426, or Executioner) to the United Bamboo.

K'ang A-yin—gang boss of the Tu Sun *tong*.

K'ang Yeh-su—nephew of K'ang A-yin.

Kant—runner for K'ang A-yin.

Li Chin—"Li the Lidless"; Big Boss of the Wo Shih Wo.

Li Pai Shung—nephew of Li Chin; heir to the Wo Shih Wo.

Ling Wo—Chief Advisor to K'ang A-yin.

Liu Tong—lieutenant to Li Chin.

Lo Han—*tong* boss.

Lu Ming-shao—"Whiskers Lu"; Big Boss of the Kuei Chuan.

Man Hsi—*tong* boss.

Meng Te—lieutenant to Lu Ming-shao.

Ni Yueh—*tong* boss.

Peck—lieutenant to K'ang A-yin (a *ying tzu*, or "shadow").

Po Lao—Red Pole (426, or Executioner) to the Kuei Chuan.

Soucek, Jiri—lieutenant to K'ang A-yin.

Visak—lieutenant to Lu Ming-shao.

Wong Yi-sun—"Fat Wong"; Big Boss of the United Bamboo.

Yan Yan—*tong* boss.

Yao Lu—lieutenant to Stefan Lehmann.

Yue Chun—Red Pole (426, or Executioner) to the Wo Shih Wo.

Yun Yueh-hui—"Dead Man Yun"; Big Boss of the Red Gang.

YU

Anne—*Yu* assassin.

Donna—*Yu* assassin.

Joan—*Yu* assassin.

Kriz—senior *Yu* operative.

Mach, Jan—maintenance official for the Ministry of Waste Recycling; former *Ping Tiao* member and founder of the *Yu*.

Vesa—*Yu* assassin.

OTHER CHARACTERS

Ainsworth, James—lawyer for Charles Lever.

Ascher, Emily—past member of the *Ping Tiao* terrorists.

Barratt, Edel—SimFic employee at Sohm Abyss.

Becker, Hans—sidekick of Stefan Lehmann.

Bonner, Alex—Chief Negotiator for the P'u Lan Finance Corporation.

Bonnot, Alex—Scientific Supervisor for SimFic at Sohm Abyss.

Campbell, William—Regional Controller of SimFic's North Atlantic Cities.

Carver, Rex—Reformer candidate for Miami *Hsien* and friend of Charles Lever.

Chan Long—security guard, working for Lever and Kustow.

Chang—guard on the Chung estate.

Chang Li—First Surgeon in the Boston Medical Center.

Chiang Su-li—Master of the House of the Ninth Dragon Tea House.

Chung, Gloria—heiress; daughter of the late Representative Chung Yen.

Curval, Andrew—leading geneticist; employee of the ImmVac Corporation.

Dann, Abraham—steward to Charles Lever.

Deio—Clayborn friend of Kim Ward from "Rehabilitation."

DeValerian, Rachel—alias of Emily Ascher.

DeVore, Howard—ex-Major in Security, and Dispersionist.

Dunn, Richard—business rival of Old Man Lever.

Feng Lu-ma—lensman.

Feng Wo-shen—protein designer and scientific assistant for SimFic at Sohm Abyss.

Fisher, Carl—American; friend of Michael Lever.

Fisher, James—financier and friend of Charles Lever.

Gratton, Edward—friend of Charles Lever and Reformer candidate for Boston *Hsien*.

Haller, Wolf—sidekick of Stefan Lehmann.

Harrison, James—employee of Charles Lever.

Hart, Alex—Representative at Weimar.

Hartmann, William—friend of Charles Lever and Reformer candidate.

Hay, Joel—leader of the Evolutionist Party of North America.

Henty, Thomas—technician.

Heydemeier, Ernst—artist; leading exponent of *Futur-Kunst*, "Science-Art."

Hilbert, Eduard—Head of Cryobiology for SimFic at Sohm Abyss.

Ho Chao-tuan—Representative for Shenyang *Hsien*.

Ho Yang—reporter for the *Wen Ming* media channel.

Hong Chi—assistant to Kim Ward.

Horton, Feng—American; a "Son"; also known as "Meltdown."

Hsiang Tian—merchant; store owner.

Jennings, Mary—alias of Emily Ascher.

Johnstone, Edward—friend of Charles Lever; father of Louisa Johnstone.

Johnstone, Louisa—long-standing fiancée of Michael Lever.

Kennedy, Jean—wife of Joseph Kennedy.

Kennedy, Joseph—American lawyer, and founder of the New Republican Party.

Kennedy, Robert—eldest son of Joseph Kennedy.

Kennedy, William—youngest son of Joseph Kennedy.

Koslevic, Anna—schoolgirl friend of Jelka Tolonen.

Kustow, Bryn—American; friend of Michael Lever.

Lehmann, Stefan—albino son of Under-Secretary Lehmann.

Lever, Charles—"Old Man Lever," Head of the ImmVac pharmaceuticals company of North America; father of Michael Lever.

Lever, Michael—son of Charles Lever; Head of the MemSys Corporation, a subsidiary of ImmVac.

Li Min—"Brave Carp," an alias of Stefan Lehmann.

Luke—Clayborn friend of Kim Ward from "Rehabilitation."

Mai Li-wen—lensman.

Marley, George—business associate of Charles Lever.

May Feng—*Hung Mao* Head of EduCol.

Milne, Michael—private investigator.

Mitchell, Bud—American; a "Son"; associate of Michael Lever.

Munroe, Wendell—Representative at Weimar.

Nong Yan—bookkeeper to Kim Ward.

Pai Mei—stallholder.

Parker, Jack—American; friend of Michael Lever.

Ping Hsiang—Representative for the Above in discussions for the re-opening of Weimar.

Reiss, Horst—Chief Executive of the SimFic Corporation.

Richards—guard at Kim Ward's *Ch'i Chu* company.

Robins—employee of Charles Lever.

Ross, James—private investigator.

Schram, Dieter—Administrator for SimFic at Sohm Abyss.

Snow—alias of Stefan Lehmann.

Spence, Graham—employee of Charles Lever.

Spence, Leena—"Immortal" and onetime lover of Charles Lever.

Stevens, Carl—American; friend of Michael Lever.

Stewart, Greg—American; NREP candidate for Denver *Hsien*.

Symons—SimFic employee at Sohm Abyss.

T'ai Cho—friend and former guardian of Kim Ward.

Tewl—"Darkness"; chief of the raft-people.

Thorsson, Wulf—settler from Iapetus Colony in the Saturn system.

Tong Ye—young Han sailor; a "morph," created by Ben Shepherd.

Tuan Wen-ch'ang—SimFic employee at Sohm Abyss.

Underwood, Harry—Representative at Weimar.

Ward, Kim—Clayborn orphan and scientist; head of the *Ch'i Chu* company.

Ward, Rebecca—Commercial Advisor to SimFic at Sohm Abyss; Clayborn friend of Kim Ward from "Rehabilitation."

Weller, John—Head of Internal Distribution for ImmVac.

Will—Clayborn friend of Kim Ward from "Rehabilitation."

Yellow Tan—lensman.

Yi Pang-chou—schoolgirl friend of Jelka Tolonen.

Yueh Pa—official in the United Bamboo heartland.

THE DEAD

Barrow, Chao—Secretary of the House at Weimar.

Bercott, Andrei—Representative at Weimar.

Berdichev, Soren—Head of SimFic and, later, leader of the Dispersionist faction.

Ch'in Shih Huang Ti—the first emperor of China (ruled 221–210 B.C.).

Chung Hsin—"Loyalty"; bond servant to Li Shai Tung.

Cutler, Richard—leader of the "American" movement.

Ebert, Klaus—head of the GenSyn Corporation.

Feng Chung—Big Boss of the Kuei Chan (Black Dog) Triad.

Fest, Edgar—Captain in Security.

Gesell, Bent—leader of the *Ping Tiao* terrorist organization.

Griffin, James B.—last president of the American Empire.

Han Huan Ti—Han emperor (ruled A.D. 168–189), also known as Liu Hung.

Hou Ti—T'ang of South America; father of Hou Tung Po.

Hsiang K'ai Fan—Minor-Family Prince.

Hwa—master "blood," or hand-to-hand fighter, below the Net.

Kao Jyan—assassin; friend of Kao Chen.

K'ung Fu Tzu—Confucius (551–479 B.C.).

Lehmann, Pietr—Under-Secretary of the House of Representatives and first leader of the Dispersionist faction; father of Stefan Lehmann.

Lever, Margaret—wife of Charles Lever and mother of Michael Lever.

Li Ch'ing—T'ang of Europe; grandfather of Li Yuan.

Li Han Ch'in—first son of Li Shai T'ung and once heir to City Europe; brother of Li Yuan.

Li Hang Ch'i—T'ang of Europe; great-great-grandfather of Li Yuan.

Li Kou-lung—T'ang of Europe; great-grandfather of Li Yuan.

Li Shai Tung—T'ang of Europe; father of Li Yuan.

Lin Yua—first wife of Li Shai Tung.

Mao Tse Tung—first *Ko Ming* emperor (ruled A.D. 1948–1976).

Ming Huang—sixth T'ang emperor (ruled A.D. 713–755).

Mu Chua—Madam of the House of the Ninth Ecstasy.

Mu Li—"Iron Mu," Boss of the Big Circle triad.

Shang—"Old Shang"; Master to Kao Chen when he was a child.

Shepherd, Amos—Great-great-great-great-grandfather (and genetic "father") of Ben Shepherd.

Shepherd, Augustus—"Brother" of Ben Shepherd, b. A.D. 2106, d. 2122.

Shepherd, Hal—Father (and genetic "brother") of Ben Shepherd.

Shepherd, Robert—Great-grandfather (and genetic "brother") of Ben Shepherd, and father of Augustus Shepherd.

Tsao Ch'un—tyrannical founder of Chung Kuo (ruled A.D. 2051–2087).

Wang Hsien—T'ang of Africa; father of Wang Sau-leyan.

Wang Ta-hung—third son of Wang Hsien; elder brother of Wang Sau-leyan.

Wen Ti—"First Ancestor" of City Earth/Chung Kuo (ruled 180–157 B.C.), also known as Liu Heng.

Wyatt, Edmund—company head; father of Kim Ward.

Ywe Hao—*Yu* terrorist.

Ywe Kai-chang—father to Ywe Hao.

PROLOGUE | SPRING 2209

In the Space Between Heaven and Earth

Heaven and earth are ruthless, and treat the myriad creatures as straw dogs; the sage is ruthless, and treats the people as straw dogs.
Is not the space between heaven and earth like a bellows?

It is empty without being exhausted:
The more it works the more comes out.
Much speech leads inevitably to silence.
Better to hold fast to the void.

—LAO TZU, *Tao Te Ching*, sixth century B.C.

WU SHIH, T'ang of North America, stood at the top of the ruined, pitted steps, looking down at the men. Behind him, headless, the huge statue sat, embedded in its chair of granite. Overhead, spotlights set into the floor of the Above picked out the figures at the foot of the broad white stairway. Five men. Five old, gray-bearded men, well-dressed and senatorial. Company Heads. *Americans.* Wu Shih studied them, his contempt barely concealed. His left foot rested on the statue's fallen head, his right hand on his hip.

One of the men, taller than the rest, stepped out in front of the others and called up to him.

"Where are they? You said you'd bring them, Wu Shih. So where are they?"

Dead, he would have liked to have said. *Your sons are dead, old men.* But it wasn't so. Wang Sau-leyan had saved their lives. There had been an agreement in Council and the traitors were to go free, unpunished, the price of their treachery unexacted. It was foolishness, but it had been decided.

"They are here, *Shih* Lever. Close by. Unharmed."

Wu Shih paused and looked about the ruins of the old city. From where he stood, high above it all, the floor of the Above was less than fifty *ch'i* overhead, a dark and solid presence, stretching away to every horizon. Facing him, beyond the darkly shadowed outline of a toppled obelisk, could be glimpsed the wreckage of the Capitol building, a huge, silvered pillar thrusting up through its ruined dome—one of many that rose to meet the smooth, featureless darkness of the City's underbelly.

He had brought them here deliberately, knowing the effect it would have on the old men. Overhead, its presence vast and crushing, lay the City that he ruled—a City that rose two *li*—almost a mile by their ancient measure—into the air, stretching from the Atlantic to the Pacific, from the coast of Labrador to the Gulf of Mexico in the south. While here below . . .

Wu Shih smiled. Here, in the darkness beneath the City's piles, lay the ruins of old America—of Washington, once capital of the sixty-nine States of the American Empire. And these men—these foolish, greedy old men—would have the Empire back; would break a century of peace to have it back. Wu Shih snorted and looked down at the massive granite head beneath the foot.

"You have signed the documents?"

A moment's silence greeted his words, then Lever answered him, the irritation in his voice barely restrained. "It's done."

Wu Shih felt a ripple of anger pass through him. It was the second time Old Man Lever had refused to address him properly.

"All of you?" he demanded. "All those on my list?"

He looked up from Lincoln's head and sought Lever's eyes. Lever was staring at the fallen stone, his face suffused with anger, his expression so eloquent that Wu Shih laughed and pressed down on the heavy stone, forcing the nose firmly into the dust that lay everywhere here.

"You haven't answered me."

Wu Shih's voice had changed, grown harder, its flattened tones filled with threat. Lever looked at at him, surprised by the command in his voice—unaccustomed, clearly, to another's rule. Again this spoke volumes. These men were far gone in their dissent—had grown fat and arrogant in the illusion of their power. Li Yuan had been right to see them as a threat—right to act against them as he had. There was no respect in them, no understanding of their true relationship to things. The old man thought himself the equal of the Seven— perhaps, even, their superior. It was a dangerous, insolent delusion.

Lever turned his head away sharply, spitting the words out angrily.

"We've signed. Everyone on your list." He beckoned to another of his party, who came forward and handed him the document.

Wu Shih watched, his eyes half-lidded, seeing how Lever turned back to face him, hesitating, as if he expected Wu Shih to come down the steps and take the paper from him.

"Bring it," he said, and put out his left hand casually, almost languidly. Wang Sau-leyan may have forced the Council to make this deal with their enemies—this "concession," as he called it—but he, Wu Shih, would show these men exactly where they stood. He saw how Lever turned, uncertainty in his face, looking toward the others as if for guidance, then turned back and began to climb. Each step was a small humiliation. Each a belittling of the man. Then, when he was only three steps from the top, Wu Shih raised his hand, commanding him, by that gesture, to stay where he was.

Lever frowned, but did as he was bid.

"Kneel," Wu Shih said, his voice soft, almost gentle now.

Lever turned his head slightly, as if he had not heard properly. "What?"

"*Kneel.*"

Wu Shih's voice had been no louder, no harder, but this time it was command not reminder.

Again Lever hesitated, half turning, the muscles in his face twitching, conscious of his fellows down below, watching him. Slowly, huffing as he did, the old man knelt, his face raised, eyes glaring at Wu Shih. This was a protocol he had clearly thought he could avoid. But Wu Shih was unrelenting. He was determined to have the form of Lever's respect if not the actuality, knowing that in such forms lay power. *Real* power. The bowing of one man before another: it was a gesture as old as it was profound. And even if true respect were not forthcoming here, he could still insist on one of its components— obedience. Simple obedience.

Leaning forward, Wu Shih plucked the paper from Lever's out-stretched hand and opened it. Its original—verified by retinal print and scan—was already on file. Yet there was more power in this—this written paper, signed by the hand of each and given here at this place where the dream of America had died—than in the purely legal form of their agreement. It was little understood by them, but ritual was more than empty show. It was power itself. Was what gave form to the relationships of men.

Wu Shih folded the paper, grunting his satisfaction. Half turning, he made a signal. At once, a brilliant light fell on a nearby building. For a moment there was nothing, then a door opened in the plain white face of the building and from the darkness within stepped a group of young men. The Sons. Gaunter, less proud for their fifteen-month incarceration. But dangerous. More dangerous than Wang Sau-leyan would ever contemplate.

Wu Shih raised his hand, dismissing the old man.

Lever backed away, moving slowly down the steps, then, at the bottom, turned and went among his fellows, making his way across the littered wasteland toward the building where the young men stood. Wu Shih watched a moment, then turned away. In his hand he held their guarantee of good behavior—their pledge to govern themselves better than they had. But he had seen the hate, the irreverence in Lever's face. Was such a guarantee worth having in the face of such open defiance?

He smiled. Yes, for it would give him the excuse to act, without the intercession of that meddler Wang.

As he made his way from there he knew for a certainty that this was not the end of this, only a temporary respite. There would come a time when he would have to face these men again.

"Americans . . ." he said beneath his breath, then laughed softly, looking back at the headless statue, silhouetted against the lights from above. *The Supernal*, they called themselves. Dwellers in the Heavens. Supremely great and excellent. Exalted.

He laughed. So they might believe, but if they so much as spat he'd make it hell for them.

━━━━━

LEAF SHADOW FELL on the pale, slatted rocks on the far side of the pool. Li Yuan, T'ang of Europe, stood on the low, humped bridge, listening to the sounds coming from the rooms across the water. Low trees obscured his view of the courtyards and the house, but the sounds came clear to him: laughter, light-headed with relief; the chatter of excited female voices; and beneath both, unremitting, the bawling of a newborn child.

He stood there, in perfect stillness, looking down at his dark reflection in the lotus-strewn water. It was a child. A son—of course a son—there would not be laughter if it were otherwise. He stood, unmoving, not knowing what to think, what feel at that moment, the world—the tiny world of tree and stone and water—suspended all about him.

A son . . . He shook his head, frowning. *There should be more than this*, he thought. *I should be glad. I too should laugh, for today the chain is forged anew, the Family strengthened.* But there was nothing—only an empty space where feeling ought to have been.

Across from him one of the nurses stepped out onto the balcony of the birth room and saw him. He looked up in time to see her turn hurriedly and go back inside; heard her warning to them and the sudden silence that followed, broken almost at once by the high-pitched cries of the newborn. He stood there a moment longer, then moved on slowly, his heart strangely heavy, for once totally un-prepared for what lay ahead.

Mien Shan lay there, a tiny figure in his grandmother's huge bed— the same bed where his father, Li Shai Tung, had come into the world. She was propped up on pillows, her dark hair tied back from her sweat-beaded brow. Seeing him she smiled broadly and lifted the tiny bundle in her arms, offering it to him.

"Your son, *Chieh Hsia.*"

He took the child from her, cradling it carefully, conscious of the others in the room watching him. With one hand he drew back the blanket and looked down at the child. Dark hair lay finely on its long, pale scalp, glistening wetly in the overhead light. Its eyes were screwed shut and its thin lips formed ugly, awkward shapes as it yelled incessantly, one thin arm and tiny hand reaching blindly, repetitively, into the air. It struggled against him as he held it, as if sensing his unease. Even so, he laughed, feeling how small, how light it was. So fragile and yet so determined. His son. Once more he laughed, and sensed the mood in the room change, growing more relaxed.

He looked down at Mien Shan and smiled. "Good. You have done well, my love." He glanced across, seeing how his other wives, Lai Shi and Fu Ti Chang, blushed with Mien Shan at the endearment, and felt an unexpected warmth. They were good, kind women. Nan Ho had chosen well for him.

He sat beside Mien Shan on the bed and turned to face her, holding the child in one arm. Behind her, on the wall above the bed, was a copy of the *Luoshu* diagram—the "magic" numbers used as a charm for easing childbirth. Normally the sight of such superstitious non-sense would have angered him. But this was no moment for anger.

"Was it hard?" he asked, lifting her chin gently with one finger, making her look at him. She hesitated, then gave the slightest nod, remembered pain in her eyes.

He took a deep breath, trying to imagine it, then nodded, his lips and eyes slowly forming a smile. "I honor you, sweet wife. And thank you, both for my son and for myself."

For a moment he looked at her, an unusual tenderness in his features, then, giving the slightest bow, he leaned forward and kissed the wetness of her brow.

He turned, facing the others in the room. Besides wives, nurses, and doctors, several of his Ministers were present—witnesses to the birth. Li Yuan stood up, still cradling the child, and took a step toward them.

"You will announce that the Families have a new heir. That Kuei Jen, first son to Li Yuan, was born this morning of his wife, Mien Shan, in good health and in a state of physical perfection."

He nodded vigorously, holding the child firmer, seeing how they all smiled at that. "A strong child. Like his grandfather."

There was a murmur of agreement and a nodding of heads. But then Li Yuan lowered his head in the sign of dismissal and, with bows of respect, the others left, leaving Li Yuan alone with Mien Shan and the child. The babe in his arms had settled and was no longer crying. Now it looked up at him, open-eyed. Huge, dark eyes that peered out from the mystery of birth. And, lowering his face gently, he kissed brow and nose and chin with a tenderness that took him by surprise.

"Kuei Jen," he said, smiling down softly at the child. "Welcome, my son. May the world be kind to you." And, looking up, he saw that Mien Shan was watching him, tears trickling down her cheeks.

THE ROOM WAS DARK, ill-ventilated. The old man in the bed coughed, a dry, hacking cough, then sniffed loudly. "Draw the curtains, Chan Yin. I want to see you all."

His eldest son went to the far side of the room and drew the heavy silken curtain back a fraction. Brilliant light spilled into the room, cutting a broad swath through the shadow.

"More," said the old man, leaning forward from his pillows. "And open the doors. It's like a sweatbox in here."

Chan Yin hesitated and looked across at the doctors, but they simply shrugged. Pulling the curtain back fully, he pushed open the bronze and glass doors that led out onto the balcony, then stood there, feeling the freshness of the breeze on his face and arms, looking out across the gardens toward the distant mountains. After a moment he turned back, facing his father.

In the sudden brightness Wei Feng was squinting at him, a faint smile on his creased and ancient-looking face. "Better," he said, easing himself back onto the pillows. "It's like a tomb. Each night they tuck me up and bury me. And yet, when the morning comes, I am still here."

Chan Yin looked at his father with concern and love. He hated seeing him like this, so old and powerless. His memories rebelled against this image of Wei Feng and would have had his father strong and vigorous again. But those were childhood memories and he himself was older, much older now. Forty this next birthday. He sighed, then crossed the room to stand with his brothers at the bedside.

Hsi Wang stood there in his Colonel's uniform, ill at ease in this situation, his usual good humor subdued. Since his father's stroke he had been only half himself, his normally untroubled face overcast. Tseng-li, the youngest, stood right beside his father, his hand resting lightly on the old man's shoulder, his beautiful face looking down into his father's. From time to time Wei Feng would turn slightly and look up at him, smiling.

The stroke had almost killed Wei Feng. Only expert surgery had saved him. But pneumonia had set in shortly afterward. Now, a month from the first heart attack, he was much better, but the experience had aged him greatly. The left side of his skull was shaved bald and his right arm lay useless on the covers. There had been a blood clot and certain areas of his brain had died, among them those which controlled certain of his movements. Not even expert prosthetics could bring back the use of his right arm.

"My sons," he said, smiling, looking from one to the other, the simple words heavy with emotion. For a moment the coughing took him again, and Tseng-li bent his huge, tall body, kneeling, holding the old man's hand more tightly until the spasm passed. Then Wei Feng spoke again, looking mainly at his heir, Chan Yin.

"The doctors tell me I shall live." He smiled sadly, then nodded. "Even that seems strange now . . . the thought of living." He took a long, shuddering breath, then spoke again. "But being such a friend to death these last few weeks, I have had the chance to study him—to look him in the face and come to know him. Like an enemy one comes to respect for his great skill and cunning."

Hsi Wang laughed shortly and Wei Feng looked up at him, smiling, indulging his laughter. "It is good to hear you laugh, Hsi. I have missed your laughter." He licked his lips slightly, then carried on. "I have stood beside him, you see, and looked back. Into the light. Looked back and seen the shape of things, here, in this shadow world of ours."

Chan Yin narrowed his eyes, listening, watching his father's face, and saw how the old T'ang's eyes seemed to look out past Hsi, as if he really could see something that was denied to their vision.

"For the first time I saw clearly. How things are. How they will be."

Wei Feng turned his head and looked at his eldest son once more. "Which is why you are here. You especially, Chan Yin. But you also, Hsi and Tseng. As witnesses. Custodians, if you like."

They waited while Wei Feng took his breath. From the open doors came the sound of the wind in the trees and the buzzing of insects. A faint breeze moved the curtains gently, cooling the air in the room.

"There is something I want from you, Chan Yin. Something no father ought to ask of his eldest son. But I have seen what is to come. And, because I love you, I want you to swear to me that you will do what I ask of you."

Chan Yin shivered, seeing the strange intensity in his father's eyes, and nodded. "Whatever you ask, Father."

Wei Feng was quiet a while, watching him; then he sighed and looked down at his useless arm. "I want you to swear to me that you will support Li Yuan. Support him in whatever he asks, and for whatever reason he gives. *Whatever* he asks of you, do it."

He paused, a sudden ferocity in his face, as if he was seeing things again from the side of death. Looking back at the world of shadows and light.

"Do it, Chan Yin! You must! For upon Li Yuan's shoulders rests the fate of us all. Deny him and the Seven will fall, as surely as I will someday die and you inherit."

For a moment Chan Yin was silent, thoughtful, then he looked up and met his father's eyes, smiling, understanding the full import of what was being asked of him.

"I swear to do as my father wishes. To support Li Yuan, whatever he asks." He bowed low, then turned, facing his brothers. "This I swear as a sacred trust, which you, my brothers, bear witness to."

Wei Feng lay back again, relaxing, looking up at the three faces of his sons. "You are good men. Good sons. A father could not ask for better sons."

Leaning forward, Tseng-li kissed his father's brow. "It isn't chosen, Father," he said softly, smiling at him once more. "It simply is."

━━◆◆◆◆━━

LI YUAN sat at his desk, beneath the portrait of his grandfather. Across from him the face of Wu Shih, ten times its normal size, stared down at him from the wall screen.

"You talk of troubles to come, Yuan, but things have been quiet for some time now. The Lowers have not been so placid these past ten years."

"Maybe so, but things are happening down there, Wu Shih. I can feel it. We are sitting on a powder keg."

"And more powder every day, neh?" Wu Shih moved back a fraction, his features formed into a frown. "Then maybe it is time, Yuan. Time to implement what we have already decided."

Li Yuan sat there a moment, then nodded slowly. The decision had been made the day before, in Council, the terms for the "new deal" agreed among the Seven. It remained only to put it before the representatives of the Above.

In principle the package was fairly straightforward. Five changes to the Edict of Technological Control, in specialized areas. Stricter monitoring controls. Changes to the Personal Liberty Act. More money to be spent on low-level health care and maintenance support. Minor concessions concerning space travel. The reopening of the House of Representatives at Weimar. And in return, the House would set up the legal machinery for population controls.

Wu Shih sighed deeply and tugged at his plaited beard. "My instincts cry out against giving those bastards anything. But as you've rightly argued, we have a problem and it will not go away. So . . ." He shrugged and raised his hands, as if in surrender.

"We go ahead then? We ratify the document?"

Wu Shih nodded. "I see no point in waiting, Yuan. Even our cousin Wang is in agreement. Indeed, his amendments to the Edict changes were most thoughtful. It is clear the problem worries him as much as you or I."

"Perhaps . . ." Li Yuan looked away a moment, stony-faced, deep in thought, then turned back, facing the giant image of Wu Shih, meeting those platelike almond eyes. "We should have done this sixty years ago. Now . . . Well, maybe it is already much too late. Maybe we are only building walls of sand against the tide."

"Yet we must try, neh? We are Seven, after all."

The tone of irony in Wu Shih's voice did not escape the young T'ang. Li Yuan laughed, then fell serious again. "These are uncertain times, dear cousin. But whatever happens, remember that I count you as my friend. As brother to my father."

Wu Shih stared back at him, his expression giving nothing away, then he nodded. "You have my support, Li Yuan, in whatever you do. And yes. I will be an uncle to you in all things." He smiled, relaxing. "Well, so much for business. Now how is that child of yours? How is Kuei Jen?"

Li Yuan's face lit from within. "He is . . ." He hesitated, seeking the correct word, then laughed, finding nothing better than what had first come to mind. "He is beautiful, Wu Shih. Simply the most beautiful thing I have ever seen."

━━━━━
▼▼▼▼▼

MICHAEL LEVER stood there on the balcony overlooking the ballroom of his father's mansion, remembering the last time he had been there, fifteen months before, at the great Thanksgiving Ball his father had thrown for the Supernal. Outwardly, things seemed to have changed very little; the pillars and balconies of the great hall were festooned as before with red, white, and blue banners, while at the far end of the hall, beside a full-size replica of the ancient Liberty Bell, a twelve-piece band, dressed in the dark blue military uniforms of the Revolution, played the battle tunes of the old American Empire— forbidden tunes that spoke eloquently of another age, when the Americans ruled their own land and the Han were safe within their borders. Looking about him, it was easy to believe that this evening and the last were somehow connected, and that the fifteen months that had elapsed between were merely a dream, a dark delusion. But there was no connection, and those days—four hundred and sixty-three days, to be precise about it—had been no dream.

He pushed back from the edge, a feeling of hollowness, a tiredness that went beyond mere physical exhaustion, making him feel giddy for a moment. There had been a breach. Whereas, before, he had looked at this with casual, accepting eyes, now he saw it clear.

It was the same, and yet it was wholly, utterly different.

Like himself. Oh, he knew how he looked. He had stood there for a long time, earlier that afternoon, staring at himself in the full-length mirror. He was gaunter than he'd been back then, and there was a haunted, slightly melancholy look about him that had not been there before, yet otherwise he seemed the man he'd been. But he was not that man.

From the beginning they had kept him—as they'd kept all the Sons—in isolation. At first he had not been frightened, but had nursed his anger in silence, expecting his release at any moment. Yet as the days wore on, he had found his mood changing as no word came.

For several days he had bellowed at his guards and refused the food they brought. Then, changing his tack, he had adopted a more civil air, demanding firmly but politely to see whoever was in charge. Unexpectedly, his request had been granted.

He could still remember how it had felt, kneeling before the man in that tiny, awful cell. Even thinking of it made him feel cold, apprehensive. Before that moment he had never felt fear, never had to bow his head before another man. But now he knew. And that knowledge had changed him. Had made him a different man. Now, when he looked at things, he saw not a world that was his to make and shape, but a world in thrall to power and desire, a world corrupted by the dark currents of domination and submission.

In the light of which, his father's anger, earlier, at Wu Shih's treatment of him had seemed childish, almost laughable. What, after all, had he expected? Gratitude? Respect? No. For the relations of men were flawed—deeply flawed—as if they could not exist without the brutal mechanisms of power.

And now this. This celebration of his homecoming . . .

He shuddered, then turned, making his way down, knowing he had no choice; that this evening had to be faced and overcome, if only for his father's sake. Even so, he did not feel like celebrating.

I have been on my own too long, he thought, feeling a faint uneasiness as the murmur of the crowd below grew louder. *I'll have to learn all this again.*

At the turn of the stairs, he paused, trying out a brief, apologetic smile, conscious of how awkward it felt, of the way the skin stretched tightly across his face. Then, reluctantly, like a prisoner being taken to the place of punishment, he moved on, down, into the body of the hall.

CHARLES LEVER stared at his son, a broad grin splitting his face, then drew him close, holding him in a bear hug for the dozenth time that evening.

All about them, pressed close on every side, the pack of friends and relations laughed delightedly and raised their glasses to toast the two men, their joy unbounded.

"Have you told him yet, Charles?" one of them called out.

"Not yet," Lever called back, holding his son's head between his hands and staring once more, as if he could not have enough of the sight.

"What's this?" Michael asked quietly.

"Later," the old man answered. "There's plenty of time."

Much had changed, but he knew that tone in his father's voice. It was the tone he used when he wanted to avoid something awkward. Michael pressed him, softly but insistent. "Tell me. I'd like to know."

Lever laughed. "Okay. I wanted to keep it a while, but I guess now's as good a time as any." His smile broadened again. "I've asked Ted Johnstone about Louisa. He's given his consent to bring things forward. I thought we could announce it tonight—make it a double celebration."

Michael felt himself go cold. Louisa Johnstone . . . He looked down, licking his lips, then looked back at his father. "No," he said softly, almost inaudibly.

"What did you say?" his father asked, leaning closer.

"I said no. I don't want that."

"No?" Old Man Lever laughed, as if at a good joke. "Hell, Michael, you can't say no. You've been betrothed to the girl fifteen years now. All I'm saying is that we bring the wedding forward."

Michael looked about him at the expectant, joyous faces, then looked back at his father. Charles Lever had grown more solid by the year. His head rested like something carved upon a bull-like neck, the close trim of his ash-white hair accentuating the robust power of his features.

That is how I will look, forty years from now, he thought. *But do I have to be like him as well?*

"Not now," he said, wanting to let the matter drop; to save it for some quieter, less public moment. But his father was insistent. He slapped Michael's shoulder, as if encouraging a fighter.

"No, come on, Michael! It's a great time to announce it! It'll give everyone something to look forward to. And it'll help us put this thing behind us."

Michael stared at his father, then shook his head. "Please, Father. I'm not ready for it. Let's talk about it tomorrow, neh?"

Even that, that attempt at the old, father-son tone, had been hard; had stretched his resources to their limit. But it was as if Charles Lever hadn't heard. He shook his massive head and gripped his son's arm firmly.

"Don't be silly, Michael. I know how you feel, but this'll help you snap out of it. A woman, that's what you need! And sons! Plenty of sons!"

"*Help* me?" The sharpness in Michael's voice made Lever jerk his head back, surprised.

Michael glared at his father, something breaking in him. "Don't you understand? Don't you fucking understand? I don't *need* help. I need to be left alone. Sons . . . What use are fucking sons when I feel like *this?*"

The great room had gone deathly silent. A hundred faces stared at him, shocked and uncomprehending.

"There's no need . . ." Old Man Lever began, but Michael made a dismissive gesture.

"You push me, Father. You always did. But I mean it. I'm not marrying the girl. Not now, not ever, understand me?"

"*Michael!*"

But suddenly he was beyond words. He turned away, pushing through the crowd roughly, ignoring the shouting at his back; seeing only the floor of the tiny cell, the guard above him, that ugly mouth leaning close, shouting abuse, teaching him about how things really were.

PART I | SPRING 2209

Monsters of the Deep

Humanity must perforce prey on itself,
Like monsters of the deep.

—WILLIAM SHAKESPEARE, *King Lear*,
Act IV, Scene II

Go into emptiness, strike voids, bypass what
he defends, hit him where he does not expect
you.

—TSAO TSAO [A.D. 155–220], Commentary on
Sun Tzu's *The Art of War*

CHAPTER ONE

Earth

N THE CLEAR, golden light of dawn the seven "gods of the soil and grain" stood at their places on the huge earthen mound. Dressed in dragon robes of imperial yellow, each held an ancient ceremonial hand plow, the primitive wooden shaft curiously curved, the long blade made of black roughcast iron. Here, at the Temple of Heaven, at the very center of the universe, the New Year rites were about to be enacted, the furrows plowed, the sacrifices made to Hou T'u, "He Who Rules the Earth," and Hou Chi, "He Who Rules the Millet," as they had been since the time of T'ang, the founder of the Shang dynasty, three thousand seven hundred years before.

For a moment longer they stood there, while ten thousand bluecloaked servants waited silently about the foot of the mound, the seven gold-clothed figures forming a single burnished eye at the center of the dark circle of earth, and then it began, the pure tone of the bell sounding in the silence, followed by the low, monotonous chanting of the officials.

As one they bent, moving outward, pushing the plows before them, seven black furrows forming in the earth like the spokes of a giant wheel.

Turning, Li Yuan looked across the circle of the mound, seeing his fellow T'ang spread out along the rim, their dark, silhouetted figures like pillars holding up Heaven itself, their yellow-gold silks fluttering like banners in the early morning breeze. For a moment the illusion was perfect. For the briefest moment he was back a thousand years, at the very center of the ancient Middle Kingdom, the offerings made, the harvest guaranteed. But then, raising his eyes, he looked beyond his cousins, beyond the pleasant arbors and orchards of the Temple grounds.

The veil fell from his eyes. There, like a vast glacier dominating the skyline, lay the City, its pearl-white walls surrounding them on every side, towering over the lush greenery of the ancient gardens. For a moment he felt almost giddy. Then, checking himself, he stood straighter, listening to the chant, to the ancient words that spoke of the harmony between the ruler and the earth and of the balance of forces that must be maintained if the Kingdom was not to fall. For a moment he let himself be comforted by the ancient formula—by the thought that they might yet keep that age-old bargain and maintain the threefold link between Earth and Man and Heaven. But it was hard to concentrate. His eyes kept returning to the whiteness. To the giddying whiteness that encircled the tiny, earthen mound.

It was like death. Death on every side. And when, for the briefest moment, he let his attention stray, he grew conscious of the lie that lay behind their apparent unity. For in that moment of vertigo he had seen the Great Wheel break and spin aimlessly, like a cartwheel tumbling down a cliff face.

He shuddered and closed his eyes momentarily, wishing it were over, then looked down, noting the earth that clung to his boots and stained the hem of his silks. As on another day, eleven years before, when they had laid his brother, Han Ch'in, in his tomb.

Later, in the sedan returning to the *Chi Nien Tien*, the Hall of Prayer for Good Harvests, he thought of all that had happened since that day. Of the War-that-wasn't-a-War, of his father's death, and of the failure of his marriage to his dead brother's wife, Fei Yen. All had left their scars. And yet he had come through; had endured all that pain and suffering, to reach these calm heights from which he might look back. This hilltop of contentment.

Yes. And that was the strangest thing of all. For there was no doubting how he had felt these past few weeks. His child, his wives—these, more than anything, had become his comfort, his delight.

Outside the small circle of his family the storm clouds were gathering. There would be War again. Or worse. And yet he was happy. When he sat there, bouncing Kuei Jen on his knee, or carrying him against his shoulder, feeling his soft warmth and hearing the soft pattern of his breathing close by his ear, he would feel his cares fall from him. For a while there would be nothing but himself and the child, as if all else were a dream. And even afterward, when he had to go out from that magic circle and face the problems of his world, he would carry that warmth—that light—within him, like a charm against the world's darkness.

The sedan swayed gently, tilting slowly backward as the carriers climbed the broad, white marble ramp that led up to the great three-tiered tower.

Happy. Yes, he was happy now. And yet it was not enough.

Climbing down, he looked about him, attending closely to all he saw, as if this were the last time he would witness all of this. It was that thought—that strange and frightening glimpse of finality—which made him look away as Wu Shih came across.

"What is it, Yuan?" Wu Shih said softly, speaking to his ear.

He turned back, smiling, taking the older man's arm. "It's nothing, cousin. Just a fleeting thought."

Wu Shih nodded, understanding. "Then come. Let us make our sacrifices."

The Seven stood in line before the great altar, their offerings held out before them. A bell sounded, high and pure in the silence, and then the chanting began again. Candles flickered in the shadows. New Confucian officials came forward, their saffron robes whispering against the stone floor, and took the offerings from the T'ang, turning back to lay them before the statue that crouched, thrice life-size, on the altar.

Shang Ti, the Supreme Ancestor, looked down on his seven sons with blind, impassive eyes. He was *Yang*, Male, the personification of Heaven itself and the great arbiter of the weather. Appeased by sacrifices, he would provide good harvests; would look after the black-haired people. Neglected he would spurn them. Would bring plague and desolation. And death.

Or so it was said. So the officials chanted.

Li Yuan, standing there, was conscious suddenly of the great line of kings and emperors who had preceded him. Of that ghostly throng who stood with him, in his person, before the altar. Had they felt as he felt now? Or was he alone in doubting the efficacy of laying paper offerings before a blank-eyed statue?

It was not the first time he had questioned his beliefs. Often, in the past, he had looked squarely, critically at the rites and customs he, as T'ang, was obliged to perform. Yet this morning the ritual seemed more hollow than before, his actions sheer pretense. And though he had questioned things before, he had never experienced so profound a mistrust of his own words and actions.

What, after all, did they mean? What did any of it mean?

Oh, he could see the beauty in it. Could even feel some part of him stir, responding to the powerful sense of tradition, to the great weight of years that the rituals evoked. But beyond that—beyond that simple, almost aesthetic thrill—there was nothing. Nothing at all.

He watched it all happening, distanced from himself, and tried to fathom why. These three things—the darkening clouds of circumstance, the great, enduring chain of tradition, and the bright yet tiny circle of his own, individual happiness—how did they come together? Where did they meet and make sense?

As they bowed and backed away, he looked to either side of him, but on the faces of Wu Shih and Tsu Ma, of Hou Tung-po and Chi Hsing, on the broad moon face of Wang Sau-leyan and the Regent Wei Chan Yin, there was nothing but a solemn certainty. Whatever they thought of this, it was hidden from him behind the walls of their faces.

They descended the steps in silence, slowly, almost casually now that the ritual was over, making for the great tent and the breakfast that had been laid out by their host Wei Chan Yin's servants. It was there, beneath the golden awning, that Wang Sau-leyan came across to Li Yuan, addressing him for the first time since his son had been born.

He faced Li Yuan, smiling, seemingly at ease, a tumbler of *ch'a* cradled in the palm of one hand. "Well, cousin, and how is the child?"

It seemed an innocuous question—the kind of politeness one

might have expected from a fellow T'ang—yet it was as if a shadow had fallen over Li Yuan. He felt a sudden tightening in his chest and—briefly, absurdly—experienced a powerful, overwhelming fear for his son. Then it passed. He was himself again. He forced a smile, lowering his head the merest degree, acknowledging his cousin's query.

"Kuei Jen is fine. He is a strong and healthy child. Heaven has blessed me, Wang Sau-leyan."

Wang smiled, no sign of calculation in his face. "I am pleased for you, cousin. A man should have sons, neh?"

Li Yuan stared back at the young T'ang of Africa, surprised by the almost wistful tone in Wang's voice, thinking to see something in his eyes, but there was nothing. Wang nodded and turned away, his business done. And Li Yuan, left to watch his back, stood there a moment, wondering, that small, hard nugget of fear returning, like a stone within his flesh.

MAIN WAS PACKED. Thirty, maybe forty thousand people were crammed into the broad two-*li*-long concourse, banners and streamers of bright red er-silk waved energetically above their heads. At the northern end of Main, before the bell tower, a raised podium had been constructed. There the crowd pressed thickest, held back by a double line of green-uniformed Security guards.

As ninth bell sounded from the tower, the lights dimmed, a hush falling on the great gathering. A moment later, cloaked in a veil of brilliant white laser light, the huge statue of the goddess descended slowly onto its pedestal.

As the figure settled there was a strong murmur of approval. Kuan Yin, Goddess of Mercy and Fecundity, sat Buddha-like on a giant lotus, a newborn baby cradled lovingly in her arms. Her face in the brilliant white light was benign, radiant with compassion.

There was a moment's silence, then, with a great popping of crackers on every side and the creaking of rattles, the crowd began to celebrate. The sick and lame, held back by the crush, now renewed their efforts to get to the front, to receive the goddess's blessing.

On the podium nearby, separated from the crowd by a wide corridor of armed guards, the dignitaries looked on, turning in their high-backed chairs to talk among themselves. The guest of honor—the man whose money had paid for the giant statue—was a squat, balding *Hung Mao* named May Feng. His company, EduCol, had benefited from GenSyn's relaxation of food patents and—developing one of those patents—had increased food production significantly over the last twelve months, perhaps by as much as four percent throughout City Europe, winning the praise of both T'ang and people. After years of ever-stricter rationing and growing discontent, it had reversed the trend and brought new stability to these levels. But what most of those gathered in Main to celebrate EduCol's generosity didn't know was just how poor, nutritionally, the new product was, nor the amount of profit the Company had made on their new soy-substitute; for while the new process cost only one sixth of the old, the product price was roughly the same.

To May Feng's right sat a big, slightly corpulent Han named K'ang A-yin, a local gang leader, operating this and the surrounding stacks under the protection of the *Kuei Chuan* Triad. Behind K'ang stood two of his henchmen, their eyes shifting uneasily in their faces as they surveyed the massive crowd. K'ang himself was studying the merchant, noting the fashionable cut of his silk *pau*, the absence of rings on his fingers. K'ang looked away, tucking one hand under the other in his lap. He, at least, knew how much profit EduCol was making. Five hundred percent, if reports were true. And he could use a cut of that, to buy himself more muscle and finance a few schemes. But May Feng knew nothing of that yet. As far as he was concerned, K'ang was simply a businessman. The man to deal with at these levels.

K'ang smiled and looked past May Feng at his friend, the local *Wei*, or Commandant of Security, who was standing off to one side of the podium. "Well, Captain Franke. It's almost time . . ."

Franke bowed his head, then turned, calling down to his lieutenant. A moment later the great curtain which was draped across the width of Main behind the bell tower twitched, then began to draw back. From the tunnel beyond, a procession of carts, heaped with the latest range of EduCol products, began to make its way out into Main toward the crowd.

At the far end of Main, on a balcony almost two *li* from where the dignitaries were sitting, a tall, bearded *Hung Mao* lowered the field glasses from his eyes and turned, making a curt hand signal. At once the group of men and women gathered about him turned, making their way down the steps and out into the crowd below.

Mach watched them a moment, seeing how they went among the crowd, handing out the leaflets, their voices murmuring old slogans, the catchphrases of ancient discontents. And after they'd moved on, he saw how those who had glanced at the leaflets now held them out to their neighbors, angered by what they'd read, their own voices raised.

He smiled, then turned away again, moving out into the corridor. Two guards were standing there, staring up at one of the public service screens.

"You'd best get downstairs," he said, showing them his ID. "It looks like trouble."

They looked at his badge, then nodded, moving past him quickly, the noise from the crowd growing by the moment.

Mach stood there a moment longer, looking up at the screen. Li Yuan was talking to his citizens, telling them about the committee that had been set up to investigate the possibility of changes to the Edict and the reopening of the House. Mach moved closer, spitting up into the face of the young T'ang, then, drawing his gun, he turned, following the guards down.

On the podium May Feng was standing now, concerned. The noise from the far end of Main was growing all the while, ⌐ising above the sound of the firecrackers. People at the front were turning their heads, anxious, conscious that something was happening back there.

"What is it, *Shih* K'ang?" the merchant asked, fingering his girdle-pouch nervously.

K'ang frowned, trying to conceal his own concern. "I'm not sure. I . . ."

His words were drowned out as deck communications cut in, the voice harsh and accusing.

"Death to all profiteers and thieving First Level bandits! Death to all those who would steal the rice from your children's mouths! Death to those who profit from the misery and need of others! Death . . ."

The litany went on, fanatical, endless, stirring up already excited passions into a frenzy; turning fear into a sudden blinding panic that spread among the masses like a brushfire. K'ang watched as the thin line of green gave and the crowd spilled out toward the podium and the giant statue. Without thought, he turned and, his henchmen close behind, leapt from the back of the platform, making for the safety of the tunnel. It was not a moment too soon, for the front edge of the crowd, impelled by the pressure of bodies from behind, broke like a wave against the podium, bringing its supporting stanchions crashing down.

For a moment May Feng kept his balance, then he went down, his mouth formed in a perfect O of surprise before he was lost to sight, trampled beneath the stampeding crowd. There was a steady roar within the great space now, like the sound of a great wind blowing from the north. As if caught in the grip of that wind, the great statue shuddered, then, with a slow, soundless motion, it fell, crushing more than two dozen people beneath it.

All was chaos now. There was gunfire from the far end of Main and the sound of small explosions, of falling ice. And over everything was the voice, chanting its litany of death, death, death.

THERE WERE THREE of them, not counting the stallholder. Becker was standing at the back of the partitioned room, browsing the shelves of secondhand tapebooks that crowded the walls. Haller lounged in a chair nearby, staring up at the overhead FacScreen, one hand lazily holding a squeezetube of prawn-flavored protein paste.

Lehmann was talking to the owner, Pai Mei, his back to the doorway. "Don't worry," he was saying. "Just get down behind the counter when things start. And remember—no one will harm you. I guarantee it."

Pai Mei, a thin-faced, hard-looking man, hesitated. K'ang A-yin was a bastard, but who knew what this one was like? Yet if the albino failed, K'ang might think that he, Pai Mei, had put him up to it. He shuddered, then gave a reluctant nod. It was a no-win situation.

Just then the ragged curtain was tugged back and two men came in. One was tall, going to fat, the other smaller, lither, but more dangerous-looking altogether. His bare arms were heavily muscled and his head was shaved, the skull painted in an intricate pattern of red and green that indicated he was a *chan shih*, a fighter. They were K'ang's men.

The fat man stopped and looked about him. Glancing sourly at Pai Mei, he touched the *chan shih's* arm. "Move them. I want to speak to *Shih* Pai in private."

The small man tapped Haller on the shoulder, indicating that he should go and quickly. Smiling, apologetic, Haller got up and went. Becker, turning, saw how things stood and, shoving the tape back hastily, scuttled out after Haller. Only Lehmann remained, his back to the newcomers.

"You," said the fat man, coming up behind him. "Out of here! I've business with *Shih* Pai."

Lehmann turned, facing them. The *chan shih* seemed easier now that there was only Lehmann in the room. He relaxed, looking about the room, for that brief moment inattentive. The fat man, meanwhile, was staring at Lehmann curiously, as if he ought to know him. But even he, for that instant, was off his guard.

Lehmann struck. With one quick movement he kicked the *chan shih* beneath the chin, then turned to face the fat man. Panicking, K'ang's lieutenant tugged at the gun in his pocket, trying to free it. He had just leveled it when Lehmann punched it from his hand, breaking the man's wrist with the downward blow. His second punch floored the man. Lehmann stood over him, looking down, his fist raised, waiting to see if he would try to get up.

Haller and Becker stood in the doorway, smiling. They had seen already how Lehmann operated. Becker looked across at Pai Mei and laughed. The stallholder had gone white. He was staring at Lehmann in astonishment.

"I thought that all three of you . . ." Pai Mei left the sentence unfinished.

Becker stepped into the room and knelt down beside the *chan shih*, feeling for a pulse at the neck. The small man was dead. "Shame," Becker said darkly. "I would have liked to have seen his expression when I slit his throat." Haller, coming up beside him, laughed at that, but Lehmann was unmoved. He stood there over his wheezing victim, tensed, perfectly still, making sure.

"That's it, you see," Becker said, looking up at the stallholder, then drew a large, razor-sharp knife from beneath his tunic. "They never expect trouble from a single man. That's how they think. And in the moment that they least expect trouble, that's when they're at their weakest." He smiled again and looked across at Lehmann, as if to say, "Isn't that so, *Shih* Lehmann?" But Lehmann ignored him. Becker looked down again, shrugging, then got to work, cutting into the flesh at the neck, blood oozing out over the bare, unswept floor.

Pai Mei looked away, feeling sick.

He looked across. Lehmann was crouching now, talking to the fat man. K'ang's man was making hoarse, gasping noises, as if he'd damaged his windpipe, but he was listening very carefully as the albino spelt out what he was to tell his boss. At one point he laughed dismissively and turned his head away, but Lehmann grasped his chin in one long, pale hand and turned his head back savagely, forcing him to look up into his face. The fat man shut up at once, fear returning to his eyes.

Becker had finished now. He wrapped the head in a towel and dropped it into a bag. Haller, in the doorway, was looking past him, his attention on the FacScreen and the media speculation about what tomorrow's meeting of the Seven might bring for the people of Chung Kuo.

"Big things are happening up there," he said at last, looking down at Becker, ignoring the pool of blood that had formed about his feet. "Big changes are coming."

"As above, so below," said Lehmann, pulling the fat man to his feet. Then, taking the bag from Becker, he thrust it into the man's one good hand.

Watching him, the two men laughed, enjoying the fat man's discomfort. But Lehmann didn't smile. Lehmann *never* smiled.

———————

THE TONG BOSS, K'ang A-yin, sat back in his chair, drawing the back of his hand across his mouth, then looked around him at the eight men gathered in the room. The Zwickau riot had shocked and angered him, but this latest news was too much. K'ang was trembling with rage. Only with the greatest effort did he keep himself from shouting.

"Okay. What the fuck is going on? Who the fuck's this *Hung Mao*?"

There was an awkward silence from his men, then one of them—Soucek, his lieutenant—spoke up.

"We don't know. I sent a runner to Pai Mei's. He only confirmed what Feng Wo said. The pale *Hung Mao* killed the *chan shih*. The others hacked his head off. Why, we don't know."

"And no one knows the bastard?"

Soucek shrugged. "You want I should do some asking?"

K'ang looked away a moment, considering, then shook his head. "No. I've a better idea. Chao, Kant . . . I want you to find out where he's staying and hit him. When the fucker's asleep. I want him dead, him and his two sidekicks. And I want their heads, back here, on my desk, by the morning."

Soucek made to say something, to insist, perhaps, that he be given the job of killing the *Hung Mao*, but K'ang raised a hand. "No, Jiri. Not this time. I want you to go and see Whiskers Lu and find out all you can about what happened earlier. If the *Yu* are active again, it threatens us all. And if it's something else, I want to know, understand?"

Soucek nodded.

K'ang stood, looking about him, more at ease now that he was taking the initiative. "Good. Then let's get going. Let's sort these fuckers out, neh? Then we can get on with making money."

━━━━━

THEY CAME two hours later. Lehmann was expecting them. Haller's bunk was empty, Haller fifty *ch'i* down the corridor in the public washroom. Becker's was occupied, but by a dummy, while Becker crouched behind the false partition, gun in hand. Lehmann lay beneath the thin blanket on the upper bunk, masked and waiting. He too was armed.

There were no locks at these lowest levels, so it was easy for K'ang's man to pull the slide-to back a fraction and roll in the gas grenade. It exploded with a dull plop, followed instantly by the hiss of escaping gas. Lehmann counted, knowing they would make certain before coming through. Sure enough, on a count of thirty, the slide-to was heaved aside and two men came into the room, machine-pistols raised. A third waited outside.

He didn't give them a chance. Poking the muzzle of the rocket launcher from the blanket, he squeezed the hair trigger and watched the far wall explode. There was no sign of the two men. Wall, floor, and men had gone. A great, gaping hole had opened up, revealing the level below. Fractured cables sparked. There was screaming from below and the sweet stink of superheated plastics hung in the air, stronger than the gas.

From farther down the corridor two shots rang out. Haller had done his job. He appeared a moment later, gun in hand, looking across the gap into the room. "Messy," he said, grinning through his mask. "Maybe K'ang will talk now."

"We'll see," Lehmann said, sitting up and wrapping the big gun in the blanket. "Either way, he'll know now that we aren't so easy. He'll be more careful in future."

"That's good," said Haller, slipping the gun back in his shoulder-holster, "It was a bit too easy for my liking."

Lehmann said nothing. He simply looked at Haller and shook his head. They had a lot to learn.

━━━◆◆◆━━━

FROM WHERE IT soared, high above the wood, the hawk could see the figures down below, among the trees. The leading group had stopped now in a clearing, resting their mounts, their necks strained back, hands shielding their eyes as they looked up at it. Farther back, part hidden by foliage, a second group waited. These last were smaller but more numerous, and in its dark, instinctive way, it knew these to be men; knew they were on foot.

It circled patiently, its keen eyes searching for that sudden, distinctive movement that would betray its prey. For a time there was nothing, then, as the wind changed, there was a flutter of sound and a brief blur, as a guinea fowl broke cover far below.

With a cry the hawk fell, turning, straining after its prey. For a moment it seemed as if the other bird might yet regain its perch, then, with a sickening thud, the hawk struck.

A roar of triumph erupted from the men below.

In the clearing the three men leaned forward, watching the hawk spread its wings wide, slowing its fall, the fowl held tightly in its talons, then settle on the ground among the trees to their right.

Tsu Ma leaned down, patting the dark neck of his mount fondly, then turned his head, looking across at his fellow T'ang. "Well, cousins, what do you think?"

Wu Shih placed one hand carefully on the pommel of his saddle and turned slightly, inclining his head. They were talking of their cousin, Wang Sau-leyan, T'ang of Africa. "I don't trust him," he said. "He has been too quiet these past six months. Too damned polite."

"He's up to something," Li Yuan added, sitting straighter in his saddle. "Something deep. Something we can't see yet."

Wu Shih nodded. "I agree. I am not certain about much in these troubled times, but of this I *can* be sure . . . Wang Sau-leyan has not changed his nature these past few months. He is still the same devious little shit-eating insect he always was."

Tsu Ma looked past them momentarily, watching his falconer run across to where the hawk had brought down its prey, his lure out, ready to draw the hawk off, then looked back at Wu Shih.

"I think you are right," he said. "But exactly what it is . . . Well, it's very strange. My servants in his household have heard nothing. Or almost nothing . . ."

"*Almost* nothing?" Wu Shih stared at him intently.

"Just that there is a woman in his life. Or so it seems. A *Hung Mao.* He has her smuggled in. Late, when he thinks no one will see. I'm told he even visits her."

Li Yuan looked away. "How strange. I would not have thought it. A *Hung Mao* . . . And you think it is serious?"

Tsu Ma shrugged. "Maybe it is nothing. Or maybe this is why our cousin has behaved himself so well recently. Perhaps he has been distracted."

"In love, you mean?" Wu Shih roared with laughter. "The only one that ingrate will ever love is his own reflection. Love!" He shook his head, then reached down, slapping his horse's flank. "No . . . that moon-faced bastard is up to something. I guarantee it!"

"*Chieh Hsia* . . ."

A servant stood at the edge of the clearing, his head bowed.

"What is it, Cheng Yi?"

At Tsu Ma's summons, the man came across, his body bent double, and took his T'ang's foot, kissing it, before falling to his knees beside the horse.

"News has come, *Chieh Hsia*. There have been riots in City Europe. Many have died . . ."

"Riots . . ." Li Yuan urged his horse forward sharply. "What in the gods' names has been happening?"

The servant bowed his head lower, answering as if his own T'ang had spoken. "It began at Zwickau *Hsien*, *Chieh Hsia*, at the dedication ceremony for the new statue, and spread quickly to surrounding stacks."

"And many have died?"

"That is so, *Chieh Hsia*. A great number. Tens of thousands, some say. Among them the merchant, May Feng."

Li Yuan looked across at Tsu Ma, alarmed. May Feng had been a leading figure in the new peace. Had sat on committees to discuss the proposed Edict changes and the reopening of the House. What's more, he represented a whole class—of powerful First Level merchants—who had been won back to the Seven and their cause. And now he was dead.

Li Yuan leaned toward the man, anxious now. "What happened? How did he die?"

The servant swallowed. "It is not clear how he died, *Chieh Hsia*. All we know is that his body was returned to his widow shortly afterward. He had been cut open, it seems, then stuffed with dirt like a sack and sewn up again."

Li Yuan shuddered and sat back. "Do we know who was responsible?"

"It is too early yet to know for certain, *Chieh Hsia*. Early rumors attributed it to the *Yu*, but General Rheinhardt believes that the *Hun Mun* had a hand in this."

Again, Li Yuan felt a ripple of shock pass through him. The *Hung Mun*—the Triads, or Secret Societies—had kept out of things before now. But that was clearly changing. If they *were* involved . . .

"I must get back," he said, turning his horse, looking from Tsu Ma to Wu Shih. "If the *Hun Mun* are involved, I must act."

"No, Yuan," Tsu Ma said, putting out a hand to him. "I would counsel against acting too rashly. Take some measures to calm things down, by all means, but consider before you take action against the brotherhoods. Your father's scheme, for instance . . ."

"Buy them off, you mean?" Li Yuan sat back, shaking his head. "No, Tsu Ma. I will not bow to them in my own City!"

"Nor am I asking you to, cousin. Pursue your father's scheme—offer them funds, assistance, power of a kind—while all the time undermining their position."

Li Yuan narrowed his eyes. "What do you mean?"

"The new force. Karr's *shen t'se* . . ."

Li Yuan looked down, then he smiled. "You know of that?"

Tsu Ma nodded. "My cousin's business is my business. How can I know how I might help him unless I know his needs, his plans?"

Li Yuan turned, looking to the older man. "And you, Wu Shih?"

Wu Shih shrugged. "You have a special force, I take it. Good. Then use it. Do as our good cousin, Tsu Ma, says. Play a double game. Buy time. For it's time we need right now, not another war. Not yet."

Tsu Ma nodded. "Wu Shih is right, Yuan. Fight a war against the brotherhoods now and it would weaken us greatly. And who would benefit?"

"Wang Sau-leyan."

"Exactly. So do not be goaded into a futile war." Tsu Ma smiled bleakly. "Oh, the time will come—and not so long from now—when we must take on the *Hun Mun*. But let us pick that time, neh? Let us be prepared for it."

"Besides," Wu Shih added, coming alongside him, "we have problems enough already, neh? The *Yu*, the Younger Sons . . . Why add to them?"

Li Yuan was silent a moment, calming himself, then reached out, taking Wu Shih's arm. "Thank you, cousin. And you, Tsu Ma. But we must get back, neh? There is much to be done. Besides, watching the hawk has whetted my appetite for other sport."

Tsu Ma stared at him a moment, then laughed. "For once, Yuan, your meaning escapes me, but let it pass. You are right. There is much to be done. Nonetheless, we must meet more often, neh? Just the three of us."

"It shall be so," Wu Shih said, giving a brief, decisive nod. "We shall be like the three brothers of the peach garden, neh?"

Li Yuan, watching the two older men, felt the darkness subside a little. So it would be. So it *had* to be from now on. *The Three*, he thought, trying the term out in his head for the first time, and finding it not strange but strangely comforting. *Yes, we shall be The Three.*

There was a sudden flutter of sound. Behind Li Yuan, on the far side of the clearing, the hawk lifted, stretching its wings, then settled on its kill once more, ignoring the lure.

CHAPTER TWO

In the World of Levels

ELKA WAS STRETCHED OUT on the sun bed, looking out across the brightly lit expanse of tiles to where her two school friends splashed noisily in the pool. Beside her on the chair lay the compact computer notepad she had been using, its display screen lit.

For a moment she watched their antics thoughtlessly, enjoying the warmth on her skin, the faint scent of jasmine and pine from the nearby rock garden. Then, with a tiny shiver, she returned to the matter she had been considering.

Yesterday had been the last day of school; the end of her childhood, of twelve years preparing for her adult life. Ahead of her, tonight, lay the ordeal of the College Graduation Ball, and beyond that the rest of her life—fifty, sixty years of it, maybe, needing to be filled.

But how?

She turned over, lying on her back a moment, conscious of how it felt to be herself, seventeen, in a young woman's body, the future open to her.

She stretched her legs, flexing her toes, exercising the muscles of her feet and calves and thighs, as if warming up for an exercise session, then relaxed again. The Marshal's daughter . . . that was how she was known. As if she had no separate identity of her own.

Jelka shook her head, exasperated, then turned onto her stomach again. *The Marshal's daughter* . . . If she had been his son, her future would have been mapped out long before today. Cadet school, a commission, and then the service. Fifty years of service: of dodging assassins' bullets and attending official functions; of investigating murders and pandering to the whims of some old Minister; of unearthing corruption scandals at First Level and tidying up after riots beneath the Net. Such was her father's life, and there were far worse ways of spending one's time, but it wasn't that. It was having a say in her future. As a son to the Marshal she would have had no say in things.

Not that being a daughter had made all that great a difference. Had it not been for Hans Ebert's duplicity—for the betrayal of his T'ang and the murder of his father—she would have been married now, her future set, determined. And no way out, except, perhaps, to kill herself.

She shuddered, recollecting her aversion for the young Major. That was something her friends had never understood. Something which, when she mentioned it, brought looks of incredulity. Hans Ebert . . . why, he had been every schoolgirl's dream, surely? A prince among men. She laughed sourly, remembering how often she had heard him called that. Moreover, as heir to the richest Company in Chung Kuo, she could have expected a life of idleness, of unremitting luxury.

Yes, but Hans Ebert was also cruel, and arrogant and devious.

She looked down, recalling her father's hurt when Hans had finally been exposed; a hurt mingled with grief at the death of his brother and his wife, and of his oldest friend, Klaus Ebert. She too had felt a similar grief, but also relief that Hans was gone from her life; a relief that was like a huge stone lifted from her chest. She sighed and shook her head. Maybe that was why it was so important now to get it right; to make sure that her life from here on was her own.

It seemed simple enough, but there was one small complication. She was a woman. For her friends that seemed to pose no problems. Only five of the sixty girls in her year were not yet betrothed, and of those, three were actively pursuing a husband. Eight were already married and two—her close friend Yi Pang-chou among them—had already presented their husbands with a child. Against which, only six of her year were going on to Oxford, and in each case it was not so much to fulfill their own needs as to make them the perfect companions for their high-flying husbands.

But so it was in this god-awful world of levels. To be a woman—an intelligent, capable young woman—it was unthinkable! One had to be a drudge, a whore, an ornament . . .

"Jelka?"

She hesitated, then turned, lifting her head lazily, as if she had been dozing. "Hi . . . What is it?"

Anna was crouched beside her, toweling her dripping hair. Beyond her stood the stocky figure of Yi Pang-chou. She was grinning, a faint color in her cheeks.

"You should have joined us, Mu-Lan. What have you been doing?"

She smiled at the use of her nickname, then sat up, stretching, conscious of how her friends were watching her.

"I was thinking. And making lists."

"Making lists?" Anna laughed. "Lists of what? Men you'd like to marry? Why, you could have any man you chose, Jelka Tolonen, and you know it."

Jelka shrugged. "Maybe. But it wasn't that kind of list. I was jotting down my options."

"Jotting down my options," Yi Pang-chou mimicked, then giggled.

Jelka smiled, good-humoredly. "I know how it sounds, but here," she handed the comset across to Anna. "Go on. Have a look. Tell me what you think."

Anna studied the screen a moment, then turned, passing it up to Yi Pang-chou. "I can't see the point," she said, looking at Jelka with a slightly puzzled frown. "It's so much effort. Why not simply enjoy yourself? Take a rich husband. It doesn't mean you have to be in his pocket. These days a woman has much more freedom."

Jelka looked away. Freedom! As if Anna had any understanding of the word's true meaning. What she meant was the freedom to go to countless entertainments; to drink and play to excess and to take young officers for lovers. Beyond that she had no idea. For her this world of levels was enough. But then, she knew no different. She had not seen how beautiful it was outside.

Yi Pang-chou had been studying her list. Now she looked back at Jelka, puzzled.

"This entry for Security. I thought they didn't accept women in the service."

"They don't. Or not yet. But I thought I'd apply. I'm as qualified as any cadet, after all. And I can fight. So why not? I thought I'd apply for the auxiliary forces, specializing in space operations."

Anna raked one hand through her long dark hair, then laughed. "You're strange, Jelka. You know that? If you really want to meet young officers, you should attend a few more parties. You don't have to sign up for the service!"

"And you've a one-track mind, Anna Koslevic!" Jelka laughed, then grew serious again. "I know it's hard to understand, but I want to do something with my life. I don't just want . . . well, I don't want to waste it, that's all."

"Like us, you mean," Yi Pang-chou said, coming across and sitting beside her on the edge of the sun bed.

"No . . . I didn't mean it like that. I . . ." Again she laughed, but this time her laughter was tinged with a certain desperation. "Look, I can talk to you two. I can say things without you being hurt by them. So when I say that I want something more than what I'm being offered, it's not to put you down. It's . . ." She shrugged. "I don't know. Maybe I want something that I simply can't have, but why not try for it?" She looked from one to the other. "Do you understand?"

"Sure," Anna said, nodding. "It's simple. You want to be a man. You want to go out there and do things. You want to break skulls and ride horses. Like your 'ex,' Hans."

Jelka shook her head. "No. I want only to be myself. But why should that be so difficult? Why should I be denied that?"

"Because it's how things are," Yi Pang-chou said, stroking the back of her hand. "There's us and there's them. Women and Men. *Yin* and *Yang*. And it's a *Yang* world." She smiled sadly. "Don't fight it, Mu-Lan. It'll only make you unhappy."

She looked down. Maybe so. But she would never be at peace unless she tried. Besides, there was always Kim. He, if anyone, would understand.

Anna leaned close, placing her hand on Jelka's knee. "Anyway. Let's forget about all that for now. It's almost six and our escorts are coming at eight, so we'd best get ready."

"Escorts?" Jelka looked up, eyeing her friend sharply. "You didn't say anything about escorts!"

"Didn't I?" Anna laughed innocently. "I guess it must have slipped my mind. Anyway, let's go through. I'll lend you one of my *chi pao* . . . the blue and gray silk with the black edging. And then I'll make you up. Maybe it'll take your mind off all this nonsense . . ."

Jelka sat there, looking from one to the other, then laughed. "All right. Just this once. But I hope you haven't said anything. Anything, well . . ."

"Anything *true?*" Anna put on an earnest face, mirroring Jelka's own, then burst out laughing. She leaned across, kissing Jelka's brow. "Come. Let's get ready. Before those big, hulking *Yangs* arrive!"

THE MAIN BUILDING of the Bremen Academy for Young Women—a huge *yamen* in the old northern style—dominated the open space at the top of the stack. On the great terrace overlooking the lake, it was hot, the music loud. On the dance floor the press of young, well-dressed bodies filled the dimly lit darkness, the rich, cloyingly sweet scents of the dancers tainting the air, their drunken laughter echoing out across the water.

It was late now, almost midnight, and the Ball had reached a fever pitch of intensity. For the young women, the days of hard work were behind them, the long vacation ahead, while for the young men, cadets and commissioned officers alike, there was a sense of temporary surcease from the rigors of duty. Tonight was a night for celebration, for high spirits and wild excess. Some lay in the corridors leading off the terrace, slumped in drunken stupor, while others cavorted wildly at the edges of the crowd, howling manically, their formal jackets unbuttoned or cast aside. Most, however, had found partners and could be found pressed close in that central darkness, washed over by a heavy pulse of sound, willing victims of those old, insistent currents.

Jelka stood there at the center of that great crush, cradling an empty glass, alone at last and conscious, for the first time that evening, just how awful it was. The heat was stifling, the noise oppressive, while to every side the crowd pressed in on her relentlessly; a great tide of bodies, male and female, jerking and swaying to the ancient rhythms of the pipes and drums.

For a moment longer she stood there, hemmed in, wondering if she should wait for her escort to return from the bar, then she turned and began to make her way across. She was aware of the unnatural excitement in the faces that she passed; of the feverish brightness of their eyes, the sudden, excessive animation of their features. There was something strange and frightening about it all, a sense of primal urgency, almost of hysteria.

Outside it was cooler, quieter. Jelka stood there at the top of the steps, gulping in the cold, refreshing air and staring about her, as if waking from some dark and threatening dream. Overhead, a very real-looking moon shone down on her from the artificial sky, casting a painted light upon the distant mountains, while to her left a faint breeze rippled the dark lake's surface, scattering petals on the white stone arch of the bridge that led across to the island and the great watchtower.

Away, she thought. *I have to get away.*

She set her glass down on the steps, then made her way down, out onto the path that led to the bridge, half running now, as if pursued. Halfway down, however, she stopped and turned, staring back at it all, her mouth wide open, as if stupefied. Then, with a faint shudder, she went on.

At the foot of the watchtower she stopped again, staring up at its brightly lit face. It was two minutes to midnight. Twelve years she had been here at the Academy; twelve years, not including the time she had spent in exile with her father and that time she had been ill, after the attack. And in all that time she had never—not once—felt at home here. She had stood there earlier, listening to the other girls say how much they'd miss the dear old place; had heard them profess to a genuine love for its strange old ways and nonsensical rules, but for herself she felt nothing; only a strange relief that it was over. And a sense of emptiness—of something unfulfilled in her.

She turned briefly, looking back, wondering if she had been missed yet, then moved on quickly, climbing the broad yet shallow steps up to the open doorway. Inside, in the shadows just inside the door, a couple was leaning against the wall, kissing, her hand at his neck, his arm about her lower back. She hesitated, watching them a moment, then tiptoed by, making her way up to the first level and the little room at the front of the tower, above the clock.

She closed the door behind her, then went across and sat on the box beside the window, her elbows on the mock-stone of the window ledge, looking back across the lake at the crowded terrace. From a distance it seemed a kind of madness, a mass delirium. As if, for once, they had glimpsed the hollowness of it all. Glimpsed it and turned away, drowning themselves in this frenzy of thoughtless activity.

She rested her chin on her hands and sighed. Coming here tonight had been a mistake. She should have trusted to instinct and stayed at home. But now it was too late.

Too late? Too late for what?

That small, inner voice—that never-resting, ever-questioning part of her—was what kept her at a distance from it all; was what made her different from the others. At school she had always been something of an outsider, right from the first. Not that she had been unpopular; it was simply that she had never formed any of those close relationships that the other girls seemed to need. Some had tried, like Anna and Yi Pang-chou, but they could only get so close before she clammed up on them. "It's because of the attacks," Anna had said to her once. "It's only natural that you should mistrust the world after what happened to you." And maybe that was true to an extent. Maybe those experiences *had* shaped her. But the explanation was somehow insufficient, for she had always felt like this. From the cradle on. There had always been a space unfilled in her. A lack. But tonight it was different somehow. Tonight the sheer intensity of what she felt was new to her.

Looking back at the dance floor, she saw not celebration and the joyous blossoming of new life, but a mechanistic orgy of self-denial; of deadness incarnate. It was pretense; pretense on a vast scale. It began with the great City in which they lived and spread like a virus to infect every pore, every cell of their individual beings. And now there was nothing. Nothing but meaningless activity and a desperate filling of the hours. A willful forgetting.

She turned her head, her eyes sweeping the familiar landscape of the College grounds, taking it all in. The star-filled sky, the moon, the distant mountains; it was false, every last tiny bit of it. The arched stone bridge, the lake, the ancient building. Manufactured, all of it; a substitute for life, conjured from nothingness.

Too late.

She shuddered. It was true. Never had she felt so alienated from it all. Never so alone.

I am trapped, she thought. *Trapped in the world of levels.*

On the steps beside the dance floor there was movement. A young cadet officer had stepped out onto the top step and now stood there, looking about him, a glass in each hand.

Jelka shivered and drew her head back, into the shadows.

He looked down and spotted the empty glass, then turned back, craning to see where she had gone. Then he came on, negotiating the steps smartly, elegantly, his manner—the very way he walked—assured and arrogant. Unquestioning. On he came, along the path and up onto the gentle arch of the bridge. For a moment he stood there, looking about him casually, as if taking in the view, then he walked on, glancing up at the watchtower, as if he could see her, there in the shadows beyond the window frame.

She moved back, then stood, looking about her. There was no way out. The floor above was locked. But maybe he would go away. The couple . . .

She heard noises from below; an angry grunt and then a murmured, "Excuse me, I . . . ," followed by the sound of booted feet ringing on the stairs.

She turned, facing the doorway, watching as it slowly opened.

"Ah, there you are," he said softly, smiling at her. "I thought . . ."

He held out her glass to her, as if she should take it, but she simply stood there, staring at him. He frowned, not understanding, then, stooping carefully, watching her all the while, he set the glasses down.

The jacket of his dress uniform seemed to glow in the light from the window. The rich scent he wore filled the tiny room.

He hesitated, then came closer. "You should have said," he said gently. "I thought you liked the music."

She could feel his breath on her cheek now; could smell the sweetness of the wine. As if in a dream she saw his right hand lift and press gently against her left shoulder, as if they were about to dance.

"Don't . . ."

"Just one kiss," he whispered, his mouth close to her ear. "Just one tiny, little kiss . . ."

She moved back, shrugging off his hand. *"Please . . ."*

She saw the movement in his face. The sudden anger, softening instantly.

"One kiss," he persisted. "You know you'd like to."

She laughed sourly. "You know that, do you?"

He laughed, the uncertainty in his eyes fading quickly. "Of course. That's why we're here, isn't it? Young girls like to be kissed. It's only natural. And you're a very beautiful young woman, Jelka Tolonen. Very beautiful indeed."

He made to touch her once again, to lift her chin and kiss her, but she pushed him back sharply, the palm of her hand thudding against his chest.

"*No.* Understand me, Lieutenant? Other 'girls' might well like it, but I don't wish to be kissed. I simply want to be left alone."

He looked down at where her hand had struck his chest, then back at her, angry now. "You shouldn't have done that."

Again she laughed. Who was he to tell her what she should or shouldn't do? She glared at him angrily, then made to push past him and go down, but he grabbed her arm roughly and pulled her about.

"You'll kiss me, understand?"

She stared at him, for that brief instant seeing things clearly. Here it was again. As in that moment when she had faced Hans Ebert in the machine, the day they had been officially betrothed. Yes, and as in that moment when the wall to the practice room had been ripped aside and the three assassins had burst in. To possess her or to kill her, there seemed no other choice for them, these half-men. Like the pure *Yang* they were, they had either to dominate or destroy.

Maybe so. But she would not acquiesce in it. Would not permit it.

She lifted her chin challengingly. "Are you drunk, Lieutenant Bachman, or just suicidal?"

His right hand was clasping her wrist. Slowly he increased the pressure on it, drawing her closer, his eyes watching her all the while, his smile brutal, unforgiving now. Slowly she moved closer, drawn in toward him, until only a hand's breadth separated them.

His left hand reached up and held her shoulder, his fingers digging into her flesh, holding her there.

"Kiss me and I'll break your neck," she warned, her voice cold now, dangerous.

He laughed, unimpressed. "Oh, I've heard the rumors, Jelka Tolonen. I've heard how you fought off the assassins that time. You're a real tigress, neh? A regular Mu-Lan. But you *will* kiss me. And you'll *not* break my neck."

There was a moment's softness in his face, a moment's relaxation, and then he tugged her toward him savagely, his face pushing out at hers, his mouth straining to find hers.

And then he was gasping, doubled up, groaning where her knee had come up hard into his stomach. Jelka stood back, breathing unevenly, looking down at him, then she turned and went down the stairs hurriedly, leaping the last four and barging unceremoniously past the couple in the doorway.

"Hey . . ."

Outside, she almost ran into her friends.

"Jelka . . ." Anna said, holding her arms and looking up into her face. "What is it?"

She drew herself up straight, then shook her head. "It's nothing . . . Really."

"Are you sure?" Yi Pang-chou said, concerned. "You look dreadful. Your face . . ."

"I'm okay," Jelka answered, rather too harshly. Then, relenting a little. "Look, it's all right. I've sorted things out. Let's go back now, okay?"

Beyond the two young women, their escorts looked on, not certain whether amusement or concern was the right expression. "Where's that randy bastard Lothar?" one of them called. "Don't tell me you've worn the young ram out!"

"Enough!" Anna said sharply, turning to them. "Can't you see something's happened?"

"Too fucking true it has!"

The voice came from behind them. From the watchtower. Bachman stood there in the doorway, one hand to his stomach, his face distorted with anger.

"You should ask the bitch what she's up to, leading me on and then kneeing me in the fucking stomach!"

Jelka turned, a cold, hard anger transforming her. If he said another word . . .

"She needs a fucking beating, that's what she needs, the spoiled little brat! She needs someone to knock some manners into her . . ."

"Lothar!" one of the young officers hissed. "Remember who she is, for fuck's sake! Her father . . ."

"Fuck her father!" Bachman snarled, then straightened up and pushed himself away from the doorway. "I don't give a shit if she runs and tells her father! That's the way of these bitches, neh? The least sign of trouble and they run and hide behind their father's skirts!"

If his words were designed to provoke, they seemed to have little or no effect. Jelka stood there, strangely relaxed, as if a weight had suddenly lifted from her.

"Lothar!"

"Don't worry," she said calmly, distanced from the words. "I fight my own battles."

"Jelka, come on, this is just silly . . ." Yi Pang-chou tugged at her sleeve, but Jelka shrugged her off.

She was half crouched now, facing him, watching him approach. He was clearly not so sure now. His hurt anger had been enough until now, but suddenly it was not so good an idea. Besides, a small crowd was forming on the steps beside the dance floor. It wouldn't do to make a scene . . .

"Ah, fuck it . . . she's just a girl."

Jelka's smile was like ice. "What's the matter, Lothar Bachman? Are you scared you might be beaten?"

Anger flared in his eyes anew. Slowly, his fingers trembling, he unbuttoned his jacket and threw it aside.

"Okay," he said. "You've had your chance."

"Why, you pompous little powder monkey!"

The reference eluded him, but the tone, cold and mocking, had its effect. With a bellow he charged at her, throwing himself forward in a kick which, if it had connected, would have shattered her lower rib cage. But she was too fast for him. As he fell, she turned, her whole body describing an arc, and kicked, the satin of her dress ripping, the hard edge of her foot smashing down into his shoulder. He cried out, but she was far from done. Savagely she kicked and punched, a kick, a punch, another kick . . .

"Jelka!"

She moved back, crouched, her bent arms raised before her as if to fend off another attack, her eyes flicking from side to side.

"Gods . . ." one of the young officers said, his face pale. "She's killed him! She's fucking well killed him!"

But Bachman wasn't dead. Not yet. Not unless four broken limbs and two shattered collarbones could kill a man.

"Kuan Yin!" Anna said, kneeling over the young man and looking back at her. "What have you done, Jelka? What in the gods' names have you done?"

Nothing, she thought, straightening up slowly. *At least, nothing you'd understand.*

━━━━━━

K'ANG A-YIN, gang boss of the Tu Sun *tong,* looked about him, then nodded, satisfied that all was well. His headquarters were four decks up from the Net, on Level 50. A respectable height for a man who, not so long ago, had had nothing but the strength of his hands and the wit he had been born with. He had bought and converted one side of a corridor, turning it into a suite of rooms, some of them interconnected offices, the rest—by far the greater part—his personal quarters. Between was one long room created out of three living spaces, which was where he held his meetings and greeted his guests.

It was an oddly luxurious room for this low level. The floor was carpeted and wall-hangings covered the bareness of the ice. A long sofa, made of ersatz leather, took up the whole of the left-hand wall. Nearby was a low table, and against the far wall stood a bar. To anyone born into the Lowers, as K'ang had been, it was impressive, yet underlying its apparent luxury was a basic shabbiness. The carpet was faded and worn, the leather scuffed and shiny in places; the bottles lining the glass frontage of the bar were genuine enough, but their sour contents had been distilled in vats not far from where they now rested.

K'ang A-yin, standing in the doorway, felt a profound satisfaction in what he saw. The walls were free of graffiti, the floor swept clean. It smelled good and in many ways it resembled those images of the Above that filtered down through the medium of the MedFac soaps. As ever when he expected someone new, he was looking forward to that first look of surprise in their face. Rubbing his hands together, he laughed throatily and turned to his lieutenant.

"Well, Soucek? What do you think the bastard wants?"

K'ang's lieutenant, Soucek, was an exercise in contrast to his boss. A tall, almost spiderish man, he had a face designed for mourning: long and bony, with slate-gray eyes that were like the eyes of a dead fish, and lips that seemed drawn by the finest of needles to a tight slit. He was a man of few words.

"A deal. Maybe a partnership."

"A partnership . . ." K'ang laughed, but his eyes were cold, calculating. He had lost four men to Lehmann already, and there was the growing feeling among the rest that this new man was some kind of power. He cut his laughter off abruptly and turned away, sniffing in deeply.

He had toyed with the idea of bringing Lehmann here and killing him. That would be simplest, easiest. But something stopped him. He had failed once, and besides, maybe he *could* use him. Make him a lieutenant, like Soucek. The idea attracted K'ang. With such a man in harness who knew what he might achieve? He might even drive Lo Han back in the north and gain access to the lucrative drug trade that came down from Munich stack. And who knew what might come of that?

K'ang looked up again, meeting Soucek's eyes, a faint smile on his well-fleshed face. "Okay. Set things up. Let's meet the bastard."

━━━━━━━

K'ANG WAS SITTING on the leather sofa, cradling a tumbler of wine in his left hand, when Soucek came in.

"He's here." Soucek laughed; a strange sound coming from that humorless face. "And he's alone. There's no sign of his two henchmen."

K'ang took that in, then nodded. "Good. Bring him in. And make sure there are three or four of our best men in here with us. I don't want to take any chances. Is he armed?"

"Maybe," said Soucek. "He said he'd kill the first man that tried to frisk him."

K'ang laughed uncomfortably. Waving Soucek away, he got up

heavily and walked across to the bar. Refilling his glass, he went through what he knew of Lehmann once more, looking for a handle. The strangest thing was that Lehmann had no history. One moment he hadn't been there; the next, there he was. His two associates, Haller and Becker, were faces from the Munich underworld. They had worked for Lo Han before they'd crossed him. Somehow Lehmann had bossed it over them, then, without warning, had muscled in on his, K'ang's, territory. And that was it. The sum total. Except that Lehmann was trained. And, if the reports were accurate, he had heavy munitions. The sort Security used.

So was he a plant? A Security infiltrator? The possibility had made K'ang check through his contacts, costing him dearly for a simple "No." But even before he'd had it confirmed, he had ruled it out. Why should Security bother with the likes of him? They had bigger fish to fry. And anyway, he paid his dues—not light ones either—to keep their eyes turned aside.

Whatever he was, Lehmann didn't fit. And K'ang, who wanted some kind of peace in those stacks and levels the *Kuei Chuan* Triad allowed him to control, needed him to fit. A deal would be best, but if not a deal, then he'd try again. And again, until Lehmann was a corpse.

That thought was in his mind as he turned to face the door.

Soucek was standing there, one thin-boned hand on the jamb, his body turned away from K'ang, looking out into the corridor. From another door, behind K'ang and to his right, came three of his best men. Killers. Good men to have behind you in a situation like this.

K'ang sipped at his wine, then nodded to himself, knowing how he would play it. As he watched, Soucek backed into the room slowly and stood to the side. The shape of his gun showed clearly through the thin material of his trousers, his hand hovering close by. K'ang smiled at him, as if to say, "Leave this to me," then moved forward a pace.

At that moment Lehmann came into the room.

There was a sudden, perceptible heightening of tension in the room. Two things were evident at once. Lehmann was tall, taller even than the gangly Soucek. And he was an albino. Skin and hair were a deathly white—a pallor emphasized by the whiteness of his simple, armless tunic and his close-fitting trousers. Even his gun, which he held loosely in his left hand, the barrel pointed at the floor, was painted white. White . . . the color of death.

K'ang heard the sharp indraw of breath of the men behind him. The muscle in his right cheek twitched, but he controlled it and slowly raised a hand in welcome, meeting the albino's eyes. He smiled, exuding confidence, but at the pit of his stomach he was experiencing something he hadn't felt in years. Fear. A plain, naked fear.

―――――

AT FIRST Lehmann let K'ang A-yin do all the talking, knowing that his simple presence there, silent among them, the big gun resting in his hand, was eloquent enough. He had seen at once how it was— saw where the real power lay—and, behind the solemn mask of his face, had smiled.

"I can use you," K'ang was saying for the third time. "With me you could go far. I'd reward you well. Look after you."

K'ang was a big man, broad at the shoulders and well-muscled, but some of that muscle had gone to fat and there were definite signs of a paunch developing. K'ang had grown lazy, self-indulgent. Like most of these low-level *tong* bosses he had grown accustomed to the small luxuries that surrounded him. Moving up, he had cut himself off from the immediacy of the Lowers; had forgotten what had given him his power. Soucek, his deputy, was the real power here. Neither knew it, but the time would have come when Soucek challenged him for control. Now there was no need, for he, Lehmann, had preempted that struggle.

He let his eyes stray a moment, letting no sign of his distaste for the drabness, the sheer ugliness of the room, register on his face. This was the worst of it, he sometimes felt; not the claustrophobic *inwardness* of everything here, nor the overcrowded poverty of life in the Lowers, but the ugliness, the unmitigated absence of anything that pleased the eye. More than that he missed the mountains, the cold, sharp fresh-ness of the air. Missed the purity of the ice.

"All right," he said, the words so sudden, so out of context, that K'ang's face wrinkled up, not understanding.

"I said all right," he repeated, tucking the gun into the strengthened web holster inside the top of his trousers. "I join you as lieutenant. Equal to Soucek here." He indicated the tall, gangly man without looking at him. "My two men . . . they work with me still, right?"

He could see that K'ang didn't like that. It meant divided loyalties. For a moment K'ang hesitated, then he nodded and held out his hand to make the bargain. It was a large, strong hand, but warm and overfleshed. There were rings on three of the fingers. By contrast Lehmann's hand was like steel, inflexible and cold.

"One further thing," Lehmann said, extending the handshake unnaturally, seemingly oblivious of K'ang's unease. "Your man, K'ang Yeh-su."

K'ang looked down at his hand, then back up at Lehmann. "What of him?"

"Get rid of him."

"Why?"

"Because he warned me. Sold me information about you."

There was a movement in K'ang's face that betrayed not merely surprise but shock. K'ang Yeh-su was his nephew. His sister's son. For a moment he said nothing. Then, "Why do you tell me this?"

"Because he's weak. Corrupt. He would sell anyone for the same price." Lehmann hesitated, then added, "And because I'm your man now, aren't I?"

For a moment longer he held K'ang's hand, then, as if he had tired of the game, released it. But K'ang hardly noticed. Freed, he turned away and signaled to one of his men. "Bring Yeh-su. Say nothing to him. Just bring him."

〰〰〰

"Jelka? Is that you?"

Jelka turned, making her way back down the unlit corridor to her father's study.

"Yes, Papa?"

The Marshal sat at his big oak desk, a stack of papers to one side, a file open before him, his hands, one flesh, one golden metal, resting on the page. He looked tired, but then he always looked tired these days, and his smile at least was as strong as ever.

"How did it go?"

She hesitated. He would find out. He was sure to find out. But not yet. Not before she'd had time to think things through. "I don't know . . ." She shrugged and gave a little sigh. "It's not my thing, really. I . . ."

He laughed softly. "You don't have to tell me, my love. I know that feeling only too well. I used to think it was me, but I know better now. We're not party people, we Tolonens. Our ancestors were made of sterner stuff, neh? All that northern ice—some of it must have got into our blood!"

His laughter was warm, wonderful, and for a moment she simply stood there, basking in it. But in the morning he would be different—when he discovered what she'd done. So maybe it was best . . .

She moved closer, until she stood there, facing him across the desk, looking down at him. "I . . . I did something tonight, Papa. I . . . hurt someone."

"You hurt someone?" He frowned, trying to understand, then gave a short laugh. "What? You mean, you broke their heart?"

She shook her head. "No. One of the young officers, it was. My escort for the evening. Lieutenant Bachman. He tried . . ."

Tolonen sat forward, his face changed; suddenly stern, implacable. "What? What did he try?"

She looked away briefly, wondering how it had got to this point; why she had let it get out of control. "He tried to kiss me, Papa. Against my wishes. He . . . he was persistent."

He sat back, indignation and anger written large on his face. "Bachman, you say? Colonel Bachman's son?"

"Yes, Papa. But please . . . listen. I hurt him, you see. Hurt him badly."

"Badly? How badly?"

She swallowed. "I think I nearly killed him. If Anna hadn't shouted at me . . ."

He narrowed his eyes, then shook his head. "You mean, you nearly killed a man, and all because he wanted to kiss you?"

"It wasn't *like* that, Papa. He . . . he was awful. It was as if I didn't exist. As if he had the right . . ." She shuddered and looked down, realizing she had clenched both her fists. "Even so, in the end I provoked him. I *made* him fight me. I could have walked away, but I didn't. I don't know why . . . I . . ." She stopped, looking back at her father. "Do you understand, Papa? Something snapped in me. Something . . ."

He stared back at her a moment, then nodded. His voice was soft now, almost a whisper. "I understand, my love. It's how we are, neh? Brittle. That time I killed Lehmann in the House. It was like that then. As if I had no choice. As if I'd lost control."

For a moment they were silent, staring at each other. Then, with a tiny shudder, Tolonen looked away, fixing his gaze on the file in front of him. "He'll live, I take it?"

"Yes."

He looked up again, a strange kind of pride in his face. "So what did you do to him? Kick him in the balls? Break his nose?"

"I wish it were that simple. I . . ." She shook her head, suddenly exasperated with herself. "It wasn't even as if I was angry at that point. It was like . . . like it was just something I had to do. I . . . well, you'll think this strange, but it was like it was Hans in front of me. Hans Ebert. And I had to stop him coming after me. That's why I broke both his legs, to stop him. And his arms."

He stared at her, astonished, then sniffed in deeply. "*Aiya* . . . And were there any witnesses to this?"

"Several dozen . . ."

For a moment he sat there, deep in thought, then, remembering something suddenly, he got up and went across to the other side of the room, where a long worktop filled the alcove.

"Something was delivered about an hour back," he said, searching among the papers there. "It wasn't marked urgent and I was busy, so I left it. It's here somewhere."

She watched him, wondering what was going on in his mind at that moment. Did he really understand why she had done it? Or was he only saying that? He would stand by her, certainly, because that was his way, but for once that was not enough. She needed him to understand. Because if *he* didn't understand . . .

"Here," he said, turning back to her and slitting open the package with his thumbnail. "If it's as you said. If it was a fair fight . . ."

He fell silent, reading through the brief report. She watched him come to the end of it, then read it once again. He nodded, as if satisfied, then looked back at her.

"We'll sit down, tomorrow, first thing, and make a report. In your own words, exactly as it happened. Then I'll go and see Bachman, sort something out about his son's medical expenses. The rest . . . well, I think it's straightforward enough. It'll teach the lad manners, neh? And maybe wake a few of them up, into the bargain." He looked away, giving a tight bark of laughter. "They're growing soft, these young men. Soft . . ."

"Papa . . . ?"

He looked back at her, seeing how she stood there, close—suddenly very close—to tears, and came across, holding her to him tightly.

"It's all right, my love. It's all over now." He looked down into her face, then gently kissed her brow.

"You understand, then? You understand why I did it?"

He nodded, his grim smile fading into concern. "It's how we are, my love. Brittle. Easily angered. But strong, too, neh? Stronger than iron."

CHAPTER THREE

Fathers and Sons

L I YUAN stood inside the doorway, looking across to where the T'ang of East Asia lay in a huge, canopied bed. The room was bright and unexpectedly airy. A warm breeze blew in through the open doors that led out onto the balcony, the scent of apple blossom strong in the air. Yet underlying it was the faintest hint of corruption. Of sickness and age.

"Wei Feng . . ." Yuan said softly, his heart torn from him at the sight of his father's oldest friend.

The old man turned his head on the pillow, his voice faint, almost inaudible. "Shai Tung? Is that you?"

Li Yuan swallowed and moved closer. "It is I, cousin Feng. Shai Tung's son, Yuan."

"Ahh . . ." Blind eyes searched the darkness whence the voice had come, looking past the young T'ang of Europe. The voice was stronger now, more confident. "Forgive me, Yuan. I was dreaming . . . Your father and I were walking in the meadow. We stopped beneath a tree . . ."

Yuan waited, but there was nothing more. "How are you, cousin?" he said gently, fearing the old man had drifted back into sleep.

"Ah yes . . ." Wei Feng's laughter was weak; the merest shadow of the great roar of delight Yuan remembered from his childhood. Yuan felt his stomach muscles tighten with pain at the thought. Was it all so quickly gone?

"Where are your sons?" Yuan asked, surprised to find himself alone with the old man. "Should I summon them, Wei Feng?"

The old man's head came round, his blind eyes staring up into Yuan's face. The hair had not grown back on the half of his skull that had been shaven, and the flesh there was a pale ivory, mottled, almost transparent. One could see the bone clearly.

"No, Yuan," the old man said determinedly. Old age and sickness had robbed Wei Feng of much, but his mind seemed as sharp as ever. "It is you I wished to see. I . . ."

The old man swallowed dryly, unable to continue. Li Yuan looked about him, then saw the jug and the cup on the table behind him and went across. He poured a little of the water into the cup, then brought it back, supporting Wei Feng's head while he sipped; then, setting the cup aside, he wiped his lips for him.

"Thank you, Yuan. You are your father's son."

Once again, it was painful to see the thin, watery smile the old man gave and recall the strength of former days. It made him feel that this ought not to be—that this great fall from health and potency was a kind of sin against life itself. He looked away momentarily, robbed of words. Why had he not felt this for his own father?

There was a moment's silence and then the old man reached out, his frail hand searching for Li Yuan's. Yuan took it, clasping it in both of his, holding it firmly yet tenderly, his fingers stroking its back.

Wei Feng's face looked up into his, the clouded eyes turned inward. It was a drawn and ancient face, creased deeply by time and care, the skin blotched and discolored like faded parchment.

"I am dying, Yuan. My surgeons tell me otherwise, but I know it is only days now before my time here is done and I go to join my ancestors. That does not distress me. Life has been good. I have been fortunate, both in my friends and in my wives and sons. I look back and see much happiness. But I am not sad to be leaving the world above, for I have seen what is to come. Dark clouds are forming, Yuan. A great storm is coming. A storm so dark, so fierce it will be like nothing ever witnessed by the eyes of man."

A faint shudder passed through him. For a moment his face was pained, then it cleared, a look of wonder filling those ancient features.

"I have been dreaming, Yuan. Strange, powerful dreams. Again and again I have seen it . . ."

"Seen what, cousin Feng?"

Wei Feng laughed as if amused, but the amusement quickly faded from his lips. His voice was a hoarse whisper.

"An egg it was, Yuan. A great egg nestled in the earth. They give painted eggs to celebrate a marriage, neh? Or to invalids, to wish them a speedy recovery. But this egg was different. It was like the great egg itself—the *hun tun*—from which the ten thousand things came forth. Moreover, it was purest white, like a great stone, polished and shining in the light that came from nowhere. It lay there, nestled in the dark earth, and the people came from all around to see it. It was huge, Yuan. The biggest man seemed as a child beside it. I stood there, among the crowd, watching, waiting for the egg to hatch. Across from me, behind the bloodred curtains of her sedan, a bride sat waiting in a high-backed chair. I glanced at her, studying her in silhouette, then looked back at the egg. Between my looking away and looking back it had changed. Now it was stippled with tiny cracks that ran from base to tip. Slowly they darkened. A bell sounded—a single, perfect note, pure and high. As if at a signal, the shell shattered into a thousand tiny pieces. And now a man stood there, clothed in darkness, his back to me. He was huge, taller than any man I had ever seen."

Wei Feng paused, getting his breath, his thin, darkly blotched tongue tracing the length of his lips.

"Shall I get you more water, cousin?" Li Yuan asked, but Wei Feng shook his head.

"Let me finish." The old man swallowed dryly, then went on. "I looked across again. The curtains of the sedan were drawn back now and I could see the bride. She was smiling. The kind of smile that lasts ten thousand years. Her wedding dress hung in tatters from her bones. Nails of black iron secured her to the chair. I looked back. The man was turning. Slowly, he turned. And as he turned, all those who fell beneath his gaze dropped to the ground, writhing in agony, as if smitten by some sudden, virulent plague."

Slowly the old man's grip on Yuan's hand had tightened. Now it relaxed, a look of puzzlement coming into that ancient face.

"And the man, Wei Feng . . . did you see his face?"

Wei Feng frowned deeply, then gave the tiniest of nods. "It was *him*, Yuan. It was DeVore. But changed somehow. Enlarged. Made somehow greater than he was in life." The old man shuddered, then turned his head away. "I have had this dream a dozen, twenty times and each time I wake before he turns to face me fully. But I have no doubt. It *was* him. That profile. I could not forget it. Yes, I can see him even now, smiling, his hands outstretched, facing his bride."

Li Yuan shivered. *Dreams.* Was this where the first signs appeared—in dreams? And was all that followed merely a working out of what was first glimpsed in dream?

"What time is it, Yuan?"

Li Yuan turned, looking out. "It is late, Wei Feng. The afternoon is almost done."

"Ahh . . ." Wei Feng nodded. Then, unexpectedly, he drew Yuan's hand to his lips and kissed the great iron ring—the ring of power Li Yuan had inherited from his father and his father's father, the great seal of the *Ywe Lung*, the wheel of seven dragons, imprinted in its face.

Li Yuan frowned, disturbed by the old man's gesture. This was not something done lightly, nor on whim; he could see that by the way Wei Feng stared up at him, his sightless eyes imploring him to understand. But he understood nothing; only that this dear, kind man—this confidant and ally, this strong and friendly presence from his childhood—would soon be gone from the world. Gone, as if he'd never been.

And afterward, outside in the cold and silent corridors, he stopped and looked down, noticing for the first time that there was earth on the hem of his gown. Earth . . . He lifted his hand, staring at the great iron ring, then walked on, his movements stiff with regret, knowing he would never see Wei Feng alive again.

━━━━━━

IT WAS LATE afternoon before Li Yuan got back to Tongjiang. Stopping only to shower and change, he went directly to his study and sat there at his desk, his Chancellor, Nan Ho, before him, Chang Shih-sen, his secretary, at his side. Outside, in the Eastern Garden, his three wives sat beside the lotus pool, laughing and talking, their maids in attendance. For a moment he looked out, watching them, the shadow of his earlier meeting with Wei Feng forgotten, his eyes drawn to the new maid—the wet nurse—seeing how she attended to the hunger of his eight-week-old son, Kuei Jen. She was a pretty young thing, well-formed and with a delicate, pouting mouth. He felt his sex stir at the thought of what that mouth might do and looked down, a faint thrill of anticipated pleasure rippling through him.

He turned back, facing his Chancellor again, a faint smile on his lips.

"You wish me to arrange something, *Chieh Hsia?*"

Li Yuan laughed. "Am I so transparent, Master Nan?"

"You are a man, *Chieh Hsia*, with a man's appetites. Besides, your First Wife, Mien Shan, suggested it to me only the other day. She too, it seems, has noticed your interest."

Li Yuan studied Nan Ho a moment, then nodded. "Arrange it, Master Nan. We have but one life, neh?"

"It is done, *Chieh Hsia*. Now . . . if we might begin."

It was the kind of gentle admonishment Li Yuan had come to expect from his Chancellor. Another might have viewed it as impertinence, but he knew better. Master Nan had been with him since his sixth year, first as his body servant, then as his Master of the Inner Chambers. Recognizing his qualities, Li Yuan had sidestepped the usual channels when he had come to the dragon throne, eighteen months back, and promoted the industrious Nan Ho—a man without family connections—to his most senior administrative post. It had been a bold and unexpected move and had caused ripples at the time, but he had had no reason to regret his decision. Nan Ho had proved himself the perfect statesman, attending to Li Yuan's business as if it were his own. Indeed, there was no more loyal servant in Chung Kuo. Unless it was Tolonen.

Li Yuan sat back, staring at the great stack of state papers that were piled up to the right of his desk. This was his daily burden—the great weight he had taken on at his father's death. Reports from his *Hsien L'ing*, commissioned studies on the effects of proposed legislation, warrants to be signed or queried, petitions from senior Above citizens, preparatory drafts for Council, Security summaries, and more. Endless, it all seemed. Enough to keep a room full of clerks busy for a week.

He half turned, looking up at Chang Shih-sen. At this customary signal, Chang handed him the first paper. For the next hour or so the great pile slowly diminished, but they were far from done when Li Yuan sat back and, with a laugh, gestured for Chang to take the rest away. He turned, facing his Chancellor.

"Look at us, Master Nan, sitting here while the sun is shining outside! Let us deal with these tomorrow, neh?"

Nan Ho made to comment, then changed his mind. He could see that Li Yuan was determined not to work that day. Smiling, he bowed low. "As you wish, *Chieh Hsia.* But I must remind you that you have dinner at your cousin, Tsu Ma's, estate this evening. We must be there at nine. Wu Shih has confirmed that he will be attending."

"Good . . . Good!" The young T'ang clapped his hands. "Then come. Let us join my wives. It is a fine afternoon, neh?"

They went outside, Nan Ho sending a servant running to bring wine and tumblers. The women were beside the pool, laughing, sharing some secret joke. As the men came out, they turned, almost as one, their laughter fading, then stood, bowing their heads, the maids kneeling in their T'ang's presence.

"Where is my son?" Li Yuan asked, looking about him, surprised not to see the wet nurse there among the group by the pool.

"He is here, *Chieh Hsia,*" a voice said from just behind him.

He turned, smiling, remembering suddenly what he had agreed with Nan Ho earlier. The girl handed the child to him, then knelt, the faintest color in her cheeks. She knew. He could tell she knew.

"Kuei Jen . . ." he said softly, transferring his attention to the child in his arms. "And how is my darling little boy?"

The child stared up at him, cooing softly, his dark eyes round with curiosity, his face the tiny image of his mother's. Li Yuan looked across, laughing, and saw how Mien Shan was watching him, her eyes moist with happiness, and for the briefest moment he thought of Wei Feng and what he had said to him on his sickbed. Life *was* good, if one let it be.

He turned, facing the sun. Then, as if compelled, he lifted the child, holding him up at arm's length, as if offering him up. And when he turned back, the child cradled against him once more, he saw how they looked at him, in awe, as at that moment when he had stepped down from the Temple of Heaven, wearing the dragon robes for the first time.

"My son," he said, looking about him, fiercely proud, seeing how his words affected them, even the seemingly imperturbable Nan Ho. "My *son.*"

━━◆◆◆◆◆◆━━

ON THE EAST COAST of North America it was dawn, and amid the low, flower-strewn screens of the Tea House of the Ninth Dragon it was busy. Maroon-cloaked waiters moved between the crowded tables, their faces impassive, the heavily laden trays they bore swept effortlessly above their patrons' heads. At the tables, wizen-faced graybeards sat there in their stiff-collared jackets, smoking and playing *Chou* or *Siang Chi*, ignoring the muted screens set high up on the pillars on every side. From two big speakers set either side of the long *ch'a* counter, the romantic strains of "Love at the Fair" drifted across the teahouse, competing with the babble of the old men. It was a timeless scene—a scene as old as history itself. For three thousand years old men had gathered thus, to smoke and talk and drink their bowls of *ch'a*.

Kim sat at a small table at the back of the tea house, up a level, on a narrow veranda overlooking the main floor, a white- and maroon-glazed *chung* of freshly brewed *min hung*—"Fukien Red"—in front of him, a small bowl of soyprawn crackers by his elbow.

He had first come here three months back, to kill an hour before a meeting, and had found himself still sitting there three hours later, his appointment forgotten, the tiny notepad he carried filled with jottings, his head bursting with new ideas. Now he came here most mornings at this hour, to sit and sip *ch'a*, and think.

Sometimes he would go down among the tables and sit there for an hour or two, listening to the homely wisdom of the old men, but mostly he would sit here, looking out across the busy floor, and let his mind freewheel. Today, however, was special, for earlier this morning—after a tiring all-night session—he had put the finishing touches to the first of the five new patents he had been working on: patents he had first conceived here at the Ninth Dragon.

He smiled, wondering what the old men would have made of it had he shared some of his ideas with them: whether they would have thought him sage or madman. Whichever, there was no doubting that they would have found them strange. His idea for a new kind of protein machine that could operate in space, for instance: that had been conceived here, at this table, while watching the old men blow their smoke rings in the air.

In one sense the problem had been a simple one. For the past two hundred years, most scientific engineering had been done at the microscopic level, using two basic "tools," NPMs and NPAs. The standard NPMs—natural protein machines—that companies like GenSyn used to engineer their products, while extremely versatile, were highly susceptible to heat variations, operating within a very limited temperature range. NPAs—nonprotein assemblers—made of harder, more predictable molecules, were stronger and more stable than the NPMs and were therefore used wherever possible in the manufacture of most technological hardware. However, when it came to the more sensitive areas of genetic engineering, most Companies still used NPMs.

In terms of cost it didn't matter which one used, under normal conditions, but these days an increasing amount of manufacturing was done in the great orbital factories, under sterile, zero-gravity conditions.

At present the potentially much cheaper conditions of manufacture that appertained in the orbital factories were applicable only to non-living processes: for the production of basic "hardware." For all other processes—for food production, say, or biotechnology, where NPMs *had* to be used—the savings were partly offset by the need to maintain an atmosphere on board the factory ships and to keep that atmosphere at an unfluctuating and—relative to the surrounding cold of space—high temperature. Cut out that need and the savings would be the same as for those factories that used NPAs; that is, somewhere between fifteen and twenty percent of the total manufacturing cost.

It was a huge saving, and the development company that could patent a protein-based nanomachine that could operate in extreme cold and under vacuum conditions was certain to enjoy vast profits.

Kim drew the *chung* toward him and raised it to his mouth. Lifting the rounded lid he tilted it gently and took a sip of the sweet black *ch'a*.

It was a problem he had set himself a long time back—long before Li Yuan had given him the means to set up his own company—and for a while he had thought it insoluble. How could one make a living thing that operated in the absence of those very things that sustained it—heat and air? The two processes seemed and surely were inimical. Even so, he had persisted, and, sitting there, watching the smoke rings curl from those ancient mouths and climb the air, had glimpsed how it might be done. Now, three months on from that insight, he had finally worked it out—down to the smallest detail. He had only to write the process up and patent it.

He set the *chung* down, smiling, the tiredness in his bones balanced against the sense of achievement he was feeling. Not only was his solution aesthetically pleasing, but it also kept well within the rigid guidelines of the Edict. The principles he'd utilized were old and well documented; it was merely the way he'd put them together that was new.

Smoke rings. He laughed, and took a deep swig of the *ch'a.* It was all so very simple, really . . .

"*Shih* Ward?"

Kim turned. The Head Waiter, Chiang Su-li, stood there, his head bowed, a few paces from the table.

"Yes, Master Chiang?"

Chiang bobbed his head, then handed across a message tab. "Forgive me, *Shih* Ward, but a messenger brought this a moment back. He said I was to place it directly into your hands."

"Thank you, Master Chiang." Kim fished in the pocket of his jacket for a five *yuan* coin, then held it out, offering it to Chiang.

Chiang made no move to take the coin. "I thank you, *Shih* Ward, but it is enough that you honor us with your presence at our humble tea house. If you will allow me, I will bring a fresh *chung* of the *min hung.*"

Kim stared at Chiang a moment, surprised, wondering what he had heard, then smiled. "That would be most pleasant, Master Chiang. It is a most excellent brew."

Chiang bowed, pleased by the compliment, then turned away, leaving Kim alone.

For a moment Kim sat there, staring at the blank face of the message card, tempted to throw it away unread. Old Man Lever had made over a dozen "offers" this last year, each one more outrageous than the last. It was five weeks since the latest and Kim had been expecting something any day. So what was the old tyrant offering now? A partnership? A half share in his empire? Whatever it was, it wasn't enough. Nothing—not even the whole of ImmVac's vast holdings—could persuade him to work for Lever.

Kim looked out across the smoke-wreathed floor and sighed. When would Lever finally understand that he didn't want to work for him? Why couldn't he just accept that and leave him alone? What drove the old man that he kept on upping the terms, convinced that it was only a question of finding the right price?

Death, Kim thought. *The fear of death, that's what drives you. And you think I can find an answer to that. You've convinced yourself that I can succeed where a hundred generations of taoists and alchemists have failed, and unlock that last great secret. And maybe you're right. Maybe I could. Or at least some counterfeit of immortality—a hundred years of youth, perhaps.*

Yes, but the truth is that I wouldn't, even if I could. Not even if it meant that I too could live forever.

He shuddered, the strength of his aversion for the old man surprising him; then, curiosity overcoming his anger, he pressed his thumb against the release pad.

For a moment a combination of tiredness and false expectation made him sit there blankly, a look of incomprehension on his face. Then, with a laugh, he understood. Michael . . . The message was from Michael Lever, not his father.

Even so, it was fifteen months since he had last seen Michael Lever, that night of the Thanksgiving Ball, and though they had been friends, much had happened between times. He could not be certain that the man he had known was the same as the one who wanted to see him now. Indeed, if the rumors were true, he had changed a great deal. But for good or ill?

Besides which, Michael wanted to meet him tonight, at ten o'clock. Normally that wouldn't have been a problem, but after a night without sleep . . .

Kim smiled. There were pills he could take to keep him awake. Besides, it would do him good to have an evening off to see an old friend. And maybe Michael could give him some advice. He'd been out of circulation, sure, but things hadn't changed that much while he'd been away. What he knew about the market was still valid. So maybe . . .

Kim set the card down, watching the message slowly fade, then looked across. At the *ch'a* counter, Master Chiang was setting out his tray with careful, precise little movements that were characteristic of the man. Kim watched him a while, then looked down, smiling. Yes, it would be good to see Michael again. Very good indeed.

———————

THE DOOR WAS OPEN, the tiny reception room empty save for a dust-strewn desk and an unpainted stool. Emily Ascher stood there in the doorway, holding tight to the stack of files and boxes that was balanced beneath her chin, wondering if she had come to the right place. For a moment she thought of checking the note Michael had sent her, but there was little point; she knew what was written there. *Suite 225*, it read; *East Corridor, Level 224, North Edison stack.* Turning, she nodded to her guide, dismissing him, then went inside, putting the files down on the desk.

She straightened up and looked about her, noting the shabbiness of the place. The walls were strewn with old posters, the floor bare, unswept in months. It had the look of a repossession.

"So this is it, neh?" she said softly and smiled to herself. She had expected something grander; something more in keeping with the Michael Lever she had worked with before his arrest. But this . . .

She went across and closed the door, then turned, hearing voices from beyond the inner door. Male voices, laughing.

She slid the door open and went through, into a big, open-plan office. Michael was sitting on the edge of a long laboratory-style desk on the far side of the room. Nearby, sprawled in a chair, sat a second man; a short-haired athletic-looking man of about Michael's age. Seeing Emily, the two men fell silent, looking across at her.

"Mary . . ." Michael said, pushing up from the desk and coming across, clearly delighted that she was there. "You found us all right, then?"

She smiled, barely conscious of the use of her adopted name. "It was no trouble. I've been down this way before . . . on business."

"I see . . ." He stood there a moment, simply smiling at her, then turned suddenly, as if he had forgotten, and put his arm out, indicating the other man. "I'm sorry . . . look, I've forgotten how to do all this. This here is Bryn . . . Bryn Kustow. He's an old friend. He was at College with me. And . . . well, other things. And this, Bryn, is Mary Jennings."

Emily met the young man's eyes and gave a brief nod, understanding. By "other things" Michael meant that Kustow had been arrested. He too had been one of Wu Shih's "guests" these past fifteen months. She could see it in his eyes. Could see how much the experience had changed these young men.

"It's not much as yet," Michael went on, looking about him at the big, unfurnished room, "but we're going to make it something." He looked back at her. "That's if you're going to join us."

She narrowed her eyes. "Pardon?"

He took a step closer. "Look, I know how it is. It's a big decision. And you might think that you don't want to risk making an enemy of my father, but . . ."

"Hold on," she said, laughing. "You're not making sense. What decision? And why should I be making an enemy of your father?"

There was a moment's puzzlement in his face, and then he laughed. "Shit . . . I didn't say, did I?"

"No. You just told me to come here. Friday, first thing. And to bring what I'd need to start work at once. I thought . . ."

"You thought this was just another of my father's Companies, neh? You thought you'd still be on the payroll." He looked away, embarrassed now. "Look, I'm sorry. I'll spell it out. Then, if you don't like what you hear, you can just turn round and leave, and no one will be the wiser, okay?"

She stared back at him a moment, then looked across at Kustow, seeing how closely he was watching her; as if recruiting her for some secret brotherhood.

"You're setting up on your own, aren't you?" she said, looking back at Michael. "A partnership. You and *Shih* Kustow here. Is that right?"

He nodded.

"And you want me to join, right? As what? Personal assistant to you both?"

Kustow sat forward. "At first, yes. But hopefully it won't stay that way. We plan to run things differently. We'll match your present salary, of course. But you'll also be on bonuses. A share of profits. If things go well, you can buy in. Become a partner."

"I see. And all I have to do is break contract with ImmVac and make an enemy of the most powerful businessman in City North America?"

Michael reached out and gently touched her arm. "Look, it's okay. You can say no. And we won't blame you if you do. But just consider things a moment. It's a whole new venture. Something that won't come along twice in your career. To be in at the start of something like this . . ."

"And my contract with ImmVac? There's a hefty breach clause, you realize?"

"We've budgeted for that," Kustow said, matter-of-factly. He stood up and came across, standing next to Michael. "All you've got to do is decide whether you want in or not."

"And just what is this venture?"

Kustow smiled for the first time. "Near-space technologies. The kind of things our fathers wouldn't normally touch."

She laughed. "Too right. That field is sewn up tight."

"Right now it is," Michael agreed, "but change is coming. There are rumors that the Seven want to make a deal with the Above. A deal that'll mean a radical rewriting of the Edict of Technology. Things are going to open up, and when they do, we plan to be there, at the cutting edge."

"I see. And all I have to do is say yes."

The two men looked at each other, then back at her, nodding.

She was quiet a moment, considering. It was a big decision. If she took this step there was no turning back. Old Man Lever would make damn sure of that. No, she had seen how he'd reacted that night Michael had said no to him; had been witness to the private scenes afterward. You didn't cross swords with Charles Lever. Not unless you wanted to make an enemy of him for life. Common sense, therefore, told her to say no. To turn around and get out of there at once. But for once common sense held no sway. After all, she hadn't come to America to carve herself out a safe career. She'd come here to do something positive; to change things. It was time, then, that she stopped running; that she dug in and did something she believed in.

She looked back at them. They were watching her; somberly, expectantly. How well she knew that look. How often she'd seen it, back in the old days, in City Europe. "Okay," she said, smiling broadly. "Count me in."

"Great!" Michael said, beaming, slapping Kustow on the back. "Bloody great! All we need now is a research scientist and a patents man."

"That and a lot of money," Kustow said, grinning, his eyes meeting Emily's briefly to thank her. "A huge pile of money!"

* * *

OLD MAN LEVER strode out onto the podium of the great lecture hall and looked about him imperiously. His gaze swept across the empty tiers, then returned to the two great screens that dominated the wall to the right of where he stood.

"I like it," he said finally, his voice booming in that great echoing space. "I like it a lot. It's exactly what I envisaged."

Behind him, the four-man design team looked among themselves with expressions of relief and triumph. It had been hard going satisfying the Old Man, but now it was done, the building finished to his precise specifications. And not before time. In three weeks the hall would be filled to bursting for the inauguration ceremony. Before then there was much to do: laboratory equipment had to be installed, personnel hired and trained, not to mention the countless items of decor—Lever's "final touches"—that had to be seen to between now and then. Even so, to have reached this stage at all seemed a miracle of sorts. Six months back, when things had been at their worst, not one of them had believed the project would ever see completion, not because what was asked of them was impossible, but because of Lever's constant meddling in their work—his abrupt changes of mind and irritating refusal to trust their judgment at any stage. The pay had been good, true, but he had ridden them hard.

Not that their experience was unique. In every area Old Man Lever had not only insisted that they hire the best in the field but that he be allowed to sit in on their consultation sessions. More than once he had overridden specialist advice, determined to stamp his own view on things, only to return, each time after a long, frustrating delay, to the very thing he'd first rejected, and with never a word that he'd been in the wrong.

But so it was with Lever. It was as if the man were obsessed. As if this one project, this single huge building and what it held, consumed him, blinding him to all else. And now, standing there at the center of his creation, he glowed with a satisfaction that seemed much more than the sense of achievement one usually got from a job well done.

"Where's Curval?" he said, half turning toward them. "Has anyone seen the man?"

"I'll bring him, Mister Lever," the Architect said, recognizing that tone of impatience in the Old Man's voice.

Fourteen and a half billion it had cost. Twice the original estimate. But not once had Lever balked about the cost. "Money's irrelevant," he had said at one point, to the astonishment of the Project Accountant. And so it had proved. Never once had he skimped to cut costs. No, the problem had been one of time. Of getting the thing done in time for the ceremony. As if it were a race . . .

Curval arrived, making his way between them, the great geneticist hesitating, glancing at them uncertainly before he walked out onto the broad platform. "Good luck," one said softly, almost inaudibly. "Poor bastard," another mouthed silently as they turned to leave, bringing a knowing smile to his colleagues' faces. So it was. Their dealings with Lever were, thank the gods, almost over; Curval's, poor sod, were only just beginning.

"Ah, Andrew . . ." Lever said, turning, smiling at the man and extending his hand. "I wanted to talk to you. To make sure everything's going to plan."

Curval bowed his head and took Lever's hand, allowing his own to be pumped and squeezed indelicately.

"It all goes well, Mister Lever. Very well indeed."

"You've signed the two men you mentioned last time we talked?"

The last time they had talked had been the day before, less than eighteen hours earlier, in fact, but Curval let it pass.

"I got onto it at once, Mister Lever. The contracts were signed and verified this morning. The men will be here tomorrow, first thing, ready to get down to work."

"Good." Old Man Lever beamed his satisfaction. "That's what I like to hear. So you've got your team now? Everyone you need?"

Curval hesitated. He knew what the Old Man wanted to hear. He wanted to hear a resounding yes; that they had the best team possible—a team good enough to tackle the big questions and overcome them—but both he and Lever knew that that wasn't so.

"It's as good as we'll get, Mister Lever. If we can't crack it with this team, no one will."

Lever stared at him a full ten seconds, then gave a terse nod. "It's the boy, neh? You still think we need the boy?"

Curval took a long breath, then nodded. "I've looked over some of the things you showed me and there's no doubting it. You can't counterfeit that kind of ability. You either have it or you don't."

"And he has it?"

Curval laughed. "In excess! Why, he's head and shoulders above anyone in his field. He's quick of mind, and versatile, too. If anyone could make a quick breakthrough, it'd be Ward." Again he hesitated. "Look, don't mistake me, Mister Lever, the team we've got is good. Exceptional, I'd say. If anyone can find an answer, they can. But it'll take time. All I'm saying is that having Ward would give us an edge. It would help speed things up considerably."

"I see." Lever looked about him thoughtfully, then turned back to Curval, smiling. "Okay. I'll come and visit you tomorrow. It'll be good to meet the team at last. I can give them a little pep talk, neh?"

Curval nodded, his face showing no sign of what he thought of the idea, then, with a low bow, he backed slowly away.

For a while Lever stood there, as if in trance, a deep frown lining his grizzled features. Then, abruptly, he turned about, marching off the platform and out through the open door, his silks flapping out behind him as he made his way through the maze of rooms and corridors to the entrance hall.

Beneath the great twist of stairs—that huge, unraveled double helix that filled the north end of the massive domed cavern that was the entrance hall—Lever stopped, looking about him, as if coming to himself again.

Waving away the two servants who had hurried across, he went over and stood before the blank partition wall that rested in the center of the floor between the stairway and the huge entrance doors. This, this great screen, was the first thing that visitors to the Institute would see on entering the building, and as yet he was still to find something to fill it. But fill it he would. And with something quite exceptional.

Lever lifted his chin, then turned away, feeling a sudden rush of pride at the thought of what he'd accomplished here. Here it was, the first stage of his Dream completed. He had brought it this far, by force of will and brute determination, and he would take it even farther, right to the shores of death itself. He smiled, all trace of the uncertainty he had felt back in the lecture hall gone from him. He had a right, surely, to feel proud of what he'd done? No Emperor or President had ever done so much.

He looked about him, then nodded, suddenly determined. For some reason, young Ward didn't want to work for him. A dozen times now he had turned down his offers. But that didn't mean that he had to give up. No. If anything it made him more determined. He was used to having his own way, and he would have his way in this eventually. Because this was too important not to give it his best shot. And if that best shot meant getting Ward, he would get Ward. Whatever it took.

Yes. Because here, at this place he had specially created for the purpose, they were ready to begin. In the days to come they would take on Death himself. Would track him down and face him, eye to eye. Yes. And stare him down.

<hr />

KIM PUSHED AWAY the empty starter plate and looked about him, noting how busy the restaurant had suddenly become, then turned back, meeting Michael Lever's eyes across the table.

"It's strange, isn't it?" Michael said, a faint smile on his lips. "I'd never have thought that I'd feel awkward in a place like this, but these days . . . well, I see it with new eyes, I guess. The wastefulness of it all. The excess. Being Wu Shih's guest made me realize how much I'd taken for granted, how much I *hadn't* seen."

Kim frowned, concerned. "You should have said. Look, I'll cancel the main course, if you want. We can go elsewhere."

Michael shook his head. "No. It's okay. Besides, I'll have to get used to this again if I'm going into business on my own account. I learned that with my father. This is where the deals are made, in the restaurants and private clubs, with a full mouth and a swollen belly, over a plate of expensive delicacies and a tumbler of brandy."

Kim laughed softly, enjoying the new Michael Lever. There was a depth of irony to him that hadn't been there before his imprisonment; a sharp, self-deprecating humor that suited him perfectly. Before, he had been his father's shadow, but now he was himself; leaner but also stronger than before.

"Do you really hate it all that much?"

Michael looked down. "I don't know. It's like I said, it's hard to see it now the way they do. Being locked up all day . . . it gave me the chance to do a lot of thinking. To look at our world afresh." He met Kim's eyes again. "My father can't understand that. To him it's as if I've been away at College or something. He can't see what I've been through. He thinks . . ." He huffed out, hurt and exasperated. "Well, he thinks I'm just being awkward, willful, but it's not like that."

Kim leaned toward him, covering his hand with his own. "I understand," he said, thinking back to his own experiences of confinement. "It changes you, doesn't it? Throws you back upon yourself."

Michael nodded and looked up at him, smiling, grateful for his understanding.

"I'm sorry. This whole business with your father. It must be hard for you."

Michael shrugged. "It hurts, sure, but I've known worse. Besides," he said, brightening, "you've not told me what *you're* up to. Have you made your first million yet?"

Kim laughed. "No, but it sure as hell feels as if I've spent it setting things up!" He sat back, relinquishing Michael's hand. "You know how it is. Creatively we're strong, but financially . . . Well, to be honest with you, Michael, I could do with some outside investment, but it's a question of finding someone I can trust. Someone who won't attach too many strings."

"Ahh . . ." Michael looked away, thoughtful a moment. "You know, Kim, I thought I knew everything there was to know about business, I thought no one could teach me anything new, but I'm having to learn it all again, from scratch. Without my father's money, without the power that ImmVac represents, I'm just another face, fighting for my share of a hostile market."

"Hostile?"

"My father. He doesn't like the idea of me going it alone. He thinks I should be back home, running errands for him."

"You mean he's actively trying to stop you?"

"Actively, no. Or at least, not as far as I know. But you know how it is. The word's out that my father's angry with me, and it's a brave man who'll risk offending Charles Lever for the sake of trading with his son. I've been cut dead a dozen, twenty times these past two days alone by so-called 'friends.' But there are ways around that. Bryn and I have been working on making contacts in the East Asian marketplace. It'll cost us, sure, but at least we can do business. Here in North America things are dead as far as we're concerned."

"I see." Kim leaned back, letting the waiter who had appeared clear the plates. "So how are you funding all this?"

Michael smiled. "I've personal accounts. Money my mother left me. About fifteen million in all. It's not enough, but it'll get us started."

Kim narrowed his eyes. "That sounds ambitious."

"It is. But tell me, Kim, how much do you need? A million? Two?"

"One and a half," Kim said, as the waiter returned, setting down a plate of steaming hash before him. "One point two if we trim back to basics."

"And that covers what? R and D? Production? Distribution?"

"R and D is covered. I do all that up here." Kim tapped his skull and smiled. "No. My costing is for the initial production run, manufacture to fitting, allowing for a three-month payment schedule. We start fairly small, keep borrowing to a minimum, and finance expansion from profits."

Michael leaned toward him, interested. "You've got something ready to go, then?"

"Pretty well. I've been working on a few things this last year. Some didn't pan out, but two of them . . . Well, let's say that I'm hopeful."

"These are new inventions, I take it?"

Kim nodded.

"And you've patented them, I hope?"

"Not yet."

Michael whistled through his teeth. "But that's madness, Kim! What if someone raided your offices? You'd lose it all."

Kim shook his head. "They could strip the place bare, but they'd get nothing. As I said, it's all up here, in my head. When I'm ready I'll set it all down and take it along to the Patents Office and register it. But not before I've sorted out the practical details."

Michael smiled, impressed by the young man. "It sounds good. Better than good, in fact. Look, Kim, why don't *we* do business? You need funding, we need a bit of specialist advice. Why can't we trade? I mean, I'll have to talk to Bryn and get his agreement, but I don't see why we can't help each other out, neh?"

Kim stared at him, confused. "Wait a minute. Have I got this right? Are you offering to back me? To put up the funds?"

"Why not?"

"But I thought you needed that money for your own venture?"

"We need ten million to get us started, sure, but that leaves more than enough for what you want. And no strings. Or at least, just the one—that you look over our proposal and give us your technical advice on what we propose."

Kim was smiling broadly now, his dinner quite forgotten. "That's great. Really great. But just what is your proposal?"

"Near-space technologies," Michael answered him, looking past him momentarily, as if seeing something clearly in the air. "It's the coming thing, Kim. The coming thing . . ."

<hr />

WEI FENG LAY on the great oakwood bed, his eyes closed, his long, thin face at rest. His hands lay one upon the other above the sheets, the slender fingers stiff, paler than the white silk of the coverings, a kind of darkness beneath their pallor. At the foot of the bed stood his three sons, heads bowed, the white of their clothes in sharp contrast to the rich colors of the room.

The long illness had wasted the old man. He was a thing of bone beneath the frail white gown he wore. His right arm and shoulder had atrophied, as if death had taken that part of him earlier than the rest. His lidded eyes rested low in the pits of their sockets, and his thin-lipped mouth was a mere pale gash in the emaciated wasteland of his face. The hair on the left side of his face had not grown back, and the scars of the operations showed blue against the ivory of his skull. When Li Yuan entered the room his eyes were drawn to the stark ugliness of Wei Feng's head in death. He shuddered involuntarily, then turned to greet the eldest son, Chan Yin, with a silent bow.

Li Yuan stood at the bedside a long time, looking down at his old friend, recalling through misted eyes how this kind and lovely man had once twirled him around in the air, his eyes alight with the joy of what he was doing, and how he, Li Yuan, had squealed with delight at it. He glanced down at the narrow bones of the hands, the wasted muscles of the arms, and grimaced. Had it been so long ago? No . . . He shook his head slowly. Fifteen years. It was barely an indrawn breath in the long history of their race.

He turned away, leaving the tears on his cheeks, stepping back as if in a dream, then reached out to embrace each of the dead man's sons; holding Chan Yin longer than the others, feeling the faint trembling of the man against him.

Chan Yin stood back, a sad smile on his face. "Thank you, Yuan."

"He was a good man," Yuan answered, matching his smile. "I shall miss both his advice and his friendship. He was a second father to me."

The forty-year-old nodded slightly, for a moment seeming younger than the nineteen-year-old Li Yuan. Before this moment, power had reversed the traditional status of age between them, but now they were both T'ang, both equals. Even so, Chan Yin deferred. Li Yuan noted this and frowned, not understanding. There was no sign in his cousin that he had inherited. Only a puzzling humility and deference toward himself.

"What is it, Chan Yin?"

Chan Yin met his eyes. Beyond him his younger brothers looked on. "My father entrusted me to give you this, Yuan."

From the white folds of his mourning cloak the new T'ang took a letter. It was white silk, sealed with bloodred wax, the traditional instrument of the Seven. Li Yuan took it and stared at it, then, reluctantly, he prized the seal open with his fingernail.

Chan Yin reached out a hand to stop him. "Not here, Yuan. Later. When you are alone. And then we shall meet. Just you and I." He paused, and raised his voice as if to let it carry to his brothers. "But remember, Li Yuan. I am my father's son. His death changes nothing."

Li Yuan hesitated, then bowed his assent, his fingers pressing the hardened wax back into place. Then, with a brief, questioning glance, he turned and left the death chamber.

Waves Against the Sand

I T   W A S   L O W   T I D E. In the deep shadow at the foot of the City's wall, a flat-bottomed patrol boat made its way between the tiny, grass-covered islands that dotted this side of the river, the tight beam of its searchlight sweeping slowly from side to side across the glistening shallows. Just here, at the great Loire's mouth, the river was broad, almost three *li* wide. Downstream lay the Bay of Biscay and the gray-green waters of the North Atlantic. In the bright, mid-morning sunlight, one of the big mid-ocean vessels was making its way in the deep water channel toward the port of Nantes. On the far bank, beyond the perimeter fence and its regularly spaced gun turrets, could be seen the needle towers and blast pits of the spaceport, the pure white of the City's walls forming a glacial backdrop far to the south. As the patrol boat slowed and turned, making its way round the low hump of a mudbank, the water seemed to shimmer. Almost imperceptibly the vibration took form in the air, a low bass growl that grew and grew in strength. A moment later the sky on the far side of the river was riven by a long, bright streak of red.

On the roof of the City, two *li* above the river's surface, a group of officers watched the rocket climb the sky to the southwest. To their backs, close by, five craft were parked about an open service hatch: a big, black-painted cruiser, three squat Security gunships, and a slender four-man craft with the *Ywe Lung* and the personal insignia of the

T'ang of Europe on its stubby wings. Uniformed guards of the T'ang's elite squad stood by the ramps of each craft, heavy semiautomatics clutched to their chests, looking about them conscientiously.

For a moment the small group of officers was still, their necks craned back, following the arc of the rocket, then, as the echoing boom of the engines faded from the sky, they turned back, resuming their talk.

Marshal Tolonen stood at the center of the group, his aide close by, clutching a small documents case. Facing Tolonen stood Li Yuan's new General, the fifty-two-year-old Helmut Rheinhardt. He and most of his senior staff had come out to Nantes to see the old man off.

"I admire your thoroughness, Knut," Rheinhardt said, picking up on what they had been saying, "but forgive me if I say that I feel you're taking on much more than you need. For myself I'd have let other, younger eyes do the spadework and saved myself for the fine sifting. From what you've said, there's plenty enough of that, neh?"

Tolonen laughed. "Maybe so. But it's a principle I've stuck to all my life. Not to trust what I'm told, but to look for myself. I've an instinct for these things, Helmut. For that small betraying detail that another wouldn't spot. From here things look fine with GenSyn's North American operation, but I've a hunch that they'll look a great deal different from close up."

"You think something's amiss, then, Knut?"

Tolonen leaned closer. "I'm damn sure of it! I've been working through the official records these past three months and things simply don't add up. Oh, superficially things look all right. The numbers balance and so forth, but . . ." He sniffed, then shook his head. "Look, Klaus Ebert was a conscientious, honest man. He kept a tight rein on GenSyn while he was in control. But things were different at the end . . ."

"Hans, you mean?"

Tolonen looked away, a shadow falling over his granite features. "It looks like it, I'm afraid. Most of the North American operation and its subsidiary companies were handed over to Hans for the eighteen months before Klaus Ebert's death. And it's in that period that almost all of the anomalies occur."

"Anomalies?" It was Li Yuan's Chancellor, Nan Ho, who made the query. He was returning to the group after briefly visiting his craft to take an urgent message. Rheinhardt and his officers bowed and moved back slightly, letting Nan Ho reenter their circle.

Tolonen hesitated, then nodded. "Accounting irregularities. Forged shipment details. Missing documents. That kind of thing."

It was a bland, almost evasive answer, but from the way Tolonen met Nan Ho's eyes as he said it, the Chancellor knew that it was more serious than that. Something else was missing. Something that, perhaps, couldn't be mentioned, not even in company like this.

"Besides," Tolonen went on, changing the subject, "it will be good to see old friends again. My work has kept me in my study this past year. And that's not healthy, neh? A man needs to get out in the world. To do things and see things."

Rheinhardt laughed. "It sounds like you've been missing the service, Knut! Maybe I should find you something to do once all this GenSyn business is finished with. Or maybe you would like your old job back?"

There was laughter at that; a hearty, wholesome laughter that rolled out across the roof of the City. Hearing it, Jelka Tolonen looked up from where she was sitting on the steps of the nearest gunship and frowned. How familiar such manly laughter was, and yet, suddenly, how strange, how alien it sounded. She stood, looking out past her father's men, toward the distant horizon.

It was a beautiful day. The sun was high and, to her back, the air fresh with no trace of wind. Cloud lay to the west, high up, over the shining ocean, a faint, wispy cirrus feathering the deep blue of the sky. It was beautiful, simply beautiful, yet for once she felt no connection to that beauty, no resonance within herself; as if some part of her had died, or fallen fast asleep.

A week had passed since the incident at the Graduation Ball, but she had still to come to terms with what had happened. When she thought of it, it seemed strange, unreal, as if it had happened to someone else, or in some other life. Yet what concerned her more was the constant, nagging sense of unease she had felt these past few weeks; that sense that things were wrong, seriously wrong, with the balance of her life.

As far as Lieutenant Bachman was concerned, her father had smoothed things over, just as he'd said he would. Even so, she had slept badly this last week, haunted by dreams in which she was a machine, a dreadful spinning thing with blades for arms, scything down whoever strayed across her blind, erratic path.

And where was her softer self in these dreams? Where was the girl she knew existed beneath that hard metallic shell? Nowhere. There was no sign of her; of the girl she felt she ought to have been. Or was it true what her father had said that night? Was it simply that they were made of sterner stuff? Of iron?

Of all this she had said nothing. At home, she had acted as though nothing were happening deep within her. As if it were all done with and forgotten. Yet she knew it was far from over, for she was undergoing a change—a change as profound and as radical as any being suffered by the greater world beyond her. And maybe there was even some connection. Maybe the change in her mirrored that outer change—was some strange kind of recognition of the reality of events?

She looked down at herself, at the simple dark blue one-piece she was wearing. It was what she always wore when she accompanied her father, its neat, military cut fitting in with her surroundings. Yet today it felt different. Today it felt *wrong.*

"Jelka?"

She turned, surprised, facing her father.

"I didn't hear you . . ."

"No . . ." He smiled and reached out, holding her upper arm gently with his bright, golden hand. "You were miles away, weren't you? What were you thinking of, my love?"

She looked down. "That I'll miss you," she said, hiding behind the partial truth.

"And I you," he said, drawing her close and embracing her. "But it won't be long. Ten days at most. Oh, and guess who I'll be seeing?"

She shrugged, unable to guess.

"*Shih* Ward . . . you know, young Kim, the Clayborn lad . . . the scientist."

"You're seeing him?"

He held up a small white envelope. "I'm having lunch with him, it seems. Li Yuan wants me to deliver this personally. The gods know what it is, but it'll be nice to see the young fellow again."

"I . . ." She licked at her lips, wanting to say something, to give him some message to pass on, then shook her head. "I'll miss you," she said finally, hugging him tightly. "I'll miss you a lot."

He grinned. "Now, now. You'll be all right, my boy." Then, realizing what he'd said, he laughed. "Now, why did I say that, eh?"

"I don't know," she said quietly, burying her head in his chest. "I really don't know."

———

THE CANVAS filled the end wall of the studio, dominating the room. It was not merely that it dwarfed the other paintings—for the new piece was easily ten, maybe twenty times the size of the artist's earlier work—it was the color, the richness, the sheer scale of the composition that caught the eye and drew it in.

To the left of the canvas, what seemed at first glance to be a huge, silver-white mountain resolved itself into a tangle of bodies, some human, some mechanical, the metallic figures unexpectedly soft and melting, those of flesh hard, almost brutal in their angularity. Looking more closely, it could be seen that this great mound of bodies was formed of two great chains, linked hand to hand, like a gigantic coil of anchor rope, the whole thing spiraling upward into the blue-black darkness of deep space at the top right of the canvas: a huge double helix of men and machines, twisting about itself, striving toward a single, brilliant point of light.

In the foreground, beneath the toppling mass of bodies, was the great ocean, the Atlantic, incongruously calm, its surface shimmering in the sunlight. Yet beneath its placid skin could be discerned the forms of ancient ruins—of Han temples and pagodas, of stone dragons and palaces and the skeletal framework of a rotting imperial junk.

It was *shan shui*—"mountains and water"—but *shan shui* trans-formed. This was the new art. An art of symbiosis and technological aspiration that was the cultural embodiment of the old Dispersionist ideals: *Futur-Kunst*, or Science-Art, as it was called. And Hey-demeier, the artist, was its leading exponent.

Old Man Lever stood before the painting, some twenty *ch'i* back, his face creased into an intense frown. He had brought Heydemeier over from Europe six months back and installed him here, giving him whatever he needed to pursue his art. And this—this immense vision in oils—was the first fruit of that investment.

He turned to Heydemeier and nodded. "It's good. Very good in-deed. What is it called?"

Heydemeier drew at the thin black cigarette and gave a tight smile of satisfaction. "I'm glad you like it, *Shih* Lever. I've called it 'The New World.'"

Lever laughed briefly. "That's good. I like that. But why so big?"

Heydemeier moved past the old man, going right up to the canvas. For a while he studied the fine detail of the picture, brushing the surface of it lightly with the fingertips of one hand, then he turned back, facing Lever.

"To be honest with you, *Shih* Lever, I wasn't sure it would work, coming here to America. I thought it might be a step backward. But there's something very different about this place. It's more alive here than in Europe. You get the feeling that this is where the fu-ture is."

Lever was studying the young man hawkishly. "And that's where this comes from?"

"Partly." Heydemeier drew on the cigarette again. "Now that it exists I realize that this was what I was always striving for, even in the smaller works. What was lacking was a sense of space—of outward-ness. Being here, away from the confinement of Europe, freed that. *Allowed* it, if you like."

"I can see that."

Heydemeier half turned, indicating the great swirl of bodies. "So. There it is, *Shih* Lever. Yours. As we agreed."

Lever smiled. "It's an important work, *Shih* Heydemeier. I don't need experts or advisors to tell me that. I can see it with my own eyes. It's a masterpiece. Maybe the start of something wholly new, wouldn't you say?"

Heydemeier looked down, trying to conceal his pleasure at the old man's words, but Lever could see that he had touched his weak point—his vanity. He smiled inwardly and pressed on.

"I mentioned my advisors. Well, to be frank with you, *Shih* Heydemeier, it was on their word that you came here. They said you were the best. Without equal, and with your best work ahead of you. So it has proved. And that's good. I can use that. I like working with the best. In everything."

Lever went across, standing there face to face with the artist. "You're a clever man, Ernst Heydemeier. You understand how things are—how they work. So you'll not take offense when I say that my interest in you was strictly commercial. A Company like mine—like ImmVac—needs its showpieces, its cultural totems, if you like. And the more prestigious those totems, the better. They give a Company great face. But this . . ." He reached out and gently touched the surface of the painting, a look of genuine awe in his face. "This goes beyond that. This transcends what I asked of you."

Heydemeier turned, looking back at his work. "Maybe. But it makes you wonder sometimes . . . Whether you'll ever create anything half as good again. Whether you can ever make something more . . . original."

He turned back, meeting Lever's eyes. "But that's the challenge, neh? To surprise oneself."

Lever watched him a moment, then nodded. "It's yours, Ernst. The painting, I mean. Keep it."

"Keep it?" Heydemeier gave a laugh of surprise. "I don't understand . . ."

Lever looked past him, enjoying the moment. "On one condition. That you paint something for me."

Heydemeier looked down, then gave the tiniest shake of his head. His voice was apologetic. "I thought you understood, *Shih* Lever. I thought we'd discussed this already. I don't undertake commissions. This . . ." He looked up, meeting Lever's eyes unflinchingly. "This was different. Was my rent, if you like. Repayment of your hospitality. But what you're talking of . . . that's different again. I have to be free to paint what I want. It just doesn't work, otherwise."

"I understand. But look at that. Look at it again, Ernst Heydemeier. That's a moment in your life—in your career—that you won't repeat. Oh, you may paint things which are better technically, but will you ever recapture that one moment of vision? Besides, I could resell this tomorrow and make, what, five, maybe ten million *yuan*. As to what it'll be worth ten years from now . . ." He paused, letting that sink in. "And what am I asking for in exchange? Three, maybe four days of your time."

Heydemeier turned away, his discomfort and uncertainty evident in every muscle of his long, gaunt body.

"I don't know, *Shih* Lever. I . . ."

"Okay. I won't force the issue. Keep it anyway. Let it be my gift to you. But let me tell you what it was I wanted. Just hear me out, okay?"

Heydemeier turned, facing the old man again. Whatever he had expected from this meeting, it had not been this. He stood there, bemused, his earlier composure shattered. "All right," he said resignedly. "I'll listen, but that's all . . ."

"Of course." Lever smiled, relaxing now he had brought him this far. "It's a simple little thing really . . ."

Twenty minutes later, as Lever was climbing into his sedan, a messenger came. He tore the envelope open impatiently, knowing even before he glanced at it who it was from. This was the second time in the last twenty-four hours that his son, Michael, had written to him about the freezing of his accounts.

"Damn the boy!" he said, angry at being chased up in this manner. "Who the hell does he think he is! He can damn well wait . . ."

He held the letter out stiffly, waiting for his secretary to take it, then, changing his mind, he drew it back.

"No. Give me brush and ink. I'll give him his answer now."

"There," he said, a moment later. "Maybe that will teach him manners!"

He stepped up into the sedan again, letting the servant draw the curtains about him, but the satisfaction he had felt only moments before had gone, replaced by a blinding fury at his son. Well, Michael would learn just how decisive he could be when pushed to it. It was about time he understood how things really were.

He shuddered and sat back, reminding himself of the day's successes—of the unexpected thrill of the auction that morning, the pleasant and productive lunch with Representative Hartmann, and his "negotiations" with Heydemeier. But this last—this final matter with his son—had taken the bloom off his day.

"Damn the boy!" he said again, turning the heavy ring on his left-hand index finger, unconscious that he was doing so. "Damn him to hell!"

JELKA CRUMPLED UP the note and threw it down, angry with herself. Angry that she couldn't find the words to express what she had been feeling that night.

Or maybe it wasn't that at all. Maybe it was simply that she had wanted to hurt the young lieutenant; that, in a funny way, she'd *needed* to. But if that was true, what kind of creature did that make her?

She sat back, taking a long breath, trying to calm herself, but there was so much darkness in her; so much unexpressed violence. Why, she couldn't even write a simple letter of apology without wanting to hit out at something!

She stood, looking about her at the chaos of her room. Sketches of uniforms and weaponry, of machines and fighting soldiers, cluttered the facing wall, while to her left a number of old campaign maps covered the face of her wardrobe. A combat robe hung over the back of the chair beside her unmade bed, while nearby, in a box in the corner, a selection of flails and staffs and practice swords reminded her of how long she had spent perfecting her skills with each. Above the box, high up on the wall, was a brightly colored poster of Mu-Lan, dressed in full military armor. Mu-Lan, the warrior princess, famed throughout history for her bravery and skill.

Mu-Lan . . . the name her girlfriends called her.

She swallowed, her anger turned to bitterness. He had made her this. Year by year he had trimmed and shaped her. Year by year he had molded her, until she was this thing of steel and sinew.

Or was that fair? Was her father really to blame? Wasn't it true what he had said that night? Wasn't it simply that she was of his blood, Tolonen, with the nature of their kind? Hadn't she glimpsed something of that on the island that time? Hadn't she seen her own reflection in the rocks and icy waters of that northern place? So maybe it was true. Maybe he wasn't to blame. Even so, if she had had a mother . . .

She caught her breath. Slowly she sat again.

If she had had a mother . . . What then? Would it all have been different? Would she have turned out normal?

She laughed; a strange, bleak sound. What, after all, was normal? Was "normal" what the others were? For if *that* was so, then she didn't wish to be normal. But to be as she was, that was dreadful, horrible.

Unbearable.

She went through to the kitchen and took a refuse sack from the strip beside the freezer, then returned to her room. She stood there, looking about her numbly, wondering where to start.

Mu-Lan, perhaps . . .

She went across and ripped the poster from the wall, stuffing it down into the sack. Then, in a frenzy, she worked her way around the walls, tearing down the pictures and sketches, the posters and the maps, thrusting them all down into the sack, grunting with the effort. Finally she emptied the weapons box into the sack and tied the neck.

She stood back, looking about her at the bare walls. It was as if she had been dreaming all these years; sleepwalking her way through the days. Oh, there had been moments when she had woken—like the time she had defied him over the marriage to Hans Ebert—but for the most part she had colluded in her fate. But now all that must change. From here on she must be mistress of her own destiny.

Lifting the sack she went back through, into the kitchen. Waving the serving girl away, she stood there, over the portable incinerator, half in trance, thinking of her mother.

In some other world, perhaps, it was different. There, beneath an open sky, she was herself, complete. For an instant she pictured it; imagined the log house on the hill beside the forest, the stream below;

turned and saw, as if in memory, her father standing in the doorway, her mother—the image of herself—beside him, his arm about her shoulder. Felt herself turn, her skirts swirling out about her naked legs, her bare feet running on the sunlit grass . . .

She closed her eyes, the pain of longing almost overwhelming her. *In some other world . . .*

The click of the incinerator brought her back. She looked about her, as if coming to from the depths of sleep, then shuddered, the tension in her unabated. What wouldn't she give to be able to live like that. To *be* like that, open and whole.

Maybe so. But that was only dreams. This here was the world she inhabited. This massive, brutal world of levels. This *Yang* world, heavy with the breath of men. And what were her dreams against the weight of that reality?

Nothing.

And yet she would become herself. She *would.* For to be like them—to be "normal" in the way that they were normal—would be a living death for her. A slow and painful suffocation. And she would rather die than suffer that.

She had been running from it. All her life she had been running from it. But now, suddenly, she was awake. That moment at the Graduation Ball . . . she understood it now. That—that awful moment when she had turned and goaded him—had been the moment when she had stopped running. The moment of awakening, when she had turned, quite literally, to confront the very thing she hated.

"I'm sorry." she said softly. "It wasn't *you*, it was . . ."

She shivered, understanding finally what had happened to her that evening. It wasn't Lieutenant Lothar Bachman she had meant to hurt. It was what he represented. He . . . well, he had been like . . . She looked about her, her eyes coming to rest on the figure of the kitchen god, squatting on the shelf above the cooking utensils, and nodded to herself.

Yes. It was as if she had been confronted by the clay figurine of an evil demon; a figure that she had had to smash to be free of its enchantment.

And was she free?

Jelka looked down at her long, slender hands, seeing them clearly, as if she had never seen them before. No, not free. Not yet. But she would be. For she was awake now. At long last, she was awake.

※※※※※

"Mary? Have you got the file of old MemSys contacts?"

Emily looked up from behind the desk screen and met Michael Lever's eyes, conscious of the slight edge in his voice. This business with his father was getting to him, especially since the Old Man had frozen the accounts.

"It's here," she said, reaching into her top left-hand drawer and taking out the bulky folder. "Not that it'll do you any good. None of them will talk to us, let alone contemplate trading with us. They're all scared as hell of taking on your father, Michael. You'd be better off trashing this and starting anew."

"Maybe." He hesitated, then came across and took the folder from her. "Even so, I'm going to try each one of them again. Someone's got to give."

"Why?" There was a strange hardness in her eyes. "Your father holds all the cards. Every last one of them. And you've got nothing."

"Maybe," he said again, not challenging what she'd said. "But I've got to keep trying. I can't go back. Not now."

"No." She said it softly, sympathetically, knowing how much pressure he'd been under these past few weeks, and how well he'd coped with it. The old Michael Lever wouldn't have coped, not one tenth as well. "As for the other matter . . . I'll let you know if we hear anything, okay?"

He smiled uncertainly. "Okay. I'll get to it."

When he was gone, she sat back, combing her fingers through her short blond hair. The other matter—the freezing of the accounts—was what lay behind his current tenseness. If the Old Man refused . . . She took a deep breath, trying to see ahead. What would she do if Michael gave up and went back to his father? She'd be out of a job, for a start. Worse than that, Old Man Lever would make sure she'd never work again. Not in North America, anyway. And maybe other places too. Wherever his long arm reached.

But strangely enough her own fate didn't concern her half so much as the prospect of Michael giving up. Of him succumbing after coming this far. She'd survive. She always did. But Michael . . . If he gave up now it would destroy him—cripple him emotionally. If he gave up now he would be tied—tied forever to his father's will, whether his father lived or not.

She shuddered and looked about her at the room in which she sat. In three short weeks they had built this thing from scratch. And though it was as nothing compared to MemSys and the great ImmVac Corporation, it was at least something. New growth, not an expansion of the old.

Yes, and left alone it would have grown and grown. Michael and Bryn were a good team. Innovative, capable, resourceful. As good as any she had worked for these past three years. The Company would have been big. As it was, it was likely it would be dead, and probably within the hour.

"*Nu Shih* Jennings?"

She looked up again. It was Chan, the guard. He'd slid back the outer door and was looking in at her.

"What is it, Chan Long?"

"There's a messenger here," he said quietly, ominously. "From ImmVac. I think it's an answer."

She nodded. Chan knew as well as anyone what was going on. That was his business. And like her, he knew what it was likely to mean. She smiled tightly, feeling sorry for the man.

"Okay. Search him and show him through. But show the man respect. It's not his fault."

Chan gave a small bow and slid the door closed again. A minute or so later the door slid fully back and Chan came through, ushering in a tall, dark-haired *Hung Mao* in the bright red uniform of ImmVac's messenger service. From the way he glanced at Chan as he passed, it was clear he had not welcomed being body-searched, but Emily was taking no chances.

She stood, coming around the desk. "You have a message, I understand? From *Shih* Lever."

He hesitated, then gave the slightest nod of his head. Inwardly

Emily smiled ironically. If she had been a man, his bow would have been low, to the waist, perhaps, but as she was merely a woman . . .

"I have a note," the man answered, looking away from her, as if he had dismissed her. "It is to be given directly into the hands of young Master Lever."

She took a long, deep breath. *Young Master Lever.* How clearly those words revealed Old Man Lever's attitude toward his son. How subtly and damagingly they placed Michael.

She moved closer, until her face was almost pressed against the man's. "I will tell *Shih* Lever that you are here. If you would be seated," she pointed past him, indicating the chair on the far side of the reception room. "He is a very busy man, but he will see you when he can."

As she turned away, she could see it in her mind. The thing to do was to keep the messenger waiting—an hour, two hours, maybe even to the close of business. That way the message would get back to Old Man Lever that his son was not to be treated like a troublesome infant, but respected as a man. That was what she would have done, anyway. But she was not Michael. Michael wanted an answer. Wanted an end to the tension and misery of not knowing.

She hesitated, then slid back the door. Inside she closed it behind her, then went across. Kustow was sitting to the left behind his desk, Michael to the right. They watched her cross the floor, their eyes filled with a tense expectation.

"It's here," she said simply.

She saw how the color drained from Michael's face. He closed the MemSys folder, then turned in his chair, looking across at Kustow.

"Well, Bryn, what do you think?"

Kustow sat back, eyeing his partner somberly. "I think he's given you the finger, Michael. That's what I think."

"But he can't," Michael said quietly. "Surely he can't? I mean, it's my money. *Legally* my money. If I took the matter to court . . ."

Kustow shrugged fatalistically. "You'd win, certainly, but not for several years. You, better than anyone, should know how expert your father's lawyers are at drawing things out. And in the meantime you've got nothing. Not even this . . ."

"Maybe, but . . . ach . . . what gives him the right, Bryn? What gives him the fucking right?"

For a moment all of the anger and frustration he was feeling was there in Michael Lever's face. Then, with a shudder, he took hold of himself again and looked across at Emily.

"Okay. Show him in. Let's hear the worst."

She went back and brought the messenger through, watching as Michael took the envelope from him and slit it open. He read it through, then, his hand trembling, passed it to Kustow at his side.

"Okay," he said, meeting the messenger's eyes, his whole manner suddenly harder, more dignified. "Tell my father that I note what he says and that I thank him for his generosity."

"Is that it?" the man asked, staring back at him.

"You may go," Michael said, letting nothing of what he was feeling enter his voice. "You've done what was asked of you."

When the messenger had gone, Michael turned, facing Kustow, his shoulders hunched suddenly, his eyes miserable, the pretense of dignified defiance cast off. "That's it, then. The end of things . . ."

Kustow studied the note a moment, then looked back at him. "Is that what you want?"

"No. But what are our options? There was seventeen million in those four accounts. Without it . . ."

"Without it we start again. Trim things down. Reassess our priorities. Work out what we can do. We've still got my money."

"Two million. Where will that get us?"

"It'll get us started, that's what. As for the rest, we'll come up with something. We can borrow from the East Asian markets, maybe. Or from his major business rivals."

"But you said you didn't want to borrow. You said that that would make us vulnerable."

Kustow smiled. "True. But I said that before your father turned nasty on us." He handed Michael back the note, then put his arm about his shoulders. "Look at it this way, Michael. Your money would have given us a cushion—might have made the ride a little less bumpy—but it was never the main component of our strategy. Talent, ability, innovative ideas, that's what this Company was going to be based on, and it still can be. But I can't do it alone, Michael. I need you. And you need me."

"But what about our plans . . . ?"

"As I said. We scale things down. Put a rein on our ambitions for a time." He shrugged. "Look, this'll set us back, I don't deny it, but it doesn't have to put an end to things, not unless you want it to. So what about it, Michael? Are you going to crawl back to him, your tail between your legs, after all we've done and said, or are you going to spit in his eye and carry on?"

Michael glanced at Emily, then turned back, studying Kustow closely, his eyes recalling all they had been through those past few years. Gripping Kustow's arms firmly, he nodded.

"Okay," he said quietly. "We'll do it your way. If it fails we're no worse off, neh?"

"Not the tiniest bit . . ."

Again he nodded, a smile slowly returning to his lips. "Okay. Then let's do it. Let's spit in his eye."

IT WAS A DARK-LIT, shabby place that stank of cheap perfumes and sour liquor. The carpet underfoot was threadbare, the walls covered with inexpensive erotoprints. The girls, lined up against one of the walls, were in character; they too were cheap and worn, their faces overpainted, their bodies mere parodies of desire.

"Well?" said K'ang, turning to face Lehmann, a grin splitting his big face. "What do you want? It's my treat. I always bring my boys here, once a month. Gives them a break. A bit of fun."

Lehmann looked about him, letting no sign of the disgust he felt show in his face. "No," he said simply.

"Come on . . ." K'ang made to take him by the arm, then remembered how he felt about that and backed off. "You're sure? I mean, if it's not your thing. If . . ."

The look on Lehmann's face warned him not to say what he was thinking. K'ang shrugged and turned back to the others.

"I'll have the fat one," said Ling Wo, K'ang's chief advisor.

"Which one?" said the Madam, coming across to him and winking.

She herself was grossly fat and, like her girls, wore little or nothing about her genitals, as if such crude display could make her more desirable. Ling Wo let her fondle him and leaned close to whisper in her ear.

"Have them both!" she said and laughed raucously, slapping his shoulder. "*Shih* K'ang here will pay, won't you, dear?"

K'ang laughed loudly and said, "Of course. Have both, Ling Wo!" But his eyes said something different, and Ling Wo chose between the girls.

Lehmann, watching, saw the Madam look from one man to the other, then turn to her girls and make a face.

One by one the others made their choices, K'ang's three advisors first, then Peck, the new man from the south who had joined them only a week back.

Peck was an old acquaintance of Soucek's and had worked for K'ang A-yin years before. Now he was back, after some trouble with Security. He had come in as Lieutenant, to strengthen the *tong*. Or so the story went. To Lehmann it read otherwise. Peck had been brought in to counter him. To bring the odds back in K'ang's favor. Not that it mattered.

Then it was Soucek's turn.

"I'll pass this time, *Shih* K'ang."

K'ang laughed. "What do you mean, pass? Since when did you ever pass? You gone off girls or something?"

Soucek lifted his big, long head and met K'ang's eyes. "I'll pass, that's all."

K'ang went quiet. He looked from Soucek to Lehmann, then looked down at the floor. When he looked up again he was smiling, but his eyes, as ever, were cold. "You don't like the way I treat you, Jiri, is that it?"

Soucek shook his head. "You treat me fine, K'ang A-yin, but I just don't want it this time. Next time okay. But now . . ." His face was hard, expressionless.

K'ang looked across at the remaining girls, including the one he always had—the best of them, though it said little for her—and then smiled. "Okay. You sit here with Lehmann and chat, neh?" And at that he laughed. He turned to Lehmann. "Mind you, Stefan, you'd be better off fucking your brains out than trying to get a decent conversation out of Jiri there."

Then, laughing, the Madam on one arm, the girl on the other, he followed the others inside.

Lehmann waited a moment, then turned, looking across at Soucek. "Why didn't you go in?"

Soucek met Lehmann's eyes. "I was watching you. Seeing how you saw it."

"And?"

"You don't like all this, do you?"

"What does it matter what I like? You're K'ang's man."

"That's not forever."

"Nothing's forever. But that isn't what you meant, is it?"

Soucek was about to answer when the Madam came bursting in again. "You boys want anything? Drinks?"

Lehmann looked at her blankly, then, "Yes. Wine will do."

Soucek half-lidded his eyes, curious. He had never seen Lehmann touch alcohol before. The Madam left the room, then returned with two drinks, setting them down on a small table at the far end of the room.

"There. You'll be comfy over here."

Lehmann looked at her again, such hostility behind the blankness of his face that the Madam's smile faded momentarily, then came back stronger, as if to cover up the unease she felt in his presence. "If there's anything else you need, just call."

They waited until she went, then sat, Lehmann with his back to the wall, Soucek facing him. The two drinks rested on the low table between them.

"Tell me about Peck," Lehmann said.

"Peck?" Soucek laughed coldly. "Peck is *ying tzu.*"

Lehmann lowered his head slightly. He had heard of *ying tzu*—shadows—and their services. They were trained specialists, contracted out to gangland bosses. Like the *chan shih* they were a staple of the underworld here, though far more rare.

"That costs."

Soucek nodded and reached out to take his glass, but Lehmann put out a hand, stopping him. "Why are you telling me?"

"A warning."

Lehmann studied him carefully, his gaze penetrating. "Just that?"

Soucek smiled again, his thin-lipped mouth an ugly, lifeless thing. "No." He hesitated and then looked down. "Because you're strong."

"And K'ang isn't?"

Soucek looked up. "He's strong. In some ways. But you . . ." He shook his head.

Lehmann was silent a long time after that. Then he picked up his glass and sniffed at it. "I'm K'ang's man now."

Soucek watched him; saw him put the glass down untouched. "Now?"

Lehmann's eyes seemed to soften marginally, as if he was pleased that Soucek had understood him, but still he didn't smile. Soucek looked down at his glass and nodded to himself. In this as in all else from now on he would copy Lehmann. If Lehmann shunned women, he too would shun women. If Lehmann touched no drink, he too would do the same. For there was a secret in all this, he saw. A kind of strength. *Macht*, the others called it, in the old slang of these parts. *Power.*

"What do you want?"

Lehmann's question surprised him. *To be like you*, he thought, but what he said was different. "I don't want to be here forever. I . . ."

He stopped and turned in his chair. Six men had come into the room. Two of them had been talking when they came in, but on seeing Lehmann and Soucek there they had fallen silent. As Soucek watched, the Madam came out and, with a glance across at Lehmann and himself, leaned close to one of the newcomers and whispered something to him. Then, with a broad, false smile, she came across again.

"Well, we are busy tonight!" she said with an excessive gaiety that struck Soucek as rather odd. Then, looking at their glasses, her smile widened again. "You want fill-ups?"

Soucek turned and looked down at the glasses. They were empty. He looked up at Lehmann, surprised, but the albino's face was blank.

"Why not?" said Lehmann tonelessly, lifting the glasses and handing them to her.

Soucek watched Lehmann a moment longer, then turned in time to see the Madam usher the men out through a door she hadn't used before. She was the last to go through and as she did, she turned, taking an almost furtive glance back at them.

As soon as she was gone, Lehmann was on his feet and crossing the room toward the exit.

"What's happening?" began Soucek, jumping up.

Lehmann turned suddenly, like an acrobat, his balance perfect. "Just sit there," he said softly. "Pretend nothing's happening. If she asks, tell her I've gone for a piss. And whatever you do, don't touch the drink. It's drugged."

———

AT THE DOOR Lehmann paused, slipping to one side as it irised open. No one. He went through quickly, using the far wall of the corridor to stop and turn himself, his gun out and searching, then relaxed. The corridor was empty.

Crouching, he set the gun down, then took off his wristband and turned it inside out. Quickly he tapped out the contact code. At once the tiny screen came alight, bloodred. There was a moment's vague activity, then the screen's color changed and a miniature of Haller's face stared back at him.

"What the hell time . . . ?" Haller began, then saw it wasn't Becker. His manner changed at once. "What is it?"

Lehmann spelt out the situation, gave the location, and told him what was needed. "You've got eight minutes maximum. Bring Becker. Go in at the front. And remember, no noise."

He cut contact, put the wristband back on, and picked up the gun. Then, pausing only to look back along the corridor, he began to run. There would be a back entrance. Sealed maybe. Guarded probably. But he would face that when he got there.

It was a narrow side alley with three ceiling lamps. He stood in part shadow, looking down. There was one man, his back to him, expecting nothing yet. Unhesitant, Lehmann moved quickly between the distinct pools of light and came behind the man silently, wrapping the fine, hard wire about his neck with a graceful looping of his hands. The man's cry of surprise and pain was cut off sharply, almost before it formed. Lehmann let the lifeless body fall, the wire embedded deep in the flesh.

He tested the door's frame for weaknesses, pushing at it, then leaning hard against it. Moving back from it, he took a breath, then kicked twice, in two separate places. The door fell inward, the crude latches snapped off.

Quickly he moved through the dust cloud, conscious of the noise he'd had to make. Almost at once he was facing one of the Madam's girls who had come out of her room to see what was happening. He grabbed her, one hand about her mouth, then pushed her back into the room, looking about him. She was alone. With a quick, strong movement, he snapped her neck and lay her down. Then, shutting the door behind him, he went back for the dead man.

He had been lucky so far. No one else had heard, and no one had seen the corpse lying there in the shadows by the door. Quickly, grunting with the effort, he dragged it inside, then set the door back in place behind him.

Would they be missing him yet? Getting suspicious? It was almost five minutes now since he'd gone for that piss. Was Soucek all right?

He put the dead man in with the corpse of the whore, then came out again. For a moment he stood there, listening. Things seemed okay. He took a breath, then went on, half running down the long, dark passageway, following it around. There was a door to the left. He paused, lifting the flap. Peck was inside, naked, on his back, a busty blonde riding him vigorously. Lehmann dropped the flap silently and went on.

At the door to the reception area he stopped again, listening. He could hear Soucek's voice, and the Madam's. All seemed fine. He went through.

He saw the relief on the Madam's face, and knew at once what she'd been thinking. "I've changed my mind," he said, before she could say anything. "There's a girl down the end there, I . . ."

He saw her smile widen and again could read her thoughts. *You like to watch.* He looked away, as if he had been caught out, and stood back as she pushed past. Soucek had stood up. Lehmann nodded and signaled for him to come.

As she opened the door Lehmann came behind her and put his hand over her mouth so that she couldn't cry out. He felt her tense, could feel the sudden fear in every muscle of her body. She was staring at the two corpses wide-eyed.

"You can join them or you can help me," Lehmann said quietly. She nodded and he released his grip. She was breathing heavily, trying to control herself.

"Just do what you were going to do. Give us three minutes, then send them in."

She turned, surprised. Her mouth worked silently, its hideous rouge making ugly shapes, then she nodded. She made to step past him, but he reached out and held her. "Remember," he said, drawing her up with one hand until her face was just beneath his. "Say a thing and you're dead. Those others, they're dead anyway. My men are coming here now. But you . . . you can live. If you do what you're told."

She swallowed, then found her voice. "Okay. I'll do what you say."

He pushed her away, disgusted by the foulness of her breath, the painted corruption of her face. He would kill her when it was done.

When she was gone, Soucek turned to him. "What do you want me to do?" he said quietly. He had drawn his gun.

Lehmann reached out and took the gun. "No noise. Use your knife. Or this." He handed Soucek a garrote with short matt-black handles. "Or best of all, use your hands."

Soucek stared at him. "Are you serious?"

"Yes. Now no noise. Understand?"

"Why?"

Lehmann glared at him. "Just do it. Right?"

Soucek nodded, chastened by Lehmann's look.

They went out and down the passageway. At the turn, Lehmann stopped and pointed over to the right. "There," he whispered. "In that doorway. They'll not see you when they come around." He turned and pointed back a little way. "I'll be there, ahead of them. When they're past, you come up behind them. You should be able to take two of them at least."

Soucek's eyes widened, then, remembering what his informer, Masson, had said about Lehmann's ferocity, nodded and got into place in the doorway. He had only moments to wait.

One of them came through on his own and stood there, listening. Distinct sounds of sexual pleasure were coming from several of the rooms now. Soucek, from his hiding place, saw the man hesitate, then turn back to the door, beckoning the others through.

They moved quickly, as though this had all been planned and rehearsed. But as they turned the corner Lehmann came at them. One went down at once, a knife in his throat. A second followed a moment later as Lehmann kicked high and shattered his nose. From behind them Soucek moved quickly, thrusting with his knife, then swinging his blade high, catching the one who was turning back on him in the chest.

There was the faintest groan from one of the men, but otherwise it was a strangely silent struggle, a violent, desperate conflict, fought in the deep shadow of the passageway, as if in the blackest of nightmares. In less than a minute it was over.

Soucek stood there, panting, his arms shaking, and looked across at Lehmann, amazed.

"Mutes," Lehmann said, as if it explained everything.

Soucek laughed softly. "But they were talking. I heard them . . ."

"That one . . ." said Lehmann, pointing to the one who lay there, the big throwing knife deeply embedded in his throat. "And that one over there." The man he indicated was face down, a garrote wound tightly about his neck. "The rest had been operated on."

Soucek bent down and looked. It was true. Four of the dead men had had their larynxes surgically removed. "Why?" he asked, looking up.

"It's an old trick. I saw it at once."

From the nearest room the sounds of pleasure grew louder briefly, then died away. Then, from the end door, stepped two more figures. Soucek tensed, reaching for his knife, but it was only Haller and Becker.

"Just in time, I see," said Haller, grinning.

"Keep your voice down," said Lehmann in a fierce whisper. "You've brought the bags?"

Haller half turned. "Becker has them."

"Good. Then let's get these bodies through to the end room and tidy up."

They worked quickly, taking the corpses down and piling them onto the bed beside the whore and the house guard. Then, while Haller cleaned up in the corridor, Becker got to work.

Soucek looked away from the grisly work and stared at Lehmann. "I don't understand. What's going on?"

Lehmann watched Becker a moment, then turned to face Soucek. "Who did this, do you think? Who would set K'ang up this way?"

Soucek thought a moment. "Lo Han?"

"Exactly. It had to be Lo Han. K'ang A-yin threatens no one else. And Lo Han would have heard that both I and Peck had joined up with him. He'd be worried by that. He'd think there was a reason for it."

"Maybe. But why this? Why the silence? The secrecy?"

Lehmann looked down at Becker again. "You could say that I didn't want to inconvenience *Shih* K'ang, or interrupt his pleasure, but the truth is I want to meet Lo Han. To find out a bit more about him."

Soucek made to speak, then stopped. Lehmann turned, looking at what he'd seen. It was the Madam. She stood in the doorway, her mouth open in horror, watching Becker.

"How did he pay you?" Lehmann asked, looking at her coldly.

For a moment she seemed not to have heard him, then her eyes jerked away from what Becker was doing and looked back at Lehmann. "What?"

"What did Lo Han give you to set this up?"

"I . . . I . . ." she stammered, then, turning aside, she began to heave.

Lehmann looked away, disgusted. "Never mind. You can tell *Shih* Soucek here." He looked back at Soucek. "We'll be gone in a while. Tell K'ang that I got tired of waiting. Tell him I've gone looking for other sport."

"And if he asks what?"

"Tell him it's drugs. Tell him I've gone to get some drugs."

THE RESTAURANT had been cleared, guards posted at every entrance. Beneath the broad slatted steps, elite marksmen lay behind low, makeshift barriers, their high-powered rifles covering the approach corridors, while in the busy kitchens Wu Shih's own personal taster sampled each dish as it was presented to him, sending them through only when he was completely satisfied.

At the center of the dark, tiled surface Marshal Tolonen sat facing Kim across a table crowded with silver trays of delicacies. Briefly the old man turned away, talking quietly to his ensign, then he turned back, facing Kim again.

"I'm sorry about all this, Kim, but Wu Shih is determined that nothing happens to me while I'm in his City. It might seem a little much, but such measures are necessary these days. We live in difficult times."

"Difficult but interesting, neh?"

Tolonen laughed. "So some might say. For myself I'd prefer things a little duller and a little safer."

"And is that why you're here, Marshal Tolonen? To make things a little safer?"

"Call me Knut, boy," he said, leaning forward and beginning to fill his plate with various bits and pieces. "But yes, you might say I'm here to make things safer. Between you and me, I'm not quite sure what it is I'm looking for, but I know the smell of rottenness when I catch a whiff of it, and there's something rotten buried in these levels, you can be sure."

"Is there any way I can help?" Kim asked, reaching for a plate.

Tolonen looked back at him. "It's nice of you to ask, but until I know what exactly's been going on here, it's hard to say what I'll need. I'll bear it in mind, though, boy. And very kind of you too. Oh, and by the way . . ." The old man felt in his jacket pocket with the fingers of his golden hand, then passed a sealed note across the table to him. "Li Yuan asked me to hand this to you personally."

Kim took the note and, setting down his plate, turned it between his fingers, studying the great seal a moment. He glanced across, noting how the Marshal was busy filling his plate, then looked down again, slitting the envelope open with a fingernail.

Inside was a single sheet, handwritten in Mandarin; the message brief and familiar.

Dear Kim,

You have been much in my thoughts of late. Working on the proposed amendments to the Edict, I have often stopped and thought how helpful it might have been to have had you at my shoulder, advising me. But before you mistake me, this is no appeal for help, but a heartfelt thank you for all you have done in the past. I merely wished you to know that should you ever need help, in any way, you have only to ask. I hope all goes well for you.

With respect,

Li Yuan

He looked up. Tolonen was watching him, smiling faintly. "So . . . how's it all going?"

"Things are fine, though there's not much to report, really. I've been holding fire on the business front, while I've been working on some new patents."

"Patents, eh?" Tolonen narrowed his eyes, as if he thought the whole thing slightly dubious.

Kim laughed. "Nothing illegal, I assure you. In fact, to be honest with you, I was surprised to learn what could actually be done within the existing guidelines. I've spent a long time recently, checking out what was already on file . . ."

Tolonen interrupted him. "I'm sorry, boy, I don't understand . . ."

"At the Central Patents Office," Kim explained quickly. "It was hard work sifting through all that stuff, but worth it in the end. Originally, all I wanted was to check whether existing patents had been registered in any of the areas I was working in."

"And were there?"

"One or two, but nothing even vaguely like what I proposed. However, in looking through the register, I noticed that there were whole areas—areas permitted under the Edict—which had essentially gone undeveloped these last one hundred and twenty years."

Tolonen eyed him curiously. "Whole areas? You mean, like whole fields of research?"

Kim shook his head. "In the context of what's there—and we're talking about several billion patents on file—you'd probably consider these 'gaps' quite small, but in terms of the research possibilities, they're vast. I could have spent months there, simply locating more such 'gaps.'"

"I see." Tolonen took a mouthful of tender pork and chewed for a moment, considering. "Have you ever thought of speeding the process up?"

"How do you mean?"

Tolonen turned his head slightly, indicating the access slot just beneath his right ear. "One of these. I'd have thought it would make your job a whole lot easier."

"A wire?" Kim looked away, suddenly uncomfortable. "I don't know . . ."

The old man leaned toward Kim. "Looking at things from the outside, it strikes me that more than half your work involves what you might crudely call 'processing' information. Now, if you were to find a way of speeding that up, you'd get a lot more done, surely?"

"Maybe."

Tolonen laughed gruffly. "The only thing that surprises me is that you hadn't thought of it yourself. You're usually way ahead of me. Way ahead!"

Kim looked down, busying himself for a moment filling his plate. When he looked up again, Tolonen was still watching him.

"So what is it, lad? Are you afraid? Is that it?"

"I . . ." Kim hesitated, not wanting to say what it was. How often had he thought this one through. How often, sitting there in the Patents Office, had he yearned for a faster way of doing things, and come to the same conclusion. Yet against the logic of the thing was a deep ingrained fear of being wired—of somehow being controlled.

"The operation's simple," Tolonen said. "And I'm certain, if you wanted it done, Li Yuan's own surgeon would perform the task. Surgeon Hung is the best there is. And so he should be. He learned his skills from his father, who did this. Fifty years I've had this. Fifty years! And it's been a godsend, especially these past six months, what with all this GenSyn business."

"I don't know," Kim said, meeting his eyes again. "It would make things easier. There's no doubting that. I just wonder . . ."

"What? That it might impair some other part of you?" Tolonen laughed, and reached across, holding Kim's shoulder briefly with his human hand. "I've never had your kind of talent, so maybe I'm not the one to comment on such things, but I've found my own wire nothing but a help all these years. All I know is that I couldn't have coped without it. Seriously."

Kim gave a tiny nod. "Maybe." But he still seemed unconvinced.

"Well," Tolonen said, leaning back again, the pearl-white chopsticks gleaming in his golden hand, "you think about it, boy. And if you want it done, I'll arrange everything for you. It's the least I can do."

———

LATER, alone in his office, Kim sat there at his desk, toying with the graphics display on his comset and thinking about what Tolonen had said. Maybe he should get wired. Maybe he was just being silly about the whole thing. After all, it wouldn't hurt to be able to process things a little faster. No, nor was there any evidence that the procedure impaired creative thought. Quite the opposite, if reports were true. In fact, there wasn't a single reason not to be wired, nothing but his own irrational fear. Even so, he held back, unable, finally, to commit himself.

So what was it? What was he really afraid of?

Control, he thought, unwilling even to utter the word, however softly. *I'm afraid of losing control again.*

And maybe that was paranoia, but he wasn't quite convinced. After all, hadn't he been the one called in by Li Yuan to look at the feasibility of wiring up the whole population? Hadn't he seen for himself how easy it would be to take that first simple step?

And if he took that first step by himself?

It isn't the same, he told himself for the hundredth time. *The two things are completely different.* And so they were. The kind of wiring Tolonen had in mind was nothing like the process Li Yuan was looking into, yet his mind refused the distinction, preferring to connect them. Wires in the head. They were a means of control. And if he took the first step, who was to say that someone else might not take the next, making him their beast?

Nonsense, a part of him replied: *you're talking fearful nonsense now, Kim Ward.*

But was he? Or was his instinct sound in this?

He huffed, exasperated with himself, then turned, startled, hearing the faintest rustle of silk behind him.

A young Han stood there, head bowed, a small tray held out before him. "Forgive me, Master. I have brought *ch'a.*"

Kim relaxed. It was only his bookkeeper, Nong Yan.

"I'm sorry, Yan. I thought I was the only one here."

Nong placed the tray down beside him, then turned, smiling. "And so you were, Master. I came in half an hour ago and saw that you were working, so I thought it best not to disturb you."

"Ah . . ." Kim nodded, yet he was surprised. Had he been that deep in his thoughts, then, that he hadn't heard the door? He set the comset down and reached across, lifting the *chung* and pouring two bowls of the steaming *ch'a.* Looking up, he offered one to the young bookkeeper.

"So how are our finances, Yan? Are we in desperate straits yet?"

Nong took the bowl with a terse nod, then squatted on the edge of the desk, beside the comset. "You know how things are, Master Kim. All bills are paid, all commitments met. Even so, the underlying problem remains as before. We are undercapitalized. If we are to expand . . ."

". . . we must get new funding," Kim finished for him, studying the details of the diagram he had sketched out on the comset's screen. "I hear what you say, Yan, but until I hear from young *Shih* Lever, we must struggle on as we are." He took a sip from his bowl, then looked up at the young man again. "You're happy, I take it, Yan?"

"Happy, Master?" Nong Yan laughed, his softly rounded face lighting up briefly. "I have a fine wife and a good Master. Why should I not be happy?"

Kim smiled. "Good. Then have patience with me, Yan, and we shall all be rich men." He tapped the surface of the comset's screen with a fingernail, indicating the faintly webbed smoke-ring shape there. "Once the patent has been registered things will begin in earnest. Until then, we hang fire. You know how it is in this business, Yan. The least said in public the better."

"So it is, Master."

"Good." Kim reached across, clearing the screen, then looked back at Nong Yan. In the few moments he had been distracted by the young bookkeeper, he had come to a decision. Taking Tolonen's card from his wallet, he studied it, memorizing the contact number, then tucked it back into the top pocket of his jacket.

Setting the *ch'a* bowl down, he leaned forward, tapping out the number on the comset's pad, then turned, looking up at Nong Yan. "Thank you, Yan. If you would leave me now . . ."

As the ensign's face appeared on the screen, Kim turned back, and, with a confidence he did not wholly feel, asked to be put through to the Marshal.

The doubts remained. Even so, he would have it done. Besides, it would be good to visit Tolonen; to sit and talk to him at length. Yes, and to see his daughter, Jelka, once again.

There was a moment's delay and then Tolonen's face appeared. "Kim! It was good to see you earlier! Very good indeed!"

Kim gave the slightest bow. "I felt I ought to thank you for the meal, Marshal. It was quite excellent."

The old man laughed heartily. "It was, wasn't it!"

"As for the other matter . . ."

"You've thought it through, I take it?"

Kim nodded.

"And?" Tolonen asked eagerly.

"And I'd like to accept your kind invitation, if I might."

Tolonen leaned back, delighted. "So you're going to have it done, eh? Good! Excellent! I'll arrange everything. Just let Hauser here know when you want to come over and we'll organize it all. You won't regret it, Kim, believe me, you really won't!"

"No," he said, smiling, reassured somewhat by the old man's genuine delight. Yet when the screen went dead once more, he felt the tightness return and wondered briefly if he had acted for the good.

Too late, he thought. And even if that wasn't entirely true, he knew that he had taken a vital step toward it.

Ten days. He would have it done ten days from now. And as he framed the thought, an image came to mind: the image of a young woman, tall and straight and elegant, with hair the color of the sun and eyes the deep blue of a summer's sky.

Kim frowned, wondering if she would remember him. Whether, in the long months that had passed since they'd met, she had ever once thought of him. He leaned forward, tapping out his personal code, summoning up the diagram again, but his mind was no longer on the patent.

Does she remember me? he thought, a sudden longing to see her face overwhelming him. *Does she?*

And if she did? What then?

He looked down at his hands where they rested in his lap—tiny, childlike hands, scarred and stunted by his experience in the Clay—and wondered what she had made of him that time, remembering how her eyes had met his own. Had he been wrong, or had something passed between them in that instant?

For a moment he sat there, undecided, then, angry at himself, at the doubts that constantly assailed him, he stood and, clearing the screen once more, hurried out, calling farewell to Nong Yan as he went.

◆◆◆◆◆

THE WHITE SILK envelope lay open, empty on the desktop. The chair behind the great desk was unoccupied, the portrait of Li Kou-lung, great-grandfather to Li Yuan, looking down imperiously on a room where nothing stirred. An ornate dragon lamp cast a pool of yellowed light about the desk, throwing heavy shadows on the tiled, mosaic floor. On the desk beside the lamp, a faint wisp of steam still drifting up from its untouched surface, rested a shallow bowl of soup, the long, straight silver handle of the spoon jutting out horizontally, the dark line of its shadow dissecting the jaundiced whiteness of the silk.

Li Yuan stood in darkness beside the carp pool, Wei Feng's letter held loosely in his left hand as he stared outward, into the shadows.

He had dismissed the servants and ordered that no one should disturb him, no matter how urgent the need. And now he stood there, unmoving, deep in thought, trying to see, in that utter, impenetrable darkness, his way through to clarity: to formulate a decision—a degree of certainty—from the sudden chaos of his thoughts.

Once before he had stood where he stood now, both figuratively and literally, facing this same matter. Back then anger and frustration—and a feeling of betrayal—had formed the thought in him, "Why Seven?" and then, as now, he had passed through the anger to a feeling of peace and to the realization that he had survived the worst his enemies could throw at him. Yet there was a difference, for now he understood that such peace, such respite, was temporary. Whatever he did, however he acted, his enemies would multiply. Cut off one head and two more would grow in its place, like that in the legend. But now, with Wei Feng's letter, something new had entered the calculations of power. Now that thought—"Why Seven?"—was given more than a tentative expression.

Li Yuan sighed. The old man had seen how things stood; had seen the divisions that lay ahead if things remained as they were, and had said to him directly, unequivocally, "Take power, Li Yuan. Grasp it now, before all Seven go down into the darkness." Those, his words, had been mirrored in his son's, Chan Yin's, face. He understood now; knew what that look of deference and humility had meant. And Chan's words, "I am my father's son," they too took on a new significance.

At first he had not believed what he had read. Slowly, one finger tracing the words, he had mouthed them to himself, then had sat back, oblivious of the servant who had brought his evening soup, trying to take in the profound significance of Wei Feng's final message to him. How would he, in Chan Yin's position, have behaved? Would he, like Chan, have submitted to his father's wishes?

He frowned, realizing he did not know himself as well as that. To give away his birthright. To bow before another when there was no need. He shook his head. No, even filial duty broke before such demands. Chan Yin would have been within his rights to ignore his father's dying wishes; to have dismissed them as the addled ravings of a sick and disappointed man. But he had not.

Beyond this question of duty and birthright lay a second, more complex one: the matter of acting upon Wei Feng's wishes, and the likely political repercussions. Ignoring the morality of it a moment, he could not, even in practical terms, accept what Wei Feng had offered him. He could not *be* the new T'ang of Eastern Asia in Chan Yin's place. While the letter stated this as Wei Feng's wish, and though Chan Yin and his brothers might agree to and accept the terms of this document—two factors which might make his inheritance incontestable in law—there was not the slightest possibility that the other five T'ang would allow it. Even Tsu Ma would act to prevent it if he knew. No, if he even so much as mentioned the possibility, it would have the effect of isolating him in Council and achieve in an instant what Wang Sau-leyan had long striven to do.

Chan Yin would inherit. The chain would remain unbroken. But in the dark something else had come to the young T'ang of Europe. Some deeper scheme that might build upon what Wei Feng had freed him to contemplate. A scheme whereby the Seven might become both simpler and more effective. Might become—he dared to whisper it aloud—"Just three of us. Tsu Ma. Wu Shih. And I . . ."

And, once uttered, the idea took root in the depths of him, became a growing seed that he might now begin to nurture with the water of thought and the sunlight of action.

Returning to his study he stood there in the doorway, looking across at the portrait of his great-grandfather, a man he had never known, wondering how he would have viewed such things and whether he, in similar circumstances, would have thought or acted differently. He could ask, of course, consult the old man's hologram, yet he sensed it would do little good. Li Kou-lung's responses had been programmed in a different age; an age of solid certainties when even to think of such matters would have been considered a sign of frailty. Sighing deeply, he crossed the room and pulled at the bell rope, summoning Chang Shih-sen, his secretary.

He stood there, waiting, staring down at the shallow bowl, then reached out and, with one finger, gently breached the cold, congealed surface, thinking to himself, *Three. Just Three*, before raising the finger to his mouth.

Li Yuan turned from the desk, drawing himself up straight, as Chang Shih-sen entered.

"Call Wei Chan Yin for me," he said, all signs of tiredness gone from him, replaced by a strange excitement. "Ask him if he will come here. At once. He will be expecting my message."

Chang Shih-sen bowed and turned to go, but Li Yuan reached out and held his arm a moment. "And Shih-sen . . . ask him to bring Tseng-li, the youngest. I have a use for him. Then rest. I will not need you for a while."

CHAPTER FIVE

The Chain of Being

N THE FORMAL GARDENS surrounding the great House at Weimar, songbirds were singing in the cypress trees, greeting the dawn. The great House itself was empty, as it had been these past eight years, since Wang Hsien, father of the present T'ang of Africa, read the Seven's Edict of Disbandment, but in the pavilion to the east of the vast, zigguratlike mass of the assembly building, a conference was taking place. There, in the shadow of the nearby City, fourteen men—the seven Chancellors of the Seven and seven graybeards, ex-Representatives of the House—sat around a huge circular table, discussing the future of Chung Kuo. On the ceiling directly overhead was a huge chart of Chung Kuo, with the boundaries of the new *Hsien*, the administrative districts, marked in red against the background white, like capillaries on the surface of a clouded eye. For eleven hours now they had talked, with only two short breaks for refreshments, but now it was almost done.

Nan Ho, seated at the table, looked up from the silk-bound folder in front of him and smiled, meeting the eyes of the pigtailed old Han facing him.

"You are a stubborn man, Ping Hsiang, but not unreasonable. What you ask for is far from what my Masters would have wished. But, as I have said many times this night, we are not here to impose. No. We must come to some new compact between Seven and Above. For the sake of all."

There was a murmur of agreement about the table and from Ping Hsiang a taut smile and a single nod of the head.

"Good. Then let us agree on this final point. Let us delay the implementation of the package of measures agreed earlier until ten months after the House has passed the proposal. That way no one can say we have not been fair and open."

"And the draft of these proposals?" Ping Hsiang asked, looking to either side of him as he spoke.

"A document is being prepared, even as we speak, and will be ready for the signature of all before we leave. You will all be given copies to take with you, naturally."

Nan Ho saw the grins of pleasure at that news and smiled inwardly. He had brought them a long way this night, from open hostility and mistrust of the Seven and their motives, to a new respect, and maybe even a grudging admiration for the men who ruled them. On the way he had gained all that his masters had entrusted him, as spokesman of their negotiating committee, to gain, and had given no more—less, in fact—than they had empowered him to give. All in all, then, it had been a successful round of negotiations, and the irony was that, now that it was done, the men who sat facing him positively glowed with satisfaction, as if they had put one over on him.

But then, that was the art of negotiation, surely? From the simplest marketplace haggling to the subtle art of statecraft, the principle behind it was the same: one had to forget the value of the thing one wanted, and begin negotiations from a point beyond. To over or undervalue, that was the basis of it, the one and only secret. But to do that one had also to know, with pinpoint accuracy, just what the thing desired was truly worth. So it had been today. He had spent long months establishing clearly in his mind just what it was the two sides wanted from this meeting.

And now it was done.

Nan Ho stood, looking about him, then clapped his hands together sharply, summoning the pavilion's servants. At once, two dozen shaven-headed young men entered, heads bowed respectfully, bearing trays of food and wine. He watched them move about the table, offering refreshments, then turned away, going across to the long window that curved away to either side.

Out there a new day was beginning, sunlight glittering off the upper windows of the House, stretching down the smooth, pearled flanks of the great building toward the deep shadow at its foot. Yesterday, before the meeting, Nan Ho had had the great doors unlocked and had gone into the House, pacing its empty corridors and lobbies until he came out into the echoing vastness of the central debating chamber. There, surrounded by tier upon tier of empty seats, he had imagined it, a year from now, filled with the elected representatives of the Above—ten thousand voices clamoring to be heard above the din—and for a moment had found himself beset by doubts. Yet he knew that there was no stepping back from this course, no real alternative to this compact between Seven and Above. It was as Li Yuan argued: it was *this* or nothing. And so he had shrugged off his doubts and gone to the negotiating table with a clear, hard mind, softening his stance only when it was clear to those who sat opposite him that he was bargaining from a position of strength, not weakness. Only then had he relaxed, bowing like the reed before the wind, making unexpected concessions. The Seven's demand for a maximum of two children per married couple was softened to three. A provocative "retrospective action" clause, never intended to be part of the final package, was fought for and then abandoned. A proposal to extend the voting franchise from the top fifty to the top one hundred levels—a measure as abhorrent to the Seven as it was to the seven graybeards facing Nan Ho—was pressed and then dropped. And so it went on, false bargains being made, while real concessions were gained.

There were footsteps just behind him. Nan Ho half turned, then formed his features into a tight, polite smile. It was Hung Mien-lo, the Chancellor of City Africa, Wang Sau-leyan's man.

"Well, Chancellor Nan," Hung said softly, his voice not carrying beyond their circle, "we have what we came for, neh?"

Nan Ho looked beyond Hung Mien-lo at the graybeards gathered on the far side of the table. "So it seems," he said, mistrustful of the man. "But it is not the power we give them that worries me—for that is little enough—as that which they might yet take for themselves. There is no stepping back from this course. To close the House a second time . . . Well, it is inconceivable, neh?"

Hung Mien-lo smiled. "Maybe. And yet stranger things have happened."

Nan Ho shook his head, disturbed by the thought. "No. To close the House again is unthinkable. Our task henceforth is a simple one. We must find ways of harnessing that power."

"Like 'Pockets' you mean?"

Nan Ho narrowed his eyes, trying to gauge what the other meant by his comment. "Pockets"—*tai*—were Representatives who had been bought by the Seven, and who had, in the past, exerted considerable influence over the House. But in the period leading up to the War-that-wasn't-a-War the Seven had tried to swamp the House with "Pockets" and the institution had fallen into disrepute. The impeachment and arrest of the *tai* in the Spring of 2201 had, in effect, been a declaration of independence by the House from the Seven, and had led directly to the War.

Nan Ho shrugged. "In this, as in all else, the past shows us the way to the future."

"The past . . ." Hung Mien-lo laughed softly and leaned closer. "And when the future finally comes? What then, Master Nan? How do we block the future? How harness it? For it *is* coming. You and I know that, even if our masters don't."

Nan Ho stared back at Hung Mien-lo a moment, his face impassive, then, seeing that the scribes were finished, the document prepared, moved past his fellow Chancellor, leaving the questions unanswered.

THE TWO BODYGUARDS looked about them nervously as the sedan was set down, unused to being so far down the levels, but Michael Lever, stepping down from the carriage, seemed not to notice their unease. He looked about him, noting the stark neatness of his surroundings, then crossed the narrow hallway.

There was no entrance hall, no suite of offices isolating the inner workings of the Company from the outside world, merely a big double door, decorated, like many Company premises, with the Company logo. Lever smiled, amused by the simplicity of it all. He reached out to touch the delicate, shimmering web, then drew his fingers back sharply, surprised to find the strands warm, the background deathly cold.

He took a step back, studying the design. At the center of the web was a tiny, smiling spider, while above it was the Company name, *Ch'i Chu*—Spider—written in English and Mandarin.

This was the first time he had visited Kim at his facility and, despite all Kim had said, he was surprised to find it all so low-key. Why, there wasn't even a camera over the doorway . . .

The doors shuddered, then, unexpectedly, melted away, leaving only the logo, hovering in the empty darkness. One of the guards made to come past him, but Michael raised a hand. Then, a faint smile of amusement on his lips, he stepped through.

There was the faintest crackle of static, the feeling of having passed through the flimsiest of barriers, and then he was inside. A tall, slightly balding Han stood before him, his head lowered, his hands folded before him respectfully.

"Welcome, *Shih* Lever. We were expecting you."

Michael laughed. "I see you were." He turned, watching the door shimmer back into existence.

"Two holograms," the Han explained, straightening up. "One for the door, one for the logo. And behind them a security force field. It was Kim's idea."

Michael nodded. "It's clever. But I prefer more solid things."

"Perhaps so. But solidity is a relative thing, *Shih* Lever. If the field had been turned on, you would have found it hard enough to walk through, hologram or no. But forgive me, let me introduce myself. My name is T'ai Cho."

Michael lowered his head. "T'ai Cho . . . I am delighted to meet you. Kim has spoken often of you. He is fortunate to have such a good friend and guardian."

The Han bowed, but his face remained expressionless. "The good fortune has been mine alone, *Shih* Lever. The honor of serving so fine and talented a young man falls to few in this life. I would have counted my life as having had little meaning had I not met *Shih* Ward."

Michael nodded, impressed by the Han's words. Yet if what Kim had told him were true, he owed T'ai Cho not merely his chance in life, but life itself. When Kim had come out of the Clay, it was T'ai

Cho who—as his tutor in the Reclamation Project—had not merely recognized and fostered Kim's talent, but had interceded at a crucial moment to prevent his death.

"But let us not stand here talking, *Shih* Lever. Let me take you through. Kim is working just now—finishing something he began last night—but he will not be long. Maybe you would like to watch. If you would follow me . . ."

"Thank you, T'ai Cho. It will be a real pleasure."

He followed T'ai Cho through. There were two small offices off to the left of the corridor, but the main work space was a big L-shaped room at the end. There he found Kim, sitting with his back to the door, crouched forward, facing an experimental environment—the vacuum-sealed transparent box five *ch'i* to a side. The top half of Kim's head was hidden within a bulky headwrap, a dozen or more wires trailing off into a console to one side, while his arms were inside the box, enclosed in skintight armatures as he operated the nano-fine waldoes. Two lab-coated technicians sat on the edge of the desk nearby, so engrossed in what Kim was doing that they didn't even look up as Michael came into the room.

Michael went across and stood behind them. As far as he could see nothing was happening. Or—and the thought struck him as strangely amusing—as if Kim were only pretending to do something. The delicate appendages seemed to cut and mold the air, drawing out fine lines of nothingness, the tips of the waldoes sparking and flickering, but it was all to no apparent purpose. He felt a vague twinge of disappointment. There seemed no point to what Kim was doing; no discernible result. Michael squinted, trying to make out something he had missed, but it was no good. There really did seem to be nothing there.

He turned, looking about him. There were benches, cabinets, various items of machinery, most of them inexpensive, older models, all of it so unexpectedly shabby that he found himself making unwarranted comparisons: setting all of this against the state-of-the-art efficiency of his father's labs. It all seemed wrong somehow; too small, too cobbled-together. How could anything worthwhile be produced in conditions like this?

For the briefest moment he wondered whether he might not be

mistaken in his plans to work with Ward, but then he remembered his father's interest and what he had heard from his European contacts. And then there was what he himself knew about the boy's abilities.

The boy . . . He turned, studying Ward in profile, then looked away, conscious of how his thoughts had betrayed him. *Appearances.* With Ward it wasn't possible to judge things on appearances, for he was not what he seemed. Nineteen now, Ward seemed little more than a child, a boy of twelve, thirteen at most, his diminutive stature the result of his childhood in the Clay. That experience, down there in the darkness beneath the City's foundations, had shaped him, inwardly and out, making him—at a glance—different from those he went among. Michael smiled. Compared to the tall, well-fed citizens of First Level, Kim seemed but the unfleshed suggestion of humanity—a throwback to an earlier evolutionary stage. Physically, Kim had so little substance. But appearances were deceptive, for there was a fire in his eyes, a strength even in his smallest movement that belied that first impression. And one further thing. For Ward was reputedly the finest theoretical scientist in the whole of Chung Kuo.

He looked back. Kim was watching him, his dark eyes curious. "Michael . . ." he said softly, greeting him. "One moment and I'm done."

He watched. Where there had been nothing, a fine point of pure white light blossomed, a fine web of threads spreading out like buds from the radiant hub, then turning back on themselves until they formed a tiny, spherical net, the whole thing taking on detail and complexity until it seemed to glow with an intense energy. It began to turn, slowly at first, then faster, the glow fading and returning until it formed a regular pulse.

Michael shook his head, astonished. It was beautiful. He glanced at Kim and saw how he was leaning forward now, his lips parted, his breathing shallow. Michael shivered, then looked back, his eyes drawn to the spinning helix of light.

It spun, faster and faster, and as it spun brief, brilliant pulses of light flashed from its glowing heart, each pulse striking one of the tiny studlike targets that dotted the inside walls of the chamber. Slowly the light intensified until he had to half-lid his eyes, then turn aside, his eyes squeezed shut, one hand shielding his face. But even then he could still see it through the flesh of his eyelids, spinning at the center of the void, like a tiny, burning star, flashing magnificently.

For a moment longer it maintained its perfect equilibrium at the center of the vacuum, then, with a noisy crackle of static, the light abruptly died.

Michael turned, blinking, staring into the darkness of the chamber, then looked across. For a moment Kim sat there, perfectly still, then, with a tiny shudder, he sat back, pulling his arms from the waldoes.

"Kuan Yin!" Michael said softly, shaking his head.

Kim turned his head and looked at him, a faint, almost apologetic smile on his lips, then, tugging off the headwrap, he came across, taking Lever's hands. "Michael . . . It's good to see you. How are things?"

Michael smiled. "I'm fine. But what *was* that?"

Kim half glanced back at the empty chamber, then shrugged. "It's something long-term, that's all. A problem I've set myself. I thought I had a solution, but, well, let's just say that it's not stable."

Michael laughed. "Yes . . . but what was it? It looked beautiful."

Kim moved past him, then turned back, a rough sketch in one hand. "Basically, it's a switching device. It's meant to transmit energy at a molecular level. The trouble is, it has to be able to maintain its form and turn at phenomenal speeds—at the speed of molecular reactions themselves, to be accurate. At present, however, it's very fragile. The least molecular interference from outside and it breaks up. As you saw. Add to that the fact that it's far too big for practical use, and you can see just how far I am from solving things."

Michael glanced at the paper Kim had given him, but the equations meant nothing to him. They might just as well have been written in Shang dynasty Mandarin. "Maybe, but it's certainly impressive."

Kim laughed. "You think so? Well, maybe, but sometimes it feels like I'm grasping at nothingness itself. That I reach out and close my hand and . . . there's nothing there. And I ask myself, what if I'm wrong? Good as I am, what if I'm wrong? What if all the talent I have isn't enough? What if the universe is *different* from how I conceive it? What if it won't conform to the pattern in my head?"

"Then you change the pattern, surely?"

Kim studied Michael a moment, then looked away. "But what if I *am* the pattern?" For a moment Kim stood there, perfectly still, staring into the empty chamber, then, as if remembering suddenly where he was, he looked back, smiling. "Well, how did it go? Is it still on?"

It was Michael's turn to look away. "I'm sorry, Kim. The Old Man wouldn't budge. And without those funds . . ."

Kim reached out and touched his arm. "I understand. And it's all right. We can make do as we are for a while longer. But you . . . you needed that money, didn't you?"

Michael met his eyes and nodded.

"So? What will you do?"

Michael smiled stoically. "I've a scheme or two. The Old Man won't put bit and brace on me that easily."

Kim nodded, but he could see how disappointed—and, beneath that, how angry—Michael was at his father for freezing his accounts.

"It was such a small amount," Michael said quietly. "Less than he spends on some of the old memorabilia he buys. But that's how it is. We have to live with it, neh?" He reached inside his jacket and took out a letter. "Here. I thought this might help."

Kim took the envelope without looking at it. "What is it?"

"A letter of introduction, to the Hang Su Credit Agency."

"Credit?" Kim laughed, recalling the difficulties he had faced in going to the Credit Agencies when he had first set up *Ch'i Chu*. The message had been the same everywhere he'd turned. Find a major sponsor or forget it. That was how things worked here. Big fish and little fish. But he had been determined to keep his independence. He had struggled on, slowly using up the funds Li Yuan had given him, cutting corners and making do, trusting that his talent would be enough to pull him through. But now it was make-or-break time. He had to sell some of his ideas—to generate enough money to allow *Ch'i Chu* to live another year or two.

He shrugged. "I'm not averse to the idea, but who in their right mind would give me credit?"

Michael smiled. "Don't worry. I've made discreet inquiries and it seems that the Brothers Hang are willing to do business with you. I've arranged an interview for tomorrow at two."

Kim laughed, genuinely surprised. "Okay. But what do I put up for security? I've sunk everything I have into this place. And now that your father has tightened the reins . . ."

Michael was still smiling. "What about the patents? They're worth something, aren't they?"

"Maybe. Once they've been developed."

"Then use them. You plan to register them tomorrow, right? Good. Then go and see the Brothers straight afterward. Put the patents up as security. You'll have your funding by six tomorrow evening, I guarantee."

Kim studied the envelope a moment, then, smiling, looked back up at Michael. "Okay. I'll do as you say. And thank you, Michael. Thank you for everything."

"Oh, and one last thing. How busy are you?"

Kim laughed. "I'm always busy. But what do you mean?"

"Tonight, I mean. Could you free some time?"

"I guess so. Everything's prepared for tomorrow. What is it?"

Michael smiled, a broad, warm smile of enjoyment, undiminished by his troubles with his father. "It's a ball, Kim. A coming-of-age ball for a good friend of mine." He reached into his pocket and took out a card, handing it across. "Here. Your invitation. It's fancy dress."

"Fancy dress?"

Lever laughed, beginning to leave. "Ask T'ai Cho. And if you've any trouble rustling up a costume, contact my secretary, Mary. She'll sort something out for you."

Kim studied the gilt lettering of the invitation and nodded, recalling the last time he had been to a ball—the evening the younger sons had been arrested—and felt a tiny, unexpected thrill of anticipation ripple down his spine.

———◆◆◆◆◆———

"Sweetheart?"

Jelka stood there before the giant image of her father's face, smiling broadly. "Daddy! How are you? When are you coming home?"

The great wall of the Marshal's face restructured itself, the muscles of the mouth and cheeks rearranging themselves, the broad smile becoming a look of dour resignation.

"Something's come up, I'm afraid. A development in the GenSyn case. It's important—something I have to follow up personally—so I might be here another three or four days. Is that all right?"

She smiled determinedly. "Of course, Papa. You do what you have to do. I'll be okay."

"Good." He stared at her proudly a moment, his eyes great orbs of steel amid the craggy cliff-face of his features.

"So how was lunch?"

"Lunch?" He frowned, then, realizing what she meant, gave a broad grin. "Lunch was fine. Young Ward sends his regards. It seems he'll be coming over to Europe quite soon, to be wired."

"Wired?" She looked up into her father's face uncertainly.

"You know . . ." He touched the access slot beneath his right ear uneasily, knowing how she felt about it. "The standard thing. A direct-processing link. He says it'll help with his work. Make things easier. Anyway . . ." he cleared his throat and put on a determinedly cheerful expression, "you can talk to him directly about it when he's over. I've invited him to dinner."

She nodded, pretending a polite interest, but beneath it she felt her chest tighten, her pulse begin to quicken. "That's good. It'll be nice to see him again."

For a moment the old man's face beamed down at his daughter, drinking in the sight of her, then, with a deep sniff, he sat back slightly, his expression suddenly more businesslike.

"Well, my girl. I must get on. There's much to do here, and I'd like to get it done with as soon as possible."

"Of course. And take care, all right?"

He nodded, the movement exaggerated by the screen. "And you, my love." Then he was gone, the screen blank.

She went across and sat at her father's desk, swiveling the big chair back and forth, staring out across the room thoughtfully. *So the boy was coming here . . .*

She frowned, then gave a small, strange laugh. The boy was not a child these days. In fact, if she remembered rightly, Kim was almost a year older than her. It was just that she still thought of him like that. After all, he was so small. So tiny and graceful. So delicately formed . . .

She shivered, then stood, disturbed suddenly by the thought of him coming there. But why should that be? He was just a boy, after all. A friend and colleague of her father's. It wasn't as if . . .

She shook her head, then turned, facing the screen once more, staring at the perfect whiteness. It was just that his eyes had burned so brightly that time. As if they saw things differently.

For the briefest instant she saw once more the tiny fox, there in the cave on the island, staring back at her with its dark and feral eyes, the memory so vivid it was as if she stood there, watching it once more. And then it was gone, leaving only the plain white screen, and the memory of some wild, dark thing that did not belong in the world of levels.

———

NAN HO was flying east, over the heart of Asia, the sun behind him now, the Altai Mountains beneath. Ahead lay the great desert, beyond it, ancient China and, in the shadow of the Ta Pa Shan in Sichuan Province, the estate at Tongjiang. He had sent ahead that he was coming, but, in the wake of Wei Feng's death—announced on the media an hour into his flight—he was not certain what state things would be in.

Wei Feng had been the oldest, the last of that generation. Even Wu Shih, the eldest of them now, was but a young man by comparison.

The thought troubled Nan Ho as he sat in his padded chair, sorting through his papers. The new T'ang, Wei Chan Yin, was a good man and a sound administrator, who had proved himself already as Regent in his father's stead, but Wei Feng's death had robbed the Council of its last real vestige of experience. Without the old man, they seemed less dignified, robbed somehow of authority. It would not be said, not openly, but it was certain to be thought—to be whispered ear to ear. And, though no outward change would be evident, the Seven would be weaker. For power was something manifested not merely in its exercise, but also in how the people perceived those who ruled them.

For the third time in as many years, the Seven were diminished: first by the murder of Wang Hsien, then by Li Shai Tung's sudden demise, and now this. It was fortunate, perhaps, that they had made their "deal" with the Above before the news had broken. Or maybe not. Maybe this news—to be announced this very evening—would be seen as further weakness. As a further erosion of power.

And when power failed altogether?

Nan Ho shuddered, then pushed the papers aside, angry with himself, conscious that Hung Mien-lo's words had got to him. Yet even as he settled back in his chair, a new determination formed in him. Whatever happened from now on, he would be prepared for it. For he was warned now. It would be no one's fault but his if they faltered in the years ahead. And he, Nan Ho, son of Nan Ho-tse, would do his utmost to ensure that that did not happen. He would make it his sole concern—his life's work.

Even if death were the only payment for his pains.

———

LI YUAN was waiting for Nan Ho in his study when he arrived, the young T'ang dressed in the traditional clothes of mourning, as if it were his father who had just died. The great desk in front of him was unusually clear, only a small white envelope set to one side. Nan Ho glanced at it as he bowed, then looked again, surprised to find Wei Feng's distinctive seal set firmly in the bloodred wax.

"You have done well, Master Nan," Li Yuan said without preliminaries. "I have spoken to Wu Shih and Tsu Ma and they are pleased with the terms you have drawn up. I thought we might have had to give much more."

Nan Ho lowered his head again, but the mystery of the envelope distracted him. What message had the dead T'ang left? And was it to Li Yuan alone, or did all seven have similar envelopes?

"Now that the matter is settled, there is something else I would like you to take on, Master Nan."

Nan Ho met the young T'ang's eyes, for that brief moment bridging the great gulf in rank that lay between them. *"Chieh Hsia?"*

"I have had news from Tolonen in America. It seems he is on to something out there."

"Did he say what, *Chieh Hsia?*"

Li Yuan shook his head. "Don't you find it odd, Master Nan? I mean, it is most unlike the Marshal to keep things to himself. If he has a fault it is usually that he keeps us far too well informed."

Nan Ho laughed. "That is so, *Chieh Hsia.* But this is his old friend Klaus Ebert's business. Tolonen saw the man as a brother, and he goes about this business as a brother would."

"True enough," Li Yuan said thoughtfully. "I have noticed that already. He sees this as a debt of honor, neh?"

"That is so, *Chieh Hsia.* He did say one thing to me, however. At Nantes, before he left."

"Yes? And what was that?"

"He mentioned some anomalies in the GenSyn records for their North American operation. When I questioned him about it, he spoke of accounting irregularities, forged shipment details, missing documents, and the like. It was a bland, evasive answer. A *safe* answer. Yet when he met my eyes I knew he meant something else. Something is missing, *Chieh Hsia,* and Tolonen has gone to find it."

Li Yuan sighed. "I do not like it, Master Nan, but for once I shall have to put up with it. The Marshal is a stubborn old man, but an honest one. We shall find out when he is ready to tell us, I suppose. But in the meantime, I want you to find out what you can. I do not want us caught wholly unprepared."

Nan Ho bowed low. As ever he was already onto the matter. "As you wish, *Chieh Hsia.*"

After the Chancellor had gone, Li Yuan leaned across, drawing the envelope toward him. In five hours Wei Chan Yin would be here.

He raised the letter to his nose and sniffed, then, setting it down again, shook his head. What had he expected? The smell of death? Of fear and darkness? Whatever, there was nothing. Nothing but the neutral scents of wax and ink and paper. Even so, he had felt a kind of fear—an almost primal dread—of what lay within that slender pocket of whiteness. It was fate, written in the dark, spidery hand of a dead man. Li Yuan shivered, thinking of it, and pushed it from him.

In five hours . . .

OLD MAN LEVER stood on the podium at the center of the crowd, a full whiskey tumbler held in one big, square-knuckled hand, a red, white, and blue silk folder in the other. Behind him, a huge stars and stripes banner was draped over the far end of the vestibule, concealing the entrance to the deck. Lever smiled and looked about him, lifting his glass in greeting. They were all gathered here today— all of the original investors—fifty of the most important men in the North American Above, multibillionaires every one of them. But it had been his idea and his drive which had brought this into being. And now, at the inauguration ceremony, it would be he, Charles Lever, who would take the lion's share of the praise.

"Gentlemen . . . *Friends* . . . Welcome." Lever combed a lock of steel-gray hair back from his eyes and beamed, showing strong, slightly yellowing teeth. "You all know why we're here and what we're here for, so let's skip the formalities and go right on in. I'm sure you're all as anxious as I am to see how the money has been spent . . ."

There was a roar of approval, and as Lever stepped down from the podium and made his way across, the small crowd followed, talking among themselves.

It was not often that they met, and to all it seemed particularly auspicious that it was on such a day, when news of Wei Feng's death and of the triumph at Weimar coincided. The normally placid old men fairly buzzed with the news. It was all linked in, they said; part of the new tide, turning in their favor. From the low ebb of their humiliation on the steps of the Lincoln Memorial they had rebuilt. And now their time was coming. The negotiations at Weimar had been the first step; the elections were the next. And each step would bring them closer to their aim—of a strong and independent America, free of the rule of the Seven, taking its rightful place in the world once more. Not an empire, maybe, but a nation. And who knew what might come of that? Maybe they would take up where they had left off and reach out for the stars, the eagle stretching its wings . . .

Beneath the huge stars and stripes banner Lever turned, facing them again. "I realize that you gentlemen have been champing at the bit, wanting to know what's been going on here, but when you see what has been achieved in the past ten months, I'm sure you'll agree that it was money well spent."

He lifted a hand. At the signal, the banner drew slowly to one side, revealing a huge entrance tunnel, the walls and ceiling of which had been made to seem like marble. Over the entrance was a massive memorial stone, an inscription cut into the stone in a bold, classical face:

THE RICHARD CUTLER FOUNDATION
FOR GENETIC RESEARCH
Opened this Seventh day of March, A.D. Two Thousand Two Hundred and Nine, by Charles Alexander Lever, Head of the ImmVac Corporation of North America.

Through the archway could be glimpsed a bright space, landscaped like a great park, and in its midst something huge, like the plinth of a giant statue.

They went through, coming out into a wooded glade from which could be seen the full extent of the Foundation and its grounds.

Lever had had the top three decks "knocked into one" as he called it, so that the ceiling—a huge screen, programmed to seem like a summer sky—was a good two hundred *ch'i* overhead. But that was not what first caught the eye. In the center of the landscaped gardens was an immense building; a structure which was as familiar to the old men standing there as the stars and stripes of the Sixty-Nine States. The Empire State Building.

For a moment there was stunned silence and then an uproar as the old men clapped and yelped their approval.

"It's wonderful, Charles," his friend, the financier, James Fisher, said, slapping Lever's shoulder enthusiastically. "The architect is to be congratulated. He's caught the spirit of the old building to perfection."

Lever beamed, conscious of congratulations from all sides. "Yes, he has, hasn't he. I gave him the basic idea and he came up with the rest. He had to modify, of course, but the general effect is just what I wanted. The labs and most of the research facilities are beneath this floor, of course—the whole thing stretches down another five decks— but this is the showpiece. The reception area, the main wards, and the lecture halls are all within the main building." He smiled and looked about him once more, "As you'll see."

In front of the huge studded entrance doors Lever turned and raised his hands. "Gentlemen! One last thing before we go in. I am proud to say that only yesterday I received delivery of the latest masterpiece by the greatest painter of our age, Ernst Heydemeier."

There was a low murmur of surprise. Lever looked about him, savoring the moment, then added, "Furthermore, let me add that I have donated this specially commissioned painting to the Institute in commemoration of this inauguration ceremony. If you would follow me . . ."

As Lever turned, the doors began slowly to ease back, revealing the facing wall-screen and Heydemeier's painting. There was a gasp of surprise and then, as more and more of the giant canvas came into view, a mounting tide of applause.

At the center of the painting the giant figure of a youth, his muscular chest naked, stood atop a mountain's rugged crest, looking toward the west, the shaft of a huge banner clasped firmly in one hand. His tautly sculpted and beautiful features glowed with a vision-ary fervor. Behind the youth and the wind-furled flag, a company of youths—young gods, they seemed—climbed toward the summit, their faces gleaming, looking toward the sun that bathed the whole picture in its glorious golden light.

"Gods . . ." one of the old men murmured, staring up at the huge canvas, his mouth agape. Nor was he alone. All about Lever the old men had fallen silent as the full scope of the massive painting came into view. There was a moment's hesitation, then, slowly, with a growing sense of awe, they began to approach the screen.

Old Man Lever stood there, looking about him, knowing what they were feeling at that moment. It was what he himself had felt only yesterday when he had first seen the painting. It was astonishing. Once more Heydemeier had taken his idea and transformed it. And now that he had seen it for himself, he knew. This was the Dream. This was what had driven him these past few years. This vision of perfection, glimpsed in the golden light of a new dawn.

He shivered. If it could be done, it would be done here. And this, this masterpiece of visionary painting, was the perfect statement of intent. To be a god and live forever—what was wrong with want-ing that?

"It's astonishing," someone said close by, real awe in his voice.

"You're right, Charles," another added softly. "It's a masterpiece. I've never seen its like!"

He looked about him, smiling, accepting the words of praise that came from all sides. Then, raising his voice once more, he beckoned them on. "Come, gentlemen. Let's not stand here gawping. Let's go through. There are wonders enough within."

TWO HOURS LATER they were standing in the central lecture hall, beneath a massive reproduction of Martin Waldeseemuller's spectacular "Universalis Cosmographia," the ancient world map, dated 1507, which filled one whole end of the theater. The original woodcut, the first map to give the New World the name of America, hung in Old Man Lever's study in Philadelphia.

They had seen it all now, and had been impressed. There was no doubt that if a solution to the aging process could be found, it would be found here, for they had bought the finest state-of-the-art equipment and hired the very best men in every field. Expert after expert had met them as they'd toured the facility, giving a brief speech of explanation before they moved on, each one impressive in their own right, each building upon the general impression of competence. It looked good. Very good indeed. All that was needed was time and money . . . and a little luck. Or so Lever had claimed. Already the research had begun; each of the eight departments looking into their own highly specialized area. Everything had been thought out carefully beforehand, every base covered. Or so it seemed.

The tour completed, Lever went among the old men, talking with them, gauging their response, modestly accepting their praise. But all the while something nagged at him. It looked good. Indeed, it was good—the best money could buy. But it wasn't "the best." Nor would it be until he had Ward working for him.

He had looked about him as they toured the establishment, trying to see it all as they saw it, with fresh eyes, but all the time he was conscious that it was just a shell—a delightful piece of technological trickery, manned not by geniuses but by lesser men, schooled in old and rigid ways of thought. And he knew—because he had made it his business to know—that it all meant nothing—nothing at all— without that final tiny piece; that spark that would bring this great, magnificent engine of research to life.

It all came back to Ward. He had to have Ward. And if the man could not be bought, maybe he could be hassled into the job. Bullied and threatened and ultimately *forced* into taking on the task. Because, if his advisors were correct, there was no one else who could take on the task. No one brilliant enough to see through the obvious and come up with a wholly new solution to the problem.

Lever took another glass of whiskey and drained it at a shot. No, if Ward would not come willingly, he would come out of need: because there was nowhere else to go, no one else to turn to. And that would happen. He would make sure it would happen. Because the alternative . . .

Lever stood there, staring up at the ancient map, conscious suddenly of the billions of men and women who had lived and died since this chart had been drawn. Of all those countless souls gone to dust and nothingness. Then, drawing a long shuddering breath, he turned, smiling, and went among the crowd of old men once again, letting nothing of his unease show on the surface of his well-lined face.

───────

MICHAEL WAS SILENT for some time after Kustow had gone, studying the papers Mary had set before him, then he turned in his chair, looking across at her.

When he had hired her, three weeks back, he had not been sure how things would work out. Her record, working in middle management for MemSys, the biggest of his Companies, had been good— first rate, in fact—but she had had little experience of working as a personal assistant. Nor would he have hired her had any of the four men he had wanted been available. But they were not. Whether his father had frightened them off or simply bought them out was irrelevant. He had been left with no choice. It was Mary Jennings or no one. And maybe he had only got her because his father had thought it beneath him to buy off a mere woman. But Mary had been better— far better—than either he or his father had anticipated. She was sharp, efficient, and resourceful. Moreover, she worked well under pressure—an invaluable trait at present, when the pressure was unrelenting. In many ways she was the best assistant he had ever worked with.

He sat back, lacing his fingers together. "Em . . . ?"

She looked up, startled. "I . . ." Then she saw the look of surprise on his face and looked away.

"Why did you call me that?"

"Call you what . . . ? Oh. Em, you mean?" He held up a copy of one of her reports. "It's how you sign yourself. The letter M. I guess I've seen it so often now I've come to think of you simply as Em."

She looked down, her mind still reeling. Of course. M for Mary. Mary Jennings. How strongly she had come to associate herself with that name these past twenty-one months; yet at the slightest reminder it had been dislodged, her real name brought back to her. Em for Emily. *Emily Ascher . . .*

She shivered, articulating it clearly in her head. Emily Ascher, late of City Europe and member of the Council of Five of the now defunct *Ping Tiao*—the infamous "Levelers"—who had brought chaos to the levels and then, foolishly, she thought, had fire-bombed Bremen stack, killing over eleven thousand innocent people. It was twenty-one months now since DeVore had given her false papers and bundled her off onto an inter-City rocket to a new life. Months in which she had maintained a low profile, keeping herself to herself, building up the solid foundations of her life, all the while waiting, biding her time.

For the time would come. And when it did . . .

"You know, I think you're right."

She looked across; saw how he was watching her. "Pardon?"

He tapped the report. "About Dunn. I don't think we can trust him. He may have been my father's enemy for a long time now, but that doesn't necessarily make him my friend." He smiled. "I know how my father thinks. How he operates. He's a rich man, not averse to buying whatever he needs. And money can make a man—even a Dunn—take stranger bedfellows than his lifelong enemy, neh, Em?"

She had it on her tongue to correct him, to ask him not to call her that again, but something in the way he said it touched her. It was like that moment when he had asked her to take over as his assistant. She could have said no. Indeed, the sensible thing would have been to say no. But there had been something in the way he'd asked her—some hint, perhaps, of that vulnerability she had witnessed in him—that had made her agree. And so now.

She smiled. "It's been my experience that one should trust least those who claim alliance purely on the basis of a shared hatred. There's always a falling out."

So it was. She had seen the *Ping Tiao* destroyed for that very reason, when Gesell had allied himself with the odious DeVore. But never again. When it came to making alliances, she would set her own terms in future.

Michael was looking at her strangely. "By the way, what are you doing tonight?"

She laughed, the question catching her totally off guard. "I'm sorry . . ."

He looked away, as if flustered—as if he had overstepped some mark, then sat back, laughing. "Look, if you've something on, forget it, but I thought, if you hadn't . . . well, perhaps you'd like to accompany me to a ball."

"A *ball?* You mean, like on the trivees?"

He shook his head. "No. This is real. An old friend of mine. She's celebrating her twenty-fifth, her Coming-of-Age. Her parents died some years back and her estate's been in trust all this time, but now it's all hers and she's throwing a huge party at the family home. I just thought . . ."

She sat back, staring at him. "Why me?" she asked, after a moment. "I'm sure there must be a dozen beautiful women out there who'd be . . ."

"I thought it might be fun," he said, interrupting her. "You've worked hard for me and, well, I thought you might enjoy it. I was . . ." He laughed. "Well, I wasn't sure how you'd react. I thought you might mistake my motives. You know, a boss and his assistant . . ."

"Especially when the assistant's a woman . . ."

He narrowed his eyes, staring at her, then nodded, a faint smile of amusement on his lips. "Well? Would you like to see how the Supernal let their hair down?"

Did she? Did she really want to mix at this level? For a moment longer she hesitated, and then she smiled; a beautiful, radiant smile. "I'd like that, *Shih* Lever. I'd like that very much."

"Good. But it's Michael . . ." he said, returning her smile. "Tonight you must call me Michael."

———————

"Is that it?"

Wei Chan Yin looked up from where he sat in Li Yuan's chair and met the young T'ang's eyes. There was nothing in his face to show what he was feeling, nor had he hesitated once in drafting the document. He had sat there, handwriting it to Li Yuan's dictation, not glancing up, nor aside to where his brother, Tseng-li, stood. More like a servant than an equal. Yet Li Yuan knew, better than anyone, the strengths, the qualities of this man. He had often talked with him when they had both been Princes and when, in the final period of his father's illness, Chan Yin had acted as his father's Regent on the Council.

"Sign it at the bottom," Li Yuan said. "Then have Tseng-li put his name to it as witness. I will sign last."

Chan Yin smiled and nodded. His hand moved across the thick parchment, signing his name with a flourish of the brush. That done, Tseng-li moved up beside him and, leaning over the desk, inked his brush and signed beside his brother's name.

Chan Yin looked up and, turning the paper about, offered it to Li Yuan. Tseng-li held out the brush. Li Yuan took the brush and signed, taking a deep breath as he straightened up.

"You understand why this must be?" he said, smiling sadly at Chan Yin.

Chan Yin paused, then shook his head. "Not yet, Yuan. Not ever, perhaps. But it was my father's dying wish." His mouth formed a faint smile. "You understand?"

Li Yuan laughed. "Maybe. Maybe not. But I am grateful, cousin."

Chan Yin gave a slight bow. Beside him, Tseng-li was looking down at his elder brother, that same restraint—product of the goodness that was in them all—shaping his features. Seeing the two men thus, Li Yuan felt deeply moved. To have such sons as these. A man might die satisfied, knowing he had bred so straight and true. He sighed, the determination forming in him that he would use this document only if he must.

"Tseng-li," he said softly. "There is something else I want from you."

The youngest looked up, his dark eyes looking out from his beautiful face with a directness and openness that Li Yuan had rarely met. "What is it, *Chieh Hsia*?"

Li Yuan smiled at the honorific. "I would like your service, Tseng-li." He paused, then, "I want you to replace Chang Shih-sen and be my secretary."

Chan Yin looked up at him, for the first time a look of surprise on his face. But Tseng-li merely nodded. "As you wish, *Chieh Hsia*."

"Good." Li Yuan smiled, more at ease now that it was all concluded. "Then we might set the day for your coronation, Wei Chan Yin. It is time you too were T'ang."

CHAPTER SIX

Into Emptiness

KIM STEPPED DOWN from the hired sedan and looked about him, astonished. A red-painted wall ten *ch'i* in height enclosed the First Level mansion, a gateway, topped by an ancient bell tower, providing the only way into the grounds. The huge double doors were of burnished bronze, studded with iron, the whole thing flanked by massive dragon pillars, painted a vivid emerald green. It was brutal. Like something from the fifteenth century. A *Ming* frontier fort, complete with watchtowers. The last thing one expected to find here at the top of the City.

All around him sedans were setting down, their occupants climbing out and making their way across what seemed some kind of horse track to the gateway. The variety and richness of their costumes were fascinating. They had come dressed as gods and goddesses, emperors and concubines, notorious villains and revered sages. All of history had been pillaged for this one night. By comparison his own spider costume was somewhat dour and unimaginative. He had not realized how much time and effort these people would put into something so . . . insignificant.

He went across, then stopped, staring up at the great stone lintel that supported the bell tower. At its center, a single Han pictogram had been carved into the stone: the character *Chung*, meaning "The Arbitrator"—the name of the family who owned this great Mansion.

He frowned, conscious that his expectations had once again been turned upsidedown. He had thought it would be like that evening at the Lever Mansion, when the Young Sons had been arrested. To be honest, he had not expected any Han to be present. He turned, looking about him, watching the people filing past him. They formed a queue beneath the bell tower, waiting to enter, their invitation cards held out for inspection by two huge, bare-chested Han, who stood before the open doors, barring the way.

Kim joined the queue, catching the air of excitement that was on every side. Reaching the front, he expected the guard to take his card and pass him through, as he had all those before, but the man blocked his way, putting a hand on his chest, restraining him.

"Wait there," the guard ordered gruffly, then turned his head. "Chang!" he called, summoning the second guard. "Get the Captain over. That missing invitation—I think we might have found it!"

Kim looked down, containing his anger. He had met this before. Not often, but enough to recognize it for what it was. To them he was not another human being, he was Clay, the lowest of the low. His large eyes and diminutive stature gave that away at a glance. And some—like the guard—hated the Clay and all those who came from there with a bitter and totally irrational hatred.

He waited, his eyes lowered, listening as the guard and the Captain talked between themselves in Mandarin. Their assumption that a mere Clayborn couldn't understand the tongue was typical of their kind.

"You! Raise your head!"

The Captain's barked command surprised Kim. He jerked his head up, meeting the man's eyes. The Captain studied him a moment, then made a coarse remark in Mandarin. Behind him the guards laughed.

"Well?" he said, thrusting the invitation at him. "Where did you get this? You're not on the guest list, and one of the invitations was reported missing. It can only be assumed . . ."

"*What* can only be assumed?"

The voice came from behind the guards. They stepped back, revealing the tall figure of Michael Lever, dressed in the bright blue and white costume of an American general of the late eighteenth century.

"*Shih* Lever . . ." the Captain said, bowing low, as if acknowledging both the real and illusory gulf in rank between them. "Forgive me, but this man was trying to gain admission to the grounds. There was a report this afternoon that one of the invitations had gone missing and . . ."

"Be quiet, you imbecile! *Shih* Ward is my honored guest. He is a great man. A *ch'un tzu*. You will bow low before him and apologize . . ."

Embarrassed, Kim spoke up. "Michael, please, there's really no need. The Captain was mistaken, that's all. Besides, he was right to be cautious. These are troubled times and this is a great house. Its doors should be protected."

Michael stared at Kim a moment, then shrugged. "If that's what you want. But I think you're mistaken. I think this shit knew *exactly* what he was doing."

Almost certainly, Kim thought, *but I'll not be a party to such pettiness. Not while I've a choice in it.*

They went through, into a huge open space—a garden landscaped in the Han fashion. At the far side, beyond a pair of gently arching white stone bridges, a large two-story Mansion in the southern style rested amid tree and rock. Already, it seemed, the great house was full to overflowing. Guests crowded the veranda, talking and drinking, while from within came the muted sound of pipes and strings.

Kim turned, looking up at his friend. "I thought it would be different. I thought . . ."

"You thought it would be like last time, neh? And you're confused, because this is Han. Well, let me explain things, before we meet our hostess."

He drew Kim aside, moving toward a quiet arbor. There they sat, facing each other across a low table of sculpted stone, Michael's tricorn hat laid to one side.

"Back when the House was still open, Gloria's father was a Senior Representative—an important man, spokesman for his *tong*, the On Leong."

Kim frowned. The five major *tong* of City America shared an ancestry with the Triads of Europe and Asia, but their recent history was very different. When things had collapsed over here, after President Griffin's assassination, it was the five *tong* who had helped hold things together on the East Coast and in enclaves in California and the Midwest. And when the City was built across the continent, they had taken a major role in the social reconstruction program. Their reward was a legitimization of their organizations. They had become political parties.

"I see," Kim said, "but I still don't understand. I'd have thought that the *tong* would be your natural political adversaries."

Michael sat back, smiling. "They are. But Gloria is very different from her father. She wants what we want—an independent and outward-looking America. And she's not alone. There are many Han who think like her. Most of them—the influential ones, that is—are here tonight."

Kim looked down. "And there I was, thinking . . ."

"That I hated the Han?" Michael shook his head. "No. Only our masters. Only those who try to keep us from our natural destiny. The rest . . . well, there are good and bad, neh? What has race to do with that?"

──────

"Bryn? Can I have a word?"

Bryn Kustow excused himself from the group with which he was standing, then came away, following Michael Lever down the broad corridor and into one of the empty side rooms.

With the door firmly closed behind them, Michael turned, confronting him.

"Well, Michael? What is it?"

Michael reached out and held his arm. "I've just had news. The bankers have called in the loan."

"Ahh . . ." Kustow considered that a moment, then shrugged. "Then that's it, I guess. The game's over for the boys."

"Is that what you want?"

Kustow looked up. "No. But what's left to us? We've allocated most of my capital, and yours is frozen."

Michael hesitated, then. "What if I could get the money somewhere else?"

Kustow laughed. "Where? Your father has the money market tied up tighter than a fly's ass."

"That's what he thinks. But I've been checking out a few tips."

"And?"

"And we've a meeting, tomorrow afternoon at two, with the Clear Heart Credit Agency of Cleveland."

"And they'll lend us what we need?"

Michael hesitated. "I don't know. What with this latest development we'll need to reassess things carefully. Work out what we need to pay off the loan and fund new development. The rates are high, but it's that or go under."

"I see." Kustow looked away a moment, then turned back, a faint smile on his lips. "There is one other option. I mean, if we do have to seek alternative employment, there is one sphere we could go into."

Michael laughed. "I don't follow you, Bryn. What are you going on about?"

"I've been busy, too, Michael. Making calls. And I've set up a meeting. Just you and me and an old school friend of ours. Two days from now, out at his place."

"An old school friend?"

Kustow put a hand on Michael's shoulder. "Trust me. Meanwhile, let's enjoy ourselves, neh? And smile, damnit. The night's young and you've a pretty woman waiting for you out there!"

A FAN FLUTTERED in the pearled light. There was the scent of rich perfumes, the swish of ancient ballgowns, the rustle of silks and satins, the low murmur of conversation, interspersed with bursts of drunken laughter. Emily Ascher stood at the head of the steps, looking down into the Hall of Ultimate Benevolence, amazed by the sight that met her eyes. The great hall was a riot of red, white, and blue, decorated with all manner of Americana. Faded flags and ancient banners hung from the surrounding balconies and across the great ceiling, interspersed with huge, carved wooden eagles. At the far end a huge cracked bell rested on a raised platform—the Liberty Bell. Behind it hung a wall-size map of the American Empire at its height, most of South America shaded blue, each of the Sixty-Nine States marked with a blazing golden star. In the space between, two or three thousand garishly dressed young men and women milled about, talking and drinking.

Emily turned, wide-eyed, to her companion. Michael was watching her, a smile on his lips.

"Impressed?"

She nodded. "I didn't expect . . ." But what *had* she expected? She laughed softly. "Are these occasions always like this?"

"Not always. But then, most hostesses don't have Gloria's style. She's done us proud, don't you think?"

"Us?"

"The Sons . . ."

"But I thought this was a coming-of-age party."

"And so it is." He smiled enigmatically, then offered her his arm. "Here, let's go down. There are some friends I'd like you to meet."

Two hours later she found herself among a group of young men gathered at the far end of the hall, about the Liberty Bell. There were nine of them in all: Michael Lever, three of his close friends, and five other "Sons" who had shared the long months of incarceration at Wu Shih's hands. Like Lever, all were dressed in the style of the early republic—authentic blue and white uniforms that had been purchased at great expense. With their short-cropped blond hair and knee-length boots they brought a strangely somber note to the occasion, making a striking contrast against the other partygoers.

At first their talk had ranged widely, embracing all manner of things: from the planned reopening of the House and new research into space technologies to developments in the GenSyn inheritance case and the latest round of inter-City trade agreements. But as the evening drew on, their mood had grown darker, their talk focusing in upon the tyranny of the Seven and the corresponding failings of their fathers.

Lever's close friend Carl Stevens was talking, gesturing animatedly as he spoke. "Our fathers talk of changing things, of a return to Empire. That's something we'd all like to see, but when it comes down to it there's really not much between them and the Seven. Whichever ruled, the Seven or our fathers, we would remain as we are. Dispossessed. As powerless then as we are now."

Beside him, Bryn Kustow nodded. "Carl's right. If anything, our position would be much worse than it is now. If the Seven fell and our fathers came to power what would happen? Would they embrace us as their natural partners in the venture? No. Not for a second. We know how they think. We've all had a taste of their treatment these past years. They see us as a threat. As potential usurpers. It's sad to say, but in effect we have become our fathers' enemies."

There was a murmur of reluctant agreement, heavy with unease.

"But what can be done?" one of the others, Mitchell, asked. "They have all the power—the *real* power. All we get is the scraps from their tables. And what can we do with scraps?"

The bitterness in Mitchell's voice was mirrored in every face. Kustow looked across at Michael, then looked down, shrugging. "Nothing . . ." he answered quietly. But there was something about his manner that suggested otherwise.

Standing there at Michael's side, Emily let her eyes move from face to face, conscious of the sudden tension in the circle. Despite what was being said, something about this whole elaborate charade of "Empire" made her stiffen inwardly against them. They talked of changing the balance of power—of "liberation"—when all they really meant was grabbing it for themselves. In that they were no better than their fathers. No. Even after their experience of incarceration, they didn't understand. To them it was still essentially a game. Something to fill the hours and stave off the specter of boredom.

Even so, it was good to see this—to understand how they thought, how they acted—for in some strange way it made her stronger, more determined.

For a moment she abstracted herself from their talk, looking inward, focusing on the ideal she had worked for all these years. The ideal of Change—*real* change—free of the old power structures. Something pure and clean and utterly new. That was what she had struggled to achieve all those years in the *Ping Tiao*. A new world, free of hierarchies, where men and women could breathe new air and live new dreams. Yes, and that was what Mach and Gesell had really betrayed when they had chosen to work with DeVore.

She shivered, then looked aside. Michael was watching her, concerned. "What is it, Em?"

She stared back at him a moment, not recognizing him for that instant, surprised to find herself there in the midst of that gathering, among those she would, without a moment's thought, have destroyed. And then, as realization struck her, she laughed. And he, watching her, smiled, his smile broadening, not understanding, yet liking what he saw in that austere and sculpted face. And as he looked, a strange new determination formed in him, as if from nowhere, making his nerve ends tingle.

————

"Well, Michael? Have you enjoyed your evening?"

Michael Lever turned, embracing his hostess, holding her a moment and kissing her cheek before he stepped back. Gloria Chung was a tall, strikingly elegant young woman with the classic features of the Han aristocracy. It was said her ancestors had been related to the great Ming dynasty, and, looking at her, it was not difficult to believe. She had dressed tonight as the famous Empress Wu in sweeping robes of midnight blue embroidered with a thousand tiny golden suns.

They were alone on the broad upper balcony. Below them the last of the guests were making their unsteady way back through the winding pathways to their sedans. She moved past him, standing there at the rail, looking out over the dim, lamp-lit garden.

"I've had a good time," he said quietly, taking his place beside her at the rail. "It's been nice to think of something other than the troubles with my father."

"And the girl?"

"The girl?" He looked blank for a moment, then he laughed. "Oh, you mean Mary?"

She turned her head, studying him, as if she could see right through him, then she smiled. "I was watching you, Michael. Watching how you were together. It was . . . interesting."

He turned his head. "What do you mean?"

"I do believe you're half in love with her."

"Nonsense," he said, shocked by the suggestion; yet even as he said it, he saw the truth in it. He stood there a moment, looking at her, then pushed away from the rail, masking his slip with a laugh. "And what if I were?"

She reached out, holding his upper arm, then leaned close, kissing him. "Don't get me wrong. I'm not disapproving. If it makes you happy . . ." She moved back slightly, her eyes searching his. "She'd be good for you, Michael. I can see that. She's strong."

"Yes, but . . ." He sighed. No, it was impossible. His father would never approve.

"You've taken the first step. Why not the next?"

"What do you mean?"

"I mean, get out of your father's shadow for good. Show him you're your own man. Marry her."

He laughed, astonished. "*Marry* her?" He looked down, troubled, then turned away. "No. I couldn't. He'd cut me off . . ."

"He'd not dare. But even if he did, how could things be any worse than they are? What else could he do?"

"No . . ."

"No? Think about it, Michael. The Old Man's backed you into a corner. He's cut off your finances and tried every which way to prevent you from making a go of it on your own. As things are, you're going to have to make a choice, and soon—either to go back to him and beg forgiveness; to go down on your knees before the Old Man and agree to his terms; or to assert yourself. So why not do it now? Right now, when he least expects it."

He faced her again. "No. Not while there are still other options."

She shivered. "You mean, like the Clear Heart Credit Agency?"

He stared at her. "How did you know that?"

"Because I make it my business to know. And if I know, you can be sure your father knows. In fact, I'm certain of it."

"How?"

"Because he's the owner of the Clear Heart Credit Agency. As of this morning."

He closed his eyes.

"So what are you going to do?"

"Do? What *can* I do?"

"You could do what I said. Marry her. Be your own man. As for the money, I'll give you that. It's two million, neh? Good. I'll have a draft ready for you in the morning. My wedding gift."

He stared at her, astonished, then shook his head. "But why? I don't understand you, Gloria Chung. Why should you want to do this for me?"

She smiled and leaned close, kissing him again. "Because I believe in you, Michael Lever. And because I want to see you strong. Strong and independent. For all our sakes."

⌄⌄⌄⌄⌄

TWELVE TINY HOMUNCULI —hologram figures no more than six *t'sun* in height—were gathered in a half-circle on the desk's surface, blinking and flickering in the faint light from a nearby float-globe. In a tall-backed chair, facing them, Old Man Lever looked down at his Departmental Heads and growled.

"So what's the problem? Why can't we use someone else? Someone cheaper than ProFax? Someone more reliable?"

Several of the figures shimmered, as if about to speak, but it was one of the central holograms—the tiny form of Lever's Head of Internal Distribution Services, Weller, who answered Lever, his image hardening, glowing stronger than before, standing out from the images to either side.

The figure bowed its head. "Forgive me, Master, but we have had a good record of trading with ProFax. Our association with them goes back over twenty years. In our experience, there *is* no one more reliable."

Lever huffed irritably. "If that were true, we wouldn't be having this discussion, would we?" He sat forward, looming over them. "So let me ask you once again, what *is* the problem? I could understand it if ProFax owned the patent to this process, but they don't. And they certainly don't have a monopoly of the market. So why can't we buy the stuff elsewhere? And why can't we cut the rates we pay for it into the bargain? It strikes me that this is the perfect opportunity."

He sat back, steepling his hands. "Okay. This is how we do it. We get our legal boys to send ProFax a writ, letting them know that they're in breach of contract, then we withhold all payments for products already shipped, and send out a request for tenders to all of ProFax's major competitors. And we do all this right now, understand me, gentlemen? Right now!"

As he uttered the final words, Lever slammed his right hand down on the "cancel" button and hauled himself up out of his chair, even as the images faded from the air.

At that very moment, right across the City, his major Departmental Heads would be being woken up and told of the decision. *Yes, and cursing me silently, no doubt,* Lever thought, smiling savagely. But that's how it was in this world: one didn't look back, one got on with things. If something made sense, there was no good reason for delay. Nor was there room for sentiment. Both were weaknesses. Fatal weaknesses, if one let them be.

He went across to the drinks cabinet on the far side of the study and pulled down a bottle of his favorite malt whiskey, pouring himself a large glass, then turned, looking about him.

It was a big, ranch-style study with heavy wooden uprights and low rails dividing the room up into "stalls." To his left, beyond one of the rails, stood a mechanical horse, beneath a portrait of himself as a twenty-year-old, bare-chested in buckskins and shiny leather boots.

It was some while—months, if not years—since he had tried himself against the horse, nor had he even thought of it, but now, for some reason, he went across and, ducking beneath the rail, stood next to it, letting his left hand rest on the smooth, cool leather of the saddle while he sniffed in the heavy animal musk of the thing.

Across from him, behind the desk, set back against the far wall, was a big, glass-fronted cabinet, filled with sporting trophies: mementos of an athletic youth. Beside it, lit softly from above, was a head and shoulder portrait of his wife, her fine golden hair set like a halo about her soft, angelic face.

Earlier, he had sat in his private viewing chamber, enclosed in the darkness there, watching a hologram of his son Michael, wrestling with him beside the pool while his young wife, Margaret, looked on. It was an old film, taken shortly before Margaret had died. Michael had been eight then, he fifty-four.

He shivered, thinking of the years between. Twenty years this autumn. Long years in which he'd tried hard to forget; to steel himself against all the hurt and injustice he had felt at her death. At the suddenness of it all. He had buried himself in his work, throwing everything into the task of making his Company, ImmVac, the number one economic force in North America. But it had cost him. He had never grieved for her properly and inside he was hurting still. Even now, after all these years, he could not look at her without feeling his stomach fall away, a dryness come to his mouth. It had been hard, bringing up the boy without her, but he had done it. And for a time it had worked. For a time . . .

Lever turned his head aside, a sudden bitterness making him grimace. After all he had been through—after all he had done for the boy—how could Michael have turned on him like that? And in public too! The arrogance of the boy! The ingratitude . . .

He shuddered, then slapped the horse's rump, angry with himself. Angry, not because of what he felt, but for the weakness, the sentiment he had allowed to sway him.

Ducking beneath the rail he went across and took the envelope from the table by the door, tearing it open angrily. Inside was the letter he had written earlier: the brief note of reconciliation, forgiving Michael and asking him to come back. For a moment Lever stood there, the letter held in one trembling hand. Then, with a spasm of anger, he ripped the thing in half, then in half again, his face distorted with anger and pain.

"No," he said softly, looking about him, bewildered, frightened suddenly by the strength, the violence of his feelings. "Not now, and maybe not ever. No. Not until you come crawling back, begging my forgiveness."

And would that be enough? Would that repair what had been broken between them? No. And yet without it there was nothing. Less than nothing, in fact, for this bitterness, this anger ate at him, day by day, hour by hour, giving him no rest. Like death, he thought, and shivered again, wondering how it was all connected. Like death.

~~~~~

IN THREE DAYS Lehmann had brought the local *tong* boss, Lo Han, to the conference table. Fourteen of his men were dead and six more had joined K'ang A-yin, under Lehmann's lieutenantship. Now Lo

Han sat there, three of his henchmen behind him, facing K'ang across the table, making a deal.

"It's too high. Far too high," Lo Han said, spitting out the end of the cigar he had been chewing on.

"Fifteen percent or the deal is off," answered K'ang, turning in his seat to smile at Lehmann, as if to say, "You can fight, but when it comes to making deals, just watch an expert."

Lehmann said nothing, knowing that what K'ang was asking for was ridiculously low. The figures Lo Han was showing in his books were rigged. Even at a conservative estimate he must be raking in four or five times as much. And a sixth of twenty percent wasn't much, seeing as he had been soundly beaten on four occasions now. But it didn't matter. Whatever K'ang agreed to, he, Lehmann, would tear up when the time came, for he wanted a pure one hundred percent of Lo Han's drug trade.

In his six weeks down here Lehmann had learned much about the Lowers. He had watched carefully and listened to Soucek attentively. He knew now how they thought and what they wanted. He knew what motivated them and how far they would go to get what they wanted. He knew their strengths and their weaknesses—particularly the latter—and had come to see just how he could use both to attain his ends.

And what were those ends?

When he had returned to the City from off the mountainside, he had wanted nothing less than total vengeance against the Seven. He had seen himself as a lone figure, slipping between the levels like a shadow, bringing death to the Families and all who supported them. But that was just a dream. As a single man he could not hope to change things, yet by his very nature he was singular: he could not parcel out his thoughts, his hatreds, and share them. Even so, there was a middle way.

Singular he might be, but not necessarily alone. Already he was forming a solid corps of men about him, Soucek chief among them. Men loyal to him alone, however it appeared on the surface. Consulting no one, letting no one into his thoughts, he went about his business, winning allies by the strength of his actions, the single-mindedness inherent in his nature. He did not have to ask; men followed him, recognizing in him something they had longed for, maybe dreamed of. Men confided in him, seeking nothing in return. Trusting him. Willing to be used by him. *Wanting* to be used.

Respect and fear. Loyalty and a deep-rooted uncertainty. It was this mixed response to him—there in all who came to know him—that eventually defined for him the means by which he would come to attain that impossible, dreamlike end which was the very source, the fountainhead, of his singularity.

He would use their respect and fear, channel their loyalty and uncertainty, knowing that both aspects were necessary and, in their combination, powerful. But at the heart of things would be his own singular desire, deadly and uncompromising, shaping things, molding those who were both attracted to and appalled by him into a body—a weapon—through which his will would be done.

He held the thought in mind a moment longer, then frowned. At the table the small men were still haggling and bargaining over nothings—Lo Han's crude arrogance matched by K'ang's petty greed. He looked past them and saw how the eyes of Lo Han's henchmen had strayed to him, troubled by his changed expression. Turning away, he went to the door and tugged it open, ignoring the looks of query from K'ang and Lo Han. Outside he nodded to Soucek and walked on, conscious of his questioning glance.

Soucek caught up with him at the corridor's end. "What is it, Stefan?" he whispered, concerned.

Lehmann turned, facing the tall, cadaverous man, taking his upper arms in his hands, but for a moment he said nothing.

He knew that they had their rules, their limitations, even here where there seemed to be no rules at all, only brute force. All human life set limits to its actions. There was always a point beyond which they would not go. But he, who valued nothing, had no such rules, no limits. He was beyond good and evil. For him nothing mattered but the accomplishment of his will—the fulfillment of his singular desire.

And if that were so, why then should he wait? Why did he not act at once, not fearing the consequences? Knowing that the consequences were likely to favor him. It was this that he had been thinking as he stood there behind K'ang—this that had made him frown. He squeezed Soucek's arms and stared into his pale green eyes.

"Are you with me, Jiri?"

Soucek nodded, seeming to grasp at once what was happening. "Right now?" he asked.

"Why not? The two together. They might suspect treachery from each other, but not from us. They'll think we fear an all-out war between the *tong*. But with the two of them dead . . ."

He let go of Soucek's arms.

The tall man smiled. It was clear that the idea appealed to him strongly; that the thought of killing K'ang scratched a long unsatisfied itch. He drew his gun. "Okay. I'll take Lo Han's henchmen."

It was both clever and sensitive of him. In effect he was saying, You, Lehmann, are the leader. To you goes the honor of killing K'ang and Lo Han.

Lehmann nodded slowly and pulled the huge pearl-white gun from its webbing holster.

"Yes," he said, his voice cold, brittle like ice. "Let's do it now."

LEHMANN STOOD THERE in the Oven Man's doorway, a tall, unnaturally gaunt figure dressed in white. At his feet lay the corpses of three of the runners who had attacked them. Two more lay dead inside the room. The rest had fled, throwing down their hatchets, as if it were Yang Wen, the God of Hell himself, that faced them.

The killing of Lo Han and K'ang A-yin had shocked the local *tong* bosses. But shock had quickly led to the realization that there was a power vacuum. A vacuum that needed to be filled, and quickly. Within the hour, two of them met and decided to act. A messenger had been sent to Lehmann to set up a meeting to arrange a truce, but the meeting was merely a pretext. The bosses had decided to deal with Lehmann before he became a problem.

Lehmann had known that. In fact, he had counted on it. He had turned up with three men, unarmed, knowing how the *tong* bosses would try to play it. Fifteen runners, armed with silver hatchets. These would administer the "death of a thousand cuts"—a warning to all other potential usurpers.

But Lehmann had had no intention of dying. He had other lessons in mind.

An hour before the meeting he had set up small groups of men in the approach corridors, making sure they understood that they were not to intercede in any way, merely show themselves when the *tong* runners beat their retreat. Then, when the runners had shown up— hard-faced, arrogant little shits, dangerously overconfident— Lehmann had set his men behind him and faced them alone, taunting them, belittling them, until, one by one, they had come at him.

Soucek stared at him now, remembering.

Lehmann had straight-fisted the first runner before the man had even known the blow was on its way, the force of the punch sending the man staggering back. He was dead before he fell.

The second runner had been more cautious, but Lehmann had taken the hatchets from him as if he were a child, then had lifted him one-handed and snapped his neck. He had stepped over the corpse and made a beckoning gesture with his left hand.

Come on . . .

Three more had tried, the last with a kind of fateful resignation, as if mesmerized by the power of the man who stood before him. If man it was. And then, as one, they had broken, running from the figure in white, whose thin, emaciated limbs were paler than ice, and whose eyes were like tiny windows into hell.

He had heard the catcalls of the men in the approach corridors; the jeers and mocking laughter as they goaded the fleeing runners. And then had watched them return, to find Lehmann as he was now, framed in the doorway to the Oven Man's room.

Soucek looked about him, finding his own awe reflected in every face, there in the wide, admiring eyes of every man. He turned, facing Lehmann again, then knelt, abasing himself, laying down his neck before the man, not quite knowing why he did so, only that this was what he ought to do. And, all about him, the others did the same, letting Lehmann move between them, pressing his foot against each exposed neck. Marking them. Making them his men. *His* absolutely. Even unto death. Just as Li Yuan had done on the day of his coronation.

And when Soucek stood again, it was with a sense of rightness, of utter certainty. There was no going back from this. From here on there would be no half measures. It was Lehmann or nothing. And with that sense of rightness came another—a sense of destiny. Of things beginning. It was like being in a dream, or at the beginning of a myth. From this time on they walked a special path. And wherever it took them—to Heaven or down into the very depths of Hell—he would walk it behind the man. For that was how it was from this moment, for all of them gathered there.

It had begun.

IT WAS AFTER FOUR when Emily got back. She kicked off her shoes and went through to the bathroom, humming softly to herself. Reaching up, she placed her hand against the side of the shower unit. Good. It was hot. That meant the servant had remembered to come in earlier. She pulled the dress up over her head and let it fall onto the chair at her side, then slipped out of her chemise.

It had been a memorable evening, and an unexpectedly enjoyable one. She stepped into the shower, casting her mind back over the evening's events as she soaped herself beneath the steady fall of water.

Michael Lever really wasn't so bad, now she had come to know him better. Not that she had always felt that way. When she had first joined MemSys she had viewed the Levers with a distant loathing, not distinguishing much between father and son, seeing only the rapaciousness of the parent Company, ImmVac, and the unheeding damage it did in its eternal quest for profit. But now . . . Well, the past six weeks had taught her much. Systems were systems and they ought to be opposed, but it was not so easy with people. You had to take each person as you found them. And in many respects Michael Lever was a good man—honest, reliable, capable of instilling a fierce protectiveness and loyalty in those about him. Was it his fault that he'd been born heir to ImmVac?

Before now she hadn't been sure. She had wondered whether there really was any difference between father and son, but tonight, listening to him talk about what he wanted for the future, she had seen another side of him—one she had never guessed existed. That desire for change—that burning need in him to do something for the ordinary people of America . . . was that real or was it merely rhetoric? Despite the warmth of the water, she shivered, just thinking about it. His passion—that fierce, uncompromising fire she had glimpsed when he'd turned to her briefly—had seemed real enough. But how far would he go along that road? As far as she was willing to go, or would his courage fail him in the face of genuine change? Would he shy away from taking that ultimate step?

She cut the flow and stepped out, squeezing her hair, then wrapped it up in a towel. For a moment she stood there, staring sightlessly at the steamed mirror as she dried herself, then turned and went through into the bedroom.

The bedroom was dark. Only the light from the bathroom spilled into the opening. Even so, she saw him before she crossed the doorway.

He was sitting on her bed, a gun in his hand, covering her. A tall, unbearded Han with close-cropped dark hair and a face she had never seen in her life.

She made to step back, but he lifted the gun slightly, clicking off the safety. The signal was unmistakable. She froze, letting her hands rest at her sides, fingers apart, the gesture meant to reassure him. She was naked, the light behind her.

"What do you want?"

She said the words calmly, showing no sign of the fear she felt. He could kill her in a second. Two bullets through the heart. It was what she had been expecting every day since she had come from Europe. And now, finally, they had caught up with her.

He stood, then crossed the room, the gun covering her all the while, his eyes never leaving her. He lifted something from the dressing table and threw it across to her. It was her robe. With the barest nod of thanks, she pulled it on.

"Who sent you?" she asked, trying another tack.

The smile he gave was strange, almost familiar. And his build. She frowned, trying to place the memory. And then he spoke.

"How are things, Emily?"

She narrowed her eyes, uncertain, then laughed, astonished. "Jan . . . ? Is that you?"

The smile broadened. Slowly the gun came down. It was Mach—Jan Mach—she could see that now, despite the change of face. There was something about the way he stood there—about the way he used the muscles of his face—that could not be disguised.

"What happened?"

He took a breath. "They were onto me. We were attacked, eleven days back, at third bell. They killed more than twenty agents and took maybe thirty more, six of our cell leaders among them—comrades who knew me personally. Who could identify me."

"Karr?"

He nodded. "It must have been. I'd heard rumors he was creating a new force, but I didn't think they were ready yet." He shrugged, his features momentarily formed into a grimace as he recalled what had happened. "This . . ." he touched his face tenderly, "I had done eight days ago. It still hurts. I should have rested—should have left the bandages on a while longer—but things were too hot in Europe. I had to get out."

"Do you want to stay here?"

Mach looked at her a moment, then nodded. "It won't be long. Two days at most."

"And then?"

He looked down at the gun in his hand, then threw it down onto the bed. "I've got to go back. There's some unfinished business. An old score to settle. I've set it up, but I've got to be there to make sure it all runs smoothly." Mach looked back at her, smiling. "And you? What are you up to over here?"

She was about to answer him when there was a knock on the door. She turned, anxious, then looked back at him. "In the bathroom. Hide in the shower unit. Take the gun. I'll try and put them off, whoever it is."

He nodded, then did as she said. Only when he was inside, the door pulled over, did she go down the hallway.

"Who is it?"

"Delivery! For *Nu shi* Jennings."

She put her tongue to her top teeth. Delivery? At four seventeen in the morning? She reached out, turning the lock, drawing the door back a fraction and staring out through the thumbnail gap. A small Han was standing there, head bowed, half-hidden behind the huge basket of flowers he was carrying.

She gave a small laugh, still suspicious. Then she saw the note and at once recognized Michael Lever's neatly rounded hand. She pulled the door back. "Gods . . ."

He handed her the basket, then stood back, bowing deeply. She turned, reading the note as she pulled the door closed behind her, then returned to the bedroom.

"Well . . . ?" Mach began, coming out from the bathroom, then stopped, seeing the flowers. "A friend?" he asked, curious.

"Yes," she said hesitantly, closing her hand over the note, for some reason not wanting him to see what was written there. "A very dear friend."

They were orchids. Perfect, exotic orchids, worth a thousand *yuan* apiece, and there had to be—what?—thirty or more of them here. She frowned, disturbed by the gift, then drew the basket to her face, sniffing at them, drawing in their delicate, wonderful scent.

"A lover?" Mach asked, blunt as ever.

"No," she answered. But even as she said it, she could see him again, smiling, turning to share a joke with her; and afterward, his dark eyes burning, talking of the great changes to come.

"No," she said again. "Just a friend. A very good friend."

CHAPTER SEVEN

Smoke Rings
and Spiders' Webs

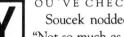

YOU'VE CHECKED EVERYTHING?''

Soucek nodded, a feral grin splitting his narrow face. "Not so much as a cockroach could get out of there unless we willed it."

"Good." Lehmann drew a long breath, then nodded. "All right. Let's go meet them."

They passed through the cordon, some of the men familiar, others strangers, all of them wary, nervous, but under strict orders to start nothing. If things went wrong today there would be war such as the Lowers hadn't seen in decades. A war that was certain to draw in the Triads.

The deck had been cleared for the meeting, and only the *tong* were present. The big men—all nine of his rival gangleaders in the *Kuei Chuan's* territory—were waiting for Lehmann in Main, standing out in the broad open space. They formed two groups, one of five men, one of four. Lehmann paused, taking in every detail, then walked on, Soucek at his side.

He could see in their faces that word had gone before him. His height, his deathly pallor, the whiteness of his clothes, his holstered gun. Some of them feigned indifference, but there was no mistaking what their eyes told him. They were afraid of him. They had only come here today because they were afraid. Like K'ang and Lo Han before them they had tried other means of dealing with him. Now they were forced to come to terms. Or risk a protracted guerrilla war that would waste their resources and distract them from the business of making money.

He raised his empty hands as if holding a large bowl, the fingers spread unnaturally wide, like long, fine needles of ice. The gesture seemed to stress his alienness; his long, thin arms held awkwardly, his whole body crouched slightly, like a fighter's. The pose was half challenge, half greeting. It distinguished him from the relaxed, almost slovenly postures of the men facing him.

"Gentlemen?"

He let the archaic word hang in the air between them, its irony unexplained, and saw them frown and look among themselves. And though it amused him, he let nothing show in his face, only an intense watchfulness—an almost machinelike attentiveness.

"What do you want?" one of them asked.

It was the first question, the *primary* question one man asked of another, openly or otherwise. Lehmann turned slightly to face the man, taking in at a glance the fact that they had chosen for their spokesman one who seemed stronger, more aggressive than the rest; a fierce-eyed, bearded man of bull-like stature. Unlike the rest he dressed simply, his fingers free of the heavy rings that seemed a mark of status down here. Lehmann raised his chin slightly, then answered.

"I want what you want. Peace. A truce. Concessions."

The bearded man smiled, showing strong white teeth. His name was Ni Yueh and Lehmann knew all there was to know about him. All that *could* be known without entering Ni Yueh's head. It was a surprise to him, however, that they had chosen Ni Yueh. He had expected to have to deal with Yan Yan or Man Hsi, one of the talkers. It made him reassess things and change his tactics. Ni Yueh was a bullyboy. An intimidator. It was obvious that this was the way they thought they could deal with him. Well, he would show them otherwise. Before Ni Yueh could say another word, Lehmann turned away from him and, changing his stance, relaxing the muscles of his face, took a step toward Yan Yan, offering his hand.

"There have been misunderstandings," he said. "Bad rumors. We need to clear the air."

Reluctantly, looking to Ni Yueh then back to Lehmann, Yan Yan took the offered hand.

Lehmann smiled. It was a charming, almost innocent smile. A disarming smile. Slowly, Yan Yan's lips formed a mirror to it, but his eyes still showed uncertainty. Lehmann closed a second hand about Yan Yan's, keeping the handshake warm and unthreatening.

"There's no need for enmity," he said reassuringly. "There's enough for all, neh? More than enough."

Yan Yan looked down at the long, pale hands that held his own, then up into Lehmann's face again, puzzled. But it was Ni Yueh who spoke.

"You say that, but why should we trust you? What's to stop you doing to us what you did to K'ang A-yin and Lo Han?"

Lehmann lowered his head slightly, his expression seeming to say, "Oh dear, that again . . ." He released Yan Yan's hand and half turned, looking across at Ni Yueh.

"I've heard the stories. Heard the tales men whisper to each other, and let me assure you, they are simply not true." There was an earnestness, a sincerity in his voice as he said it that half convinced them. A plea for belief. The very look of a wronged man. His eyes seemed pained by the misunderstanding. Regretful.

"I didn't want to kill K'ang A-yin. He was a friend. A benefactor. But he made a deal with Lo Han, and my death was part of that deal. Soucek here can vouch for that, can't you, Jiri?"

Soucek nodded and stepped forward, saying the words Lehmann had had him rehearse.

"It was halfway through the meeting. Lehmann and I had gone out to check that everything was secure in the corridors. When we came back, K'ang had moved back against the far wall and Lo Han was sitting there with his big snub-nosed gun in one hand, laughing. It seems that K'ang had given his permission to kill Lehmann. He told me to leave the room. Told me it was simply business. But I stayed."

"How loyal," said Ni Yueh in an undertone that suggested he didn't believe a word of it. But Soucek turned on him angrily.

"Maybe. But I saw it like this. A boss looks after his men. He sells one he sells them all, right? So I made a choice."

There were nods from the other big men. Soucek's outburst had impressed them. If it was as Soucek said, then Lo Han and K'ang had clearly broken the code. It was not done to betray one's own so casually, even for the sake of peace.

"So," Ni Yueh said, stepping between the two men and confronting Lehmann face to face, "there was Lo Han, sitting behind the desk with his gun out. How is it he didn't kill you?"

Lehmann held Ni Yueh's eyes. "Because I was better than him. Quicker. And now he's dead, and I'm alive. It's simple, really."

"Too fucking simple!" Ni Yueh turned to face the others. "I don't believe a word of this. I trust this bastard about as much as I'd trust shit to taste good."

There was laughter, but it was short-lived. Lehmann had split them. The three who had been standing with Ni Yueh were still glaring at him, but the others—Yan Yan and Man Hsi among them— were not happy with Ni Yueh's words. Man Hsi spoke up.

"I don't see what proof you have, Ni Yueh. We all know how things get distorted. I say we should forget the past and make things good for the future. That's why we're here, right? Not to bicker and fight. We've done too much of that already and it's got us nowhere. No. We've got to make deals. Patch things up. For all our sakes."

Ni Yueh was scowling. For a moment he seemed about to answer, then, abruptly, he shook his head and turned away, as if he'd washed his hands of it. Turning to Lehmann, Man Hsi spoke again, his voice growing softer, more conciliatory.

"So what deal have you got for us, *Shih* Lehmann? What can you offer us to make the peace?"

Lehmann looked past Man Hsi at the others, knowing how things stood. If they had wanted—if they had *really* wanted—they could have wiped him out. It would have cost them dearly, but it had been possible. They *could* have done it. But now? Inside—deep inside—he laughed. Now it was too late. Simply in agreeing to come here and meet him they had made their greatest concession. Had admitted to him their lack of will. Even Ni Yueh, for all his hostility.

Turning to Soucek, he nodded, then waited while his lieutenant brought the documents. As arranged, others brought a long, six-legged table and a stack of chairs and set them down close to where the big men stood. Then, documents in hand, Lehmann put out a hand, inviting them to sit.

There were ten copies of the treaty; one for each of the signatories. He watched as they first frowned, then, with greater interest, began to read the fifteen terms that would bring peace to the Lowers of north-central Europe. A treaty that divided the *Kuei Chuan's* territory into ten equal parts. That provided the detailed conditions by which they dealt with one another. Lehmann had modeled it on the commercial treaties he had found among his dead father's effects, but the terms were specific to the *tong*.

Man Hsi looked up, met Yan Yan's eyes, and smiled. As Lehmann had expected, they were impressed. They had never seen the like of this before and it pleased them greatly. It gave their activities the seal of legality. It made them feel like businessmen. Like Company executives. Lehmann watched each of them straighten up as they finished reading and seemed to puff out, bigger than they'd been only moments before. Kings. If only of the Lowers.

"Well?" he said, looking to Man Hsi.

Man Hsi looked across at Ni Yueh, who nodded grudgingly, not looking at Lehmann. After that it was a formality. Soucek handed out brushes and they signed, Yan Yan with a flourish that strayed over the signatures of three of his fellow bosses. Slowly the documents were passed around the table until each of the copies bore ten signatures at its foot. That done, Lehmann stood, raising his hand for silence.

"By this document—a copy of which will be held by each of us— we have peace in our part of the great City." He smiled pleasantly, and nodded. "Yes, peace and prosperity. But . . ." his face changed, all friendliness draining from it, ". . . should *anyone* break this treaty, then all the other parties must and *will* unite to bring the transgressor to account." He paused dramatically and looked at each of them in turn. When he spoke again his voice was fierce, insistent. "It is only if each one of us *knows* this and *fears* it that the agreement will work. You understand?"

There was a moment's hesitation, then nods and a murmur of agreement.

"We understand," Ni Yueh said, his voice heavy with sarcasm. But his eyes showed something different now. The treaty had affected him; had made him question what he had earlier believed. And though the bantering tone remained, deep down he was far less certain. Lehmann had impressed him despite all.

"Good," said Lehmann, releasing Ni Yueh's eyes. "Then our business here is done."

THE CORRIDOR was packed. People had been gathering for the last thirty minutes outside the offices of the *Ch'i Chu* corporation, curious to see who had ordered such a grand sedan. Old men and children, young wives and idle youths, Han and *Hung Mao* alike, all stood there, gawping and chattering. Some busied themselves examining the sedan, feeling the thickness and quality of the green er-silk coverings or peeking inside at the big, luxuriantly cushioned chair. There were jokes about how big a man the chair might carry, and then sudden laughter as one of the young boys acted out a mime, pretending to be a fat official, his pomposity matched only by his grossness as he waddled across to take his place in the chair. Others, meanwhile, had formed a crowd about the squatting pole-men, trying to strike up a conversation, but long experience had made the carriers taciturn. The four men waited patiently, saying nothing, their eyes downcast, conscious of the runners who stood nearby.

There was a murmur of surprise as Kim appeared, dressed simply, a slender folder tucked beneath his arm. Many looked beyond him, waiting to see who else was to come, but there was no one, only the employees of *Ch'i Chu*, who came out and stood there under the arch of the entrance.

Many in the crowd had seen the boy, either in the tea house, or walking the corridors late at night. Few, however, understood who he was, or what his role in the strangely named *Ch'i Chu* corporation was. They had thought him just a boy. A messenger, perhaps, or the nephew of a rich man. But now they looked at him anew, redefining him. Or trying to.

Kim stopped, glancing about him uncertainly, then turned back, a smile coming to his face. Bright red good-fortune banners had been draped over the doorway to the offices. Beneath them, all six of his staff had formed up, to say good-bye and wish him luck.

"Here," T'ai Cho said, coming forward and handing him a small, sealed box. "You'll need this."

"What is it?"

"Lunch," T'ai Cho explained, smiling broadly. "From what I'm told, it will be a good few hours before they process the patent, and I know you. You would forget to eat."

Thanks, Kim mouthed, touching his arm briefly, then looked back at the others. The two middle-aged Thais he had hired as researchers were grinning broadly now and waving, excited as children. Beside them, to their right, his assistant, a fresh-faced young Han named Hong Chi, was looking about him, wide-eyed, clearly enjoying it all. Seeing Kim watching him, Hong smiled, then lowered his head, blushing.

Kim's guard, a stocky young *Hung Mao* named Richards, met his eyes proudly and shouted a gruff "Good luck!" while Nong Yan, his bookkeeper, called out, "Go now! Make us all rich!" which brought a huge shout of laughter from the rest.

"I shall," Kim said softly, feeling warmed by the smiling faces that surrounded him on every side. "Be sure I shall."

With a bow to them all, Kim turned, climbing up into the sedan. As the pole-men lifted the heavy chair, he leaned out, waving good-bye, his voice drowned by the cheering of the crowd and the shouts of the two runners as they cleared the path ahead.

Sitting back, Kim felt a shiver of anticipation ripple through him. So this was it. He looked down at the folder in his lap and gave a little laugh of surprise. Some days he would simply sit there, staring at his hands, astonished that he had survived the darkness of the Clay to come to this. And he would count himself blessed that it was so, in spite of all that had happened in between. Even so, today was special, for today it all came together at last.

"Smoke rings . . ." he said quietly, then laughed again, feeling the sedan sway and bob beneath him. "Smoke rings and spiders' webs."

EMILY TURNED quickly, the narrow beam of the overhead light picking out the false image in the mirror, then flipped backward, ignoring the hologram that appeared suddenly to her right, facing the shadowed figure by the door, the knife held out before her. The blade flashed, sank deep into the upper rib cage, then jerked back. She took a step back, breathing deeply, then sheathed the knife, satisfied.

"Cut," she said quietly. At once the lights came up, the apartment's computer registering her command.

Shuddering, Emily wiped the back of her hand across her forehead. It had been a hard workout. For the first time in a long while she had forced herself to the very limit.

She looked about the room—at the bloodied figure of the manne-quin; at the darted targets she had set up on the walls; at the ceiling-mounted projectors; at the mats and traps and trip wires—and real-ized she had missed the excitement of all this. It was time she did something. Time she started organizing once again.

Quickly she went about the room, tidying up, stashing the equip-ment in the storage box at the far end of the room and covering it all over with a pile of sheets and old clothes. Then she went through to the shower, standing there under the flow until the water ran out, considering the way ahead. Mach was out, meeting contacts and making deals: doing what he was good at. She had barely seen him for more than twenty minutes since he'd arrived that night. As for herself, it was two days now since she had been in to the office.

She had called in sick. A brief message on Michael Lever's personal comset. He had called back, less than a minute later, asking if she needed anything; saying that he'd call if she wanted him to. But she had sent back that it was all right. It was just a virus. Nothing serious. Just one of the new forty-eight-hour things that had been sweeping the levels recently. She would keep to her bed and come in when she felt better. His second message was brief, almost businesslike, except for the way he'd signed it. "Love Michael."

So where did that leave her? She walked about the apartment, toweling herself, recalling how Michael had looked at her the other evening at the ball, and how she'd felt, watching him as he talked, conscious of a growing admiration for him. In the hallway she stopped, standing before the flowers he had sent, and lifted one of the perfect pink and white orchids to her nose. The blooms were still fresh, their scents rich. With the faintest shiver she turned away, returning to the bedroom. There, she stood before the wardrobe, wondering what to wear. She was going down level, so it would have to be something basic. The kind of thing her alias, Rachel De Valerian, might wear.

She looked across. The false ID was on the bed, where she'd left it earlier. A permit card. Employment details. False retinas. Everything she'd need if she were to be stopped and questioned by Security. DeVore had thought it all through. Had made sure to do a fine job for her. But why? Because he knew she would eventually begin again, agitating, causing trouble for the Seven? Was it simply that? Or was it something else? Had he some other purpose that was as yet hidden from her?

Whatever, it was time to take a few risks. Time to make good on the promises she had made herself.

She had changed and dried her hair when a knock came on the door. Three raps, a pause, a single rap, a pause, and then a further three. Mach. He was back.

She studied herself in the mirror a moment, composing herself, then went through, slipping the bolt from the door, then pressing the key-open. As the door began to slide back, Mach came through, barely looking at her, making straight for the bathroom.

"Hey!" she called after him. "What's the hurry?"

She followed him along, then stood there in the doorway watching as he undid his jacket and took out three high-powered Security automatics, each handgun wrapped in sheet ice, and placed them in the now empty water-cabinet above the shower.

That done, he turned, grinning at her, his new face still a shock to her each time she saw it.

"That's good," he said, noting at once how she was dressed, his careful eyes not missing that her eye color had changed, but registering it by the movement of a finger to one of his own eyes. "Who arranged that for you? DeVore?"

She stared at him, something of her old hostility returning. "Well it wasn't you, was it, Jan? You wanted me dead."

Mach laughed strangely. "Did he tell you that?" He shrugged. "He told me you'd slipped the net. That he'd tried for you, but that you'd been too good for him."

She shivered, thinking back. No, it hadn't been like that. DeVore had found her easily enough, and—if he'd wanted to—he could have killed her. But he hadn't. And here she was, two years on, ready to begin again.

"They killed him, you know," Mach said, moving past her, heading for her bedroom. "I tried, at Nantes Spaceport, but his man—that red-eyed albino bastard, Lehmann—buggered things up for me. Killed three of my best men. But then the T'ang's man—that big man from the Net, Karr—finally got him. Smashed his head open with a rifle butt, so I've heard."

Again she followed him through, watching as he took his things from the bottom of the wardrobe and placed them quickly but carefully into a holdall.

"I didn't know," she said. Then, "What are you doing?"

He turned, still half crouched, looking back at her. "I'm moving on, Em. Fresh fields. New ventures. You know . . ."

She shook her head. "You surprise me, Jan. You always did. You're so resourceful. So flexible."

He stood, then laughed softly. "Do I detect a note of disapproval in that last comment, Emily Ascher?"

She met his eyes clearly, trying to see him through the mask of new flesh, then nodded. "We want different things, you and I. We always did, only it took me a long while to see that."

He studied her a moment, then looked away, pressing the lips of the holdall together and hoisting it up over his shoulder. "No, Em. It isn't what we want, it's what we're prepared to do to get it. That's what makes you and me different. But now we can go our own paths, neh? Now we've the opportunity to see whose way is best." He met her eyes again. "I'll not lie to you, Em. If you'd stood in my way, I'd not have hesitated to have had you killed. But you didn't. And I don't think you ever would. If I did, I'd never have turned up at your door two nights back. So, whether you believe me or not, let me tell you that what DeVore said simply wasn't true. I didn't want you dead. Nor do I now. And if there's anything you need—if there's any way I can help, then just call me. I owe you one, right?"

She stared at him, then shook her head. "So where are you going? Back to Europe? Or do you plan to move down-level here?"

His smile stretched the new skin about his mouth tight in what seemed almost a parody of a smile. "Neither, Em, my dear. I'm going to be a house guest. That's where I'm off to right now. I'm staying with Old Man Lever down in Richmond."

━━━━━

OLD MAN LEVER was standing beside the pool, drying himself, as the two men were led in to see him. He turned, relaxed, watching them approach him around the pool's edge, then threw the towel down, stretching out a hand to greet them.

"Milne . . . Ross . . . It's good to see you again. You'll have a drink, I hope?"

The two men hesitated, looking to each other, then nodded.

"Good." Lever turned, snapping his fingers. At once the Steward went across and busied himself, preparing drinks. Lever took a light silk jacket from the back of a chair and threw it across his broad shoulders, then turned, facing them again.

"Well? What have you got for me?"

"Nothing much, I'm afraid," Ross said, one hand going up to draw a thin wisp of strawlike hair across his balding pate. "She's a regular Miss Goody-two-shoes from what we can make out. Good at school. A clean College record. And not a mention of her ever appearing, even as witness, before a deck judicial hearing. In short, the public record backs up the Company file. *Nu Shih* Jennings is what she says she is. It's all there, except . . ."

He hesitated, looking down.

"Except what?"

"Except that it doesn't make sense," Milne finished in his quick, nervy fashion. "It's all too pat. Too neatly structured. Like someone made it all up. It's . . ." He squirmed, his shoulders moving as if he had something up the back of his jacket. "Well, it's lacking anything distinctive. You know, the kind of things that shape a life. That give it its flavor."

"Hmmm," Old Man Lever nodded to himself. "But it all fits?"

"On the surface," Ross answered, lifting a hand slightly, signaling the dark-haired Milne to keep quiet. "But we could dig a little deeper, if you want. We could go back to Atlanta Canton. Speak to a few people who knew her before she moved out. Find out what she was really like."

Lever was silent for a time. Then, taking a long swig from his glass, he shook his head. "What reason could there be for those records being wrong?"

Ross looked at his companion, then shrugged. "No reason. Just that it feels wrong. We've been doing this job near on twenty years, Mister Lever, and you get to know the smell of wrongness. And this . . . well, this just *stinks* of wrongness."

Beside him, Milne nodded emphatically.

"Okay," Lever said, setting his glass down. "Let's assume the records *have* been doctored. Let's say that someone's done a number on her official files. Fine. But let me ask you just two questions. Who did it? And why?"

"I don't know," Ross said, meeting the old man's piercing gaze. "I just know that someone has. As Milne says, it's just too neat."

But Lever was shaking his head. "No. It makes no sense. It takes a lot of clout to change those records. A *lot* of clout." He laughed, then, leaning closer, added softly, "And who should know better than me, neh?"

He moved between them. "No, gentlemen. Thanks, but let's leave it at that. I was hoping you might dig up something I could use against the woman—a string of ex-lovers or something—but it looks like I'm just going to have to plain invent something." He laughed. "Hell, maybe I should just have done that in the first place!"

"And our file?" Ross asked tensely.

"I'll keep that," Lever said, meeting his eyes again. "You'll be paid well, *Shih* Ross. Very well indeed. But this thing is closed now, understand me? Closed."

━━━━━━

WHEN THEY WERE GONE, Lever turned, looking up at the balcony overlooking the pool. From behind the cover of a vine, a man emerged and leaned against the rail, looking down at him.

Lever called up to him. "Well, Mach? What do you think?"

Mach smiled. "It's as you said, Mister Lever. It makes no sense. If this Jennings woman were a sleeper, put in by some rival of yours, she'd have stayed on where she could have done most harm, not gone to Michael."

Lever nodded. Those were his thoughts exactly. Even so, Ross's conviction had shaken him. He'd used Ross and Milne often these past ten years, and their instinct was generally sound. So what if . . . ?

For a moment he entertained the thought, trying to think of a reason—any reason—why her records might have been doctored, then shook his head, dismissing it again. No. It made no sense. No sense at all.

"Well, that's it, then," Milne said, cradling his *ch'a* bowl and squinting at his partner across the table of the low-level tea house. "Another file closed."

"Maybe," Ross said, his eyes following the progress of one of the serving women. "And maybe not."

Milne watched his face, waiting, knowing that Ross was chewing something over.

"I've been thinking," Ross began in a lazy drawl, turning his attention back to Milne. "Thinking that we could do with a holiday. And with what Mister Lever's paid us, I reckon we could have ourselves a hell of a fun time in Atlanta."

"Atlanta . . . ?" Milne stared back at him blankly a moment, then laughed, understanding dawning on him. "*Atlanta!* Hell, sure. Atlanta."

"Good," Ross said, sitting back and nodding, a smile of satisfaction splitting his face. "And maybe we can do a little digging while we're there. I mean . . . what harm can it do?"

LI YUAN was at the far end of the gallery, standing beneath one of the five huge portraits that filled the midnight-blue walls. As the great doors opened, the young T'ang turned, looking toward them, then smiled, beckoning Tolonen across.

"Knut," he said, offering the ring finger of his right hand for the old man to kiss. "You are well, I hope."

Tolonen came to attention, his head bowed, his close-cropped steel-gray hair presented to his T'ang. "I am fine, *Chieh Hsia.* I . . ."

He stopped, conscious of something odd in Li Yuan's manner. Of a strange thoughtfulness in that young, unbearded face, an unnatural stillness to his bearing, that reminded him suddenly of the boy's father, Li Shai Tung. So the old man had been at times, as if something had lodged in his thoughts, like a rock in the middle of a stream.

Tolonen turned, looking up at the portrait Li Yuan had been studying and gave a small smile of recognition. It was Ch'in Shih Huang Ti, the First Emperor. The unifier of ancient China. The tyrant, so-called. In the portrait he was standing on the shoreline of Shandong, staring out toward the east—to P'eng Lai, the Isle of the Immortals. Tall, bearded, and arrogant, the peach of immortality clutched in his left hand.

"I have been thinking," Li Yuan said, moving past Tolonen to stand beneath the portrait once again. "Trying to see some pattern in the flow of time."

"A pattern, *Chieh Hsia?*"

"Of what men are, and what they do, and why they never learn."

Tolonen looked down. "Do you really think that's so, my Lord?"

Li Yuan nodded. "I do, Knut. Take our friend here. In many ways he was a great man. A military genius and a visionary administrator, whose actions shaped our land for two thousand years. And yet, as a man, he was ultimately flawed, for he wanted more than life could give him. He wanted to live forever, and that destroyed him. All the good he had done was undone by that. His great empire lasted but a year or so beyond his death."

The young T'ang moved on, his booted footsteps echoing on the tiled floor, until he stood beneath the second of the portraits. Of the five, this was the most famous, for copies of it hung in every deck, at every level of the great earth-spanning City.

"Wen Ti . . ." Li Yuan turned, looking back at Tolonen, a strange, sad smile on his lips. "How many times have you heard old men and schoolboys praise him for his virtue? How many times has his name been used like a charm to castigate an errant child or a poor official? In the history books he is portrayed as a rock, a mountain of a man, as just as he was compassionate, as fair as he was stern, and yet, under his rule, the Middle Kingdom almost faltered. Incursions by the northern barbarians, the Hsiung Nu, twice forced him to make accommodations—to cede land and make huge tributary payments. Why, his capital, Ch'ang-An, almost fell to them! And like Ch'in Shih Huang Ti, only a year or so after his death the empire was in chaos, rebellions sweeping the provinces."

"He did his best, *Chieh Hsia* . . ."

"Maybe so, Knut, but it gives one pause for thought, neh? Ch'in Shih Huang Ti was a tyrant, yet beneath him the empire thrived. Wen Ti was a good man, yet beneath him the empire suffered. Which, then, should I model myself upon?"

"Is the choice that simple, *Chieh Hsia?*"

Li Yuan smiled, then moved on to the next painting, looking up at the image of an elegant-looking middle-aged man in golden silks. "No, Knut. It is never that simple. Take the case of Ming Huang here, sixth of the great T'ang emperors. He was a great man. A wise ruler and a powerful warrior. His reign was a golden age, it is said. The great poets and painters of our history—Li Po, Tu Fu, Wang Wei—such men thrived under his rule. It was a time of great culture, of prosperity and peace, and yet all that was destroyed, the empire torn apart by rebellions, and why? Because of his weakness. Because of his infatuation for a woman."

Tolonen looked down, uncomfortable with this sudden turn. "So it was, *Chieh Hsia.* So history tells us, anyway. But what is your point?"

The young T'ang turned. "My point? Why, that emperors are men, not figureheads or abstract forces, and that what they are shapes the destiny of those they rule. They stretch out a hand and the shadow falls across a continent. So it is. So it has always been. And I, Knut. In what way am I different?"

He turned back, staring up at the handsome features of Ming Huang a moment longer, then, with a small shake of his head, went across to the fourth of the portraits.

"Mao Tse Tung," he said quietly, his eyes taking in the familiar icon. "First of the great *Ko Ming* emperors. The Great Helmsman himself. Like Ch'in Shih Huang Ti—his idol—Mao could be ruthless and tyrannical. Beneath him, the Middle Kingdom was unified again, all invaders cast out. And yet, like Wen Ti—whose values he tried to overthrow—Mao tried hard in his early years to give the people peace and prosperity, to end corruption and reform the bureaucracy. To make the Middle Kingdom strong and healthy after decades of suffering and neglect. In many ways he seems the perfect balance between the two men. And yet he too was flawed. Flawed by a belief in his own infallibility. In his Great Leap Forward, tens of millions died, Knut. And for what? Simply to prove him wrong."

Tolonen looked down, frowning. "But you are not any of these men, *Chieh Hsia*. You are yourself. Surely you can learn from their mistakes and be what they were not?"

Li Yuan glanced at the old man questioningly, then turned, making his way across to the last of the five great canvases. For a moment he stood there, staring up at the powerful image of the man his own ancestors had overthrown. Tsao Ch'un. The Tyrant. Founder of the City. Of Chung Kuo itself.

"Coming here, seeing these men, their faces, it makes me wonder. Can I learn from their mistakes? Or am I doomed to take the same path? To go down in history as a weak and foolish man? Or as a tyrant?"

Tolonen went across and stood beside him. "Does it worry you, Yuan?"

"Worry me?" Li Yuan laughed, then turned, facing his father's General once again. "Yes, Knut. It worries me. But not as others might think. It worries me that my weakness might prove the death of millions. Or that some excess of desire or pride, arrogance or cold-heartedness might turn my face to tyranny. I look at these faces, these giant figures from our past, and I ask myself. Am I strong enough? Wise enough? You said of Wen Ti just now, 'He did his best.' Well, will *my* best be good enough? Have I, within me, what it takes to mold and shape a world and all its people? Or will ignorance and desire destroy me, as they have destroyed so many in the past? I am determined, yes. But what if determination fails, Knut? What then?"

The old man sniffed deeply, then shrugged, clearly disturbed by the young T'ang's words.

"Never mind . . ." Li Yuan looked down, unclenching his fists and staring at them a moment, as if to comprehend them. Then, as if coming to once more, he looked back up at the old man, his dark, hazel eyes less intense than a moment earlier. "So tell me, Knut. What *did* you find in my cousin's City?"

"Something strange," Tolonen answered, his voice suddenly clear and resonant. "Something strange and horrible."

<hr/>

IN WHAT HAD ONCE BEEN K'ang A-yin's offices, Soucek stood at ease, waiting to be acknowledged. The place had been redecorated since K'ang's death, a simple elegance replacing K'ang's cheap ostentation. A minute passed, then, finally, Lehmann looked up from the screen on his desk, noted the two men his lieutenant had brought back with him, and nodded.

"Good. Did it go well?"

Soucek sniffed. "I don't think they like us much. But as for our money . . . well, that's a different matter, neh? Money is money, Above as Below."

Lehmann switched off the screen, then came around the table. Ignoring his lieutenant, he studied the two newcomers carefully, reaching out to check the tight, flickering bands about the neck of each. Satisfied, he stepped back.

"Welcome," he said simply. "My name is Stefan Lehmann, and you'll be working for me."

Soucek could see the fear and uncertainty in their faces, just as earlier he had noted their clear disgust at their new surroundings. Lehmann too must have noticed it, for he seemed quick to reassure the men.

"I understand how you're feeling just now. You weren't expecting to come down here, were you?"

They nodded.

"No. Well, I know that what you've seen so far is pretty bad, but I've had special quarters prepared. Something more like what you're used to."

Soucek narrowed his eyes, fitting another piece into the puzzle. Lehmann hadn't told them yet what he was up to. The first Soucek had known about this was when Lehmann had handed him a special clearance pass and sent him up to Level 180 to meet with a Company Broker. All the documents and payment certifications had been in a sealed package. Soucek had only to ensure that the broker handed over the two men; Lehmann could do all the rest from his newly installed desk console. But Soucek had glimpsed the figure the broker had tapped into his comset and had whistled to himself. Why, they had paid more than two months' profits for a year's contract on each man!

"There's a lot to do here," Lehmann was saying, "but I want you to familiarize yourself with the details of our operation before you get down to things. And I want your input, understand? If you see that a thing can be done better, I want to know how, okay?"

The strangers, still more intimidated than reassured by the look of the tall albino, nodded hastily.

"And understand this . . . I've added an extra clause to your contracts." Lehmann paused, looking from one to the other. "It's very simple. You do well for me and I look after you. You help me increase my profits and you get a cut. A small one, but significant. And it's nondeductible against your lessee's contract."

Soucek saw how that changed things. The two men glanced at one another, then looked back at Lehmann, smiling.

"Good," Lehmann said, turning away, retreating behind his desk. "Now get some rest. We'll start tomorrow. My lieutenant here will show you your quarters. He'll get you anything you want."

Lehmann sat, leaning forward to touch the screen, bringing it alive. The audience was over. Soucek ushered the men out.

Walking back to the special area, one of them, a fair-haired man in his early twenties, turned to Soucek and asked him who Lehmann was.

Soucek shrugged. "He runs things down here."

"You mean he's a Deck Magistrate?"

"No. Judges he can buy by the dozen."

He saw how thoughtful they were. How their initial disgust had turned to puzzlement and to a new kind of respect.

Yes, thought Soucek. *After all, he had the clout to bring you two down here. Why, I don't yet know. But I shall soon.*

"And what are you, *ch'un tzu?*"

It was their turn to laugh. "You mean you don't know?" the blond-haired one said, stopping. "I thought you understood. We're commodity slaves." He touched the flickering band at his neck. "That's what this means. Your boss has bought our services for a year."

Soucek drew in a breath. He didn't like to be thought ignorant. "I know that," he said, brazening it out. "I meant, what do you do?"

"Whatever he wants us to do. But our specialties are computers and drugs synthesis. I'm the computer man."

Ah, thought Soucek, *so that's it. But why does he want specialists? What is he planning?*

They walked on, coming to the special area. Guards let them into corridors that had been newly carpeted at great expense. The walls were freshly painted, the two suites furnished with pieces brought down from the Above. It was all in stark contrast to the corridors and rooms through which they had passed. Here it was cool and quiet. No crowds of people crushed against each other. No ragged urchins tugged at you, their dirty faces pleading for a coin, or for something to eat. Now that he had seen it for himself, Soucek saw how like the Above this was. Ordered. Elegant in its simplicity. And Lehmann had known that. Had known what K'ang had only guessed at. As if he had experienced it himself.

Later, alone in his room, stretched out on his bunk, he thought things over. He had known Lehmann only weeks now, but in that brief time he had had the opportunity to study him better than he'd studied anyone before. Even so, Lehmann remained something of an enigma, forever hidden behind those glassy, blood-pink eyes. At times he felt like asking him right out, "What are you thinking?" but knew how it would be. Lehmann would turn and look at him, then look away, saying nothing. As if to say, "What business is it of yours?" And yet, for all that, he respected Lehmann more than he respected any man. Maybe even loved him in some strange way. But what *was* Lehmann? Who was he?

He had not seen it at first. Only slowly, gradually, had he begun to notice all the things that were different about him. Not the immediate, obvious things—his height and gauntness, the color of his skin, his eyes—but other, less readily discernible things. Things seen in contrast only. His scorn for luxuries. His innate austerity. Things that contrasted sharply with the other *tong* Bosses. Unlike them he had never even considered moving up the levels. He had laughed contemptuously when Soucek had suggested it. "They'll pay for their softness," was all he'd said. But Soucek had thought long and hard about the meaning of those words and had heeded them. Copying Lehmann, he had given up alcohol, drugs, and meat, and had begun to spend more time in the practice rooms, honing his fighting skills.

After the meeting with the other nine Bosses, Lehmann had sent him up to see Ni Yueh alone, with gifts and letters of friendship. He recalled sitting in Ni Yueh's plush offices and seeing it all with Lehmann's eyes, noting the waste—the "fat" as Lehmann called it. And he had looked at Ni Yueh anew—perhaps even as Lehmann saw him—seeing not merely his strength and brutality, but also the softness, the small signs of weakness. "Desire is a chain," Lehmann had said. "Only will and discipline can break it." Well, he had looked at Ni Yueh now and seen a man in whom desire was stronger than will. And had said nothing. That too he had learned from Lehmann. The weak man babbled his thoughts to any that would listen. The strong man kept his silence.

Ni Yueh had liked the gifts, the letters, and he, Soucek, had returned with other gifts and written promises. But Lehmann had scorned the presents and pushed them aside, more concerned with Soucek's view of things. He had listened attentively, then turned away suddenly, nodding to himself. "We'll bait him," he had said. "Hook him and draw him in." And though Soucek had not understood the exact meaning, he got the drift of it. "How far can you trust him?" he had asked, and saw how Lehmann turned, studying him closely. "Trust?" he'd answered. "I trust no man, Jiri. Not even you. If it were a matter of life and death, a question of choice—of my life or yours— could I trust you? Could I *really* trust you?"

He had wanted to say yes, but with Lehmann's eyes upon him he had not wished to answer glibly, insincerely. He had hesitated, then bowed his head. "I don't know . . . I . . ." But Lehmann had only shaken his head and taken his arm, as if to console him. "Have no illusions, Jiri. Strip what you feel bare. Look hard at yourself. All else means nothing."

It was the closest he had come to Lehmann, and the moment had seared itself into his memory, but it was the closeness of utter strangers. Even at that moment, he had sensed the utter cold of the vacuum that surrounded Lehmann and kept them separate. Where there were no illusions there could be no warmth. And love, even love, became a thing of ice.

━━━━━━━

WHISKERS LU'S FACE filled the big overhead screen, his left eye staring down blankly from the pink, crab-mottled rawness of his melted face, his narrow, lipless mouth formed into a fierce grin.

"Wong Yi-sun! Welcome! Come inside! We are all here now."

Fat Wong hesitated, then, with a nod to his bodyguards, passed beneath the great lintel of the House of the Ninth Ecstasy, entering Lu Ming-shao's territory. Inside, he looked about him, surprised by the understated elegance of the place. When he had first heard that the meeting of the Council was to be held in a singsong house he had been outraged, wondering whether this were some subtle insult on Whiskers Lu's part, but his advisors had reassured him that this was where Lu Ming-shao did most of his business from these days, and so he had accepted the invitation. Now, seeing it for himself, he understood. Lu's First Level contacts would feel at home in a place like this. It was a good place to do business. Even so, it was of a piece with Lu Ming-shao that he should run the Black Dog Triad from a whorehouse.

There was the faint rustle of a curtain to his left. Fat Wong turned, facing it, one hand on the knife at his belt, then he relaxed. A scantily dressed young woman stood there, her head bowed.

"Might I take your cloak, Wong Yi-sun?"

Fat Wong studied the girl, noting how delicately she was formed, wondering briefly whether that delicacy were a product of chance or of human manufacture, then he nodded, letting her take the silk from his shoulders. As he turned back, Whiskers Lu appeared on the far side of the room, coming across to embrace him.

"Yi-sun . . ." he said, holding Fat Wong at arm's length, as if he had not seen him in a long while. Then, with a flourish of his arm, he turned, inviting Wong to go through.

Again Wong hesitated, the habit of suspicion shaping his response, then let himself be led through. In a room at the center of the House the other four Bosses were waiting, sitting about in huge, comfortable chairs, drinks and trays of sweetmeats on low tables at their sides. As he entered, they called out, greeting him, as if they were old friends and this a chance to drink and eat and talk of women and past times, whereas the truth was that what they were to discuss today was of the utmost importance, heralding a new phase in their relationship with the Above.

Fat Wong smiled, letting himself fall into the role, accepting the tumbler of wine Whiskers Lu held out to him, knowing that his stomach implant would neutralize its effects. He sat, looking about him, conscious yet again of the refinement of the decor. He had had his advisors dig back into the history of this place and had learned what had happened here with the old Madam, Mu Chua, and the Minor-Family Prince, Hsiang K'ai Fan. It was Mu Chua who had built this place and established its reputation, running the House for more than thirty years. Her death—her throat slit by Hsiang K'ai Fan even as he was fucking her—might easily have been a disaster for Whiskers Lu, but the intercession of Li Yuan's General, Hans Ebert, had saved Lu's skin. In a secret deal negotiated by Ebert, the Hsiang family had agreed to pay Lu Ming-shao twenty-five million *yuan* in compensation, provided he took no retributive action. With those funds Whiskers Lu had rebuilt the House of the Ninth Ecstasy and installed a new Madam. He had also imported one or two "oddities," things accepted from the Hsiang family in lieu of cash. Among those oddities were one of the GenSyn ox-men and five of GenSyn's famous "Imperial Courtesan" line—the model with the two additional orifices. Such "treasures" had won a new clientele to the House and things were almost as they were.

Whiskers Lu came close, leaning over Wong, his voice lowered to a whisper. "If there is anything you would like to try while you're here, Yi-sun, you are most welcome."

Fat Wong smiled, as if pleased by the offer, but it was yet another instance of Lu Ming-shao's poor breeding. Or his naivete. He studied Whiskers Lu a moment, noting the changes that this last year had brought. Gone was the ragged fur he had once sported about his shoulders; gone too the wild-barbarian look. Lately he had taken to wearing his hair slicked back, his mustache trimmed and waxed. Lu thought it made him look more refined, but the truth was otherwise; it only made his masklike face look more artificial, more foolish. Wong smiled inwardly, then looked past Lu. There, in the corner of the room, was a *wei chi* board, set up as if midway through a game. He had heard that Lu Ming-shao had recently taken up the game and this seemed to confirm it. Rumor had it, however, that Whiskers Lu was very bad at the game and had killed two opponents in fits of temper. If so, it was but another thing against him. The time was coming fast when Lu Ming-shao would prove too great an embarrassment to the *Hung Mun*, and when that day came he, Wong Yi-sun, would be the first to act.

It was another hour before they came to business. Between times there was the usual sparring—the sounding-out of positions before the hard bargaining began. This once, however, there was little to debate and they came quickly to agreement. The matter was a simple one. In a year's time the House at Weimar would be reopened. Before then, candidates had to be selected, elections held. It was an ideal opportunity for the *Hung Mun* to buy their way in. Rumor had it that the new House would have real power, real influence. If so, it was to the advantage of them all to gain a foothold. The only question was how big a foothold and how much that would cost.

Li the Lidless was speaking, reading from a special report he had had his advisors draw up.

". . . it is also felt that any attempt to spread our net too wide might not only prove a strain upon current resources but might also result in a diminishment of effective influence. It is suggested, therefore, that each of the six brotherhoods concentrate on acquiring the friendship of five Representatives. The resultant pressure group within the House—funded centrally and with the capacity to 'extend' its influence on certain matters within the House; that is, to buy the votes of responsive members—ought to provide a solid foundation for our continued expansion up the levels."

Li Chin sat back, looking about the circle of his fellow 489s. "Long years we have waited in the darkness down below. Now our time has come. We must climb. Up, into the light."

Fat Wong leaned forward, conscious of the receptive mood Li's words had created. "Then we are agreed? Thirty Representatives, to be controlled directly by this Council. Policy and funding to be as outlined in Li Chin's report."

He looked about the circle, seeing how enthusiastically they nodded; how willingly they embraced this next step. For once the potential benefits for all outweighed the petty needs of individual Triads. But how long would that last? How long would it be before one or the other of them tried to win a greater share of influence than their fellows? Once already he had had to deal with such divisions, enlisting Li Yuan's aid to crush his rival, Iron Mu. But next time would be more difficult. Next time he might have to fight them all. Which was why it was important to pacify them just now, to seem to be working with them closely, hand-in-hand, so that he might build up his strength.

Because ultimately he did not want what Li Chin wanted. No. He wanted it all.

Fat Wong turned, looking across at Whiskers Lu once more, and, smiling, his manner deceptively casual, said what had been on his mind all along.

"I hear there has been trouble among your *tong*, Lu Ming-shao. They say there is a new man, cutting in. I wondered . . ."

He saw the agitated movement of Lu's good eye, the sense of turmoil beneath the glassy mask of his face, and knew he had touched a nerve. But when Whiskers Lu spoke, it was in the same almost-bantering tone he always used.

"It is so, Wong Yi-sun, but when is there not trouble among the lower orders? Besides, the matter is already settled, a new balance found. One must let the little men fight their battles, neh?"

They were good words, and Fat Wong bowed his head, acknowledging them, but all there were aware of the significance of the exchange, for while the rest of them had worked their way up the levels of their respective brotherhoods, Whiskers Lu alone had won his post by conquest. He had not entered the brotherhood as a child, nor was he steeped in the ancient rituals of the *Hung Mun*. No. Like the "new man" Wong had mentioned, Whiskers Lu was an outsider, a usurper, and had bullied his way into a position of power. The reminder was thus unwelcome.

"Well, brothers," Whiskers Lu said, standing, his whole manner suggesting that he had already forgotten what had just been said, "now that we are agreed, let us retire to the next room. I have arranged an entertainment. Something rather special. Something . . . *different.*"

His lipless mouth grinned broadly, but as he turned away, Wong noted how Lu's left hand was clenched, the tendons showing at the wrist, as if all of his anger—anger that could not be expressed on the masklike nullity of his face—had been channeled down into that hard, bunched node of flesh and bone. And, seeing it, Fat Wong smiled.

Yes. Step by step he would undermine them, even as he seemed to be working with them. Step by step, until he was ready. And then there would be war. War such as the lowers had never seen.

WHISKERS LU let the door close, the last of his guests departed, then turned, his thin smile fading, and glared at the three men who remained in the room.

"How *dare* the fucker discuss my private business in my House!"

Lu Ming-shao kicked out, sending one of the low tables flying, tumblers and bowls of food scattered across the carpet.

"The toad! The fucking insect! What the fuck does he think he's playing at?"

The three men looked to each other but said nothing. When Whiskers Lu was like this, it was best to keep one's head low and wait for the storm to pass.

Lu Ming-shao shuddered, his one good eye burning in his glassy face. "If it had been any other man, I'd have slit his fucking throat! But I'll have him. See if I don't!"

He turned, anger making his movements jerky, angular. "Po Lao . . . Why was I not told what was going on? What the fuck are you up to, keeping me in the dark?"

Po Lao, Whisker's Lu's "Red Pole," his second-in-command, bowed his head, accepting the criticism, but inside he was fuming. Lu Ming-shao *had* been told about the new man, and not once but several times, but he had been too busy preparing for the Council meeting—closeted with designers and entertainers—to pay any attention.

"It's not fucking good enough," Lu went on, standing close to Po Lao, the pink, crab-mottled flesh of his melted face pressed right up against Po's. "I want you to go down there, *personally,* and see to the matter. To sort things out for good and all, because I don't want any more trouble, understand me? And I particularly don't want any word of what's happening in our territories getting out to that cunt Fat Wong."

Po Lao felt his face burning beneath its rigid exterior. For a moment he was giddy with suppressed anger. Then, with a curt bow, he turned away. But at the door Whiskers Lu called him back again.

"And Po Lao. No fuck-ups. I want it settled. Right?"

Po Lao turned back, meeting Lu Ming-shao's good eye, letting nothing of what he was feeling show. "I understand, Master Lu."

"Good. Now go. I want to hear from you tonight."

✦✦✦✦✦

"*Shih* Ward?"

Kim looked up, beginning to smile, then checked himself, realizing that it was not the young official he had been dealing with earlier, but the Supervisor of the section. Beyond the stoop-backed old graybeard stood two departmental guards, their side arms held across their chests.

"What is it?" he asked, standing, puzzled by the look of stern anger on the elderly Han's face.

In answer the man thrust a folder at Kim—the same folder he had submitted only four hours back at the counter on the far side of the waiting room.

"It's all done, then?" he asked, staring down at it, wondering momentarily where the completed patent certificate was.

"Are these your documents, *Shih* Ward?" the Supervisor asked, ignoring Kim's comment.

Kim glanced at the folder again. "Yes. Of course. Why? Is there a problem?"

The man's smile was cold, ironical. "You might say that. But first let me confirm two things." He reached across and opened the folder, drawing out the slender, microns-thick official form. "Is this your signature at the bottom of this patents application form?"

"Yes."

"And you understand that this form is to be used only for new patents originated by the signatory?"

Kim nodded, concerned now; not understanding why the man should need to ask, nor why he should feel the need to have guards present.

"Then I am afraid to say that this form is invalid, being in breach of Section 761 [D] of the Patents Protection Laws. Moreover, *Shih* Ward, it is my duty to arrest you for making a fraudulent application, infringing a patent already registered at this office."

Kim laughed, but it was the laughter of disbelief, not amusement. "It isn't possible. I checked. A week ago. Here at this very office. There was nothing. Nothing even vaguely like it!"

The official smiled, clearly enjoying his role, then produced a copy of a patent protection form. He let Kim study it a moment, watching as the young man's face drained, then took it back from him.

Kim stood there, his hands shaking, his mouth agape. "Someone stole it," he said quietly. "They must have."

The official turned, handing the folder to one of the guards, then turned back, puffing out his chest, as if to display the big, square badge of office there. "Your comments have been noted, *Shih* Ward, and, along with the recording of this interview, will be submitted to the Hearing in two days' time. Until then, I am afraid you will have to be detained."

"Detained . . . ?" Kim shook his head, disbelief tilting over into a kind of stupor. He felt sick and dizzy and hardly heard what the man said next, but then, suddenly, his hands were being pulled behind him. He felt the restraint-lock click into place about his wrists, then he was being pulled backward out of the room.

"You must send word!" Kim called out, trying to make the official listen. "You must tell T'ai Cho!" But the Supervisor had already turned away and was talking to the other guard. And then the door slammed shut in front of him and he felt a sharp, sudden blow on the back of his head. And then nothing.

CHAPTER EIGHT

Dynasties

T HE GIRL WAS ASLEEP, her long, auburn hair fanned out across her naked back, the thin sheet draped across her buttocks like a shroud. For a moment Old Man Lever studied her, conscious of the contrast between them. Her flesh was so smooth, so *new*, like silk over the taut frame of bone and muscle, no sign of age marring its perfection. He sighed, then pulled himself up heavily, stretching the tiredness from his bones. Suddenly he felt old. Very old. He looked about him, at the simple luxury of the room, a luxury to which he had been born, and shook his head, as if he didn't understand whence all this had come, then looked down at himself again, at thinning legs and a stomach gone to paunch, a chest to flab—at the changes and distortions time had brought to the landscape of his flesh. All these years he had kept himself trim, had fought Time itself, fleeing from it, like a swimmer in dangerous waters, but Time, patient as a shark, had waited in the depths, staring up at him with cold, impersonal eyes, biding its time, knowing there was no escape.

He shuddered, then padded across to the armchair in the corner of the room and pulled on the dark blue silk dressing gown he had thrown there earlier. The girl had been good—very good indeed— and she had finally brought him off, but it had been a long, uphill struggle, and he had almost sent her away at one point, ashamed of his failure.

It had happened before, of course, and he had blamed it on tiredness or an excess of wine, but it was neither—he knew that now. He was simply getting old.

He drew the sash tight about his waist, then went across, standing there at the mirror, looking at himself clearly in the light from the overhead lamp. In four weeks' time he would be seventy-four. One year older than Tolonen. An old man. Powerful, as old men went, but old all the same.

He turned away, angry with himself. Only an hour ago he had been full of life, buoyant after the news from the Patents Office, standing there, whooping at the screen. Yes, just an hour ago he had felt as though he could run ten *li* and then take on a pair of serving girls, one after the other, as he'd done in his youth. But now he knew. It was only the adrenaline rush. Only the ragged tide of feeling through an old man's head.

Going across to the room's comset, he tapped out a code irritably. "Get me Curval on the line," he said, even before the picture had properly formed. "And get him *now*, whatever he's doing."

He looked across at the girl again. She had turned and was lying on her side, one breast exposed above the sheet. Lever shivered. No, it wasn't her fault. She had tried. Had tried her damnedest to be sweet to him. Besides, the girl was mute. So maybe he would keep her. Maybe he would have her assigned here, to his private rooms.

He turned back as Curval's voice came through.

"Curval . . . I want you to come here at once. I've a job for you. I want you to go up to Boston for me and see the boy again. I'll brief you when you get here."

Curval made to answer, but Lever had already cut him off. Turning away, he crossed the room quickly and stood over the girl, shaking her until she came awake.

"Quick now," he said, pulling her up. "You must help me dress. I've things to do."

And as she busied herself about him, he began to feel better; began to shrug off his earlier mood. No, it was no good skulking and sulking. One had to *do* something. First he'd draft a note—an answer to the T'ang of Africa—to be sent by way of Mach, agreeing to his offer. Then he would arrange a meeting of the major shareholders to the

Institute and force them to agree to an increase in funding. Last, but not least, he would see Curval, and brief him. For Curval would be his key.

He smiled, letting the girl fuss about him, wondering why he had not thought of it before. At present Curval was Head of the Institute, his reputation as the leading experimental geneticist of his age unchallenged. But Curval, good as he was, wasn't good enough, not when it was a question of squaring-up to death. He had as much as admitted to Lever's face that he considered the problem unsolvable. Even so, he might be the means by which Ward could be wooed back to the fold. Yes, where money and threats had failed, maybe a play at Ward's natural scientific curiosity might succeed. If Curval could show him how wonderful a challenge it was. If he could fire him with a new enthusiasm.

Especially now, when the boy was down and vulnerable.

Lever looked down. The girl had stopped, staring at the fierce erection he now sported. He laughed, then drew her close, forcing her head down onto him.

Yes, he would be young again. He *would* be young.

━━━◆◆◆◆◆━━━

TWO HUNDRED *LI* to the north, in the boardroom of a small company, four men sat about a long oak table, talking.

Michael Lever had been silent for some while, listening, but now he leaned forward, interrupting the stream of talk.

"Forgive me, Bryn, but the point isn't whether it *can* be done, but whether it *ought* to be done. I don't know about you, but I don't want to live forever. It's bad enough thinking of being fifty, let alone being fifty forever."

Bryn Kustow was hunched forward at the far end of the table, facing Michael, his elbows pressed against the polished surface, his long forearms stretched out along the wood, meeting in a handclasp. His ash-blond hair was cut aggressively short, but the style suited him. He looked like a soldier, sitting there.

"Fifty, no, but what if you could be twenty-five for the rest of time? Wouldn't that tempt you?"

Michael shook his head. "I know how I feel. Besides, I want sons of my own, and I want those sons to love and respect me. I don't want to be a barrier in their way."

Kustow nodded and leaned back in the big wheel-back chair. Between him and Michael, to either side of the table, sat their friends and longtime companions, Jack Parker and Carl Stevens. They were dressed simply and sported the same aggressive hairstyle as Kustow. It gave them a kind of uniformity. One look was enough to place them. *Sons*, they were. Part of the new movement.

"It sounds like you hate him," Stevens said, leaning toward him. "Has it really got that bad?"

"No. It's not as simple as that. For all he's done to me these past few weeks, I still don't hate him. But this obsession of his with immortality. Well, it's gone too far. All his energies seem to be channeled into the search for a new serum or for some new way of switching off the aging process." He looked across at Kustow, his face filled with hurt. "I've seen it grow in him these past few years, like a sickness. And I don't want to be that way. Not ever. I don't want to be old in the way he's getting old. Hanging on like a beggar. There's no dignity in that."

"My father's the same," said Parker, looking about him at the circle of his friends. "He's got no time for anything else, these days. The day-to-day stuff he delegates, then goes off to jaw with the old gang." He paused and shook his head. "And you know what they're talking about? They're talking about spending a further fifteen billion on the Institute. Fifteen billion! And who loses out?"

"Sure. So what do we do about it?"

They stared at Kustow, as if he'd said something that was difficult to grasp.

"Do?" Stevens asked, shaking his dark, cropped head and laughing. "What *can* we do? It's like Mitchell said the other night at Gloria's. They've got all the money, all the real power. All we have is the vague promise of inheritance."

"Vaguer by the day," said Parker, nudging him and laughing.

But Kustow and Lever weren't laughing. They were watching each other. Kustow narrowed his eyes in a question, and Michael nodded.

"Okay . . . we'll come clean," said Kustow, standing up and walking around the table until he stood behind Michael. "The paperwork, earlier . . . that was a front. Michael and I called you over today for a special reason. Not to make deals, or anything like that, but to work on this thing that's bugging us all. To see if we *can* do something."

"We're listening," Parker said, leaning back, assuming an air of businesslike attentiveness. Across from him, Stevens nodded.

It was Michael who spoke.

"Essentially, you're right, Carl. They have got all the real power. But let's not underestimate ourselves. What have *we* got? Let's look at it. Let's see what we can rustle up between us."

He separated his hands and sat back, using his right hand to count the fingers of his left. "One, we've got our personal allowances. Not inconsiderable. There's many a small company who would welcome the same figure in turnover. Don't be offended, but Bryn and I have been checking up. Between the four of us we could count on a figure of some one and three quarter million *yuan*."

Parker laughed. "And where would that get us? Your accounts are frozen, Michael, or had you forgotten?"

"Hold on," said Kustow. "Michael's not finished yet."

Michael smiled, his handsome face showing patience and determination. "Two, there's what we could divert from those funds we control on behalf of our fathers' companies."

Parker frowned. "I don't like the sound of that. It sounds vaguely criminal."

"It is. But let's face that when we have to. From such funds we could probably command upward of twenty million *yuan*."

Stevens whistled. Personally he was in charge of three small production companies that serviced his father's near-space development corporation, but they were minnows—sops his father had given him to keep him quiet; more a hobby than a job. He was an engineering graduate and the eldest of them at twenty-eight, but in himself he felt like a boy still, playing when he should have been acting in the world.

"Three, there are Trusts we could borrow against. Even at the most pessimistic rate we could expect to raise something like fifteen million *yuan*."

Parker interrupted him. "They'd know." He laughed briefly, then shook his head. "Don't you see? If we set about realizing all of this they'd know at once that we were up to something."

Lever smiled. "Good. Then you're thinking about it seriously?"

The young man sat back, chewing on some imaginary straw, then nodded. But there was a hesitancy in what he said next. "I think I see what you're getting at. We have the money, so that's not it. That's not our key, right? Because we can't use money against them. They've got it tightly bottled up as far as money's concerned."

Kustow came forward and leaned over the table, facing him. "That's right. But the very fact that we *have* the money gives us an edge. The fact that if we wanted to, we could call on some forty to fifty million between us, *that* gives us power."

Stevens took his hand from his mouth. "I don't see it, Bryn. How? If we can't use it, how does it help us?"

Kustow half turned and looked at Lever. Again, Lever nodded. Slowly, Kustow straightened up, then, without another word, he left the room.

"What's going on?" Parker asked, laughing uncertainly. "What is this, Michael? Some kind of revolutionary cell we're forming here?"

Lever looked at him calmly and nodded. "That's just what it is, Jack. But we're joining, not forming it."

Stevens had tilted back his head and was scratching beneath his neck. For a moment he said nothing, then, slowly, he began to laugh, his laughter getting stronger. "Well, I'll be. . . ."

Kustow was standing in the doorway again. "Gentlemen, I want you to meet an old school friend of mine. A man who, we hope, will someday make America great again." He stood back, letting a tall, dark-haired man step past him, into the room.

Stevens had stopped laughing. Parker, beside him, gasped and half rose from his seat.

"Hello," said Joseph Kennedy, smiling and putting out his hand. "It's good to meet you. Bryn's told me a lot about you two."

<hr/>

KENNEDY LEANED BACK in his chair and stretched out his arms, yawning and laughing at the same time. The table in front of him was cluttered with half-filled glasses and empty wine bottles. Around the table the young men joined in his laughter, pausing to suck on their cigars or drain a glass, the air dense with cigar smoke.

They had all known Kennedy, of course. You could hardly grow up in the North American Above and not know the Kennedys. Even after the fall of the Empire, a Kennedy had overseen the period of transitional government and, through his influence and skill, had prevented the great tragedy from becoming a debilitating catastrophe. This was that man's great-great-grandson, a figure familiar from the elite MedFac channels. When his father had died, eight years back, he had inherited one of the biggest legal firms on the East Coast and had not hesitated to step into his father's shoes at once. Now, however, it seemed he was tired of the legal game. He wanted something bigger to take on.

Which was why he was there, speaking to them.

Joseph Kennedy was a big, good-humored man, handsome in the way that all the Kennedys were handsome, but with something else behind the good looks; something that made people look at him with respect, perhaps even with a degree of awe. He was powerful and charismatic, like an animal in some ways, but supremely intelligent with it. His mind missed nothing, while his eyes seemed to take in more than the surface of things.

Though he was a good six years older than the men he had come to meet, there was a youthfulness about him that made him seem one of them. He had made them at ease quickly and with a skill that was as much inherited as his vast personal fortune. But he did not play upon his charm. In fact, the opposite was true. When he spelled out what it was he wanted from them, he made certain that they knew the cost of their involvement. It would be bad, he told them. In all likelihood they would be disinherited before the year was out, estranged from their families. At worst there was the possibility that they would be dead. The stakes were high, and only a fool went blindly into such a game.

That said, however, he reminded them of their breeding, and of what there was to gain.

"Freedom," he said. "Not just for you, but for all men. Freedom from the old men who chain you, but also freedom from the Seven."

"We will make deals," he said. "At first our enemies will think us friends, or, at worst, accomplices. But in time they will come to know us as we really are. And then they'll find us worse than in their darkest dreams."

And when he said that he paused and looked at them, each in turn, measuring how each one faced him and then, as if satisfied, nodded to himself.

There was more, much more, but in essence they knew what he wanted of them. Loyalty. Obedience when the time came. Support—covert at first, but then, when he asked it of them, out in the open. When the time was right they would mobilize all their resources; four out of hundreds across the great continent who would rise up and change the face of North American politics for all time.

Behind them were discussions about the Edict, about the immortality treatments and the latest terrorist attacks in Europe. Now, at the tail end of the evening, they were talking of other things. Of women and ball games and mutual friends. Kennedy had been telling them an anecdote about a certain Representative and the daughter of a Minor Family. It was scandalous and close to the knuckle, but their laughter showed no fear. They were as one now; wedded to the cause. And when, finally, Kennedy left, they each shook his hand and bowed their heads, mock solemn, like soldiers, but also like friends.

"Was he always like that?" Stevens asked Kustow when he had gone. "I mean, was he like that at College, when you knew him?"

Kustow stubbed out his cigar and nodded. "Always. If we had a problem we went to him, not to one of the teachers or the Head. And he would always sort it out." He smiled, reminiscing. "We idolized him. But then, in my second year, he left, and everything changed."

There was a moment's silence, an exchange of glances.

"Does anyone fancy a meal?" Parker said, breaking the silence. "I don't know about you guys, but I'm starving."

"Sure," Kustow said, looking to Stevens, who nodded. "And you, Michael?"

Michael hesitated, then shook his head. "Another time, maybe. Right now I've got to sort something out."

"Mary?"

He looked back at Kustow, wondering how he knew, then laughed. "I spoke to her earlier. Said I'd see her sometime this afternoon. I . . ."

There was a hammering at the outer door.

"What the hell?" Kustow said, turning to face the sound.

"Do you think . . . ?" Stevens began, looking to Michael.

"No," Michael said quietly as the hammering came again. "But whoever it is, they sure as hell want to see someone in a hurry."

He went across quickly and slid the door back, then strode out across the plush expanse of carpet in the reception room. The three men followed him, standing in the doorway, watching as he slid back the bolt and stood back, pulling the double doors open.

Outside, in the dimly lit corridor, stood a Han. A tall Han in plain green silks with mussed hair and a distraught expression.

"T'ai Cho!" Michael said, surprised. "What in the gods' names are you doing here?"

"It's Kim!" T'ai Cho said breathlessly, grasping Michael's arm. "He's been arrested!"

"*Arrested?* For what?"

"At the Patents Office! They say he stole the patent he was trying to register! You have to do something, *Shih* Lever! You must!"

"What is this, Michael?" Parker asked, but Kustow touched his arm and gave him a look, as if to say "leave it."

"I'll come," he said, looking across at Kustow. "Bryn, will you get word to Mary. Tell her that I've been delayed. I . . ." He turned back. "T'ai Cho . . . has Kim got legal help?"

"No . . . no, he . . ."

"Okay." He patted T'ai Cho's arm, as if to reassure him, then looked back at Kustow. "Do you know where Kennedy was off to, Bryn?"

"Just home, I think."

"Good. Then contact him. Tell him I need him. Tell him . . . tell him a good friend of mine is in trouble and that I'd appreciate his advice and help."

Kustow smiled and nodded.

"And Bryn . . . tell Mary that I'll see her when I can."

◆◆◆◆◆

"So what happened?"

Kim had been standing at the far end of the bare detention room, facing away from where Michael Lever was sitting on a narrow, pull-down bench, but at Michael's words he turned and came across, kneeling beside the taller man.

"It was my bookkeeper, Nong Yan," he said, looking up into Michael's face. "It had to be."

"How do you know?"

Kim shrugged. "No one else saw it. No one else had even the vaguest idea what I was working on. Even so, I don't know how he did it. He could only have had the briefest glimpse of it. I . . ."

Again his eyes drifted off, as they had once or twice already; as if this were a scientific puzzle, to be analyzed and solved. Not that it really mattered now.

In less than three hours it had all come apart. The patent was gone—stolen—and with it any chance of securing terms from the Hang Yu Credit Agency. Indeed, news had reached the bankers fast, for a handwritten message had reached Kim an hour back, expressing the regretful apologies of the Brothers Hang. But that was not all. Acting on the news, Kim's present bankers had recalled their development loan and taken immediate action to recover the debt, stripping the facility of all its equipment. At the same time, news had come that a third party had bought up all of the surrounding units—units Kim had made offers for only days before—at four times the normal rental, effectively preventing any physical expansion of Kim's operation. Not that it made any difference now.

"I should have realized . . ." he said, after a moment. "Realized what I was up against."

"My father, you mean?"

Kim nodded. "He's toyed with us both, neh? And for what? In my case, so that he might use me to pursue some addlebrained notion of postponing the inevitable. Even though I couldn't do it."

"He thinks you could. He thinks you could find a way of prolonging life. Of extending it, three, four hundred years. Maybe indefinitely."

Kim took a long breath, then looked up again, his expression suddenly intense, his eyes burning.

"Technically, perhaps. But that's not what I mean. I couldn't do it because I *couldn't* do it. I wouldn't let myself. The consequences are unthinkable. Once in my life already I've meddled in things that should have been left well alone, but this time I have a choice. So no.

The dream of living forever must remain just that. A dream. I mean, just think of it! Unlink the great chain of being, and what would follow? It would be a curse, Michael. Nothing but a curse!"

Michael shuddered, then looked away, disturbed by this sudden glimpse of the young man's potency; by the dark, intense power locked away in his taut, diminutive form.

"So what will you do now?"

Kim smiled. "It depends on what your friend Kennedy can arrange. I was going to go to Europe next week, but what's the point? Whatever I do, your father blocks me. He's obsessed."

"You should go," Michael said quietly. "Really, Kim. You can't let him beat you. This . . ." He shivered, then stood, beginning to pace the room. "He's been like this all his life. If he wanted something, he'd get it, no matter what. If someone stood in his way, he'd crush them. And no thought for the consequences. Once . . . not long ago, really . . . I thought that that was how things were. That it was normal to behave that way. But now . . ."

He stopped, turning to look back at Kim. "Look, Kim. If I could help you, I would. You know that. Whatever you needed. But he's fucked me too. Boxed me in. It's how he works. Destroy and control. There's no subtlety to him. No compromise, either. But he doesn't have to win. Not unless we let him."

Kim smiled. "Okay. I'll go to Europe. Just as soon as all the legal stuff's sorted out. But I'm finished here. Look . . ."

He took the four handwritten letters from his pocket and handed them across. Michael studied them a moment, then looked up again, his eyes pained. The stamped timings on the resignation letters showed they had come within an hour of his arrest. Kim took them back from Michael, staring at them a moment, as if they were a mystery he couldn't solve, then pocketed them again.

"I keep trying to tell myself that it's understandable. That I'd do the same. But it's not true. I . . ." He looked away, close, suddenly, to breaking down. "What's happening, Michael? What in the gods' names is happening?"

"It's this world," Michael answered softly. "That's why we have to change it. You in your way, me in mine. We've got to fight the old men who want to keep things as they are. Every step of the way. Because if we don't . . ."

There was a knocking on the door. A moment later a lock drew back and the door swung inward. It was Kennedy. Behind him two men stood to attention, like an honor guard.

"Michael . . . Kim . . ." Kennedy stepped into the room, tall and imperious, offering his hand for Kim to take. "Okay. It's all dealt with. I've filed bail for fifty thousand *yuan*, so you're free to go. However, the hearing has been brought forward, to eleven tomorrow morning. Which means we'll have to get our act together, fast."

"So what do we do?"

Kennedy smiled broadly. "We produce files. Experimental notes and the like. Things that'll prove beyond all doubt that the patent's your development."

Kim shook his head. "They don't exist. It was all up here, in my head."

"All . . ." Kennedy gave a small laugh, then looked to Michael. "I guess you were right, Michael. He *is* different."

"Even so," Kim said, as Kennedy returned his attention to him. "I doubt that they've got anything either. In fact, I'd guarantee that they don't even understand yet what they've got, let alone how it works."

"I see. But how do we use that? The burden of proof is on us, not them. They registered first. We're the ones in default."

"Unless we counterclaim? Sue them for false registration?"

Kennedy smiled, the smile growing broader by the moment. "Hey, now that's a good idea. A very, very good idea."

But Michael was shaking his head. "It's not on, Joe. I mean, Kim's broke. How can he sue when he's broke?"

"Maybe," Kennedy answered. "But I'm not. And I'm sure as hell not letting your father get away with this one, Michael. Unless you've any personal objections?"

Michael looked down, then looked back at the two men, smiling. "No. None at all, as it happens."

"Good. Then let's go and get something to eat and talk this through. Somewhere where your father will get to hear of it. The Kitchen, maybe."

Kim stared at Kennedy a moment, then nodded. "Yes," he said quietly, remembering the first time he had visited Archimedes Kitchen, and Old Man Lever's joke about the shark meat they had eaten. Well, now he knew. Finally he understood what the Old Man had meant that evening. They had stripped him bare. Down to the bone. Even so, he had lost nothing. Nothing of substance, anyway. So maybe this was a good thing. To be taught this lesson. To progress from it and build anew. And maybe having the wiring implant put in—maybe that too was serendipitous. Maybe that too was *meant*.

He gave a little shudder. Just for now he was beaten. Things here were finished for him. But now was not forever. He turned, looking about him at the bareness of the room, remembering all the times he'd been incarcerated, then, smiling, put out a hand, touching Michael's arm.

"Okay. Let's go and be seen."

◆◆◆◆◆

SOUCEK STOOD in the mouth of the cave, watching while Lehmann moved among the deep shadows within, gathering together his belongings. Out here he was afraid—possibly more afraid than he had ever been—but he showed nothing, conscious that Lehmann was watching him. To his back was the slope, that awful uneven surface, shrouded in treacherous whiteness, that in places fell sheer a thousand *ch'i* to the rocks and icy water below. He would not look there, not now, lest his courage fail him. No, the warm darkness of the cave was more to his liking—to the habit of his being. He had never, until two hours back, set forth beyond the City's walls. Had never suspected that such a place as this existed. But now he knew. This was where Lehmann had come from. This place of cold and ice and fearful openness.

Lehmann moved quickly, almost effortlessly about the interior of the cave, taking things from ledges and from small niches hacked into the rock face. Weapons and clothing, tools and food, and, most surprising of all, a complex communications system—unlike anything Soucek had ever seen—in an all-weather case, the logo of SimFic impressed into the hard plastic in the bottom right-hand corner.

"That's it," Lehmann said, coming out into the brightness once again. "I'll destroy the rest, then we can get out of here."

Soucek moved back, taking care with his footing, recalling how unpleasant it had been to fall, then watched as Lehmann set the timer on a small device and gently lobbed it into the cave. He turned at once, as if unconcerned, and began trudging back up the mountain-side, following the ragged line of deep indentations they had made in the snow coming down. Soucek followed, glancing back once and then a second time. They were thirty *ch'i* up the slope when it blew, the sound startlingly loud, echoing back and forth between the great peaks, rock fragments scattered far into the valley below. Soucek stopped, looking about him anxiously, his fear getting the better of him momentarily. Across from him, half a *li* distant on the facing slope, a huge spoon-shaped wedge of snow slid, slowly, as if a giant, invisible hand were scooping it up, then settled, throwing up a fine cloud of whiteness, the snow packed high against the tree line.

Soucek turned, looking up the slope at Lehmann. The albino stood there, perfectly at ease, gazing about him, an expression of awe—something Soucek had never expected to see on that narrow, unsmiling face—transforming his features, making him almost handsome. And Soucek, seeing that, understood. Here was Lehmann's home. This his element. Yes, it was this, this fearful emptiness, that had formed him; that was reflected in the icy mirror of his being. It was from here that he drew his strength, and it was this—this place of stone and ice and sky—that made him singular; made him utterly different from the rest.

Soucek turned back, forcing himself to look around, fighting down the fear that threatened to engulf him, trying—*willing* himself—to see it as Lehmann saw it. And for a moment, for a single, fleeting moment, he saw the beauty, the sheer inhuman beauty of it all.

"Look!" Lehmann said, his voice strangely excited. "There, Jiri! There, above that peak to the far left of us."

Soucek turned, looking, shielding his eyes against the brightness of the sky. For a moment he saw nothing, nothing but the empty peaks, the pale blue sky, and then he spotted it—saw the dark speck circling high above the point of rock.

"It's an eagle, Jiri. A T'ang among birds! Look how magnificent it is."

But Soucek had turned, and was watching Lehmann, seeing only him; seeing only how powerful the man seemed, here in his natural element.

"Yes," he answered. "Magnificent."

▂▂▂▂▂

WHISKERS LU'S "RED POLE," Po Lao, had left ten minutes back, having shouted at Lehmann for the best part of an hour. Now Lehmann sat there, at his desk, silent, staring at his hands. Soucek, standing in the doorway, could feel the tension in the room. They were all there—all of his lieutenants—and all had witnessed the dressing-down Po Lao had given him. He had expected Lehmann to act—to answer Po Lao with a knife or a gun, perhaps—but he had done nothing, merely stared incuriously at the man as he ranted, letting him spend his fury in words.

And there was no doubting that Po Lao had been furious.

He had been waiting for them on their return, sat in Lehmann's chair, his feet up on Lehmann's desk, his runners scattered about the corridors, making sure Lehmann's men made no move against him. And for once the legendary patience of Po Lao had given way to temper, and to an outburst of anger that was a clear sign that Whiskers Lu had been riding him hard.

Lehmann had opposed nothing Po Lao had said, yet there had been a stillness to him—a rocklike imperviousness—that had impressed even Po Lao in the end. Soucek had seen it with his own eyes. He noted how the Red Pole's eyes went time and again to Lehmann's face, conscious after a while that here was a man he could not intimidate. And with that realization he had lowered his voice and become more reasonable, more conciliatory, until, at the end, it had seemed almost as though he and Lehmann had come to some strange, unspoken agreement between them.

For a moment longer Lehmann sat there, deep in thought, then, with a strange, almost lazy motion, he drew a sheet of hardprint toward him and, taking the ink brush from the pot, drew the schematic outline of a running dog on the back of the paper, the figure starkly black against the white. He looked up, his eyes moving from face to face, as if measuring each of them, then, taking his knife from his belt, he nicked the top of his right index finger, so that a bead of blood appeared. Slowly, applying the gentlest pressure to the cut, he placed the tip of his finger against the paper, drawing a bright red circle about the figure of the dog.

Soucek, watching, looked about him, seeing the understanding, the sudden excitement in every face and felt his heart begin to hammer in his chest.

* * *

OLD MAN LEVER turned from the screen, speechless with fury, then hurled his goblet into the old stone fireplace.

As a servant scrambled to clear up the shattered glass, the old man paced the room like a wounded cat, cursing, his eyes blazing, oblivious, it seemed, of the men who stood in the shadows to either side, watching.

"How could he?" Lever said, stopping before the screen once more. "How *dare* he!" He clenched a fist and raised it, looking about him, as if searching for something to hit out at. "And Kennedy . . . what's Kennedy's involvement in this?"

There were blank expressions on all sides, shrugs and apologetic bows. But no one knew. This had come as a surprise to them all.

Lever raised his voice. "Does no one know *anything?*"

"There are rumors that Kennedy plans to move into politics," Curval answered, stepping out from beside one of the pillars.

Lever fixed him with one eye. "Politics?"

"They say he wants to form his own party. To challenge the old guard when the House reopens."

Lever studied the geneticist a moment, then began to laugh; a scornful, dismissive laughter that was like the braying of a wild beast. In an instant the big room was filled with laughter as Lever's men joined in, sharing his joke. But beneath the laughter was relief that the old man's rage had been defused, his anger deflected. For the time being.

"Politics!" the old man exclaimed, wheezing with amusement. "Who would have believed it? And my son?" He turned back, facing

Curval again, his eyes suddenly much colder. "Is my son involved in this?"

Curval shrugged. "I wouldn't have said it was Michael's thing. But if Kennedy stood bail for Ward, maybe there's something in it. I mean, why else should he get involved?"

Lever stared at him a moment longer, then went across and sat down behind his desk. For a while he simply sat there, deep in thought, then, looking up, he set to work.

"Okay. Harrison . . . I want you to find out all you can about young Kennedy and his plans. James . . . I want a team posted to cover my son's activities. I want to know where he is and what he's doing every hour of the day from now on, understand? Robins . . . I want you to compile a list of all Kennedy's contacts—business and personal—along with their financial strengths and weaknesses. Spence . . . I want you to take over the winding up of Ward's business affairs. I don't want any last-minute hitches, okay? Good. And you, Cook, I want you to find out a bit more about this trip to Europe our young friend is apparently making. I want to know if he has any plans to set up over there. If he has, I want to know who he meets and what's agreed."

Curval stepped forward, catching Lever's eye. "And my meeting with the boy? Is that still on?"

Lever shook his head. "Not now. Later perhaps. When things are better known. Right now it might prove . . . counterproductive, let's say. Ward has ridden this one. He's survived. Right now he has friends, supporting him, buoying him up. But that won't last. Besides, there's nowhere for him to go now. No one to turn to after this. We have only to isolate him once more. To harry him, like dogs at his heels, until he tires and falls. And then . . ." Lever smiled, broadly, savagely, like some wild thing scenting victory. "And then we'll have him."

———

SOUCEK STOOD THERE over the cot, rocking it gently, cooing to the now-sleeping child. Across from him, Lehmann was tidying the room. The woman lay face down on the bed, as if asleep, the single stiletto wound to the back of the neck hidden beneath her long black hair.

Lehmann had explained nothing, simply told him to come. As on the last occasion, when they had gone outside, Lehmann had taken him into the service shafts, this time climbing the pipes fifty, maybe a hundred levels, until Soucek had begun to wonder whether they were going up to the roof itself. But then Lehmann had turned off, following the map in his head, finding his footing easily, confidently. They had come out thirty *ch'i* from here, in a maintenance corridor. There Lehmann had handed him a uniform from his pack, then put one on himself. The orange of deck maintenance. ID in hand, he had come directly to this door, as if he'd done it several times before, and knocked. There had been the sound of a baby crying, a woman's spoken query, and then they were inside, Lehmann talking to the woman, reassuring her. A moment later she was dead.

Soucek had watched as Lehmann turned the woman over. He had taken a thin sheet of printout from his pocket—a sheet with her picture on it—and checked it against her. Then, satisfied, he had lifted her and placed her facedown on the bed. When the baby began to cry halfheartedly, Lehmann had turned, looking directly at Soucek, and made a rocking gesture.

What are we doing here? Soucek wondered, looking about him. It was a normal Mid-Level apartment, modestly furnished. And the woman. She was simply a wife, a mother. So what the fuck was Lehmann up to? What did he want here?

His answer came a moment later. There were footsteps outside in the corridor, then a brisk knocking and a cheerful call.

"Sweetheart! It's me! I'm home!"

Lehmann signaled for Soucek to go out into the kitchen, then went across. Moving to one side of the door, he pressed the lock. As it hissed back and the man came into the room, Lehmann moved between him and the door, his knife drawn.

He was a tall, almost cadaverously thin man, with dark, short-cut hair and of roughly the same height and build as Lehmann.

"Becky?" he asked, confused, seeing the woman on the bed, apparently asleep. Then, understanding that someone else must have operated the door lock, he jerked around.

Soucek, watching from the kitchen, saw, in the mirror on the far side of the room, the look of horror in the man's face; saw Lehmann glance at a second paper. Then, letting the paper fall from his hand, he leaned in toward the man, as if embracing him. A moment later, the man fell back, the smallest sound of surprise escaping his lips.

As Lehmann knelt over the body, Soucek stepped out into the room again.

"Who is he?"

"There," Lehmann said, concentrating on what he was doing. "The paper on the floor."

Soucek went across and picked it up. It was a printout giving brief personal details of the man. Thomas Henty. *Hung Mao*. Married. One child. Age thirty. A technician. Soucek turned back, looking across, then grimaced. Lehmann was using a narrow scalpel now, and was carefully cutting the man's eyes from his head. As Soucek watched, he severed the optical nerve and gently dropped the eyeball into a special tubelike carrier he had taken from his pack. There was the faintest hiss as the soft eye slid into the cold compartment, then the lid clicked over. Moments later the other eye joined its companion in the narrow box.

Eyes. He was stealing the man's eyes.

"What about the child?"

Lehmann leaned back, looking across at Soucek. "Forget the child. He's dead. They're all dead now." And, as if in explanation, Lehmann took a small device from his pack—an incendiary—and, setting the timer for sixty seconds, placed it between the two corpses on the bed.

"Quick now," he said, going across to the door. "We've another call to make and only forty minutes to get there."

But Soucek paused at the door, looking back into the room. The sight of the dead couple on the bed and the soft snuffling of the sleeping child tore unexpectedly at his feelings. For the briefest moment, he stood there, as if paralyzed, wondering what special torments the demons of hell would have in store for him when his life above the Yellow Springs was done. Then, with a tiny shudder, he turned away, following Lehmann out into the corridor.

THAT NIGHT the dream came once again.

Again, as once before, she stood alone upon that tilted, shattered land, trapped beneath a low, impenetrable sky of steel. It was dark, an oppressive, elemental darkness lit now and then by sudden flashes of light. All about her the storm raged violently, growling and shrieking at her with a voice of primal evil. Before, she had felt only fear; a gut-wrenching fear that had rooted her to the spot. This time, however, it was not fear she felt but excitement.

Excitement, and a sense of expectation.

Beneath her the tower slowly climbed the slope, its wooden, spiderish limbs folding and stretching inexorably, its dark mouth grunting and wheezing as it came on. With each searing flash of light she saw it gain on her, its shattered, glasslike eyes glittering malevolently, its jagged, toothless maw crammed with splintered bone.

Closer it came, and closer yet, and as its foul breath rolled up the hill toward her, she cried out, her voice high and clear above the noise of the storm. There was a moment's silence, a moment's utter stillness, and then, as once before, the earth between her and the tower cracked and split.

She shivered, watching, knowing what would come. Knowing and yet fearful in case, this time, it would be different.

Slowly, like a shadow forming from the dark mouth of the earth, he emerged: a stooped little creature with short, strong limbs and eyes that burned like coals. Turning, he looked at her, his wet, dark skin glowing with an inner light.

She smiled, greeting him, recognizing him for the first time. It was Kim.

For a moment he was still, watching her, his dark yet fiery eyes seeming to pierce her to the bone. And then, slowly, his lips parted in a smile, like a pocket opening in the blackness of his face, light—a brilliant, burning light—spilling out, falling like molten gold from the mouth of a furnace.

He smiled, and then, with an agility that surprised her, he spun about, facing the tower, his arms held up before him, as if to ward it off.

"Avodya!" he said clearly. *"Avodya!"*

Slowly the tower heaved itself up, creaking beneath its own bloated weight, a furious whispering and muttering coming from within its hideous maw. Then, with a rush, it came up the slope at him, its cracked eyes glinting, its thin legs straining, a low moan rising to a screech as it ran.

"*Avodya!*"

On it came and on, rushing at him through the half-dark. On, like some vast, unstoppable machine, until, with a fearsome cry, it threw itself at him.

And as it fell, the darkness seemed to explode. Where the small, dark creature stood was now a web of brilliant, coruscating light that pulsed between the fingers of his outstretched arms.

Slowly, ever so slowly, the tower fell, tumbling, shrieking, into the fierce, pure fire of the web. And where it touched it sparked and vanished, flickering into nothingness.

For a moment longer, its shrieks echoed across the shattered land, flapping like bats against the ceiling of the sky. Then, as they faded, a pure, high ringing tone grew, until it filled the sudden stillness.

She blinked and looked, but he was gone. Slowly, fearfully, she went across. The earth whence he'd come no longer gaped, but was smooth and seamless. And beyond it, there where he'd stood—there, where the tower had tumbled shrieking into the fiery web—was nothing. Nothing but a huge circle of ash.

Jelka shuddered and then woke, remembering. Kalevala and the storm. And the morning after—the circle of darkness in the woods and the seven charred tree stumps. And Kim. All of it linked somehow. All of it tied in to the future. But how or why she did not know. Not yet.

CHAPTER NINE

Plucked Eyes and Severed Heads

OLONEN WAS STRIPPED to the waist, exercising, when Kim came into the room. He turned, nodding to Kim, then continued with his routine, bending to touch his toes, then throwing his arms up above his head, twisting his torso once, twice to either side, before ducking down again. It was a vigorous, impressive routine that even a much younger man would have found strenuous, but at seventy-five the old man made it look easy. He was in fine physical condition and, but for the bright, golden sheen of his artificial arm, he seemed in perfect health.

Kim waited, watching respectfully, in silence. Only when the old man had finished and was standing there, toweling himself down, did he cross the room and stand by the broad oak desk that dominated the study.

"Hello there," Tolonen said, coming across. "How are you, boy?"

He reached out with his good hand and held Kim's hand a moment, meeting his eyes squarely, challengingly, as he always did.

"I'm fine," Kim answered, taking the seat the Marshal offered him. "I wasn't sure you'd have time to see me."

Tolonen smiled, making his way around to the other side of the desk. "Nonsense. You're always welcome here."

Kim bowed. "Thank you. But I wouldn't dream of keeping you from your business."

The old man laughed. "There's no chance of that, my boy. I've got to be off in twenty minutes. Li Yuan himself has summoned me. I'll have to shower and change before then, but we've time for a chat, neh?"

Tolonen turned, taking a tunic from the back of the big, leather-backed chair, then pulled it on in one swift motion. To Kim, watching wide-eyed from his chair, he seemed like a god, there was so much power and authority in every movement.

He turned back, facing Kim again, and sat, leaning toward Kim across the broad expanse of the desk's surface. "So how's business? Did you finally get around to registering those patents?"

Kim hesitated, not wishing to burden the old man with his problems. "There were difficulties," he said, after a moment. "Complications with the patent . . ."

"Complications?" Tolonen sat back slightly. "You mean the thing didn't work, after all? But you were so confident."

"No . . ." Again Kim held back, loath to discuss the matter. But Tolonen was staring at him now, curious. "The device works. That's not the problem. The problem is that someone beat me to it. They registered a day before me."

"I didn't think anyone was working on the same lines. I thought you said . . ." Tolonen stopped, his face changing, suddenly realizing what Kim was actually saying. "But that's outrageous! Does Li Yuan know of this?"

"Not yet."

"Then maybe he ought. We should *do* something . . ."

Kim looked down, shaking his head. "Forgive me, Marshal, but I would rather the T'ang knew nothing of this. He has much on his mind as it is. Besides, the problem is mine, not his, and I shall find ways and means to solve it."

Tolonen stared back at the young man a moment, taking in his words, then gave an emphatic nod. "All right. But if this should happen again . . ."

"I'll let you know . . ." Kim smiled. "But enough of my troubles. How did your investigations go?"

Tolonen gave a small sigh and put his hands together, metal and flesh interlaced. "They say that those who look shall find, neh? I can say very little just now, I'm afraid. I . . ." He stopped, studying Kim's

face a moment, then reached into the drawer to his left and took out a
slender computer file, placing it on the desk between them.

"Can I trust you to be discreet, Kim?"

Kim narrowed his eyes. "This has to do with what you found?"

"It has. At present only three people know what is in that file. With
yourself and the T'ang, it'll make five. And so it must remain, for the
time being. You understand me?"

"I understand."

"Good. Then take the file and read it. And let me know what you
think. In return I shall have a special team investigate this matter of
the patent." He lifted a hand to still Kim's objections. "I heard what
you said, my boy, and I respect you for it, but sometimes it does not
hurt to have a little outside help, neh? All I ask is that you keep the
information in that folder to yourself and return it once you have had
time to consider its significance."

Kim leaned toward the old man, about to ask him about the file,
when the door to his right swung open and Jelka came hurrying into
the room. She was talking, already three or four steps into the room,
when she stopped and fell silent, realizing that her father was not
alone.

She bowed her head. "Forgive me, Father. I didn't realize you had
company."

Jelka turned, looking across at Kim. He was sitting there, like a
large-eyed child in the big, tall-backed chair, the very smallness of
him making her frown involuntarily, then look back at her father.

Kim smiled, amused, not hurt by her reaction. Across from him,
Tolonen stood, turning to his daughter with a kindly, indulgent smile.

"This is Kim," he said. "Kim Ward. A valued servant of Li Yuan.
And this, Kim, is my daughter, Jelka."

Kim stood, offering his hand, seeing how she had to bend slightly
to take it. Her hand was warm, its pressure firm against his own,
enclosing his, her eyes friendly, welcoming.

"I know who Kim is, Daddy," she said, releasing Kim's hand. "He
was on the Project."

Kim's eyes widened, surprised that she remembered. But Tolonen
merely laughed.

"Of course! I'm forgetting, aren't I?" He came around, putting an arm about his daughter's shoulders. "Why, you might almost say that she found you, Kim, after the attack. We had given up any hope of finding survivors, but Jelka insisted that you'd escaped. She made us search the vent for signs that you'd got out that way. And you know what? She was right!"

Kim stared, his mouth open. He hadn't known.

He looked down, suddenly abashed. That first time he had seen her—when she had come with her father to visit the Wiring Project—he had stared at her in awe, thinking her some kind of goddess. Never, even in his wildest imaginings, had he thought she would remember him. But she had. More than that, she had made them look for him.

Kim looked down at his hand. He could still feel the gentle warmth, the firm but pleasant pressure of her hand enclosing his, and shivered, surprised once more by the strength of what he felt. And when he looked up, it was to find her watching him still, a strange intensity in her vividly blue eyes.

The file lay on the desk beside him. For a brief moment both men had forgotten it, but now Tolonen reminded Kim, pointing to it.

"Take it with you, Kim. And look at it closely. You don't have to answer at once. The end of the week will be soon enough."

Kim stared at the file a moment, then, impulsively, answered the old man. "I don't need that long. I'll give you my answer tomorrow." He smiled. "Whatever Li Yuan wants, I'll do. If I *can* . . ."

At that Tolonen laughed, and, as if letting his daughter in on a joke, began to explain. "Kim here is a physicist. Our experts say he's the best, despite his years. Maybe the best we've ever had."

He could see how she glanced at him, then back at her father, as if she couldn't quite take it in. Indeed, to Kim, sitting there watching her, nothing seemed more implausible than the fact that men like Tolonen and Li Yuan should need him, seeing in him something that they could not match, and using words like "the best." To the part of him that was Clayborn—that had come up from the darkness beneath the City—it seemed absurd. And when this girl, so tall and beautiful that she seemed somehow unreal, narrowed her eyes and asked him if it were true, if he *was* the best, he could only laugh at her and nod, watching her face change slowly until it mirrored his own delight at the absurdity of things.

"If I can . . ." Tolonen murmured, echoing Kim's words, then laughed. But Kim didn't hear. He was still staring at the girl, seeing how she looked away from him, then back, something strange happening in her face even as he watched.

He looked down at the unopened file and nodded to himself. But the gesture had nothing to do with what was in the folder. Had nothing to do with physics, or projects, or Li Yuan's needs. It was the girl. In an instant he had decided something, irrevocably and without further doubt. He would not rest. Not until he had married her.

———

IN THE IMPERIAL SHOWER ROOM of Tongjiang, the maids of the inner household, Fragrant Lotus and Bright Moon, were preparing to wash the young T'ang's hair. Taking soft woolen towels from the big cupboards above the sinks, they laid them out beside the glazed bowls of unguents and shampoos, the silver combs and brushes, the trays of brightly colored beads and silken thread; then, returning to the sinks, they opened the great dragon mouths of the taps and sprinkled a fine, nut-brown, aromatic powder into the steaming crystal fall.

As they worked, Li Yuan watched them from his chair, at the center of the great tiled floor, enjoying the sight of the two young women, the sound of the ancient songs they hummed as they busied themselves about him, the sweet scent of their softly veiled bodies as they brushed past.

He sighed, for once not merely content but happy. For a long time he had denied himself such things as this, attempting to harden himself against the world, but now he understood. This too was part of it. Without these moments of soft luxury—of surrender to the senses—there was no balance to life, no joy. And without joy there could be no real understanding of the flow of things. No wisdom.

For a long time he had struggled to be what he was not. To be some purer, finer creature. But it was all in vain. From the day of his betrothal to Fei Yen, the balance of his life had been lost. Casting off his maids, he had cast off that part of him that needed warmth and comfort, a mother's touch. He had tried to shape himself, as a tailor cuts cloth to make a gown, but the gown he'd made had been too tight. It had stifled and disfigured him.

He looked down, remembering those times. To have one single, perfect love; that had been the dream. To have a woman who was all to him, just as he was all to her—like *Yin* and *Yang*, or night and day—that had been the dream. But the world was not a dream. The world was harsh and true to itself alone. In it there was falseness and betrayal, sickness and hatred, cruelty and loss. Loss beyond the strength of hearts to bear.

And yet there was this. This simple light of joy to set against the darkness of the times. The joy of a woman's touch, a child's embrace, the laughter of a loving friend. These simple things, weightless as they seemed in the great scale of things, were the equal of a hundred deaths, a thousand cruel blows. Feathers and iron. Joy and grief. Balanced.

Li Yuan laughed softly, then looked up, conscious suddenly that the maids had finished and were standing there before him, watching him.

"*Chieh Hsia* . . ." they said as one and bowed low, their smiles betraying how much they too enjoyed these moments alone with him.

"Here," he said, standing and putting out his arms to them. "Hsiang He. Ywe Hui. Come here, my little blossoms. Come here and tend to me."

━━━━━

TOLONEN WAS WAITING for him in his study, standing by the door to the eastern garden, his golden hand glinting in the sunlight as he turned to face his master.

"*Chieh Hsia*," the old man said, bowing low. "Forgive me if I came too early."

Li Yuan shook his head and laughed. "Not at all, old friend. The fault is mine. I spent too long in the shower this morning and now everything is running late."

"Then I will be brief, *Chieh Hsia*, and come directly to the point. You asked me to have my discovery checked out and analyzed. Well, I now have the preliminary findings and they are most disturbing. Most disturbing indeed."

Li Yuan looked across and saw the folder on the edge of his desk. "Is this it here, Knut?"

"That is it, *Chieh Hsia.*

Li Yuan stared at the Marshal a moment, then went around his desk and sat. Drawing the thickly padded folder toward him, he flipped it open. On top of the pile was a picture of the thing he had seen last time Tolonen had visited him. The thing he'd brought back with him from North America. In the picture it looked like a giant walnut, the size of a young child's hand. Just looking at it, Li Yuan could recall the scent of the original, the dry spicy mustiness of it.

A brain it was. An artificial brain. Smaller and less complex than a human brain, but a marvel all the same. In many ways it looked like the brains GenSyn produced for many of their top-range models, but this was different. GenSyn brains were limited things, grown from existent genetic material—painstakingly nurtured in baths of nutrients over a period of years. But this brain had been made. Designed and built, like a machine. A living machine.

When he had seen it first, a week ago, he had been unimpressed. The thing was long dead—the only one of five to have remained in its storage case. But the experimental notes—a small library of computer records—had been saved intact. Using them, Tolonen had spent the last week piecing together what had happened. Now, reading through his summary, Li Yuan felt himself go cold.

"Kuan Yin!" he said, looking up at Tolonen. "What put you onto this?"

The old man bowed stiffly. "Gaps in the record, *Chieh Hsia.* Things that didn't make sense. There was too much wastage of basic materials, for instance. The percentages were far higher than in previous years, so I did some digging, found out where the "waste" was being shipped, and followed the trail. As I suspected, it was being sold off cheaply, the funds being used to finance a small R and D establishment in the far south. That's where I found it all. Untouched. The room sealed up."

"A mistake, do you think?"

Tolonen shook his head. "I think we were just lucky. My guess is that whatever this was, it was almost ready to go. And the only reason it didn't is because we hit them first."

Li Yuan frowned. "What do you mean?"

"Look at the dates on the final research entries. They're all late autumn 2007. That's significant. That means this thing was coming to fruition at the same time that we dealt with Hans Ebert and DeVore. If I'm right, we settled with them before they could get this under way. Before they could *use* one of these things."

"I see. So you think this was Hans Ebert's doing?"

Tolonen sniffed deeply. "I'm certain of it. Not only are his initials on a number of the documents, but the whole thing has the twisted feel of one of his schemes. That said, I think he was making these things up for DeVore. Maybe even to DeVore's specifications. From the shipping documents we've found, they were going to be shipped to Mars."

"Mars?" Li Yuan stood, then walked slowly across to the window. "Why Mars?"

Tolonen turned, watching the young T'ang. "I'm not sure, *Chieh Hsia*, but I feel sure it has something to do with those copies that came in from Mars that time."

"But my father's investigations drew a blank."

"Maybe so. But perhaps we should look again. More thoroughly this time. Send Karr perhaps."

Li Yuan glanced at him, then looked back out at the sunlit garden. "Perhaps."

Tolonen hesitated a moment, then spoke again. "There is one other thing, *Chieh Hsia*. Something which isn't in the summary. Something we're still working on."

"And what's that?"

"The brain. It wasn't like anything else GenSyn ever produced. For a start, it wasn't connected to any kind of spinal cord. Nor did it have to be sited in a skull. Moreover, it's a lot more compact than a normal human brain, as if it was designed for something else. It makes me think that this was only a single component and that the rest was being made up elsewhere, maybe at sites all over Chung Kuo."

"To be sent to Mars for assembly, you think?"

"Maybe." The old man frowned and shook his head. "Maybe I'm just being paranoid about this, *Chieh Hsia*. Maybe it's all dead and gone, like the brain itself. Maybe we killed it when we killed DeVore.

But I'm not so sure. The fact that this could be built in the first place worries me immensely. If you were to put a number of these inside *Hei* bodies, for instance, you could do a lot of damage. No one would be safe. Not if those performance statistics are correct."

"So what do you suggest?"

"That you meet with Wu Shih and Tsu Ma and let them know of this at once."

"And the rest of the Council?"

Tolonen shook his head. "For once I think you need to keep things tight. Master Nan will need to know about this, certainly. But if Wang Sau-leyan were to find out, who knows what he would do? If this thing was built once, it could be built again. And in our cousin's hands, who knows what evil might result?"

"That is so," Li Yuan said quietly. "Yet why not simply destroy all record of it? That would be simplest, surely?"

"Maybe it would, *Chieh Hsia*. But can we take the risk? Can we be certain that these are the only records of the experiments, or are there copies elsewhere? On Mars, perhaps? Or somewhere else, hidden away?"

Li Yuan looked down. "So we must live with this?"

"It seems so, *Chieh Hsia*. At least, until we can be sure."

"Sure?" Li Yuan laughed bleakly, recalling with surprise his earlier mood of joy. When could they ever be sure?

———————

OLD MAN LEVER turned, the dark, curly-haired head held firmly between his broad, square-fingered hands, and smiled.

"Well, what do you think?"

Lever held out the severed head, as if offering it to the three men who stood before him, but they merely grimaced, their fans fluttering agitatedly before their faces.

"Really, Charles," one of them, a tall, morose-looking man named Marley, answered. "It's grotesque. What is it? GenSyn?"

Lever shook his head, but the smile remained in his eyes. He was enjoying their discomfort. "Not at all. It's real. Or was. As far as I know there are only three such heads in existence, but this is the best. Look at it. Look how well preserved it is."

As he thrust the head out toward them, there was a sharp movement back; a look of revulsion in their faces so profound it was almost
comical.

Lever shrugged, then turned the head in his hands, staring down
into the dark, broad features. Lifting it slightly, he sniffed the black,
leathery skin.

"It's beautiful, neh? Slaves they were. Negroes, they called them.
They were brought over to America from Africa four, five centuries
ago. Our forefathers used them like machines, to toil in their fields
and serve in their mansions. They say there were once thousands of
them. Subhuman, of course. You can see that at a glance. But men,
all the same. Bred, not made."

Marley shuddered and turned away, looking about him. The room
was cluttered with packing cases from a dozen different auction rooms,
most of them unopened. But those that were open displayed treasures
beyond imagining. Clothing and furniture, machines and books,
statues and paintings and silverware. Things from the old times none
of them had dreamed still existed.

He turned back. Old Man Lever's eyes were on him again, as if
studying him, gauging his reaction to all this.

"I thought we might have a special exhibition suite at the Institute,
George. What do you think? Something to boost morale. To give us a
renewed sense of our heritage. As Americans."

Marley shot worried glances at his fellows, then looked back at
Lever, a faint quiver in his voice. "An *exhibition*? Of this?"

Lever nodded.

"But wouldn't that be . . . dangerous? I mean . . ." Marley's fan
fluttered nervously. "Word would get out. The Seven would hear of it.
They would see it as a kind of challenge, surely?"

Lever laughed dismissively. "No more than the Waldeseemuller
map that already hangs there. No, and certainly no more of a challenge than the Kitchen. Besides, what would our friend Wu Shih do if
he knew? What *could* he do?"

Marley averted his eyes before the fierce, challenging gaze of the
other, but his discomfort was evident. And maybe that was why Lever
had invited them this morning—not to show off his most recent
acquisitions but to sound out their reaction to his scheme. The

ancient map of the world that hung in the great hall of the Institute, that was one thing, and Archimedes Kitchen and its anti-Han excesses, that was another. But this—this scheme for an exhibition, a *museum* of ancient Americana—was something else entirely. Was an act of defiance so gross that to ignore it would be tantamount to condoning it.

And Wu Shih could not afford to condone it.

So why? Why did Lever want to bring things to a head? Why did he want a confrontation with Wu Shih? Was he still burning at the humiliation he had suffered on the steps of the ancient Lincoln Memorial, or was this something else? In setting up this exhibition was he, perhaps, attempting to create some kind of bargaining counter? Something he might trade off for some other, more worthwhile concession?

Or was that too subtle a reading of this? Mightn't the old fool simply be ignorant of the likely result of his proposed action? Marley stared at the severed Negro head in Old Man Lever's hands and shuddered inwardly. It would not do to offend Lever, but the alternative for once seemed just as bad.

He met Lever's eyes firmly, steeling himself to ask the question. "What do you want, Charles? What do you *really* want?"

Lever looked down at the head, then back at Marley. "I want us to be proud again, that's all, George. Proud. We've bowed before these bastards all our lives. Been *their* creatures. Done what *they* said. But times are changing. We're entering a new phase of things. And afterward . . ." he lowered his voice, smiling now, "well, maybe they'll find occasion to bow their heads to us, neh?"

Yes, Marley thought, *or have ours cut from our necks . . .*

He was about to speak, about to ask something more of the Old Man, when there was a banging on the door at the far end of the room. Lever set the head down carefully, then, with a tight smile that revealed he was loath to be interrupted, moved past them.

While Lever stood there at the door speaking to his First Steward, Marley looked to his two companions—like himself, major contributors to the Institute's funds—and saw his own deep reluctance mirrored there. But how articulate that? How convey their feelings without alienating Lever?

He turned, looking back at Lever, and caught his breath, surprised by the look of unbridled anger in the old man's face.

"Send him up!" Lever barked, dismissing the servant with a curt gesture. Then, composing himself as well as he could, he turned back, facing them again.

"Forgive me, *ch'un tzu*, but my son is here, it seems. I forbade him to come without my express permission, but he is here nonetheless."

"Ah . . ." Marley looked down, understanding. The rift between Old Man Lever and his son was common knowledge, but until now he had not known the depth of their division. Things were bad indeed if Lever had barred his son from the family home.

"Should we leave, Charles? This matter of the exhibition . . . we might speak of it another time. Over dinner, perhaps?"

He had hoped it would be enough to extricate them from a potentially embarrassing situation and buy some time to discuss the matter privately among themselves, but Lever was shaking his head.

"No, George. If the boy has the impertinence to disturb me while I am in conference with my friends, he is hardly to be rewarded for it with a private audience, neh?"

Marley bowed his head slightly, the bitterness and determination in Lever's voice warning him against pursuing the matter. A moment later the son himself was there in the doorway; a tall, athletic-looking young man so like his father that they might easily have been taken for brothers.

"Father," the young man said, bowing his head dutifully, waiting to be asked into the room. But Old Man Lever gave no word, made no gesture of admittance. He merely stood there, stone-faced and implacable.

"I asked you not to come. So why are you here, Michael? What do you want?"

Michael Lever looked to the three men, then back to his father, as if expecting something of him. Then, understanding how things were, he lowered his head again.

"I had to see you, Father. To speak to you. This thing between us . . ." He hesitated, finding it hard to say the words, then looked up, meeting his father's eyes. "I wish to be reconciled with you, Father."

Old Man Lever stood there a moment, unmoving, silent, as if

carved in granite, then, turning away abruptly, he gave a tight little laugh. A derisory, dismissive laugh.

"Then you will marry Louisa Johnstone, after all?"

"Marry her . . . ?" The younger man faltered, at a loss. He glanced uncertainly at the others, then took a step toward his father. "But that's behind us, surely, Father? I'm talking of the future. Of being your son again, your hands . . ."

"My *hands!*" Old Man Lever whirled around, his face ugly now, one angry look from him enough to make his son step back beyond the room's threshold again. "And if my hands will not do as I ask them?" He shook his head contemptuously and waved the young man away. "Pah . . . Go and play with your dreamer friends, boy. Go sleep with your low-level whores. I'll have nothing to do with you, boy. Nothing at all!"

For a moment the young man said nothing. Then, with one final, precise bow—a bow that showed immense self-control—he withdrew. "So be it, then," he said softly, turning away. "So be it."

But Marley, standing there, had seen that initial look of angry bewilderment on the young man's face and knew he had been witness to a final breach. Whatever the rights and wrongs of this—and Lever was certainly right to insist that his son obey him—there was no doubting that the old man had set out to deliberately humiliate his son, speaking thus to him before those who were not of his kin. He turned, looking at Lever, expecting to see that stern and unrelenting expression maintained on his features, and found, to his surprise, not anger but regret and—underlying all—a hurt so profound, so all-embracing, that it threatened momentarily to engulf the old man.

For the briefest unguarded moment it was so, and then, as if a steel door had slammed down over it, it was gone.

"Well, *ch'un tzu*," Lever said, clearing his throat, "as I was saying . . ."

WHILE MILNE STOOD at the counter, asking questions of the clerk, Ross looked about him at the walls and furnishings of the Records Office, as if they might give some kind of clue.

It was a dirty, shabby place, empty drink-bulbs and crumpled paper forms littering the spittle-stained floor, while on the walls of the public space were torn and faded posters, overpainted with slogans and graffiti, one symbol—a simple black palmprint—dominating all others.

"Who's this?" Ross asked, leaning over an old Han seated on the bench. "Are they popular here in Atlanta?" But the ancient stared straight through him, as if he weren't there.

"Terrorists, I guess," Ross murmured, straightening up and looking about him once more. Not that there was much to know about places like this. They were all much of a muchness these days.

He went back across, standing beside Milne at the counter. A young Han clerk was talking animatedly to Milne in Mandarin, running his finger along the open page of one of the big official Records books.

"So what have we got?" Ross whispered. "Anything good?"

The clerk glanced at Ross, then, removing his finger, slammed the book shut. "That's it," he said, in halting English. "That's all there is."

"Shit," said Milne quietly. "Just our luck."

"What's the problem?"

Milne looked away nervously. "There was a deck fire, three years back. All of the local records were destroyed. Backups, too, in a separate fire. The deck itself was cleared. Reseeded with new settlers. They've been rebuilding the files ever since, but there's not much. Only what we've seen already."

Ross looked down. "Hmm. Bit of a coincidence, neh? I mean, when was the last time you heard of something like that? Two fires?"

"It's not impossible. Fires happen."

"Maybe. But it's all too neat, don't you think? I mean, if you wanted to put in a sleeper, what better way?"

"And you think that's what happened? You think Mary Jennings is a sleeper for one of Lever's enemies?"

"And you don't?"

Milne hesitated, then gave a reluctant nod.

"Right. So what we do is this. We find out where the survivors of the fire were moved to, and then we go and speak to some of them. Find out what they remember about our friend Mary Jennings. That is, if they remember anything." Ross turned back, facing the counter again, a fifty-*yuan* bill held out between his thumb and forefinger. "And then?"

Ross looked back at his partner and smiled. "And then we do something we should have done right at the start. We make a facial check on our friend. Not just here in North America, but right across the seven Cities." He laughed. "It's time we found out just who Mary Jennings really is."

———

EMILY SAT before the mirror in her room, brushing out the long dark tresses of the wig. It was a tight fit, but that was good. Unlike the other she had bought, this one looked natural. As well it might, for it reminded her of how she had once looked, twelve years ago, when she was seventeen.

Seventeen. It was not long as the world measured things, and yet it seemed another lifetime. Back then things had seemed so simple. So black and white. She had known then where she stood in the world and what she wanted. Meeting Bent Gesell, she had become his woman, faithful to him alone, sharing his ideals; that vision of a better, purer world. A world without levels, free of hatred and corruption. For eight years that vision had sustained her. Had driven her on. But then Gesell had been seduced: won over by the dream of power DeVore had seeded in his head.

The vision had died. And yet DeVore had saved her. After the debacle at Bremen, it had been DeVore who had come to her, offering her a new identity and a passport to a new life—that same life she had led these past twenty-one months.

Yes, but what had she done in that time? What achieved?

Nothing, came the answer. For almost two years now she had sat on her hands, serving her natural enemies, doing nothing for the cause she'd once believed in.

So maybe it was time to begin anew. To go down the levels and organize again.

She stood, looking about her at the tiny room. Her bag was packed, her jacket laid neatly across it. Beside it on the bed rested the second of the two IDs DeVore had given her. Stooping, she picked it up and studied the tiny image within. *Rachel DeValerian*, it read. *Maintenance Engineer.*

She smiled. Even Mach knew nothing of this. Only DeVore. And he, if Mach could be believed, was dead now, his skull smashed into tiny pieces by the T'ang's man, Karr.

Only she didn't believe that. From what she knew of the man, she couldn't believe he would have let himself be caught so easily. No. He was out there somewhere. Waiting. Biding his time.

And Michael?

She sighed. The note had gone by messenger more than three hours back. He would surely have read it by now. In fact, she had been expecting him to call these last few hours. But nothing. It was as she'd thought—as she'd said in the letter—he was too preoccupied with other things to see what he had done to her. Too bound up in his father's business. For a while she had thought him cured of all that, changed, free to pursue his own straight path through life, but she had been mistaken. Kennedy's visit had opened her eyes to that.

Yes, and the news that he had gone to see his father—to beg forgiveness and become his "son" again—had hit her hard. Had woken her to the reality of her life.

She had delayed too long. Had let herself be blinded by her love for him. Well, now she knew. It was no good waiting for Michael Lever. No use relying on any man. Surely she had learned that lesson once already in her life, with Gesell?

Even so, some instinct kept her here, waiting for him to call, to knock on the door and tell her it was all a mistake. That what he'd said to her was true. That he *had* changed.

That he loved her.

"Ten minutes," she said softly to herself, glancing at the timer on her wrist. Ten more minutes, and then she would go.

She tucked the ID into the inner pocket of the jacket, then went across and stood before the mirror once again, carefully removing the wig and replacing it in the carrier.

She had booked her flight already, under the name of Mary Jennings, taking the rocket to the West Coast and then a fast-track south. There, in the teeming lowers of old Mexico, she would switch identities. To begin again. As Rachel DeValerian.

She looked about her nervously, going through all she had done these past few hours. All bills were paid three months ahead, all commitments met. Only Michael would miss her. And then maybe not.

She closed her eyes, wishing, hoping against all reason, that he would call, at this late hour, and put things right between them. That he would simply walk through the door and take her in his arms and . . .

There was a banging on the outer door, so sudden that it made her jump.

Michael . . .

She went across and stood there, trying to calm herself, but her pulse was racing, her heart pounding in her chest. As the hammering came again, she called out, her voice tiny, barely in control.

"Who is it?"

"It's me! It's Bryn!"

Bryn? And then she understood. It was Bryn Kustow, Michael's partner.

Thumbing the lock, she stood back, letting him in.

"You've got to help me," he said breathlessly. "Michael's gone. He went to see his old man and they had a big bust up. I got a call. I don't know who it was. One of the old man's cronies, I suspect. Marley, maybe. But it seems that Michael was very upset. The Old Man really gave it to him. Making demands. Insisting that he marry the John-stone girl. Humiliating him in front of strangers. I tried Michael's apartment but he wasn't there. No one's seen him for hours!"

Taking his arm, she made him sit on the edge of the bed, then stood over him, her mind in a whirl, trying to take in what had happened. "Okay. Slow down. Let's think this through. You say you went to his apartment. Had he been there?"

"I think so. I mean yes. Yes, he had. The manservant said he'd called in. Very unlike himself. Very distressed."

"And did he take the note?"

"The note?"

"I sent him a note. It's important. It might explain things."

Kustow shrugged. "I don't know. I . . . Yes. Hang on. The man said something about . . . about a special messenger coming."

"Shit." She shuddered, knowing now that she had got it wrong. Whatever Michael had been doing, going back to see his father, it had had nothing to do with her. And that was Kennedy's fault. Kennedy who had misled her.

"Look," she said, "he won't have gone far. I know what he's like. He won't want to face anyone he knows. Not now. I reckon he's gone down. Down to the lowers. If I were you, I'd check the bars in all the local stacks. Somewhere dark and anonymous, where he's not likely to be known. That's where you'll find him."

"Michael? Down there?" Kustow laughed, but then he saw how she was looking at him and his laughter died. "You think so?"

She nodded. "Yes. And when you find him, tell him this. That the note was a mistake. I didn't understand. I thought . . ." She shrugged. "Look, just tell him that I'll wait for him. If he wants me, he knows where I am. And Bryn . . ."

"Yes?"

"Tell him that I love him. And that I need him, even if his father doesn't. Tell him that, neh?"

———◆◆◆◆◆———

KIM WAS STANDING with his back to her when she came into the room, his dark head tilted forward as he looked down at something in his hands. She set the tray she was carrying down noiselessly, then, quietly, knowing he had not heard her, went across and stood there, behind and slightly to the side of him, looking down at the object he was holding.

It was a globe of yellowed ivory, carved with intricate towers and ornamental bridges, crowded with tiny figures, yet small enough for him to cup in one of his tiny, childlike hands. She watched him set it back carefully, then half turn, realizing suddenly that she was there.

"I'm sorry, I . . ."

She smiled and shook her head. "No, don't apologize. Handle them if you want."

He looked at her strangely, his lips parted, the pupils of his eyes forming large dark circles that surprised her with their intensity. There was a wild, untamed quality about him that both frightened and attracted her. His eyes seemed to fix and hold her with a power she didn't quite understand, yet when she found her voice again all that she said was, "You've nice eyes. They're so dark . . ."

"They're green," he said, laughing, looking up at her.

"No . . . not their color . . ."

She hesitated. She had been about to say that they were like the surface of the northern sea; that their greenness seemed to mask an unfathomed depth of darkness. But he knew nothing of seas and so she kept silent, watching him, knowing only that she had met no one like him before. His dark hair was cut neat against his large but not unattractive head, and his skin had the pale smoothness of a child's. He was dressed simply, so simply that in that single respect alone he was distinct from anyone she knew. Even her father's young soldiers wore jewelery and made up their faces. Yes, even the austere and distant Axel Haavikko. But Kim wore nothing special, added nothing to his natural self.

He looked past her at the tray. "Is that *ch'a?*"

"Yes." She laughed, feeling a sudden warmth come to her cheeks. She had forgotten. For that brief moment she had forgotten every-thing. "There are some sweetmeats too. But you'll stay for dinner, I hope. My father should be back . . ."

He nodded, then moved around her, bending down to take one of the sweetmeats from the tray.

She turned, watching him. In some indefinable way he was beauti-ful. Quite beautiful. Nor was it the kind of beauty she was accustomed to. He was not tall, nor broad, nor handsome in the classical Above sense of that word. Even so, something shone out from him. Some quality that was more sensed than seen. Some powerful, uncom-promising thing that simply wasn't there in other people. She felt that he was somehow . . . *in touch.* Was that it? In touch. But in touch with what? She shook her head, watching him bend to take another of the sweetmeats, his smallest movement different, somehow *connected.* She watched, frowning with the intensity of her watchfulness, but she could say no more than that.

He turned, looking back at her, smiling. "Won't you join me?"

"I . . ." She laughed, embarrassed, realizing how awkward, how gawky she must have appeared at that moment, but he seemed not to notice. He merely stood there, smiling, one hand raised to her in invitation, waiting for her to come to him.

She crossed the room and took his hand, the movement so easy, so natural, that it seemed to her that she had somehow always done it. But the feel of his palm against her own stirred her so deeply that she shivered and glanced down to where their fingers met and interlaced. When she looked up again he was watching her.

She frowned, suddenly conscious of how frail, how small he was beside her, how her hand enveloped his, her strong, slender fingers thicker, longer than his. Like a mother with her child.

His face was serious, unsmiling now, his eyes still questioning her. Then, unexpectedly, he lifted her hand to his lips and kissed it, brushing it with his lips gently before releasing it. Again she shivered, then turned away quickly, a sweet but painful sensation filling her, physical in its intensity. And as she turned, the memory of her dream came back to her, so that she saw it vividly—saw again that small, dark creature, whose eyes burned like coals and whose wet, dark skin shone with an inner light. She saw it climb from the darkness of the cracked and scarred earth and lift the mirror at the tower. Saw it and gave a small cry, as if in pain. But it was recognition.

She turned back. He was watching her, concerned, not understanding why she had made the sound.

"Are you all right?"

She made to speak, but at that moment there were noises in the hallway outside. Kim was still watching her, confused, unable to comprehend the pain, the sudden intentness of her glances at him. "I . . ." she began, but it was all she could say. It was *him*. Now, the dream returned to her, she saw it. Saw how his eyes saw through her to the bone and the darkness underneath. Saw it and knew—even as her maid came into the room—that this was her fate. This childlike man. This fierce and gentle creature.

"Jelka?" He was looking at her strangely now. "Are you all right?"

She took a breath and nodded. "I . . . I'm fine." But she felt faint, felt both ice cold and fiery hot, as if a sudden fever had taken her.

Forcing herself to be calm, she looked across at her maid and smiled, as if to reassure the girl.

"You'll stay for dinner, *Shih* Ward?"

"If you want me to."

She nodded. "I . . . I must go now," she said, looking down. "But please, make yourself at home. My maid . . . my maid will see to you." Then, with one final glance at him, she turned and left the room.

And after, as she lay on her bed, thinking back on what had happened, she saw him differently: saw not the man nor the creature of her dreams, but the two transposed, inextricably mixed. And knew, with a sudden certainty that surprised her, that she wanted him.

THREE HOURS had passed and now Kim sat there in the Marshal's study, listening to her talk. Jelka was standing on the far side of the room, beside the huge window wall, staring out into the artificial depths of the past and re-created country of Kalevala, a wistfulness in her face that seemed to mirror the light in the other land. And as she talked, he leaned in toward her, entranced, hanging on her every word.

"You can't help yourself, that's the worst of it. It's like a constant betrayal of yourself. You feel nothing, and yet you go on smiling, talking, laughing, all to fill the vacuum, to mask the nothingness you're feeling all the time." She glanced at him. "At least, that's how it was." She laughed, showing her perfect teeth, her chin slightly raised.

Kim, watching her, caught his breath, pained by the beauty of that one small movement. She was like something from a dream; so tall and straight and lovely. Her hair was like a screen of golden silk, her eyes the blue of the sky in the land beyond her. And her mouth . . .

"As for the rest of them, they don't even seem to notice how things are. It's as if they're dead to it all. I mean, perhaps they really can't tell the difference between this and real life. I don't know . . ." She shrugged, her eyes suddenly pained, "But it seems to me that there's a falseness, an intrinsic *flaw* in them. It's as if the City's swallowed them. Eaten them up, souls and all. And yet they seem happy with that. It's as if they really don't need anything more."

She turned, facing him, a fierce determination in her eyes. "That's how it is here, Kim. Like a living death. Yet when I saw you I knew at once that you were different." She shivered, the intensity of her words forcing her face into a grimace of pain. "Do you understand what I'm saying? It's not your size. It's not even what you do—that talent that my father values so highly. It's *you*. You're different from the rest of them. And I want that. I want it so much that it hurts me to think that I might not have it . . ."

She looked away, her eyes releasing him. But her words had seared him. He looked down at his trembling hands, then answered her.

"You have it," he said, meeting her eyes. "All of it." He laughed strangely. "I think I wanted you from the first moment I saw you. Your eyes . . ."

She turned, surprised. "Then it wasn't just me? You felt that too?"

"Yes . . ." He was silent a moment, then, quietly, "I love you, Jelka Tolonen. I have done from the first."

"You love me?" She laughed, surprised. "You know, I thought all that was done with. That nothing would ever touch me again. I thought . . ."

Again she shivered, but this time she came across and knelt beside him, taking his hands.

"You see, I wasn't expecting anything. I didn't think that anything more could happen to me. There was the engagement to Hans Ebert, of course, but, well, it was as if I was living inside a kind of shell, in a magic theater where things only seemed to happen, and nothing real ever took place. I thought that that was all there was ever going to be. And then I saw you . . ."

He turned his face, meeting her eyes. It was like looking into the sky. He could sense the depths of blackness beyond the blue and remembered suddenly his vision—of that great web of brightness spinning out through the surface of her eyes into the darkness beyond.

"And your father?"

Her eyes moved away, then came back again. "Papa . . . ?" She shook her head, real anguish behind the tiny movement. "He's a darling really. I just can't tell you . . ."

He nodded. He had seen for himself how Tolonen doted on his daughter. "And yet?"

"Well, it's just that he can't see that there's a difference. To him it's all politics. Deals. Who's in and who's out. And death underpinning everything. I love him, but . . ."

He saw just how much that "but" had cost her and touched a finger to her lips to prevent her from saying more. She smiled, grateful to him, and gently, tenderly kissed his fingers. It was the prelude to a proper kiss. Their first. He broke from it, surprised, his eyes wide, seeing his own astonishment mirrored in the perfect blue-black of her pupils.

"You're beautiful," she said, her fingers touching his cheek. "So dark and perfect."

He laughed softly. "And you're mad. Utterly mad."

She nodded, but her eyes were filled with that same fierce determination he had witnessed earlier. "Maybe. But I'd fight the whole Above to have you."

THE TWO MEN stood before the unmarked door, waiting to be admitted. Soucek turned, reading the plaque on the wall nearby. LEVEL ONE HUNDRED AND EIGHTY-SIX it read; NORTH 2 STACK, CANTON OF DUSSELDORF. He looked about him, trying to get some clue as to what they were doing, why they were here, but there was nothing. This far up the levels the Seven were still firmly in control. Things were neat and tidy. As if the chaos of the lowers were a dream and nothing else but this existed.

For a moment Soucek stared past his feet, trying to picture the levels stacked up beneath him, layer above layer; to imagine all those people—young and old, Han and *Hung Mao*—eking out their lives in the packed and degenerating strata of the City. Narrow, blighted, desperate lives. He had not really thought of it before, not until he had begun to travel between the levels on Lehmann's business, but now he could not shake it from his mind. He had seen the City from outside; had gone up the levels and seen what existed up Above, and knew—with a certainty he had never had before—that it was wrong. There had to be a better way.

He looked back at Lehman, seeing how patiently he waited; how he held the flask loosely in one hand, as if it contained nothing of value.

And yet three men had died, not counting the woman and her child, to get what it held.

Soucek shuddered, remembering. But just then the door hissed back, and a tiny, boyish-looking Han in a black, er-silk *pau* stepped through. He smiled, offering both hands in greeting to Lehmann. Tiny golden hands that were like the hands of a mechanical toy. His head was shaven, a faint purselike scar just behind and beneath his right ear revealing that he had been wired. He wore a sweet, aromatic perfume, but beneath it one could discern the strong scent of chemicals.

"Feng Lu-ma," Lehmann said, acknowledging the man, but he ignored the offered hands.

The Han shrugged, then moved past them, looking up and down the corridor before he ushered them inside.

"You're early," Feng said, toying nervously with the tiny lenses that hung like a necklace of delicate glass pendants about his neck and shoulders. "I didn't expect you until four."

He led them down a narrow, unlit passageway and out into a bright, crowded workshop. The walls were covered with row upon row of tiny translucent box files, while the nearby work tops were cluttered with dissecting instruments and culture dishes, stacks of slender ice-covered folders, and strange, spiderish-looking machines. Four young Han—thin-faced, malnourished-looking youths—glanced up from behind their high desks on the far side of the room as they entered, then quickly returned to their work, delicate, silvered instruments flashing between their fingers. There was the sharp, almost tart odor of chemicals, the original of the scent that lay beneath Feng's perfume. Moreover, it was cold; surprisingly so after the warmth of the corridors outside, but that was to be expected. Soucek looked about him, taking it all in, surprised to find this here. Before now he had only been guessing, but now he knew. It was a lens shop.

He turned, looking at Lehmann, seeking something more—some final piece to the puzzle. On the surface of things it made no sense coming all the way up here to a lens shop. No, if Lehmann had wanted a lens shop there were plenty beneath the Net who would do as good a job and ask only a tenth of what they charged at this level, so why come here? But even as he asked himself he began to understand.

It was of a piece with the murders. Lehmann had gone to inordinate lengths in selecting his victims. He had read the files Lehmann had handed him. Besides the physical match, Lehmann had gone out of his way to ensure that all of them, even the married technician, had been without complicating family connections. That meant, of course, that there was no one to mourn their deaths. No one to ask awkward questions. After which, it had been simplicity itself to bribe an official and falsify the public record—to make it seem as though the men were still alive.

Which, of course, was necessary if Lehmann were to use their eyes. For no matter how good a copy might be made of their retinas, no one—no, not even a Plantation Guard—would pass a dead man through a checkpoint.

Anonymity, that was what Lehmann sought. That was why he had chosen his victims so carefully; why he had come here rather than trust to the dubious "confidence" of one of the Net shops. Yes, he had heard tales of how certain *tong* bosses had bought information about their rivals, then had had them tracked and trapped.

But Lehmann was too clever to have that happen. That was why the official at the public record office had subsequently had his throat cut; why his colleagues had been pacified by an anonymous "sweetener."

He watched as Lehmann haggled with the man, then handed over four large denomination credit chips and the flask. The Han took the flask around to the other side of the nearest work top and sat, unscrewing the lid and tipping the frozen eyes out into a sterilized cold dish. He poked at them delicately with his tiny golden fingers, lifting each in turn and studying it beneath the light. Then, satisfied, he looked back at Lehmann.

"These are fine. There's two, three percent damage at most. Certainly nothing I can't repair. You haven't, by any chance, the original retinal mappings?"

Lehmann took the copy files from the inner pocket of his tunic and handed them across. All references to names and whereabouts had been removed. Again, Lehmann had taken great care not to let the lensman know any more than he had to.

Soucek saw how the man's eyes narrowed, scanning the files, noting the erasures, then returned to Lehmann. "I should charge you more."

Lehmann stared at him impassively. "I can take them elsewhere if you wish, Feng Lu-ma. To Yellow Tan, perhaps. Or your friend, Mai Li-wen. Maybe I should . . ."

The Han studied Lehmann a moment longer, then looked down. "When do you need them by?"

"Tomorrow."

There was a moment's pause, then. "All right. You'll come your-self?"

"No. My man here will come."

"But you ought . . ."

Lehmann leaned across the work top threateningly. "I know what I ought to do, *Shih* Feng, but I'm a busy man. Besides, I've worn lenses before. I don't need your help to fit them. You just do your job and everything will be fine, neh?"

The Han stared at him thoughtfully, then nodded. "Tomorrow, then. After ten."

But Soucek, watching him, could feel the weight of curiosity at the back of the man's words and knew—without needing to be told—that he would have to kill the man.

━━━◆◆◆◆━━━

BRYN KUSTOW stood there in the doorway of the crowded club, looking about him anxiously as customers elbowed past. It was dangerous this far down the levels and normally he wouldn't have come here alone, but just now things weren't normal. Michael was down here somewhere.

Kustow squinted, trying to make out faces in that long, ill-lit room, but it was hard. The Blinded Eye was packed tonight, the noise from the big speakers in the corners deafening. *Ta*, it was—"beat"; a stripped-down form of Han folk music, amplified heavily; the music of these parts. Kustow stood there, grimacing against the sound, searching the crowded tables for a face he knew, but they were mainly Han here. Ugly little bastards too. *Tong* runners and minor criminals, for sure. As he craned his neck, a big, pug-nosed Han planted himself directly in front of him.

"What you want, fuck face?"

"A friend," he shouted back, keeping his tone measured. "I'm looking for a friend. A big guy. Short blond hair."

The man glared at him a moment, then turned, pointing across the room. On the far side of the bar a light flickered fitfully. Beneath it, at a packed gaming table, a tall *Hung Mao* was slumped across the table, face down. To either side of him, eager Han faces watched the dice fall and tumble across the baize, ignoring him.

Kustow felt his stomach tighten. Was it Michael? And if it was, was he all right? He reached in his pocket and took out a ten-*yuan* chip, pressing it into the big man's hand, not certain it was the right thing to do down here. But it seemed it was. With a glance at the ten piece, the man stood back, letting him pass.

"Over there," he said again, as if Kustow hadn't taken it in first time. "Take the fucker home, neh? Before he gets his throat cut."

Kustow made a tiny bow, then, pushing through the crowd, made his way across. As he came out in front of the table, another Han, smaller yet more vicious-looking than the last, barred his way.

"What you want?" he shouted against the wall of sound.

Behind the thin-featured Han the gaming had stopped. A dozen Han faces were watching Kustow coldly.

"My friend," Kustow shouted back, indicating the slumped figure of Michael Lever. "I've come to take him home."

The Han shook his head. "Your friend owe money. Five hundred *yuan*. You pay or he stay."

Kustow looked about him, trying to read the situation. Was it true? Had Michael lost that much to them? Or was the Han trying it on?

"You have his paper?" he yelled back, meeting the Han's eyes once again.

The Han sneered. "What fucking paper? He owe me money. You pay or you fuck off!"

Kustow took a long breath. Five hundred. He had it on him. Twice that, in fact. But it wouldn't do to let them know that. He felt in his pocket, separating out three of the big fifties and three tens.

"I can give you one-eighty. It's all I have. But I can give you my note for the rest, if that's okay?"

The Han hesitated, eyeing him suspiciously, then nodded. "Okay.

But get him out of here right now. And don't come back. Not if you know what good for you!"

▬▬◆◆◆◆◆▬▬

FORTY MINUTES LATER and a hundred levels up, Kustow held Michael Lever steady as he leaned over the sink, heaving. Michael's hair was wet where Kustow had held his head beneath the flow, but the two tablets he'd forced down his throat were beginning to take effect.

Michael turned his head slightly, looking back at his friend. "I'm sorry, Bryn. I . . ."

Kustow shook his head. "It doesn't matter. Really it doesn't. But what the fuck were you doing down there? You could have been killed."

Michael turned back, staring down into the bowl again. "Maybe that would have been for the best."

"Don't say that. It's not true."

"No?" There was a strange movement in Michael's mouth and then his whole face creased in pain. "It's finished, Bryn! It's all gone fucking wrong!"

"No, Michael. No. There's the Movement, remember? And there's Mary . . ."

Michael shook his head. "She's gone. I got her note."

"No, Michael. You're wrong. She wants you. She told me so. The note . . . it was a mistake. She didn't understand what had happened."

Michael snorted. "She understands all right! I'm washed up! A failure! And my father hates me!" He shuddered violently. "There's *nothing*, Bryn! Nothing!"

Kustow gripped his shoulders firmly. "You're wrong, Michael. You don't know how wrong. She needs you, even if the old man doesn't. And I need you, too, you silly bastard. Don't you understand that?"

Michael turned, looking up at him uncertainly. "She *needs* me? Are you sure about that? What did she say?"

"She loves you, Michael. Don't you understand that? She loves you. So stop all this bellyaching and go to her. And for fuck's sake do it before you end up dead in some clapped-out, five-piece drinking den!"

Michael stared at him. "Do what?"

Kustow stared back at him a moment, then laughed, surprised at his naivete. "Why, marry her, of course. Marry her. Now, before it's too late."

"*Marry* her?" Michael laughed sourly and shook his head. He shivered, then, straightening up, pushed away from the sink. Kustow tried to stop him, but, breaking free of his friend's grip, Michael stumbled toward the door. For a moment he stood there, his forehead pressed against the door's surface, then he turned back, swaying unsteadily, meeting Kustow's eyes.

"Look, I know you mean well, but just leave me alone, Bryn, understand? Just fucking leave me alone!"

CHAPTER TEN

Monsters of the Deep

T HE SWEEPER PAUSED, leaning on his broom, staring across at the scene outside Hsiang Tian's Golden Emporium. Black dog banners were everywhere one looked, the triangular silks fluttering gently in the false wind generated by the big fans sited above the storefront. There was a low buzz of expectation and then the crowd began to move back, Triad runners pushing them back from the front of the store. There was a moment's angry jostling and then the crowd settled again, watching as Whiskers Lu strode out, his stylishly cut black silks glistening in the bright overhead lights.

Lu Ming-shao was a big, exceedingly ugly man, with a melted, misshapen face and an air of uncouth brutality. He spat, then turned, summoning Hsiang Tian from within. Hsiang came, his head lowered, ingratiating himself, yet uncomfortable all the same.

"Bring them out," Lu Ming-shao ordered, his rough voice booming. "The four I liked best. I want to see them out here, in the light."

Hsiang turned, snapping his fingers. At once there was hurried movement within. A moment later the first of the sedans emerged, a long, sleek model with delicate satin coverings, carved dragon-head lamps, and a high-backed "wooden" chair, designed to seat two; a *tien feng*, or "Heaven's Wind." It was carried by six of the Emporium's runners, their dark mauve one-pieces emblazoned front and back with the bright red pictogram, a box within a box, *hsiang*, and their status number. Setting the sedan down close to Whiskers Lu, they knelt, heads bowed, waiting patiently while he mounted the chair and settled his huge bulk across both seats. Then, at Hsiang's signal, they lifted slowly, taking the sedan in a slow, smooth circle.

Whipped up by the Triad runners, the crowd yelled and cheered, genuinely enjoying the sight, but when Whiskers Lu stepped down, it was with a curt shake of his head.

"Next!" he barked, turning his back on Hsiang.

There was a further commotion inside, and then the second sedan appeared. This was a bigger, seemingly more substantial model, an eight-man *yu ko*, or "Jade Barge." It was broader and squatter than the previous model, and Lu Ming-shao looked less out of place in its huge, thronelike chair. What's more, the extended canopy, with its blood-red er-silk covering, gave the whole thing a slightly regal appearance, reminiscent of the state carriages of the Minor Families. Even so, when Whiskers Lu stepped down again, it was with an expression of distaste.

Seeing that look, Hsiang turned quickly, summoning the next sedan. As it came out under the bright exterior lights, the sweeper made his way across and, pushing his way through the fringes of the crowd, stood near the front of the press, close to the line of runners, watching as Lu Ming-shao mounted the sedan.

He had heard many tales of Whiskers Lu, of his legendary fearlessness, of his heartlessness and casual brutality, but his eyes saw something else. Whatever Whiskers Lu might once have been, he was no longer the man of legend. Sharpness had given way to self-indulgence, brutishness to a kind of uncultured hedonism. Oh, there was no doubting that Lu Ming-shao was a big, fearsome-looking monster of a man, and not one to casually make an enemy of, yet those special qualities that had made him a 489—that had allowed him to wrest power from the hands of his deadliest rivals—were phantoms now. He saw how Whiskers Lu looked about him, aware not of the possible danger from the crowd—the ever-present danger of assassination— but of the impression he was making on them. He noted the big expensive rings the man wore, the elegant First Level fashions and understood. Three years of unopposed leadership had changed Lu Ming-shao. Had made him soft. Worse, they had made him vain.

As he watched, Whiskers Lu climbed up into the wide, deeply cushioned seat and settled back among the padded silk. Yes, only a fool paraded himself this way before the *hsiao jen*, the "little men." Only a fool closed his eyes, relaxing, when an assassin's bullet lay only a fraction of a second from his heart.

Lehmann turned, then made his way back through the throng, satisfied. He had seen enough. It would be easy to take Whiskers Lu. Easier than he'd anticipated. But it was best not to be too cocksure. Best to plan it properly and make sure the odds were wholly in his favor.

Returning to his cart, Lehmann folded down the handle of his broom and fixed it to the two clips on the side. Then, for all the world like a common sweeper going off shift, he swung his cart in a sharp half-circle and began to push slowly toward the side corridor, making for the down transit.

━━━◆◆◆━━━

THE NURSE handed Jelka back her pass and came around the desk. Behind her, in the glass-fronted booth that overlooked the spacious reception area, the clinic's security guard relaxed, returning to his game of chess.

"Is he expecting you?"

Jelka smiled. "No. But I think he'll be pleased to see me."

"Well, follow me. He's awake, but he may be working."

"Working?"

The nurse laughed. "He never stops. The morning after the operation he was sitting up, looking at files. But we've kept him from using the input as yet. It takes a while for the implant to take, even with the latest drugs."

Jelka gave a vague nod, frowning. It sounded horrible. Behind her, her bodyguard, Zdenek, looked about him, ill at ease without his gun. Only Jelka's strongest pleas had made him agree to come in here.

"Were there any problems?"

"No. It's a standard enough operation, these days. More than three million last year, they reckon. But he has to rest. Otherwise he'll be back in here with an embolism. And that would be very serious."

"Ah . . ." But Jelka was far from reassured.

"He's a friend of yours?"

It was none of her business, but Jelka answered her anyway, aware that Zdenek was listening, and that whatever the bodyguard heard would be reported back to her father. "He works for my father. And for Li Yuan."

The nurse glanced at her, her eyes widening, then nodded. "Ah, so that's why he's here." She laughed. "I thought it was strange."

They came to the end of the corridor and turned left. At the second door the nurse stopped and tapped out a code on the panel beside the door. A screen lit up at once, showing an overhead image of a patient in a bed. It was Kim. Leaning forward slightly, the nurse spoke into the grill.

"*Shih* Ward, you have a visitor. Jelka Tolonen. Will you see her?"

Kim smiled broadly, looking up at the camera. "Of course. Please . . . show her in."

As the door slid back, the nurse stood aside, letting Jelka go inside. Zdenek made to follow, but Jelka turned, facing him. "Please, Zdenek, stay here. I'll be ten minutes, that's all."

He hesitated, then shook his head. "I'm sorry, *Nu Shih* Tolonen, but your father would have me court-martialed if I did. My orders are never to leave you alone." He paused, clearly embarrassed at having to be so heavy-handed. "You understand why . . ."

She was quiet a moment, then turned to the nurse again. "Have you an audio unit? Just the earphones."

The nurse hesitated, then nodded. "You want me to get a pair?"

Jelka nodded, then turned back, smiling at Kim. "I'm sorry. This won't take a moment."

He smiled, drinking in the sight of her. "That's all right. It's really nice to see you. How did you know I was here?"

She glanced at Zdenek, then smiled broadly. "I'll tell you . . . in a moment."

The nurse returned, handing Jelka the headphones and a small tape machine, an under-ear sling. Jelka handed it to Zdenek. "Will you wear this for me?"

The big man looked at the earphones and laughed, relenting. "Okay. But when your father asks me I want to be able to tell him something. All right?"

She smiled and leaned forward, pecking his cheek. "I'll make something up. Okay?"

Zdenek nodded, then went to sit in the far corner, the earphones balanced awkwardly on his large, close-shaven head. Satisfied, Jelka went across. She pulled out a chair, sitting beside the bed, her back to the guard.

Kim was sitting up in bed. The comset he'd been working on was pushed aside on top of the bedclothes. He leaned forward, intending to kiss her, but she made the smallest movement of her head.

"What's the matter?" he asked quietly, then looked past her at the guard. "Is this your father's idea?"

"He thinks it's necessary when I travel."

"And you?"

She nodded. "They've made three attempts on my life already. It's unlikely they'll stop now. They can get at him through me. That's why it's best to take no chances."

"I see." But it was clear that he hadn't realized before just how tightly circumscribed her life was.

She smiled, her mood brightening. "Anyway. How are you?"

He looked past her briefly, then met her eyes again, smiling. "I'm fine. It's still sore, and the headaches are bad, especially at night, but they say it's healing well."

She leaned closer, looking at the silvered stud that jutted from the flesh beneath his ear. The skin surrounding it was red and chafed, but the single, thread-thin scar above it looked good. Even so, the thought of the implant made her feel queasy. She had never been happy about her father's, and though he had had it long before she was born, it still seemed unnatural. More so than his artificial arm.

"Well?" he asked softly.

She drew back her head and looked at him. The uncertainty in his voice was clear. He hadn't been sure how she would take it. After all, he hadn't even told her he was going to have it done.

"You *need* this?"

He looked at her intently a moment, then nodded. "It'll make my work much easier."

She looked at the silvered stud again. "It's a neat job."

"The best. Li Yuan's own surgeon."

"Then I'm glad. Really I am." She hesitated, then looked down. "Your work . . . it means a lot to you, doesn't it?"

He was quiet, watching her.

"No . . . I mean, I know it does. My father said. But more than that, I can see it in you. It's what you are. You can't separate yourself off from it."

He let out a long breath. "And you don't mind?"

She looked up, meeting his eyes. "No. Why should I mind? It's what you are. It's what makes you what you are. I can see that."

"Can you?" He watched her a moment, then nodded. "Yes. I can see that."

They were silent a moment, then she reached out and took his hand. "I understand. I . . ." She lifted her shoulders slightly, looking away from him, then met his eyes again. "It's like my father, I suppose. He loves me, fiercely, almost possessively, but there's more to him than that. He *has* to do what he does. When he was exiled—when he couldn't be General anymore—it was like he was dead. Or like a shell, paper-thin, the mere pretense of a man. Seeing him like that made me understand. Like you, he is what he does. The two things are inseparable. Without it . . . well, maybe he would be less of a man than he is. And maybe I'd love him less than I do."

"Maybe," he answered, his eyes watching her carefully, a strange tenderness in their depths. "And you?"

She laughed and sat back, cradling his hand now in both of hers. "Me?"

"Yes, *you*. Isn't there something *you* want to do? Some part of you that needs something more?"

She shook her head slowly, squeezing his hand between her own, her face suddenly more serious. "No. There's nothing I want to do."

"Nothing?"

She smiled. "No. I've already found what I want."

━━━━━

FROM HIS SEAT in the corner Zdenek watched everything. Jelka had her back to him so he could see nothing of what passed on her face, but he could see the Clayborn Ward clearly. He saw how the child-man smiled, and looked down, disturbed, knowing he would have to tell what he had seen.

And then?

He felt sorry for Jelka. This would hurt her. Badly, perhaps. But it was necessary. Her father would end this thing, for there was no way she could marry Ward, and a mistake here might spoil her chance of marrying well elsewhere. Besides, Ward was Clayborn, and Clay was Clay, it could not be raised.

And Jelka? He watched the back of her head, seeing how the overhead light caught in the golden strands of her hair. For a moment he was distracted by it, then, smiling, he looked down at his big, ugly hands. Jelka Tolonen was something special. Something high and fine and . . . well, above Ward, anyway. Far, far above him.

━━━━━

"Well? What should we do?"

Tsu Ma turned, facing his cousins, his broad, manly figure framed in the moon door. Beyond him, through the broad circle of the entrance, the sun lit up the western garden. "To be frank with you, Yuan, I think we should dig much deeper. Find out where the brain came from, and who designed it. What Tolonen says makes sense. We should send Karr out to Mars again. Have him turn the Colony inside out until he finds what's going on out there. This . . ." he shook his head, "this frightens me, Yuan. The fakes that came in to kill your brother, they were bad enough, but these!"

"I agree," said Wu Shih. "Tolonen's findings are the most significant thing to have come to our notice these past twelve months. To think that they were so close to developing and using these things. It only goes to prove how right our forefathers were in clamping down on research into these areas. Indeed, it makes me have second thoughts about our plans. We must be careful how we change the Edict. Careful what we permit within our Cities."

Li Yuan looked from one to the other, then nodded. "Then we are agreed. We will keep this to ourselves. As for Karr, I will think the matter through. Just now he is doing important work for me, keeping an eye on what is happening down below. But that may have to wait.

As you say, cousin Ma, we must find out where these things came from, and it may well be that Karr alone can do that for us."

They walked on slowly, following the path toward the lake.

"And this evening?" Wu Shih asked quietly. "Shall we still go ahead, as planned?"

Tsu Ma looked up, meeting his eyes. "Our path is set. The announcement must be made. Even this cannot alter that."

"Maybe so," said Li Yuan somberly, "but I have slept badly since learning of these things. It is as if we are being warned." He sighed, then stopped, turning to face his fellow T'ang, the great expanse of the lake behind him. "Our ancestors argued that there can be no compromise with Change. So we were taught to believe, from the cradle on. Yet now we seek to make a deal with Change. To let it run, like a fish on a line. But what if the line breaks? What if we lose control?"

"There is no option," Tsu Ma answered bluntly. "You know that, Yuan. If we falter now we are lost. A deal must be made. Something given, something taken back. No one has said it will be easy. But that is why we are T'ang. To make such decisions and carry them through. And to face the problems as they arise. It is our great task, and I, for one, will not shirk from it."

Wu Shih reached out, touching his arm. "We did not say you would, cousin. I am merely thinking that perhaps we ought to delay a while—to give us time to find out more about this other matter—before we announce the reopening of the House."

"And if we did?" Tsu Ma shook his head. "No, cousin. Too many people know of this already. Ministers and their assistants. Representatives and leading businessmen. To delay would have them question our determination. It would cause more problems than it would solve. No. Our path is set. We must grasp the reins and hold on for dear life!"

"So it is," Li Yuan said, acknowledging the truth of what Tsu Ma had said. Yet in the last day his reluctance had taken on a clear and solid form. It was as he'd said. Tolonen's discovery was like a warning. A sign of things to come. The step they were about to take—the changes to the Edict and the reopening of the House—were irrevocable. And while they might think they knew what would transpire, there was nothing in past experience to say for certain what would happen. From here on the future was unknowable, like a page from an unread book.

Once before the world had fallen into chaos. Once before . . .

He shuddered and turned away, staring out across the ancient lake toward the orchard. And as he looked, the image of a sprig of white blossom snagged in the darkness of his memory, then blew away, turning, turning in the wind.

"And that's all you heard?"

When Zdenek nodded, Tolonen sat back, his left hand placed flat against the desk, his right rubbing at his neck, metal against flesh. There was no doubt that Zdenek's report had disturbed him, but the old man's response was not quite what the bodyguard had anticipated. For a while he simply sat there, his granitelike face clouded, uncertain. Then, sniffing deeply, he shook his head.

"I don't know. I simply don't know."

There was a kind of precedent, of course. Once before Tolonen had interfered directly in his daughter's life. Then he had tried to marry her—against her will—to Klaus Ebert's son, the traitor, Hans. The old man had been wrong, and he knew it, but was that what was affecting him now? Or did he hesitate for another reason? After all, it seemed he rather liked the young man, Clayborn or no. Admired him—for as much as he could admire someone who wasn't a soldier. But was that important when the question was one of marriage to his daughter?

"You will keep this to yourself."

It was command, not question. Zdenek bowed his head curtly, coming to attention again.

"Shall I continue to watch them, sir?"

Again Tolonen seemed in two minds. A bodyguard was necessary in these troubled times, but he had not foreseen the need for a chaperon. Zdenek had his own thoughts on the matter, but kept them to himself. It would have been impertinent of him to say more than he had already.

Tolonen was frowning, his top teeth pulling at his lower lip. Then, as if the indecision were too much for him, he stood and came around the desk, stopping an arm's length from where Zdenek stood, looking at him steadily.

"You will do as you have done in the past and no more. Understand?"

Zdenek parted his lips, as if to speak, then gave a curt nod. Tolonen was silent a moment, then spoke again, his voice softer than before.

"I'll admit that what you say makes me . . . uneasy. If her aunt were living still . . ."

Tolonen's voice trailed off. He turned away abruptly, going back around his desk. Seated again, he looked up at Zdenek.

"All right. That's all. And Zdenek . . . thank you."

~~~~~~

ALONE AGAIN, Tolonen went and stood by the viewing wall, thinking things through. For a while he stared sightlessly away through the artificial landscape of trees and mountains, then turned and went back to his desk, his decision made. This time he would be subtler. Yes, he would let time be the cure of this.

Leaning forward, he spoke into the intercom, summoning his private secretary. The young equerry came into the room a moment later, coming to attention in the doorway, his head bowed.

"General?"

"Come in, lad. Close the door and come over. I want to ask you something."

The young soldier hesitated, then did as he was told, surprised by the unusually personal tone in the General's voice. "Sir?"

Tolonen smiled, indicating that he should take a chair. "At ease, lad. I need to pick your brains."

The equerry drew up a chair and sat. It was the first time in eight months' service with Tolonen that he had done so, and he sat up straight, as if at attention, his head held rigid.

"You come from a good family, Hauser," Tolonen began, smiling warmly at the young soldier. "Your uncle was a Major, was he not?"

The equerry nodded, then found his voice. "In the colonies, sir. And the mining satellites."

"And your eldest brother . . . he's there now, isn't he?"

"Yes, sir. On a five-year tour of duty."

"And does he like it out there?"

The young soldier smiled for the first time, relaxing. "He loves it, sir. Says it's beautiful out there."

Tolonen sat back, studying his equerry with some care. The young man sat up even stiffer than before, conscious of the Marshal's eyes on him.

"Have you ever thought of a colonies posting?"

The equerry looked down, his tongue touching his top teeth momentarily; a gesture Tolonen had noticed before.

"Well, lad?" he coaxed, more gently than before.

The young soldier met his eyes. "I do what is asked of me, sir. But . . . well, yes, I would welcome such a posting if the opportunity arose."

"And if it arose now?"

The young man allowed himself a smile. "Now, sir?"

Tolonen laughed. "Let me explain . . ."

———————

IT WAS COLD in the Dissecting Room, colder than Maryland in January, yet Old Man Lever stood there, bareheaded and without a jacket, staring down at the row of corpses laid out on the long slab. Nearby, Curval, the Chief Geneticist, stood watching him. The two men were alone in the room, the investigation team dismissed for the moment while the Old Man saw things for himself.

"What went wrong?" he asked, turning, meeting Curval's eyes.

"We're not sure," Curval answered, looking past Lever at the eleven shaven-headed bodies. "It seems like some kind of virus, but we're not certain."

Lever licked dryly at his lips. "Why not?"

Curval shifted awkwardly. "Because it might not be that. All of the corpses show traces of the thing, but the virus itself doesn't seem harmful. My personal belief is that it's a long-term side effect of the drug treatment. But we'll know that for sure as soon as we've tested a few of the living immortals."

Immortals . . . Old Man Lever shuddered and turned back, staring down into the blank face of one of the dead. There had been deaths before, of course, mainly from accidents, but nothing on the scale of this. No. Once this got out . . .

"Does anybody know? I mean, apart from the staff here?"

Curval nodded. "I'm afraid so. The clause in the original contracts allowed us to bring all the bodies back here—for tests—but there's been trouble with some of the relatives. I got a team onto it at once, but it looks like a group of them are going to go public, tonight at ten."

Curval waited, tensed inside, for the Old Man to explode with anger, but there was nothing. Lever simply stood there, as if in shock, staring down at the nearest corpse.

"There's no choice, then," he said, after a moment. "We have to go public before they do."

"Is that wise? I mean, what will we say?"

"That the treatment is a failure. And that we're working on something new. Something better. Something that we've just invested a further ten billion *yuan* into."

Curval blinked. "We've got new sponsors?"

Lever shook his head. "No. The money will come direct from ImmVac. At the same time we'll be making substantial payments to all those on the present program to ensure that they receive the best medical treatment possible in the coming days."

Curval bowed his head. "I see."

So the rumor was true: some of the major sponsors *had* pulled out. If news of that broke at the same time as this, then the Project was as good as dead. And even if it survived, it would be the object of wide-scale public derision. Faced with that possibility, Old Man Lever was willing to double the stakes and risk all on a further throw of the dice. To make a brave face of it and ride out the present storm, hoping to limit the damage.

And who knew?—it might even work.

Curval looked up again, meeting the Old Man's eyes. "So what do you want me to do?"

"I want some kind of research outline. Something that'll sound impressive. And I want some visuals of our best men at work in the labs. You know the kind of thing."

Curval nodded. "And the boy? Ward?"

Lever stared back at him, eyes narrowed. "Offer him what he wants. *Whatever* he wants. But get him."

———

WHEN CURVAL HAD GONE, Lever walked slowly up the line, then back, stopping beside the last of the corpses, that of a fifty-seven-year-old woman.

For a long time he stared down at her, at the cold, pale shape of her, unable to take in what had happened. Her name was Leena Spence and she had been one of the first of his "immortals." He had slept with her once or twice, before she'd had the treatment, but lately, tied up in the business of the Institute, he had seen little of her.

And now it was too late.

He shivered, the cold beginning to get to him at last. So this was death. *This.* He swallowed, then leaned closer, studying the fine blue tracery of lines that covered the pale, smooth flesh of her skull like the hand-drawn pictograms in an old Han notebook.

He reached out, running his fingers over the faint blue lines, as if to gauge the mystery of it, but it was like a map he could not read of a country he did not know. Queequeg's back, Curval had called it once, for some reason, and that came back to Lever now, making him frown, then shake his head, as if to deny what had happened here. But they were dead. His immortals were dead. Eight yesterday, a further five today, like machines being switched off one by one.

A virus, Curval had said. But what kind of virus? Something harmless. Harmless and yet deadly. If that *was* what had done this.

Old Man Lever drew his hand back, shuddering, then turned and walked swiftly away, rehearsing words and phrases in his head, beginning at once upon the task that lay ahead.

———

ROSS LAY on the narrow bed, reading, files scattered all about him. Nearby, at the table, Milne was hunched over his comset, working through the transcripts of the interviews they had done that morning.

The stay-over was a small, spartanly furnished room that had cost them ten *yuan* for the week. Not that they planned to stay a week.

No. For with what they'd got that morning, they could probably wrap things up that evening.

They had tracked down more than thirty of the former inhabitants of Mary Jennings's "birth-deck," including a midwife who had worked there more than forty years. Not one of them had any knowledge of the girl. That, in itself, might not have been conclusive. There were between five and ten thousand people in an average deck, and it was possible—just possible—that their sample was insufficient. But the results of the facial identification check had confirmed what they had suspected all along. Mary Jennings was a fake. In reality she was Emily Ascher. A European.

"Listen to this," Ross said, sitting up, then turning to face his partner. "It seems that her father was involved in some kind of scandal. He was an official in the *Hu Pu*, the Finance Ministry. It looks like he made some kind of mistake on the interest rates. There was a Hearing and he was kicked out. The family fell. One hundred and twenty levels. Six months on, the father was dead. The mother had to cope with the child on her own."

Milne looked down. "How old was she?"

"Nine, I think."

"Then maybe that's why."

Ross frowned. "Why what? I don't follow you."

"Why she became a terrorist."

Ross laughed. "Are you serious, Mike? I mean, what evidence have we got?"

"Instinct," Milne said, glancing at him nervously. "I've been thinking about it. She's not your usual kind of sleeper. I mean, she's a woman for a start. And most industrial espionage is short-term. The sleeper gets in, does his job, and gets out—as quick as possible. They're in a year at most. I've not known one to be in there as long as her. And then there's the background. Maintenance and economics. The combination fits the profile. Remember that report we read about the makeup of the *Ping Tiao*. I reckon that's what she was. *Ping Tiao*. The timing fits too. She vanished only weeks after Bremen. And then here she is, over here, in the Levers' employ. There has to be a reason for that."

"Coincidence," Ross said, putting his feet down onto the floor. "For a start the *Ping Tiao* had no foothold over here. Besides, it would take real clout to destroy a deck and all its records."

Milne shook his head. "I think the fire was genuine. An accident. But someone took advantage of it. Someone with Security training, perhaps. And a lot of influence."

Ross's eyes slowly widened. "DeVore? You mean DeVore, don't you?"

Milne nodded. "They say he was working with them at the end. So why not this? It's the kind of thing he was good at."

"But why? What's his motive?"

"I don't know. Just that it all fits. Her background. The timing. The nature of the deception. And it makes sense, too, of the spare ID of Rachel DeValerian. I think she was put in as a terrorist sleeper. Biding her time. Waiting to set up over here, when the time was right."

Ross was quiet a moment, considering things, then he nodded. "It would certainly make sense of why she left Old Man Lever to join up with the son. That was bothering me. But if DeVore put her in over here . . ." He laughed. "Hey. Maybe you're onto something."

"Then maybe we should get it all written up and get back to Richmond straight away."

Ross looked down. "You think we should take this to Lever, then?"

"Why, who were you thinking of?"

"Wu Shih, perhaps?"

Milne laughed uneasily, but before he could answer there was a faint rapping at the door.

Ross looked at Milne tensely, then stood. Drawing his gun he crossed to the door.

"Who is it?"

"Room service!"

Ross glanced at his partner. *Did you order room service?* he mouthed. Milne shook his head, then stood, drawing his own gun.

Ready? Ross mouthed. Milne nodded. Moving to the side, Ross reached out and thumbed the door lock. As the door irised back, a tall Han stepped into the room, carrying a fully laden tray, covered in a cloth.

"Compliments of the management," he said, setting the tray down on the bedside table, then turned, a look of surprise and shock coming into his eyes as he saw the drawn guns. *"Ch'un tzu?"*

Ross looked to Milne then back at the Han. Only then did he lower his gun and, with a faint, embarrassed laugh, went across and lifted the cloth from the tray. There were six bowls of steaming food.

"I'm sorry," he said, turning back and meeting the Han's eyes. "You can't be too careful. I thought . . ."

The movement of the Han's arm was deceptively fast. Ross felt himself being lifted and turned, something hard and acid-hot slicing deep into his back. There was the sound of a gun's detonation, followed instantly, it seemed, by the searing pain of a bullet smashing into his collarbone. Then he was falling toward Milne, the darkness enfolding him like a tide.

━━━━━

MACH LOOKED about him at the room, then, setting the detonator on the incendiary, stepped back. He had what he'd come for. The rest could burn.

For a moment he paused, smiling, pleased with himself. His instinct was still good, despite what had happened in Europe. If he had not followed these two, the game would have been up for Emily. And for him too, perhaps. As it was, he knew now what had happened that time with DeVore.

Yes. Milne had been right. A clever man, Milne, but no good with a gun. As for Emily, what he'd found out today might one day prove invaluable.

"Rachel DeValerian," he said softly, noting how closely the surname mimicked the form of DeVore's own. He laughed and tapped the file against his side, then, turning away, he thumbed the door lock and stepped out into the corridor. Richmond was two hours away.

━━━━━

THE PLACE STANK. But this was not the normal stink of the Lowers, this was a powerful, strongly animal stench that seemed to fill and thicken the close, warm air, pressing like a foul cloth against the mouth and nostrils. Soucek had gagged at first and turned to look questioningly at Lehmann, but the albino had showed no reaction.

"Gods, what is this place?"

Lehmann glanced at him. "It used to be a pen." He indicated cages, the silvered snouts of the feeding tubes, retracted now into the walls. "Some friends of mine have emptied it for a while."

Soucek nodded, understanding. He had never seen one of the great meat animals—the *jou tung wu*, as they were called—but he had seen pictures. He looked about him, imagining the huge, brainless creatures, one on each side of the central walkway, the vast pink bulk of each crammed tight into the rectangular mesh, the dozens of tiny, eyeless heads guzzling at the trough. He made a noise of disgust. No wonder the place stank.

He was about to say something more when he saw the figures at the far end of the pen; three of them, each of them holding a hand up to his mouth. He almost laughed, but checked himself, letting nothing show on the blank of his face. It was a sign of how much he had changed since knowing Lehmann. *Show nothing*, he thought, recalling what Lehmann had said. *The man who shows what he's thinking is weak. He allows his opponent an advantage.* And never more so than when the stakes were as high as they were today.

There was a moment's hesitation as the three men looked among themselves, then they came forward. They were big men, their bare arms heavily muscled. Together they seemed to form a type, but no one knew better than Soucek how different from each other these three were.

The three stopped a body's length from where Lehmann and he stood. Everything about them was wary. They had committed themselves heavily simply by coming. If Whiskers Lu found out, they were dead. But that didn't mean they were won over. Far from it.

"You've chosen a sweet place for our meeting, *Shih* Lehmann."

The speaker was Huang Jen. As lieutenant to Po Lao, Red Pole of the *Kuei Chuan*, he was the most senior of the three. It was not surprising that they had chosen him as their spokesman. But the bovine look of him was misleading, for he was a clever, subtle man—though not entirely. He had a reputation for sadism. To his left stood Meng Te, a big Han with a large, shaven head who had joined the

Kuei Chuan from one of the northern *tong* a year back. Making up the three was a sullen-faced *Hung Mao* named Visak.

"Sweet enough," Lehmann answered, stepping forward, taking each of them in turn by the hands. "Like what we do here, neh?"

Lehmann was holding the hands of Visak as he said this, and Soucek, watching, saw how the man's eyes widened marginally, trying to fathom the albino. Visak was the most interesting of the three. It was rare—almost unique—for a *Hung Mao* to rise in the ranks of the Triads and said much for his ruthlessness and ability. Though beneath Huang Jen and Meng Te in the Triad hierarchy, he was, without doubt, the most dangerous of the three. Before Lehmann had asked him to sound the man out, Soucek would have considered him the most loyal of Whiskers Lu's henchmen. Fiercely loyal. But here he was.

Security-trained, Visak's prowess in hand-to-hand fighting was legendary throughout the Lowers. In stature he was one of the few men Soucek had met who were as tall as Lehmann, and seeing the two of them together, he noted how big Visak really was, for the sheer breadth of his chest and shoulders made the albino seem frail. But Lehmann appeared undaunted. He met the other's gaze unflinchingly.

"You understand the need for secrecy?"

Huang Jen lifted his chin disdainfully. "Your man promises much, if I take his vague inferences to mean anything. Will you spell it out for us? Make it clear?"

Soucek glanced at Lehmann uneasily. What if this were a trap? What if Whiskers Lu knew about their meeting? It would mean war, surely, for all Lehmann said of Lu's softness, his lack of will. But Lehmann seemed contemptuous of such fears.

"I am the coming force," he said, looking from one to the other. "The very fact that you are here means that you understand this. That you know where the future lies."

He stood there imperiously, relaxed but commanding, as if every word he said were incontestable fact. And though Soucek had seen this side of him before, he felt his nerve ends tingle with a strange excitement as he listened. At these moments it was like hearing the voice of some dark, unnatural power. It both terrified and awed him.

"In time it will all be mine. From the north to the south. From west to east. Every last corridor. You know this. You hear what is whispered among your men. Even now they see it clearly. Lehmann, they say. Lehmann's the one. And they're right. You know they're right."

Visak glanced at the others, then laughed. But Soucek could see that even he was awed.

"I want proof," he said. "Something more than words."

The words seemed strange, rehearsed, and Soucek, watching, narrowed his eyes suspiciously. Was Whiskers Lu behind this? Was he listening even now? But Lehmann was shaking his head slowly.

"No, Visak. No sideshows. No games. What we do we do in the utmost seriousness. You are here because you have already chosen. Children want proof. Children and old men. But men such as you and I . . . we work in certainties, neh?"

Visak raised his chin challengingly, then relented, giving a grudging nod. Huang Jen, who had been watching him, looked back at Lehmann.

"You are right, *Shih* Lehmann. There are whispers. But you have still not answered me. What do *we* get out of this? And what do you want from us?"

Lehmann was silent a moment, his pink eyes seeming to hold and judge each one of them in turn. Then, satisfied, he answered.

"I want you to swear loyalty to me. Here. Right now. I want each one of you to be my man. To serve me. And, in the time that is to come, to do what I ask of you."

"And in return?"

"You live. You rule with me."

Huang Jen smiled. "And that's all?" But the smile quickly faded.

"The choice is simple," Lehmann said coldly. "All or nothing. Which is it to be?"

For a moment there was silence, stillness. Then, hesitantly, Meng Te went down onto his knees and bowed his head. Slowly, and with one final questioning look at the albino, Huang Jen also knelt.

For a time it seemed that Visak would choose against, but then, with a suddenness that was strange, he too knelt and lowered his head. Only then did Lehmann go down the line, offering his foot for them to kiss, speaking the words he would have them offer him in token of their loyalty.

He moved back, calling on them to stand.

"I want you to prepare yourselves. To gather about you those loyal to you and put aside those who might waver. When things are ready, I'll send and tell you what to do."

Soucek shivered, understanding how they were feeling at that moment. He too had knelt and sworn his loyalty. *Yes*, he thought, watching them bow and turn away, *I understand this better now*.

It was not simple force or cunning they responded to, but something stronger, deeper than those; something so different from what they were used to that to encounter it was to be changed, as he, Jiri Soucek, had been changed. To be in Lehmann's presence was to cast off all masks, all illusions. It was to grasp the raw essence of things. It was like . . . like pressing through the flesh and touching bone!

All . . . or nothing. It was so potent an offer that to refuse it was almost impossible for men such as they. Even so, he wondered whether it were enough. Whether they were bound to Lehmann as he himself was bound.

He turned, looking at Lehmann. The albino was staring at the tunnel's mouth, concentrating, his features fixed, like a mask. Then he turned, looking at Soucek. "That will make Whiskers Lu think, neh? He'll try to kill me, I warrant."

It was so unexpected that Soucek laughed. "Then Visak was acting?"

Lehmann shook his head. "Not all the time." He sniffed loudly, then cleared his throat. "Still, times are sad when such *hsiao jen* are legend. You'll watch him, neh?"

Soucek nodded, but he was thinking through what had happened, trying to see it all anew.

Lehmann turned, starting toward the tunnel's mouth. "Come, Jiri. Let's go. It stinks here."

Soucek looked up, his eyes widening, surprised that Lehmann had even noticed.

TO THE SOUND of martial music, the golden curtains swept back, revealing the dragon throne, mounted on a platform of seven broad steps. To each side, vast pillars rose up into depths of darkness, while in the great chair itself Wu Shih, T'ang of North America and spokesman for the Seven, sat cloaked in silks of imperial yellow. As the camera panned in, his face grew until it filled the screen, its stern authority staring out at the watching billions.

"People of Chung Kuo," he began, his dark eyes clear and certain. "Today I have great news to tell you. An announcement of the utmost importance to everyone in the seven Cities. For the first time since the dark cloud of war fell over our great civilization, there is peace in the levels. Both high and low can look forward to a future of safety and prosperity, of growth and stability. But to ensure that stability, certain measures must be taken."

Wu Shih paused, his lined and bearded face emanating a strength, a calm assurance that was impressive. Rocklike and yet fair he seemed at that moment. A father to his people.

"First of all, the State of Emergency which has been in place these past nine years is immediately revoked. From this day on, the law will be as it was before the troubles began. Furthermore, all political prisoners will have their cases reviewed by civil tribunals, these matters to be concluded, at the latest, six months from now."

There was a faint softening to the features, the merest hint of a smile. "Secondly, the House of Representatives at Weimar will be reopened one year from now, elections to be held in three stages in the six months prior to that. Further announcements regarding the dates of such elections and of franchise rights will be posted throughout the Cities in the days to come."

He paused once more, letting that sink in, then continued, his eyes staring out unblinking at the gathered masses, commanding their attention.

"Thirdly, and perhaps most significantly, we have decided upon a package of revisions to the present Edict of Technological Control. In five important areas we shall be allowing new developments. Developments which, it is hoped, will be of benefit to everyone living within our great society. Changes."

Throughout Chung Kuo there was a murmur of surprise. *Changes.* Never had they thought to hear the word from the lips of a T'ang. But Wu Shih was not finished.

"Finally, there is one last great matter we must face as a people.

One challenge which we must let unite us in the years to come. For many years now we have chosen not to speak of it. To ignore it, as if by itself it would go away. But it will not go away. And so, finally, we must tackle the great question of our time. Are we to be a single people, free and safe and prosperous? Or are we to see ourselves riven by division, our great Cities destroyed, our institutions falling into anarchy and chaos?"

There was a slight upward movement of the great T'ang's head. His eyes burned now with a fierce challenge.

"We cannot let that be. We cannot let our children suffer. Therefore we must confront the fact that has stared us in the face too long. Our numbers are too great. Chung Kuo groans beneath the burden of that weight. That is why, in the years to come, we must work together, People and Seven, to find a solution to this last great problem that confronts us. This is a new beginning. A new chance for us to set things right. People and Seven. Our chance to be strong again. To ensure stability and a good life for all."

As the final words echoed out across the great world of levels, the camera panned back, revealing once more the dragon throne, the pillars, and the steps. Slowly the golden curtains closed.

Wu Shih rose from his seat and, coming slowly down the steps, made his way through the kneeling technicians and out into the hospitality suite at the back of the studio. Guards opened the doors before him, their heads bowed low. He went through. Inside, his fellow T'ang, Tsu Ma and Li Yuan, were sitting on the far side of the room, facing a giant screen. They turned as he entered, standing up to greet him.

"That was good," Tsu Ma said, coming across and holding Wu Shih's arm briefly.

"Yes," added Li Yuan, smiling. "The people will sleep soundly tonight, knowing what is to come."

"Maybe so," Wu Shih answered, taking a seat between them, "and yet for once the words felt hollow even as I uttered them. All that talk of a new age. Of peace and stability and of working together, People and Seven. I would that it were so, that we could call on them and they'd respond, yet I fear we must face dark days before things get any better."

Tsu Ma looked down thoughtfully. "Maybe. And yet to say as much would only bring it that much quicker. No, you spoke well tonight, cousin. For once we must pray that what we say will come about, even as we prepare ourselves for the worst."

"Prayers, cousin Ma?" Li Yuan laughed gently. "Has it come to that?"

Tsu Ma met his eyes somberly. "Maybe that's the answer, Yuan. Prayers and chanting, bells, icons and incense . . . as in the old days."

Wu Shih, watching him, frowned. "Are you serious, Tsu Ma?"

Tsu Ma turned, smiling bleakly. "No, my dear friend. I would sooner allow our cousin Wang to cut my throat than have us return to those dreadful times. Yet from recent reports it seems that such thinking is rife, even as high up as the Mids. There is a need among them. Something that the City does not satisfy."

Li Yuan nodded. "I too have heard such things. Of new cults, new movements in the lowers. My forces try the best they can to uproot such growths, yet the garden is long untended, the weeds many. I fear the day will come when we must relinquish such regions to the darkness."

Wu Shih sighed. "I confess that is how I also feel. I tell myself that we *must* prevail, yet in my heart of hearts I am uncertain."

Tsu Ma nodded. "We must face the truth, cousins. It is as Wang said, that day at Astrakhan when we first saw how things were to be among us. We live in new times. There are new ways of thinking and behaving. It is said that in my great-grandfather's day everything under Heaven, yes, even the *wan wu*, the ten thousand things themselves, would bow before the sound of his voice, the solemn glare of his eye. But now?" He laughed sourly. "Well, our eyes have lost their fierce glow, our voices their terrifying power. Or so it would seem, neh? And our Cities . . . our Cities are filled with the shadows of fear and ignorance and hatred. And how can one fight such shadows?"

"And yet we must."

"Yes, cousin Yuan. And we must also guard against these other, inner shadows—the shades of fear and despair. For we who rule are not as other men. If we fall, who will stand in our place? If we fall, all is lost."

A heavy, brooding silence fell, and then, unexpectedly, the screen behind them lit up once more.

"Cousins . . ."

It was Wang Sau-leyan. His moon-shaped face filled the great screen, smiling, as if he saw them.

"Wu Shih . . . you spoke well tonight. Indeed, you spoke for us all when you said that this was a new beginning, a new chance to make things right. So it is, cousin. So it is. But time alone will show just how important this moment is. It is a joyous moment, a truly great moment for the Seven and for the people of Chung Kuo. Let us go forward from this moment and build upon that vision of a new age. I, for one, will not hesitate to strive toward that goal. You can be assured of my continued support in Council for all measures designed to bring that aim about."

The smile broadened momentarily, like a fracture in that pallid expanse of flesh, and then, unexpectedly, Wang bowed his head.

"And so I bid you good night, cousin Wu. Likewise to my cousins, Tsu Ma and Li Yuan. May the gods protect you and your loved ones."

The screen blanked. Below it the three T'ang sat in stunned silence, staring at each other. At last Tsu Ma broke the spell.

"Now what in the gods' names was that about? What is that calculating bastard up to now?"

"Whatever it is," Wu Shih said irritably, "you can be certain of one thing—that our effusive cousin means not a single word of what he said."

"Maybe not," said Li Yuan thoughtfully, "but now, at least, we are forewarned."

"True," said Tsu Ma, leaning back in his chair, a sudden twinkle in his eye. "And there's one, at least, who casts a shadow large enough to fight."

━━━━━

THERE WAS A SUDDEN, violent banging at the door. Emily woke, groping for the gun she always kept at her bedside, her heart hammering. For a moment she thought herself back in her tiny apartment in Munich *Hsien*, then she realized where she was—America—and sat up, suddenly alert.

There was no gun, only the bedside timer. It was after four and the apartment was in total darkness. For a moment she sat there, breathing shallowly, listening, wondering if she had imagined it, and then it came again.

Mach. It had to be. Security wouldn't have bothered knocking.

She hissed out her anger, then got up quickly and threw on a robe. He had better have a good excuse for waking her at this hour. A fucking beauty of an excuse.

She stabbed the view button angrily, studying herself briefly in the wall-length mirror beside the door, then looked back at the screen.

"Michael . . ."

Michael was leaning against the wall beside the door, his closely cropped head lowered, his body slumped forward, as if he were ill. As she watched he swayed back slightly and looked up at the camera, bleary eyed.

No, not ill. Drunk.

She studied herself in the wall-length mirror, wondering what he wanted of her, then, with a tiny shudder, slammed her hand over the door-release pad.

He stood there unsteadily, simply looking at her. She made to chastise him, then stopped, catching her breath.

"Michael . . ." she said, pained by the sight of him. "What is it?"

He looked away, then looked back at her, tears welling in his eyes.

She had never seen him like this. Never seen him anything but strong, resourceful, positive, even when things had seemed hopeless. But that look in his eyes had been dreadful. She had never seen such misery, such a vast, despairing sense of loss.

"Come on," she said gently, putting her shoulder under his arm to support him. She drew him inside and closed the door behind them. "Let's have some *ch'a.* You can tell me all about it."

"It's finished," he said, shuddering, his face screwed up in sudden torment. "There's no going back. It's ended between us."

She stared at the side of his face, wondering what he meant.

"Who . . . ?" she began, then understood.

"He pissed on me, Em. The old fucker pissed on me."

The words were angry, accusing. But the anger of the words was underlaid with a raw hurt that genuinely surprised her.

She sat him down in the kitchen in one of the big chairs, then began to prepare the *ch'a*, her mind racing.

"It was Kennedy," he said, telling her what she already knew. "It was his idea. He thought it would help things. Take the pressure off. Give us some breathing space in which to raise some funds and develop our campaign. It seemed like a good thing to do at the time. But I didn't . . ."

Again his voice broke, betraying him. He closed his eyes, squeezing the lids tightly shut, but still the tears came, defying his every effort to hold them back.

"I didn't know," she said softly, sympathetically. "I thought you hated him."

"Hated him?" He laughed and opened his eyes again, staring at her almost soberly. "I could never hate him, Em. Never. He's my father. He's . . ."

Again he could not go on.

"So what happened?" she asked, coaxing him gently. "What *did* he say?"

He took a deep, shuddering breath, then shook his head. "It wasn't what he said, it was how he did it. He had his cronies there. You know, that crowd he's roped in to fund his immortality project. I wanted to speak to him alone, but he wouldn't have it. He wouldn't even let me into the room. And then . . ." He licked his lips, then carried on. "Well, it was hopeless. He doesn't want to know." He looked up at her forlornly. "He wants me to be a slave to him—to do everything he says. And I can't do that, Em, I can't! He asks too much. He always has."

"I see . . ." But she didn't. Not yet. This was something specific. Something he was holding back from her.

She turned away, busying herself a moment, pouring the *ch'a*. When she turned back it was to find him leaning forward in the chair, watching her strangely.

"What is it?" she said, setting the bowl down on the table beside him. "What aren't you telling me?"

He laughed, but it was a strangely forlorn sound. "You're a good woman, Em. And not just good at your job. There's something about you. Some quality . . ." He shrugged and sat back slightly, his movements awkward, slightly exaggerated, as if he were trying hard to control himself. "I saw it from the first. Even before you started working for me. I noticed you. Did you know that? I used to look out for you in my father's offices. I . . ."

He looked down at his hands, as if it were suddenly hard to say what he was about to say, then looked back at her again, his whole manner suddenly changed.

"Gloria Chung . . . remember her, Em? The hostess at that party we went to. She told me something that night. Something I should have known for myself but hadn't really seen until then. Well, to-night, facing my father, what she said came back to me. You see, I had to make a choice. Oh, I don't think the Old Man was even aware of it. Anything else he'd have asked of me I would have done. Anything. But *that* . . ."

Emily shook her head, suddenly exasperated with him. "*What*, for the gods' sakes? What the hell are you talking about, Michael?"

"It was you," he said, his gaze suddenly piercing her. "That's what it was all about. He wanted me to marry the Johnstone girl and I refused. As before, only I didn't know it back then. But tonight I was certain of it. Anything else, and I'd have agreed. Anything. But to lose you, Em . . . No. I couldn't do that. Not that."

He stood unsteadily, taking her hands. "Don't you understand it yet? I want to marry you, Em. To spend my life with you."

The words surprised her; caught her totally off guard. She was silent a moment, then recollecting herself, she shook her head. "But what about your father? You love him, Michael. You need him. If you marry me, he'll cut you off for good."

He shuddered, the full weight of his hurt there briefly in his eyes. "Maybe. But it's done already, Em. It's finished between us. Really. There's no going back. So now it's just you and I. That's if you'll have me. That's if you feel even the tiniest bit the way I feel toward you."

She laughed, but beneath her laughter was a kind of numbed surprise—almost awe—that he had done this for her; that he had cast it all off simply to have her.

"I'll have you, Michael Lever," she said quietly, surprised by the strength of what she felt for him at that moment. "Just you and I. For life. And no going back, neh? No going back."

CHAPTER ELEVEN

Lost

I T H A D B E E N a long time since they had entertained, and Jelka felt awkward, unpracticed in her role as hostess. Their guests, the Hausers, were friends of her father's from years back, the husband ex-Security and a onetime Colonial Governor, the wife a soldier's wife, silent and dutiful in all things. Their son, Gustav, had come to work for the Marshal as his equerry and was shortly to be reposted. Jelka often saw him about the house, though he kept much to himself. He seemed a pleasant enough young man, though, like all of them, bred with a certain stiffness to him.

At the table she busied herself, turning to have a word with the servants, making sure things went smoothly, then turning back to ensure that the conversation kept flowing. Not that there was any real problem with that, for the two men monopolized the talk. First it was pure reminiscence, then, after their wineglasses had been topped up and the dessert was out of the way, they moved on to that perennial topic among the old: How things had changed.

"It was far simpler back then," Hauser began, nodding and looking to his wife. "Values were stronger. Positions were much clearer cut than now." He sipped and leaned forward, giving Jelka the benefit of his gaze. "There was no question of divided loyalties. A man was what he said he was."

She wanted to question that. It struck her that men had always been as they were now—a mixed bunch, and some more mixed than others—but she kept her silence, smiling, as if she agreed.

Hauser smiled back at her, pleased by her acquiescence. "Our job was simple, back then. We rounded up a few malcontents. Made sure things ran smoothly in the levels. None of this 'Who's my friend? Who's my enemy?' business."

Tolonen sighed and wiped at his lips with his napkin. "That's true, Sven. Why, if I could but tell you . . ." He shook his head sadly and reached for his glass. "Honor is not a thing you can buy. It must be bred. Must be there from birth in the immediate environment of a man. And if it's not . . ." He drank deeply, then set his glass down again, pursing his lips.

Jelka, watching him, thought of Kim. Was it true, what her father said? Was honor simply a thing to be bred into a man? Couldn't a man be naturally honorable?

"Unfortunately," continued her father, "we live in an age where such standards are vanishing fast. Young men like your son are rare, Sven."

She looked down once more, keeping the smile from her face. The old Governor had pushed out his chin at her father's remark and nodded sternly, the gesture so like a character in a trivee historical that she had it on her lips to remark about it. But there were rules here, and she would obey them, dislike them as she might. She said nothing, merely looked past the governor's wife to the waiter, indicating that he should fill the woman's glass again.

"You must be excited."

Jelka looked back at the ex-Governor and realized he had been talking to her. "I beg your pardon, Major Hauser?"

"About the trip. It must be wonderful. Seeing all that so young. I was in my late forties before I first went out."

She still wasn't following him. Confused, she looked to her father for explanation, but the Marshal was staring fixedly down at the table, as if deep in thought.

"Yes," went on the Governor, "I can remember it clearly, even now. Seeing the moons of Jupiter for the first time."

She laughed. "I'm sorry. I'm afraid you must be mistaken."

It was the old man's turn to look confused and turn to her father. "What's this, Knut? I thought you'd settled things?"

There was a slight color to Tolonen's cheeks. He met his old friend's eyes firmly, but his voice was quieter than usual. "I haven't told her, Sven. Please . . ."

"Ah . . ." There was a moment's clear embarrassment, then the old man turned and looked back at Jelka. "Well, as it's out, I guess you might as well know. I suppose your father wanted to surprise you, neh?"

Jelka had gone cold. She was looking at her father steadily. What had he done now? "A trip?" she asked, ignoring their guests momentarily.

"I would have told you," Tolonen said, still not looking at her. "Tonight. When our friends here had gone."

There was a slight emphasis on the word *friends* that was meant to remind her of her duty as hostess, but she ignored it.

"You're doing it again, aren't you?"

She could sense how both their guests had stiffened in their seats. Her father, however, had turned to face her.

"Doing what?"

"Interfering . . ." She said it softly, but the impact of the word couldn't be softened. She was thinking of Hans Ebert and her father's pressure on her to marry him. He had been wrong then, and he was wrong now. She *loved* Kim. And she would not be separated from him. Not for some soldier!

She shivered, realizing the point to which her thoughts had brought her. Did she really hate all this talk of duty and breeding? Hate all this soldiering?

"Jelka . . ." her father said softly. "You must listen to me. In this I know best. Really . . ."

She folded up her napkin and threw it down on the table, then stood. Turning to the Governor and his wife, she gave a small bow and a faint smile of apology. "I'm sorry. I really don't feel well. If you'll excuse me . . ."

She made to turn away, but her father called her back.

"Where do you think you're going, girl?"

She took a deep breath, then turned to face him. He was angry with her. Furiously angry. She had never seen him quite like this. But the sight merely steeled her to what she was doing. She faced him out, for the first time in her life openly defying him.

"What is it?"

He waved a hand at her, indicating that she should sit. But she remained as she was, standing away from the table, the chair pushed out behind her. He saw this and narrowed his eyes.

"You'll sit down, and you'll apologize to our guests for your behavior."

She opened her mouth, astonished by him. Slowly, she shook her head. "No. I'll not go."

"Sit down!"

There was real menace in his voice this time. She sat, slightly away from the table, making no effort to draw her chair up. "I'll *not* go," she said again, as if he had not heard her the first time.

Hauser was silent, looking from her to her father. But his face was the mirror of her father's.

"You'll go because I tell you to. Understand?"

She went very still. Then, looking up at him again, she shook her head.

This time he stood and yelled at her. "You'll go, dammit! Even if my men have to bind you and carry you on board. *Understand?* You're still my daughter, and until you're of age, you do what I say!"

She shuddered, looking away from him. He was so ugly like this. So . . .

Not meaning to, she laughed.

It went very quiet. She could feel the chill of the atmosphere about her. She looked up at him again. He was looking at her strangely, almost as if he didn't recognize her.

"What are you afraid of?" she asked.

"What?" He didn't seem to understand. "Afraid?"

"Kim," she said. "Why are you so afraid of him? Why would it be so wrong if I married him?"

She had said nothing before now, but this was the nub of it. The reason for all this heavy-handedness.

Her father laughed oddly. "You'll not marry him. Not *him*."

She met his eyes and saw that he was determined in this. But he had reckoned without her opposition. Like before, he had thought she would bow meekly to his wishes.

"I have your blood," she said softly. "If needs be, I'll fight you on this."

"You'll go," he said, with an air of finality.

For a moment longer she hesitated, then nodded. "I'll go," she said, "because you make me go. But it will change nothing. I'll marry him, see if I don't."

His eyes widened and his mouth opened as if he were going to argue more with her, but then he nodded, and sat down. He had her agreement. That, for now, was enough for him. The rest would take its course. Why fight tomorrow's battles before they came?

"Now may I go?" she asked, still sitting there.

He looked back at her again, then across at his guests. The ex-Governor gave a tight little nod and a half-smile. Beside him, his wife sat stiffly, looking down at her hands, as if in shock.

"Go on, then," Tolonen said softly, and stood for her, as if nothing had happened. But, watching her go, he knew that something had broken between them. Some last link of childish trust. He shivered, then turned back to his guests.

"I'm sorry, Sven," he said. "I should have warned you . . ."

━━━━━

THE BOARDROOM was tense, silent, as Old Man Lever, at the head of the table, read through the figures on the loan document. To his left along the great oak table sat the financiers, eight in all, to the right his team of advisors. All eyes were focused on the Old Man as he turned the page and, looking up, tapped the document in front of him.

"The top-up's too high. I thought we'd agreed on two point six."

"Two point eight, Mister Lever," Bonner, the Chief Negotiator, answered quietly. "I have it minuted."

Lever stared at him a moment, as if Bonner had taken leave of his senses, then, taking his ink brush from the stand beside him, he put a line through the figure and wrote the new figure beside it, initialing the change.

There was the briefest exchange of glances to his left, a small shrug of acceptance from Bonner. The matter was decided. As ever, Lever had gotten his way.

"And what about this matter of extended term insurance?" Lever added casually. "I think we should share the expense, fifty-fifty. What do you think?"

Bonner looked down. "It's unusual, Mister Lever. The borrower usually bears the cost of any loan insurances, but if that's what you want." He looked back up at Lever and smiled. "Besides, I'm sure the project will come in on time."

Lever smiled, then reached out to pat Bonner's arm. "Good. Then we'll get this signed and witnessed, neh?"

Bonner let out a breath, the tension draining from him. The two points on the top-up would cost them over fifty thousand, and the insurance might add up to one hundred and fifty thousand more, but in terms of the total deal that was nothing.

Eight billion *yuan!* Bonner's mind reeled at the thought of it. It was the biggest loan his Finance House had ever set up. And even at the fine rates Lever had insisted on, it would bring handsome profits. Personally, as Chief Negotiator, his own share was a quarter point, but a quarter point on eight billion was nothing to sneer at.

And every last *fen* secured by prime ImmVac stock, the best on the market. Bonner stood, bowing to the old man. Behind him, in a line, his team did the same, keeping their heads lowered as Bonner walked around the table to append his signature to the bottom of the agreement, then flicked back, initialing the two changes. A second copy of the document would be retinally imprinted and registered later in the day, but for now their business was concluded, the deal done.

Old Man Lever turned and, looking across at his Chief Steward, clicked his fingers. At once, the Steward turned and pulled open the doors. Waiting there in the corridor beyond were six servants, bearing trays of wine and delicacies. Quickly they went about the table.

"Come," said Old Man Lever, looking about him with a broad smile, "let's celebrate! For today the Cutler Institute for Genetic Research is mine. Lock, stock, and barrel, as my grandfather used to say."

He laughed, then nodded to himself. Standing, he took a wine cup from the nearest servant and raised it. "This is a great moment, and nothing . . . *nothing*, can spoil it!"

All about the table, cups were lifted, voices raised in the traditional toast. *"Kan pei!"*

"Mister Lever . . ."

The Steward stood at Lever's shoulder, leaning close, his voice a whisper, low but insistent.

Lever turned a fraction. "Yes?"

"News has come, Master. Moments back. It's Michael, Mister Lever. He's married. Married the Jennings woman."

MACH AND CURVAL were standing in the anteroom when Lever came storming out, his eyes bulging with anger. They had heard the tray go crashing down, and Lever's angry shout, but the sight of him, his face set into a fierce grimace, his fists bunched tight, surprised them both.

"What is it?" Mach said, catching up with the old man. "What in hell's name has happened?"

Lever stopped abruptly and turned, facing Mach. "It's Michael. He's betrayed me."

"Betrayed you?"

Lever shuddered. "He's married her. The bastard's gone and married her!"

Mach stared at him, shocked. Emily, he meant. Michael had married Emily Ascher.

"It's not possible," he said, after a moment. "She wouldn't. I mean . . ." He shook his head, unable to explain it. "Are you certain?"

"Not certain, no, but fairly sure. I'd put a trace on him, you see. I . . ." Again Lever shuddered. "He's betrayed me, Jan. Pissed on me! First with the Ward boy, and now this!"

"Maybe they've got it wrong. Maybe . . ."

"No. This time he's really done it. Done it to spite me. To piss on me. My *son* . . ."

"Charles . . ."

"No. This is my fault. I should have expected this. Should have known he'd do this." He shivered, lowering his voice. "I should have had her killed."

Mach glanced at Curval, then shook his head. "No, Charles. It would have solved nothing. You have to live with this. To show him it means nothing to you."

"*Nothing?*" Lever closed his eyes, the sudden pain in his face something awful to see. "That boy meant everything to me. *Everything.* And now . . ."

"You must show him he means nothing," Mach said, insistent now. "It's the only answer, Charles. The only answer."

━━━━◆◆◆◆━━━━

WHISKERS LU, Big Boss of the *Kuei Chuan*, stood, letting out a great roar. Fat Wong's handwritten note lay on the desk before him, its curt, six-word summons the reason for his anger.

"How *dare* that jumped-up little cocksucker tell me what to do! How dare he summon me like one of his runners!"

Lu's men kept their heads lowered, their eyes averted. They had been poring over a plan of the lowers, discussing the recent incursions by the 14K in the eastern stacks and the movements up-level of the Red Gang to their north, trying to work out countermoves, but this had pushed all that from Lu Ming-shao's mind. For ten minutes now he had raged, taxing the limits of his invention with the names he had called the United Bamboo's 489. And yet everyone there knew that Whiskers Lu would go. He had to. For Fat Wong was currently strong, his alliances in Council secure, whereas the last year had seen the decline of the *Kuei Chuan's* fortunes, the erosion of their once firm links with their neighboring Triads.

Yes, and that too had been Fat Wong's doing, no doubt. Lu Ming-shao had no proof of it, but how else could it have happened? Why else would the 14K have dared encroach on *Kuei Chuan* territory unless Fat Wong had given his tacit agreement? And now this.

"Why not kill him?" Visak said suddenly, speaking into the stillness between Lu's rages.

Whiskers Lu laughed humorlessly and fixed Visak with his one good eye. "Kill him? *Kill* Fat Wong?" He laughed again, this time in disbelief. "How?"

"An assassin," Visak said, meeting Lu's ferocious stare. "I know a man. He's special."

"Special?" Whiskers Lu leaned forward, holding the edge of the table, and laughed. "He'd have to be a ghost and walk through walls to get Fat Wong."

Visak lowered his head. "With great respect, Master Lu, this man *is* special. He could get Wong Yi-sun. Wong and all his top men."

Whiskers Lu was breathing shallowly now, his hands gripping the table's edge. His mottled, masklike face twitched violently. Then, relaxing, he pushed back again, composing himself, drawing his silks tightly about him. He turned, making a show of studying the glass cases on the wall behind his desk—the cases that contained the heads of his three great rivals—then nodded.

Lu Ming-shao took one of the heads down, studying it a moment, a brief smile flitting across his glasslike features as he recalled the moment he had killed this one—that look of dumb incomprehension in the man's eyes as he had choked the breath out of him, and the great surge of satisfaction he had felt afterward. Unconsciously he smoothed the tip of his thumb across the surface of the blinded eye, then reached up again, setting the head back in its place.

"All right. But it has to be tonight. Understand? I'll be fucked if I'll let that bastard live to see another day. Not after the way he's insulted me. Contact your man at once. Offer him whatever he needs. Then bring him here, understand? I want to see this ghost. An hour from now if possible, but tonight, at any rate. Before the meeting."

He turned, meeting his lieutenant's eyes. "Oh, and Visak. You will make sure of your friend, won't you? Very sure."

Visak nodded, then, bowing low, turned away. Whiskers Lu watched him go, then sat, thoughtful now, his rage spent. For a moment he was silent, staring at the handwritten note, then, reaching out, he crumpled the note into a tiny ball, popped it into his mouth, and swallowed.

For a moment there was nothing. Then, as if all the tension in the room had been suddenly dispelled, Whiskers Lu began to laugh, his laughter echoed back at him.

━━━━━

LU MING-SHAO pushed the young girl aside unceremoniously, then eased his huge bulk up off the bed. He pulled on the robe his man was holding and tied the sash tightly about his waist, eyeing his lieu-tenant.

"So he's here, then?"

Visak lowered his head. "In the audience room, Master."

"Unarmed, I hope."

"Yes, Master. And under guard."

"And the task I want of him. He understands what it entails?"

"He does, Master."

"Good. How did he react?"

Visak hesitated, his eyes straying briefly to the young Han girl on the bed, who lay there, naked, watching the exchange, her eyes curious. He looked back at Lu Ming-shao, meeting his one good eye.

"Our friend is rather a cold fish. He is not one to . . . *react*."

Whiskers Lu stared at him a moment, then laughed delightedly. "Good! I warm to him already."

They went through, Visak leading the way, Whiskers Lu's runners kneeling, bowing low before him as he approached. The door to the audience room was barred by two of his best men, Meng Te and Huang Jen.

"Okay," Lu said, looking about him and smiling. "Let's meet our special friend."

Inside, the unexpected. A tall man dressed totally in white, his back to them, his head tilted slightly, looking down, as if he was cradling something. As he turned, they saw what it was. A baby.

Whiskers Lu glared at Visak, angry that he'd not been prepared. "What is this?"

The tall man looked down at the baby, then, looking back at Whiskers Lu, threw it at him.

Lu Ming-shao, taken totally by surprise, raised his arms in reflex, catching the child. As he did, the man drew his gun and fired twice. Whiskers Lu heard the choked cries and felt the floor shake as the bodies fell either side of him, but he himself still stood there, un-touched.

The stranger put the gun away. "The unexpected is a powerful tool, don't you think, Lu Ming-shao?"

Lu Ming-shao swallowed, his anger something cold and hard. "What the fuck do you think you're doing, *friend*?"

"Those two were traitors," the tall man answered calmly. "They made deals behind your back. They sold you to another."

Lu Ming-shao turned, looking down at the fallen bodies of Meng Te and Huang Jen. Was it possible? Yet even as he asked the question he knew that it was perfectly possible. After all, he was the outsider here. There were no blood ties as existed between the other 489s and their men. They were his men through force alone, not loyalty.

He looked down at the child that rested, strangely silent in his arms. A *Hung Mao*, it was. An ugly little brat, weeks old at most. He lifted it slightly, as if to test its weight, then threw it back at the stranger.

The tall man stepped back, letting the child fall, screeching, to the floor. He had a knife in his hand now. A huge, wicked-looking thing with a white pearl handle.

Whiskers Lu drew his own knife and, bellowing loudly, lunged at the other man, knowing now that he had been set up. But he had taken only two steps before he sank down onto his knees, his breath hissing painfully from him, Visak's knife buried to the hilt in his upper back, Visak's weight bearing him down.

The baby was silent now. It lay beneath Lu Ming-shao, crushed by the weight of the two men.

Visak got up and moved away, leaving the knife embedded in his former Master's back, his eyes going to the tall man.

The stranger moved closer, standing above Whiskers Lu, listening to the pained wheezing of his final breaths, the soft gurgle of the blood in his pierced and damaged lung. Then, with the sole of his left boot, he forced Lu's head down brutally into the floor, turning his foot, the heel gouging into the melted, masklike face of the dying man, cracking open the brittle mottled plastic of his flesh, as if he were crushing an insect.

Lehmann looked up past the dying man, meeting Visak's eyes. "Summon the Red Pole, Po Lao. Bring him here at once. And if he asks, tell him only that things have changed. That he has a new Master."

━━━━━

MAIN HAD BEEN EMPTIED. Beneath the clock tower, the decapitated bodies of those who had opposed Lehmann were laid in rows, more than three hundred in all, their severed heads stacked in a huge pile close by.

Lehmann stood there, gaunt yet imperious, looking about him at the heartland of his new territory, his face betraying nothing at that moment of triumph. Twenty *ch'i* away, in the shadow of the tower, stood Soucek, Visak at his side. The two men had fought hard these last few hours, quelling the last pockets of resistance; making sure no news of this got out before its time. Now it was done, Lehmann's rule made certain. At a signal from the albino, Visak bowed and went across, calling the men in from the main corridor.

The runners crossed the great floor slowly in a great tide, approaching the tower timidly, their eyes wide, staring at the rows of headless corpses, the gruesome stack of bloodied skulls nearby. Then, at Visak's shouted command, they went down onto their knees, lowering their foreheads to the floor. More than four thousand men in all. *Kuei Chuan*, every one.

Lehmann stood there a moment, looking out across their lowered backs, then went among them, lifting this man's chin and staring into his face, and then another's, moving between them all the while, fearless and magisterial, like a T'ang, his every movement emphasizing his command.

For long minutes there was silence; a silence in which, it seemed, they dare not even breathe, then, coming out from their midst, Lehmann went over to the stack of heads and, taking one in each hand, turned to face the watching mass.

"These were my enemies," he said, his voice calm and cold and measured. "And this will be the fate of all my enemies, from this day on. But you . . . you have the chance to be my friends. My men."

He set the heads down and took a step toward them.

"There is a price for disloyalty. So it is. So it has always been among our kind. But loyalty . . . how do you earn that? What is *its* price?" Lehmann turned his head slowly, his pale pink eyes encompassing them all. "I understand your shock, your confusion over what has happened. But I know that many among you were unhappy with how things were under Lu Ming-shao. That many of you welcome change. As for me . . . well, you do not know me yet. Only, perhaps, by reputation. That, too, I understand. You might fear me right now, but there is no reason for you—any of you—to owe me any loyalty. Not yet. But in the months to come I shall ask much of you. Things Whiskers Lu never dreamed to ask. And in return?"

Lehmann paused and nodded slowly, thoughtfully, as if in reverie; yet when he spoke again, his voice was suddenly powerful, echoing across the great open space. "In return I will give you everything. Everything you ever dreamed of."

━━━━━

KIM REMOVED THE JACK from the face of the terminal, letting the wire coil back into the stud beneath his ear, then sat back, breathing shallowly. "It's good. Very good. And easy to use. I thought it would take a while to get used to."

The surgeon smiled. "Everyone thinks that. And there's a degree of truth to it. What you've just experienced—that's just the beginning. You see, while it uses the same skills you've always had—you can't, after all, slow down the speed that messages travel at in the nervous system—you're used to limiting your thought processes to the speed at which you can read or speak language. Once those limitations are removed, the brain can process raw data at phenomenal speeds. Anything up to a thousand times as fast as it could unaided. But it takes a while to adapt."

Kim nodded, his eyes looking inward. He was remembering how it had felt: the *power* of that feeling. Information had flashed into his head at an almost frightening speed. He had had a feeling of exultation, of tightness—of utter clarity. He had felt himself grow by the moment, achieving a degree of sharpness he had never experienced before. Sparks of pure insight had flickered between points in his head, like electrical discharges, and he had struggled to hold on to them as others filled his head.

He looked at the surgeon again. "You should do this yourself. It would help you, surely?"

The surgeon laughed. "They all say that. We call it conversion syndrome. Those who haven't got it, fear it; those who have, have a proselytizing urge to make others have the operation. But I don't have it because I can't."

"Why?" Kim's fingers traced the shape of the stud unconsciously. It was a gesture that betrayed the newness of the implant. The surgeon saw it and smiled.

"For you there are no drawbacks. You're a theoretician, not a practitioner. But experiment has found that there's a slight decay of motor control. A loss of sharpness in that area. As if the increased use of the memory draws upon other sections of the brain and weakens their functions. A sort of compensatory effect, if you like. As a surgeon I can't risk that. My work is with my hands as much as with my knowledge of the mind's workings. I can't afford to impair my motor responses. Besides, they'd not allow me to."

Kim nodded, considering. "There would be other difficulties, too, wouldn't there?"

The surgeon smiled. "Interfacing," he explained quickly. "That's the term we have for it. From old computer jargon. Interfacing is the difficulty you experienced moving from one state to another. Why you couldn't say anything for the first few seconds. The mind has grown accustomed to responding at what is, for it, a more natural speed. Dropping down from that it stumbles and finds great difficulty in adjusting. The effect lasts only five to ten seconds, but it would be utterly debilitating for a surgeon.

"You only get that effect when you cut out, and there seems no way of preventing it. When you plug in, the mind speeds up gradually. It's almost two seconds before it reaches its full operating speed. Cutting out, there's no gradual assimilation. The change of state is immediate and, to an extent, shocking."

"Harmful?"

The surgeon shook his head. "The mind's a resilient machine. It defends itself against damage. That's what the interfacing effect is—a defense mechanism. Without it there *would* be damage."

There was a knock on the door. A moment later an orderly entered and, after bowing to the surgeon, handed Kim a "sealed" notecard, the tiny slip of plastic winking blankly in the overhead light.

"Excuse me a moment," Kim said, getting up from the chair and moving away from the terminal.

"Of course," the surgeon answered. "I'll make my other calls, then come back later, if you like."

Alone again, Kim placed his thumb to the seal and activated the release. At once a message appeared on the blank plastic card. He read it slowly, moving his lips to form each word, realizing, even as the message sank in, how painfully slow this normal way of doing things was. Then that was forgotten. He read it through again, astonished, his mind struggling to understand what had happened.

"He can't . . ." he said, turning sharply to face the door, his whole stance suddenly changed; his body tensed now, crouched like a fighter's. "No . . ."

The message was brief and to the point, signed with Tolonen's personal code.

Shih Ward,

You are not to see my daughter, nor should you try to see her. There is no future for the two of you, and certainly no possibility of a match. You will keep away from my living quarters and deal with me only through my office in future. Finally, let me warn you. If you persist in this matter, I shall do all in my power to break you.

—Knut Tolonen.

The hairs on his neck bristled as he read the note again. He threw it down and went to the terminal. Sitting there, he tapped in the "Reach" code she had given him. Her private code, known only to her and him. He waited, anger and fear and something else—something he knew but could not put a name to—churning in his stomach. For a long time there was nothing. The screen remained blank, the delay pulse the only sign that the machine was attempting to connect them. Then, almost imperceptibly, the screen changed, showing not her face, as he'd hoped, but a message. Briefer than Tolonen's and less personal, but something: a sign for him that she had no part in this.

Nanking. South Port 3. *Meridian.*

Nanking was the great spaceport that served the colonies. South Port 3 must be the departure point, the *Meridian* the ship. But why had she given him these details? Unless . . .

He went cold. Quickly he signed off, then summoned up details of departures from Nanking, South Port 3, and found the *Meridian* listed on the second page. He shivered. Seven hours. Less than seven hours, in fact. That was all the time he had to get to her and . . .

And what? He sat back, his heart hammering in his chest, his hands trembling. He could do nothing. Tolonen would make certain of that. Even now, perhaps, he was being watched. But he would have to try. He would never forgive himself unless he tried.

He stood up slowly, feeling weak. Turning, looking down at the tiny slip of card where it lay on the floor across the room from him, he recognized at last what the feeling was he had failed to put a name to. It was dark and vast and empty like a pit; a feeling so dreadful and debilitating that it seemed to drain him even as he stood there; making him feel hollow and close to death. It was loss. He had lost her.

But even as it swept over him, another feeling grew—of anger, and determination. No. He would try. He would go after her, Tolonen's threats notwithstanding. He would try. Because nothing else mattered to him as much as Jelka. Nothing in the whole vast universe.

━━━◆◆◆◆◆━━━

SOUCEK WAS WALKING beside the sedan, Po Lao and Visak several paces in front of him at the front of the procession as they approached the end of the corridor and the rendezvous point beyond. Lehmann had handpicked the tiny force that marched along beneath the black dog banners, yet there were only two dozen of them, including the pole men, and Soucek felt uneasy, hideously exposed, here in Red Gang territory.

The meeting had been rearranged at short notice. The note sent to Fat Wong had stated bluntly that the Big Boss of the *Kuei Chuan* would meet him on Red Gang territory or not at all. It had specified a time and a place, and had informed Wong Yi-sun that copies of the note were being delivered simultaneously to each of the other four Bosses. That last was an elementary precaution, yet if Fat Wong *was* contemplating a move against the *Kuei Chuan*, this seemed as good a place as any to make it. If what Visak had said were true, the last six months had seen Fat Wong's United Bamboo Triad grow very close to Dead Man Yun's Red Gang. Why, they had even gone so far as to support Red Gang encroachments on *Kuei Chuan* territory. To

Soucek, then, this seemed a strange thing to do—tantamount to putting one's head in the tiger's mouth. But Lehmann had ordered it.

They slowed, Soucek not alone in counting the guards on the barrier up ahead and noting the great array of banners beyond. They were all here—14K and Yellow Banners, United Bamboo, Red Gang, and Wo Shih Wo—and here in some force too. The *Kuei Chuan*, a meager two dozen fighting men, were clearly the last to arrive.

He felt his pulse quicken, his chest tighten at the thought of the encounter ahead. For once he felt a slight uncertainty about what Lehmann was doing. This was a different league. A different league entirely. It was one thing to kill a Big Boss, another to establish oneself in his place. And yet Po Lao, like Visak, had bowed to Lehmann, accepting the inevitable. So maybe . . .

A figure appeared at the barrier. A small, dapper-looking Han in cream-and-lilac silks. Behind him four other middle-aged Han waited, watching the sedan come on.

"That's Fat Wong at the front," Visak said quietly, talking from the corner of his mouth. "The bald one to his left is Dead Man Yun, our host. The pop-eyed one next to him is Li Chin, Boss of the Wo Shih Wo—Li the Lidless as he's known. The starchy old man is General Feng, Boss of the 14K. Beside him—the tall one with the crippled hand—is Three-Finger Ho, Boss of the Yellow Banners."

Soucek narrowed his eyes, taking it all in. He had never thought to see these men, not separately, let alone together like this, but here they were, gathered at his Master's summons. His fear now was a solid thing at the pit of his stomach and part of him wondered if he would ever see another morning, but the thought of letting Lehmann down made him keep his fear in check; made him look about him with cold, clear eyes.

They were powerful men, there was no doubting it. He could see it in their stance, in the calm aura of superiority that hung about them as they waited, and in the cold, passionless depths of their eyes. Men died at their slightest whim, at their smallest gesture. And yet they were men, for all that. They could be killed. As Whiskers Lu had been killed.

And Lehmann? He too could be killed, for he was simply a man when it came down to it. And yet the thought of someone bettering Lehmann seemed wrong somehow—almost an impossibility—and that sense of wrongness gave Soucek new confidence, for at bottom he believed in Lehmann.

They stopped ten paces from the waiting group. Slowly the sedan set down. Soucek tensed, seeing how Fat Wong's hands were clenched, how his eyes were hard and cold. Lehmann's counter-summons—that terse, unsigned message—must have angered Wong Yi-sun greatly. Coming here was, in itself, a kind of loss of face. And yet he had come.

There was the rustle of heavy silks as the plain black curtain was lifted by the two attending pole men, and then Lehmann stepped out from the darkness within, straightening up slowly, his tall, emaciated figure ghostlike in the glare of the overhead lights. As ever he was dressed from head to toe in white.

White, the color of death.

A great gasp went up from the men manning the barriers. A gasp of fear as much as surprise. In front of them Fat Wong, his mouth fallen open, shook his head slowly in disbelief. For a moment he was at a loss, then he turned, looking to the Red Pole of the *Kuei Chuan* for an explanation.

"What in the gods' names is going on, Po Lao? Where is your Master? And who the fuck is this?"

But Po Lao held his tongue. He merely turned, his head bowed low, facing his new Master, his whole manner subservient.

"Our good friend, Whiskers Lu, is dead," Lehmann said, stepping forward, Wong's slur seemingly ignored. "So let me introduce myself. My name is Stefan Lehmann and, as of two hours ago, I became the new Big Boss of the *Kuei Chuan* brotherhood." He turned slightly, meeting Fat Wong's eyes from no more than an arm's length away, his voice soft, his face unsmiling. "Fat Wong . . . it's good to meet you at last." His eyes held Wong's a moment longer, then he looked past him at the others gathered there. "And you, *ch'un tzu*. It's good to meet you all. I've heard so much about you . . ."

Moving past Wong Yi-sun, Lehmann joined the circle of the 489s, looking about him coldly, imperiously, defying them to contradict his claim to power. And Soucek, looking on, saw how they stared back at him, impressed despite themselves, maybe even awed—even the great Wong Yi-sun. In a few moments he had won through sheer audacity what no force of arms could ever have achieved: their respect.

Soucek shivered. It was done. Lehmann, the *Hung Mao*—the usurper—was one of the Six now. A Boss. A 489. One of the great lords of the underworld.

And in time he would be more. Yes, Soucek burned now with the certainty of it. In time he would be more.

———————

THE BARRIERS were down, the ship sealed. Kim stood there, staring up at the departures board, the figures on the clock, his stomach falling away as he realized that he was too late. Then, forcing himself to go on, to carry things through to the very end, he crossed the big lounge quickly, making for the Security desk in the corner.

The young guard looked up at him as he approached and frowned. "What do you want?"

Kim held out his all-levels pass. "I've got to get a message through!" he said breathlessly. "It's vitally important."

"What ship is it?" the guard asked, studying the pass a moment, then looking back at Kim, eyeing him curiously; clearly recognizing him for a Clayborn.

"The *Meridian*. South Port 3."

The guard smiled and sadly shook his head. "I'm sorry, *Shih* Ward, but it's too late. The *Meridian* is already sealed."

"I know," Kim said, impatient now. "But I have to get a message through. It's terribly important."

"I'm sorry," the guard began again, all politeness, "but that's simply not possible. Not until the ship is in orbit."

Kim looked away, wondering what he could do, what say, to persuade the guard to help him, then turned back, leaning across the barrier, deciding to confide in the young officer.

"The truth is that the girl I love is on board the *Meridian*. Her father wants to prevent us from getting married, so he's sending her off to the Colonies. I only heard about it a few hours back, so I must speak to her before she goes. I simply must."

The young guard sat back slightly. His chest patch showed that he was a lieutenant, but from his manner Kim could tell he was not long out of cadet school.

"I'd like to help you, *Shih* Ward, really I would, but I can't. The communications of the *Meridian* are locked into the launch sequence now. Even the great T'ang himself couldn't communicate with the *Meridian* right now—not unless he wished the countdown canceled."

"I see." Kim turned away, a sense of futility sweeping over him. It was loss. He had lost her.

"*Shih* Ward . . ."

Kim turned back, staring at the guard, hardly recognizing him. "Yes?"

The young man came from behind the barrier, his eyes softer than before, strangely sympathetic. "I'm off duty here in five minutes. If you want, I can take you up into the viewing tower. You can watch the ship go up from there. As for your message, well, maybe I can pass something on for you. Among the technical stuff. Fifty words maximum, mind you, and I can't guarantee it'll get through, but it's the best I can do."

Kim shivered, then bowed his head, a feeling of immense gratitude flooding through him. "Thank you . . ."

Twenty minutes later, watching the tiny point of flame disappear into the upper atmosphere, Kim shivered and looked away, touching his top teeth with his tongue thoughtfully. Seven years. Seven years he'd have to wait until she could be his. Yet even as he thought it, he knew what he would do. Knew just how he would fill those seven long years of waiting. They would be hard, but he would get through them. And then she would be his, meddling old men or no. *His.*

PART 2 | SUMMER 2209

The Interpreted World

Who, if I cried, would hear me among the angelic
    orders? And even if one of them suddenly
pressed me against his heart, I should fade in the
    strength of his
stronger existence. For Beauty's nothing
but beginning of Terror we're still just able to bear,
and why we adore it so is because it serenely
disdains to destroy us. Every angel is terrible.
And so I repress myself, and swallow the call-note
of depth-dark sobbing. Alas, who is there
we can make use of? Not angels, not men;
and even the noticing beasts are aware
that we don't feel very securely at home
in this interpreted world.

—Rainer Maria Rilke, *Duino Elegies*; First Elegy

CHAPTER TWELVE

The Beginning of Terror

———————

O N T H E Q U A Y S I D E of the old town two knots of men stand before the Blind Dragon Inn, drinking and laughing, a space of twenty *ch'i* separating them, their voices carrying in the still early evening air. Out in the center of the broad estuary three large junks are moored, their quilted sails furled, their familiarly rounded shapes bobbing gently in the strong tidal current. Downriver, two hundred *ch'i* out from the enclosed square of the fishing harbor, a large three-masted *Hung Mao* merchantman rests, heavily laden, its long hull low in the water.

For a moment the sea breeze drops. There is an instant's perfect stillness; a stillness filled with the sun's late warmth. Then, as the wind picks up again, the high, tormented calls of seabirds rend the air, echoing across the old stone houses of the town.

At the edge of the farther group, a young Han turns, shielding his eyes, looking out past the party of *Hung Mao* sailors crowding the nearby quayside, his gaze traveling across the cobbled square toward the streets that climb the hillside, searching out the pale-cream facade of one particular house: a small, terraced cottage with a tiny, enclosed garden in which the moonlight dances in his memory and the smell of jasmine is strong.

"What're you staring at, chink?"

The *Hung Mao* is a big, barrel-chested man, the muscles of his arms like the thickly corded ropes that secure a ship at anchor. He stands over Tong Ye menacingly, his bearded face dark with mockery and loathing.

Behind Tong Ye there is a low murmur. Wine cups are set down hastily. There is the rustle of cloth and cheap silk as weapons are drawn from hidden places. All other talk is forgotten. There is a tension in the air now, like the moment before a storm finally breaks, and at the eye of that storm is Tong Ye, his eyes staring back uncomprehendingly at the big man, his mind still half in reverie.

"Beg pardon?"

The tar, gap-toothed and pugilistically ugly, his red hair tied in a pigtail at his unwashed neck, leans forward, placing a calloused hand firmly on the young Han's shoulder.

"You know fucking well what I mean, you slanty-eyed little scumbag. We've seen you, sneaking about after dark. And we know who you've been calling on. But you're going to stop that, understand me, boy? You're going to keep to your fucking ship from now on, or you'll be missing the means to piss on your boots."

The young Han swallows, then moves back a pace, shrugging off the hand. He is frightened—shaken by the revelation that his visits to his lover have been observed. Even so, he brazens it out, facing the big man unflinchingly.

"Forgive me, *ch'un tzu*, but there is no law against it, surely? And the young lady . . . if she does not object to my calling on her . . . ?"

The tar turns his head and hawks a fat gobbet of phlegm onto the cobbles. His head comes round, his eyes half-lidded now, his body tensed. One fist is already clenched, the other feels among the padded cloth of his jacket for the spike concealed there.

"Maybe not, but I do. The very thought of one of our own being touched by one of you . . . *ah-ni-mals.*"

The word is barely out, its rounded, nasal tones, heavy with a lifetime's stored resentment, still lingering in the air, as the first Han sailor throws himself at the big man, a thick stem of bamboo making an arc in the air toward the big man's head. A moment later, all hell has broken out.

On the cobbles before the inn, a single group of men are locked in struggle, their angry voices carrying in the still evening air. Out in the estuary the lookouts on the junks have paused in their task of lighting the mooring lamps and stare out across the water anxiously. On the merchantman there is frantic activity as a boat is prepared for lowering. A tall, dark figure sporting a tricorn hat stands briefly at the prow of the merchantman, a telescope raised to his eye, then he turns, making hurriedly for the boat.

On shore, the young Han is down, a steel spike embedded deeply in his guts. Beside him lies the red-haired tar, his skull split like an eggshell. Others lie on the cobbles as the fight continues, its viciousness unabated, long centuries of hatred fueling every blow. With a piercing shriek one of the Han falls backward from the quay and tumbles, slowly it seems, into the glassy water.

There is the blur of arms, fingers clenching and unclenching, the steady grunt and moan of blows given and received. And then there is a moment's stillness as the Han break off and, one after another, launch themselves from the high stone wall of the quay and into the water. And as they clamber aboard the shoreboats, they stare back at their adversaries, wide-eyed with shock and excitement, their hatred mixed with a strange, inexplicable longing.

There is a moment's silence, a moment's utter stillness as the android mannequins go limp, their programs ended, and then, from behind the barrier, applause.

From where he stood, half hidden behind the bank of monitors on the roof of the Inn, Ben Shepherd turned in the bulky VR harness, the faintest hint of a smile on his lips, and gave a small bow of acknowledgment to the four soldiers seated just beyond. It was the best take yet. Those last few adjustments—that tiny change of emphasis and the decision to focus on the single red-haired sailor—had made all the difference.

Beside him, his sister, Meg, looked up from the replay monitors.

"Well?" he asked, "did we get it all?"

She nodded, but he could see that she was still unhappy. She wanted Tong Ye to live. Wanted a happy ending, the lovers reunited. Whereas he . . .

"Maybe she can nurse him," she said quietly.

He shook his head. "No. We have to experience all that built-up anger and resentment. To feel it in our blood and understand exactly what it means—what all of this results in. If Tong Ye lived it would take the edge off things. We would have no sense of tragedy. As it is . . ."

"As it is, I feel angry. Denied something."

He stared at her a moment, then gave a single nod. "Good. We'll build on that. Feed that tiny spark until it's a roaring flame. We'll start tonight, after dark, while we're in the mood."

She watched him as he struggled out of the silvered harness. Ben had filled out this last year; had gained weight to match his height, shrugging off the last vestiges of childhood. Now he was a man, sun-bronzed and tall, his movements easy, confident. Even so, he still lacked something. Was still somehow less than his dead father. But what was it? In what did that crucial difference lie?

Ben hung the exoskeleton on the rack, then turned back. There, stacked on their sides in a long, reinforced metal frame, were his notebooks—thirty huge, square-shaped, leather-bound volumes that he called his "roughs." Embossed into the spines, as in the center of each cover, was a single word in an ancient gothic script, *Heimlich*, followed by a number. Unerringly, he reached out for the volume numbered fourteen and lifted it from the rack, his artificial hand coping effortlessly with the book's weight.

They had worked hard these past six weeks, taking advantage of the long days, the perfect light. Most of the "internals"—the sensory matrices that constituted the major part of Ben's Shell experience—had been completed long before. These "externals"—brief, carefully choreographed scenes which owed much to the ancient cinematic art—were the final stage, providing a backdrop to the rich, sensory data flow. When the two were paired the work would be complete. That was, if Ben was satisfied.

It was a big if.

"Here," he said, setting the book down beside the storyboard he had been working from and opening it up. "I reckon we can simplify things."

Meg moved closer, leaning over him to see.

The open pages of the rough were covered in a jumble of brilliantly colored lines and symbols, Ben's neat, tiny handwriting boxed-in in places where he had made subtle changes to his scheme.

She smiled, realizing how familiar all of this had become. Until a year back he had not let her share this, but now she was his constant helper, there at his elbow at every stage of the work. She studied the rough. Eighty-one lines crossed the page, each representing one of the eighty-one input nodes in the brain and body of the ultimate recipient of this artificial reality "experience."

"The experiencing viewpoint is predetermined," he said, tapping the page. "We can't change that without restructuring the whole of the internal for this section. But we can cut things to the nub when it comes to the external. Have one man set the fires, not three. Likewise, we can cut the number of guards. It'll save time setting up. We'll only have the seven morphs to program, not twelve."

She nodded. "I agree. It'll make things tighter, more direct. And why not make Tong Ye's friend our focus—the fire-setter?"

Ben looked up. "Yes. I like that. Maybe we can add something earlier. A small moment between the two just to emphasize things."

"And the girl?"

Ben shook his head. "I know what you think, Meg, but what happens to her *has* to happen. Without that . . ." He shrugged, staring away across the twilit estuary, touching the black pearl that hung on a golden chain about his neck, then looked back at her, his green eyes dark, thoughtful. "Just wait, my love. You'll understand. I promise you. You'll see why I did it like this. Why it *had* to be like this."

━━━━━
ᐁ ᐁ ᐁ ᐁ

STILLNESS. Silence. Moonlight on velvet blackness. And then the surface breached. A head, its fine dark hair slicked back. The inverted image of flame in a bright, black-centered eye. And gone. The surface dark, still. Footsteps on stone cobbles. Booted feet in movement, patterns of light and shadow on the folds of leather, gold and midnight black. The flutter of naked flame in a metal brazier. Shadows dance, revealing the whorled grain of ancient oak. Silence, then the creak and slow groan of a heavy door opening. A sudden spill of light, golden and warm. Laughter. A chapped and pudgy hand, the flesh pale, blotchy, plain silver ring on the index finger, wiped against a beer-stained apron. The scent of jasmine. Darkness. A head surfacing, fish-mouth gasping for air. And gone. The slosh of water against the stone steps of the quay. Booted feet turning. The brief flash of lamplight on a musket stock. And laughter. Uneasy, guilty laughter.

The camera eye draws back.

The landlord stands there a moment, hands on his ample hips, half in shadow, watching the woman leave, her long skirts rustling, whispering in the early morning silence. He turns, looking out across the water toward the distant hills. Out in the center of the estuary the junks rest silently, their mooring lamps reflected in the darkness of the water. Downriver, the merchantman is quiet, the shape of a guard silhouetted against a bulkhead lantern.

He yawns, stretches his arms. Behind him the brightness of the doorway darkens with a second presence. The constable leans languidly against the solid oak beam of the doorpost and points out toward the junks, his words a low, indistinguishable murmur, heavy with insinuation. The landlord laughs quietly and nods, then turns away, returning inside, pulling the heavy door closed behind him. There is darkness, the click of a latch being lowered, then silence. A moment later footsteps sound on the cobbles. The moon is high. It is an hour before the guard will be relieved.

The camera angle changes, giving a view of darkness. Slowly the dark resolves itself. A young Han crouches on the smooth, worn stone of the Pilgrims' Steps, his slender form concealed from the guard by the stone lip of the quay. Behind him lies the still, black surface of the water. For a moment he seems frozen, carved from the darkness, then, as the footsteps recede, he draws the oilskin bag from about his neck and unseals the pouch. Something small and bright gleams briefly in the moonlight, then is gone inside the sodden cloth of his shirt.

The camera draws slowly back, revealing the steps, the nearby inn, the pacing guard. A patch of quartered light reveals an unshuttered window in the narrow alleyway beside the inn. All is stillness, then, to the left of the picture, a shadow slips over the stone lip of the quay wall and melts into the darkness beyond. Farther along, the guard has stopped and stands at the edge of the quay, staring out across the water at the junks.

The remote tide drifts slowly in. There is the flicker of light on a musket stock, a glimpse of wide, curious eyes, a smoothly shaven cheek, and then it is past, skirting the wood-and-plaster frontage of the inn.

The alleyway seems empty: a narrow length of blackness framing a rectangle of yellow light. But then the darkness grows, sheds a form. A head bobs into the light beneath the sill. There is the glimpse of dark, sodden cloth, of slightly built shoulders and the sleek curve of a back.

The camera eye moves inward, taking a line into the darkness, then turns, looking past the crouching figure into the lamplit room.

Six pale, naked bodies lie on a trestle table. The constable, his back to the window, quaffs deeply from an ale pot. Beyond him sits the landlord, talking, one plump, pasty hand resting on the thigh of the dead Tong Ye.

It is time.

There is a click, the brief flare of a tinder. Inside, the constable half turns, disturbed by the noise. Then, from the quayside, comes a shout.

The landlord starts up, spilling his beer. "What in the gods' names is that?"

"Fuck knows! We'd best go see, neh?" And, setting down his mug, the constable follows the landlord through the open door.

The room is empty now. From beneath the sill comes a gentle, crackling hiss as the oil-soaked cloth ignites. And then the crash and tinkle of breaking glass, the sudden flare of oil as the bottle shatters on the stone flags inside the room. At once the legs of the trestle table catch. Flames lick the frayed edge of grease-spattered curtains, gnaw hungrily at the dry timber of the door frame. In a moment the room is ablaze, the pale skin of the corpses gleaming brightly in the garish, unnatural light. As the camera closes in, the flesh of the nearest begins to sweat and bubble.

The camera moves back, clearing the blackening sill, then climbs the outer wall, up into darkness. Here, in the upper rooms, more than forty men are sleeping; half the crew of the merchantman, spending their last night ashore.

The camera moves out, over the smoldering inn. Farther along the quay the guard has turned, facing the innkeeper and the constable.

"The junks!" he cries. "The junks are leaving!"

Out in the center of the estuary the three Han vessels have doused their mooring lights and are moving slowly toward the mouth of the river. There is the noise of oars being pulled through the water, the sound of singsong Han voices calling encouragement to the rowers.

For a moment the three stand there, staring outward, then, as one, they turn, conscious of the growing light at their backs, the sharp hiss and pop and crackle of burning. The heat. The sudden stench . . .

The landlord, his mouth agape, takes a step toward the burgeoning light. As he does, a figure dashes past him, black cloak flapping, a spill of golden hair gleaming, flashing in the infernal light.

"No!" he cries. "For the gods' sakes, woman, don't! The bugger's dead . . ."

He takes two faltering steps toward the heat, then stops. It is too late. For an instant the black of her cloak is framed against the brightness of the opening, then she is gone.

Thick smoke drifts across the water. The whole of the inn is on fire now, flames leaping from the timbers of the roof, piercing the restful dark above the town. There are screams—high-pitched, agonized cries—and then nothing. Nothing but the furnace-roar of air and flame, of cracking beams and the splintering of glass.

In the alleyway, a tall, silvered figure moves slowly through the haze, like something glimpsed in dream, its smooth, high-domed head gleaming like a mottled egg, its torso smooth, sexless, veined like polished marble. And its face . . . its face is featureless save for two tiny button eyes that gleam amid the swirl of smoke and light.

At the charred window it stops, leaning across the sill to stare through layers of thick, choking smoke into the fire-blackened room, then climbs inside, bare feet sizzling on the red-hot flags. A moment later it returns, a limp, dark figure in its arms.

At the front of the inn a crowd has gathered. As the figure emerges from the alley a great gasp goes up. Of surprise, and disbelief, and awe. It is the crippled man. John Newcott's boy. The loner. They watch him come on, stumbling now, close to collapse, his clothes smoldering, the limp form of the woman cradled in his arms.

As he reaches the edge of the crowd, two men come forward, taking his burden from him.

The camera eye moves closer. A man's lined and bearded face winces, pained by what he sees. He looks up, tears in his eyes, meeting his fellow's gaze, then shakes his head. The camera turns, looks down into the ruined face of the woman. Slowly it moves inward, until the charred and blistered surface of her flesh fills the screen.

And then darkness.

———————

ON THE FAR SIDE of the estuary a lone figure crouched in the deep shadow beneath the trees, staring across at the happenings on the waterfront. For a moment he was still, concealed amid leaf and long grass, then, with a strangely decisive movement, he started down the steep slope, making his way between the trees to the water's edge.

There he paused, staring out again, his large, dark eyes filled with the light of the distant fire. Then, with the faintest shudder, he reached down, untying the rope that secured his boat, and stepped into the hollowed trunk, pushing out from the bank with a quick, practiced motion.

For a moment he did nothing, letting the boat glide out into the current, his head turned, his eyes drawn to the distant blaze, a mixture of fear and fascination making him crouch there like a frightened animal, the short wooden paddle clutched defensively against his chest; then, stirring himself, he dug the paddle into the flow and turned the boat, steering a course parallel to the bank.

This changed things. Up ahead of him, out in the central darkness of the river, the junks were leaving. What's more, the merchantman was making no attempt to pursue them. It was still there, at anchor in the offing, its load untouched.

The man grinned crookedly. His scarred fingers scratched at his neck, then combed long, lank hair back from his face. Satisfied, he dug the paddle deep into the flow, once and then again, switching from side to side, hastening his strokes, knowing that it was urgent now.

———————

IT WAS LATE. Ben stood there at the water's edge, looking out across the bay, the satisfaction of a solid day's work like a physical presence in his blood. He closed his eyes, relaxing. For a moment it was perfect. For one brief yet timeless moment he lapsed out of himself, melting into the eternal blackness of the night. Then, with a tiny shudder, he returned to himself, conscious of something lost. Of something denied him.

He turned, looking back at the low, familiar outline of the cottage, embedded in the hillside. A light was on upstairs, in Meg's room. From where he stood he could see her, moving about inside, brushing out her dark long hair, then turning to study herself in the mirror. He smiled, then let his gaze move upward, over the thatched roof of the cottage, following the narrow road that climbed the hillside. Beyond the line of cottages—dark now; sensed more than properly seen—the land climbed steeply. At its summit, silhouetted against the paleness beyond, was the old church of St. George's. Beyond that, less than half a *li* distant, the City began again, a huge wall of whiteness, vast and monumental. Ben shivered, then turned full circle, aware suddenly of its presence, there on every side of him, encircling and containing the valley—containing *him*—like the walls of a giant box.

Reducing cottage, town and trees, roads, walls and human figures. Reducing all to toys. Toys in a giant playbox.

The moon had sunk beneath the edge of the wall. For a moment his eyes traced the silvered line where the whiteness of the wall met the black of the sky, then he turned back, facing the bay.

Out on the river it was dark, the surface smooth, like a mirror; a huge lens, reflecting the vastness of the star-filled night.

What was it like, that immensity? What did it *feel* like? Was it just a simple nothingness, a lapsing out? Or was there something beyond that brief moment he had experienced just now? Something *more* to be had?

He turned from the water, climbing the hill, making his way across the lower meadow, away from the cottage, toward the sapling oak that marked his father's grave.

Today he had felt close to it. Had felt at moments almost as if he could reach out and touch it. Standing there among the figures on the waterfront, he had caught the briefest, most transient glimpse of it, there in the raging fire's heart. And for a moment the unnameable thing had been there, on his lips, almost articulate, like a scent. But when he had opened his mouth to utter it, it had flown, ineffable as ever, evading all attempts of his to bring it back.

Ben sat, the young tree at his back, looking out across the bay to the river beyond. It had gone well today. For the first time in weeks his inner doubts had been silenced, his imagination caught up in the play of images. This was his tenth month working on the Shell, his two hundred and ninety-seventh day spent struggling with the material, and finally he felt close to capturing what he had first envisaged, all those months back.

He smiled, remembering where this had begun, back there in those few months before his father, Hal, had died. Hal had wanted to create something for his wife—something she could remember him by. Ben had proposed a "sense-diary"—a "within the skin" kind of thing—but Hal had wanted more.

"No. She has to see me too. From the outside. She'll need that, Ben. It'll comfort her."

And so he had broken with habit, switching from intense sensory fugues—moments which captured the experience of what it felt like to be Hal Shepherd—to colder, sense-distanced externals, using older, more conventional techniques.

He had expected to be bored by it, at most disappointed, yet from the first it had been different, unexpectedly challenging. Exciting.

In the three months he had worked with his father on the Shell—months in which he had seen Hal transformed, hollowed out by the cancer that had been planted in him by Berdichev's assassin—he had learned more about his craft than in the previous three years.

He had had to make compromises, of course. Had had to let go of his vision of making it all realer-than-real. The cuts, for instance, between the internals and the externals—those mind-jolting leaps of perception he had termed the "discontinuity effect"—had, until then, always been a stumbling block. Before then, he had always argued that by drawing the viewer's attention to the artificiality of the medium, one destroyed the power of the illusion. Forced by his father to confront the problem, he had discovered otherwise; had evolved all manner of ingenious and subtle ways of using that moment to make the illusion stronger, more powerful than before.

It had surprised him. He had always thought that jolt—that moment when one went outside one's body and turned, looking back—

destructive. And so it was if one thought in pure terms. Yet if one cheated—if one made the fiction work for you—if one embraced the suprareal . . .

He laughed softly, remembering those days, recalling how his father would watch him, fascinated, his eyes burningly alive in that wasted face. His father-brother. Amos's seed.

"Ben?"

He let the moment fade—let the intensity wash from him—then turned, looking up at his sister's shadowed form.

"I thought you were tired?"

She sat beside him, leaning back, her arms out behind her. "I was," she said quietly. "But then I saw you out here and I thought . . ."

He turned, looking at her. It was dark, her face in deep shadow, and yet he had no need for light to see her. He had only to close his eyes and he could see her, as a child, a girl, and now—these last few years—a woman.

"You're tired, Ben. All this . . . it's too much. You need help. More than I can give you. Technicians. Someone to help you with the setups. Someone to take some of the basic programming work off your hands." She paused, then, exasperated by his silence, added, "You think you can do it all, Ben, but you can't! It's wearing you down. I see it day by day."

He laughed, but as ever he was touched by her concern. "I'm all right, Megs. Really I am."

Ben lifted his face to the night. From where he sat he could smell her; could almost taste the salt-sweet scent of her skin, feel the silk-smooth warmth of her beneath the soft cotton of her dress.

He turned, kneeling, facing her, for a moment content simply to be there in the darkness with her. Then, gently, he pushed her down, onto her back, one hand lifting her dress, his fingers tracing the smooth length of her inner thigh until they met the soft warmth of her sex, the small noise she made, the tiny shiver in her limbs, enflaming him, blinding his senses, making him jerk like a puppet and push down against her urgently, thrusting at her even as she struggled to unfasten him.

And then darkness. Violent, searing darkness.

———

IN THE FAINT LIGHT of dawn he woke. The house was still, silent, and yet he lay there stiffly, as if alerted, not knowing why.

He went out, into the corridor, standing in the deep shadow, looking toward the far end of the long, low-ceilinged space. The door to his mother's room was closed. To the right, beside it, light from the casement window fell onto the wall, illuminating the portrait there.

Slowly he went toward it.

Every day he passed it. Every day he glanced at it, giving it no more thought than he would a blade of grass or a leaf fallen on the path. But now he stood, studying it intently, trying to see beyond its familiar shapes and colors to the feelings that had formed it—that had here been channeled into canvas, oil, and brush. He closed his eyes, letting his fingertips explore the surface of the canvas, then stood back, squinting at it, trying to see it fresh.

It was himself. Or, rather, Catherine's vision of him. He stared at the dark, fragmented face, at the flecked and broken flesh and nodded gently. She had seen the doubleness in him. Had seen and captured it perfectly. For a moment he let his vision dissolve, admiring the abstract play of red and green and black, deriving a rare aesthetic thrill from the composition; then, focusing again, he saw it whole once more. No. Even Meg didn't know him this well. Even Meg.

Catherine . . . They had been students together at Oxford. Friends and, ultimately, lovers. He had not thought of her in some while; had shut her out, choosing not to remember. But now it all flooded back. The way she rested, like a cat, in her chair, her legs drawn up beneath her. The way her hair fell, a cascade of golden red, each strand a fine, clear filament of flame. The touch, the taste, the smell of her. He closed his eyes, the memory perfect, overwhelming, then, shivering, he turned, going down the narrow twist of stairs.

Downstairs the curtains were tightly drawn, the darkness intense. He made his way blindly to the door and raised the latch, stepping out into the freshness of the new day, his bare feet treading on the dew-wet grass.

Bird calls sounded from the trees across the bay, and then silence.

He moved out across the close-cut lawn, then turned, looking up at the window to his mother's room. The quartered space was dark, the curtains drawn, like a lid over an eye.

For a moment he stood there, thoughtful. She had seemed much happier these past few days, as if, at last, she had come to terms with Hal's death. No more did he wake to hear her crying in the night. And at breakfast yesterday morning he had been surprised to hear her singing softly in the garden.

He turned suddenly. There had been a noise. A high, keening noise that came from the darkness on the far side of the bay. It could have been an animal, but it wasn't. No, for there was nothing in the Domain that made a sound like that.

He shivered, a strange excitement filling him. It was the sound that had woken him, he realized. A strange, unearthly noise.

"Intruders . . ." he said quietly, a faint smile lighting his features. There were intruders in the valley.

CHAPTER THIRTEEN

Intruders

H E S A T at his father's desk, his great-great-grandfather Amos's keyboard—a strange, semicircular design—resting in his lap. The curtains were drawn, the door locked. Across from him, pulled down in front of the crowded, untidy bookshelves, a huge flatscreen showed a view of the lower valley; of a tree-covered hillside, a wide expanse of sunlit water.

Ben had sent out the remotes an hour ago; a dozen tiny, insectile "eyes" that even now scoured the valley from the creek in the far north to the castle at the river's mouth, searching for signs of intrusion. On one of two small, desk-mounted screens to Ben's left the remotes appeared as pinpoint traces on a map of the Domain, following preprogrammed search patterns. Ben sat there patiently, switching from view to view, alert for anything unusual, but as yet there was nothing.

As if he'd dreamed the sound. But he hadn't dreamed it. And that meant one of two things. Either there'd been an unprecedented breach of security, or someone high up in Security had let the intruders in.

The obvious course of action was to call Li Yuan and ask him to send someone in. Karr, perhaps. But that was the last thing Ben wanted, because it would be a shame if he didn't find a way to use this—to harness it for his art.

Behind him the brass doorknob half turned, then rattled.

"Ben? Are you in there?"

It was his sister, Meg. He glanced at the timer. Six fourteen. She was up early. Very early, considering they had been working so late.

"I'm working," he called out, knowing even as he said it that it wouldn't satisfy her. "Make breakfast. I'll be down in a while."

He could sense her hesitation, could almost feel her curiosity through the wooden door, then there was the creak of floorboards as she made her way back down the passage.

He sat back, considering his options. If Meg knew what was going on she would want to call in the troops. She would be frightened, concerned for their safety. And there was no need. He could take care of this himself.

He stared at the map a moment, then, looking back at the keyboard, began reprogramming the remotes, one by one sending the tiny eyes shooting southward, out over the town and its tiny harbor, out past Warfleet Cove and the ancient castle, and on, toward the sea.

Out there, they'd be. Somewhere out there. At the Blackstone, maybe, or Castle Ledge, or sheltering by the Mew Stone . . .

No. He dismissed the thought. There wasn't shelter for a family of mice out there, let alone a human settlement. Not a single island or outcrop from Start Point in the south to Exmouth in the north, only the smooth, white walls of the City, towering over the land and dropping sheer into the sea. There was the odd rock, of course, jutting a dozen yards or so above the rough waves' surface, but there was no chance they might have settled one of those. The first high tide would have washed them away. Even so, he had to look, because the intruders must have come from somewhere.

He looked up at the screen once more, watching as the remote skipped above the surface of the wind-ruffled water. Slowly, like a shadow looming at the back of things, the great Mewstone grew, its jagged spine silhouetted sharply against the morning sky.

For a moment he was struck by the simple beauty of the scene; by the interplay of light and dark; the exhilaration of pure movement. He could use this, maybe. Tie it in somehow.

Sunlight winked, winked again, then flooded the screen with light. And then darkness. Sudden, absolute darkness, as the remote went beneath the wall of rock that rose forty yards above the water.

He slowed the eye, widening the aperture to let in as much light as possible, getting the computer to enhance the image, but there was nothing. Nothing but sea and rock.

He switched, impatient now, picking up one of the remotes he had sent south past the Dancing Beggars. At once he saw it, there, some two or three hundred yards off, slightly to the left. A boat. A strange, incredible boat.

The deck was a broad, ungainly raft of railway sleepers lashed tightly together, the weight of the hull—more a decorative border than a true hull—making the craft dip dangerously low in the water.

He moved the remote closer, scanning its length. Broken TV sets and car fenders, refrigerator doors, hubcaps and radios, their innards gutted, had been tied together with electric cable. Computer keyboards and anglepoise lamps, vacuum cleaner hoses, video machines and coffee percolators, satellite receiver dishes, steering wheels and electric toasters, all had been welded into a single mass that formed a low wall about the raft.

It was like a collage, a great collage of once-familiar things. Things from that great, sprawling, dynamic, intensely technological world that had existed before the City.

Ben laughed softly, delighted, then, with a grunt of satisfaction, he gave the eye full power, skimming it quickly past the raft and on.

Out here it was. Somewhere out here. But what? A man-made island, perhaps? An ancient sailing vessel? Or was it something else?

To his right the City dominated the skyline, a smooth wall of whiteness following the coast in a long, staggered zigzag, its unnatural cliffs towering two *li* above the breaking waves. To his left the sunlit sea was calm and empty. As the seconds passed, excitement dulled to uncertainty. What if there were nothing but the raft?

And then he saw it, low and far to the left, its outline glinting in the sunlight, a faint wisp of smoke going up into the brightness. He slowed the remote, changing its direction, sending it out on a path that would skirt the vessel to its south.

Again he felt his heartbeat quicken, his mouth grow dry with anticipation. A raft, it was—a raft! But bigger, much bigger than the other. So big, in fact, that he sat back with a small laugh of surprise. And not just one, but several. Huge things, bigger than anything he'd

ever seen or imagined could exist. Slowly he lifted the remote, climbing the sky, until he was hovering high above the strange armada,
looking down.

There were five of them: massive constructs, perfectly hexagonal,
like patches from a giant quilt, a *li* to each side, loosely stitched
together by rope bridges in a dozen places. Moored here and there at
the edges were a number of smaller rafts, like the one he had seen in
the estuary.

Ben stared, fascinated, at the nearest of the rafts, taking in its
details. Earth had been piled onto the raft, covering its surface to
some depth—tons, thousands of tons, of earth. Dark, fruitful earth
that was covered now in places by lush green grass, in others by orderly
rows of plants and vegetables. At the center was a tiny settlement of
thirty huts, clustered in a circle about a central meetinghouse. Paths
went out from the settlement; paths dotted here and there with
storehouses and water storage towers.

He tilted the remote, looking. All five of the rafts were organized
on the same ancient principle, the only distinguishing feature being
the size of the meetinghouse of the central raft.

There, he thought; *that's where I'll get my answers.* And, moving his
hand gently, carefully over the controls, he sent the remote down, in a
long, lazy spiral, toward the broad, low ceiling of the meetinghouse.

━━━━━━

MEG STOOD on the bottom lawn, looking out across the bay, angry
with him. Two hours had passed since he'd said he'd come and still
there was no sign of him.

The tide was in. Beneath her feet, at the bottom of the tiny runged
ladder that was set into the concrete bank, the tiny rowboat bobbed
gently. She had been tempted to take it out and damn him, but
beneath her anger was a burning curiosity. For almost a year now he
had included her, at every stage and in every decision, but now—for
no apparent reason—he had locked her out again: *physically*, the door
barred against her entry.

She looked about her at the wooded slopes, the cottages, and
beyond them all the Wall. Some days she felt so lonely here, so
isolated, and yet it never seemed to touch Ben. Never. It was as if he

enjoyed the empty streets, the lifeless simulacra that, apart from the three of them and the guards, were the sole inhabitants of the Domain. As if this were enough for him. But she had realized, long ago now, that she was missing something.

She touched her top teeth with her tongue, then shook her head. It was as if she couldn't even think it, for to think it would be close to saying it, and saying it would seem a betrayal of Ben. And yet the thought remained.

She wanted someone else to talk to. Someone less harsh, less forbidding than her brother. Someone to share things with.

A tiny shudder passed through her at the thought. *Someone to share things with.* She had been sharing things with Ben all her life. Had learned to see the world through his eyes. But suddenly it wasn't enough. Not that she was unhappy as things were. She enjoyed Ben's company and loved to see him working. It was just . . .

She smiled, realizing that she had come to the edge once more, both literally and metaphorically. Beneath her naked feet the ground fell away sharply, the water ten feet below where she balanced. Another step and she would have fallen.

The thought of it brought back to her the day he'd saved her life; the day he had dived into the cold, incoming tide and dragged her unconscious body from the waves, then had breathed the life back into her. Without him, she realized, she was nothing. Even so, she wanted something more than him. Something different.

She turned, walking back slowly to the cottage, enjoying the sun on her back, the faint, cooling breeze on her neck and arms. Back in the kitchen she cleared the table, scraping Ben's breakfast into the garbage, then busied herself tidying the place up. She was preparing the dinner, peeling the potatoes, singing softly to herself, when Ben finally appeared.

She didn't hear him. The first she knew was when he put his arms about her and turned her to face him.

"I'm sorry," he said, kissing her brow. "I wanted to try something out, that's all. A new idea . . ."

She smiled, relieved that he was back with her; yet at the same time she knew he was withholding something from her.

"And the next scene? I thought we were going to start on it early."

"Ah . . ." He looked past her; out through the latticed window toward the bay. "I thought we might leave that for a while. This new thing . . ." He looked back at her, then kissed her nose. "Let's go out, huh? On the river, maybe. It's been some while since we took the boat out."

"I'd like that," she said, surprised how, as ever, he seemed to anticipate her mood; to read her better than she read herself.

"Good. Then leave that. I'll help you later. Let's pack a picnic. We can go to the old house."

She looked at him strangely. "Why there, Ben? It's an ugly place. There's nothing there now. Even the foundations . . ."

She stopped, realizing that he wasn't listening; that he was staring past her again, his mind elsewhere.

"Why there?" she asked again, softer this time.

"Because," he answered quietly, then laughed. "Just because."

━━━━━

BEN STOOD in the brilliant sunlight, his feet on the dark and glassy surface where the old house had once stood, looking about him. On every side of the broad, dark circle nature had proliferated, but here the green had gained no hold. He crouched, then brushed at the surface, wiping away the layer of dirt and dust. It was over eight years since he had lost his hand, here, on this spot. Beneath him the fused rock was mirror smooth. He stared into the polished darkness, trying to see his face, then turned, looking across at Meg.

Meg had laid the cloth down on the edge of the circle nearest the river, beneath the overhanging branches. She moved between sunlight and deep shade, the dark fall of her hair and the mottling of leaf shadow on her arms reminding Ben of childhood tales of wood nymphs and dryads. He stood there a while, watching her, then went across.

She looked up at him and smiled. "I was thinking of the last time we came here . . . before the accident."

"The library," he said, anticipating her. "And the secret room beyond."

"Yes." She looked about her, frowning, as if surprised not to find it all there, surrounding them.

"Where does it go, Ben? Where does it all go?"

He was about to say, "*Up here,*" and tap his skull, but something in her manner stopped him. It was not a rhetorical question. She wanted to know.

"I don't know," he answered. *Into the darkness, maybe.*

She was still looking at him, her brown eyes wide with puzzlement. "Is it all just atoms, Ben? Atoms, endlessly combining and recombining? Is that all there is, when it comes down to it?"

"Maybe." But even as he said it he realized that he didn't really believe it. There *was* something more. That same something he had felt only last night, in the flames and afterward in the darkness beside the water. Something just beyond his reach.

He shivered, then looked about him again, conscious of the old house, there, firm in his memory. He had only to close his eyes and he was back there, eight years ago in the spring—there in the room with the books; there in Augustus's secret room, reading his journal, and after, in the walled garden, standing beside Augustus's tomb.

His brother, dead these eighty-eight years. Part of old man Amos's experiment. Amos's seed, *his* son, like all of them.

"*Oder jener stirbt und ists.*"

Meg looked up at him, curious. "What was that?"

"It's a line from Rilke. From the Eighth Elegy. It was carved on Augustus's gravestone. 'Or someone dies and *is* it.' " He nodded, finally understanding. Augustus saw it too. He too was in search of that same *something*—that terrible angel of beauty.

Ben sat, facing his sister, then reached across and took a bright green apple from the pile. As he bit into it, he thought back over what he had seen that morning, remembering the dark, wind-tanned faces of the raft-dwellers. Savage, barbarian faces, the teeth black or missing in their mouths, their long hair unkempt, their ragged furs and leathers greasy and patched. Some had worn ancient metallic badges with faded lettering, like the names of ancient tribes.

He had assessed the speed of the raft armada and estimated that it would be at least eleven hours before they reached the headland at Combe Point. That would bring them there roughly at sunset. Until then he could relax, enjoy the day.

He finished the apple, core and all, then reached across to take another.

"Ben . . ."

Meg's look of admonishment, so like his mother's, made him withdraw his hand. For a moment he was silent, watching her, then he laughed.

"I've decided to change things," he said. "I've been thinking that maybe you were right. Maybe the Han should live."

Her face lit with delight. "Do you think so? Do you really think so?"

He nodded, then leaned closer, conspiratorially, including her again. "I've been thinking through a whole new scenario. One in which Tong Ye is kept prisoner in the inn after the fight. He's badly injured, close to death, but the girl nurses him. And afterward . . ."

———

SHADOWS WERE LENGTHENING in the valley as Ben sat down at his father's desk once more, the curtains drawn, the door locked tight behind him. It was dark in the room, but he had no need for light. Memory guided his fingers swiftly across the keyboard. At once twin screens lifted smoothly from the desktop to his left, glowing softly.

He called up the map of the Domain, homing in on the four grid squares at the mouth of the estuary. As he'd thought, the raft armada had anchored off the Dancing Beggars, just out of sight of the guard post at Blackstone Point.

He turned, facing the big screen as he brought it alive. It brightened, then settled to a dull reddish-brown, littered with small, ill-defined patches of darkness. The camera eye of the remote was looking directly into the portico of the meetinghouse, but in the late evening shadow it was hard to make out what, if anything, was happening.

He switched between the three remotes quickly, then returned to the first image, widening the aperture and enhancing the image until the dull orange haze to the right of center resolved itself into an ancient iron brazier filled with coals, the long, dark-barred shape behind it into the struts and spars of the meetinghouse. In the last of the daylight a dozen elders stood about the darkened doorway, talking animatedly. In the space before them, a large crowd had gathered, waiting cross-legged on the dark, smooth earth.

Ben eased back, breathing shallowly, his eyes taking in everything.

It was perfect. Just perfect. His fingers moved over the surface of the keyboard. There was the faintest click as the tape began to run. At the top left corner of the screen the "record" trace began to wink redly.

The sun was low now, to the west, above the hills of Combe Point. Moment by moment the light decayed, until, at a signal from one of the elders, torches were brought—ancient oil-soaked rags on poles— and lit from the brazier. At once the scene took on a different aspect.

In the unsteady flicker of the torchlight, the faces in the crowd seemed suddenly strange, almost demonic. Turning the remote slowly, he panned across the sea of faces, noting how drawn, how emaciated each seemed. Thin lips parted like a wound, neck muscles tensed. An eye moved shiftily, uncertainly in a sunken orb, the pupil flickering darkly like an insect on a pale egg. Beyond it a jaw lowered, exposing blackened canine teeth that snarled and then laughed. Ben stared, fascinated. It was as if the half-light brought out the truth of these faces. Reduced them to a cipher to be read. Again he was conscious of how unlike the faces of the City-dwellers these faces were. Inside, the face was a mask, a wall, built to conceal. Here, in these savage, simple faces, all was offered at a glance. One had only to learn the language.

He was panning back across the crowd when the picture swung about violently. A moment later the screen went black. At once Ben switched to the second remote, turning it to focus on the malfunctioning eye. For a moment he searched fruitlessly, then he saw it, there in the hand of one of the guards. The man had plucked it from the rafters of the hut where Ben had set it; had crushed the soft-cased machine as one would crush an insect. Now, however, he was staring at the thing in his hand, realization dawning in his savage, bearded face that it was not a living creature.

Cursing softly, Ben tapped out the auto-destruct sequence. As he watched, the remote glowed hotly in the guard's hand. With a small cry, the man dropped it, then went to tread on it. But even as he did, the remote caught fire, scattering sparks like a falling cinder.

For a moment there was commotion. A small crowd formed about the tiny, melted shape, their voices briefly raised, before one of the elders shooed them back to their places.

Ben sat back, relieved. If, even for a moment, they suspected he was watching them, it would all be undone. His whole plan depended on the advantage his eyes gave him; on his superior information. It was the only real edge he had.

He switched between the two remaining remotes, testing each in turn, boosting the image, the sound, almost to distortion. It was too late to reposition them. He would have to trust now that whatever happened next took place within sight of them, which meant outside, in front of the meetinghouse. He daren't risk a second incident.

He had barely finished when there was a faint humming in the air—a sound which grew by the moment. It was an aircraft; a Security cruiser by the sound of it. He tilted the first remote, searching the darkness above Combe Point.

He saw it at once, there, coming in from the east, flying low, its headlamps cutting a brilliant path across the dark waters. He cut to the now standing crowd, to the elders gathered on the portico—seeing the awe, the feverish anticipation in every face—then switched back. The cruiser was coming in noisily, ostentatiously it seemed, making enough of a display to be seen clearly from the guard post.

Ben glanced at the empty screen to his left, then keyed in his father's access code. All was ready now. He had only to see who it was. To find out why and what they wanted. Then he could act.

The cruiser slowed, passing over the raft armada once and then again, its searchlights playing on the crowd below, figures peering down from within the craft. Then, slowly, it descended.

As it came down, the crowd moved back, away from the sleek black shape that settled in their midst. A gun turret swiveled about, then was still. A hatch hissed open skyward, like a wing unfolding. A moment later, six masked and suited guards came down the ramp, heavy automatic weapons held close to their chests.

Whoever it was, he was taking no chances. He knew better than to trust this rabble. His men fanned out, taking up defensive positions about the ramp, eyeing the crowd warily, as if expecting an attack. A moment later he appeared at the top of the ramp. As he paused, looking about him, Ben focused in, until the man's head filled the screen, his features so close that the image had almost begun to break up.

Ben clicked, taking a copy of the image, then clicked again, transferring it. The computer search took less than a second. On the screen to Ben's left, the boxed image from the large screen was relocated at the top right of the picture, a second image—the official file copy, updated only eleven weeks back—dominating the screen, the name of the officer printed underneath in English and Mandarin.

Major Per Virtanen.

Virtanen. Ben nodded, understanding. The face had meant nothing to him, but the name . . .

Ben returned his attention to the big screen, watching the man come down the ramp, then turn, looking about him, conscious of the impression he was making. He was a tall, silver-haired officer in his mid-fifties, his features strong, decisive, his eyes a penetrating blue. His magnificent azurite-blue dress uniform was cut elegantly, the embroidered silk patch on the chest—that of a third-ranking military officer—depicting a leopard snatching a bird from the air. All in all, he seemed the very picture of refined strength—the perfect representative of the T'ang's authority—but Ben knew better.

Eight years ago, when Virtanen had first come before the Appointments Board to be considered for the post of Major, only one man had opposed his promotion, Ben's father, Hal. In normal circumstances, Virtanen would have been appointed, for there was no need for the Board's decision to be unanimous. But Hal Shepherd had gone directly to Li Shai Tung, the present T'ang's father, and had the appointment nullified.

Ben remembered it vividly. Remembered how angry his father had grown when telling his mother of it. How he had stood there in the kitchen, his fists clenched, his dark eyes blazing.

It was not unheard of for officers to "buy" their appointments—indeed, it was more the rule than the exception—nor was the use of family connection really frowned upon. No. What made Virtanen's case exceptional was his use of Triad connections, the illicit drug money, to buy influence. That and the suspected "murder" of a rival for the post, hacked to pieces in his sedan by a *tong* assassination squad. Nothing could be proved, of course, but the circumstantial evidence against Virtanen was considerable. In the words of the old Han saying, Virtanen was a toad masquerading as a prince. A man unsuited for the task of upholding the T'ang's law.

Accepting Hal's advice, Li Shai Tung had upheld the objection and refused the appointment, giving no reason. For Virtanen, confident of his promotion, it had been a severe loss of face—not to speak of the expense—and it was rumored that he had raged for days, cursing Hal Shepherd to anyone who'd listen.

And now, eight years on, Virtanen had finally been appointed Major. Eleven weeks ago, to be precise, in the wake of Li Yuan's deal with the Triad boss, Fat Wong.

Ben scrolled the file quickly, scanning Virtanen's orders for the past eleven weeks. Under the guise of restructuring his command, he had removed all of those officers familiar with the running of the Domain and replaced them with his own men, leaving the foot soldiers—the actual guards who served in the Domain—until the very last. At the same time he had had all Security reports for the Western Isle—for what was once called Great Britain—routed through his office.

Ben let his breath out slowly, watching the elders come on, their heads bowed, their eyes lowered before the great man.

Everything made sense. All but one thing. Were Virtanen successful then there was sure to be an inquiry; an in-depth investigation under Li Yuan's direct control. And, as things stood, the finger would point directly at Virtanen.

And that didn't make sense. A man like Virtanen, used to dealing with snakes—to making deals and covering his ass—had to have some kind of get-out.

Ben sat back, pondering the problem; considering what *he* would do in Virtanen's place. The man looked so confident, so totally at ease. He had to have a plan. He wasn't the kind to sacrifice himself simply for revenge. No, not after waiting so patiently to bring it about. He had had eight years now to brood on the question, so what had he come up with? What devious little scheme was he hatching?

Ben waited. One moment there was nothing, the next . . .

Of course, he thought, his eyes widening as, up on the screen, the elders knelt before Virtanen.

Two of the guards came across, moving between Virtanen and the elders, their guns raised threateningly. There was a moment's angry murmuring and then the elders backed off. As they did so there was a movement behind them, in the doorway of the meetinghouse. A man emerged, half hidden in the shadows; a tall man, maybe a full foot taller than Virtanen and broad at the shoulders. He wore dark silks and his hair was braided. In his hand was a slender silver rod.

Ben smiled, recognizing what it was. It was a piston. A piston from an old combustion engine.

As the man stepped down, a chant began from among the crowd. A low, almost bestial sound that filled the flickering darkness.

"Tewl . . . Tewl . . . Tewl . . ."

Ben switched between the remotes, setting one to track Virtanen's face, the other to focus on the newcomer. Halving the screen, he watched as the two approached each other. Finally they stood there, face to face, no more than an arm's length between them.

The chant died.

Seen from close up, Tewl was an ugly bastard. His broken nose seemed overlong, while his mouth, paralyzed on the left side, seemed to form a perpetually crooked smile. His eyes, however, were hard, and the look he gave Virtanen was like the cold, calculating gaze of a deep ocean predator.

Virtanen, clearly unused to such fierceness, looked aside momentarily, then forced himself to meet that unflinching stare.

"Tewl . . ."

The crooked smile widened, and then Tewl moved closer, embracing Virtanen.

"You came," Tewl said, moving back. And Ben, watching from the darkness miles away, mimicked the sound, the shape that twisted mouth made.

Virtanen's smile was forced. "Your people are ready, Tewl? They know what they have to do?"

Tewl looked past Virtanen at the crowd and nodded. "We know what we have to do. But you? You will keep your promise to us? There will be no more trouble from your forces?"

Virtanen lifted his chin slightly, clearly put out. "You keep your part of the bargain, Tewl, and I give my word. No one will trouble you. The valley will be yours."

Ben nodded. Yes, and as soon as Tewl and his people had taken the Domain, Virtanen would send in his troops. Too late to save the

Shepherds, of course, but the intruders would be punished. Conveniently eradicated, down to the last man, woman, and child.

There would be "suicides" among the ranks of those who had served in the Domain; a serious fire at the Central Records Office. Crucial pieces of information would go missing. And a culprit from among the staff of Security would be found, his records conveniently doctored. And he too would be found to have swallowed cyanide rather than face questioning.

And in the end, the T'ang's inquiry would show that Virtanen had acted swiftly and correctly. That he had done all he could to try to save the Shepherds. A slight taint of suspicion would remain, but not enough to spur the T'ang to action. At least, not now when Virtanen's connections with the Triads were so important.

Ben studied the man. There were small signs of tension and unease, but no more than would be natural in such a situation. No. You might take Virtanen at face value. If you knew no better, you might even believe that his word was worth something.

If you knew no better.

Leaving the first remote focused on Virtanen, he switched to the second, turning it slowly, panning across the crowd, the guards, the elders. He was about to pan back when a movement on the far side of the clearing—in the doorway of one of the surrounding huts—caught his attention. He zoomed in.

The girl was standing just inside the door, one pale and slender hand resting on the upright. For a moment he wasn't sure whether it had been a trick of the light, but then, as she emerged again, he saw that he had not been mistaken. That same flame-red hair. Those same green, catlike eyes.

He caught his breath, astonished by the likeness. She was thinner and a good few inches shorter; even so, she could easily have been her sister.

"*Catherine* . . ." he whispered, staring into her face as if he stood directly before her.

It was as if she was staring past him. Looking out past his shoulder at what was happening on the far side of the clearing. Then, as if dismissing it from her mind, she turned away.

For a moment Ben stared at the empty screen, then he leaned forward, activating the remote, lifting it high above the clearing, then settled it, there on the upright of the doorframe where her hand had rested only moments before.

Across the clearing the two men were still talking. As the tiny, insectlike remote crawled slowly into the dark interior of the hut, Ben tapped into the audio output from the other eye.

Virtanen's voice seemed calm, but there was a tightly restrained anger underlying the words.

"You shouldn't have done it, Tewl. Sending in the raft . . . It could have been dangerous. If you'd been seen . . ."

"I had to see," Tewl answered gruffly. "I had to be sure. Besides, my men were careful."

"Maybe so, but you must do what I say in future. One wrong move and all is undone. You understand me, Tewl?"

Inside, the darkness was intense. Ben boosted the image. Slowly the shadows took on a grainy, reddish form. The girl was in the far corner, seated on a low camp bed, her hand up to her neck. As he watched, she shook out her hair and, stretching her head forward, began to comb it through.

Silence. As the comb draws through the flamelike hair, Ben sits there in his father's study, watching, the past alive, vividly alive—in him.

And then darkness. A violent, searing darkness.

<hr>

THE BANGING woke him. Ben turned his head, then winced, the pain intense just above his left ear. Slowly he raised himself, letting his eyes grow accustomed to the darkness. The chair lay close by, the keyboard dangling from its arm. He pulled himself up, conscious of the tart smell of sickness in the room, the hiss of static from the neglected screens.

Like Time, bleeding from the darkness.

It was late. After eleven. He had been out for over two hours this time. It was over two weeks since the last fit, and then he had blacked out for two, three minutes at most. But this had been quite different.

Ben shivered, then put his fingers gently to the wound. The gash was deep, almost an inch long, but there seemed to be no real damage. The blood had clotted well. It felt more tender now than painful.

The banging came again. "Ben! Open up! Please!"

"Coming . . ."

He straightened up the chair and set the keyboard down on the desktop, then cleared the screens. He had no idea whether the remotes were still functioning, or whether anything had been recorded after his fall, but that would have to wait. First he had to see to Meg.

He unlocked the door and tugged it open. Meg was standing there, her face anxious.

"Ben! It's Mother. I don't know . . ." She stopped, seeing the blood matted in his hair. "God Almighty, Ben . . . what happened?"

"I had a fall," he said, coming out into the hallway and pulling the door closed behind him. "I blacked out a while, that's all. Now what's all this about Mother?"

"I can't find her, Ben. I've looked everywhere. I've even been down to the meadows and called, but there's no sign of her. And that's not like her, Ben, is it? I mean, she always says where she's going."

"Okay . . ." He put his arms about her, drawing her close, reassuring her by his touch. "Okay. Now tell me when you last saw her. She was there when we got back from the old house, wasn't she?"

Meg looked up at him. "Yes. In the rose garden."

"Right. And that was shortly after seven. So she can't have gone far, can she? You say you've looked everywhere?"

"Three times at least. I even took a torch down to the bay."

"Okay." He kneaded her shoulders. "There's probably a perfectly good explanation. Look, why don't you go down to the kitchen and make us some supper while I check the house again. And don't worry, Meg. It'll be all right."

She nodded and turned away, happy to have something to occupy her mind, but Ben, watching her go, felt a tightness at the pit of his stomach. What if he was wrong about Virtanen? What if he'd miscalculated and the man had taken her? What if he had her now?

He began, searching the upper rooms. In his mother's room he stood there a long time, staring into her wardrobe, trying to work out what it was that was missing. Her robe. The red silk ankle-length bathrobe that she used to wear before his father's death. Everything else was there. All of her dresses, every one of her coats and long jumpers.

He turned, looking about him at the smooth white surface of the quilt, the jars of creams and perfume bottles on the dressing table, surprised by how tidy, how orderly the room was. If Virtanen had taken her there'd be some sign of a struggle, surely? Unless he'd come upon her in the meadow. But then, why would she be wearing her bathrobe in the meadow?

He went down. Down, past the old dresser in the hallway, and left, ducking under the low lintel and into the lounge where he and his father had entertained Li Shai Tung on that spring evening eight years past.

On the far side of the long oak table was a small, black-painted door, set back into the whitewashed wall. Ben went across and put his ear to it, then gave it a gentle push.

It swung back noiselessly, revealing a flight of steps, leading down. It ought to have been locked. In fact, it had been locked. He had locked it himself, only yesterday.

He turned, listening, hearing Meg at work in the kitchen, then turned back. He went down five steps, then reached back to pull the door closed behind him. Ahead was the faintest glow of light, like a mist over the blackness.

At the foot of the steps he stopped, his pulse racing. He had known. Yes, even as he had been entertaining those absurd notions about Virtanen kidnapping her, somehow he had known she would be here.

He looked about him at the shadowy rows of standing shelves that filled the cellar workplace; at the crowded racks and gaunt machinery that stood untended on every side.

She was here. Her scent was in the air. He walked on slowly, silently, moving between the shelves toward the source of light at the far end of the cellar. Turning the corner, he stopped, taking in the scene. Ten feet away, the morph was slumped in its metal frame, just as Ben had left it yesterday. But about its shoulders now was draped a red silk bathrobe.

Ben moved on, slower now, more reluctantly, knowing now what he would find; knowing, even before his eyes confirmed it, why his mother had been so happy these past few days. Why she no longer cried in the night.

He stopped, letting his fingers move absently across the smoothly lacquered surface of the Shell. He had made changes to it since his father's time, but it still looked like a giant scarab beetle, its dark, midnight-blue lid not quite opaque. Peering close, he could just make out her form, there inside the coffinlike interior; could see from the rise and fall of her breasts as much as from the flicker of the control panel just below the catch, that she was living out the dream.

He looked down at the panel. She was more than halfway through the three-hour sequence. It would be another hour, maybe more, before she was back with them again.

Ben turned and went across to his desk. Seated there, he took a notepad from the drawer and tore two sheets from it. The first note was to his mother. "I'm sorry," it read. "I didn't realize. I hope it brings you comfort, Love, Ben."

He folded it and set it aside, then began the second. On one side of the paper he wrote "Ben & Meg" in a small, neat hand that was unlike his own. On the other side he quickly penned a note from his mother, telling them that she had gone to see an old friend and that she would be back after midnight. He signed it with a flourish, then folded it lengthwise, the way his mother always folded her notes to them.

Satisfied, he got up and, setting the fake note in his pocket, he took the other across and slipped it into the pocket of the bathrobe, ensuring it would be seen.

He had never told his mother about the Shell he and his father had made for her. In the wake of Hal's death he had thought it best to keep it from her, lest it upset her even more. But he had been wrong. Just looking at her through the darkness of the glass, he could see how happy she looked, how at peace.

Ben stood there, staring at the Shell, understanding, perhaps for the first time, just how powerful this was. The Shell could heal. Could turn misery to song and make whole the wound of death. It was a powerful medium—the most powerful the world had ever seen—and it had been trusted to him to make it work.

He touched his tongue to his top teeth, the way his sister Meg did, then, with a tiny laugh, he went back up, pulling the door to behind him. As he came out into the dining room, he called out to her.

"Meg! Meg! I've solved the mystery!"

She came to the kitchen door, her face half smiling, half anxious, then took the note from him.

"Thank God!" she said, looking back at him. "I knew it had to be something like that. Even so, it's odd, don't you think? I mean, it's not her way to go off without telling us."

"Maybe she's got herself a lover," Ben said mischievously. "A dark-eyed soldier with a waxed mustache."

Meg looked at him, surprised. *"Ben!"*

He laughed. "No. I'm serious, Megs. I mean, haven't you noticed how she's been these last few days? Haven't you heard her singing in the garden?"

Meg went silent for a moment, her eyes thoughtful. "Yes, but . . ."

Ben reached up and lifted her down the four steps, twirling her about. "Besides, while she's away, I could make love to you. Upstairs. In her bed. She'd never know. She'd never ever know."

CHAPTER FOURTEEN

The Hole in the Dark

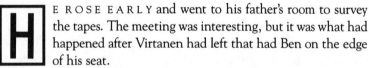

HE ROSE EARLY and went to his father's room to survey the tapes. The meeting was interesting, but it was what had happened after Virtanen had left that had Ben on the edge of his seat.

The elders, silent throughout the exchange between Tewl and the Major, had gathered about the big chieftain, gesticulating wildly, their faces filled with a fierce passion. But it was not their animation that fascinated Ben, so much as the language they used; a crude, alien tongue that he had never heard before. For a while he had sat there, letting the strange music play in his head, sending ripples down his spine. Then, calling up Amos's Universal Lexicon, he requested an aural trace on four words that had cropped up often during their exchanges: *Omma, Gwayteea, Nans,* and *Golow.*

At once a list of close matches in more than fifty languages appeared beneath each word, the spellings as varied as the meanings given, but in only eight instances did all four appear within a single language set. He cleared all but those, then fed in a fifth: the word the crowd had chanted; the word engraved on the pendant that hung about the chieftain's neck.

Tewl.

Ben smiled. *Of course . . .*

For the next hour he worked patiently through the file, learning the basics of the language, giving himself enough of a vocabulary to go back to the tape again and listen, this time with an ear attuned to what the elders were saying.

Today. They wanted to attack today. This very afternoon. To go from here—*omma*—into the valley—*nans*—while it was still bright—*golow*. But there were those who wanted to wait—*gwaytya*—until it was dark—*tewl*.

And Tewl, the dark man himself, what did he want?

Ben watched the chieftain consider what had been said—watched him a second time, understanding this time why his eyes narrowed, why his frown intensified. And then that tiny, hesitant nod of the head. They would go in early, before Virtanen's men, and consolidate their position, because Tewl, like many there, did not trust the Major.

And because they were warriors, unbowed beneath the sky; ashamed to skulk like rats beneath the cover of darkness.

Meg touched his arm, drawing him back from his reverie. "And the Shell, Ben? Are we going to work on it today or not?"

He looked up at her, the image of the tall, dark-robed chieftain still vivid before his eyes, then nodded.

"Yes," he said, a smile forming on his lips. "But there are a few things I have to do first. Some preparations."

"Preparations?" she said, eyeing him warily.

"Trust me," he said, his smile suddenly like the Cheshire Cat's, dark and enigmatic. "Just trust me."

———

MEG SAT on the turn of the stairs, eating an apple while she slowly turned the pages of the book. Beside her, the tiny casement window was open, the late morning sunlight filtering down through the leaded squares, misting the dark fall of her hair with gold. It was a warm, still day, the air filled with birdsong and the low hum of insects, while from below came the sound of Ben, moving from room to room.

It was a perfect day. A day for thoughtless dreaming. But in that instant Meg was unaware of it. For a moment she was there, outside herself, the weather cold and bleak, the hillside bare, exposed to the harshness of the elements. For a moment she saw the faces of the villagers clearly, etched starkly in the fierce light of the great bonfire, like wooden masks, moving from dark to light, from light to dark.

Catching her breath, she looked up, one hand resting briefly in her tightly braided hair, then called down to him. "Ben?"

There were footsteps, and then his face appeared at the foot of the stairs. "What is it?"

"This book I've found. It's wonderful. Listen."

She looked down at the page, then began to read, tracing the words with a finger.

"Not a plow had ever disturbed a grain of that stubborn soil. In the heath's barrenness to the farmer lay its fertility to the historian. There had been no obliteration, because there had been no tending."

His voice cut in, low but resonant.

"It seemed as if the bonfire-makers were standing in some radiant upper story of the world, detached from and independent of the dark stretches below. The heath down there was now a vast abyss, and no longer a continuation of what they stood on; for their eyes, adapted to the blaze, could see nothing of the deep beyond its influence."

She stared at him, then nodded. "You know it, then."

"And the rest," he said, smiling up at her. "But it does give me an idea. Maybe we could use Hardy's scene. Rework it and use it as a kind of counterpoint to the burning of the inn."

She looked down. Something was going on. The very vagueness of his suggestion told her as much. Why else would he want to distract her?

"The preparations . . . are they done?"

He laughed. "No. Not all of them."

"So what were they for? What's going on?"

She saw his lips begin to form the shape of the word; saw him hesitate, then look away, and knew she had been right. *Nothing*, he'd been about to say, but, faced by her, he had been unable to lie to her. She looked down, smiling.

"It's like this . . ." he began. Yet even as he said it, the air was rent by the sound of an explosion; a low, reverberating noise that shook the house and rattled the casement window.

She stood, dropping the book. "What in God's name . . . ?"

But Ben was smiling, grinning almost, with delight. "It's begun," he said, turning away from her. "It's finally begun."

━━━━━

BEN STOOD in the sunlit meadow, the glasses to his eyes. To the far left, where the valley tapered to a point, a plume of smoke rose slowly, dark against the pearled whiteness of the City's walls.

"What is it?" Meg asked, leaning gently against his back.

"The seal," he answered. "They've blown the seal."

"Who?"

Ben shook his head, then laughed. "I'm not sure. But I'm going to find out."

She watched him turn and walk back toward the house, knowing he was holding something back. But why? She looked back at the slowly climbing coil of smoke, frowning at it, then, knowing she had no choice, she turned back, running up the slope after him.

Ben was upstairs in their father's old room, staring down at the flatscreen, his fingers flying across the console.

She stood there a moment, looking across at him, conscious of a strange, almost feverish excitement in the way he crouched there over the keyboard, then went across. "What's happening, Ben? Come on, you have to tell me!"

He turned. "It's happened, Megs. After all these years, it's finally happened. Someone's come for us."

"Come . . . What do you mean, come?"

"We've been invaded, Megs, that's what. The communication lines to the guard houses are dead, the seal's been blown, and there are intruders at the river's mouth."

She stared at him, appalled. "Then you must let the General know. He must get someone here, at once."

"No." He said it clearly, firmly, then turned back to the screen, beginning to tap out a new sequence on the keys. "I want to deal with this myself."

She let out a tiny moan. "For God's sake, Ben, what do you mean? There are intruders in the valley. They have to be dealt with. We can't do that. We don't know how!"

"I didn't say 'we.' I want you to lock yourself in the cellar."

"You want . . ." She stopped suddenly, another thought dislodging what she'd been about to say. "Where's Mother, Ben? Where in God's name is she?"

"I've sent her away," he said, concentrating on the message he was typing onto the screen. "I asked her to get me something from the City. She left two hours back. So you don't have to worry . . ."

"Don't have to worry?" She gave a high-pitched, nervous laugh, horrified by what he was saying. "Don't you understand what's happening, Ben? We're being *attacked*! The Domain is being invaded!"

"I know," he said calmly. "And I promise I'll be careful. But you needn't worry. I'll deal with it."

She shuddered, looking at him as if she didn't recognize him, then shook her head, for the first time in her life surprised, genuinely surprised at him. "So what are you going to do?"

He turned slightly, tapping the SEND button as he did so. "I'm going to fight them, Meg. That's what I'm going to do."

"Fight them? How?"

He looked away, a gleam of excitement in his eyes. "Something like this doesn't happen every day. I've got to take advantage of it."

She stared at him, sudden understanding dawning on her. So that was it. He was going to film it all. To make a great adventure of it. She shook her head. "No, Ben. You can't."

"No?" He cleared the screen, then turned back to her, his eyes piercing her with their intensity. "Just watch me."

For a moment she thought of fighting him, of going behind his back on this and letting the General know, but standing there, looking back at him, she knew she wouldn't.

"Okay," she said quietly. "Fight them, if you must. But you have to let me help you, Ben. You *have* to."

"Good," he said, smiling, squeezing her arm gently, as if that was what he had wanted all along. "Then come quickly now. We've a lot to do."

━━━◆◆◆◆◆━━━

THEY LAY in the long grass, a hundred *ch'i* from the opening in the wall, the ground firm beneath them. Where the seal had been was now a perfect circle of darkness, five times a man's height, the pearl-white wall surrounding it smoke-blackened and misted. The seal itself was broken. It lay on the grass beneath the great hole, its perfect circularity shattered like a broken mirror, long shards of pure white ice fanned out upon the green.

It was still and warm. From the woods on the far side of the creek a blackbird called, its piping song echoing out across the open space between the walls. But from the hole itself there came no sound, no sign of movement.

The field glasses lay on the earth beside Ben's elbow. For the past few minutes he had been silent, listening to the receiver he had cupped against his right ear.

Meg watched him a moment, then leaned closer, whispering. "What are they doing, Ben? Why aren't they coming out?"

"It's too bright for them," he whispered. "Tewl wants them to come out, but they won't. It hurts their eyes, so they're going to wait until it's dark."

She stared at him, bewildered. "*Who*, Ben? Who are they?"

"The Clay," he said, pronouncing the word as if it had some mysterious significance. "The men from the Clay."

She looked down. The Clay! Wild savages they were. Vicious, ugly little brutes. And they were coming here!

"How do you know?"

He handed the small black cup of the receiver to her. She stared at it, reluctant to place it to her ear, hearing the tiny, growling voice that buzzed like an insect in the dark interior.

"They've been talking," Ben said quietly. "Communicating back and forth. Tewl . . . he's the chief of the raft people . . . he wants them to attack at once. But they're refusing. And without them he won't commit his own forces. Which is good. It gives us time. Another twelve hours. It ought to be enough."

"Sure, but what's happening, Ben? I mean, why don't they just come in anyway? If there's only us . . ."

He smiled. "They're not interested in us. We're only small fry. No. They want to take the town."

"The town?" She almost laughed. "But there's nothing in the town."

"You know that. And I know that. But they don't. Don't you understand, Meg? They think it's all real."

Real. She shivered. Never had anything seemed so unreal as at that moment.

"Meg . . ." He nudged her, pointing toward the seal, then handed her the glasses. "Look!"

She looked. Two of the creatures could be seen now, leaning across the lip of the seal, their dark, misshapen forms like something glimpsed in a nightmare. She shuddered and handed the glasses back to Ben.

"So what are we going to do? How are we going to fight them?"

Ben lifted the glasses to his eyes, focusing on the naked figures that crouched there, shading their eyes, peering reluctantly into the brightness of the valley. Compared to the men from the raft, these were smaller and more wiry, their bodies flecked with scars, their eyes large and bulging in their bony heads. He had seen their like before, fattened up and dressed in the fine silks of the Above, but never like this; never in their natural state.

Even so, it was not that that excited him, looking at them. It was something else. Ben shivered, then nodded to himself, knowing that it was true what had been said. Sealed into the darkness, the Clay had reverted, its inhabitants regressed ten, twenty thousand years, to a time before cities and books. In these Clay-men there was no refinement, no culture, unless pure instinct was the ultimate refinement.

They were like animals. Thinking animals. Or like some strange genetic throwback. Ben grinned, the old words coming to his lips.

> Man . . . who trusted God was love indeed
> And love Creation's final law—
> Tho' Nature, red in tooth and claw
> With ravine, shrieked against his creed.

"What is that?" Meg asked, pulling him down, afraid he would be seen.

"Tennyson. Though what the old bugger would have made of this . . ." His voice trailed off. "Look. They're going back inside. Good. For a moment I thought Tewl might have persuaded them, but they're going to sit it out after all."

He turned his head, smiling at her, then began to get up. "Come on, then, Megs. There's no time to lose. Twelve hours we've got. Twelve hours to do it all!"

———————

THE GRASS had grown tall before the old barn. Huge swaths of nettle and wildflowers blocked the entrance, forming a barrier fifteen feet wide in front of it. Ben threw the sack down and knelt, pulling out the ancient scythe and testing its edge on a nearby blade of grass. Then, stripping to the waist, he set to work.

Watching him, Meg was reminded strongly of her father. How often she had watched him standing there, just so, his body moving effortlessly from the hips, like one of Adam's sons in the early morning of the world.

She studied him, seeing how he moved, like some mindless, perfect automaton. Saw the green fall before the silver, and frowned.

He turned, throwing the scythe down, a broad path cleared in front of the big double doors.

"I don't understand," she said, looking past him at the dilapidated old building. "If we've only got twelve hours . . ."

"Illusions," he said, meeting her eyes. "Surely you of all people should know how fond old Amos was of illusions. This . . ." he turned, indicating the barn, "is just another of them. Come . . ."

Ben went up on tiptoe, placing his eye against a dark whorled knot in one of the wooden planks, as if trying to see inside. There was the faintest sound, like the soughing of the wind through the grass, and then he stepped back, lifting the rusted latch and easing one of the huge doors back.

Inside was brightness, cleanliness. She stepped past Ben, wide-eyed with astonishment. It was a storehouse, a huge storehouse, packed with all manner of things. Six broad shelves lined the wall opposite, while at the far end, to her left, a number of large machines squatted on the white-tiled floor.

She went across, the smell of machine oil and antiseptic strong in that big, high-ceilinged room. Under the glare of the overhead lights she pulled one of the plain white trays from the second shelf. Inside, sealed in see-through plastic and neatly labeled, were a dozen mortar bombs. She glanced at one of the labels, noting the familiar oak tree logo and the date, then looked closer, surprised to find Ben's handwriting on the label.

Ben's? No. She noted the initials—"A.S."—and understood. Amos. Great-great-great-grandfather Amos.

Quickly she looked, going from tray to tray. Rope ladders, absailing harnesses and power-packs, land mines, mortars and ammunition, handguns and rifles, rocket launchers, flash bombs and hunting knives, decontamination suits, bulletproof vests and gas masks. And more. Much, much more. The supplies of war, all of it neatly parceled in see-through plastic with Amos's neat handwriting on the label.

She turned. Ben was standing by the door, looking through a hard-covered file marked "Manifold."

"What is this, Ben?"

He hung the Manifold back on the peg by the door, then looked across at her. "This? This is the intestines of the beast."

He walked across, his boots clicking on the dust-free tiles, and pulled down two sleds from where they hung on the end wall, bringing them back across.

"Here," he said, handing her the smaller of the two. "I want a rocket launcher, a dozen shells, two handguns, one rifle with ammunition—better make it two hundred rounds—two lightweight gas masks, a dozen flash bombs, and two of those vests."

She stared at him in disbelief. "What are we doing, Ben? What in Christ's name are we doing?"

"We're being Shepherds, Meg, that's all. Making preparations. Now come on. You said you'd help."

She watched as he drew the big sled across and began to load it, pulling down things from the shelves as if he knew where everything was.

"You've been in here before, haven't you?"

"No."

"Then how did you know about all this?"

He reached up and took a long, dark package from the shelf, placing it in the sled, then looked back at her. "This place has defenses no one knows about but us. We Shepherds have been preparing for this for near on two hundred years now."

It was not the words so much as how he said them. That "us"

seemed to exclude her. Seemed somehow masculine. *"We Shepherds . . ."*

She turned away from him, facing the shelves once more, doing as he'd asked, filling the sled with guns and bombs and bullets, her mind strangely detached from what she was doing. She had read the passages in Amos's journal: had read about his preparations for the Great Third War he believed was coming, but never for a moment had she thought all this existed.

The intestines of the beast . . .

She shuddered, then looked down again, checking the handwritten label, ensuring she had the right ammunition for the rifle.

THE CUT TURF was laid neatly on its back, beside the dark square of earth. Nearby, forming a staggered line across the lower garden, a further five patches showed black against the green.

Meg stood over Ben, watching him take two of the small devices from the bag at his shoulder, noting how carefully he embedded them in the earth. Earlier he had shown her how the flash bombs worked, going through the remote-trigger sequence twice, to make sure she understood.

"Hopefully we won't have to use them," he said, setting the turf back firmly and looking up at her. "The speakers should do the trick. But if you have to, don't hesitate. And remember, the object is to take the little buggers alive. We use force only as a last resort."

She looked back at the cottage. It was late afternoon now, but most of it was done. Using special panels from the storehouse, they had sealed the kitchen end and the dining room, and blocked the stairway, leaving only the entrance to the living room free, the door down to the cellar open. Helping Ben fix the screens over the doors and windows, she had understood for the first time what all the fastenings on the frames were for. From childhood she had thought them merely decoration, but now she knew. It was as Ben had said. Amos had prepared thoroughly for this day.

We Shepherds . . .

He handed her the bag. "Here. You do the rest. I'll finish off in the cellar."

She nodded, standing there a moment, watching him return inside, then turned back, facing the water. It was only three hours now until sunset. The thought of it made her throat constrict, her stomach muscles tighten with fear, but she had said nothing to Ben. Not that it would have made any difference.

"Well, fuck you, Ben Shepherd," she said quietly, moving across to the next of the cut squares and kneeling down, the awkward shape of the handgun pressing into her side. "Fuck you and Amos and all your pigheaded breed."

▬▬▬▬

"Ben?"

He turned, looking back at her from the saddle of the old green bicycle. "What?"

"What if they come while you're gone? What should I do?"

"They won't," he said, reaching back to check the towrope. "Besides, I'll be back before it's dark. But if it makes you feel any better, why don't you go up to the old church and sit on the wall. You get a good view of things from there. And if they *do* come, you can hide in the tower until I get back. Okay?"

She nodded reluctantly, watching him draw the pedal back, preparing to set off. "Ben. . . ?"

He laughed. "What now?"

"Take care."

He smiled, then was gone, his strong legs powering him up the steep slope between the hedges, the tightly packed sled rattling along behind him on its casters.

Ten minutes later he was on the level above the ferry road. Resting the bike against the wall by the old postbox, he unfastened the sled and, letting it run on in front, made his way down to the landing stage.

The rowboat was where he had left it ten days before. Loading the sled into the middle of the long, narrow boat, he pushed it out into the shallow water, then jumped aboard, picking up the oars and setting to, pulling himself across the narrow strait.

The path up to the old railway track was difficult, the stone steps slippery, overgrown in places. The sled seemed to grow heavier as he climbed, more awkward, but finally he was there, fifty feet above the river, the ancient track stretching away between the trees.

He set the sled down, slotting the groove in its base onto the rail, then squatted down, taking the slender case of the comset from his back and unfolding it. Activating the screen, he quickly checked on the remotes. In front of the breached seal there was no activity. Out on the raft armada, however, there was plenty. Five of the smaller, steam-powered rafts were being prepared, stockpiles of precious fuel being loaded on board, along with great stacks of weapons—crude spears, swords, and clubs for the main part.

Satisfied, he switched the comset off and secured it to his back. Then, attaching the towrope to his belt, he set off once more, running between the tracks, heading south toward the guardhouse, the sled sliding smoothly along behind him.

THE SLED LAY to his right, hidden in the dense undergrowth. Above him, some twenty-five feet up the embankment, was the blockhouse, its windows lit up brightly. From where Ben lay, the assault rifle held against his chest, he could see that one of the windows was open. From within, music spilled out into the air. It was the *Yueh Erh Kao*, "The Moon on High."

For a moment he found himself distracted; found himself wondering what it was like to be a guard—a Han—here in this strange land, listening to this most Chinese of melodies, and thinking of home. Of China, half a world away. What did that feel like?

He listened, knowing that he was wasting time, but unable to move, the music touching him as it had never done before. Breaching him. He looked up, his eyes finding the pale circle of the moon, there, like a ghost in the early evening sky.

The moon. He closed his eyes and saw it, full and bright, like a hole in the darkness, and saw, at the same moment, its negative, there at the valley's far end, the Clay-men huddled beyond it, waiting to emerge.

The moon . . .

Opening his eyes, he felt a pain of longing pass through him. A longing to be something else—something *other* than he was. To be a Han, a river pirate, a Clayborn. To be . . .

To be other than he was . . . Yes, that was it. That was what drove him on.

He turned slightly, looking out across the valley, for the briefest moment held by the beauty of what he saw. In the fading light, a flock of birds seemed to float in the air above the river, the tiny specks of their bodies folding back upon themselves time and again, like a veil fluttering in the breeze. How many times had he seen that? How many times had he looked and not seen the beauty in it?

The music ended. He turned back, beginning to climb. In the sudden silence he could sense the stillness of the valley all about him. Could feel it waiting, like a lover, for the darkness.

There was the murmur of voices from above. Han voices. And then music, the sound of strings and flutes—of *p'i p'a*, *yueh ch'in*, *ti tsu*, and *erhu*—echoing out across the English valley, reminding Ben of that moment, eight years before, when Li Shai Tung had sat at table with them, his carved ivory face in strong contrast with the simple English-ness of everything surrounding him.

The world we've made, he thought, edging toward the open window.

He pulled himself up, slowly, carefully, until he stood there, his back to the wall, the window to his right. Again he waited, listening, letting the song play itself out. Then, in the silence that followed, he moved closer, looking in at an angle through the open window.

The voices came again, but he understood now. A radio rested on the cluttered desk beside the window. Beyond it the room was empty.

Slowly he moved his head around, looking in, searching the big room with his eyes, the gun raised, ready.

No, not empty. There, on the floor in the far corner, lay one body, and there, behind the table to the right, was another. But there were five guards in all. Where were the others?

Coming around the corner of the blockhouse, he had his answer. A trestle table had been set up in front of the main doors. A jug of wine rested at its center. Chairs and broken wine bowls lay scattered all about it.

One guard lay slightly down the embankment, on his back, his mouth open in surprise. Another still sat in his chair, a neat hole through his forehead. Nearby, in the doorway itself, a third was slumped against the wall.

Ben walked toward the scene, his eyes taking in everything. He had known these men. Only yesterday they had sat behind the barrier and applauded him. And now they were dead.

He stood before the man in the chair, looking down at him. His name was Brock and he had been shot from close range. Ben put the rifle down and crouched, studying the wound, then moved behind the dead man, examining the mess the bullet's exit had made, putting his fingers into the shattered cranium. The flesh was cold, the blood congealed.

He went through, examining the bodies in the guardhouse, then came out again, looking about him, picturing it in his mind. The duty guard, Cook, had been strangled at his desk, the other, Tu Mai, had been knifed in the back. Had one man done that? An officer, perhaps? Someone they had no reason to suspect? Whoever it was, he would have had to have killed the duty guard first, quickly, silently, and then Tu Mai, gagging the young Han with a hand, perhaps, as he dragged him down.

Ben turned. Yes, and he would have needed to have had the door closed while he did it, too, else he'd have been seen by the men at the table.

He closed his eyes, seeing it clearly. The officer had come out and turned, facing Brock, drawing his gun, giving Brock no time to get up out of his chair. He had fired once, then turned to shoot the second guard, Coates. The last of them, the young lieutenant, Mo Yu, had backed away, stumbling back over the embankment. He had been shot where he fell.

Ben frowned, wondering why he had not heard the shots, then understood. He and Meg must have been down in the cellar, getting things ready. Which meant this had happened two, three hours ago at most.

But why? Unless, perhaps, Virtanen knew that Tewl planned to go in early. Knew and was using that to firm up his alibi. Ben had checked. These five were all that remained of the old guard. The others—in the guardhouses in the town and at the mouth of the river—were Virtanen's men.

Yes, it all made sense. This was the communications post for the valley: the Domain's main—if not only—link with the outside. Virtanen, questioned by an inquiry, would claim that Tewl's men had attacked and overrun it. Which meant in all probability that Virtanen intended to delay only long enough for Tewl's men to be successful before he counterattacked, sweeping the intruders from the valley, strengthening the evidence in his favor.

All of which put pressure on Ben to tie things up quickly. The question was, how long would Virtanen delay? An hour? Two?

He went back inside. The duty officer's log lay there on the communications desk in the corner. It was open, the last entry noted but not initialed. Frowning, Ben scanned the record quickly. It was as he'd thought. They had to call in every four hours.

Every four hours . . . And yet the last message had been sent out thirty minutes back.

Virtanen? Had Virtanen himself been here? It was unlikely. No, in all likelihood Virtanen was at dinner right now, somewhere public and in the company of important people—*ch'un tzu* of the first level. Some place where he could be reached "urgently" and summoned back to deal with this. Where he might make a great show of his concern, his "anxiety" for the Shepherds.

No. Not Virtanen, but one of his servants. One of his Captains, perhaps. Someone who could sit there for two hours with the bodies of the men he'd butchered, waiting to send a signal.

Ben closed the log, then set to work, doing what he'd come to do. Moving back and forth between the sled, he positioned a dozen of the big flash bombs along the shore beneath the guardhouse, setting their remote-trigger combinations. Then, climbing up onto the roof of the blockhouse, he set up the two wide-angle cameras, focusing one upon the quayside, the other on the mouth of the river, looking out beyond the anchored junks.

Finished, he looked up, noting how high the moon had climbed since he'd last looked, how bright it had become. The light was dying. In thirty minutes it would be dark.

He turned, looking back at the silent figures on the terrace outside the blockhouse. It was strange how little he felt. He had liked the men, enjoyed their company, but now that they were dead he felt no sadness, no sense of outrage. It was almost as if . . . well, as if they were merely machines now, like the morphs he used, or like Amos's automatons that peopled the town across the river. Whatever had animated them was gone. Had flown, like frightened birds.

No, what he felt wasn't sadness, or pity, but a fascination with their newly transformed state. A curiosity that was as powerful as it was new.

What was it like to be dead? Was it simple nullity? Or was there more to it than that? Placing his fingers within the guard's shattered skull, he had felt something wake in him; something dark and ageless.

He laughed, a strange, uncertain laugh, then bent down, picking up the rope. *Darkness*, he thought, setting off once more, making his way back down the slope toward the track. *Ultimately there is nothing but the dark.*

━━━━━

THE MOON was high. Ben stood among the gravestones in the churchyard, looking out past his sister at the broad sweep of the valley. Beneath them, the houses of the village fell away, following the steep curve of the road in a jumble of thatched roofs and chimney pots, their pale white walls gleaming brightly beneath the circle of the moon. Beyond lay the river, a broken sheet of silvered blackness, flanked by the soft roundness of the hills. Hills overshadowed by the vast, glacial presence of the City.

Meg sat on the old stone wall, her feet dangling out over the drop, her dark hair lustrous in the moonlight. It had been dark now for almost fifteen minutes, but still there was no word from Tewl, no sign of the intruders in the valley.

"What do you think it's like in there?"

"I don't know," he answered quietly. "Like hell, I guess."

She half turned, looking back at him. "I mean, what do they eat? Nothing grows in there. So how do they survive?"

"Insects," he said, smiling at her. "And slugs and other small things that crawl in from the outside." *And one another*, he thought, but didn't say it.

"It must be awful," she said, turning back. "The most awful thing there is. To be trapped in there. To know nothing but that."

"Maybe," he said, but her comment made him realize just how much the Clay was like his Shells. There, too, one was confined, cut off from normal life. In such conditions the senses grew hungry for stimulation—for the sweet water of dream and illusion. The mind was thrown inward. Untended, it fed upon itself, like the monsters of the deep.

He rested his good hand on the stone beside him. A tall, leprously pale stone, its tapered surface spotted with mold. "I wonder what they dream about?"

"Do you think they dream?"

He nodded, his fingers tracing the weathered lettering on the ancient stone. "I'm sure of it. Why, the darkness must be filled with dreams. Vivid, lurid dreams. Imagine it, Meg. Eternal night. Eternal blackness. Waking they must see their dreams. Live them."

"I'd go mad," she said quietly.

"Yes . . ." But there were many kinds of madness. And was the City really so different? In some ways the Clay seemed far healthier. There, at least, they dreamed. Up above, in the glare of that eternal artificial light, they had forgotten how to dream. Or when they did, their dreams were pale and powerless; had shrunk to a ghostly insubstantiality, worn down by the relentless onslaught of a thousand cheap illusions, ten thousand bright distractions.

One needed darkness. One needed the respite of dream. Else life was but a mechanism.

He shivered, Shakespeare's words coming suddenly to mind. *If I must die, I will encounter darkness as a bride, And hug it in mine arms.*

Meg turned to him, suddenly impatient. "Why don't they come? What are they waiting for? I thought you said they'd come when it was dark."

"Soon," he said, soothing her, his good hand reaching out to touch and hold her cheek. "They'll come here soon." And even as he said it he heard the insect buzz of voices in the earpiece, the gruff sound of Tewl giving his instructions.

"Wait," he said, his hand going to her shoulder and squeezing it. "At last. They're coming out."

Moving past her, he jumped up onto the wall and, spreading his arms, leapt out into the darkness as if embracing it, landing in the long grass a dozen feet below.

"Come on!" he called, turning to her, his moonlit face alive with a strange excitement. "Quickly now!" And, turning away, he began to run full tilt down the steep slope of the meadow, heading for the sea.

CHAPTER FIFTEEN

Nature Red in
Tooth and Claw

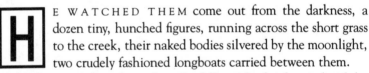

HE WATCHED THEM come out from the darkness, a
dozen tiny, hunched figures, running across the short grass
to the creek, their naked bodies silvered by the moonlight,
two crudely fashioned longboats carried between them.

As they ran, they glanced up fearfully at the bright circle of the
moon, astonished to find it there, and, gritting their teeth, fought
down the urge to flee from its all-seeing glare.

They set the boats down at the water's edge, then crouched, huddled close together in the space between the canoes, staring back at
the hole. A full minute passed and then a second, larger wave of Clay-
men emerged, slowly, hesitantly, looking anxiously about them at the
silvered darkness of the valley. Some turned and tried to flee, back
into the dark, but one of their number stood before the hole, a dagger
in one hand, a whip in the other.

"There," Ben said softly, pointing him out to Meg, who was
crouched beside him behind the low stonewall, the glasses to her eyes.
"That one there. He must be the chief. Look how he's gathering them
up. And see, at his waist. There's the handset he was using."

"They're all so ugly," Meg whispered, lowering the glasses. "There's
one there has had half his face eaten away. You can see the shape of
the skull. And there's another who's got only a stump for an arm."

Her voice fell silent. In the silvered dark below, the Clay-men moved slowly across the open ground between the wall and the creek, their shadowed forms like broken fragments of the darkness.

For a moment the silence was complete. Then, from the center of that shadowy host came the crisp chatter of the handset. Standing toward the back of the group, the chief froze, surprised by the voice at his waist. He twitched, then, looking about him, lifted the handset to his ear, holding it there as if, at any moment, it would bite. All about him, his men had stopped, crouched low, as if to press themselves into the earth. There was a moment's silence, and then the chief answered, his voice low and guttural.

"It's Tewl," Ben whispered, leaning toward his sister, translating what he could hear of the exchange. "He's telling the Clay-men to get a move on. But the chief's not budging. He's saying they didn't know there'd be a moon. It's spooked them. They thought it would be black, like inside. He's telling Tewl his men need time, to get used to it."

"So what's going to happen, Ben? Are they going to attack?"

"Yes. But this makes things tight. It looks like Tewl's boats have set off already. The tide's against them, fortunately. Even so, unless we deal with this end of things quickly, we won't get to the harbor in time."

"In time for what?" she asked, staring at him, curious now.

"For the show," he said, looking back at her, the moon's bright circle reflected clearly in the liquid darkness of his pupils.

"The show?"

"I . . ." Ben fell silent. Down below, the chief had finished talking and had tucked the handset back into his belt. Looking about him, he picked out six of his men, then pointed up the hill toward the cottage.

"*A-wartha!*" he said fiercely, thrusting his hand out once again, as if to emphasize what he was saying. "*An chy. Kherdes! Tenna dhe an chy!*"

"What is it?" Meg asked, a ripple of fear passing down her spine at the sound of that awful, bestial tongue; at the threat implicit in that thrusting, grasping hand. "What did he say?"

But it was as if Ben hadn't heard her. "Come on," he said, touching her arm. "Quick now. We've work to do." And, ducking down, he turned and started back toward the cottage, his body hunched, his movements almost furtive, mimicking the figures who, even as Meg looked back, peeled off from the main body of the Clay-men and started up the slope toward her.

━━━〰〰〰〰〰━━━

THEY CAME ON slowly, sniffing the air like dogs, their short, wiry bodies hunched low and twitchingly alert as they approached the cottage. In the shadows of the lower garden they stopped, huddled together, the low growl of their voices carrying to where Meg lay in her perch above the potting shed, watching.

Like a pack, she thought, as one of them—a bull terrier of a man— leaned over one of the others, his head twisted slightly, as if to bite the neck of the creature. Nearby, the rest looked on, making cringing gestures of abasement, like the young wolves she had seen in the film Ben had shown her.

She shivered, her hands trembling as she widened the angle of the shot. It was a wonder they still used language, their gestures were so eloquent. It was just as Ben had said. Their bodies spoke.

Do as I say, the leader seemed to be saying. *Don't have any ideas of your own.*

She watched the other stoop and lick the creature's hand subserviently, then straighten up, his face filled with a pathetic eagerness.

"*Ena . . .*" The terrier-man said, pointing at the cottage. "*Ena ha ena!*"

There was a moment's hesitation, and then they came on again, spreading out as they approached the earth border of the rose garden. *Two more steps*, she thought, remembering what Ben had said. Two more steps . . .

The whispering began.

At first it was like the wind rustling through the leaves of an ancient, autumnal forest; a dry, soughing noise that seemed half-articulate. Yet if there were words amid that sound, they were as much imagined as discerned. Then, as the noise grew slowly louder, the clear hard shape of words formed from the confusion, like seeds falling to the earth.

"*Of ancow . . .*"

The Clay-men froze, half turned toward the sound, their eyes wide with sudden fear.

"*Of ancow . . .*"

A low moan rose from the dark, huddled shapes on the slope. Yelping, they threw themselves down, burrowing into the earth, as if to merge with the darkness, but the moonlight was unrelenting; it beat down on them mercilessly, pitilessly, forcing them to turn their heads and look back at it.

"*Gwelaf why gans ow onen lagas . . .*" the voice whispered, as if from the air itself. "*Ow golow lagas dewana why!*"

There were barks of fear and whimperings and a long, low moaning that was horrible to hear, like the sound of an animal in pain.

"*Ow enawy a-vyn podrethes agas eskern . . .*"

At that the whimpering grew frantic. The Clay-men were baying now, in torment, their fear so great that Meg could sense it from where she lay; could smell its sharp, distinct odor in the air. Their squat, ugly faces were distorted now, like the faces of the mad she had glimpsed in her brother's sketchbooks. Fear had given way to something else—to some darker, more primeval force.

For the briefest moment she hesitated, filled with a sudden, unexpected sympathy for the creatures, then, quivering slightly, not knowing what to expect, she pressed the switch.

The air beyond the Clay-men shimmered. And then, as if forming from the air itself, four massive figures stood there, palely outlined against the dark. Four ancient, ghostly warriors, their armored breastplates glinting in the moonlight, long, wicked-looking blades in their mailed fists. And their faces . . .

Meg shuddered, recognizing them. Ox and lion, they were, man and eagle, their features harsh and unforgiving. *Angels*, she thought, glimpsing the great wings—six in all—that rose from their broad, muscular backs. *Ben has conjured up the angels . . .*

Briefly they stood there, powerful and malevolent, and then, as one, they stepped forward, raising their swords.

"*Dyesk-ynna!*" said the Ox-faced angel, beckoning the Clay-men, his voice booming like thunder in the silence. "*Dyesk-ynna!*"

Until that moment the Clay-men had crouched there, paralyzed by the sight, but now, their nerve broken, they turned and ran, shrieking, toward the safety of the cottage.

And Meg, watching, ran with them in her head, her spine tingling with a fear she had never, ever thought to feel.

"I know your works," she said softly, fearfully. "You have the name of being alive, and you are dead."

———

MEG SAT at the bottom of the cellar steps, watching through the tight-fitting mask as her brother bound the last of the unconscious Clay-men. Beyond him stood the morph, inactive now, the nozzle of the empty gas cylinder dangling loosely from its polished hand.

Ben turned, smiling up at her through his mask. "There," he said, the words muffled. "All we have to do now is get them upstairs, into the small barn, then we can get down to the town."

"Upstairs?" She shivered. Even the thought of touching one of the grotesque, childlike creatures horrified her, let alone lifting and carrying one. "Can't we leave them here?"

He shook his head. "I can't risk it, Megs. Think of the damage they'd do down here if one of them got loose. Up there it doesn't matter. The small barn is secure, and there's nothing they can damage."

"Isn't there something you can give them to keep them out a bit longer? You know . . . a drug or something?"

"And if it killed them? No, Megs, I can't risk that. I want these . . . these *men*. I need them for my work. That's why I bothered with all this, so as not to harm them."

She looked away, finding no words to explain her aversion.

He smiled. "Look, I'll put them in sacks, if you like. If that makes it any easier. But it has to be done. And the sooner the better. Now, are you going to help me, or do I have to do it all on my own?"

"I'll help," she said, finally, meeting his eyes again. "But not this, Ben. I can't. I simply can't."

He studied her a moment, then, with the tiniest little nod, turned away. Bending over one of the limp Clay-men, he lifted it, balancing it over his left shoulder. Then, stooping to lift another, he draped its wiry frame over the other shoulder before turning to face her again.

"The keys are hanging by the door. Go ahead and open up, then get your brown waist-length coat and a bicycle from the shed. Wait for me by the postbox above the ferry road. I'll be there as quickly as I can."

She nodded, knowing he was disappointed in her, but for once there was nothing she could do. Nothing in heaven or earth would make her touch one of them. Nothing. Not even Ben's disapproval.

"Okay," she said. "But don't be long, Ben. Please. I couldn't bear it if they attacked me. I just couldn't."

"No," he said, his face softening. "Nor I."

MEG STOOD there on the veranda of the old naval college, looking out across the river. At the foot of the hill, the water stretched away to either side, a broad, uneven sheet of moonlit darkness, its reflective brightness framed by the solidity of the hills. To her left, beyond the scar of the Old Mill Creek, the dark flank of the land hid any sign of the village and the cottage beyond. It was there, on the far bank, that the darkness was most intense, the primal blackness of the woods pressed against the water's edge threateningly. To the south—to her right as she turned, looking out across its sprawl—the lamps of the old town glowed in the dark, each point of light distinct. Beyond it the castle was dour and solid on its rock foundations, guarding the river's mouth. Fishing boats were clustered in the old harbor, their masts like winter saplings. Close by, lying alongside the cobbled quay, the big merchantman rested at anchor, its sails furled, the oil lamps that ringed its hull forming a necklace of light in the surrounding water.

All seemed well. All seemed . . . *familiar*. And yet, just beneath where she stood, on the far side of the river, the Clay-men were waiting, their log canoes tucked in against the bank, beneath the overhanging trees.

She turned back, looking to see how Ben was getting on. He was standing before the middle of the three big control panels, the porta-ble harness he was wearing making him seem strangely inhuman—more machine than man. To his right, concealed from the river by the wall of the veranda, a bank of screens—four wide, three deep—gave a dozen different views of the valley.

In many ways it was all as before. The cameras were in place, the tapes rolling. Lights winked and flickered on the boards. Nearby, on the flat top of the tape-storage unit, one of the big notebooks lay open, Ben's neat hand covering the pages. Outwardly there seemed little difference between this and other times. Yet what she felt was different. Was as distinct as it could possibly be.

And why was that? Why was the thought of this—of *using* this situation—so disturbing? Was it simply personal fear, or was it something much deeper than that? Something she couldn't face without questioning all that Ben did, all he *was*?

She studied her brother, as if to discern some difference in him, something she had never noticed before that moment, but there was nothing. He had always been like this: a lens, taking it all in. Assimilating and transforming it. Recasting the world in his own dark image.

As now.

"That's it," he said, straightening up. "All we need now is to position the cameras properly and we're ready."

She nodded, yet for once she felt herself distanced from him, out of sympathy with what he did. Before it had all been a game: endlessly fascinating, yet a game for all that. Now it was real. Real men would be hurt down there. Real blood spilled. And yet Ben acted as if the game went on. As if there really *was* no difference.

"Take number three," he said, not even glancing at her, his eyes fixed on what was happening on the screens. "I want a tight focus on the quay in front of the inn."

She went across, adjusting the position of the camera until she heard him grunt his satisfaction.

"Good. Now two."

"Ben?"

He looked across at her, distracted. "What?"

"What are we doing, Ben? Why do you need this?"

His eyes met hers, then quickly moved away. It was the briefest of contacts, but it was long enough for her to understand. He didn't know. And the not-knowing was why. Was a reason in itself.

She shivered, then looked past him, noticing for the first time the rocket launcher that lay on the grass beside their bicycles, its brutal heaviness emphasized by the thick leather strap.

"Two," he said again. "Please, Meg. We don't have much time."

She did as she was told, focusing in on the tiny crowd that stood in front of the old Castle Hotel, drinking.

Drinking . . . Or pretending to drink. Just as they pretended to think and breathe and talk. It was all one vast pretense. And Ben behind it all, working his dead puppets for all he was worth.

Dead, she thought. *It's all dead. And maybe that's why he needs this. To bring it alive. To give it breath and substance.* But somehow the explanation didn't satisfy. Her unease remained, and with it a growing feeling that she should have defied Ben and called Tolonen in. But now it was too late.

"Look," Ben said quietly, pointing up at the top right-hand screen. "There, beyond the junks."

She went and stood behind him, watching as the first of the steam-powered rafts came into view, laboring through the water, its deck packed with dark and threatening shapes. Seeing it, she felt her fear return; a sharp, cold thing that seemed to sap her will. How could they fight these creatures? How prevail against such odds?

"Let's hear what they're saying," Ben said, reaching out to touch one of the pads on the panel beneath the screens. At once a soft, guttural murmuring began. Hearing it, Meg shivered and turned her head, looking up at the moon. *What if it all ends here?* she thought. *What if it all goes wrong?*

But Ben was clearly harboring no doubts. "Okay," he said, turning to her. "It's just as I thought. They're going for a frontal assault on the town. The Clay-men have been told to land just upriver of the merchantman, the raft people farther down, by the steps of the old Customs House. Tewl plans a pincer movement. He wants to herd all of the townspeople into one place, then deal with them there."

"So what's going to happen? What will you do?"

Ben smiled. "My morphs are going to fight."

"Fight? But how can they? They're not programmed to fight!"

"Of course they are. We've choreographed more than eighty different moves."

She stared at him, astonished that he couldn't see it. "Yes, but . . . well, those others won't be programmed, will they? They'll do things that are . . . unexpected."

"That's right."

"But they'll cut them to ribbons!"

"Maybe. Some of them, anyway. But not all. I'll be working some of them through the harness here. The big tar, for instance, and the Han with the limp. And others too. Switching from body to body. Hitting back where they least expect it."

Meg frowned, trying to understand, to work out what he wanted from this madness, but there wasn't time. Ben had turned and was leaning across the central board, making minuscule adjustments to the settings, while across the river, in the deep shadow beneath the overhanging trees, two canoes were pushing off from the bank, moving with silvered quickness across the darkness of the water.

THERE WERE SHOUTS in the valley. Hideous, unearthly sounds. On the cobbles outside the ancient coaching inn, the crowd fell silent, looking across the harbor toward the quay beyond. There, in the shadow of the three-masted merchantman, two figures were struggling beneath the lamp, as if locked in an embrace. For a moment there was only that, and then, like demons crawling from a gap in hell itself, a dozen of the Clay-men appeared over the lip of the river wall, whooping and screeching, their dark, stooped figures making for the town.

There were shouts, the first murmurings of panic, and then the crowd broke, some running toward the merchantman, but most to the right and the safety of the Customs House. These last had not gone far when a group of savage-looking creatures—maybe half a dozen in all—burst from the shadows of one of the seafront houses, confronting them. Big, crudely armored men with notched swords and vicious-looking clubs.

"Back!" someone shouted. "Get help from the inn! There's weapons there!" But even as the shout went up, the invaders rushed the front of the crowd, laying about them savagely. Screams filled the air. Awful, pitiful screams, like the sounds of real men dying.

At first the crowd was forced back by the viciousness of the onslaught, several of them falling beneath the rain of blows, their limbs hacked from their bodies or their skulls crushed by hammer blows, but then, encouraged by the efforts of the young watchman from the castle, they began to fight back. Using whatever weapons they had at hand, they began to push the raft-men back step by step toward the Customs House. Yet even as they did, more of the raft-men joined the raiding party, swarming up the steps and out onto the lamp-lit quay.

Observing it all from the safety of her vantage point above the town, Meg set the glasses down and turned, facing her brother.

For a moment she watched as Ben kicked and swung, then ducked and came up sharply, aiming a vicious punch into the air, his eyes never leaving the screen in front of him. Down below, she knew, on the cobbles before the Customs House, the morph of the watchman would have kicked and swung, then ducked and come up quickly, aiming a vicious punch, his movements the perfect duplicate of Ben's.

She shivered, frightened by the sight; by the sheer physicality of it, the uncompromising violence of each movement. "There's too many of them," she said quietly. "Your plan will never work, Ben. They'll overwhelm the morphs before there's time."

"Wait," he answered, moving back slightly, his eyes never leaving the screen even as his hands made small adjustments to the control panel at his side. "It's far from over yet."

She saw him lift his arm, as if to ward off a blow, then duck and twist, as if he threw a figure through the air. From the town below, the shouts and screams continued.

The screens were alive with activity. Close-ups of flailing arms and agonized faces were juxtaposed against long-range shots of tiny figures struggling beneath the harbor lamps. Metal bit deep into flesh—some real, some *made*—while blood flew like the spray of some dark fountain.

Close up and context, she thought, swallowing, recalling the number of times they had done this kind of thing with the morphs. But this time it was different. This time it was real. Or half real, anyway.

She studied the varied images of the struggle. The Clay-men had been held on the quay beside the merchantman. In the opening moments of the fight, Ben had had the crew pour down the wooden ramps and throw themselves at their attackers, the morphs lashing out in a frenzy. At first they'd been successful and several of the Clay had gone down, badly hurt, but things were turning fast. More than thirty of the morphs lay there on the quay now, inert or badly damaged, while a dozen or more floated facedown in the water below. Less than half their number remained standing. In a minute or two, they would be overwhelmed, the left flank lost.

Meg turned back, lifting the glasses to her eyes, trying to make out what was happening elsewhere. One of the strange, steam-driven rafts was docked beside the Customs House steps. Out on the river, four more of the rafts formed a staggered line across the water, their dark shapes drifting slowly in toward the shore. The second was no more than fifty yards out now, yet unless the first raft moved it would be hard for the raft-men to disembark.

Unless they used the ferry ramp.

She turned slightly, focusing on the raft. There was feverish activity on board; a great deal of pointing and shouting. As she looked, one of the warriors—the steersman, maybe—slapped one of his fellows down, then, jabbing his finger in the direction of the ramp, forced the two rudder men to bring the unwieldy craft hard about. She watched as the raft swung slowly around, avoiding the moored craft narrowly as it made for the gap in the wall.

For a moment it glided in, the prow perfectly positioned for the ramp, then, suddenly, there was a huge explosion.

Meg felt her chest tighten. In the echoing silence that followed she could hear the splashing of things falling back into the water. Could see the tiny shapes of stone and metal, flesh and splintered bone, falling, tumbling through the broken darkness.

On the quay beside the Customs House the fight had stopped. The raiders staggered back, staring out at the falling wreckage, horrified.

"What happened?" Meg asked, thinking for a moment that the raft's boiler must have gone up. But when she turned, she saw that Ben was smiling, and understood. He had mined it. Mined the ferry ramp.

Sympathy, that was it. That was what he lacked. That was the thing her father, Hal, had had, and he, Ben, did not. The thing she had looked for and not found in him, that moment before the old barn, watching him use the scythe. Simple human sympathy.

Ben clenched his palm, briefly breaking the circuit that connected him to the watchman as he took three paces back. Then, unclenching, he let out a bloodcurdling yell, and half ran, half lunged at the screens.

From the town below, she heard the echoing yell the watchman gave, the high, chilling scream of a badly wounded man, and turned to look. One of the raft-men was down, on his knees, the watchman's sword embedded to its hilt in his chest.

"Ben . . ." she whispered, feeling a shiver of pain pass through her. "What in God's name are you doing, Ben?"

But he was unaware of her. As she watched, the sky lit up again. The junks moored in the middle of the river had burst into flames and were swinging around into the path of the last of the rafts. She heard the shouts of panic, the splashes as some of the raft people threw themselves over the side, but for most of them it was too late. As the first of the junks collided with the raft, a rain of embers and burning cloth fell over it, smothering the craft in a great sheet of roaring flame.

Meg groaned, appalled.

On all sides the morphs were getting up from where they lay, crawling and limping, hobbling or simply dragging themselves toward their foes, ignoring the blows that rained down on them as they threw themselves at their attackers, struggling to subdue them.

In front of the Customs House, the young watchman had sunk to his knees, his head hacked cleanly from his shoulders. Yet even as he toppled over, another of the townsfolk took his place—a big, corpulent-looking fellow that Meg recognized instantly as the inn-keeper. With a bellow, the innkeeper swung his sword about his head and brought it down savagely, an inhuman strength cleaving the astonished raft-man from temple to waist.

At that a great cry went up. Until moments before it had all been going well for the attackers, but now two of their rafts were lost, and instead of timid townsfolk, they found themselves faced by demons. Men who did not lie there, as the dead were supposed to, but stood and joined the fight once more, not heeding the frightful wounds they'd suffered.

Out on the river, the rafts were turning, heading back toward the river's mouth and the safety of the sea. They had seen with their own eyes how things were shaping. Even Tewl, who had stood there on the prow of the third raft watching, gave a small shudder and turned away. "*Nag-us genys*," he was heard to mutter. "*Ny harth o mlath nag-us genys.*"

The unborn . . . We cannot fight the unborn . . .

"Enough!" Meg said, angry with him suddenly. "For God's sake, Ben, *enough!*"

But Ben could not hear her. Ben jumped and kicked and spun, fighting the air, his eyes transfixed, chained to the images on the screens.

IT WAS OVER. The captives were huddled in the space before the ruined inn, sixty or so in all, a cordon of battle-scarred sailors forming a loose circle about them. Coming this close to them, Meg shivered. The scent of them was strong, almost overpowering. A musty animal smell. Looking down at the dark, painted faces of the raft-men, the bowed heads of the Clayborn, she could remember how hard, how viciously they had fought. Just now, however, they were frightened and subdued, especially the Clay among them. The sight of the scarred and mutilated dead rising from the ground had unnerved them. As well it might. Ghosts they had been fighting. Yes, and one dark, form-shifting spirit, who had fled each time they'd tried to cut him down, only to return, renewed and twice as deadly.

And now that spirit stood before them, his human form encased in a shimmering, silver mesh. A powerful magician, who commanded the unborn and spoke their language with a skill not one of them possessed.

Ben leaned toward them, his voice soft, conciliatory now that he had won, their strange and ugly language transformed in his mouth so that it was almost beautiful. Above his head floated three of the remotes, their lens-eyes taking in each detail of this scene, each twitch and furtive gesture of his captives.

On tape, she thought. *You'd have it all on tape if you could, wouldn't you, Ben?* Yet the sourness she had been feeling earlier had drained from her. What she felt now was a kind of tiredness, a dreadful weariness that was in the bone itself. She had to get away. Far away from all of this.

It began to rain. Out on the river there was a loud hissing as a mist of steam rose from the smoldering junks. A low, fearful moan rose from the Clayborn, who hunched even tighter into themselves, trembling, but the raft people merely looked up, as if greeting an old, familiar friend.

It was only then, as they looked up, their faces tilted to the night sky, their weather-sculpted features revealed in the lamplight for the first time, that Meg noticed. There were women among them. And not just one or two, but a number of them, maybe eight or nine in all. Meg narrowed her eyes, the shock she felt profound.

Her brother had been fighting women. Killing and maiming women. She wondered if he had known that.

And if he had?

She looked down, suddenly frightened by what she was thinking, what feeling at that moment.

There was a noise. A grunt of surprise. She looked up, and saw that Ben had moved, had gone right up to the captives and was crouched there, his hand reaching out to lift one of their chins and turn the face toward him.

"Jesus!" he said, lifting the strap and tugging the battered helmet from the warrior's head.

Long, red hair spilled out from within the helmet's crest. Green eyes looked up past him, meeting Meg's. Green eyes in a pretty, Slavic face.

Meg caught her breath. Catherine! It was Catherine! Or someone so like her as to be her twin.

Ben stood, shaking his head, then turned, looking back at Meg. "I saw her," he said, frowning, trying to piece things together. "I picked her up on one of the remotes. In the village on the big raft. But I never thought . . ."

He turned back, staring down at her, then put out his hand, as if the woman should take it. But she drew back, her fear of him mixed with a natural defiance.

"*Dos, benen!*" he said, ordering her. But the words were barely uttered when the sky to the south of them lit up, the old castle silhouetted briefly against the brilliance. A moment later, two loud explosions rent the air.

"The rafts," Ben said, facing the fading glow. "Virtanen has destroyed the rafts."

How do you know? she wanted to ask, but she was sure he was right.

Besides, she could hear the cruiser's engines now, could feel the faint vibration in the air.

"Over there!" Ben said urgently, pointing past her toward the steps. "In the gap . . . the ferry ramp!" And, not waiting to see whether she obeyed, he went across, lifting the rocket launcher from where he'd left it on the wall and slipping it over his shoulder.

He turned back, facing the captives. Some had stood. Others were glancing nervously at the sky, as if they knew what was to come. From the look of them, they would try to run at any moment.

"*Tryga!*" Ben said, his voice powerful, commanding. "*Tryga omma!*" Yet even as he said it, there was a shadow on the moon and the dark shape of a cruiser swept across the sky above the river, the sound of its engines reverberating in the sudden stillness.

There was a murmur of fear from among the captives. The cruiser had been unlit; had been like a giant beetle, whirring across the sky. A dark, malignant thing, heavy with threat.

"Go!" Ben said, turning to her again, and shooing her away. "For God's sake get out of sight! It'll be back any moment!"

This time she went, crouching between the sloping walls, halfway down the cobbled ramp, the dark edge of the river only yards below. But what about Ben? What was he going to try? To bargain with Virtanen? To make him confess to what he'd done?

Madness, she thought, not for the first time that day. *All of this is madness. Our lives are in danger, and all because my brother wants excitement!*

It was not strictly true. Virtanen had started this. But Ben could have wrapped things up much quicker if he'd wanted. If what she suspected were true, he had gotten his evidence against Virtanen long ago. All this was simply games.

The murmur of the cruiser's engines had faded, now it came back, stronger than before, and, from the disturbance of the water below her, she could tell that it was hovering out there, above the river.

Slowly she crept up the ramp again, until she could poke her head above the brickwork and look across.

The captives were still there, huddled together tightly now, every head turned to face the threat of the cruiser. All about them, the morph-sailors stood impassively, their weapons raised, their faces vacant.

There was no sign of Ben.

She turned her head, trying to make out the cruiser. At first she couldn't see it, then, with a suddenness that surprised her, it turned its searchlight full on, the beam's brilliance startling her, making the captives cry out with fear.

For a moment everything seemed superreal, picked out in stark relief, heavy with shadow.

"Shepherd!" a voice boomed down. "Ben Shepherd! Are you there?"

Don't answer, she pleaded silently, staring across at the cruiser as if mesmerized. *For God's sake, Ben, don't answer.*

"I'm here, Major Virtanen!" came a voice from the far side of the river. "Down here at the water's edge!"

She watched, her heart hammering, as the cruiser slowly turned, its lamps sweeping across her and out, searching the far bank. And as it did, she noticed a tiny speck—one of Ben's remotes?—float up, away from the passageway beside the Customs House, lifting rapidly toward the hovering cruiser.

Slowly the cruiser turned back, the brilliant light from its searchlight scouring the quayside. "Why the games?" the voice asked from within that glare. "We came to help you, Shepherd. To save you from the raft-men."

There was a moment's silence, a moment's utter stillness, and then laughter. Laughter that grew in volume until it seemed to fill the Domain, echoing back and forth between the hills. Ben's laughter.

The detonation was unexpected. She felt herself thrown back; found herself rolling, tumbling down the slope until she hit the coldness of the water. Heat . . . the air had been full of heat. And the light. For the briefest moment the light had intensified, as if . . .

Her ears were ringing. She sat there, waist deep in the water, and understood. Virtanen had fired a missile.

And Ben? Where was Ben?

She pulled herself up and hurried up the slope. Through the swirl of smoke she could see that the quayside was a ruin, as if a great chunk had been bitten from the stone. Beyond that, where the captives had been, was nothing. Nothing but a charred depression. She stared at it, numbed, then sank down, her knees giving way beneath her.

"God help us . . ."

Smoke swirled in the beams of the cruiser's lights. From the darkness beyond that great circle of light, a figure emerged, moving slowly through the veils of smoke until it stood there, at the center of the charred and smoking depression, its arms and legs, its chest and head, encased in shimmering silver. It was Ben, the rocket launcher held loosely in his artificial hand, as if it weighed less than an old man's cane.

No! she wanted to scream, but her mouth was dry, her throat constricted with fear. *No!* She could barely look she was so afraid for him.

"Virtanen!" Ben called, his voice cold, unlike she had ever heard it before. "Why don't you come down here and face me? Or are you afraid of that? Do you always prefer to kill people without warning?"

There was silence, and then a background muttering, which cut out quickly.

"Rockets not working?" Ben inquired, coming forward a few paces, and hefting the launcher. "I wonder why that is?"

From the craft there was silence. A heavy, brooding silence.

Ben was looking down, studying the launcher, then, slowly, almost lovingly, he lifted it to his shoulder, eyeing along the sights. "It's a little trick of mine. Or should I say ours. You see, we Shepherds have been expecting this for years now. Preparing for some evil-minded bastard like you to come along."

Meg stood, knowing what he was about to do, knowing also that even if it were justified, it was wrong to do it this way. Trying to keep calm, she began to walk toward him.

"Ben! You can't!"

"Stay there," he said, raising a hand to stop her. "I wasn't going to do this. But the bastard killed her. Without a moment's thought. He just went and killed her."

She stood there, in the shadows, looking across at him, surprised by the intensity of emotion in his voice. It was as if Virtanen had killed the real Catherine. As if . . .

She licked at her lips, then spoke again, trying to keep her fear for him out of her voice; to bring him back from the darkness where he suddenly was. "Maybe so, Ben, but this isn't right. Let Li Yuan sort this out. Let *him* make the decision."

He looked at her, meeting her eyes in a long, clear gaze, then returned his left eye to the sight, tilting the mouth of the launcher up toward the cruiser.

"*Be-enn!!*"

The explosion knocked her off her feet, throwing her back against the low wall that surrounded the ferry ramp. No, she kept thinking as she lay there. No, it wasn't the way. But in that last clear meeting of their eyes she had understood. He was mad. Her brother Ben was mad.

The Coast of Darkness

Thither he plies
Undaunted, to meet there whatever Power
Or Spirit of the nethermost Abyss
Might in that noise reside, of whom to ask
Which way the nearest coast of darkness lies
Bordering on light; when straight behold the throne
Of *Chaos*, and his dark pavilion spread
Wide on the wasteful Deep! With him enthroned
Sat sable-vested *Night*, eldest of things,
The consort of his reign; and by them stood
Orcus and Ades, and the dreaded name
Of Demogorgon; Rumour next, and Chance,
And Tumult, and Confusion, all embroiled
And Discord with a thousand various mouths.

—John Milton, *Paradise Lost*, Book II [v.954–67]

CHAPTER SIXTEEN

Circles of Light

I T WAS DAWN in Karnak and Wang Sau-leyan, T'ang, ruler of City Africa, stood on the broad and deeply shadowed balcony, his back to his two companions, looking out across the wide, slow river toward the Valley of the Kings.

Early sunlight lay like a stain on the clifftops opposite, a band of reddish-gold atop the blackness below. To the south lay Luxor, ancient Thebes. There the City began again, its walls, smooth white cliffs of ice, lifting two *li* into the morning sky. On the river a bird circled low above the surface, dark against the dark, then dropped soundlessly into the water.

Wang Sau-leyan turned, leaning lazily against the rail. Chi Hsing, T'ang of the Australias, was to his right, staring downriver toward the City. Hou Tung-po, T'ang of South America, stood in the arched doorway, looking back at him, smiling. They had been talking all night, but now it was done; the matter agreed among them. Tomorrow they would begin their campaign.

Wang returned Hou's smile, then tilted back his head, enjoying the freshness of the morning. It was simple really. Li Yuan had begun the process a year ago, when he had presented his package of changes to the Council. Now he, Wang Sau-leyan, would push things farther, letting his "friends" in the Above know that he supported their demands for new, more extreme changes to the Edict. At the same time, Chi Hsing, Hou Tung-po, and he would finance a faction in the newly reopened House to press for those changes: changes which Li Yuan could not afford to grant.

"What will he do?" asked Hou, coming out onto the balcony.

Chi Hsing turned, looking back at them. They were all equals here, yet it was to Wang Sau-leyan that they looked for guidance.

Wang's moon face looked away as he spoke. "Li Yuan will oppose us." Then, turning back to face them, he added, "He and his friends Tsu Ma and Wu Shih."

"And then?" Chi Hsing asked, concerned. They had gone over this ground three times already, and yet still he wanted it fixed. "With Wei Chan Yin sure to support them in Council, they could simply overrule us, four to three."

"Maybe so. But I think our cousins will think twice before being so hasty. Much has been said about the autonomy of the new House—of it not being an instrument of the Seven. Well, we can use that, neh? The people will be watching things closely in those first few weeks. They shall want to see whether the Great Promises will be fulfilled, the bargain between People and Seven properly made. The last thing our cousins want is for their words to seem empty. A demand for further changes, made publicly—constitutionally—in the House, will be a great embarrassment to them. They will have to oppose it, of course—they have no choice but to oppose it—but they will find it awkward doing so."

Wang smiled, looking from one to the other. "Our purpose is not so much to oppose Li Yuan as to make him show his hand in public. To force him to intervene. For our part we must cultivate a reasonable air, conceding the difficulty of change while acknowledging its necessity. That way we might, at first, lend tacit support to the idea while not committing ourselves to it."

He paused, then pushed away from the rail. "As for Li Yuan, we must find other ways of isolating him from his allies in Council. We must make him seem unreasonable, his schemes harebrained, disastrous in their consequences. Tsu Ma, perhaps, might stay with him, but Wu Shih is his own man and might be swayed. As for Wei Chan Yin, he is his father's son and, like his father, will vote to maintain the stasis. Within the year things will have changed. It will no longer be four against three, but two against five. And then we shall use the Council itself to bridle our young cousin."

Hou nodded enthusiastically, but Chi Hsing was still hesitant. In spite of his fears he liked and respected the young T'ang of City Europe, and his blood had sung with satisfaction when Li Yuan had acted against the rebellious sons of the Above. Yet what he wanted most of all was peace. Peace, so that his sons might live and grow to be men. And Li Yuan, for all that he liked him, threatened that peace. Chi Hsing met Wang's eyes and nodded. "So be it," he said.

Wang smiled. "Good. Then I shall begin at once, wooing our cousin Wei. Rumor has it that something has been eating at him. Some secret inner grief, connected to Li Yuan. Perhaps a private meeting between us will reveal just what seed of bitterness he nurtures."

"And Wu Shih?" Chi Hsing pushed out his chin as he spoke. It was an almost belligerent gesture, one Chi Hsing himself was entirely unaware of, but to Wang Sau-leyan it was revealing. He knew that Chi Hsing disapproved of his lifestyle—particularly of the *Hung Mao* concubines he kept—but this was rooted elsewhere. Seeing that gesture, he understood that he would not be able to trust Chi Hsing completely. If it came to a crucial choice Chi Hsing might yet side with Li Yuan.

Again he smiled. "As I said, Wu Shih is his own man. He will vote as before. For tradition. And to preserve the functions of the Seven." He shrugged. "As for Tsu Ma, he is Li Yuan's shadow. But two against five cannot carry policy. Li Yuan will see this and, in his frustration, seek to circumvent us."

Wang Sau-leyan looked from one man to the other and smiled, a great feeling of satisfaction washing over him. Each had their role to play. Hou Tung-po would placate the Minor Families, wooing them with new concessions—concessions that Wang Sau-leyan would draft and present to the Council of the Seven as legislation, principal among them a guarantee of posts in all the major Ministries—posts they had, in effect, been denied this last half century.

And Chi Hsing? He was to penetrate the higher levels of Li Yuan's administration—to buy and blackmail those nearest the young

T'ang. For they must know for certain what he was thinking, what planning in the months to come.

Only reluctantly had Chi Hsing agreed. Yet he *had* agreed, and his agreement bound him to this conspiracy. As time passed, circumstance would bind him much closer to their cause. He would be shaped by his actions until he became what he acted. And all the time his actions would be *against* Li Yuan.

"Come inside," Wang said, embracing the two men. "Let's drink to peace. And to a freer, happier world than this."

Chi Hsing smiled and nodded, but before he went in, he turned, looking back at the darkness of the river, wondering.

LI YUAN leaned forward, spreading his hands along the cool wooden balustrade, and looked across the lake toward the distant hills. He had thought never to come here again, but here he was, not three years passed since his last visit, his heart hammering in his chest at the thought of the meeting to come.

The day was hot and still, unnaturally so, even for this southern climate, but where he stood, on the north balcony of Yin Tsu's summer palace, there was shade of sorts. Two body-servants stood behind him, their heads bowed, the long-handled fans moving slowly, indolently in their hands.

Li Yuan breathed deeply, trying to prepare himself, but there was no preparing for this moment. He heard her soft footsteps coming down the broad twist of steps behind him and turned, suddenly awkward, moving between his servants to face her. Fei Yen had stopped, six steps from the bottom, her head lowered.

"*Chieh Hsia*, I . . ."

Her hesitancy was a new thing. When she had been his wife there had been a natural arrogance about her which had somehow awed him. Back then he had always felt inferior to her, but the years had changed that. He was older now and T'ang. And she was a cast-off wife, exiled from the Court. Twice exiled, he thought, remembering the two years mourning for his brother.

He took a step forward, holding out his right hand to her. She came down the last few steps and knelt, taking his hand and pressing her lips to the great *Ywe Lung* ring, her small, dark head bowed beneath his gaze. He bade her get up, then stood silently, staring down at her.

She was still as beautiful as ever. That same porcelain delicacy he sometimes dreamed of was still there in her, undiminished.

"How have you been?"

She had been looking down all this while, her eyes averted. Now she glanced up at him. "I am well, *Chieh Hsia*."

"Ah . . ." But he had heard otherwise. The man who had been here when he arrived was but the latest of a long line of lovers she had taken. As if there were some lack in her that she could keep no man for long.

"And Han?"

"He has grown, *Chieh Hsia*." She paused, then. "He is with his nurses just now."

Li Yuan sighed. This too he had heard. As if the mother shunned the son who had brought her fall from grace. The last time he had seen the child, Han had been barely nine months old. And now the boy was almost three. For a moment old feelings stirred in him. Looking at Fei Yen he frowned, wondering where he had gone wrong with her. But he had thought this through many times. The blame was not hers. The mistake had been marrying his dead brother's wife. All wrongness flowed from that.

He had come with no intention of seeing her, thinking her at Hei Shui in the north, but she had come here with the man only hours before his craft had landed, and so his scheme of seeing the boy without her had come to nothing.

"Can I see him?"

She tensed, silent a moment, then answered him. "I would rather not, *Chieh Hsia* . . ."

It was said softly, deferentially, but with a firmness that said much about her feelings on the matter. It was as he'd expected. Despite her unchanged looks, the last two years had hardened her. This new exile wore at her worse than the last. For her it was a kind of death, and she blamed him for it.

He looked away. "I have a gift for him."

"Leave it, then. I'll see he gets it."

He noted the impoliteness and turned on her, suddenly angry. "You will bring him here at once. I wish to see the boy, and I shall." He drew a breath, then, more gently, "I'd like to see him, Fei Yen. To meet him."

She looked up, her eyes burning, their relative status momentarily forgotten. "Why? You have your son, Li Yuan. What's my child to you?"

He bit back the words that came to mind, turning from her sharply, his hands clenched with anger and frustration. Finally, he looked back at her, his chin raised commandingly. "Just bring him. Down there, beside the lake. I'll see him there."

"As my T'ang commands."

The words dripped with bitter irony. Turning from him, she ran back up the steps, her own anger evident in her every movement.

He watched her go, touched strangely by the familiarity of that anger, then went down and waited at the lake's edge, looking across at the ancient orchard. It was some while before the child came. He had been changed and groomed. A nurse brought him down the steps, then left him there, at the edge of the grassy slope that led down from the summer palace to the lake.

Li Yuan turned, facing the boy squarely, and raised a hand, summoning him. The child came slowly, but not hesitantly. Despite his age, he carried his head proudly and walked like a little prince. His fine dark hair was neatly cut and combed, and he wore fine silks of gray and blue and black. Two *ch'i* from Li Yuan, he stopped and bowed low, then looked up again, not certain what was required of him beyond this formality.

The boy's dark eyes were proud but curious. He met Li Yuan's gaze unflinchingly and when the T'ang smiled, his lips formed only the faintest echo of a smile, as if maintaining seriousness were the greatest art. A lesson he'd been taught.

"I am Li Yuan, Han. Your T'ang."

"Yes," the boy said clearly. "Mama said."

"You know it is your birthday soon?"

The boy nodded, then waited, moving slightly on his feet.

"Good. And did your mama tell you that I've a gift for you?"

Again he nodded; a strong, definite movement of his neat and perfect head. Seeing it, Li Yuan shivered and pressed his teeth together. This was harder than he'd thought. Simply to see the boy was painful. So perfectly named. So very much like his murdered brother.

He nodded to himself, then took a pouch from the inner pocket of his jacket. Tugging open the leather cord, he spilled the tiny object into his other palm, then knelt, indicating that Han should approach him.

The boy stood close. Li Yuan could feel his breath on his forehead as he took the warm and tiny hand and slipped the ring onto the second finger. Moving back, Li Yuan noted how the boy was staring at the ring, puzzled by it.

"What does it mean?" Han asked, looking directly, frighteningly into his eyes from only a hand's width away.

For a moment Li Yuan felt overwhelmed by the depth of the child's eyes, by his closeness, the warmth of the tiny hand that rested in his own. He wanted to hold the boy close and kiss him. Wanted, for one long, almost unbearable moment, to pick him up and carry him from that place. To take him back with him.

The moment passed. The boy stood there, watching him, awaiting his answer.

He sighed, staring at the ring. "It's a kind of promise, Han. A promise I made myself. Each year I shall bring you such a ring. Until, when you're a man, full grown, there will be one final ring to keep. One final token of that promise."

Looking up, he saw that the boy had made nothing of what he'd said. Li Yuan smiled and patted his head. "Never mind. One day I'll explain it better to you."

He let go of the tiny hand and stood, looking back across the lake. "It's strange," he said, talking as much to himself as to the child. "It reminds me of the orchard at Tongjiang. I used to play there as a child, with my brother, Han."

For the first time the boy looked up at him and smiled. "Han? Like me, you mean?"

Li Yuan looked down and nodded, letting his left hand rest gently on the crown of the boy's head, his fingers in the dark, fine hair. "Yes, Han. Like you. Very much like you."

━━━━━━━

THE TWO visiting T'ang were about to depart when Wang Sau-leyan's Chancellor, Hung Mien-lo, appeared at the doorway, the Captain of Chi Hsing's elite guard two paces behind him.

"What is it, Chancellor Hung?" Wang asked, turning to him.

"Forgive me, *Chieh Hsia*," Hung answered, lowering his head first to his own T'ang and then to the others, "but it seems there is some trouble with the great T'ang, Chi Hsing's, craft. The preflight checks have shown up faults in the computer backup systems. I am advised that it would be unwise for the great T'ang to attempt the return flight until such faults have been rectified."

Wang turned, looking back at Chi Hsing. "Well, cousin, what would you like to do? You are more than welcome to stay here until the repairs are made."

Chi Hsing stroked his neck with one hand, considering, then shook his head. "No, Sau-leyan. It would be pleasant, most pleasant indeed, but I must get back."

"Then why don't you use one of my craft?"

Chi Hsing smiled broadly, delighted by Wang's offer. "I would be most honored, cousin. But what about my own craft?"

Wang turned, looking past Hung Mien-lo at the Captain. "I shall have a team of my best technicians aid your crew, cousin. As for the security aspect, your man, here, might stay, perhaps, to oversee the work?"

Chi Hsing beamed. "Excellent! But you are certain you can spare a craft, Sau-leyan? I can always send for my second ship."

Wang reached out and took his arm. "And waste four hours? No, dear cousin. You are right. I have already kept you from your business far too long. You will be missing your sons, neh?"

Chi Hsing laughed and nodded. "Even one night away from them seems too long, sometimes."

"Then let us part. Come, cousins, I will see you to your craft . . ."

━━━━━━━

HE WAS SAYING his farewells to his onetime father-in-law, Yin Tsu, when Fei Yen burst in at the far side of the hangar.

"Li Yuan!" she called angrily. "What is the meaning of this?"

Yin Tsu turned, aghast, trying at one and the same time to apologize to his T'ang and remonstrate with his daughter, but she swept past him imperiously, standing at arm's length from Li Yuan, her hands on her hips, glaring up at him.

"Come now, Li Yuan! I *demand* an explanation!"

He laughed coldly, taken aback by her outburst. It was years since anyone had spoken to him like this.

"An explanation? For what?"

"For *what?*" She laughed scornfully. "Why, for the guards, Li Yuan! Am I to be a prisoner in my own father's house? Am I to be followed and hounded every second of the day?"

Li Yuan looked to Yin Tsu, then back at her. "I have already explained to your father why the guards are here, Yin Fei Yen," he said patiently, but she would have nothing of his reasonableness. She moved closer, almost shouting the words into his face.

"Have I not been humiliated enough, Li Yuan? Have you not made me suffer enough for my mistake? Must you continue to hound me and meddle in my affairs?"

The word was unfortunately chosen, but still Li Yuan was patient. He would not, at this last moment, be drawn by her.

"You misunderstand me, Fei Yen," he said, leaning close, letting his voice carry only to her. "I know all about your lovers. But that is not why I am doing this. We live in troubled times. The guards are there for one reason only—to keep Han safe. As for you, my once-wife, I have no wish to meddle in your life. And you are quite wrong if you think I want you to suffer. No. I wish you only happiness."

For a moment she stood there, her dark eyes watching him. Then, with the faintest rustle of her silks, she turned away, walking quickly across the hangar and out into the early afternoon sunlight.

And Li Yuan, watching her go, felt a part of him drawn out after her, as if on a fine, invisible line, and knew, as he had not really known before, that he was not quite over her.

━━━━━

THE CAPTAIN sat at a table, a bottle of Wang Sau-leyan's best wine open before him. A serving girl stood behind him, her fingers gently massaging his shoulder muscles while he watched the men at work on the far side of the hangar. The two craft looked identical from where he sat and, not for the first time, he found his thoughts turn uneasily to the question of why the T'ang of Africa should want a perfect copy of Chi Hsing's craft.

While servants set out the meal, the Captain turned his head, looking across to where Wang Sau-leyan was deep in conversation with a tall, odd-looking Han. The Han seemed central to all of this somehow. It was to him that the technicians came with their queries, and it was to him alone that they would defer, as if the great T'ang were invisible to them. That intrigued him—that absence of any mark of respect for Wang Sau-leyan. When he'd first seen it, he had been shocked, for it went against all instinct. But now he thought he understood.

He returned his eyes to the men, busy at work inside the right-hand craft, Chi Hsing's original. They had been at work now for over three hours, and in that time they had been most thorough. A team of six technicians had taken the control panels apart and painstakingly rebuilt them. Meanwhile, two of their colleagues had broken down the access codes to the craft's computer records and stripped them bare, making copies of everything—of security keycodes, pilot trans-missions, field distortion patterns, and all. He had listened to their excited chatter and felt his unease grow. The copy craft would not simply look like Chi Hsing's, to all intents and purpose it would *be* Chi Hsing's. And Chi Hsing himself would know nothing of its existence.

Unless . . .

He felt the tension return to his muscles and tried to relax, to let the young girl's fingers work their magic spell, but it was difficult. Too much was going on inside. He looked at the bowls of delicacies that had been set before him, conscious of how, at any other time, he would have fallen upon such rare culinary delights, but just now he had no appetite. When Wang's agent had brought him, he had not expected any of this; had not really asked himself why Wang Sau-leyan should wish to delay his cousin's craft, accepting the man's reassurances. But this . . .

He shivered, then reached out to take some of the duck in ginger, forcing himself to eat; to act as if nothing were wrong. But beneath the outward mask of calm, he felt a sense of panic, knowing he had got himself in out of his depth. Why should Wang Sau-leyan go to such lengths to copy his cousin's craft unless he wished to use it? And why should he do that?

Moreover, the presence of these men—political terrorists, he was certain, if only from the way they pointedly refused to bow to the great T'ang—added a whole new dimension to things. To find such men here, at the heart of the T'ang's palace, what did *that* mean?

Across from the Captain, Wang Sau-leyan leaned back, nodding his satisfaction, then turned and came across. The Captain rose at once and bowed low, keeping his eyes averted.

"You have everything you need, Captain Gustavsson?"

He kept his voice calm, clear of the fear he felt deep down. "All is well, *Chieh Hsia.* I am honored to be of service to you."

It was not what he had meant to say, but it would do. Moreover, it reflected something true about the situation. He had not understood before, but, in taking Wang Sau-leyan's money, he had become Wang's man. There was no turning back from this. No way of excusing himself. Inadvertently he had committed himself to whatever was being done here.

If I had known . . .

But it was too late now for such thoughts. And when Wang put out his hand, he took and kissed the great ring of power, knowing that it was this or death, and there was his family to think of—his sons and baby daughter, his wife Ute, and his invalid mother. Wang knew that. He was sure to know it. It was why they had chosen him. Why it was even possible that Wang's agents had been in some way responsible for his money troubles. Certainly, he had never had so bad a night at *Chou* as that session six weeks back when he had lost eight thousand *yuan* at a single sitting. Even so, it had been his decision, and now he must live with it.

"If there is any further service I might offer, *Chieh Hsia.*"

Wang smiled, his plump, moonlike face taking on an air of great benevolence. "Maybe there is something. For now, however, you have my gratitude, Captain. And my protection."

The Captain looked up, surprised, then quickly lowered his head once more. "I am deeply honored, *Chieh Hsia.*"

"Well . . . let me keep you no more. Enjoy your meal while it is hot, Captain. Such pleasures are rare in life, neh?"

Rare indeed, he thought, looking through his lashes at the back of the retreating T'ang. He sat, his skin strangely cold, a new tightness at the pit of his stomach. *Eat*, he told himself. *Enjoy the feast that's spread before you.* But though there were dishes there he had never dreamed he would taste, things that only a T'ang might afford, he found himself picking at them dispiritedly, chewing the richly flavored foods listlessly, as if they were but tasteless copies of the things they purported to be.

He looked about him, as if waking, seeing the men working on the craft, the odd-looking Han standing nearby, supervising them, and nodded to himself, understanding. Lifting one hand, he put the fingers gently to his mouth, feeling once more the cold, hard pressure of the *Ywe Lung*—the Wheel of Dragons—against the warm softness of his lips, then drew them back, as if the flesh were bruised.

━━━━━

WANG SAU-LEYAN stood at the rail, the dark stillness of the Nile beneath him, and looked up at the full and shining circle of the moon. For so long now he had held himself in check, containing his natural impulse to oppose and destroy. But now—finally—his patience would be rewarded.

He smoothed his hands over his ample stomach, then smiled broadly. It was strange how far he had come these past few years. Stranger still that he had not seen this in himself from the first. But it had always been there, since his first conscious moments.

They had never understood him. Not one of them. His father had disliked him from the start, repulsed by the pudgy little creature he had sired. His mother had persevered for a time, but had thought him a stubborn, willful child. Dismayed by his behavior and unable to control him except by the strictest measures, she had cast him from her side before he was three, having nothing further to do with him. Her sudden death, when he was seven, had left him curiously unaffected, unable to share in the general grief, but it had given him a strange, unchildlike understanding of his nature. From that moment on he had known it was his fate to stand outside that bright circle of human connectedness; to be an onlooker, cut off from kith and kin. A Han, a son, but really neither; more some alien creature born into a fleshy form. And from that moment's realization had come the urge to oppose, the impulse to destroy all that he touched.

No, and no one, not even Mach, understood how deep that impulse ran in him; how strongly that urge to destroy tugged at him, sweeping him along, like a smooth white stone caught in the dark ocean's undertow. It was not power he wanted, but the opportunities that power brought: the chance to meddle and corrupt, to smash and overturn. To break . . . well, a whole world, if he so wished.

A whole world . . . No, not even Mach wanted that. Even he would stop short at some things.

The oxygen generators, for instance. Those huge pumping stations that reached down deep into the earth's mantle to tap the reservoirs of energy and convert the basic building blocks of life into the most precious thing of all—air. Mach knew of them, secret though they were. He knew that, since the destruction of the rain forests, life on Chung Kuo would have been insupportable without them—as intolerable as the icy wastes of Mars. But never—not even for a passing moment—would he have considered acting against them. *Destroying* them. It was unthinkable. No, what Mach wanted was an end to the old—to Seven and Cities and the stifling world of levels. And afterward? Well, to be blunt about it, Mach hadn't really thought it through. His vision of the new order was vague; a thin tissue of ideals, with no more substance than the words he breathed into the air. Necessarily so. For had he pictured what it would be like—what it would *really* be like—when the Cities fell, he would have quailed at the thought of the misery and devastation to come.

But he—Wang Sau-leyan, T'ang of Africa—had thought long and hard on the matter. Had pictured in his mind the long, straggling lines of skeletal figures stretching out across that bleak, unending wasteland. He had seen them, there in the clear, gray light of dawn, trudging from nowhere to nowhere, tongues black in their wizened heads, blank eyes staring straight ahead, while to every side, the dead were heaped in rotting piles, all trace of human warmth, of human connectedness, leached from their wasted forms. And at such moments his nostrils would twitch with distaste, as if sensing the overwhelming stench of putrefying flesh. And he would smile.

Yes. He saw it clearly. A dying world, its foul, unregenerated air filled with the darkness of corruption. And afterward, nothing. Nothing but rock and wind and salted oceans. Nothing for a million years.

He lowered his eyes, looking out across the dark surface of the river toward the ancient Valley of the Kings. Here death was close at hand. Was a dark companion, ever-present, more intimate than any lover. He could feel its breath upon his cheek, its hands caressing his softly rounded flesh, and shivered at the touch, not from fear but from a strange, inexplicable delight.

No. Not one of them knew him. Not one. Hung Mien-lo, Li Yuan, Jan Mach—each saw but the surface of him; the softly rounded mask of flesh. But beneath that—beneath the tissue of his physical self— was something hard and unyielding; something wholly inimical to life.

He turned, hearing the rush of wind, the beating of wings overhead, then laughed, delighted. Birds filled the air suddenly, returning to their nests on the far side of the river, their long, dark shapes swooping and circling high above the moonlit darkness of the Nile. And then, one by one, they plunged into the dark water, exploding in sudden circles of light.

Like messengers, he thought, and felt a strange unearthly thrill pass through him. *Messengers.*

━━━━━

IT WAS A PLACE of pools and paths and ancient stones, of pleasant bowers and gently flowing streams. Birds sang in the sunlit branches of time-twisted junipers while below, amid the lush green covering, cast-bronze statues of long-extinct animals—bright red pictograms cut into their flanks—lolled peacefully, as if shading themselves for the fierceness of the late afternoon sun. It was a scene of great tranquillity, of a long-cultivated harmony that was almost indolent in its nature. But today, the Garden of Reflective Quiescence gave Li Yuan no sense of inner peace as he walked along its paths. For once, his eyes skirted the surface of things, seeing nothing of the delicate balance of form and color and texture the garden's designers had striven so hard to create, focused only on the hard nugget of unrest deep within him.

Returning from T'ai Yueh Shan, he had ridden out, urging the horse on madly, as if to purge what he felt from his blood, but it had been no use. At the ruined temple he had turned, looking about him, seeing her image everywhere he looked.

And the child?

He stopped, realizing suddenly where he was. He had strayed from the path and was among the flower beds. Earth clung dark and heavy to his pale kid boots while his hand had closed upon a flower, crushing it, scattering the bloodred petals. He looked down, appalled, then backed away, turning, his hurried steps echoing off the flagstones as he ran back down the path toward the Southern Palace.

Li Yuan leapt the steps in threes, then ran across the grass toward the open doors of the Great Library. The ancient, Chu Shi-ch'e, looked up, startled, from behind his desk as Yuan burst into the room, and began to get to his feet.

"Sit down, Master Chu," Li Yuan said breathlessly, crossing the broad, high-ceilinged room. Behind, Chu, his assistant, twenty years his junior, looked on, wide-eyed, as the young T'ang dragged the ladder along the rail, then began to climb.

"*Chieh Hsia* . . ." protested Chu, coming around his desk. "Let the boy do that . . ."

"I am grateful for your concern, Master Chu, but it is a T'ang's prerogative to do exactly as he wishes."

"That may be so, *Chieh Hsia*," the old man answered, tugging at his long white beard, "but of what use is a servant who is not allowed to serve?"

Li Yuan turned on the ladder, looking across at the *Pi-shu chien*. Chu Shi-ch'e had been appointed Inspector of the Imperial Library by his grandfather Li Ch'ing, more than sixty years earlier, and in all that time he had never missed a day's service from ill health. Moreover, it was said that Chu Shi-ch'e's knowledge of the archives was encyclopedic. If his movements had grown slower with time, his mind had remained as nimble as ever. Li Yuan hesitated a moment longer, then relented, coming down, letting Chu's assistant—the "boy," a stoop-backed old fellow of a mere sixty-four years—climb in his place.

"What was it you wanted, *Chieh Hsia?*" Chu asked, coming alongside, his bent head a sign as much of age as of respect for his T'ang.

Li Yuan drew a long breath. "There is a tape I saw once, years ago. It was of my brother Han, when he was a child. A very young child. In the orchard with my mother, Lin Yua."

Chu stared at him a moment, his eyes narrowed, then turned away, firing two rapid phrases of Mandarin at his assistant. Almost at once the "boy" was clambering down the steps again, a long, narrow case with a golden cover in one hand.

The case was part of the official archives—the daily record of the Li Family, dating back more than two hundred years. Here, stacked floor to ceiling on these walls, were the complete holographic records of the Family, each case embossed with the great *Ywe Lung*, the Moon Dragon, symbol of the Seven.

Li Yuan watched as the assistant handed the case to Chu Shi-ch'e, then backed off, bowing deeply. Chu opened the case, checking the contents, then, clicking it shut, turned, offering it to Li Yuan.

"I think this is what you want, *Chieh Hsia.*" Again the old man's eyes seemed to pierce him; to see through to the innermost depths of him. And maybe that was so, for of all the Family's retainers, no one knew half as much about his masters as Chu Shi-ch'e. The old man gave a wintry smile. "If you will forgive us, *Chieh Hsia*, we will leave you to view the tape."

"Thank you, Master Chu," Li Yuan said gratefully. "I will summon you when I am done."

He watched them go, then turned, facing the black, lacquered platform at the center of the room—a big circular stand six *ch'i* in width, its surface carved in the form of a huge *Ywe Lung*, the whole thing resting on seven golden dragon heads. Here he had come, long years ago it seemed, to sit at his father's feet. And, as his father talked, telling him of his long and dignified heritage, the ghostly images of his ancestors would walk the earth once more, their words as strong and vibrant as the hour they had uttered them. It had always seemed a kind of magic—much more so than the computer-generated trickery of the ancestral figures in the Hall of Eternal Peace and Tranquillity, for this was real. Or had been. Yet it was some while since he had come here. Some while since he had let himself be drawn back into the past.

It was a weakness, like the business with Fei Yen, yet for once he would indulge it. And then, maybe, the restlessness would go from him, the dead mouth of the past stop speaking in his head.

He looked down at the case in his hands, studying the date embossed into the hard plastic beneath the *Ywe Lung*, then flipped the catch open, taking out the hard green disc of plastic that held that day's images. For a moment he simply stared at it, reminded of that moment in the tomb, twelve years before, when he had carried the first of the ritual objects to his father. That had been the *pi*, symbol of Heaven, a large disc of green jade with a small hole bored at its center. This here was like a smaller *pi*, lighter, warmer to the touch, yet somehow related, even down to the tiny hole at the center.

Li Yuan looked about him at the layers of gold-bound cases that lined the walls, a tiny shiver passing through him at the thought of all that time, all those memories, stored there, then crossed to the garden doors. He pulled them closed, then tugged at the thick silk cord that hung from the ceiling, drawing down the great blinds that shut out the daylight.

He went across, leaning across the platform to place the disc onto the spindle at the hub of the great circle of dragons, then stepped back. At once the lights in the room faded, a faint glow filling the air above the platform.

"I am Li Yuan," he said clearly, giving the machine a voice recognition code, "Grand Counselor and T'ang of Ch'eng Ou Chou."

"Welcome, *Chieh Hsia*," the machine answered in a soft, melodious voice. "What would you like to see?"

"The orchard," he said, a faint tremor creeping into his voice. "Late morning. Lin Yua with my brother, the prince, Han Ch'in."

"*Chieh Hsia* . . ."

The air shimmered and took shape. Li Yuan caught his breath. The image was sharp-edged, almost real. He could see the dappled shadow of the leaves on the dark earth, the dust motes dancing in the sunlight, yet if he reached out, his hand would pass through nothingness. He walked about it slowly, keeping to the darkness, looking through the trees at his mother, her skirts spread about her, her face filled with sunlight and laughter, his brother Han, nine months old, crawling on the grass beside her. As he watched, she leaned out and, grabbing Han's tiny feet, pulled him back to her, laughing. She let Han get a few *ch'i* from her, then pulled him back again. Han was giggling, a rich baby gurgle of a laugh that brought a smile to Li Yuan's face even as his chest tightened with pain. No, he had not been mistaken. This was what he had remembered earlier, deep down, beneath the level of conscious thought. This moment, from a time before his time, and a child—his brother—so like his own that to call them different people seemed somehow wrong.

He stared into the magic circle of light, mesmerized by this vision of that distant yesterday, and felt a kind of awe. Could it not be so? Could not a person be reborn, a new vessel of flesh fashioned for the next stage of the journey? Wasn't that what the ancient Buddhists had believed? He closed his eyes, thinking of the ruins in the hills above the estate, then turned away.

Weakness, weakness . . .

He shook his head, bewildered. What was he up to? What in the gods' names was he doing? Yet even as he turned back, meaning to end it—to kill the image and get out—he stopped dead, staring into the light, bewitched by the image of his mother cradling his brother, by that look of love, of utter adoration in her face. He groaned, the ache of longing so awful, so overpowering, that for a moment he could not breathe. Then, tearing himself free of its spell, he breached the circle of light and lifted the disc from the spindle.

As the room's lights filtered back, he stood there, trembling, horrified by the ease with which he had been seduced. It was as he had reasoned that time, in those final moments before Ben Shepherd had come. This longing for the past was like a heavy chain, binding a man, dragging him down. Moreover, to succumb to that desire was worse than the desire itself. Was a weakness not to be tolerated. No, he could not be T'ang and feel this. One had to go on, not back.

He let the disc fall from his fingers, then turned, going to the door. There was work to be done, Ministers to be seen. The unformed future beckoned. And was he, its architect, to falter now? Was he to see it all come to nothing?

He threw the doors wide and went out, hastening down the corridor, servants kneeling hurriedly, touching their heads to the floor as he passed. Back in his study he took his seat behind the great desk while his servants rushed here and there, summoning his senior officials. But it was neither Nan Ho nor his secretary, Chang Shih-sen, who appeared in the doorway moments later; it was his eldest wife, Mien Shan.

He looked up, surprised. "Mien Shan . . . What is it?"

She came two steps into the room, her head lowered demurely, her whole manner hesitant. "Forgive me, husband, but might I speak with you a moment?"

He frowned. "Is something wrong, Mien Shan?"

"I . . ." She glanced up at him, then, lowering her head again, gave a small nod. There was a faint color at her cheeks now. She swallowed and began again. "It is not for myself, you understand, *Chieh Hsia* . . ."

"No," he said gently. "But tell me, good wife, what is it?"

"It is Lai Shi, husband. This hot weather . . ."

He leaned forward, concerned. Lai Shi, his Second Wife, was four months pregnant. "Is she all right?"

"She . . ." Mien Shan hesitated, then spoke again. "Surgeon Wu says that no harm has been done. She was unconscious only a short while. The child is unaffected."

"Unconscious?" He stood, suddenly angry that no one had told him of this on his return.

Mien Shan glanced at him again—a timid, frightened look, then lowered her head once more. "She . . . fainted. In the garden. We were playing ball. I . . ." Again she hesitated, but this time she steeled herself to say what she had to say, looking up and meeting his eyes as she did so. "I begged Master Nan not to say anything. You are so busy, husband, and it was such a small thing. I did not wish you to be troubled. Lai Shi seemed fine. It was but a moment's overexertion. But now she has taken to her bed . . ."

Li Yuan came around the desk, towering over the tiny figure of his First Wife. "You have called Surgeon Wu?"

She bowed her head, close to tears now; afraid of her husband's anger. "He says it is a fever, *Chieh Hsia*, brought on by the air, the heat. Forgive me, husband. I did not know . . ."

"I see . . . and this fever—is it serious?"

"Surgeon Wu thinks it will pass. But I am worried, *Chieh Hsia*. The days are so hot, and the air—the air seems so dry, so lacking in any goodness."

Li Yuan nodded. He had noticed as much himself. For a moment he stared at her, conscious of the simple humility of her stance; of how different she was from Fei Yen in that. Then, touched by her concern, he reached out and held her close, looking down into her softly rounded face.

"Go now, Mien Shan, and sit with Lai Shi. I shall finish here and come as quickly as I can. Meanwhile, I shall give instructions to Nan Ho to have the Court removed to the floating palace. I cannot have my wives troubled by this heat, neh?"

Mien Shan smiled broadly, pleased by the news. Yet her smile, which ought to have warmed him, merely made him feel guilty that he could not return it with a matching warmth.

He sighed, suddenly tired of everything. "Forgive me, Mien Shan, but there is much to be done."

She drew back, bowing her head. "Husband . . ."

He watched her go, then turned, shaking his head, angry with himself. Why was he so cold with them? Weren't they, after all, the best of wives—kind and loving, solicitous of his health? Why then should he show them such disrespect? Such indifference?

Or was it simpler than that? Wasn't it just as Ben had said that time? Wasn't he still in love with Fei Yen?

For a moment he stood there, breathing deeply, conscious that, for the first time since he had cast her from him, he understood. He loved her, yes, but that meant nothing now. His duty was to his new wives. He had not faced it before now. Not properly. He had let things slide, hoping that time would cure him, that things would come good of their own accord, but they never did. It was that simple—he had not worked at things. He had lacked the will. But now . . .

He nodded, determined. From now on it would be different. From this moment on he would work at things. Would make them right again. Beginning this evening, at Lai Shi's bedside. And in time . . . in time these feelings would subside and the dark, hard stone of pain would be washed from him.

He unclenched his hands, letting the past go, letting it fall from his fingers, then went back behind his desk, making a start on the pile of documents; selecting only those that needed his urgent attention.

FEI YEN stood on the terrace beside the lake, barefoot and alone. It was late now and the day's heat had finally dissipated, but the air was still warm and close, and as she paced the cool, lacquered boards, she gently fanned herself.

His visit had disturbed her deeply. At first she had thought it simple anger and irritation at his meddling, but it was more than that. Even after she had calmed herself—after she had bathed and had her serving maids rub scented oils into her back and legs to relax her—she had felt that same strange tension in her gut, and knew it had to do with him. She had thought it finished, all emotion spent between them, but it wasn't over yet; she knew that now.

She turned her head. To her right, on the far side of the lake, there were lights on in the hangar. Faint noises carried across the dark and silent water, the sounds of her father's servants preparing the craft for her departure in the morning.

She sighed and, pushing away from the rail, descended the narrow steps that led down to the shoreline. There, beneath the brilliant circle of the moon, she paused, staring down into the dark mirror of the lake. Beneath her feet a huge, white polished stone gleamed in the moonlight, making her reflection—darker, less discernible than the stone—seem almost insubstantial.

Fading away, she thought. *I'm slowly fading away, like a hungry ghost.*

She shuddered and turned, trying to push the thought away, but it persisted, nagging at her until she had to face it. In a sense it was true. The life she should have had—her "real" life, as wife to Li Yuan and mother of his sons—had ended years ago. She had killed it, just as surely as if she had taken a knife and slit her throat. And this life she now had—this succession of empty days, which she filled with passing lovers and idle pursuits—was a kind of afterlife, lacking all purpose and all reason.

A pang of bitterness—pure and unalloyed—struck her at the thought. It was all her own fault. And yet, what would she have changed? What would she have done differently, given the choice? She took a long breath, then turned, confronting her reflection once again, leaning forward to study the image closely.

She had changed a great deal these past few years. Gone were the excesses of former years. She wore no jewelry now. Likewise her clothes were simpler—a plain *chi pao* was all she ever wore these days. As for her hair, that was brushed back severely from her face; plaited tightly and secured in a tiny bun on either side of her head.

I look like a peasant girl, she thought. Yes. And so she had dressed that morning, three years ago, when she had broken the news to him.

For a moment she was still, remembering. *What would you say if I told you I had fallen?* she had asked him, thinking he would understand. But he had looked back at her blankly, puzzled by her words. And she had had to make it clear to him. A child. A son. And for a time they had been happy. But that time had been brief. As brief, it seemed, as an indrawn breath.

She knew now she had been wrong to take Tsu Ma for a lover. But it had been hard being alone all that time; hard to be a woman and to be ignored. In any case, she had been beside herself. Tsu Ma . . . just the thought of him had swayed her from her senses. Those afternoons, stretched out beneath him, naked on his blanket in the ruins of the ancient temple . . . that had been sweetness itself. Had been a taste of Heaven.

Yes, and though it had been wrong, it was as nothing beside what Yuan had done. To kill his horses . . . She shivered, the memory of it still fresh. How could he have done that? How could he have killed those wonderful, sensitive beasts? She had never understood.

And now he had returned; older and more impressive than he had been. A T'ang in every word and action. Yes, it was true. The child she had known was gone; dead, almost as if he'd never been. And in his place was a stranger. Someone she ought to know but didn't.

She turned, looking back toward the terrace. A figure was standing there; a small, hunched figure that she recognized after a moment as her father.

"Fei Yen?" he called softly. "Is that you down there?"

He came down the steps and joined her beside the water.

"Father," she said gently, embracing him. "I thought you had gone to bed."

"And so I shall, but not before you, my girl. What are you doing out here? It's late. I thought you were leaving early in the morning?"

"I am. But I had to be alone a while. To think."

"Ah . . ." His eyes met hers briefly, then looked away. "I too was thinking. Han needs a father. This life is no good for him, Fei Yen. He needs a stronger hand. Needs balance in his life."

It was an old, familiar lecture, and as ever she smiled, knowing that her father wanted not to judge her, but only what was best for the child. She studied him a moment in the moonlight. He was old now, his gray hair receding, his powers as a man waning, yet when he was with Han it was as if the years fell away. No, she had never seen him laugh so much as in the past few weeks.

She leaned close, kissing his brow tenderly. No one else in the world loved her as her father did. No, and no one else forgave her, whatever she did.

"He has his uncles," she said, as if in answer, but Yin Tsu gave a dismissive snort.

"And a fine lot of good they are." He laughed; a short, sharp sound, full of disappointment. "I had such hopes, Fei Yen. Such plans for them. And what have they become? Drunkards and wastrels. Drains on the family purse, one and all."

It was harsh, and, to a degree, unfair, but she let it pass. Her brothers could fight their own battles. Right now there was Han to think of. Han and herself.

"And these guards?" she asked tentatively. "You think Li Yuan was right to do that?"

Yin Tsu considered it a moment, then shrugged. "I do not know, *nu er*. It is . . . unusual. But Li Yuan has his reasons, I am sure, and if it helps set his mind at rest, then that must be good, neh? He carries a heavy burden, that young man, and carries it well." His eyes shone with admiration. "Would that he were a son of mine . . ." Then, realizing what he had said, he looked away again, but not before she saw the regret, the brief flash of bitterness that had crossed his features.

She looked up. In the distance, above the hills, two geese flew slowly across the sky, their wings beating silently as they headed south, toward the sea. The sight made her clench her fists, remembering that time on the lake at Tongjiang with Li Yuan, Tsu Ma, and her cousin Wu Tsai, on the tiny island, beneath the colored lanterns. The night she had played the *p'i p'a* for them and sang the refrain from "Two White Geese."

And now she was alone. *Like grass on a lonely hill, knowing it must wither and die.* The words made her shudder, then turn back, facing her father.

"Come," she said, laying her hand gently on his arm. "Let us go back inside."

After kissing him good night, she returned to her rooms; to the faint, enchanting flicker of aromatic candles and the sight of her maids busying themselves, finishing the packing for the morning. Waving them aside, she went through to where Han slept and stood there, looking down into the cot.

It was only at moments like these, when Han lay there, his limbs spread idly in sleep, his dark hair tousled, that she realized just how much she loved him. Not mildly, or casually, but with a fierce mother love that was as protective as the mother wolf's for her cubs.

She reached down, brushing the hair back gently from his eyes, then pulled the blanket up about his chest. She was selfish, she knew. The men who came to pay court to her—hollow clowns and dandies all—took up too much of her time. Kept her from him. But that would change. She would spend more time with him.

She took her hand back, slowly, reluctantly, then blew a silent kiss. *Let him sleep,* she thought. *Let him dream his pleasant, childish dreams.* For tomorrow would be a long day. A long, long day.

Distant Thunder

KIM REACHED ACROSS and took the ink brush from the stand. Inking the brush, he drew the document toward him and signed his name at the bottom of the final sheet.

"There," he said, sitting back. It was the final touch; the last of the formalities. Now he was theirs.

He looked up and saw how Reiss was smiling. SimFic's Chief Executive, more than any of them gathered there, had wanted this. To rebuild the Company's reputation and put it back up there among the Hang Seng's top ten. Yes, and he had paid more than twice what Kim's broker had estimated to bring Kim back into the fold.

And so here he was again. In Berdichev's old office, nine years later and ninety-nine years wiser. Or so it felt.

"Welcome back to SimFic, *Shih* Ward," Reiss said, bowing his head and offering Kim both his hands. "I am delighted that we've signed you."

Kim stood, forcing himself to smile and take the man's hands. *Two years*, he was thinking, *was that it all it was?* And yet, strangely, it didn't feel like it had before. Back then, he had had no prospect of being free, whereas now, at least, he had a contract. Five years—six, if he took up the bonus option—and he would be free again. And rich.

He turned back, watching as one of Reiss's men "sanded" his signature, then removed the papers into a special folder. It was a long document, twenty-four pages in all, and he had gone through it carefully with his broker yesterday, but in essence it was simple. He was their slave now. For the next five years he would do what they said when they said. That was, as long as it did not endanger his life or seriously threaten his health. And providing it was legal. Not that they had any intention of placing him in any danger; not after the fee they had paid to sign him.

He touched his tongue to his lower teeth thoughtfully. Twenty-five million *yuan* had been placed in an account in his name already. And there was more to come. Much more. Fifteen million a year, for five years, and a further twenty-five if he stayed on that extra year. And then there were the performance bonuses, the two percent cut on any inventions subsequently manufactured from his original patents, and the sliding scale payments for developing any of SimFic's existing patents to "manufacturing standard."

All in all, he could come out of this exceedingly well. Rich enough, if things worked out, to start again; older, wiser, and with the capital, this time, to expand. Rich enough, perhaps, to marry a Marshal's daughter.

He looked back at Reiss and smiled; a gentler, more relaxed smile. "I'm pleased to be with you, *Shih* Reiss," he said, conscious of the dozen or so senior executives ranged at the far end of the office, watching their exchange. "I hope our partnership will be a fruitful one."

His echo of Reiss's words from earlier that day brought a smile to the Chief Executive's lips. "I hope so, too, Kim. I really do. But come, let's go through. It's time."

Kim nodded, then allowed himself to be turned about, a faint sensation of heaviness in his limbs. In the next room the technician was waiting beside his machine. Kim, entering the room, studied it with a detached interest, conscious of the sudden feeling of hollowness—maybe even a trace of fear—at the pit of his stomach. The machine was a kind of gantry, attached by a thin coil of wire to a slim, black-cased comset. On the surface it looked fairly harmless, yet it would provide them with the means of controlling him for the next five years.

A slave, he thought. I'm going to be a slave again. A thing that thinks. A puzzle-solver. Not a person but a commodity. To be used as the Company desires.

He shivered, then stepped forward, letting the technician help him into the brace.

It took only seconds. Then he stepped back, the collar pulsing gently about his neck. He could feel its warmth, its energy, almost as if it were alive, and, though he had meant not to, he found his left hand had traveled up, unbeknownst to him, to touch and gently tug at it.

"It'll not harm you in any way," Reiss said, as if to reassure him. "We'd have preferred not to, but the legal formalities . . ." His voice trailed off, then, "Look on it as a safeguard. Company life can be hard and very competitive, as you know." He laughed awkwardly. "Well . . . it'll help us take good care of you. That way we'll all be happy, neh?"

Kim nodded, giving Reiss the best smile he could manage; but suddenly the reality of it was on him. This was his life for the next one thousand eight hundred and twenty-six days. *This . . .*

Reiss turned and took a folder from one of his assistants, then turned back, handing it to Kim. "Here are the details of your first assignment. We thought we'd give you something familiar to begin with. Something you can get your teeth into straightaway."

Kim took the folder and opened it. Inside were four flimsy sheets of paper. On the first were four handwritten equations. On the second was a tiny, neatly drawn diagram, the notations in a different hand from the first. The third sheet was filled with notes, some by the author of the equations, but most of them by whoever had drawn the diagram.

"Molecular switches," Kim said quietly, feeling a pulse of excitement pass through him. "It's what I've been working on."

"I know," Reiss said, watching him carefully. "We've been working on the same lines for some time now. And this is the closest we've got. They're unstable . . ."

"Yes," Kim flicked back, studying the equations a moment, then looked at the final sheet. It was headed up with SimFic's double helix logo. Beneath it, in a neat printer face, were the details of his assignment.

"Sohm Abyss," he said, looking up at Reiss, wide-eyed. "You're sending me to Sohm Abyss!"

THE PHILADELPHIA NIGHTCLUB was almost empty. It was just after seven in the morning and the four young men sat about one of the central tables, the top buttons of their *pau* loosened, their jackets on the backs of their chairs. It had been a long night but a successful one and they had raised more than a million *yuan*. Enough, for now, to keep the movement from bankruptcy. Kennedy had left more than two hours back, more tired than usual, the new security men he'd hired shadowing him closely. That was but one of the changes they had noticed. Small things that made them think back to what Kennedy had said to them that first time and reassess. Overnight, it seemed, the mood of things had changed.

It was four days to the first round of voting and things looked good. Michael Lever was up even on the more dubious EduVoc polls, and talk was that his father's man, Edward Gratton, would be lucky to pick up more than a third of the vote. All night people had been coming up to Michael and slapping his back, congratulating him, as if the count were a formality. It had made him uneasy. It felt like tempting the gods.

"You worry too much, Michael," Kustow was saying. "What can Gratton do in four days? They've flung every last bit of dirt at you they could find and it still wasn't enough. It's our time, and nothing can prevent it. The tide has turned against the old men. People want change. And by the gods, they're going to get it!"

Parker and Fisher laughed, but Michael was silent, brooding. His own seat looked safe, it was true, but things weren't going quite so well across the board. Indeed, if things didn't improve, they'd be lucky to take four of the thirty seats they were contesting. But he was also thinking of something Kennedy had said—something he had whispered to him earlier that evening—about the possibility of a deal. He had warned Michael to be careful. To be *very* careful.

"A lot hangs on this one, though," said Fisher. He turned in his seat to summon a waiter for more *ch'a*, then turned back. "You know, there's a whole clutch of seats that are vulnerable in the second round. Forty or more, I reckon. And each and every one ripe for the picking."

"That's provided we get a good vote first time out," Kustow added more cautiously.

"Sure . . ." Fisher leaned forward, looking from one to another. "I think we will. I think we'll do better than the poll showings. Much better. That's why I've asked Kennedy if I could run for one of those seats."

Michael looked up. "That's good, Carl. What did he say?"

Fisher laughed. "He said yes."

All three congratulated him at once. "Damn the *ch'a*," Kustow said, getting up unsteadily from his chair. "This calls for another bottle of that special wine!"

"Where are you going to run?" Michael asked, pulling Kustow down from his feet.

"Miami *Hsien*. Against Carver."

Miami was Fisher's home stack. The place where his father's Company was registered. Like Michael, he was going to be running directly against his old man's candidate.

Michael looked down. "Is that wise?"

Parker and Kustow were watching Fisher closely now. Both knew what Lever meant. The day after Kennedy had been nominated to run in Boston, Fisher's father had disinherited him: had frozen the funds to all three of his son's companies. Fisher had been forced to lay off his work force. Some had found other jobs, but more than a hundred families had "gone down." The local media had had a field day, and Representative Carver had returned from a business trip in City Europe to fly back and be interviewed in the home of one of those families that had suffered through, as he termed it, "the irresponsible management of a young and untried man." Going down—with all its social stigma—was the one thing all voters feared in common, and in the minds of the voters of Miami, what Carl Fisher had done was unforgivable.

"I want the chance to put my case," Fisher said. "I want the opportunity of facing Carver and telling him to his face that he's a liar and a cheat. That for eighteen years he's been in the pocket of my father."

Kustow whistled. "You'll say that to his face?"

"He'll sue," said Parker.

Fisher smiled. "Kennedy's hoping he will. He wants to fight the case himself. I've given him all the stuff I had. Accounts books, file numbers, memory copies of conversations."

For the first time since the crowds had left the club, Michael sat forward and smiled. "You've got all that stuff?"

Fisher nodded. "I got it all together first thing. After I'd first met Kennedy. Thought I might need some insurance."

Slowly, but with gathering force, Michael began to laugh. And in a few moments they were all laughing. The waiter, when he brought the *ch'a*, looked around at them, then shrugged and walked away, keeping his thoughts to himself.

———————

EMILY TURNED, looking about her, trying to estimate the scale of the problem at a single glance, but it was hard to take it all in. The eye was drawn constantly to the smaller details: to the distressed face of a wheezing ancient, or the empty, hopeless eyes of a silent, uncomplaining child; to the weeping sores of a young blind beggar or the mute suffering in the face of a mother who yet cradled her cold, long-dead baby. In the face of all this individual misery the greater picture just slipped away. This much suffering was, quite literally, unimaginable. She had thought Europe bad, but this . . .

She was down at Level Eleven, immediately above the Net, at the very foot of Washington *Hsien*, here to publicize the newly launched "Campaign for Social Justice." It was their plan to fund and build fifty "Care Centers" across the City to try to deal with the problem of low-level deprivation, but from the moment she had stepped out into Main here, she had known how pathetic, how woefully inadequate their scheme was. It would take a hundred times what they proposed even to scratch the surface of this problem. Why, there were more than fifty thousand people crammed into this deck alone—fifty thousand in a deck designed to hold eighteen thousand maximum!

When she had been voted Chairwoman by the committee of Young Wives, she had thought that this might—just might—be a way of getting something done. For the past six months she had thrown herself into the task of organizing meetings and raising funds. But now, seeing it for herself, she understood. She had been fooling herself. There was only one way to change all this. From the top. By destroying those who allowed this to go on.

She walked among the crowds, feeling a thousand hands brush against her, or tug briefly at her silks, a thousand eyes raised to her in silent supplication. Feed me! Relieve me! Free me from this Hell!

Above her the tiny media cameras hovered close, capturing the scene, focusing in on the expression in her face. And as she returned to the great platform, with its banners and waiting guests, a reporter pressed close, clamoring for a statement.

"Just show it," she said. "And let everyone in the Mids know that this is how the people down here have to live. Every day. And"—she steeled herself to say the lie—"and that they can help. That if they give only a single *yuan* to the Campaign, it'll help relieve some of this suffering."

She turned away quickly, lest her anger, her bitterness, made her say more. No. It would help no one for her to speak out in public. Least of all these people. What it needed now was action. Action of the kind she had held back from until now.

It was time for her to organize again. To adopt the false ID DeVore had prepared for her all those years back and become someone new. Rachel DeValerian. Terrorist. Anarchist. Leveler.

Yes, it was time for the *Ping Tiao* to be reborn.

＊＊＊＊＊

FROM WHERE KIM STOOD, high up on the viewing gallery, two *li* above the great ocean's surface, the events of the great world seemed far off, like the sound of distant thunder. The night was calm, immense, the darkness stretching off in all directions. Without end. Literally, without end. He could move forever through that darkness and never reach its limit.

Darkness, he thought. *In the end there's nothing but darkness.* And yet, all his young life, he had sought the light. Had striven upward toward it, like a diver coming up from great depths.

Far off, the waves broke in a staggered line of white along the encircling breakwater. That line seemed frail and inconsequential from where he stood, yet he had flown over it earlier and seen the great ocean's swell; had seen waves fifty *ch'i* in height smash with ferocious power against the angled breakwater, and had felt more awe in him at that than at the sight of the great mid-ocean City they had built here over Sohm Abyss.

He turned. Above him, beyond the great spire of the central block, the night sky seemed dusted with stars—a billion stars that burned incandescently, like nothing he could ever have imagined. That too—so different somehow from the simulations—awed him. The reality of it. Until now it had all been in his head, like some complex three-dimensional chart. But now, seeing it with his own eyes, he understood what had been missing. Its vastness; its awe-inspiring vastness. It was something he had known but never grasped. Not until now.

He turned back, conscious of the faint yet discernible motion of the viewing platform. Down below, among the levels, one felt nothing, almost as if one were on dry land, but here the tidal swell of the great ocean could be sensed, despite the breakwaters, the huge chains of ice that kept the City anchored to the ocean's floor, ten *li* down.

He looked down thoughtfully. Something in him responded to that: to the thought of those vast, unlit depths beneath the fragile man-made raft of the Ocean City; to all that weight and pressure. Something dark and antithetical to his thinking self, that looked back at him sometimes in the mirror, sharp-toothed and snarling.

He placed his hands flat against the thin layer of ice that separated him from the vastness outside and shivered. Darkness and Light. How often it came back to that—the most simple of all oppositions. Darkness and Light. As in the great Tao. And yet, ultimately, he did not believe in the Tao. Did not believe that dark and light were one and the same thing. No. For it seemed to him that the dark and light were locked in an ageless, unending struggle for supremacy: a struggle that could end only when one canceled out the other, in a blinding flash of searing light or in the abnegation of total nothingness.

And then?

He stepped back, amused. So what *had* existed before the universe? And what would be there after it was gone? These seemed logical enough things to ask, and yet, at the same time, they were nonsense questions. A grasping after straws. What pertinence did they have on the here-and-now of daily life? What use were they as tools?

No use at all. And yet he felt the need to ask them.

"*Shih* Ward?"

Kim turned. A Han was standing in the shadows beside the open door to the service elevator, his shaven head slightly bowed. His green SimFic one-piece was emblazoned with the number four, indicating his status within the SimFic hierarchy at Sohm Abyss.

"Is it time?" Kim asked, finding himself suddenly reluctant to leave the safety of the darkness.

The Steward looked up, meeting his eyes. "They are waiting below, *Shih* Ward. You must come now."

Kim bowed, then went across. Yet at the safety gate he stopped, looking down into the brightly lit heart of the Ocean City. Sohm Abyss was typical of the mid-Atlantic Cities. The thick outer wall formed a giant hexagon, linked by flexible walkways to a central hexagonal tower, topped by a slender communications spire. From above it had seemed like a bright and gaudy brooch cast thoughtlessly upon the darkness of the waters, but from where he stood it was more like a vast cat's cradle, the silvered walkways like the threads of a giant spider's web . . .

"*Shih* Ward!"

The slight sharpness in the Steward's voice reminded him of what he had become that morning. A thing. An entry on the SimFic Corporation's balance sheet. Turning back, he bowed apologetically, then stepped into the narrow cage. Obedient. Their servant.

Yet even as the gate irised shut, he realized suddenly that what they had purchased was but a part of him, and that that same unknown, uncharted darkness that lay beneath this great man-made artifact lay beneath all things, large and small alike.

Yes, and as for consciousness itself, what was that but a brightly lit raft, afloat upon the dark waters of the subconscious? A tiny, fragile edifice of man-made reason.

As the elevator began to descend, Kim turned and, looking up, studied the smooth curve of the Steward's shaven head, the folds of the green cloth covering his back, and wondered briefly whether the man was ever troubled by such thoughts, or whether status and material standing were his only measure of things.

If so, what was it like to be like that? To be content with how things seemed and not to question how things really were? What deep pool of inner stillness did one have to tap to become so inured to the greater mysteries? How did one let go of thinking and just *be*? Or was it that? Was it not so much "letting go" as never properly grasping hold?

For a moment longer he picked at the problem, like a monkey poking inside an ant's nest with a twig, then he relented.

Curse or blessing, it was what he was. What SimFic had paid him for. To question it was pointless. No, what he had to do over the next five years was to find a way to use it without using himself up. To keep from becoming the thing they thought he was—a mere puzzle-solver and generator of ideas. In doing so, he would have to give them what they wanted, but at the same time he would also have to keep back something for himself. One thing, perhaps. One pure and singular vision.

The elevator slowed, then stopped. As the door irised open, admitting the babble of conversation from the room beyond, Kim recalled the silent, star-spattered darkness up above and smiled, knowing what it was.

◆◆◆◆◆

KUSTOW WALKED BACK with Michael to the apartment he had hired on the south side of the stack, overlooking the fashionable Square. On the way they talked of many things—of Kennedy's new bodyguards and the significance of the new set of changes to the Edict—but mainly about whether Kustow too should run.

"Is that what you want, Bryn?"

"I guess so," Kustow answered. "Anyway, it doesn't look like there's much else open to me now. We're all out of favor as far as the Market is concerned, and we can't live off moonshine."

Michael turned, facing him. "That's not what I asked, Bryn. Is it what you really want?"

Kustow looked down, considering. "If I hadn't wanted to get involved, I guess I wouldn't have taken the first step, would I?" He looked up at Michael ruefully. "I think we both knew where this would lead. And Joseph Kennedy didn't pull any punches or tell any lies, did he?"

"I guess not."

"So that leaves me two options, to be precise. Both of them political. I can remain behind the scenes, as a shaper, or I can put myself up front."

"And you want to be up front?"

Kustow took a deep breath. "I'm not sure. I've liked what we've been doing. I mean, I've enjoyed working with you and Carl and Jack. We make a good team. But going it alone, with a new team . . ." He shrugged. "I just don't know."

Michael was silent a moment. "People will expect you to run. As the party grows you'll lose status unless you're a Representative. You'll lose whatever you currently have. No, if you don't run you might find yourself muscled out, Bryn. At least, that's how I see it."

Kustow dropped his head, then nodded. He was frowning, looking down at his feet. When he looked up again there was a painful indecision in his face. "You know what it is, Michael? I'm afraid."

Michael laughed shortly, then frowned. Kustow was the biggest of them. The strongest. The most extroverted. It wasn't possible that he could be afraid. "Afraid of what?"

"Of the whole business, I guess. Of power and politics. I don't want to become another Carver, or Gratton, or Hartmann."

Michael shook his head. "You won't! Goddamnit, Bryn, isn't that what we're about? To get rid of the old guard and bring in new ways— better ways?"

Kustow shivered. "Maybe. I don't know. I just looked at things from the outside tonight, that's all. Looked at all that backslapping and fund-raising and the bodyguards and the whispering between friends, and I wondered if we were really going to be any different from the rest."

There was a moment's silence between them, then Michael took his old friend's arm. "Come on. My apartment's only up the corridor. Let's get a few hours' sleep, then talk again."

Kustow smiled gently and nodded. "Okay. Lead the way."

Outside his door, Michael turned and looked at Kustow again.

Maybe Bryn was right. Maybe it would turn out just as he feared. But if they didn't try, if they just left it, that, surely, would be just as bad?

Michael thumbed the lock and touched out the combination with his other hand. As the door began to open, Kustow smiled drunkenly at him and stumbled past.

The explosion was deafening. Michael was thrown back across the corridor and fell awkwardly, blacking out. When he came to, what seemed only a moment later, there were Security guards everywhere and two medics were leaning over him, doing something to his legs. His legs were numb.

"Where's Bryn?" he asked, trying to sit up. But he couldn't sit up and the words came out as a kind of dry cough. He realized then that his chest hurt. One of the medics leaned close to his face and told him to relax, it would be okay. What would be okay? he wanted to ask, but his hold on consciousness was weak. He kept slipping back into blackness. Each time he woke things seemed to have jumped. Bit by bit he began to piece things together. He was strapped to a trolley, his head propped up slightly by cushions. To his right a big blunt-faced man was talking into a handset and listening to the responses. He was muttering something about a bomb. Someone had been killed.

It was only later that it hit him. *Someone had been killed.* Bryn. But by that time he was lying in a hospital bed, under armed guard, and there was nothing he could do. Again and again he saw Bryn smile and stumble past him, unsteady from the wine he'd drunk. He wanted to put out his arm and stop him. To call him back. To warn him somehow. But there was nothing he could do. Bryn Kustow was dead.

━━━━━━

KIM STOOD at the head of the steps, looking out across the sunken floor of the reception hall, surprised by the sight that met his eyes. The air was cool, the lighting a subdued shade of blue that seemed to fill the huge, high-ceilinged room with moving liquid shadows.

He smiled, amused by the effect. It was like being at the bottom of a pool. A huge pool filled with the soft, slightly echoing murmur of voices. There were three, maybe four hundred people down there, gathered in groups between the pillars. The Steward, two steps down from Kim, turned and looked back at Kim impatiently, then continued down the steps. A moment later, Kim followed.

A group of about thirty people—men for the main part—were gathered beside what seemed like a large glass table set into the floor. The Steward made his way across to them, then stepped back, beckoning Kim to come forward.

At the center of the group stood a big, bearlike man in his early sixties with an unfashionable goatee beard, neatly trimmed ash-white hair, and an elegant cut in silks. He was William Campbell, SimFic's Regional Controller for the North Atlantic Cities and, as he greeted Kim, he leaned toward the young man.

"Forgive the informality, Kim, but it's how I like to do things. You see, out of all eleven of SimFic's Regional Controllers, I have the biggest administrative area and the smallest staff. Like the plankton, there's a lot of me, but I have to spread myself very thin!"

Kim smiled, then took Campbell's offered hands, shaking them firmly. He stepped back, looking about him, conscious of how all eyes were on him.

"I'm delighted to meet you, Controller. And your friends, the *ch'un tzu* here . . . are they all SimFic employees?"

Campbell looked about him, his casual ease contrasting strongly with the tenseness of the men surrounding him. "Not at all. We have these evenings once a week. Anyone who's anyone in Sohm Abyss comes along. But quite a number here are SimFic. I'll take you around in a moment. Put names to faces."

"Thanks," Kim smiled, warmed by Campbell's manner. Yet at the same time he was conscious of a strange tension in the air about him, as if things weren't quite as they seemed. He set the thought aside, determined to be sociable. "I was up on the viewing gallery just now. It's a beautiful place. I don't know why they don't build more of these Ocean Cities."

Campbell laughed. "Economics, Kim. Pure economics. The cost of the City itself is fairly negligible, but to site one of these little beauties—to carry out all of the necessary surveys and secure the seven great tether-cables—that costs a phenomenal amount. We just couldn't justify it these days."

Kim nodded thoughtfully. "And yet it was done."

"Oh, sure. But as far as SimFic is concerned we've a different strategy these days. I mean, why build these things new when you can acquire them? Take Sohm Abyss, for instance. Right now we own twenty-five percent of the facility. It's the most we *can* own under present legislation. But things are changing." Campbell looked about him. "It would be nice to fly the SimFic flag over one of these Cities, don't you think?"

There was a nodding of heads, a strong murmur of agreement.

"But enough of that." Campbell reached out, laying one large, bearlike hand familiarly on Kim's shoulder. "Let me take you around. Introduce you to the people you'll be working with."

Kim let himself be turned and led away. "Who were they?" he asked, glancing back at the group they had left.

"Company men," Campbell said quietly, stroking his goatee thoughtfully. "Administrators for the most part. By the way, would you like a drink?"

Kim hesitated. "I . . ."

Campbell stopped one of the waiters and took a wine cup from his tray. "Oh, that's right. You don't drink. That's good. Some of them out here drink far too much. And other things besides. They think I don't know what goes on, Kim, but I've my own sources. Take the guy in the gray, for instance."

Kim turned, looking back, noting a tall, thin-faced man in gray silks.

"You've got him. Good. That's Bonnot. Alex Bonnot. He's the Scientific Supervisor here. Your direct boss. A good man according to the records. Reliable. Honest. But I've my doubts. So watch him, eh, Kim? And let me know if he oversteps the bounds."

Kim's eyes flicked up to Campbell's face and then away, not quite understanding what was meant. But this whole thing felt odd. Why, for instance, hadn't Campbell introduced him to them? "I don't follow," he said after a moment. "I thought *you* were in charge of things here."

Campbell smiled. "Overall, yes. But Sohm Abyss is Bonnot's. At least, the science side of things. The fish-farming, cold-storage, and star-gazing part, as we like to call it. The administrative side is run by the man standing next to him, Schram. Dieter Schram. He fancies himself as a bit of a scholar, but he's hardly in your league, Kim. Dull, too, unfortunately. Which is probably why he got this posting. As for myself, I spend most of my time traveling between the Cities. I've eight in my region, though I'm actually based at Cape Verde."

"So I take my orders from Bonnot?"

"And Schram. But they take their orders from me." Campbell turned slowly, relaxedly, drawing Kim on through the crowd, ignoring the staring faces, moving toward a group who were standing beside one of the pillars. "Oh, I know what goes on in places like this. I also know what's happened to you in the past, Kim. I've read your file thoroughly. But you can be sure that nothing like that will happen here. In fact, you have my word on it." He slowed, looking down at Kim. "Oh, I'll work you hard enough, Kim Ward, but I'll be fair with it. And if we get results, I'll be generous to you. Outside the terms of your contract, understand me?"

Again Kim wasn't quite sure that he did, but he nodded and, responding to Campbell's broad, generous smile, grinned back at him, reassured.

"As I see it," Campbell continued, "if I can keep you happy, you'll produce the goods. If you produce the goods, SimFic makes profits. And if SimFic makes profits we all grow fat. So it's in my best interest to keep you happy, neh?"

"I guess so."

They had stopped just before the group. The five men had turned to greet Campbell as he approached and now they stood there, their heads slightly bowed, waiting for the Controller to introduce them.

"This here is Hilbert, Eduard Hilbert. He's Head of Cryobiology and an expert in biostasis procedures . . . cell repair and the like. Our experiments are at an early stage, but we're hopeful, neh, Eduard?"

Hilbert bobbed his head. He was a thin, dark-haired man in his mid-thirties with the slightly haunted look of a man who preferred the laboratory to social gatherings. Kim extended his hand. "It's good to meet you."

"And you." Hilbert looked away, embarrassed, yet his brief smile had been friendly enough. Moreover, in turning he had revealed the pulsing collar about his neck. He too was a commodity slave.

"And this," Campbell continued, introducing a young Han in his early twenties, "is Feng Wo-shen. His background is in protein design, but he'll be working with you, Kim, as one of your assistants."

Feng bowed his head low in what was a very formal way. Straightening up, he met Kim's eyes, a natural enthusiasm burning in his own. "I am delighted to be working with you, *Shih* Ward. We are all very excited about the work ahead."

Kim returned his bow, then looked up at Campbell. "Assistants?"

The big man smiled. "Of course. We don't expect you to do all the experimental work yourself. You'll need assistants for that. To start with I've allocated you four. If you need any more . . ."

Kim laughed. "No, no . . . four's quite enough. It's just that . . . Well, I didn't expect to be treated quite so well."

Campbell looked genuinely surprised. "Why the hell not? Look, Kim, we've made a huge investment in you. It would be downright stupid not to get the best out of you. You're a theorist, right? That's what we bought you for, neh? Well then, it makes sense surely to free you to do what you're best at. To utilize your talents to their maximum capacity."

Kim thought briefly of geese and golden eggs, but merely smiled and nodded. "I take your point, Controller. Yet a great deal of my work is, of necessity, experimental. Feng Wo-shen and the others . . . they'll be of great help, but you must understand . . ."

Campbell raised a hand. "Whatever you want. And whichever way you want to do it. Just get me results, eh? Results." He turned back, putting out an arm to indicate the next in line. "Now, this here . . ."

For the next half hour Kim moved about the reception hall, meeting the people he was to work with, coming back, finally, to the group about the glass-topped table—a table which he saw, suddenly, was no table at all, but a huge display tank, its occupant, if occupant it had, hidden beneath a screen of greenery and rock. While Campbell went through the business of introducing him formally to Bonnot and Schram, Kim thought of the task ahead. At last he was to be given everything he'd been denied before: good equipment, well-trained staff, and whatever was needed to develop and manufacture a marketable product. The only real difference was in how the profit from the venture was distributed.

He smiled inwardly. What Campbell had said earlier was true. If he did well, they would all be happy. And who knew, he might even enjoy the work. Yet it wasn't quite as simple as that. He could see it in the way Bonnot and Schram looked at him, with a jealous hostility and a deep-rooted contempt for his stunted Clayborn body. Well, he could live with that. Besides, there was always Campbell's promise of protection.

As soon as was polite, he moved to one side of the group and leaned over the tank, looking down into its depths, his fingertips resting gently against the glass. The surface of the tank was cold, the ice thick, reinforced, as if the water within were being kept at a different pressure from the room.

For a time there was nothing, then, as if it had been waiting for him, it appeared, slowly at first, one appendage coiling like a snake about the rock, blindly searching with its tiny suckers. And then, with a dreamlike slowness that was mesmerizing, it hauled itself up through the concealing layers of weed, until its vast bulk seemed to fill the tank . . .

He stared at it, fascinated. It was like a spider. A giant aquatic spider, its long arms coiling sinuously along the restraining walls of the tank. As he watched, the mottled dome of its head turned through the shadows until it faced him, its huge eyes blinking slowly, then meeting his own in a cold, incurious stare that seemed to sum him and dismiss him.

Kim moved back, shivering. Once more mere knowing had failed him, for to be in the presence of such a creature—one of the ancient monsters of the deep—was to experience a sense of primal fear. Yes, simply to meet those eyes was to stare into something vast and dark and eternally alien, eternally withheld.

It was a deep ocean creature. How, then, had they trapped it? How brought it here? How kept it? As it turned, slipping back beneath the masking layers of weed and rock, he tried to estimate its length. Fifty, maybe sixty *ch'i* it was. Huge, even by the measure of its kind.

Kim turned, sensing another presence just behind him. It was Campbell. He stood there, one hand tugging at his goatee thoughtfully.

The Controller looked past Kim at the disappearing monster, then met his eyes again. "Well? What do you think of our pet? Impressive, neh? One of the deep-level units found him, more than a year back, some six *li* down in the center of the Abyss. They stunned him, then put him in a temporary capsule with a few tidbits while they decided what to do with him. In the end we had to build a special pressure chamber. Even then it took us almost two weeks to bring him up—a *ch'i* at a time, it seemed. But here he is. Our pride and joy." Campbell turned, looking back at Kim. "You're very fortunate, Kim. He doesn't deign to visit us that often. Most of his tank's down there, beneath the City. A huge thing it is. You can visit it sometime, if you want."

Kim gave a vague nod, then looked away. Six *li* . . . Which meant that the pressure in the tank had to be phenomenal.

"Has he a name?"

Campbell nodded. "We call him Old Darkness. Among other things. But look, let's talk about it later, eh? There's someone else I'd like you to meet. She'd have been here earlier, but her flight was delayed. Come, she's waiting over there."

Kim stared at the tank a moment longer, then followed Campbell across, giving the briefest nod of acknowledgment to Schram and Bonnot as he passed.

"Here," Campbell said, ushering him into a circle of people. "Barratt and Symons you met earlier, but I'd like to introduce you to our new Commercial Advisor. I understand you know each other already . . ."

But Kim was no longer listening. At the first sight of the short, dark-haired woman, he had moved past Campbell and embraced her, holding her against him tightly, fiercely, his eyes brimming with tears. "Rebecca . . ." he said, amazed, moving his face back to stare at her, as if at a long-lost sister. "The gods forgive me, I thought you were dead . . ."

◆◆◆◆◆

THINGS HAPPENED FAST. Within an hour of the attack, Gratton was on all channels, coast to coast, expressing his shock and sadness. His image was intercut with pictures looking down on the operating table as the surgeons tried to put Michael Lever back together again. Only the intercession of Kennedy got the floats out of there—under threat of expensive legal actions. Then, before three hours had passed, Kennedy himself spoke to reporters—calling a news conference in the anteroom at the hospital, a white-faced Carl Fisher standing at his shoulder as he talked.

Various terrorist organizations had been quick to disclaim the incident. The Black Hand had even gone so far as to condemn the action. A MedFac poll, taken half an hour after Kennedy's abrasive statement, expressed the general attitude: Gratton was sunk . . . if Lever lived.

Kennedy had accused no one. He had stood there, red-eyed, genuinely moved by what had happened, and denounced violence as a political means. Eloquently, he had outlined what had happened to these young men who had only stood up for what they believed in. The disinheriting, the double-dealing, the embargoes by the old men. And now this. He phrased it cleverly, so that no one could accuse him of making too direct a link between the attack and the old men who were out to stop them, but the mere fact of juxtaposition gave his words a power that forced his listeners to consider whether this act had come from the same hands that had shaped the rest of it.

Charles Lever's writ against Kennedy was served an hour later. The floating cameras, following him all the while now, caught the moment and broadcast it, along with Kennedy's sad, regretful smile and his few words. "Tell Mr. Lever I'm sorry he's more concerned for his own political hide than for his son's life."

Those channels that hadn't had a camera there bought tapes and showed them repeatedly throughout the remainder of the night and for the whole of the next day. But by then they had fresher material to work on.

Security, conscious of how sensitive the matter was, had put two Special Services units onto the case and results were already coming in. Representative Hartmann had been taken in to Security Headquarters in Washington for questioning, and three men from his political entourage—all ex-Security—had been making statements all afternoon. Hartmann had smiled at the cameras gathered overhead, but the smile had been sickly—the smile of a man who knows the trap has been sprung. News soon leaked out that they had taken him from an off-planet shuttle in Denver.

After Kennedy's response to the writ, Charles Lever had locked his doors against the media. At the Cutler Institute, they refused to comment on the situation. Meanwhile, a southern network had followed up the Bryn Kustow connection and was showing an hour documentary on the dead man's life, together with an interview with his grieving mother. His father had shut himself away and was refusing to comment.

At eight thirty, three hours after he had come out of the operating theater, Michael Lever opened his eyes. Emily was seated at the bedside, leaning over him. On the far side of the room, Kennedy, Fisher, and Parker sat on hospital chairs, waiting. Overhead, a single camera captured the moment for later transmission.

At first there was nothing in Michael's face, only a vague disorientation. Then, as memory came back, he began to sob. Emily leaned closer, whispering words of comfort and holding his hand tightly. Behind her, the three men were standing now, tears streaming down their faces. The camera's second lens caught this also.

After a moment Kennedy came across and stood beside Emily, looking down into Michael's heavily bandaged face. He wiped his eyes and cheeks with a surgical rag, then moved back slightly, giving the camera a better view.

Michael shuddered. "Who did it, Joe? Do they know who did it?"

Kennedy shook his head. "Not yet." He said nothing about Hartmann. Nothing about his father's writ.

Michael closed his eyes and swallowed. When he opened them again they were moist with tears. "I feel numb, Joe. From the waist down."

Kennedy glanced at Emily, then looked away. From above it seemed as if Kennedy were finding it hard to say what he had to. He turned his head to the side, his shoulders giving a tiny shudder; then he faced Michael again, bracing himself. "They say that there's nothing they can do about that, Michael. Fragments of the device passed through your chest and lodged in the base of your spine. You're paralyzed, Michael. From the waist down."

Michael's face was blank a moment, then he nodded. It was clear he was still in shock.

"They say you were lucky," Kennedy went on. "You'd be dead if you'd been alone."

Again Michael nodded, but this time a flicker of pain crossed his face. "I loved him . . ." he said softly, his voice ending in a tiny sound that tore at the listener like a barb. Then he turned his face aside. A single tear traced its way down his cheek, the camera lens switching to close-focus to follow its progress.

Bryn Kustow had taken the full brunt of the explosion. It had, quite literally, torn him apart. But his body had shielded Michael from the blast. Even so, the explosion had broken both of Michael's legs, cracked his skull, and caused extensive internal injuries. Fragments of hot metal as well as bone from Kustow's right arm had lodged in Michael's flesh, severing blood vessels, musculature, and nerves. His most serious injury, however, was his damaged spine. It was not impossible that he would walk again—bioprosthetics could cure almost anything but death itself these days—but it would be some while before he would be on his feet. And the election was only three days away.

One enterprising channel, having shown a diagram of the relative positions of Kustow and Lever, gave their viewers a full hologrammic reconstruction of the explosion. Billions watched as computer simulations looking remarkably like the two short-haired and handsome young men were blown apart by the explosion. Then, moments later, it showed it once again, varying the viewpoint and slowing the action.

Another channel, deploring the taste and, maybe, regretful that they had not had the idea first, set up a fund to pay for Michael Lever's bioprosthetic treatment, taking the opportunity to comment on the fact that, by rights, a certain Charles Lever should be footing the bill. They, too, found themselves served with a writ within the hour.

Hartmann was charged with conspiracy to murder on the morning of the election, but by then the damage had been done. Gratton had pulled out the night before. When the polls closed, Michael Lever had been elected almost unopposed, collecting ninety-seven percent of the votes cast. More significantly, the New American Party, buoyed up by the sympathy vote, had won no less than twenty-six of the thirty seats they had been contesting.

The cameras were allowed briefly into Michael Lever's hospital room to get his reaction. From his bed he smiled dourly up at the cluster of floats and made a short speech of thanks. Then, clearly tired, he lay back with the help of a nurse and, even as the cameras watched, he closed his eyes and slept. It was left to Representative Joseph Kennedy to read the prepared speech on Lever's behalf.

A THOUSAND *LI* northeast of where Michael Lever lay sleeping, Charles Lever stood in a darkened room, watching the image of his son. It had been a bad week, not least in the markets. But now, looking at his son lying there, so vulnerable, so badly hurt, the old man softened. "I didn't mean . . ." he said, in a whisper. At least, he hadn't wanted to push things quite this far.

He reached out to touch and trace the image on the big screen, his fingers following the strong line of Michael's cheek, just as once he'd touched the sleeping child.

Things change, he thought, turning away. And maybe there was a reason for that. A lesson in it. He shivered and stood there, facing away from the screen, then turned back, hearing the commentator mention his name.

". . . whose silence has been taken by many to be, perhaps, more meaningful than any words he could have offered."

He felt that same tightening in his chest, the anger coming back. None of them had the guts, the balls, to come out openly and say it. But the innuendo was clear enough. Lever spat out his disgust and took a step toward the screen. As he did so, the image changed and in place of his son's sleeping face was his own: a hard, uncompromising face; the face of an old man. He breathed in sharply, as if stung, then stormed across the room to the comset. Grunting with anger, he tapped out the code for his lawyer. Then, while he waited for the connection, he turned to listen to the commentary again.

". . . and while Hartmann's confession makes no explicit allegations, many leading figures on the Index are surprised that the Security investigations have ended with Hartmann and his close associates. Is vengeance the motive, as Hartmann claims? Or is there something deeper and darker behind this whole business?"

Even as the commentator finished, Lever was through.

"Dan? Is that you? Good . . . Look I want you to arrange an exclusive interview with EduVoc. Usual terms. We have the right of veto . . ." He listened a moment, then huffed out irritably. "You think that's wise?" Again he listened. "No. Of course not! There's no link whatsoever!" He took a deep breath, calming himself. "Look, Dan, all I know is that I'm sick to death of this shit . . . this innuendo. I want it ended, right? If you can't get veto, we go ahead without and sue the bastards if they play any tricks on us."

Kennedy's face was on the screen now, a kind of sad dignity in his expression as he read out Michael Lever's speech. But all the old man saw was its smug self-righteousness, its falseness. *You*, he thought. *You're the bastard who did all this!* Yes . . . the more he thought about it, the more he realized what had happened. And maybe . . . well, maybe Kennedy had even arranged this little stunt. To win support. To make martyrs of his young men and turn a losing position into a winning one.

As soon as he'd had the thought he was convinced of it. It made perfect sense, after all. Michael's death—like Kustow's—served no one but Kennedy.

Finishing his call, Charles Lever put the comset down, laughing sourly. He could prove nothing yet, but given time he'd make the charge stick. First, however, he had to clear his own name and turn opinion around. And if that meant canning his feelings of betrayal, he would do that. He'd act a part. And in time, maybe, he would get his son back. Not the son he'd had. No, nothing could bring that back now. But something. A son in name. Yes, he'd have that much.

———

KIM WOKE SUDDENLY, kicking the cover away from him, his naked body sheened in sweat. He had been dreaming. Dreaming of his time in Rehabilitation.

He had been back there, in the Unit, the night that Luke had died, feeling that same tightness in his chest, that same awful, devastating sense of loss.

He sat up, setting his feet down on the warm, uncarpeted floor, then took a long, shuddering breath. The memory was so powerful, so vivid, that he had to remind himself where he was. Rebecca. Meeting Rebecca again had brought it all back. She had been there that night, along with Will and Deio. And the bird. The dead bird . . .

Five of them, there'd been. Clayborn. Escapees from that vast, uncharted darkness beneath the City's floor. Each one of them a product of the "Program"; an argument against the old saying that Clay was Clay and could not be raised.

Yes, he could see them even now as if they sat about him in the darkness. Deio, dark-eyed and curly-haired, to his left; the big, North European lad, Will, lolling beside him, the fingers of one hand combing through his short blond hair. Across from them sat Luke, his strong Latin looks reminiscent of an ancient *Ta Ts'in* emperor, a restrained, almost leonine power in his every movement. And finally Rebecca, silent, thoughtful, defensive, her oval face cupped between her hands as she stared back at Kim.

Slowly his breathing calmed. Slowly the ghosts faded from the room, until he alone remained. He leaned across, switching on the bedside lamp, then stood, looking about him, refamiliarizing himself with the tiny room. Anchoring himself to the here and now.

It was some time since he had dreamed so vividly. Some time since he had felt such fear, such loss, such longing. It was four years now since he had left the Unit, and in all that time he had never once looked back. Not that he'd forgotten those times. No, for it seemed he was incapable of forgetting. Rather, it was as if he had built a wall about them. A wall his conscious mind refused to climb.

Until now.

He went across to the tiny galley and stood at the sink, sluicing himself down, letting the cold water run down his face and chest and arms. And as he did he looked back again, remembering.

Rebecca. What did he remember of Rebecca?

Mostly her intensity, and the way she used to look at him, her dark eyes staring relentlessly, her whole face formed into a question. She had such a strong, intense face. A face perfectly suited for austerity and suffering. She was always the last to understand Deio's jokes; always the last to smile or laugh.

One would have thought that their shared experience would have bound them tight, yet she had always been the outsider among them, even after what had happened. And yet he had felt drawn to her even then—to the vulnerability he had sensed beneath that facade of imperturbability. Forgetting nothing, he remembered her words clearly, as if she had spoken them only yesterday. Recalled how angry she had felt at being "cheated":

"It's all just as Luke said. A trade. A crude exchange. Our lives for what we can give them. And the rest—all that pretense of caring—is nothing but hollow words and empty gestures."

Did she still believe that? Or had she forgotten what had happened back then? Last night, talking to her, it had been hard to tell. She had seemed so different; so outward and self-assured. But was that simply another mask?

After Rehabilitation she had signed on for three years with the giant CosVac Company as a commodity slave, working as a Technical Design Consultant, but had bought out her contract six months early to take up an offer from SimFic. She had worked for fifteen months in their East Asian arm, then had moved here three months back, reporting directly to Campbell.

She had done well for herself. To all intents and purposes she was her own boss; a free woman, defining her own aims, carving her own path up the levels. Yet standing there, listening to her, watching her laugh and smile, Kim had felt that, beneath it all, something was missing. Or was it memory playing tricks? Was it simply that he remembered how vulnerable she had been that day they had taken Will and Deio? Was it simply that he could see her still, sitting there alone in the common room, desolate, her tiny, doll-like hands trembling, afraid that they would come for her too?

Kim straightened up, studying himself in the mirror above the sink. Maybe he was wrong. After all, he himself had changed a great deal since those days. Four years. It wasn't long, but a lot could happen in that time.

He turned slightly, frowning. Something, perhaps the play of light on the water, reminded him suddenly of how the dream had begun. He had been in the pool, floating on his back, staring up at the ceiling, at the red, black, and gold of the ancient Tun Huang star map.

He narrowed his eyes, remembering. Slowly the colors melted, fading into black, while all about him the edges of the pool misted into nothingness. And suddenly he was alone, floating on the surface of the great ocean, a billion stars dusting the darkness overhead.

There was a moment's peace, of utter, perfect stillness, and then it happened.

With a noise like a vast sigh the surface of the water shuddered and became a massive field of earth; of moist, dark clay that stretched to the horizon. He began to struggle in the soft, dark earth, but the more he struggled the more the clay clung to his limbs, tugging at him, slowly sucking him down into its black, suffocating maw.

He cried out, and woke, on his back at the bottom of a deep, dark well. It was still and silent. Far above him the moon sat like a blinded eye in the center of the sky. Lifting his hand, he saw it appear far above him, like a vision, floating there in the darkness, the fingers groping for the light.

There was a noise nearby. A scrabbling, scratching sound. Turning, he saw, part embedded in the curving wall of the well, the faces of his friends Will, Deio, and Luke. From the clay beneath each face a pair of arms extended, hands clawing blindly at the clay that filled each eye, each choking mouth.

He looked back. His hand had floated free, beyond his grasp, but it didn't matter now. Lifting his bloated body, he began to climb, flexing his eight limbs quickly as he climbed the wall. Up, into the light.

At the top he turned, looking back. His friends had freed themselves. They lay there now, exhausted, at the foot of the well. Seeing him, they called out plaintively. *Save us, Lagasek! Save us from the darkness!*

He turned his great abdomen about, meaning to help them, to cast a silvered thread down through the darkness and let them climb to safety, yet even as he turned the earth heaved like a great sack and folded in upon itself. And they were gone.

He cried out . . . and woke a second time, back in the room, in Rehabilitation, himself again, listening to Will describe what he had seen on the plain below the ruins of Bremen. A tribe of men. Of blue-black men with teeth of polished bone.

Kim shuddered, remembering, then pushed back, away from the sink. He looked up, meeting his eyes in the mirror, conscious suddenly of a faint pulsing glow from the other room. He turned. The comset in the far corner of the bedroom had come on-line, the RESPOND key flashing a dull, insistent red.

He went through, leaning across the chair to tap in his personal access code. At once the message spilled out onto the screen.

> Meridian. Departing Titan: 15. 10. 2210 CKST
> Can route messages via SimFic's Saturn Rep.
>
> [Campbell]

He pulled out the chair and sat, the dream forgotten. *Jelka* . . . Jelka was on Titan! He imagined her out there and laughed, astonished. The gods alone knew how Campbell had found out, but he had. Kim shivered, a moment's doubt assailing him, then shook his head. No, he would grab this chance to speak to her—to let her know what had been happening. And to tell her that he would wait for her. However long it took.

CHAPTER EIGHTEEN

East Winds

Y OU'RE FAMOUS NOW, '' Kennedy was saying. "People expect things of you, Michael. Big things. You've been close to death, and that means something to them."

Michael Lever smiled faintly and looked away. He was propped up in bed, a small hill of pillows behind him. It was a large, private ward and on tables to one side were dozens of sprays of flowers from well-wishers. He looked back at Kennedy, a warmer expression on his face. "I appreciate what you're saying, but . . . well, it's just that I don't want to think too much about it yet." He looked down. "Not yet . . . okay?"

Kennedy sat back. "I understand, Michael. I'm not here to push you. Just to let you know how things stand. Right?"

"Right."

Later that afternoon Kennedy was flying off to Chicago. There, this evening, he would be making a speech on the matter of the proposed new population legislation—in particular on what they were calling the "Euthanasia Bill." The attack on Lever had meant that more than the normal media attention would be on the speech. Already several channels had been clamoring for Michael's reactions and comments. Thus far Kennedy had fended them off, but they both knew that, denied some kind of response, the media could well turn hostile. Kennedy was here to try to persuade Michael to make a limited comment.

"I'm sorry that it had to happen this way, Michael. This kind of life . . . it's hyperreal. They want you to live every second in the lights. And they're hungry. Like sharks. Feed them some blood—the other guy's blood, if you can—and they're happy. But you can't keep them out of the water. And you can't make friends with them. Not in any real sense. So you have to deal with them on their own terms."

Michael looked up. He was less pale than he had been, but he still looked drawn. "I understand, Joe." He sighed and reached out to scratch at his useless legs. "Let's compromise, huh? Tell them I'm tired now—sedated, maybe—and that I'm going to see the playback of the speech in the morning and speak to them then. How about that? That way you could get back here, maybe . . ." He leaned back again, looking up hopefully at the older man.

Kennedy smiled. "Okay. We'll do it your way. And I'll try and get back for the conference."

"Try?"

"I'll be here, Michael. Okay?"

Michael nodded and let his head relax, closing his eyes. Kennedy, watching him, felt the weight of all the unsaid things press down on him briefly. The last week had been the hardest he had known, the demands on him exhausting; but it would all be worth it in the long run. For a moment he sat back and closed his eyes, pressing at his face and yawning. He needed sleep, a whole week's worth of sleep, but there wasn't time just now. This was a crucial moment: make or break time.

Only two days ago Charles Lever had come out of his self-imposed isolation and spoken to the media about his feelings of grief and anger at what had happened to his son. Kennedy had made sure that Michael hadn't seen it, nor heard anything of the rumor circulating that Charles Lever had organized the attempt on his son's life. But things were in flux. The bombing had acted as a catalyst—fragmenting popular opinion into two diametrically opposed camps. They had benefited from the initial public outcry, and their fortunes had risen dramatically on a tidal wave of emotional reaction, but in the week that followed the old men had fought back. The media stories about Kennedy and the other young men were vicious and often quite unabashedly libelous. To even try to answer some of the grosser charges was impossible. Cornered, their opponents were throwing mud. And some of it would stick.

Strangest of all that had happened that week were two separate and quite unexpected developments. First, two days back, at the same time that Charles Lever was talking to the media, Kennedy had been approached by an old acquaintance, a young man who claimed to be representing the "Sons"—the group formed from the old Dispersionist faction. Michael Lever and his friends had once been members of the group, but had broken with them when they had linked up with Kennedy. Now, it seemed, the Sons wanted to meet and come to some kind of arrangement.

Only an hour after that visit, someone else had come to see Kennedy—Fen Cho-hsien, Wu Shih's chief minister.

He had sat there for a long time afterward, wondering if the two events were somehow connected—were an elaborate setup, designed to trap and expose him to the media—but eventually he decided that it was a genuine coincidence; one of those tiny twists of fate that made life both unpredictable and interesting. The Sons had not said what they wanted, and he had committed himself only to a meeting. But Fen Cho-hsien had been specific. Wu Shih wanted a deal.

He had hoped to talk to Michael of this. To sound him on it. But Michael wasn't ready yet. Bryn Kustow's death was too close. He was still shocked; horrified by how personal this business was; astonished that someone—anyone—should want him dead. A veil had been torn aside and he had glimpsed what all of this was really about.

Kennedy opened his eyes and looked at the now sleeping Lever. He would be a better man for this personal knowledge. Harder, less easy to fool. Though the loss of Bryn was tragic, what they had gained might yet make up for it.

And for himself?

As a Kennedy he had always known how things stood. He had been taught, from his family's long history, how naked power was, and how frail the flesh that wielded that power. And now Wu Shih had made that history personal. If he said, "Come, make a deal," then he would need to go and do as he was told. What other choice was there?

He shivered and stood up, leaving Michael to sleep. Perhaps it was best that things were as they were. That way he alone could be blamed. He alone take the responsibility.

━━━━━━

DEAD MAN YUN pulled a piece of steaming pork from the pot and popped it into his mouth, then turned, facing Fat Wong.

"Aren't they beautiful, Wong Yi-sun? Aren't they just peaches?"

Fat Wong smiled, looking across to where the three young boys sheltered in the skirts of their mother, Yun Yueh-hui's daughter.

"They are little emperors, Yueh-hui. If they were my grandsons I would want no more from life."

Dead Man Yun's face creased into a rare smile. He laughed, then slapped Fat Wong's back robustly. "That is so, Wong Yi-sun. I am a blessed man. The gods have truly smiled on me."

Fat Wong reached out, embracing his old friend briefly, touched by his words. One could not count on much in this life, but Yun Yueh-hui had been a staunch ally these past ten years. As safe as T'ai Shan.

"You know what to say?"

Yun nodded, his face impassive. "I know my part in this, Yi-sun, and I am happy with it. We have no choice. We must cleanse ourselves of this scourge before it overwhelms us."

"Indeed." Fat Wong moved back, watching as Yun turned, giving final instructions to his servants. Then, at Yun's signal, they went back into the dining room, the two of them following the servants and their heaped trays.

The others were waiting for them there: Ho Chin, Feng Shang-pao, and Li Chin, the three Bosses looking up from their places at the great oval table. It was a long time since they had met like this, and Fat Wong, looking about him, felt a vague sadness that this should pass. But pass it must. The Great Wheel had turned. Change was inevitable. And he could not let old friendships stand in the way of that. Not unless he wished his family's banner to hang in another's hall.

Fat Wong sat, smiling at each of his fellows in turn, then watched as the servants set out the bowls—thirty courses in all—at the center of the table.

"Why, this is excellent," Three-Finger Ho said, speaking for them all. "It is many years since I ate snake and monkey-brains."

Yun lowered his head slightly. "I am honored that you like my humble fare. But come, *ch'un tzu*. Let us begin. Before the rice grows cold."

They had met tonight to deal with Lehmann, to settle things, once and for all, but for a time their talk steered clear of the matter, as if it were a jagged rock. Fat Wong was happy with this, savoring the meal, the flow of casual pleasantries, but as the servants began to clear the bowls, he turned the conversation, bringing it directly to the point.

"So what are we to do about this upstart? How are we to rid ourselves of this *pai nan jen?*"

The term brought smiles from about the table; but they were tense, nervous smiles that faded quickly. "The white man." It was how they had come to talk of Lehmann among themselves, as if the term distinguished him from the other *Hung Mao*. Moreover, it was apt. For everywhere he went, death—the White T'ang—seemed to follow.

"Let us kill him," Three-Finger Ho said bluntly. "Hire a *shao lin* to assassinate him."

"It has been tried," General Feng said, wiping his fingers on the wet cloth, then handing it to the servant behind him. "Whiskers Lu tried it, but our friend was too clever for him. No, if we are to strike, it must be through someone close to him. Someone he trusts."

"Difficult," Li the Lidless interjected, sucking at his fingers noisily. "He lets few come close to him, and those are fiercely loyal. I doubt we would find one among them who would take our blood money. No. We would be better off fighting him."

"A war?" Fat Wong asked, eyeing Li from across the table. "An all-out war, to the death?"

Beside him, Dead Man Yun looked down.

"Exactly," Li Chin said, leaning across to take the last few cashews from one of the bowls before the servant cleared it. "Five against one. How could we lose?"

Fat Wong looked down, suddenly apprehensive. If Li Chin's idea took hold he was in trouble. The agreement he had reached with Li Yuan—whatever its merits in the long run—depended in the short term on him maintaining peace down here in the Lowers. Were he to break that agreement, who knew how Li Yuan might react? Had his preparations been more advanced he might have risked it. But he was not ready yet. He could not afford to antagonize Li Yuan.

"Is that wise?" he asked quietly, meeting Li's staring, egglike eyes with a show of apparent openness. "I have some sympathy for your view, Li Chin, but think of the cost, the disruption to our enterprises. Have we not always said that it is better to make money than fight wars? Is that not why we have thrived while others have gone under?"

"Maybe so," Li answered. "But when the east wind blows, the wise man bows before it. We must bow to the inevitable, Wong Yi-sun. We must fight the *pai nan jen*, before it is too late."

"Is war the only course left to us, brother Li?" Dead Man Yun asked, gesturing for his servants to leave the room. "Have we exhausted every other option?"

Li Chin turned, facing Yun. "Every day that passes makes him stronger. Can you not see it, Yun Yueh-hui? We can delay no longer. We must act. At once."

Yun nodded. "Of course. That is why we are here tonight, neh? To deal with this problem before it becomes insoluble. But we must think hard before setting out on such a venture. War is like a fire, easy to start, but hard to control. I do not rule it out. No. But we must save it for our final option, when all else has failed."

Li looked about him, seeing how the others were nodding in agreement and sat back, shrugging. "So what do you propose?"

Yun glanced briefly at Wong Yi-sun, then looked back at Li, his dark eyes staring back unblinkingly from his death-mask face. "I say we starve him out. Destroy his markets. Attack him indirectly, through his middlemen. Undermine him and make his rule untenable."

"And if that fails?"

"*Then* we fight him."

Li considered a moment, then nodded. "Okay. But how long do you propose we give ourselves? Six months? A year?"

"Six months," Fat Wong said, hiding his satisfaction. Yes, and then there would be war. But not against Lehmann. No. For by that time he would have swallowed Lehmann up, pearl-handled knife and all.

"East winds . . ." he said, lifting his wine cup and looking about the table. "Here's to east winds!"

◆◆◆◆◆

FROM WHERE THEY STOOD, high up on a Fourth Level balcony, overlooking the busy thoroughfare, the two men could see the loaded carts being wheeled back toward the interdeck transit elevator. Lehmann's men were everywhere, keeping the inquisitive at bay, making sure the operation went smoothly and without a hitch.

"You've covered yourself?" Lehmann said, not looking at the man beside him, his eyes taking in everything that was happening down below.

"Naturally," the Major answered casually. "It'll be weeks before they sort out the mix-up. And even then they won't be certain just what happened."

"And your Captains know nothing?"

The Major smiled broadly. "No more than the men. As I said, it's all a question of overlays. Of contradictory information. My man's good. One of the best when it comes to manipulating the records. When the *T'ing Wei* come to investigate the matter, they'll find two sets of information—two versions of events—and both will be corroborated."

Lehmann glanced at the officer. "And the money?"

"Don't worry, my friend. It's salted away where no prying eyes will find it. As I said, I'm a patient man. Six years from now I can take early retirement, if I want it, that is. When I do, I can look forward to a nice little nest egg, neh? And all this will have been forgotten by then. No one will notice if I live like a T'ang. They will think merely that I have invested wisely over the years."

He laughed, but Lehmann, beside him, was silent, thoughtful. He had paid the Major two and a half million to set this up. A further two and a half was due once this was done. In return he got munitions worth half that much, maybe even less. But it was worth it. Because this way no one would know they had them. This way no rival Boss would get to hear what he was up to.

Lehmann turned from the balcony. "Let's go," he said, touching the Major's arm. "I want to be out of here before those alarms start sounding."

The Major nodded, studying Lehmann a moment, an unasked question on his lips, then turned, following the albino back down the stairwell toward the waiting lift.

━━━━━━

THE CROWD in the great hall had fallen silent. Only a faint murmur of silks could be heard as heads turned to see who it was had come among them. A thousand faces, Han, aristocratic, looked toward the giant, jade-paneled doors at the far end of the hall. Two men stood there.

The *Hung Mao* stood between the towering doors, looking about him. There was the faintest trace of a smile on his lips, but his eyes were keen, sharply observant. For a *min* he held himself well; proudly, as if he too were *ch'un tzu*. Beside him was the Chancellor, Fen Cho-hsien, looking impatient, clearly put out by the fact that he had to accompany the man. "Come," he said distinctly, and started forward, moving between the lines of guests. The *Hung Mao* walked behind him, looking from side to side quite openly, his head making small bows, his face lit by the mildest, most innocuous of smiles, as though he realized his presence was offensive and wished to minimize that insult.

When Chancellor Fen reached the smaller doors on the far side of the hall he turned abruptly, and signaling to the musicians, whose instruments had fallen silent with the rest, he spoke a few words in the mother tongue to those nearest him. At once heads turned back and conversation began to pick up. The orchestra started up a moment later.

"I am sorry to come among you thus," said the *Hung Mao* quietly.

Fen Cho-hsien studied him a moment, then nodded, placated by the modesty of the man. He was not like most of the others. There was a subtlety, a grace about him that was rarely found among them. Most were like apes, crude in the expression of their needs. But this one was different. Fen Cho-hsien bowed slightly and turned to face the doors again, knocking firmly on the carved and lacquered panel.

Two guards opened the doors and they went through, into an

anteroom, then down a narrow corridor where a ceiling scanner rotated in its flexible cradle, following them. At the far end of the corridor, more guards were waiting. The *Hung Mao* had been searched already, but now they repeated the process, checking him thoroughly while the Minister waited, his eyes averted. Satisfied, one of them spoke into a handset and pressed out a code. Behind them, the doors to the inner sanctum opened.

Wu Shih came forward, hands extended. "Representative Kennedy, it is a delight to meet you at last. I have seen much and heard much about you." He took the American's hands and pressed them firmly, his eyes meeting Kennedy's with an expression partway between greeting and challenge. "I felt it was time that we met . . . and talked."

The room was a delicate blue, every piece of furniture chosen to complement its soft, relaxing shade. When they sat it was on low chairs with silk cushions of a rich, deep blue, speckled with petals of peach and ivory and bronze. Kennedy's dark business silks seemed intrusive, a foreign element. He sat there, trying not to feel discomfort. There had been no time to change. The summons had said "At once," and you did not argue with the word of a T'ang. Not yet, anyway.

Wu Shih leaned forward, the silk folds of his long, flowing gown whispering softly. He seemed soft, almost effeminate beside the big, hard-featured *Hung Mao*, but his eyes were like the eyes of a hunting bird and his hands, where they showed from the soft blue silk, were hard and dark and strong.

"I am sorry I gave you so little time. In such matters it is best to act quickly. This way no one knows you are here."

Kennedy made a small, turning movement of his head, as if to indicate the crowded hall outside, but Wu Shih simply smiled.

"No one but you and I. What I tell my people not to see they do not see."

Kennedy smiled, understanding, but remained on his guard.

"You wonder what I want. Why I should ask you here today."

"You'll tell me," Kennedy answered matter-of-factly.

Wu Shih sat up a little, reassessing things. Then he laughed.

"Indeed. I am forgetting. You are a realist, not an idealist. You deal with real things, not dreams."

There was truth as well as irony in the words. Wu Shih had been doing his homework. But then, so too had Kennedy.

"The attainment of real things—that can be a dream, can it not?"

Wu Shih gave a small nod. "Not like other dreams, neh?"

He was referring clearly to the Cutler Institute. To the dreams of the Old Men.

"*Yu Kung!*" Kennedy said. *Foolish old men.*

Wu Shih laughed and clapped his hands. "You know our tongue, then, *Shih* Kennedy?"

"Enough to understand. Perhaps enough to pass."

The T'ang sat back, studying him. "There's something that was not in your file. Where did you learn the *Kuan hua?*"

"My father had many dealings with your servants and your father's servants. A little knowledge of your ways was helpful. It was one of the great secrets of his success."

"And your father taught you?"

Kennedy smiled and nodded. At that moment he seemed his most boyish and charming and Wu Shih, looking at him, felt some element of warmth creep into his calculations. He liked this particular American. So unlike the crabby old men and their shriveled dreams of forever.

"Then perhaps my intuition is better than I first thought."

Wu Shih hesitated, then stood and turned away from the American. Kennedy, aware of protocol, got to his feet, waiting silently to find out why Wu Shih had summoned him. After a minute or so, the T'ang turned back to face him.

"I must choose to trust you, *Shih* Kennedy. And that is no light thing for a T'ang to do. We trust few to know what lies within our minds, and you are a stranger here. Even so, I will trust you."

Kennedy gave the slightest bow, his eyes never leaving the other's face.

"You are a clever man, Joseph Kennedy. You know how things are. Where the power lies in this City. And you know how to use power, how to manufacture the raw stuff of which it is made." The T'ang

allowed himself a smile. "And no, not money. Not just that. Something deeper, more dependable than money. Loyalty. I see you and I
see those about you and I recognize what it is that binds them to you."
He paused. "You are a strong man, *Shih* Kennedy. A powerful man.
My ministers have told me I should crush you. Find ways to dishonor
you. To entrap you and buy you. They have proposed a dozen different
schemes to break you and humiliate you."

Kennedy said nothing. He stood there, his head slightly lowered,
listening, his watchful eyes taking in everything. Wu Shih, noting
this, smiled inwardly. Kennedy was no fool. His strength came
from deep within—from a self-confidence that, like his own, was
innate.

"However, what I see of you I like. I see a man who thinks like a
man ought to think. Who puts his people before himself. And I like
that. I *respect* it. But as a practical man I must ask myself a question.
Can there be two Kings in City America? If I let this man—
yourself—continue thus, will I not, in time, fall prey to his success?"

He was quiet a moment, then, "Well?"

"I am the T'ang's man," Kennedy answered, no hesitation or trace
of uncertainty in the words. "I speak not against the Seven, but
against the Old Men."

Wu Shih narrowed his eyes a moment, then nodded. "So you say
now, Joseph Kennedy. But what when America is yours? What when
the people come to you and say, 'You, Representative Kennedy, are
the man who should be King. You are American. Let us be ruled by an
American!' How will you answer them? Will you turn to them and say,
'I am the T'ang's man'?" He laughed. "I like you, and I do you the
honor of trusting you with these thoughts, but I am no *yu kung, Shih*
Kennedy. I too am a practical man."

Kennedy was silent a moment. Then, with what seemed almost a
sigh, he spoke again. "What do you want from me, *Chieh Hsia?* What
can I give you to ensure my loyalty?"

Wu Shih came closer until he stood almost face to face with the
American. "I want a hostage."

Kennedy frowned, not understanding.

"There is a new technique my friend Li Yuan has been perfecting.
A means of control."

"Control?"

"It is a simple technical device. It does no harm, I assure you, and the operation is perfectly safe."

"And you want me to . . . to undergo this operation?"

Wu Shih shook his head. "No, *Shih* Kennedy. I see you still don't understand. I want no martyrs. No, nothing like that." He smiled and reached out to lay his hand on the American's shoulder. "I mean your wife, your sons. That's who I mean."

———————

EMILY CLOSED THE DOOR and turned, facing Michael, alone with him at last. She felt raw, her nerves exposed by all that had happened these past few days. The pace of events had left her no time to come to terms with what she felt, but now, facing him, it all came welling up; all the grief and hurt and naked fear.

She went across and stood there, looking down at him. He was asleep, his face pale and pinched, his left hand, where it lay above the cover, flecked with tiny scabs. She had seen the detailed pictures of his injuries, of the horrific damage to his legs and lower back; had stood there in the background while First Surgeon Chang had explained to Kennedy what needed to be done. And had felt nothing, only a sense of numbed unreality. Of shock that this should have happened now. Now when she had finally decided to commit herself.

She took a long breath, then shook her head, reminding herself that all of that had ended. To organize one needed anonymity, and in the space of twenty-four hours she had become famous coast to coast, a "face," "Michael Lever's wife." So now that option was denied her. If she wished to do something—to shape this god-awful world for the good—she must find another way.

She looked down at him and sighed, then put her hand out, touching his brow gently, reassured to find it warm.

His wife. But what had that meant so far? That she shared his bed. And beyond that?

Beyond that it had meant nothing. Kennedy had made sure of that. Yes, for it was Kennedy who had made sure she stayed at home whenever Michael traveled about the City; Kennedy who had insisted that she sit with the other wives and girlfriends while the men discussed matters of moment. For, after all, wasn't this a man's world? And wasn't that her role—to be the quiet, dutiful wife?

She shuddered, realizing that she had been lying to herself this past year. Oh, she had been happy enough, even when Michael had been away, for their reunions were moments to savor, to look forward to with sweet anticipation. Yet it had never been enough. And now, faced with the prospect of living without that, she understood the price she had paid for her happiness; how much of herself she had denied.

Kennedy. It all came back to Kennedy.

Since the day she had married Michael he had made sure that she was shut out of things; her voice silenced, her views ignored. Almost as if he sensed that there was something that distinguished her from the women of his own social circle, his level. Something more than a simple question of breeding.

And Michael? Michael had accepted it all, as if there were nothing wrong with it. And maybe, in truth, he really couldn't see it, for he too had been bred to accept things as they were. But all that must change. She was determined on it. From now on she would be at his side at all times, offering advice and support, discussing each issue with him as it arose, challenging his inbred notions of the world and its ways, whatever Kennedy and the others thought of it.

She shivered, suddenly indignant, recalling all the times that Kennedy had snubbed her. "My dear," he called her condescendingly. Well, she would show him from here on.

"Em . . . ?"

Michael was looking up at her, a weak yet somehow radiant smile lighting his features. Seeing it, all thought evaporated. She reached down and hugged him, gently, carefully, laughing as she did.

"How are you feeling?" she said, kneeling beside him, her face close to his own, her hand clasping his.

"Tired," he said, "and a little numb. But better, much better than I was. I'm glad the cameras have gone, that's all. It was hard. Bryn's death . . ."

She smoothed his brow. "I know. Don't talk about it now. Let's talk about us, eh? About what we're going to do about all this."

There was a flicker of pain in his eyes, a moment's uncertainty, and then he spoke, his voice strangely quiet. "If you want a divorce . . . ?"

She shook her head, strangely moved by the directness of his words, by the blunt honesty of the man.

"It's still there, isn't it?" she said, a faint smile on her lips. "They didn't blow it off, did they?"

He smiled grimly. "Not that I know of."

"Shall I take a look?"

"Em!" He laughed, his laughter shading into a cough. "Behave yourself! The cameras!"

"Bugger the cameras," she said quietly. "Besides, it might give the bastards something to smile about, neh?"

For a time they were silent, looking at each other, then Michael turned his head aside, a slight bitterness, or was it self-pity, registering in his face.

"It'll be hard," he said. "Harder for you, perhaps, than for me. I've only got to get better. You . . ."

"I'll survive," she said, squeezing his hand. "Besides, I've something to do now, haven't I? Something to take my mind off things."

He looked back at her. "What do you mean?"

She smiled. "I'm your wife, Michael. That means something now. Much more than it did before this happened. It gives me a voice."

"And you want that?"

She considered a moment, then nodded. "I've seen things," she said. "Down there in the Lowers. Things you wouldn't believe. Suffering. Awful, indescribable suffering. And I want to do something about it. Something positive."

He stared at her a moment, then nodded, a smile coming to his face. "You're a good woman, Em. The best a man could have. And if that's what you want, then go ahead. Besides, I think you're right. Joe's looking at how this affects the elections, but it's bigger than that, isn't it? I've been thinking, Em. Bryn's death . . ." A flash of pain crossed his face. "Bryn's death has got to mean something. Something good has got to come out of it. So maybe you're right. Maybe we should use this opportunity. You in your way, me in mine."

"And Joseph Kennedy?"

"You don't get on, do you? I've noticed it. From the first, I guess. But it didn't seem to matter before now. He's a good man, Em. I'd vouch for it. But you do what you have to. And if he opposes you, tell me. I'll back you. You know I will."

She smiled, then leaned closer, kissing his brow. "I know. In fact, I've always known it. But as you say, it didn't matter much before now."

━━━━━━

LI YUAN CROUCHED there in the shallows of the lake at Tongjiang, his silks hitched up to his knees, facing his fifteen-month-old son.

Kuei Jen was leaning forward as he splashed his father, giggling uncontrollably, his chubby arms flailing at the water, his dark small head beaded with bright droplets.

A ragged line of servants stood knee-deep in the water close by, guarding the deeper water, the sunlight gleaming off their shaven heads, their faces wreathed in smiles as they watched their T'ang playing with the young prince.

On the bank, a picnic had been set up. From beneath the gold and red silk awnings, Li Yuan's wives looked on, laughing and smiling at their husband's antics. Lai Shi and Fu Ti Chang were sitting at the back, on a long seat heaped with cushions, but Mien Shan, Kuei Jen's mother, stood almost at the water's edge, her laughter edged with concern.

Kuei Jen turned, looking across at his mother, then jumped, a funny little movement that brought laughter from all about him. The infant looked around, wide-eyed with surprise, then, seeing the smiles on every face, clapped his hands and, giggling, jumped again.

"That's right!" Yuan yelled delightedly, encouraging him. "Wriggle, my little fish! Wriggle!" And, throwing back his head, he roared with laughter.

But Kuei Jen was beginning to get overexcited, and this time, when he jumped, he stumbled, throwing out his tiny hands as he fell, a brief cry of surprise escaping him before he went under. Quickly, Li Yuan bent down and scooped the spluttering Kuei Jen up, holding him close against his chest, there-there-ing him, and kissing his face.

For a while Kuei Jen howled and howled, but slowly Li Yuan's gentle words had their effect and the child calmed, nuzzling in close to his father's chest.

"There!" Li Yuan said, lifting him and holding him up, above him, at arm's length. He laughed softly. "No harm done, eh, my little fish? No harm."

For a moment longer he hugged his son, kissing the dark crown of his head. "You're a good boy, neh?" he murmured. "A good boy." Then, turning in the water, he waded across to the shore and handed Kuei Jen to his mother.

Mien Shan took her son, looking past him at Li Yuan and smiling broadly. "Thank you, Yuan," she said quietly. "And you are a good father to your son. The very best of fathers."

She turned, summoning her maids. At once they were at her side with towels and dry clothing, tending to the child.

Li Yuan smiled, touched by her words, then stepped up onto the bank, letting one of his body servants towel down his legs while another brought a fresh tunic and fussed about him, dressing him. As they finished, he turned and looked across. Lai Shi and Fu Ti Chang were watching him, their heads close, talking. He smiled, then went across, planting himself between them, putting his arms about their shoulders.

For a moment he sat there, silently enjoying the day. Out on the lake the men had begun to play a game with a stuffed ox's bladder, batting it about and diving to catch it, throwing up great sprays of water, to the amusement of all. Even Kuei Jen had stopped whimpering and had turned to watch them, a smile of amusement lighting his tiny features.

Watching it all, Yuan felt a shiver of contentment pass through him. This was enough, surely? Enough for any man. To have this day, this sunlit, happy hour forever, that *surely* was enough?

He waited, silent within himself, but for once there was no dark voice to counter that first strong feeling of contentment. So maybe this was it—the balance he had been seeking all these years. Maybe it was simple after all. A matter of relaxing. Of letting go.

"Yuan?"

He turned his head, looking into the dark and pretty eyes of his Second Wife, Lai Shi.

"What is it, my love?"

Her eyes slipped away, meeting Fu Ti Chang's on the other side of him, then returned to his. "It's just that we were talking. Wondering . . ."

Something in her face, maybe the slightest hint of mischievousness in her mouth, told him at once what they had been talking of.

"Wondering whose bed I would come to tonight, is that it?"

Lai Shi nodded.

For a moment he studied her. Lai Shi was not the prettiest of his wives. No, for there was something about her features—some irregularity in that long northern face—that did not quite meet the conventional standard of beauty. Yet when she smiled, when her eyes sparkled with mischief, there was a sensuality to her face, a voluptuousness, that made her by far the most attractive of his wives.

Saying nothing, he turned, facing his Third Wife, Fu Ti Chang. She was the tallest of his wives but also the youngest; a long-legged willow of a girl with breasts like tiny pears and an elegance that, at times, he found intoxicating. She sat there, letting him study her, her large eyes meeting his openly, that modesty that was so ingrained a part of her character staring out at him.

"You wish for a decision?"

Fu Ti Chang nodded.

He turned. "And you, Lai Shi?"

"Yes, husband. But before you do, let me say something. That ten days is a long time for us to be without you. Last night you went to Mien Shan's bed. And before that . . ."

"Before that I was away." He laughed. "I understand, Lai Shi. A woman is a woman, neh? She has her needs."

Lai Shi smiled, while Fu Ti Chang looked down, a faint blush at her neck.

"Well, a decision you shall have. But first let me say what it is I most like about each of you. Why the choice is such a difficult one."

"Husband . . ." Lai Shi protested, but Li Yuan shook his head.

"No. You will hear me out. And then I shall tell you my decision."

He lay his head back on the cushions and stared out across the lake, considering a moment. Then, with a brief laugh, he began to speak.

"If we are to believe, as the ancient Buddhists once believed, that every soul has been upon this earth before, then Fu Ti Chang was once, I am convinced, a horse. A beautiful, elegant horse, with a good, strong rump, long, fine legs, and the stamina of a Thoroughbred. Many a night have I had her in the saddle until dawn, and never once has she complained of tiredness!"

There was a giggle from Lai Shi, but Fu Ti Chang herself was still, listening to his every word.

"But what I like most about my sweet Fu are her hands. For my youngest wife has the gentlest hands under Heaven. If Kuan Yin ever made love to a mortal man, then I am certain it was in the form of my darling Fu Ti Chang."

Fu Ti Chang gave a slight bow of her head, clearly touched by his words.

"Now, as for Lai Shi, well, what am I to say? That she is the naughtiest of my girls, the most willful?"

"Tell me what creature I was, husband. In my former life . . ."

He laughed. "Why that's easy, Lai Shi. You were a bird. A mischievous magpie, the bringer of good news and joy."

"A magpie!" She laughed delightedly.

"Yes," he said, smiling broadly, enjoying the game. "With a wicked, teasing mouth that, many a night, has settled in my nest."

She smiled, her dark eyes sparkling. "Can I help it if little *niao* needs to be fed . . ."

He roared with laughter. "Maybe so, Lai Shi. But eaten?"

He stood, then turned back, looking down at them. "Nan Ho chose well for me, neh? Too well, perhaps, for how am I to choose? Thoroughbred or magpie, which is it to be? I feel as if I ought to have a copy made of myself."

"Two copies," Fu Ti Chang said, ever practical.

He turned, looking across to where Mien Shan was standing at the lake's edge, the now-sleeping Kuei Jen cradled against her shoulder. "Of course. I had not forgotten Mien Shan. But as for tonight . . . well, why don't you both come to my bed?"

"Both?" Fu Ti Chang stared back at him, shocked, it seemed, but, beside her, Lai Shi was grinning broadly. She leaned close, whispering something to Fu Ti Chang. For a moment Fu Ti Chang looked puzzled. She frowned intently. Then, unexpectedly, she let out a peal of raucous laughter.

"Yes," he heard her whisper, and found himself intrigued.

They turned back, facing him again, suddenly very formal, sitting up straight-backed in the long seat.

"Well?" he asked. "Is it a satisfactory answer?"

"Whatever our husband wishes," Fu Ti Chang said, bowing to him, her face cracking as Lai Shi began to giggle at her side. "*Whatever* our husband wishes."

He was about to comment, to ask them what was going on, when a movement to his right distracted him. He looked across. His Master of the Inner Chambers, Chan Teng, was standing there, his head bowed.

"What is it, Master Chan? Is something wrong?"

"No, *Chieh Hsia*. All is well."

"And the packing? That goes well?"

"We are almost done, *Chieh Hsia*."

"Good. Then it is something else, neh?"

Chan Teng bowed. "That is so, *Chieh Hsia*. Marshal Tolonen is here, for your appointment."

Li Yuan shook his head. "I did not expect him until four. Is it that late, already?"

"I am afraid so, *Chieh Hsia*."

Ah, he thought; *then the afternoon is almost done.* He looked about him, savoring the sights that met his eyes; the servants playing in the lake, his wives, his sleeping son. *There must be more days like this*, he thought. *Days of ease and happiness. For without them, what is life?*

Nothing, came the answer. *Less than nothing.*

He turned back, facing his Master of the Inner Chambers. "Thank you, Master Chan. Go now and tell the Marshal that I will be with him in a while. I must have a final word here."

Chan Teng bowed, then backed away, turning and hurrying off toward the great sweep of steps and the palace beyond. Li Yuan watched him go, then turned back, looking at his wives. It would have been nice to have gone with them tomorrow, to spend a few more days with them before duty called him back, but that was not to be. There was far too much to do, down here on Chung Kuo: the GenSyn Hearings were due to start shortly, and then there were the preparations for the reopening of the House.

A copy . . . He laughed, remembering what had been said. Yes, it would have been good to have had a copy—a twin—of himself these past few years. One to work and one to play. Two selves to share the joys and burdens of this world.

He turned. Mien Shan was watching him, smiling, real love there in her eyes as she held the sleeping child. He went across and held her, kissing her brow, then, bending down, carefully took Kuei Jen from her.

For a moment he closed his eyes, lulled by the gentle warmth of his son pressed close against him, then, with a final, tender kiss on the infant's cheek, he handed him back, smiling at Mien Shan.

"Ten days," he said, a faint sigh escaping his lips. "Ten days, that's all, my love, and then I'll join you up above."

THIS FAR into United Bamboo territory, Fat Wong's runners seemed to outnumber the common people by two or three to one. Young men wearing the emerald-green headbands of the Triad moved past Lehmann constantly as he walked the packed corridors, while in the great thoroughfare of Main, groups of young affluent-looking Han, their green silks displaying the hand and bamboo cane symbol of the United Bamboo, sat around tables, relaxed, drinking and playing *Chou* or *Mah-Jongg*, for all the world like young aristocrats.

He had heard that Fat Wong was the biggest of his rivals and now, through the false lenses he wore to mask his true identity, he could see it was so. Here, in the cluster of stacks that formed the heartland of the United Bamboo, the wealth of the brotherhood was on open display. A dozen great cinnamon trees rested in massive ornamental bowls along the central aisle of Main, while to either side the balconies were festooned with bright red slogan banners and garlands of colorful flowers, as if in celebration. The shops along the central mall were full, the products cheap—a fifth the price you'd find anywhere else in the City—while everywhere he looked there was an underlying

sense of orderliness he had seen nowhere else in the City at this low a
level.

Indeed, if he had not known better, he might have thought himself
a good twenty decks higher, up near the top of the City.

Lehmann looked about him as he went, his eyes taking in everything, the tiny cameras, implanted into the cornea of the lenses,
recording every detail.

He had read the secret Security report the Major had obtained for
him. At the last reckoning Wong Yi-sun's annual turnover had been
more than one hundred and twenty billion *yuan*. It was a massive sum;
one that, to be frank, had surprised him, for it dwarfed his own
turnover by a factor of twenty to one. That was worrying, true, but no
cause for despair. No, for if anything it made his task easier. Only the
Wo Shih Wo and Dead Man Yun's Red Gang could compete with the
United Bamboo in terms of market share and the two of them
combined were only half Fat Wong's size. It was little wonder, then,
that his spies had reported back that the other Bosses were growing a
little wary of their erstwhile friend. Indeed, after what had happened
to Iron Mu, they were right to be suspicious of Wong Yi-sun's motives.

So much so, in fact, that, after their dinner at Dead Man Yun's,
three of the Bosses had met again, hours later, to discuss their own
secret agenda. An agenda that, had he known of it, would have
outraged the birdlike Wong.

At the gateway between the stacks, Lehmann waited at the barrier
to show his documentation to one of the guards. As before, the
regular Security men were shadowed all the while by United Bamboo
officials who checked their work and made their own unofficial checks
on who went through into their territory. Thus far Lehmann had
passed through all five gates with only the minimum of fuss, but this
time, as the guard made to hand him back his card and pass him
through, one of the officials—a bald-headed Han with a deeply
scarred chin and a short, slightly corpulent figure—took the card
from the guard's hand and, pushing him aside, placed himself directly
in front of Lehmann.

He glanced down at the card, then looked back at Lehmann, his
whole manner hostile. "What are you doing here, *Shih* Snow? What is
your business in this stack?"

Lehmann lowered his head, as if in respect, and held out the papers he had had prepared, offering them to the Triad official. "Forgive me, Excellency, but I have a routine maintenance call to make. The documents will explain."

From beneath his lashes, he saw how the man deliberately ignored the papers, disdaining to take them.

"Who asked you to come? Which official did you speak to?"

"It was Yueh Pa. He informed our office two hours back that there was a malfunction in one of the junction boxes. In the east stack, Level 34."

That much was true. Indeed, he had been waiting three weeks for something to go wrong so that he might pay this visit. But once in, he had no intention of putting the fault right. At least, not in the sense they wanted it done.

"Yueh Pa, eh?" The Han turned, offering a few words of Mandarin to his colleague, then turned back to Lehmann, letting the card fall from his fingers. "You can pass through, *Shih* Snow, but I will have one of my men assigned to you all the while you are here, understand? I do not like strangers. Especially *Hung Mao*. So keep your eyes to yourself, do your job, and go."

I understand, pig's ass, Lehmann thought, bowing low to retrieve his card, then maintaining the bow as he circled the man and ducked under the half-raised barrier. Not that it would help them, even if they attached a dozen runners to watch him.

He waited there, head lowered, while the official called across a young thin-faced runner and gave him his instructions. Bowing low to his Master, the young Han turned and, coming across to Lehmann, barked at him in Mandarin, showing him the same contempt his Master had shown. With a bow, Lehmann handed his papers across to the young brute, showing nothing of what he felt, then followed on behind the man. On into the very heart of Fat Wong's territory.

———————

"*Shih* Kennedy! *Shih* Kennedy! Is it true what you said in your speech tonight about the so-called Euthanasia Bill?"

Kennedy stood on the rostrum of the Press Room, elegant and powerful, facing the crush of media men and reporters. Remotes buzzed about his head like giant bugs, hovering in the bright, over-head lights, their hungry lenses capturing his every word, his every gesture, but it was to the men below that he played, addressing them by name, leaning toward each questioner as he framed his reply, as if confiding in them.

"It's true, Ted," he said, his features stern, responsible. "They'll deny it, naturally, but we have copies of the study documents. Fas-cinating stuff it is too. Like I said, this is no brief memorandum we're talking about here, but a report of near-on six hundred pages, detail-ing every little circumstance. Moreover, they've costed the exercise down to the last *fen*. And why do that if it's merely—and I quote—'an option we're considering'?"

The reference was to the statement issued by the *T'ing Wei*, the Superintendent of Trials, immediately after the speech. Stung by Kennedy's accusations—or "caught out" as some commentators had put it—the *T'ing Wei* had backpedaled furiously, at first denying that there was any such document, and then, when it became clear that no one was going to accept that, putting out a revised statement, admit-ting the document's existence, but denying that it was anything more than a study.

As for the speech itself, that had been a sensation. A revelation. Not in living memory had an audience responded so enthusiastically, so passionately, to anyone. Kennedy had had them eating out of his hand. Throughout the ninety minutes of the speech there had been a kind of buzz in the great hall, a sense of something new happening right there before their eyes. Kennedy had stood there at the front of the stage, handsome, charismatic, like a king in exile. Scorning notes, he had addressed the great crowd from memory, his deep, resonant voice washing like a tide over their heads. And his words, simple yet powerful, had touched a raw nerve. You could see that. See it on the faces in the crowd; faces that filled the screens throughout the great City of North America. This was his moment. The moment when he came of age.

And afterward, the crowd had stood there, cheering wildly, ap-plauding Kennedy for more than twenty minutes, bringing him back time and again to the stage, a great roar going up each time he reappeared, followed moments later by the chant:

"Ke-ne-dy! Ke-ne-dy! Ke-ne-dy! Ke-ne-dy!"

And all the while he had stood there, smiling and looking about him, applauding his audience just as they applauded him, his boyish modesty there for all to see.

"*Shih* Kennedy! *Shih* Kennedy!"

Kennedy leaned forward on the rostrum and pointed down into the crush of media men, singling out one of the many who were calling him. "Yes, Peter. What is it?"

"Are you aware that a number of surveys done over the last six months have revealed that quite a large percentage of people are actually in favor of limited euthanasia proposals?"

Kennedy nodded somberly. "I think *limited* is the word, Peter. I've seen those surveys—you're talking about the Howett Report and the Chang Institute paper, I assume . . . Yes? Well, all I can say is that one should look very carefully at the questions that were asked in those surveys and see how they actually relate to these new proposals. I think you'll find that there's very little correlation between them. What the new 'Study' reveals is that the actual proposals are far more radical, far more deep-reaching. Besides, there's a hell of a difference between thinking that something might just possibly be a good idea and actually going out and doing it. A hell of a difference. I mean, what we're talking about here is killing people. And not just one or two, but millions. Tens of millions."

Kennedy put his hand up to his brow, combing back a lock of his dark hair, an expression of deep concern in his steel-gray eyes.

"No, Peter, what I think those surveys show is that most people recognize that there's a problem. But this isn't the solution. At least, not one that any decent person should be contemplating."

There was a buzz of sympathy from the floor. But at once the clamor began again.

"*Shih* Kennedy! *Shih* Kennedy!"

"Yes, Ho Yang . . ."

The young Han, a reporter for the all-Han station, *Wen Ming*, glanced at his hand-held comset, then looked up, addressing Kennedy, an immediate translation going out across the airwaves.

"In your speech you seemed to imply that, as far-reaching as the Study document was in terms of the upper age group, this was merely the thin end of the wedge, and that we might expect such preliminary measures to be followed by a whole package of population controls. Could you amplify on that?"

Kennedy smiled. "Certainly. And, once again, this is not a matter of mere speculation. These discussions are going on right now, in secret rooms throughout the seven Cities. Deals are being made, proposals drawn up. Proposals that, if we're not careful, will be presented to the House and voted on by men whose interests are not necessarily ours."

"And what exactly do you mean by that, *Shih* Kennedy?"

Kennedy leaned forward slightly. "I mean that there are men—rich, powerful men, if you like—who put profit before family, individual gain before the common good. And it's these men—these *hsiao jen*, these 'little men'—who are at present dictating things. I don't know about you, Ho Yang, but I think that's wrong. I think that a matter of this importance should be debated publicly and decided publicly. Something must be done, yes. We all recognize that now. But it must be done openly, in the light, where all can see."

And so it went on, for almost two hours, until, with a smile and a wave, Kennedy stood down. But even then—even after the lights had gone down and the remotes had been packed away—Kennedy wasn't finished. After speaking with his advisors, catching up on the latest news, he went out among the media men, shaking hands and stopping to say a word or two here and there, suddenly informal, a friend, not just a "face."

"How's Jean?" one of them asked.

Kennedy turned. "She's fine, Jack. Fine. In fact, she's going off with the boys for a week or so, to escape all of this politicking. She's always complaining that I work her too hard, so I thought I'd give her and the boys a break, before things get really hectic."

There was laughter at that. All there knew just how hard Kennedy worked. Phenomenally hard. In that he was like his father.

"Okay, boys, so if you'll excuse me now . . ."

Kennedy went through, into the anteroom. There, in a great cushioned chair on the far side of the room, sat Jean, his wife, her arms about their two young sons. They were looking away from him, unaware that he had come into the room, staring up at the big screen in the corner of the room.

He stood there a moment, looking across at them, torn by the sight. There was such pride in young Robert's face as he stared at his father's image. Such undemanding love. And Jean . . . He could barely look at her without thinking of the deal he had made with Wu Shih.

For a time out there he had almost forgotten. The deal had seemed as nothing. But now, facing his family once again, he felt the hollowness flood back into him, leaving him weightless, like a leaf in the wind.

He shuddered. What was it they said? *When the east wind blows, the wise man bows before it.* Well, he had bowed, sure enough. But not like a reed. More like a great tree, its trunk snapped and fallen in the face of the storm.

"Joe!" Jean saw him and came across, embracing him. Moments later he felt his two sons holding tight to him, one on either side. "Dad!" they were saying. "Dad, it was wonderful! You were brilliant!"

He steeled himself. "I'm sorry, Jean. If there was any choice . . ."

She drew her head back, looking at him, then reached out to wipe the tears that had come, unbidden, to his eyes. "It's all right. I understand. You know I understand. And I'll stand by you, Joseph Kennedy. Whatever you do."

"I know," he said. "Maybe that's what worries me most. That you're so understanding. If I could only . . ."

She put a finger to his lips. "There's no alternative. We both know that. Remember what you said, all those years ago, that night in your father's house, that year we first met? You said . . . that it didn't matter how it got done, only that it got done." She smiled. "That's still true, isn't it, Joe? And what you did tonight . . . that's a big step toward it."

"Maybe . . ."

"No. No maybes about it. Tonight you started something. Something that even Wu Shih can't stop."

He looked down. To either side of him his sons were looking up at him, trying to understand what was going on.

"It's all right," he said to them, holding them tightly against him. "Everything's going to be all right. You'll see."

There was a knock. He freed himself, then turned and went across, pulling back the door.

A tall Han waited there. One of Wu Shih's men, the number seven—*ch'i*—embroidered in Mandarin on the chest of his powder-blue silks. Beyond him the press room was empty, except for two shaven-headed Han.

"Are they ready?" the tall Han asked.

Kennedy turned, looking at his wife, his sons, then turned back, giving a nod. "They're ready," he said, trying to keep the pain, the anxiety he suddenly felt, out of his voice. But the tears betrayed him.

He had had his moment. It was gone now. Ahead lay only hollowness.

CHAPTER NINETEEN

Weimar

NINE YEARS . . .'' the ancient murmured, tears forming in his watery eyes. "Nine long years I've waited for this day."

His companion, a distinguished-looking graybeard of seventy-five years, nodded somberly. He looked about him at the tiers of empty or sparsely populated benches that stretched away on every side of the House, then leaned closer to his fellow, placing a thin, fly-speckled hand on his friend's arm. "Do you remember the last time we were here, Johann?"

"Like yesterday," the ancient replied, a faint light appearing in his eyes. "That was the day we voted down the Seven's veto, neh? The day Secretary Barrow indicted the *tai* . . ." He sighed heavily, his deeply lined face filled with a sudden pain. "Ach, had we but known what sadness would follow . . ."

"Had we but known . . ."

For a moment the two were silent, watching as, below them, at the center of the Great Hall, the officials of the Seven prepared the central rostrum for the ceremony to come. Then, clearing his throat, the younger of the two spoke again, drawing his powder-blue silks about him as he did.

"They were sad years, true enough, but maybe they were meant to be. Maybe that day and this were foreordained." He smiled morosely and patted his companion's hand. "You know, the more I think of those times, Johann, the more I feel that the conflict was inevitable. That the War . . . well, that the War was necessary."

The ancient shrugged, then laughed; a dry, asthmatic sound. "Maybe so. But we survived, neh? We few."

The graybeard looked about him again, conscious that, of the three and a half thousand Representatives who had packed the House that day, nine years before, a mere handful—two hundred at most—had lived to see this day.

"Few indeed," he said, feeling a sudden weight—not bitterness, but a mixture of regret and the inexorable workings of fate—descend on him.

Once more silence fell. Far below them, out on the central rostrum where the Upper Council sat, a group of gray-haired dignitaries were seating themselves.

There was a moment's brief delay and then the ceremony began. At the central lectern the elderly Representative for Shenyang *Hsien*, Ho Chao-tuan, cleared his throat and began to read from the prepared statement, formally dissolving the House. Overhead, a dozen remotes hovered in the air, relaying their images back to the watching billions.

With the faintest rustle, Ho Chao-tuan set the statement aside and began to read from the list of standing members. As each name was read, a shouted "Yes" would come down from one or other of the elders scattered about the massive chamber. Eventually, all one hundred eighty-three surviving members had responded. With a terse nod, Ho backed away from the lectern, his part in the ceremony concluded.

As Ho Chao-tuan moved back, a tall, middle-aged Han with a plaited white beard stepped forward. This was Ch'in Tao Fan, Chancellor of East Asia. Looking all about him at the near-deserted tiers, he thanked the members, then, with a dramatic flourish, unfurled the official scroll and began to read.

On the benches high above Ch'in Tao Fan, the ancient placed his hand on his friend's arm and smiled sadly. "Our day is done," he said quietly. "It is up to others now to finish what we began."

"So it is," the graybeard answered, sighing, helping his fellow to his feet. "So it is."

Down below them, Ch'in Tao Fan spoke on, talking of the days to come, and of the great step forward, while behind him, on the far side of the great chamber, in the broad ceremonial corridor beyond the great double doorways, the first of the newly elected Representatives, more than eight hundred in all, waited silently in their powder-blue silks, ready to take their places at the empty benches.

———

THREE HOURS LATER, their business in the House done, three of the new Representatives stood in the doorway of the private dining rooms above the Great Hall. At their appearance one of the House Stewards came across, his maroon silks embossed with the number thirty-five.

"*Ch'un tzu,*" he said, bowing deeply. "You are most welcome here. Your guest has asked me to apologize on his behalf. He has been delayed, I fear, and will be a few minutes late. Refreshments, however, have been provided. So, please, if you would come in."

They entered, looking about them and exchanging glances.

The room was large yet not imposing, the decor and furniture clearly chosen with great care and with the most exquisite taste. Four tall Ming dynasty officials' chairs dominated the left-hand side of the room. Close by, on low Ching dynasty tables, bowls of lychees, plums, and strawberries had been laid out. At the far end, in front of a huge picture window that overlooked the formal gardens, a high scroll-legged table was laden with porcelain jugs and bowls, while to the right of the room, beyond a long, head-height screen of carved mahogany, a table had been set for six, western silverware set at each place beside the cloth-wrapped chopsticks.

"What will you drink, *ch'un tzu?*" the Steward asked, turning to face them again. "Will it be your usual, Representative Underwood? Or would you prefer a cordial?"

Underwood laughed, intrigued. "I'll have my usual," he said after a moment.

"And you, Representative Hart? A cool black dragon wine? Or is it too early in the day?"

Hart lowered his head slightly, both amused and impressed. "That would be fine, thank you. But tell me, Thirty-five, is it normal for the Stewards to know what each member drinks?"

The Steward looked at them, smiling politely. "It is not always so, no. But my master is a meticulous man. He likes to do things properly."

"Your master . . . ?" Hart looked to the other two. This grew more curious by the moment.

The man had contacted them a week back, using an intermediary, and had "bought" a meeting with them. Each had been informed that the other two would be present, but beyond that they had been told nothing. Nothing but the man's name. Li Min.

The Steward brought their drinks, then bade them sit. He smiled and bowed to each in turn, then took two small steps backward. "As I said, *ch'un tzu*, my master will be a little delayed. But please, be at your ease until he comes. I must leave you for a short while to supervise the meal, but help yourself. The fruit is fresh from the Plantations this very morning."

With a final bow, the Steward turned and went.

"Well . . ." Underwood said, sipping at the ancient malt whiskey the Steward had handed him. "If that doesn't beat it all! What do you think our man, Li Min, wants?"

Munroe laughed. "What do they all want? Advantage. Someone to make deals for them. To give them face."

"And is that why we're here?" Hart asked, reaching down to take one of the large, blue-black plums from the bowl beside him. "To make deals? And to give some Han merchant face?"

"I'm told it's what politics is about," Munroe said, straightening up again. "But what do you think this one wants? I mean, it's odd, don't you think? A Han, asking three *Hung Mao* Representatives to a meeting on the morning that the House reopens. You'd think he'd choose three of his own kind, neh? You know what they're like, these Han."

"Only too well," Underwood said, setting his drink down. He picked up one of the lychees and sniffed at it, then bit deep, lifting his pocket silk to his chin to dab at the trickle of juice. "That's exactly what I meant. I mean, I've heard there's been a lot of this kind of thing going on these past few months, but this feels different. The fact that he went out of his way to buy our time, for instance. Now why should he do that?"

"To make sure we came?" Hart said thoughtfully.

"Yes, but why?"

Underwood had barely uttered the words when the door swung open and a tall, extremely pallid-looking *Hung Mao* came into the room, followed closely by two soberly dressed assistants, both of whom wore the telltale flashing collars of commodity slaves.

"Gentlemen," the *Hung Mao* began, putting out his hands to beg them to remain seated. "Thank you for coming here. I am Li Min."

Underwood set the half-eaten lychee down. Across from him Hart and Munroe looked equally stunned.

Munroe sat forward. "*You?* Li Min?" He shook his head. "But we were expecting . . ."

"A Han? Yes, well, forgive my little subterfuge, gentlemen. It was . . . necessary, let's say." The man turned, giving a curt hand signal to one of his assistants who proceeded to close and lock the door.

Underwood was on his feet. "Is that really necessary, *Shih* Li?"

The man turned, facing him. "If you wish to leave, Representative Underwood, you may, of course. I have locked the doors not to keep you in, but to keep others out."

"Then what the hell is going on?" Munroe asked, on his feet beside Hart and Underwood. "I want to know who you really are and why we're here, and I want to know it right now or I'm walking."

"That's right," Hart said.

"Please, gentlemen. I shall do as you ask. But be seated. You are at Weimar. In the great House itself. No harm can come to you here."

Mollified, the three men sat again, the tall *Hung Mao* taking the vacant seat facing them.

"All right," he said, looking from one to the next, his frost-white face expressionless. "You wish to know who I am and why I have asked you here today. Well, the answer to the first is that I am Stefan Lehmann, only son of Under-Secretary Lehmann."

Hart laughed, astonished. Beside him Munroe shook his head slowly. Underwood just sat there, his mouth open.

At Lehmann's signal, one of his assistants brought a case and handed it to him. He opened it and took out three files, offering one to each of the men.

"Inside those files you will find genetic charts and other material that will verify my claim. But as to what I want from you, that depends very much on what you yourselves want."

Lehmann fell silent a moment, watching the three men study the material; then, when it seemed they were convinced, he began again.

"You wondered earlier how it was that the Steward knew what each of you drank. Well, he knew that because I have made it my business to find out about each of you. Oh, you were no strangers to me, or at least, your fathers weren't. But I wanted to know a great deal more about each of you before I came and sat here facing you. I wanted to be sure."

"Sure about what?" Hart said, his composure regained somewhat now that he had had a little time to digest what was happening.

"About whether I could trust you." Lehmann paused, then, lifting his left hand casually, pointed at Munroe. "You, Wendell. Your father was disbarred from the House eight years ago and your whole family sent down fifty levels. He never got over that, did he? He died eight months later, some say of shame, others of poison." Lehmann turned slightly, his hand swinging around until it pointed at Underwood. "And you, Harry. All of your family property was confiscated, neh? If it hadn't been for friends, you'd have ended up below the Net. As it was, your father took his own life."

Lehmann let his hand fall back into his lap, his eyes on Hart once more. "As for you, Alex, you had to suffer the humiliating indignity of a pardon. Or at least, your father did. But it rubs off, neh? In this world of ours, what happens to the father happens also to the son." He paused again, nodding slowly to himself, knowing he had their full attention now. "But when I look at the three of you, what I see is not the sons of traitors but good, strong, hardworking young men. Men who, through their own efforts, have regained the positions of preeminence taken from them by the Seven. There is no doubting it. You are Great Men once more. And yet the taint remains, neh?"

Munroe let out a long breath, then leaned toward Lehmann, his hands clasped together in front of him. "So what's your point, *Shih* Lehmann? What do you want from us?"

To either side of him, Hart and Underwood were staring openly at Lehmann now, an intense curiosity burning in their eyes.

"As I said. It's not so much what I want, as what you want." He sat back slightly, looking from one to the next. "You are Great Men, certainly. Representatives. It would seem, to the outward eye, that each of you has everything he needs. Status. Riches. Power. Together with the Seven, you plan to make this world of ours great again. Or so the media tells us. But knowing you—knowing each of you as well as I do—I would not have thought that there was any great love in your hearts for the Seven."

Munroe stared back at him a moment longer, then looked down. "So?"

Lehmann paused. "So this. I wanted to let you know that it's not over. That the War didn't end. That it's still going on, DeVore or no, Berdichev or no. That I am my father's son and that the things he stood for live on in me."

"Dispersionism . . ." Hart said, in an awed whisper.

Lehmann nodded. "Yes, Dispersionism. And something else. Something wholly new."

IT WAS DONE secretly, quietly. In the media the news was that his wife and children had gone away on a brief vacation while Kennedy worked on campaign details. Then, for a week, there was nothing. When Kennedy saw them again it was on the afternoon of the elections, at Wu Shih's private clinic on the West Coast. They had been treated well—like royalty—and he found them in the solarium, beneath the tiny artificial sun, the two boys playing at the pool's edge.

He went across and knelt beside her chair. "How are you?" he asked, kissing her, then searching her eyes for some sign of difference.

"I'm fine, love. Really. I've never felt better." She laughed, and for a moment there really did seem nothing wrong, nothing intrinsically different about her. Her skull was shaved, yes, but otherwise she seemed her normal self—perhaps even bubblier than usual. "They're going to give me some injections to speed up hair growth. In the meantime I've been given the most delightful selection of wigs. I've spent the whole morning just trying out different colors and styles."

He smiled bleakly. "You're sure you're okay?"

She nodded. "Really. And the boys too." But now, in her eyes, there was the faintest intimation that she understood what they had done. "Don't . . ." she said softly, seeing the pain in his eyes. "It's better than having you dead. Much better."

He nodded and smiled, as much to reassure himself as her. Then, after kissing her again, he went and sat with the boys at the poolside, not fussed by the fact that their small hands left dark, damp patches on his silks, delighted simply to see them again.

Robert, the eldest, was babbling happily to his father, showing him the new scar beneath his ear where the input socket sat, more proud than fearful of its meaning. "Just wait till the other boys see this," he said. "I betcha they'll all want one! And the doctor says I could have a special unit put in so's I can see all the vids direct." The youngster looked away, laughing, then launched himself into the pool, not seeing the strange look of unease that crossed his father's face.

"Maybe . . ." Kennedy said to himself, hugging his youngest boy's head against his leg. But his heart was strangely heavy and, for the first time in his life, he was uncertain.

———

OLD DARKNESS stretched sinuously at the bottom of his tank, his great eyes closed, his long, gray-green tentacles coiling lazily in sleep. About the tank, a scattering of rock and plant gave the huge, glass-walled enclosure a false air of normality, the look of some giant display case. But things were far from normal here. Within the tough, reinforced layers of ice, the water was kept at a pressure that would crush a frailer, human form like powdered clay.

Nearby, looking into the tank at the vastness of the sleeping leviathan, Kim drifted, suspended in the water, his thoughts dark. To his right, some twenty *ch'i* distant, was Rebecca, her hands pressed tight against the outer glass.

Behind them, the early morning sunlight filtered down through the shadowed outline of the City overhead, forming broad shafts of gold in the pale blue water, while below them the endless depths stretched down, into dark, unseen realms of perfect blackness.

"He's beautiful," Rebecca said, her eyes, half glimpsed behind the face-plate of her mask, gleaming with a strange delight. "So strong and graceful, don't you think?"

Kim half turned in the water, moving back, away from the menace of the slumbering form. Powerful it was, and strong. But beautiful? He turned, looking back at it, then shook his head. No, even in sleep, Old Darkness was inimical. A deadly, hostile thing, lacking all warmth, all sympathy with human life.

Looking at it, at the dark, repulsive bulk of it, he felt the deep stirrings of unease. Inimical it was, and yet connected. The first time he had seen the creature he had recognized it, but here, alone in the water with the beast, that feeling was much stronger. Old Darkness . . . it was aptly named, for the light of intelligence, of love or connectedness, had never touched this creature. It was a thing of nightmare. And yet . . .

He shuddered, then forced himself to formulate the thought. It was as if he were staring back at himself. Or not *himself* exactly, but a part of him: that part that was forever hidden from the light. Here, in the figure of Old Darkness, it was given solid form, cold and gargantuan.

It's hideous, he thought, *and yet the thing exists. It has a purpose in the scheme of things. Like darkness itself, it exists because, without it, there would be no light, no warmth. Because, without it, there would be nothing.*

"What does it eat?"

Rebecca's laughter came ringing through the earphones of his mask. "Anything we give it," she answered, turning toward him, smiling through her mask. "The deep survey teams bring it back tidbits from the deep. Strange things with glowing eyes and spiny fins, bloated things with heavy, scaly bodies and huge, hinged mouths."

Again he shuddered, imagining it down there in its natural element, and wondered whether it was like that in the deepest recesses of the mind; whether there were creatures there like Old Darkness, vast leviathans of the imagination, gliding silently, dark against the darkness, their long tentacles coiling and uncoiling as they preyed upon the deformed progeny of the undermind.

"Seen enough?" Rebecca asked, kicking up toward him, her right hand trailing lightly along the surface of the glass.

He nodded. Enough for thirty lifetimes. "You're right," he said. "In a strange way he is beautiful. But frightening too."

For a moment she was close, beside him in the water, her hand on his arm. "Maybe that's what beauty is. Something that frightens us." And then she was gone, moving up, past him, toward the hatch, some fifty *ch'i* above.

━━━◆◆◆◆━━━

REBECCA SHOWERED and dressed, then came through to where Kim sat on the bench in the men's room, cradling a bulb of *ch'a* between his cupped hands. It was quite early—not yet nine—and they were alone there in the big, echoing room.

"Well?" she said, sitting on the bench across from him. "How's it going?"

Kim smiled. "Fine," he said. "Bonnot's a bit of a pain. Schram too. He can't keep his nose out of things, can he? Whatever I do, he has to know about it. But I've known worse."

She nodded thoughtfully. "You and I both."

"Yes . . ." For a moment he looked at her, realizing how lonely he had been, how pleased to see her familiar face. But it was more than that. They had come from the darkness of the Clay, he and she; had struggled to make their way in this world of light, failing once and yet surviving. Coming through. They both knew what it was to be a "thing," owned bone, blood, and flesh by another, their very existence subject to the whims of petty men. And that had formed them, just as much as their experience of the Clay. Yes, and made them different, separate from the rest. Physically and mentally different.

"Do you ever think of those times?" he asked quietly. "You know, back in Rehabilitation?"

"Sometimes." She looked down. "Do you remember the bird?"

He nodded. After Luke had defied them—after they had taken him away that first time—the powers-that-be had given the four of them that remained a bird. A strange, artificial thing, he realized now. Something made, not born. A product of GenSyn's labs.

The bird's eyes had been amber, the pupils black. It had gazed into the far distance, proudly, arrogantly, barely deigning to acknowledge their presence there outside its cage. Strong, three-toed claws had gripped the metal perch, the talons stretching and tightening as if impatient. And when it had spread its wings, the vivid emerald feathers unfolding like twin fans, it had seemed a gesture of dismissal.

Kim shuddered, remembering that first moment. Will, like himself, had thought it beautiful, and Deio had likened it to a song made flesh. Only Rebecca had not been moved by it. "It's too bright," she had said, and he had turned, staring at the bird, wondering how anything could be "too bright."

From that day on, Will had been obsessed. Each morning, the big North European lad had fed the bird, talking to it through the bars of its cage.

And each night he had pressed close to the cage, whispering to it. Always the same. Four lines of poetry in the ancient guttural tongue of his part of the Clay. Closing his eyes, Kim could still hear him saying it, even now, four years on.

> Mit allen Augen sieht die Kreatur
> das offene. Nur unsere Augen sind
> wie umgekehrt und ganz un sie gestellt
> als Fallen, rings um ihren Freien Ausgang.

The words had moved him, thrilled him, long before Will had told him what they meant.

> *With all its eyes the creature-world beholds*
> *the open. But our eyes, as though reversed,*
> *encircle it on every side, like traps*
> *set round its unobstructed path to freedom.*

So it was, for all of them, bird and Clay alike. And then Luke had died. Suddenly, awfully.

Will had been devastated. Kim remembered that too. Remembered the sight of him sitting on Luke's empty bed, still, dreadfully still, hunched into himself, his big, changeling's body forced into a much smaller area than it was used to, as if he was trying to fit himself into Luke's skin, into his smaller, subtler form.

Kim looked up, his eyes moist. Rebecca was watching him, her eyes wide, as if she too saw what he saw. "Why did he do it, Kim?" she asked. "I thought he loved the bird?"

He shrugged, but the memory was so strong, so vivid, it was as if he could see it there before him.

The bird lay at the bottom of its cage, its golden eyes dulled, unseeing, its soft neck broken. Emerald wing feathers littered the floor beside the damaged cage, evidence of a struggle, while in a chair nearby sat Will, dull-eyed yet breathing, his hands resting loosely in his lap.

"I don't know," he said, the image slowly fading. But it was untrue. He knew why Will had killed the bird.

She came close, crouching beside him, looking up into his face. There were tears in her eyes now, pain in the lines of her mouth. "I never understood it. Never. Luke, Will, Deio . . . there was no reason for their deaths. No point."

"No," he said, putting his hand over hers comfortingly. "It was awful." He shivered, the pain raw in him, as if it had been yesterday. "You know, I've blanked it out since then. I couldn't live with it. Couldn't face it until now. I feel guilty, you know that, Becky? Guilty that I survived and they didn't."

"Yes," she said, looking up at him again, grateful that he had said it, her hand squeezing his gently. "I know. I understand."

"Yes . . ." He wiped a tear away, then stood, pulling her up, holding her a moment. "But here we are, neh? We came through."

Her dark eyes stared back at him, momentarily intense, looking through the surface of him, it seemed, into the raw darkness beyond. "We did, didn't we?" she said quietly, resting her head on his shoulder. He felt the shudder that ran through her, the warmth of her lips as they gently brushed his neck.

She moved back, away from him, offering him a small, apologetic smile. "What are you doing tonight?"

"Tonight?" He shrugged. "My shift ends at eight, but after that, nothing. Why?"

Her smile broadened. "We're having a party, that's why. Election night, and all that. Why don't you come? It won't start until ten. You could pick me up then if you like. It should be fun."

He stared at her a moment, thinking once more how different she was, how assured this older Rebecca was, then nodded, smiling back at her.

"Why not?"

ALL DAY, right across City America, people had been voting to send Representatives to the newly reopened House. Almost a tenth of the seats were up for grabs in this round and there were already signs that the old status quo was about to be shaken. In Miami central stack a huge MedFac multiboard filled one end of the crowded, buzzing Main. Below it, more than twenty thousand people were packed in, staring up at the eighteen large screens. The scenes on most differed little from that in Miami. Large crowds jostled noisily beneath a thick mass of banners, and, from time to time, a huge cheer would go up as another local stack declared.

Over each screen was the name of the *Hsien* being contested, and at the bottom, superimposed on the screen, was a list of candidates and the number of votes polled for each. As the evening drew on these figures built up, and as they did the excitement in the crowd increased accordingly. Change was in the air.

Two central screens showed something different. On the left was a map of City North America, its distinctive, lopsided face divided up into the four hundred and seventy-six Representative districts, colored by party. To its right was a pie chart showing the relative strengths of the seven parties that currently dominated North American politics. Largest of these by far was the Reformers, who held eighty-seven seats. But all eyes were on Kennedy's New Republicans, who had begun the contest without a single seat in the old House and had won thirty in the first round of voting.

The campaign had been harder and, in some ways, dirtier than anyone could remember. Early on, Kennedy had declared that he would not put up candidates for the three seats held by Evolutionist incumbents. It was an unexpected but greatly popular move. Though the Evolutionists were a long-established party, they were a steadily diminishing power, and the New Republicans could have won the seats. Within a week, however, Evolutionist candidates for nine of the remaining contestable seats had withdrawn and urged their supporters to vote for New Republican candidates.

The Reformers had hit back hard. Questioning the reliability of the "new alliance," they had launched a campaign to discredit Joel Hay, the Evolutionist leader, using material they'd been holding for some time. It was vile stuff that struck at Hay's most intimate behavior. Even so, for a day or two Hay fought back. Then, realizing the damage he was doing to his party, he announced his resignation.

There was jubilation in the Reformer camp, but, only a day later, their smiles turned to frowns as Kennedy, who had maintained a strict silence on the matter, now stepped forward to announce a formal merger of the two parties under his own leadership. The press conference, with New Republican and Evolutionist candidates lined up behind Kennedy as he made his speech, went out worldwide. Overnight, without the need for an election, the New Republicans had become City America's third largest power, with forty-two seats.

It had not ended there. The next day the campaign against Carl Fisher had begun in earnest with the appearance on a nationwide network of two of Fisher's school friends, accusing him of homosexuality and a whole string of other perversions. Fisher, shaken and angry, had reacted with an unexpected bluntness that had done him no harm.

"Let them say it again to me, face to face, and I'll bust their jaws!"

Overnight it became his campaign slogan. Carl "Jaw-Buster" Fisher went up five points in the polls, while Carver, the Reformer incumbent, found himself the butt of a thousand cartoons, all depicting him rubbing at a loosened jaw. Few, looking at the athletically built and handsome Fisher, paid attention to the accusations. He was pictured everywhere, surrounded by good-looking women, punching a bag, knocking back a glass of beer after exercise. Carver, older, flabbier, showed poorly by comparison.

Reformer claims of inexperience and political naivete carried little weight, it seemed. Change was in the air, and the young men of the New Republican and Evolutionist Party, the NREP, were an attractive alternative to the old style Representative people had grown accustomed to. But it wasn't only image. Kennedy picked his candidates well. These new young men were the very cream of the emergent ruling caste; the sons of powerful men and bred to power themselves. They were well educated and quick in argument. And backing them up was an elite of political researchers and writers attracted by the promise of power. Reformer money couldn't buy such backing, try as it did.

As the night drew toward its climax, it grew clear that a minor political sensation was happening. With five seats still to be settled, the Reformer vote was in tatters. The NREP had gained nineteen districts. They needed only three of the four remaining Reformer-held seats to become the second biggest party in North America, passing the On Leong and the Democrats. In Carl Fisher's campaign suite, the Party leaders gathered, watching the EduVoc channel, excitement like wine in their blood. At the center of this small, select group, Michael Lever leaned forward in his wheelchair and pointed at the screen.

"Who's he?"

To the left of the picture, behind Greg Stewart, their candidate for Denver *Hsien*, stood a gaunt-faced, steely-eyed young man, some inches taller than Stewart. He was shaven-headed and had the look of a paid assassin.

Kennedy bent down beside Michael, speaking softly to him. "That's a guy named Horton. Calls himself Meltdown."

Michael narrowed his eyes, then nodded. Now that Kennedy had given him a name, he recognized him. "He was incarcerated, right? I never met him but I heard about it. He was on a hunger strike, wasn't he?"

Kennedy nodded. "That's right. His father is a friend of your father."

"And he's working for us now?"

"We've come to an agreement, let's say. They'll be working closely with us from now on."

Michael frowned. He wasn't sure about this. When Wu Shih had rounded them all up—that evening of the Thanksgiving Ball—they had all been outraged, but he saw now how dangerous the "Sons" had been. He had wanted change, but not by such means as some of them had subsequently proposed. Their tactics were the same as those that had killed Bryn. And he wanted no more of that.

"Are you sure we want this?" he asked quietly.

Kennedy smiled. "I'm sure, Michael. And listen, I know what I'm doing. We're in charge, not them. They need us, so they play by our rules."

"And if they don't?"

"They will. Don't worry."

Kennedy straightened up. On the screen there was news from two of the last five seats to declare. They had won Mexico City. Vancouver had stayed On Leong.

Parker, standing behind Michael, laughed. "So not a rout, then!"

Michael half turned and looked up at him. "No. And it'll be harder next time. They're learning from us all the time. There'll be new candidates next time around. Younger men. And they'll be tailoring their campaigns to look like ours. We've had it easy so far. They'll not be so arrogant in the future."

"And we will?"

There was a faint hint of annoyance in Parker's voice, and a number of people were looking down at Michael strangely, as if he were an uninvited guest. But Kennedy spoke up, calling for order.

"Michael's right. First time out we got the sympathy vote. This time we took them by surprise. They'd written off our first-round victories as a sentimental anomaly—a flash in the pan. But from now on they'll be on their guard. As Michael says, they'll change their ways. Same old policies, but new ways of presenting them. New faces too. Maybe even men who might have served us well. They'll be buying heavily."

He paused and looked around. The room had gone quiet. Only the sound from the screen went on. They were all watching Kennedy now as he stood at Michael's side, his hand on the invalid's shoulder.

"But we're not going to be stopped. The mood for change is genuine, and change itself is long overdue. It'll be harder to win in the future, and the contest will be much closer than tonight. But we'll win. And we'll keep on winning, because those we oppose are a dead force—an old, stinking corpse. We've got to show people that. But it'll get harder to do, I warn you, because the harder we push the more devious they'll get, the more disguises they'll use."

Again Kennedy stopped and looked around, nodding slowly. "We'll strip them naked, neh? To the bone . . ." And then he laughed, showing his strong white teeth, and the suite was suddenly full of laughter. From the far side of the room came the sound of popping corks, and on the screen the news that they had won the last three seats.

Michael looked up at Kennedy. "And what of us, Joe? Will *we* be young forever? Will no one strip us bare?"

He said it softly, so that it carried no farther than Kennedy. For a moment Kennedy seemed not to have heard, then he looked down at Michael, his face different, more serious, perhaps more tired than Michael had ever seen it, and nodded. "To the bone." And his eyes, so dark and normally so strong, seemed filled with the pain and certainty of his words. As if he saw and knew.

━━━━━━

KIM SAT at a table in the restaurant, his empty *ch'a* bowl set to one side, the letter he had been writing held loosely in his left hand as he read it through a second time.

It was an hour since he'd come off shift and he really ought to have gone back to his rooms to shower and change, but he had put off writing to Jelka far too long now. So first this. Even if he had to start it all again tomorrow, trying to get the words down right. To say all those things that kept bubbling up from deep within.

The restaurant was filling up. Already the tables nearest Kim were full, the talk alive with the news of what was happening in City America, but Kim's attention was elsewhere, thinking of Jelka out on Titan. In a year she would be on Mars, heading back in toward Chung Kuo. If he sent the letter there, it might reach her quicker, perhaps, than trying to get a message out to Titan in time. But first he had to get it right.

He sat back, thinking suddenly of Rebecca, and of that moment in the changing rooms earlier. He had said nothing of that to Jelka. Nothing of what he'd felt; of the pain he'd suffered at the reopening of that wound . . . nor of the catharsis. But why?

Maybe it was because it confused things. Because it would give her the wrong idea. He huffed, annoyed at himself, his fingers going to the pulsing torque about his neck, then, flipping back to the start of the letter, he began to read it through once more.

"Excuse me . . ."

The voice was soft-spoken, very polite. Kim looked up. A tall Han was standing there, holding a tray, his head slightly bowed. The man smiled, the smile vaguely reminiscent of T'ai Cho, then tilted his head, indicating the empty seat across from Kim.

"Would you mind?"

Kim shook his head, smiling back at the man. "No. Please do . . . I'll be going in a while, anyway."

"Ah . . ." The Han bowed again, then began to set out his meal. "It is very kind of you. Some people, they . . ." He stopped, his face suddenly apologetic. "Forgive me. Am I disturbing you?"

Kim laughed, then folded the letter and slipped it into his pocket. "Not at all. Kim Ward," he said, offering his hand across the table.

"Tuan Wen-ch'ang," the Han answered, bowing a third time. He took Kim's hand, shaking it vigorously. "I note we are both employed by the great SimFic corporation, and yet I have not seen you here before."

Kim nodded, noting for the first time the double-helix logo on the shoulder of the Han's light-green tunic. "That's not surprising," he answered. "I haven't been here long, and I've spent most of my time in the lab."

"Ah . . ." Again the Han smiled. Again the smile reminded Kim of his old tutor and guardian, T'ai Cho.

"Where do you come from, originally?" Kim asked, strangely drawn to the man.

"Originally?" The Han laughed, showing slightly imperfect teeth. Again that was like T'ai Cho, and the thought of it made Kim realize that he had not contacted his old friend since he had been at Sohm Abyss.

"Originally my clan is from Ning Hsia, in the northwest. We are Hui, you understand. Not Han." Again he laughed. A pleasant, warming sound. "As for me, I was born on Mars. In Tien Men K'ou City, in the south. My clan were settled there, you understand, after the Third Colonial War. We helped build that City. That and many others."

"Mars . . ." Kim nodded, his thoughts briefly returning to the letter and to Jelka. "It must be wonderful."

Tuan Wen-ch'ang shrugged. "Sometimes, yes. But mostly it is a bleak and desolate place. Life is hard there. Very hard. Here . . ." He laughed. "Well, let us say that life is much easier here. One need not fear the cold, for instance."

"No," Kim said absently, then, suddenly realizing what time it was, he leaned forward across the table. "Look, Tuan Wen-ch'ang. I'd like to talk more to you—it has been pleasant, most pleasant— but right now I have to go or I'll be late. There's someone I promised to meet."

"Of course." Tuan Wen-ch'ang stood, bowing low, as if to someone high above him in status, then looked back at Kim, smiling his imperfect smile. "I am here most nights, *Shih* Ward. If you see me, come and sit with me. It is good to talk, neh?"

"Very good," said Kim, smiling, and with a final shake of the tall Hui's hands, he left, stopping only at the door to glance back at the man, reminded, even in the way the tall Hui sat, crouched forward over his food, of T'ai Cho.

TUAN WEN-CH'ANG sat there a moment, waiting, watching the reflection in the glass beyond the table. He saw the boy turn and look across at him, then turn back, hurrying to his appointment. Tuan waited a second, then, leaving the untouched plate of food, made his way quickly to the door on the far side of the restaurant—the door Ward hadn't taken.

So far so good, he thought, taking the cast from his mouth, and slipping the false teeth into his pocket. It had been easy, winning the boy's trust. The softness of his voice, the simple mimicry of the boy's friend, had been enough. And the rest? Tuan Wen-ch'ang jabbed at the buttons of the interlevel elevator, then, as the doors slid back, went inside, a cold, malicious smile lighting his features. The rest was simple.

WU SHIH sat back and breathed in deeply, pleased with the way things had gone. The "State of the Parties" print-up was on the screen, and he looked at it with a sense of deep satisfaction.

Reformers	94
NREP	65
On Leong	53
Democrats	42
Hop Sing	22
Innovators	10
Ying On	4

In the last month Kennedy had come from almost nowhere to become the most important man in North American politics. Wu Shih had read the situation perfectly and had acted in good time. Now he might congratulate himself. Li Yuan, he knew, would be delighted. Unlike the Reformers and the Democrats, Kennedy was for Population Controls. His success would soften the others' attitudes, and that would mean that things would go much easier in the House. And that was good.

Young men, he thought. *They think all things are new.* Laughing, he stood up and walked across to where he had left the draft of the new Edict he had been working on. *As if history were myth and men could change their natures.* Again he laughed, and this time a servant came to the door at the far end of his suite, inquiring dumbly if there were anything he needed, but Wu Shih waved him away.

"We are born old," he said softly to himself, picking up the comset. "And perhaps that is bad. We do not hope for things the way these young men do."

It was true. He thought them naive, even a touch ridiculous at times. But he admired their hope, their optimism, their *energy*. Yes, the last above all. Confucianism had never really touched them here in North America. Elsewhere it had thrived, like some strange debilitating bacillus, but in North America it had been grafted on superficially. Like a mask, ready to be removed at any moment.

Which made them dangerous, though not uncontrollable.

A third time he laughed, thinking of what Li Yuan planned for them. To make their desire for change the vehicle for stasis, that was a stroke of genius!

It was crude as yet, and the tests were not yet complete, but it promised much. If this worked then nothing was beyond them. Why, they might yet spread out and take the stars.

He looked at the comset and smiled knowingly. The best designs were always the simplest, the most direct. Like a well-glazed dish, they pleased the eye immediately, yet satisfied more deeply with each reacquaintance. So with this.

Wu Shih sat again, his smile widening. Americans! He'd wire them all!

———————

IT WAS FIFTEEN MINUTES after midnight when, beneath a barrage of bright lights, the leader of the New Republican and Evolutionist Party, Representative Joseph Kennedy, emerged from the count, smiling and waving to the crowds gathered in the Main below. Behind him, in the long, high-ceilinged room, he had left a shocked and somber group of people gathered about the losing Reformer candidate. Outside, however, beneath banners and awnings that stretched across the wide Main, there was no doubt of the popularity of the NREP's success. At the first sight of Kennedy a great roar of approval and delight went up from the crowd.

To the far right of the balcony, Kennedy's closest associates looked on happily. Like the crowd below, they cheered and clapped enthusiastically, carried away by the emotion of the moment.

Kennedy leaned over, looking out, shielding his eyes with one hand, the other arm about the shoulders of his pretty wife, Jean. Turning to his friends, he gestured for them to come across and share the spotlight. As the young men slowly made their way to him, Fisher pushing Michael in his wheelchair, a huge cheer went up, louder than the first. Kennedy greeted each in turn, introducing each to the masses below, hugging each of them to him delightedly.

They smiled, conscious of the floating cameras overhead catching every word, every nuance of expression. They had grown accustomed to it these past few weeks; even so, it wasn't easy, not knowing what was to come. As Michael turned his chair, he saw how Kennedy's wife moved back, out of the way, as if she understood.

This was the moment when they burned their bridges. The moment when they started something new. Michael eased his wheelchair back, watching as Kennedy stepped forward and, putting out a hand, indicated to the crowd below that he wanted to speak. On huge screens the length of Main, the cameras focused on his tall, handsome figure, panning in on his by-now-familiar features. For a moment the buzz continued, then, slowly, it subsided. Kennedy looked about him, smiling, then leaned toward the crowd.

"We are all, here in this great hall, Americans. And proud to be Americans. And Carl Fisher, our new Representative for Boston, is a fine American, from a fine old American family."

There was a huge roar of approval at that. Kennedy waited for it to subside, then carried on.

"Today, however, we did much more than elect a good candidate, though Carl Fisher is certainly that. Today we launched a new campaign. A new era. A new sense of ourselves as a people."

The cheering went on, beneath Kennedy's voice, greeting every sentence, growing more and more enthusiastic by the moment as the crowd worked itself up. *Yes, and in tens of millions of households it will be the same,* Michael thought, looking up at Kennedy. *They know something is happening here. And they expect something of him. Something . . . different.*

Kennedy put his right hand up to his brow, sweeping back his hair with that characteristic gesture of his. "It might seem a small start," he said quietly. "A mere sixty-five seats in the House. But there is still another round of voting. There are still one hundred and eighty-six seats to be contested next month. And that's enough. Enough, if we can take a good number of them, to give us a firm foothold in government—to allow us to wield the kind of influence we need if we're to bring effective change to this great City of ours."

For a moment the cheering was deafening. Kennedy leaned forward again, raising a hand for silence.

"Carl Fisher, your candidate, elected by you here tonight, is more than just another Representative, however. He is one of the first of a new breed of men—good, committed young men—who are set to change the face of politics on this continent. Men who will kick out the old gang and their tired old ways. Men who pledge themselves to get rid of the wheeling and the dealing, the vested interests and the power groupings, and return us to a sense of our greatness as a people."

Kennedy smiled and, for the briefest moment, looked up into the overhead camera, as if he could see Wu Shih and the Old Men looking on.

"This is our time," he said, a sudden power in his voice. "A new time. Time for us all to realize what was once great about our country. What was truly great about America. It's time for us to call it all back. To have back what we've been denied all these years. To grasp it and hold it and use it. For America. As Americans."

He paused, getting his breath. What he had just said had not been uttered publicly before. Indeed, his words had been close to treason. But no one made to gainsay him. He put out a hand, leaning out over the balcony, looking about him at the great mass of people below. The tension was palpable. When he paused this time he could feel all of them there below him, waiting for his words, powered, just as he was powered at that moment, by the great tidal flow of his rhetoric.

"Americans," he said simply, and felt the great ripple of emotion that the word conjured up roll out from him and roll back like a giant wave. "We *are* Americans."

He stood there silently a moment, then raised both of his arms, palms open, accepting the wild applause from below.

Michael, watching from his side, felt that great tide of wild emotion sweep over him, and found himself crying suddenly, in love with the man; with his sheer strength and vitality, and with the invigorating spirit of change he had brought to them all.

Change. It was coming. At last, after all these years, it was coming. And nothing—absolutely nothing—could stop them now.

━━━◆◆◆◆◆━━━

KIM STOOD at the window, staring out across the bright-lit center of Sohm Abyss, the music pounding in his head, merging, it seemed, with the steady pounding of his heart. It was late and the celebrations were growing wilder by the moment. There was a sense of exhilaration in the air, a feeling that change had come at last, that a new age lay ahead for everyone.

For once he had joined in with the party mood, accepting the drink his host—a plump, middle-aged Han he had met briefly that first night—had offered him. Three refills later he was feeling light-headed, but also curiously lucid. Not that it mattered how he felt. Not now. Campbell's "decree" had come two hours back, announcing that tomorrow was to be a day of rest for all SimFic employees. In celebration of that evening's momentous events.

Kim smiled, staring out through his reflection at the great web of walkways that linked the outer hexagon of walls to the spirelike inner tower, their graceful arcs beaded with lights, then turned fractionally, sensing a movement just behind him. In the glass a face appeared beside his own, the head overlarge, the eyes slightly too big. A Clayborn face. A moment later he felt a warmth against his back and, closing his eyes, breathed in the scent of jasmine.

"Becky . . ."

"I wondered where you'd got to," she said, her mouth close against his ear. "Don't you want to dance?"

"I'm tired," he said, turning his head so that she could hear him above the music, her face only a hand's length from his own. "I thought I might go soon."

"Tired? *You* tired?" She smiled, her eyes searching his own. "It's early yet. Besides, you heard what Campbell said."

"I know, but . . ."

"Here." She took his left hand, then pressed something small into his palm.

"What's this?"

"Something to help you loosen up. Go on. Just pop it in your mouth."

He stared at the tiny blue tablet a moment, then shook his head. "Thanks, but . . ."

She hesitated, then took it back from him. "Okay. But stay a little longer, neh? Another hour. I mean, what's the harm?"

"No harm," he said, mirroring her smile. "But no drugs, eh? I like to be in control."

"I know." She leaned close, kissing his cheek, then reached down and took his hand. "I remember well."

They danced. For a while he lost himself in the music and the rhythm, the flashing play of lights. Bodies crowded the center of the floor, moving in a strange abandonment on every side, like particles in violent motion.

Later, in a moment of lucidity, of sudden silence, he looked about him and found that Rebecca had gone. He was about to go and look for her, when she reappeared, two small, porcelain *ch'a* bowls held out before her.

"What's this?" Kim asked, sniffing at the faintly opalescent liquid.

"It's *ch'a*," she said, laughing. "What did you think it was? I thought you needed something to sober you up a bit before you went."

"Ah . . ." He let himself be turned about and led toward a small table in the far corner of the room. But even as they made their way across, the music began again, the people all about them erupting in a frenzy of sudden activity.

He squeezed through, holding the bowl up above his head, then sat unsteadily. Setting the bowl down, he leaned toward her. "I think I've spilled some."

"Never mind," she said, moving around until she sat beside him on the heavily padded sofa. "Here, have some of mine."

He watched her pour some of the sweet-scented *ch'a* into his bowl, then, encouraged by her, lifted the bowl and drained it at a go.

"Good," she said. "You'll feel better for that."

"It's good," he said, looking past her, his voice raised to combat the assault of the music, the squeals and shouts of the celebrants. "I don't think I've ever . . ."

He stopped, sitting back, then put his hand up to his throat.

"What's the matter?" she asked, concerned.

"I . . ." He felt the bile rise in his throat and swallowed hard. For a moment he had felt nauseous, as if he'd eaten well and then someone had gone and punched him in the stomach.

"Are you all right?" she said, her hand resting lightly on his thigh. "Maybe you shouldn't have drained the bowl like that."

"Maybe," he said, but the nausea was passing, a strange feeling of euphoria washing over him. "I . . ." He laughed. "You know, Becky, I think I'm drunk. I think . . ."

She put a finger to his lips, silencing him, then leaned close, speaking to his ear once more. "I think I should get you home, that's what I think."

He nodded. Home. Yes, but where was that?

"Come on," she said, pulling him to his feet, then turning him to face her, her smile strange, enigmatic. "Now. While you can still walk."

━━━━━

HE WOKE, feeling strange, disoriented, a bitter taste in his mouth, the scent of jasmine in his nostrils. It was dark where he lay. Whatever light there was came from a doorway at the far end of the room, to his right, while from beyond it came the sound of running water, the hiss of steam.

He turned his head; too fast, it seemed, for the pain that shot from the surface of his eyes to the back of his skull was fierce, as if a spike had been driven through his head. He groaned and closed his eyes, wondering what in the gods' names he had done to himself.

Not my room, he thought. *This isn't my room.* He made to grasp the thought and push at it, but his mind refused to push. The thought slipped from him and was gone. *Dead*, came the thought. *It feels like I've died and gone to hell.*

"Kim?"

He opened his eyes, slowly this time, turning his head a fraction at a time, until he could see where the voice had come from.

Rebecca was standing in the open doorway, the light behind her. A towel was draped loosely about her shoulders, but otherwise she was naked. In the half-light he could see a thousand tiny beads of water covering her flank, her breasts, the soft curve of her upper thigh.

"Are you awake?"

He made to answer, but his mouth was dry, his lips strangely numb. He groaned and closed his eyes, but he could still see her, standing there, her breasts small but prominent in the half-light, the nipples stiff.

For a while there was nothing, only silence; a silence that before had been filled with the sound of running water, the hiss of steam. Then, suddenly, he sensed a presence beside him on the bed, felt a small, cool hand brush his cheek. Gently, solicitously. The voice, when it came, was soft, like the touch of the hand. It lulled him.

"I didn't realize you'd drunk so much, my love. I'd have not given you it if I'd known."

The words passed him by. He felt himself gathered up, *focused*, in the touch of her hand against his cheek, the sweetly perfumed scent of her.

"Here," she said, lifting his head gently.

He felt something small and hard being pressed between his lips. A moment later, he felt the smooth edge of a glass against his lips. He swallowed reflexively, letting the cold, clear water wash the tablet down.

"There," she said, letting his head fall back. "You'll be all right in a while."

He lay there for a time, thoughtless almost, the warmth of her hand against his chest comforting, reassuring him. And then, slowly, very slowly, like waves lapping gently against the sand, thought returned to him.

The tablet. She had given him the tablet.

He opened his eyes, looking up at her, yet even as he did, the nausea returned, stronger than before, making him retch.

He turned his head, leaning out, away from the bed, as the spasms came, unable to help himself, the bile filling his throat, choking him almost.

Rebecca moved back sharply, turning from him, hiding her anger, her momentary disgust, listening to him retch. Then she turned back. "I'm sorry," she said, collecting herself, one hand combing through her short dark hair. "It's all my fault. I should have known."

"Known?" He stared at her, not understanding.

There was the strong, tart smell of sickness in the room.

She stood, looking back at him from the foot of the bed, then forced herself to smile. But it was a faint, halfhearted smile. "It doesn't matter. Look. Let's get you cleaned up. You can shower if you want. I'll sort this out."

Kim sat up, wiping at his mouth. "I'd better go. I . . ."

He stopped, staring at her, mesmerized, it seemed, by her naked form, as if he had not noticed it before that moment.

He looked down, suddenly embarrassed, but she had seen the movement in his eyes, the uncertainty in his face.

Letting the towel fall from her shoulders, she moved up, onto the end of the bed, moving toward him slowly, crawling on all fours, her breasts swinging gently beneath her, her eyes watching him all the while.

"Becky . . ." he said, the sound of it strange, almost pained, but it was too late. His need betrayed itself. She leaned over him, slowly unlacing his tunic.

"It's all right," she said softly, smiling down at him, her fingers caressing the smooth warmth of his chest. "You're home now, my love. Home."

Total War

OUT OVER THE GREAT northern ocean a storm was gathering. Air moistened and made lighter by the unseasonable heat began to rise rapidly, leaving behind it a low-pressure area that drew more air in along the surface of the ocean. That air in turn was moistened and warmed, rising in a great swirling chimney, spiraling in a counterclockwise direction, heading east on the North Atlantic Current, toward the great walled shores of City Europe.

From high above Chung Kuo, a satellite eye noted the buildup of cloud, the ominous shape, and passed impersonal warnings down to its land-based station. There, senior officials of the *Ta Ssu Nung*, the Superintendency of Agriculture, studied the computer-enhanced infrared images and consulted among themselves. It was a big storm, true, even at this stage, but as yet there was no need for alarm. The front was some two and a half thousand *li* out, approaching the Biscay Abyssal Plain, and the computer prediction of its course showed that it would in all probability strike the great uncharted island to the west of the Western Isle. There was an objection to this prediction. A very junior official suggested, in the most humble terms, that the area of high pressure moving slowly down from Iceland might push the great storm south. At the same time, a second area of high pressure, over the Iberian Peninsula, was moving north. The effect of this might be to channel the storm into a narrow corridor between the two—a corridor of moist, hot air that would serve only to feed the hurricane and increase its fury.

In the magnificently decorated offices of the *Ta Ssu Nung* there was a moment's consultation among the senior officials and then a deci-sion was made. If the area of high pressure currently over Iceland *were* to move south, the cold air that the storm would entrain on its western flank might indeed add fuel to the developing storm, but it would also induce the low to turn to the northeast, thereby missing continental Europe. There were nods all around. All agreed that the storm constituted no threat to the City. In all likelihood it would spend itself over the uncharted island. And even if it was forced south, there was little real chance of damage. The walls of the City were sound, no agricultural regions lay in the path of the storm, and the sea defenses of the great ports of Brest and Nantes were adequate. A warning would be sent to the latter if necessary, but otherwise no action need be taken. There was no need to involve the T'ang or his staff.

Out at sea, however, the storm was gathering force. Six days of unrelenting heat had created unprecedented conditions in the North Atlantic. Moreover, the second area of high pressure, near the Iberian Peninsula, was beginning to feed warm air into the storm system, gradually strengthening the jet stream. Like a great mouth feeding upon the hot, moist air, the great swirl of the hurricane grew, increas-ing in speed as it went. And as it moved east, so too did the area of high pressure over the Icelandic Basin, changing direction, pushing the storm slowly, inexorably south.

━━━━━

IT WAS SIX MINUTES to four, and in the dimly lit silence of the corridors surrounding Ujpest stack, Soucek crouched, surrounded by three thousand of his men. Fifty *ch'i* along the corridor, out of sight beyond the left-hand turn, was the barrier. At this early hour only two men were manning this, the northwestern entrance to the 14K's heartland. Beyond the barrier, eighteen thousand of General Feng's best men slept on, unaware of what the dawn would bring.

Soucek looked about him and smiled, encouraging those nearest. They had planned long and hard for this, and now it was almost time.

Seventeen hundred *li* to the west, Visak and four thousand men were waiting, positioned about the Wo Shih Wo's heartland in Milan Hsien. Three thousand seven hundred *li* beyond that, in the corridors surrounding the Canton of Saragossa, Po Lao and a further three thousand men waited to infiltrate the heartland of the Yellow Banners. To the northeast, Lehmann himself led the largest of their forces, an army of fourteen thousand men, crouched in the corridors surrounding Metz, ready to take on Fat Wong and the United Bamboo.

They would hit at once. Four armies, taking on the full might of the *Hung Mun* at one go, outnumbered eight to one, but with the advantage of surprise. Surprise, and perfect planning.

Communications to the four heartlands would be cut at fourth bell. Minutes later, hallucinogenic and disabling drugs—small capsules placed in the ventilation systems weeks ago—would be pumped into the stacks.

At five minutes past four the first of the false broadcasts would be made, using the taped voices of their enemies' most trusted men; broadcasts that would override the local media stations, feeding deliberately contradictory messages directly into the heartlands.

At ten minutes past, the first of the bombs would go off—the first of many—spreading chaos and panic throughout the enemy stacks. Five minutes later, a series of chemical fires would be set off. Elevators would be shut down, exits blocked.

Maximum disruption, that was Lehmann's aim. Standing there yesterday, after putting the final touches to the plan, he had turned from the map and faced them, quoting Sun Tzu:

"Speed is the essence of war. Take advantage of the enemy's unpreparedness; travel by unexpected routes and strike him where he has taken no precautions."

And so it was, though the hours to come would tell just how unprepared their enemies were.

Soucek looked down at the timer on his wrist. Three minutes to. He turned, giving the signal for his men to put on their masks.

Key men had been bought in their enemies' camps. Men like the two on the barrier; like the guards to General Feng's private rooms. Already assassins were going about their work, creeping silently, stealthily into forbidden rooms. Making it easier. Reducing the odds against them. Even so, it would be hard. Lehmann had said as much. For this was no skirmish, no simple test of strength, this was war, total war. A war for survival. By the end of today things would be different here below. Changed for all time.

Soucek shivered. And himself? Would he survive this day?

Fifteen seconds . . .

He raised his arm, tensed, looking about him hawkishly, his whole self gathered in the gesture, then brought it down sharply, hurling himself forward, a great wave of men following him down the corridor toward the barrier.

THIRD OFFICIAL K'UNG sat back in his chair, heaving a sigh of relief. It had been a tiring night tracking the progress of the storm, worrying that the high pressure area moving down from Iceland would push it farther south. But his worst fears seemed not to have materialized. The Icelandic high had drifted east, and after a worrying three hours the storm appeared to have stabilized, holding its course. Latest estimates showed that it would make landfall somewhere out over the southwestern tip of the Western Isle.

K'ung yawned, then looked about him, glad that he would be going off shift shortly. All about him his staff had their heads down, making reports and compiling information. But decisions . . . Well, he was glad he had not had to make a decision this night.

Leaning forward again, he tapped through to the *Ta Ssu Nung's* office in the Western Isle and gave them the storm warning, quoting the latest computer predictions for wind strength, sea height, and time and location of landfall. That done, he stood, stretching his weary muscles. His relief, Wu, would be here in ten minutes. In the circumstances he might as well take advantage of his seniority to use the shower first, while the water was still hot, and grab a bowl of *ch'a* at the restaurant.

He looked up at the huge, wall-size chart once more, seeing the great swirl of the storm, prominent in the upper left-hand corner of the screen. In the hours since the crisis meeting, the storm had grown considerably. Estimates of its size now put it at over two hundred and fifty *li* from tip to tip. But it was not so much its size as its direction that had concerned K'ung. The front of the storm was now only three hundred *li* from landfall, moving north-northeast at a rate of a hundred and forty *li* an hour.

He went to move away, then stopped. In his tiredness he had almost forgotten. Brest and Nantes were still on Code B alert. He would need to give them the all-clear before he went. Wu, certainly, wouldn't think to check.

Seating himself, K'ung keyed in the security code for the day, then tapped out the message quickly, holding down both destinations at once.

Done, he thought, not waiting for the acknowledgment. It had been a hard night. It would be good to shower the tiredness from his bones.

FAT WONG STOOD THERE, staring up at the empty bank of screens, then tried the keyboard again. Nothing. The board was dead.

"What the fuck is going on?"

Wong Yi-sun turned, looking about him at the men who were crowded into the compact space of his central control. These were his most trusted men. His "sons." He studied their familiar faces a moment, noting the fear—the real fear—in every face, and understood its source. Word of mouth was that the attack had come on three fronts; that runners from the Yellow Banners, the Wo Shih Wo, and the *Kuei Chuan* were involved. Thousands of men, attacking with heavy armaments and using gas. But the rumors were patchy, unconfirmed. With the communications net down and bombs going off all over the place, it was hard to say just what was happening. All he knew was that he had woken to find two assassins in his room: men they had later identified as Yellow Banners *chan shui*—Three-Finger Ho's men.

There had been panic when he had first come into the room, but now they were quiet, watching him expectantly. His children.

"Hui Tsin," he said, addressing his Red Pole, taking control of things. "I want you to send a dozen of your best runners out to each front. West, south, and east. They will be our eyes, our ears in this battle. I want them masked and armed, each squad divided into six teams of two: one messenger, one guard. Each guard must be willing to lay down his life to allow the messenger to get through, you understand?"

"Yes, Master." Hui Tsin bowed and hurried off. Wong turned, facing another of his men.

"Hua Shang, I want you to get word to Yun Yueh-hui. Tell him that we are being attacked and that the United Bamboo would welcome help from their brothers of the Red Gang."

"Master . . ."

"Oh, and Shang . . . Send off a dozen runners, by different routes. Instruct each one to contact Yun's headquarters by whatever means they can. Speed is of the essence here."

Hua Shang bowed his head and was gone. Fat Wong turned, facing the others. They waited, tense, yet almost content now that there were things to be done, tasks to be accomplished, their faces open to him, expectant.

"Good," Wong said, beaming back at them. "You understand, my sons. The day has come. It is war. So now we fight. Whoever comes against us."

LI CHIN LAY on his back, beneath the silken bedsheets, his eyes, which had never closed in life, staring sightlessly at the ceiling mosaic. His face was ash-pale, the pillow beneath his head dark, almost black with his blood.

The eighteen-year-old, Li Pai Shung, stood there a moment, looking down at his uncle. He had returned only yesterday, after a year at College in Strasbourg *Hsien*, and had spent the night with his uncle and friends, feasting until the early hours. And now Li Chin was dead, murdered in his bed. And Li Pai Shung was suddenly 489. Boss of the great Wo Shih Wo.

He shivered, then turned, summoning the Red Pole across to him.

"You have the men who did this, Yue Chun?"

The big Han bowed to his new master. "We cornered them, Master, only fifty *ch'i* from here, but the assassins killed themselves. Arsenic capsules, it seems."

"Ah . . ." Li Pai Shung looked away, his eyes returning once more to the tiny stiletto wound at the side of his uncle's neck. "Then we do not know who sent them."

"They were Fat Wong's men, Master. My lieutenant, Liu Tong, recognized them."

Li Pai Shung turned, surprised. "Wong Yi-sun?" Then he laughed. "No. Fat Wong wasn't ready. My honorable uncle was wrong about many things, but not about that. Wong Yi-sun would never have moved against us unless the odds were heavily in his favor. Unless he was certain of victory. No, Yue Chun, this is something else."

"General Feng?" Yue asked, frowning.

"It is possible," Li Pai Shung said, recalling the intense rivalry there had been with General Feng's 14K on their northeastern borders over the past year. Possible but unlikely. There was a great deal of difference, after all, between that kind of ritual muscle-flexing and all-out war. And there was no doubting that, whatever else was happening, this was a war. Already the Wo Shih Wo had lost six stacks and more than three thousand men.

He turned back. Yue Chun was waiting with that perfect patience that characterized the man.

"All right," Li Pai Shung said finally. "Whoever it is, let's hit them back. And let's hit them hard."

———————

THE CORRIDOR AHEAD was blocked with the bodies of the dead. Here, at the entrance to the central stack of Budapest *Hsien*, the 14K had made a stand. More than a thousand men had died here in the last hour, in hand-to-hand fighting that was fiercer than anything Soucek had ever thought to see.

He stood there, getting his breath, while his men brought up the heavy armaments. Despite this setback, things had gone well for them these past six hours. The first assault had won them eight of the twenty-six stacks controlled by the 14K. After that it had been steady fighting, stack by stack, floor by floor.

So far, Lehmann's tactics had worked perfectly. Prisoners had been taken, but they'd been bound and drugged, then left in rooms behind their lines, freeing his own men for the fight. Those enemies that had continued to resist had been shot out of hand. Where things had been difficult—where resistance had been particularly fierce—they had used bombs and flamethrowers to clear rooms and corridors.

Momentum had been the secret. For four hours they had pressed forward relentlessly, enclosing their opponents, panicking them, forcing them to flee or surrender. But now they would have to fight a very different kind of battle, for now they were on the death ground. This was the final stack. Here the 14K either fought or ceased to exist as a brotherhood.

The death ground . . . Soucek shivered, remembering the words Lehmann had drummed into each of them. The words of the great Sun Tzu. Words that were more than two and a half thousand years old.

In death ground I could make it evident that there is no chance of survival. For it is the nature of soldiers to resist when surrounded: to fight to the death when there is no alternative, and when desperate to follow commands implicitly.

So it was here, at this hour. Unless, as Sun Tzu suggested, he gave them that small chance of escape—that narrow corridor of light through the darkness—that would undermine their will to fight. But first he must push them to the edge. Must make it clear to them that there was no question of compromise; that it was his intention to eradicate them, down to the last man.

He turned, watching as the two big guns were wheeled into place, signaling his men to take up positions on either side of the corridor, some twenty *ch'i* back from the barrier of corpses. Then, when all was ready, he gave the order.

FAT WONG SAT DOWN heavily, staring at the note that had come. There was no doubting its authenticity. It was Yun Yueh-hui's hand, and the coded phrases were those they had agreed on long ago, should this situation arise. But the words . . .

He let the note fall from his hand and looked up, searching the faces of his men as if for explanation.

"He says he cannot come. *Mei fa tzu,* he says. It is fate."

Wong shook his head, numbed by what was happening. It was as if T'ai Shan itself had fallen. In the last hour news had come of the murder of General Feng, his throat cut by his concubines in the bath, and of Li Ch'in, stabbed in his own bed by two *chan shih* of his, Wong's, brotherhood. From Three-Finger Ho in Saragossa there was no word, no answer to his angry query about the two Yellow Banner assassins. Not that it was important now. No, for he knew now who he fought. It was the *pai nan jen*, the "white man," Lehmann.

Already he had lost more than two thirds of his heartland to the *Kuei Chuan*. And though he had fought off the latest enemy offensive, it had cost him dearly. Lehmann had only to keep on pressing and the prize would be his. Which was why the news from Dead Man Yun was so bad. With the Red Gang at their back, the United Bamboo would have swept the *Kuei Chuan* from the levels. But Yun had betrayed him.

Wong stood, his anger spilling over, and waved his men away, slamming the door shut behind them. Alone, he let all of the hurt and bitterness flow out, raging at the empty room. Then, feeling better for that purging outburst, he sat again, letting his thoughts grow still.

Was it lost? Was all that he'd worked for gone? Or was there still a tiny chance? Some way of turning things?

Wong Yi-sun closed his eyes, concentrating, clearing his head of all sentiment, trying to see through the great swirl of events to the clear hard truth at the center of things. Just why had Yun Yueh-hui betrayed him? Why, in his moment of utmost need, had his brother failed to come?

He opened his eyes again, staring down at his tiny, almost feminine hands, using his fingers, like a child, to enumerate the facts.

One. Yun Yueh-hui's Red Gang, alone of the five brotherhoods, had not been attacked by the *Kuei Chuan*.

Two. Dead Man Yun, his ally, who had given his sacred word to aid him if attacked, had refused to come to his help.

Three. The Red Gang had not joined in the attacks, but had stayed within their borders.

Fact one suggested a deal with the *Kuei Chuan*—an agreement, perhaps, to share the spoils of war; maybe even to divide things up after it was over. But if such a deal had been made, then surely the Red Gang would have joined the *Kuei Chuan* in this venture, attacking the

United Bamboo from the north? Indeed, an alliance in which one partner did the fighting, while the other sat at home, made no sense at all. Yet if it wasn't an alliance, then what in hell was it? As far as he could make out, Lehmann had neutralized the Red Gang. But how in the gods' names had he done that? What possible inducement could he have offered Yun Yueh-hui to make him stay within his borders?

Fat Wong groaned, letting his head drop. He had been wrong last time they'd met. He should have done as Li Chin said and destroyed the *pai nan jen*. Now it was too late. Now there was nothing he could do.

Nothing. Except to endure.

━━━━━━

LEHMANN STABBED a finger at the chart, indicating where the fast-track bolt ran through the center of Fat Wong's heartland, then looked back at his two lieutenants.

"That's where you go in, along the track itself, even as our main force is attacking the south entrance here. I want each of you to take in a team at either end. Six of your best men. Men who are good with knives and garrotes. The lights will be cut, so I want everyone blacked up. You travel fast and silently. If a man falls, the rest go on. The aim is to get to Fat Wong, and we won't do that unless we hit him before he knows we're coming. The attack should distract his attention, but don't count on it. Wong Yi-sun is a good fighter, an experienced general. He will be expecting us to try at him again."

"And if we get him?"

Lehmann straightened up. "If you get him, we've won. Wong is the head. And without the head, the United Bamboo is nothing."

There were smiles at that, as if the thing were already done. "When are we to go in?"

He glanced at the timer on the desk nearby. "In thirty-eight minutes. We hit them four minutes before tenth bell. You go in three minutes later, so I want you in position well before then."

There were nods; then, when Lehmann said no more, both men bowed and left.

Lehmann turned, summoning the messenger across.

Until now things had gone well. Word from Budapest was that the

14K were close to capitulation, while the news from Saragossa was that only a handful of isolated stacks held out. Three-Finger Ho had been taken, his Red Pole killed. But things were slowly changing. In Milan, Li Ch'in's nephew, Li Pai Shung, had mounted a vigorous counterattack, pushing Visak back and inflicting heavy losses. And here, in Metz, his forces had found themselves bogged down in fierce hand-to-hand fighting in the corridors, their progress slowed almost to a standstill. It was time, then, to push things further.

Lehmann dismissed the messenger, then turned, studying the chart again. This was his last throw. All of his reserves had been called up for this attack. If it failed, that was it, for there was nothing more to call upon. But it was close now. Very close.

Leaving the map, he went through, into the anteroom, then stood there, looking through the one-way mirror into the room where Dead Man Yun's daughter and her three boys were being held. The boys were in the makeshift beds, sleeping; the woman sat in a chair beside her youngest, her hand stroking his forehead gently, her face care-worn, prematurely aged by worry.

Yun Yueh-hui had been the key. If he had been there, at Fat Wong's back with the full force of the Red Gang behind him, there would have been no chance of success today. As it was, he, Stefan Lehmann, was within hours of a famous victory, the like of which had not been witnessed in the Lowers. Good planning had brought him within sight of that victory, but planning could take you only so far: audacity—sheer daring—was needed, if you were to go all the way. Audacity . . . and luck.

━━━━━

THE STORM HAD TURNED. The high-pressure area to the north, which had been dormant these past few hours, had begun to move south once more, pushing the storm before it, channeling it into a narrow corridor of warm, moist air over the north of Brittany.

In the central control room of the *Ta Ssu Nung's* European office, a red warning light glowed fiercely on the panel of the Controller's desk, but for once there was no one there to see it. Third Official K'ung had gone home and his replacement, Wu, had called in sick. A replacement was on his way, but he would be an hour yet.

Between times the storm gathered speed and power, pushing a great wall of water before it, heading now for the coast of France and the port of Nantes.

———

ON THE FAR SIDE of Chung Kuo, at Tongjiang, Li Yuan sat in his study, reading the handwritten message that had come an hour back. Scattered on the desk nearby were the other contents of the package: audiovisual files, a folded piece of lilac paper, a ring.

He looked up, his eyes straying briefly to the open doors and the garden beyond, troubled by what he'd read, then turned, looking directly at his Chancellor.

"What do you think? Are these documents genuine? Is it as this Li Min claims? Has Wang's man, Hung Mien-lo, come to some arrangement with Wong Yi-sun?"

Nan Ho considered a moment, then gave a sigh. "This troubles me, *Chieh Hsia*. It troubles me greatly. As you know, latest reports indicate that there is some kind of struggle going on in the lowers of our City. The full extent of it we do not know as yet, though first indications are that it is of some considerable scale. In the circumstances, this message is of profound significance, for it provides us with a much clearer understanding of what is happening."

Li Yuan drew the ring toward him, then picked it up between his left-hand thumb and forefinger, studying it, troubled by something familiar about the design inset into its face.

"Maybe so. But what do we know about this Li Min? Where does he come from? And how has he come by the power to take on the rest of the brotherhoods?"

Nan Ho hesitated, then gave a tiny shake of his head. "It is a great mystery, *Chieh Hsia*. We have heard conflicting reports this past year. One story tells of a tall *pai nan jen*—a pale man—who killed one of the Big Bosses, Whiskers Lu, and usurped his position. Certainly Lu Ming-shao has been killed, but how or why has been hard to ascertain. As far as the usurper himself is concerned, it has been difficult getting any word of who or what he is. Either no one knows or no one wishes to say. Either way, our investigations have drawn a blank. As for this Li Min, we have no word at all. This is the first anyone has heard of the man."

Li Yuan set the ring down, then picked up the handwritten paper once again, his eyes drawn to the printed "chop" at the foot of the page and the bright red signature to its right. The top character, Li, was the same as that used by the son of K'ung Fu Tzu, and denoted a carp. The underlying character, Min, meant "strong" or "brave."

"Brave Carp," he said quietly, then set the paper aside. "An adopted name, I would say, wouldn't you, Master Nan?"

"It is possible, *Chieh Hsia*."

"If so, then might this not be the kind of name our friend, the *Hung Mao* who killed Whiskers Lu, would adopt?"

Nan Ho shrugged. "Again, it is possible, *Chieh Hsia*. But is this significant? Does it matter who Li Min is? Surely the important thing here is Wang Sau-leyan's involvement? If it is true . . ."

Li Yuan raised a hand. At once Nan Ho fell silent.

"As you say, if our cousin Wang *has* tried to make a deal with Fat Wong, then that is indeed significant. But not as significant, perhaps, as what is going on right now in the lowers of the City."

He sat back, his eyes resting on the scattered files and papers a moment, then got up and went across to the open doorway, standing there, contemplating the afternoon sunlight, his back to his Chancellor.

"I must be honest with you, Nan Ho, I have never been entirely happy dealing with Wong Yi-sun and his "brothers." Given the circumstances it was a necessity, and yet my instinct has been against it from the first. I recall only too well my father's attempts to come to terms with the *Hung Mun*. And his failings in that regard. Failings which, to be frank, have colored my own endeavors."

Li Yuan turned back, looking at his Chancellor. "Which is to say, I suppose, that Hung Mien-lo's advances do not surprise me. I do not trust our friend, Wong Yi-sun. Moreover, I have known for some time now that my cousin Wang seeks to undermine me by whatever means possible. In the circumstances, some kind of alliance of self-interest has seemed to me not merely possible but inevitable.

"All of which is worrying, I agree, but not half so worrying as this matter with Li Min. I mean, why should a man we have never heard of before today go out of his way to attack a vastly superior enemy? And why should that same man, confidently assuming that he will emerge from this conflict triumphant, write to me in such terms, pleading necessity and assuring me of his loyalty? It makes little sense, wouldn't you say, Master Nan? That is, unless there is much that we do not know."

Nan Ho bowed his head. "It is strange, I agree, *Chieh Hsia*, but for myself I had put little store by the man's words. It was solely their context that interested me, and the light they seemed to throw upon a murky situation." He cleared his throat, then moved a little closer to his T'ang. "It might well prove that I have misread the situation, *Chieh Hsia*, but from what we know, it seems most unlikely that Li Min will prevail."

"Then what does he want?"

"To draw you into this conflict, *Chieh Hsia*. To win you over to his side and—by providing you with evidence of Fat Wong's duplicity—to get you to throw in your *Hei* against the United Bamboo, as you did once before against Iron Mu and the Big Circle."

Li Yuan laughed. "Then why does he quite explicitly beg me not to intervene?" He went across to the desk and picked Li Min's letter up, quickly locating the passage. "Here! I quote you, Master Nan. 'I most humbly beg His Most Serene Highness not in any way to be drawn into this conflict . . .' " He looked up at his Chancellor. "Is that not clear? Or am I to read his words some other way?"

"Forgive me, *Chieh Hsia*. I know how it reads, yet it makes no sense unless one interprets it otherwise."

"Unless Li Min really *does* think he can defeat his enemies. Unless he really is concerned that I might intervene on Fat Wong's behalf and turn the tables against him."

"But *Chieh Hsia* . . ."

Again the young T'ang raised a hand. "I am loath to contradict you, Master Nan, but for once my instinct is strong. Something is going on down there that we do not understand as yet. Something of profound and lasting significance to the future of my City. My gut instinct is to act, and at once, but without further information it would be foolhardy to commit myself. So that must be our priority: to

gather information; to find out all we can about this Li Min—
whatever it costs—and to monitor the situation down there closely. To
that end I want you to instruct General Rheinhardt to mobilize a
special force to go down there and find out what they can. And I want
Rheinhardt to report back to me, personally, every hour on the hour."

Chancellor Nan bowed low. "As you wish, *Chieh Hsia.*"

"Then go. There is no time to lose."

Li Yuan stood there a moment after Nan Ho had gone, deep in
thought, staring at the lacquered surface of the door, then he turned
back, looking across at the surface of his desk, his eyes returning to
the ring. That design, like a pike turning in the water: where had he
seen that before? He went across and picked it up again, trying to fit it
on his finger and noting, as before, how narrow it was, as if made for a
woman's hand. Yet it was clearly a man's ring, the rough-cast iron
almost brutal in its *yang* masculinity.

He glanced down at the signature on the paper, then looked back at
the ring. A carp, a pike. The two things reminded him of his father's
words that time, about the City being a carp pool without a pike. Well
maybe that was it. Maybe that was the clue to it all.

A carp, a pike. For a moment longer he stood there, staring at the
two things, as if to free their significance from the air, then, with a
sigh of impatience, he turned and went out into the early afternoon
sunlight, determined to enjoy it.

THE BITTER SCENT of burning silk hung in the air as Fat Wong
made his way down the narrow steps, his tiny feet moving briskly, a
handful of his men following after. The sound of fighting was close
now, the rapid stutter of small-arms fire punctuated by dull concus-
sions that made the whole deck shudder. Wong's face was set, his
movements urgent. Time was against him.

At the foot of the steps he turned right. Ahead, twenty *ch'i* along,
the corridor was blocked by a makeshift barrier, manned by his own
men. Wong Yi-sun approached it at a run, waving the guards aside as
he clambered up over the barrier and dropped down nimbly onto the
other side, hurrying on, not waiting for his men. Farther up the
corridor, in a large room to the left, a temporary headquarters had

been set up. Going in, he went straight to the central table, pushing aside the men who stood there. Looking down at the hand-drawn map of the United Bamboo's heartland, he studied the position of the brightly colored squares on the hexagonal grid, taking the situation in at a glance.

Lehmann had split them in two, as neatly as if he had brought an ax down on a log. To the west things looked particularly desperate. There, his own forces were surrounded, cut off and heavily outnumbered now that five of his *tong* had gone over to Lehmann. Here in the northeast, the position was nowhere near as bad, yet it was only a matter of time. Once Lehmann had dealt with Wong's western forces, he would turn and the final battle would begin.

"What news is there?" he asked, looking about him.

"This came, Master," one of his men said, bowing low and handing him a sealed note. "It came in from the north, ten minutes back. From Red Gang territory."

Wong Yi-sun laughed, then ripped it open anxiously, his hopes rising. At last, Yun Yueh-hui was coming! At last! But it was not from Dead Man Yun. It was from Li Pai Shung, the new Boss of the Wo Shih Wo, greeting him and assuring him of his friendship and loyalty.

He crumpled the note and threw it down, a wave of bitterness washing through him. The gods were mocking him. Raising his hopes and then dashing them. For Li Pai Shung was already dead, the Wo Shih Wo destroyed. And his old friend and ally Yun Yueh-hui still sat on his ass in his rooms, doing nothing.

"*Why?*" he asked for the hundredth time that hour. "Why doesn't the Dead Man come?"

But there was no answer, only the dull sound of an explosion close by, rattling the plastic counters on the map.

＊＊＊

LEHMANN WALKED slowly through the ruins of the deck, surprised by the extent of the damage. When he had last seen it, this had been a luxurious, orderly place, the balconies festooned with bright red banners and garlands of colorful flowers, the shops and restaurants busy with affluent young Han. Now it was empty, desolate, the great floor littered with debris, the shop fronts gutted, the tables over-turned.

The heart, he thought. *I have plucked the heart out of the beast.* Yet still it fought on, stubbornly, defiantly, like a badly wounded bear, refusing to die.

He turned, looking down the length of Main toward the bell tower, remembering how it had once looked. Twelve great cinnamon trees had stood along the central aisle, brightening the great space with their broad green crowns. Now the aisle seemed bare. The ornamental bowls were cracked and charred, the trees gaunt, blackened stumps, embedded in ash.

Death, it all said. Death has come.

Lehmann sighed deeply, tired to his bones. The United Bamboo was broken. Once their banners had flown proudly over this place: banners on which nine long, thick canes of bamboo were gripped by a single giant hand, ivory yellow against a bright green background. But now that hand had been hacked from its arm, its tight grip loosened. And he had picked up the canes and snapped them, one by one.

He turned, clicking his fingers. At once his men spilled out from the corridors where they'd been waiting, slowly filling the Main. In the midst of them, six men carried a bulky field communications unit on a litter between them. Setting it down where Lehmann indicated, they got to work. While they did so, Lehmann looked about him, taking advantage of the lull in the fighting to think things through.

His assassins had failed, but then, so too had Fat Wong's counter-attack. And now the United Bamboo were backed up into three decks just north of where he stood, all exits from those decks sealed top and bottom. At best they had four thousand men. Half of those were wounded, all of them tired and hungry, but they were no less dan-gerous for that. When the final battle came, they would put up fierce resistance. Besides which, his own men were close to the limit now. He had tried to rest them when he could, to make sure they were properly organized and supplied with food and ammunition, but it had been difficult of late. Moreover, in the chaos of battle much had gone wrong. Take Hui Tsin, for instance. They had surrounded Fat Wong's "Red Pole" in one of the western stacks, cutting him off and then slowly closing in. Lehmann had taken great care, sure that they had him, but Hui Tsin had slipped the net, audaciously cutting his way through the *Kuei Chuan* lines with a mere handful of fighters, while his main force struck elsewhere.

A good man, Lehmann thought, feeling something akin to admiration for Hui Tsin's ability. *It is a pity he has to die.*

He turned, looking across. The rig was prepared. The technicians were standing there, heads bowed, awaiting him.

He went across and stood beside the desk, his tall, white figure standing out against the soot-stained blackness of his surroundings. For a moment he simply looked about him at his men, noting how they looked to him, eager now, unquestioning, their tiredness set aside, and inwardly he smiled, knowing he was close.

"Come," he said, tersely, unsmilingly. "Let's finish the job."

〰〰〰〰〰

"Gods . . ."

Hui Tsin moved back sharply, a look of disgust, maybe even of horror on his face. Fat Wong's Red Pole had seen many things in his life, but never anything quite so vile as this. The three boys had been trussed up—bound tightly hand and foot—and hung from hooks. Then, while their mother watched, they had been killed, their eyes poked out, their throats slit like pigs.

He turned, looking about him at the empty, blood-spattered floor, his eyes finally coming to rest on Dead Man Yun's daughter. She sat there in the far corner, unnaturally still, her knees drawn up to her chest, her face ashen, her eyes staring into emptiness.

He shuddered, angered and sickened by what had happened here. If he had known he would not have killed the guards, but taken them. Yes, and made their last few hours in this world a living hell. As it was, there was little time. The final assault would begin any time now and Leipzig was two hours distant. If there was any chance of saving the United Bamboo, he had to leave here now. To get this evidence to Dead Man Yun and wake that aged dragon from his slumbers.

Hui Tsin looked about him, then nodded. "Cut them down and bring them," he said quietly. "And be gentle with the woman. What she has suffered here today we cannot even begin to imagine."

No, and yet it was the way of War, the way he had chosen long ago, when he had first uttered the sacred oaths and partaken of the rituals of the brotherhood. How many mothers' sons had he sent to their deaths? How many days of grief and bitterness had his knife hand carved from the whiteness of the years?

The gods help me, he thought, *for my earthly soul will surely sink down into the earth-prison when I am dead, to rot in eternal torment, while my spirit soul roams the upper regions, forlorn, a hungry ghost.*

Maybe so. But before that happened, there was one final score to settle; one last, earthly battle to wage.

Lehmann. He would hang Lehmann on a hook and gut him. Or die trying.

IT WAS THE WIND that hit first, pushing ahead of the great storm like a company of outriders, wreaking havoc wherever it struck.

At Nantes Spaceport, it struck without warning, effortlessly ripping the perimeter fence from its foundations and whipping it across the open space like a giant, deadly length of ribbon. Buildings exploded. Small ships were lifted from their pads and thrown about like toys, while in the deeper pits, the big interplanetary craft were rocked and buffeted, their service crews picked up and crushed like ants against the walls and safety doors.

As the wind moved on, channeled up over the roof of the great City, there was a moment's silence, a moment's calm. From the toppled ruins of the central spire, a handful of survivors hobbled out, blessing their luck, then stopped, conscious of the growing darkness of the storm. There, filling the sky from horizon to horizon, was a wall of solid blackness. And a growing noise, a noise which, as it came nearer, seemed to sound not merely in the air, but in the earth itself, in every atom of one's body, a single, organlike note of such intensity and scale that it seemed like the voice of Hell.

For the briefest moment they stood there, transfixed, their hands pressed to their ears, and then the storm surge hit, a giant wall of water sixty *ch'i* in height, that powered its way ashore, scouring the great port clean before it hit the wall of the City with a force that threw it back upon itself.

Slowly, unheard beneath the great storm's roar, a segment of that whiteness tore itself away from the surrounding stacks. Slowly, with a dreadful, dreamlike slowness, it collapsed, tumbling into the surging darkness of the waters. And as it did the second wave struck, smashing into the breach with a force that made that great wall shudder and begin to split apart.

━━━◆◆◆◆◆━━━

DEAD MAN YUN stood there, his normally placid face twitching with emotion as he looked down at the corpses of his daughter's children. Their tiny, bloodless bodies had been laid out on the huge bed in Yun Yueh-hui's room; that selfsame bed where they had so often played, leaping about with gay abandonment while he, smiling, had looked on. If he closed his eyes he could hear them still: could hear their childish laughter, their shrieks of joy echoing throughout his rooms.

Ah, yes, he thought, clenching his teeth against the memory. *But all that ended—all joy, all love, all happiness—when these, my beauties, died.*

Yun shuddered, tears running freely down his cheeks, then reached out to gently touch and stroke each darling face, as once he'd done to comfort them in sleep. But there was no comfort anymore. No, and nothing safe. Nothing but pain and grief and bitterness.

"My beauties . . ." he said, the ache of longing in his voice dreadful to hear. "My darling little ones . . ."

"Master Yun," Hui Tsin said softly, loath to break into the old man's grief. "Forgive me, but there is little time."

Yun turned, staring at Fat Wong's Red Pole almost sightlessly, then gave a tiny nod. "Good boys, they were, Hui Tsin. Such darling little boys. They were my life. Without them . . ."

Hui Tsin bowed his head, embarrassed by the rawness he had glimpsed in the old man's face, the frightening openness. Whatever else he'd expected, it had not been this. Anger, he'd thought there'd be, and maybe even rage, but this . . . this *womanly* response . . . He took a long breath, then spoke again.

"Forgive me, Master Yun, but unless we act now it will be too late. The *pai nan jen's* forces are attacking and Wong Yi-sun . . ."

Yun raised a hand, silencing the Red Pole, his manner suddenly more firm, much more the Yun Yueh-hui of old.

"I understand, brother Hui. And I shall act. But not yet. Not until I have properly grieved my daughter's sons. Return to your Master. Go now, at once, and tell my brother Wong that the Dead Man will come. But do not push me, Hui Tsin. You have no sons, no grandsons, and so do not understand how I feel, nor what I have lost this day." Yun moved closer, towering over the Red Pole, a fierceness now behind his eyes. "I see how you look at me, Hui Tsin, but you are wrong. Do not mistake my grief for weakness, nor my tears for sudden softness. When I come I shall come as an avenging demon. And then I shall crush the *pai nan jen*. Were the legions of Hell lined up behind him, I would crush him."

Connections

RADITION HAD IT that when the first frosts came the Li Family would close up the estate at Tongjiang and move wives, sons, and daughters to Yangjing, their floating palace, 160,000 *li* above City Europe. It was an annual occurrence—a tradition that stretched back to the earliest years of the Seven when the huge geostationary environments had first been built. Li Yuan had spent a dozen childhood winters thus, not knowing snow until, at thirteen, he had stood there by the frozen lake at Tongjiang, looking up in wonder at the falling whiteness. Each spring the Family would move back, in time to witness the first buds sprout from the seeming deadness of the branch, to see the miracle of blossom in the orchard.

This once, however, they had come early, to escape not the frost but the unseasonable heat of these late autumn days. Li Yuan stood in the half-light of the shuttle hangar, smiling to himself, Kuei Jen cradled warm against his shoulder, as he watched the unloading. At such moments he felt his father move in his bones. So many times he had looked up from playing among the unloaded crates and, through a child's eyes, had seen his father, even as he himself stood now, supervising the unpacking.

Satisfied, Li Yuan turned and went through. Kuei was fifteen months old now and babbling his first half words. Li Yuan laughed tenderly, delighted by the ill-formed nonsense, and nuzzled the child, nodding to the guards who stood there, heads bowed at the door to his rooms. Inside, things had been prepared. A tray of sweetmeats rested on a low table. Beside it was a bowl with food for Kuei Jen. A nurse waited, eyes averted, ready to feed the boy.

Normally Li Yuan would have handed Kuei Jen to her and gone through to his own suite, to rest or to do some work, but on whim he dismissed the woman and, setting Kuei Jen in a low chair, knelt down, beginning to feed the boy himself. He was almost done when there was a faint cough behind him. His cousin, Wei Tseng-li, knelt in the doorway, his eyes lowered.

"Come in, Tseng-li. Please. I am almost done here."

Conscious of protocol, Tseng-li hesitated, then, bowing low, he crossed the room in a crouch and knelt across from the T'ang and his son, not presuming to be standing while the T'ang knelt. But, seeing the smile of pleasure on Li Yuan's face, he ventured a smile of his own.

"He is a healthy boy, Highness. He will be a fine athlete, a good horseman when he is older."

Li Yuan looked to him, his smile widening. "You think so, cousin Tseng?" He laughed, then turned back, pushing another spoonful of dinner into the waiting mouth, careful not to let Kuei Jen grab the spoon. "Is there anything of importance to be dealt with?"

"A few matters, Highness. But nothing so urgent that you cannot finish here."

Wei Tseng-li had been Li Yuan's private secretary for more than six months now; a post he had filled better than any expectations. In the past weeks Li Yuan had come to rely on him more and more as the demands on his time had increased. Now, with the House open, they could relax a little.

"Good," Yuan said, straightening a little. "I'll finish, then we can go through."

The bowl was almost empty. Li Yuan scraped the spoon around its edge to catch the last of it, tucking it neatly into his son's mouth.

"You have the way of it," Tseng-li said, laughing. "When I try I have it everywhere!"

Li Yuan glanced at him, then set the bowl aside. "You feed him often, then?"

Tseng-li smiled broadly, for the moment wholly unselfconscious.

"Only when Mien Shan permits. They are all quite jealous of the task. There is a regular contest between your wives as to who will tend to young Kuei. A loving jealousy, you might call it."

"Ah . . ." Li Yuan looked thoughtful a moment longer, then slowly got to his feet. He hadn't known, and he wasn't sure exactly how he felt about it. He had thought only the nurses fed the child.

"Wait here a moment, Tseng-li. I must give the child back to the nurse."

He lifted Kuei Jen from the seat, turning away from his secretary, then paused. The child, at his shoulder, was looking past him at Tseng-li, smiling in that open way that only young children have. His dark and liquid eyes held two perfect, tiny images of Tseng-li. Li Yuan took a slow, deep breath, then began to move again, aware that in that brief moment he had both weighed and decided something.

Tseng-li. He could trust Wei Tseng-li. Maybe even with his life.

＊＊＊＊＊

LI YUAN THREW HIMSELF forward, arms out in a dive, and cut the water crisply. He pushed hard with his legs underwater, his arms pulling him forward strongly, smoothly through the cool and silent medium. At the far end of the fifty-*ch'i*-long pool he surfaced, gasping for air, then rested there, one hand holding the tiled overhang while he got his breath back.

Throughout the three hours he had spent with Tseng-li at his desk he had thought of this. Of the cool silence of the pool, the flicker of shadows on the plain white walls, the gentle lapping of the water against the metal rungs. More of his time these days was taken up with official business, and though he sought to delegate as much as possible, it still left him little time that was his own. So often, recently, he had found himself thinking of something other than the matter at hand. He would catch himself imagining this: the long, weightless glide after the plunge; the pattern of light and shade on the water's mottled surface.

For a long while he floated there, thoughtless, the water rising either side of him, following the curve of the palace. Then, coming to himself, he pushed away and began to swim, a leisurely breaststroke

that took him to the other end. Turning, he started back. He was
halfway down when he heard the door behind him slide back. Slowing, he turned and, floating there, his arms out, his legs slightly
raised, looked back at the doorway.

The figure in the doorway had knelt and bowed low, in *k'ou t'ou*,
forehead pressed to the floor. It stayed there, awaiting his acknowledgment.

Li Yuan frowned and pushed with his legs, moving closer. "Who is
that?"

The head lifted slowly. It was Tseng-li. "Forgive me, Highness, but
I thought the pool was empty. I did not know you came here."

Li Yuan laughed, relaxing. He had been angry, but seeing Tseng-li
he softened. "You came to swim?"

Tseng-li bowed his head again. "I will go, Highness. Forgive me."

"No . . . stay. Come join me, Tseng-li. There's room for two."

Still the young prince hesitated.

"Tseng-li! Your T'ang commands you! Now join me in the pool!"

He said it sternly, sharply, yet he was smiling. It would be good to
relax in Tseng-li's company. Besides, there were things he wanted to
say to his young cousin; things he had found difficult to say earlier.

Tseng-li got up slowly, and, after bowing one last time, stripped off
quickly and jumped into the water. Li Yuan watched him surface,
then strike out firmly with a bold, aggressive backstroke. He followed
him slowly down, coming alongside him at the far end of the pool.
Tseng-li hung there by one hand, looking back at him and smiling.

"Highness?"

"You swim well, cousin. The curve doesn't bother you."

Tseng-li laughed and looked past Yuan at the steep curvature of the
water. In the artificial gravity of the palace things behaved differently
than on Chung Kuo. Li Yuan's great-great-grandfather, Li Hang Ch'i,
had had them build this pool, in defiance of the strangeness of the
place. He, too, had been fond of swimming. But Li Yuan's father had
never used it. He had felt the pool unnatural, odd.

Tseng-li looked back at Li Yuan. "I came here earlier and saw it. All
day I've thought of coming here."

"*All* day?" Li Yuan looked mock stern at him, and Tseng-li blushed, realizing what he had said. But then the T'ang laughed and nodded. "You were not alone in that thought, cousin. My mind was also drawn here. But tell me, you don't mind its strangeness?"

"No, Highness. I like new things. Strange things."

"And the old?"

"That too. We live in constant flux. Things persist, and yet they also change. Is that not the law for all time?"

Li Yuan laughed. "Now you sound like my father."

Tseng-li joined his laughter. "Like all our fathers!"

For a time they rested there, in the water, laughing. Then Li Yuan pushed away from the ledge. "Swim by my side, Tseng-li. There is something I must say to you . . ."

———

IT WAS JUST AFTER TEN in the morning when Kennedy reported to the duty captain at Plainsborough garrison. After searching him thoroughly, the two guards placed an audio-wrap over his head and led him to their craft. That first part of the journey took an hour, then he was led up a short set of steps and strapped into an acceleration couch. Minutes later he felt the firm, steadily accelerating pressure of the shuttle's climb.

Only when it docked, some eighty minutes later, did a gentler pair of hands release his straps and take the bulky wrap from his head. Kennedy sat up, feeling slightly nauseous, and rubbed furiously at the two welts that the wraparound's harness had left across his forehead and beneath his eyes. It had been a tighter fit than he was accustomed to. Ironically—and, again, perhaps deliberately—they had been showing an old historical saga, about the fall of the Sung dynasty before the onslaught of the Mongol generals. A heavy-handed piece of Han propaganda.

Kennedy cleared his throat and looked up at his liberator. From the touch, the faint trace of scent, he had expected a woman, but it was not. A middle-aged man, slender and finely featured, bowed and introduced himself. He was dressed in silks of salmon-pink and lemon.

"I am Ho Chang, your valet. It will be some while before the T'ang can see you. Meanwhile I shall prepare you for your audience."

Kennedy made to say something, but Ho Chang shook his head. "Wu Shih has given specific orders. You must do exactly as I say."

Kennedy smiled inwardly, understanding at once how things stood. Beneath the perfect manners ran a streak of raw hostility. Ho Chang did not like him. Nor did he mean to like him.

He let himself be bathed and dressed. The cut of the silks felt strange; far stranger than he had thought they would feel. They were elaborate and heavy, like the silks the Minor Families wore, and he felt overdressed in them. As he stood there, studying himself in the mirror, Ho Chang fussed about him, taking great care to mask his natural smell with scents.

"The very smell of you offends our noses," Ho Chang said bluntly, in response to Kennedy's unspoken query. "You smell like babies. Your skin . . ." He wrinkled his nose. "It stinks of milk."

Kennedy laughed, as if he took it as a joke, but beneath his laughter he felt real anger. Unlike many of his kind, he took great care not to touch milk products. Why then should Ho Chang insult him, unless as a foretaste of the audience to come? Was that why he had been summoned here: to be humiliated?

Ho Chang took him through to an antechamber, a great cavernous place where shadows lay on every side and dragon pillars rose up into the darkness overhead. There, insisting that Kennedy kneel, he lectured him on the proper etiquette to be followed. It was all very different from the first time he had met Wu Shih. This time full protocol was called for. He would kneel on the stone before the raised dais and strike the floor with his forehead three times. Not looking up at the great T'ang, he would stand, then repeat the process, prostrating himself three times in all before Wu Shih. This, the *san kuei chiu k'ou*, was the ultimate form of respect as laid down in the ancient Book of Ceremonies; a form reserved only for the Sons of Heaven.

And afterward? Afterward he would stay there, on his knees before Wu Shih, not daring to lift his head and look upon his master until the T'ang permitted. Nor would he speak. Not unless Wu Shih said he might.

For a long time they waited there in the cool penumbral silence. Waited until Kennedy felt certain that this, too, was deliberate; a ploy to make him understand his own insignificance in the scheme of things. Then, finally, it was time. Ho Chang led him to the great doors and, bowing once, moved back, leaving him there. Slowly the doors eased open. At once Kennedy knelt, as he'd been shown and, lowering his head, shuffled forward until he came to the foot of the steps.

Wu Shih sat on his throne. Behind him giant dragons of gold and green were emblazoned on huge banners of red. Wu Shih wore yellow, the color of imperial authority, the nine dragons—eight seen and one hidden—emblazoned front and back. He watched silently as Kennedy went through the *san kuei chiu k'ou*, then nodded his satisfaction.

"You may lift your head, *Shih* Kennedy."

Kennedy looked up, surprised by the power, the resonance in Wu Shih's voice, and, at a glance, saw how things were. Here his victories in the recent polls mattered nothing. Here, knelt beneath the dragon throne, he understood.

Wu Shih stared down at him a moment, then laughed; humorlessly, imperiously.

"Things have changed since we last spoke, *Shih* Kennedy. You are more dangerous, more attractive than you were. How strange that seems, yet it was not wholly unexpected. Your success has merely hastened things. Has made it necessary for me to act a little sooner than I wished."

Kennedy looked for Wu Shih's hands and found them among the folds of yellow cloth. They were as he remembered them. Not soft, like his facial features, but hard and strong. The T'ang's face was deceptive, for it suggested that one might deal with this man, but not the eyes, the hands. They revealed the kind of man Wu Shih really was. A man of great power. Ruthless and uncompromising.

"I'll not prolong things, *Shih* Kennedy," Wu Shih said, leaning forward slightly, his omission of Kennedy's official rank the most casual of insults. "I take you for a clever man, one who can see how things are, therefore I'll not insult you with evasions, nor humor you with airy promises. No. I have brought you here for the simplest of reasons. To make a contract between us."

Kennedy opened his mouth slightly, then closed it, bowing his head.

"Good. I respect a man who understands how things really are. Such good sense saves time in explanations, and right now I am an impatient man."

From Wu Shih's smile, Kennedy understood that some irony was intended, but it passed him by. "I shall agree, of course, to whatever you ask, *Chieh Hsia*, but if it is to be a contract, might I know what consideration I should expect?"

The T'ang smiled tightly. "Of course." He paused, then nodded. The smile had gone. "For your part you will continue as you are, speaking out against the policies of the Seven and opposing our measures in the House. Seeming to be what you are not."

There was a moment's silence between them; a moment in which Kennedy, for the first time, understood exactly what was required of him. Feeling cold suddenly, alienated from himself, he slowly bowed his head, listening, knowing what was to come.

"You will continue to campaign as now. In fact, you will act in all respects as though no contract existed between us. Short of open insurrection, that is."

"And in return?"

"In return I will pay off all your campaign debts. More than that, I am prepared to fund an expansion of your activities and any incidental expenses that occur. Your friend Michael Lever's medical bills, for instance."

Kennedy looked down, surprised, trying to make sense of things; but for the moment Wu Shih's purpose evaded him. There was a moment's silence, then Wu Shih spoke again.

"Your wife . . . how is she?"

"She is fine, *Chieh Hsia*."

"And your sons? Are they well after their treatment?"

He nodded, feeling a tightness at the pit of his stomach.

"That's good. I like them." Wu Shih laughed; a softer, more generous sound than before. "Indeed, I like *you*, Joseph Kennedy. You are a good man and I wish you no harm. However . . ."

Kneeling there, Kennedy felt that "however" hang in the air above him, like a vast weight about to fall.

"Well, let us be plain, *Shih* Kennedy. I am not blind to the currents of our times. I can see, for instance, that you are the man of the moment; that what you presently stretch your hand out to grasp will shortly be there within your palm."

Wu Shih leaned forward, his voice raised the slightest fraction. "Oh, and don't mistake me, either. I know how you see us. Cut off from things. Isolated behind a screen of Ministers and minor bureaucrats. Yet the truth is other than you think. Because we spend so much of our time up here you think we are out of touch. Secluded. But our history is full of events that warn of the dangers of seclusion, and we have made it our business to avoid this error—to trust no one and to know everything. This is Wu Shih you are dealing with, *Shih* Kennedy, not Han Huan Ti!"

For a brief moment Kennedy met the T'ang's dark, hawkish eyes and saw, rather than the scorn he'd expected, something that was almost respect.

Han Huan Ti, as every schoolchild knew, was an Emperor of the ancient Han dynasty who had ruled through his court eunuchs and had been totally cut off from the realities of his great empire. His reign had been an evil time, characterized by popular uprisings and opposed by scholars and soldiers alike. The point was not lost on Kennedy. "Then you know I have another meeting, *Chieh Hsia?*"

Wu Shih nodded. "Three days from now. With my old friends, the 'Sons.' I understand they wish to join your organization."

It was more than Kennedy knew. "Perhaps," he said. "And you would oppose that, *Chieh Hsia?*"

"Not at all. It would make sound political sense, after all. And with you to keep an eye for me . . ."

Kennedy's knees were beginning to ache. He shifted his weight gently. "Then this . . . contract makes no difference, *Chieh Hsia?*"

"On the contrary, it makes all the difference. For there will come a moment—a single moment—when you will think you have outgrown me."

Wu Shih paused, then stood up. Slowly he came down the steps until he stood there, over the American, his foot raised, touching the brow of the other.

"It is then, at that very moment, that our contract will find its meaning. Then, when you think it matters least, that it will bind you."

It had been the very lightest of touches, the merest brush of the T'ang's silk slipper against the flesh of his forehead, but behind that almost tender contact was such a depth of brutality that Kennedy shuddered and felt his stomach tighten, his testicles contract, the naked reality of what he was doing hitting him.

"Come," said the T'ang, stepping back. "The machine is ready."

———

CHARLES LEVER strode about the room, red-faced and angry. He had been drinking heavily, and his temper hadn't been improved by the news his accountant had brought him.

"*How much?*" he demanded, turning back to face the sour-faced man who sat there in the chair in the corner of the room.

"About eleven million in all. Most of it drawn against bonds payable on his inheritance. High rates, but what does he care?"

Lever went to the table and poured another glass of brandy from the decanter, swilling it down thoughtlessly. "The scheming little bastard! And to think I wasted my sympathy on him!" He laughed unpleasantly. "Well, they won't see a *fen!* I'll disinherit the little shit! Then they can chase *him* for satisfaction!"

His lawyer, standing by the door, sighed and looked away, holding his tongue. There would be time later, when the old man had calmed down, to explain the difficulties of disinheriting Michael, not least of which was the fact that there was no one else to inherit. Not without tracing the most distant of relations.

"Will you see Hartmann now?" asked Lever's private secretary, poking his head around the door. It was the fourth time he had asked.

"Fuck Hartmann! What use is the bastard now?"

The head disappeared; went off to tell the ex-Representative— released pending trial on Lever's personal bond for twenty million— that his master was indisposed and could not see him yet.

Lever strode up and down, unable to rest, his whole body tense with anger, with the feeling of betrayal. At first it had hurt, seeing Michael there in his hospital bed, speaking out against him. He had stood there before the screen, shocked and frightened by the transformation in his son, as if all these years he had been sheltering a viper in his bosom. And now the snake had turned and he had been bitten.

"Well, damn him. Damn his black hide!" Lever's voice was almost hysterical, on the edge of tears. But when he turned back to face the young man his voice was calmer, more threatening than before. "Well, that's it, eh? A fine reward for a father's love. Spits in my face. Insults me. Questions my integrity." And with each statement he tapped his chest with the stiff-held fingers of his right hand. His large, double chin jutted out aggressively as he spoke and his eyes glared, challenging anyone to gainsay him. "He's *not* my son. Not now."

He turned to the lawyer. "Draw up the papers. Start now. I want him *out*! I don't want him to get a single *yuan*, understand? And if you need a new beneficiary, leave it all to the Institute."

The lawyer opened his mouth as if to query that, then closed it without saying a word. He nodded and turned to go.

"And Jim," said Lever, calling him back a moment. "Arrange to meet those bonds. In full. I'll have no one suffer for my son's treachery."

Alone, finally, Lever stood there by the window, looking out across the lawn toward the bright circle of the lake, seeing nothing but his son's face, younger, much younger than it was now, smiling as it looked up at him, so bright and eager and loving. He shuddered and, unseen, let the first tear fall. Not love nor money could bring that back now. Not love nor money.

━━━━━

AT THAT SAME MOMENT, in the great floating palace of Yangjing, in geostationary orbit high above City Europe, Li Yuan was talking to his fellow T'ang, Wu Shih.

Wu Shih's face leaned in toward the surface of the screen, his features grave with concern. "The rumors are strong, Li Yuan. More than forty channels have carried something in the last few hours. And MedFac has gone so far as to declare that there is a war going on in your City."

"A *war* . . . ?" Li Yuan laughed, but beneath his laughter was concern. He had had General Rheinhardt report to him regularly since he had received Li Min's package, but now it seemed that the initial assessment of the situation had been wrong. There was indeed a war going on down there in the Lowers of his City, if not one which, as yet, threatened him. But if Wu Shih were growing concerned then it was time to act—firmly, decisively—to bring the thing to a quick close.

He smiled. "I am grateful for your concern, Wu Shih, but the matter is already in hand. Indeed, I hope to be able to issue a full statement to the media two hours from now; one that will reassure them and put an end to speculation."

Wu Shih smiled broadly. "I am glad it is so, cousin. It would look ill to leave the matter any longer."

"Indeed."

Li Yuan leaned across and cut the connection, then sat back, taking a long deep breath. He had held back from acting until now, adopting a course of *wuwei*—inaction—hoping that the matter would resolve itself. But from the latest report it seemed that the sides had reached a kind of stalemate. And that was dangerous.

So far the fighting had been limited to the Triad heartlands and to the lower fifty. Locked in a stalemate, however, one or both of the sides might look to escalate the conflict and bring in other, outside elements. And who knew where that might lead? No. He had to act, and now.

He leaned forward and tapped out the code that would connect him with Rheinhardt, then sat back, waiting for his General to appear.

"Helmut," he said without formalities. "I have a job for you. I want you to prepare the *Hei* for action. They are to go in an hour from now. It is time we settled this matter . . ."

━━━◆◆◆◆◆━━━

STANDING THERE in the frame, Michael Lever looked about him. For the first time in weeks the big hospital room seemed cramped and crowded. Besides the two doctors and four attendants, others had come to see him take his first steps since the bombing. He looked across at them, smiling uncertainly, and feeling even less confident than he looked.

"Take your time," one of the doctors said, making a last check of the frame.

"Don't fuss," he said, looking briefly at the manual controls on his chest, hoping he would not need them.

At the far end of the room Kennedy was watching him, Mary and Jack Parker close by. As he met Kennedy's eyes, the older man's face creased into a smile. "Go for it," he said softly. "You can do it, Michael."

He nodded, pleased that they were there, then looked back at the doctor. "Ready?"

The doctor stepped back. "Whenever you are, Michael. But don't strain for it. The connections have to develop. Work them too hard and you'll have difficulties."

He had been told all of this before, but he listened, knowing how hard they had worked to get him here so quickly: standing, about to walk again. He turned his head and smiled at Mary. "Here goes, then."

It was an odd sensation, like wishing, and at first, like most wishes, nothing happened. He was used now to the numbness of his body; had grown used to the ghostly, disembodied sensation of not having his legs or arms respond to the messages he sent them. This, then, was strange. A calling upon ghosts.

He tried again, the message he sent—the *desire*—almost tentative. There was the faintest tingling in his muscles, but no movement. *Not enough*, he thought. *Not quite enough*. He closed his eyes, resting. The frame, keeping him upright, was a comfort, but he was still afraid. What if it didn't work? What if, after all that delicate and painful surgery, the machine malfunctioned? What then?

They had warned him about this. He would feel fragile, alienated from his own body. The bioprosthetic implants would seem intrusive, maybe even hostile to him. But they were not. They were simply undeveloped. He had only to trust them.

Opening his eyes, he turned his head again, looking to the doctor. "It's hard," he said. "It feels like there's no power there. No pressure."

"There's a tingling?"

"Yes, but it's very faint."

The doctor smiled. "Good. Work on that. Bring that tingling on a bit. Develop it. But remember, your muscles have done no work at all these past weeks. There'll have been a slight atrophy. Nothing damaging, but enough to make it seem at first that you're getting nowhere. Keep trying, though, and it'll come."

He turned his head back. Then, gritting his teeth, he tried again. The tingling grew. Then, suddenly, he felt the frame lift and then settle again. He had moved his left leg forward about four inches.

There was a cheer in the room. He looked up. Everyone was smiling at him. He laughed, relief flooding in.

"That's great," said the doctor, coming closer to check on the frame. "That's really excellent, Michael."

The frame had done it, exaggerating his movement mechanically and taking his full weight, but that did not lessen the sense of achievement he felt. After so long he was connected again, linked up to his own body. He shivered and felt tears come to his eyes. As he developed the connections, the *control* he now had over his body, the doctors would slowly diminish the supportive power of the frame. And eventually, if all went well, he would discard the frame altogether. He would walk again.

Mary came across and held him awkwardly, one arm reaching through the frame to take his shoulder, the other caressing his cheek. "I'm so glad, my love. Really I am." She stood back, grinning widely. "I can't wait to see you walk into the House and take your seat."

He grinned back. All of the fear he had been feeling these past few days had dissipated. Slowly, conscious of the awkward, rather stilted movements of the hydraulics, he raised his left arm and moved it until his hand rested on his wife's shoulder. "Just now I feel a bit like a maintenance machine," he said, laughing.

Mary leaned forward to kiss his forehead, then moved back as Kennedy came across.

Kennedy leaned close, whispering, "I'm proud of you, Michael. You don't know how proud. It's hurt me to see you lying there, day after day."

"Thanks . . ." Then, more hesitantly. "You don't know what it's meant. I think I'd rather have been dead than lie there any longer."

"I know . . ." Kennedy made to step back, but was held there a moment longer, the arm of the frame trapping him.

"One question, Joe."

"Go on."

"Who paid for all of this?"

Kennedy was about to answer, but Michael spoke again, quickly. "Look, I know how much in debt we were after the last campaign, even after the money I raised." He searched Kennedy's gray eyes. "So?"

Kennedy hesitated, then shook his head. "It's paid for. Let's leave it at that, huh?"

For a moment Michael considered persisting, then he nodded. "All right. I'll leave it. For now." Slowly, but less awkwardly than before, he moved his arm away. "But I want to know who to thank."

There was a strange movement in Kennedy's face, then, slowly, he smiled again. "I can't," he said, shaking his head. "Really, Michael. Just accept it."

"Was it my father?"

"Your father?" Kennedy laughed abruptly, as if the very idea was absurd. "No . . . Look, Michael, I'm sorry, but don't ask me. Please. I just can't say. Okay?"

"Can't?"

"Can't." There was a finality to the way he said it that made Michael frown. For some reason the subject had touched Kennedy personally, and at some deep and hidden level. Why should that be?

"Okay," he said after a moment. "I won't ask again."

"Good," said Kennedy, stepping back out of his way. "Now let's see if you can get that right leg going too."

———————

LATER, alone with Parker, he asked again.

"Don't ask me," said Parker, sitting down at his bedside and leaning across him to take his hand. "Joe saw to all that stuff. Anyway, what does it matter? It's paid for. That's all that counts."

"Is it?" He was silent a moment, then, "You know, I've felt helpless in more ways than one, Jack. All the while I've been here it seems as though things have been kept from me. As if there's something you haven't told me, any of you. Is there a reason for that, Jack? *Is* there something you haven't told me?"

Parker looked down. "Like what?"

Michael took a deep breath, then shook his head. "I don't believe this. Look, Jack, it's me, Michael, your best friend. What can't you tell me?"

Parker met his eyes. "You want to know?"

"Of course I bloody want to know. It's driving me crazy all this not knowing. Sure I'm an invalid, but don't treat me like a mental cripple too, Jack. You know me better, surely?"

"Maybe," said Parker. It was an odd thing to say. They had known each other almost twenty years.

"So?"

"They know who planted the bomb."

Michael went cold. How often had he thought about this? A thousand times? More? And he had always assumed that they didn't know. "When did they know?" he asked. Not who, but when. At that moment it seemed more important.

"Later that day. They . . . they got him almost straightaway."

Michael shuddered and looked away. There was a slight tingling in his limbs. The frame was hanging in its bracket at the far end of the room. For a while he stared at it, conscious of how large and clumsy it looked without him in it. Then he looked back at Parker. "Who was it?"

Parker smiled wearily. "Hartmann."

"Hartmann?" He laughed disbelievingly. Then, with a suddenness that took his breath, he realized what that meant. "No . . ."

Parker was watching him, a look of deep concern in his eyes. "There was a lot about it in the media those first few days. Since then it's been embargoed. Which is . . ."

"Why I hadn't heard," Michael finished. Again there was that tingling in his limbs, as if in response to some involuntary command, a tensing of the muscles, a ghostly bunching of fists. "Who placed the embargo? I didn't think anyone had enough clout."

Parker blinked and looked away. When he spoke again it was almost in a whisper. "Wu Shih. Who else?"

"Wu Shih?" Michael was confused. "Why? I mean, why should he want to do that?" Then, "Look, Jack, what's going on here? I don't understand . . ."

Parker smiled bleakly. "Nor me. At least, not all of it. But between us I'd say that our friend Kennedy has been making deals."

"Deals? With Wu Shih?"

Parker shrugged. "Let's just say that things have been a lot easier these past few weeks. Too smooth. And I've been doing some thinking."

"And?"

"Look, Michael, I'm sorry. I know how it seems. Your father's man tries to have you killed. It's not a nice thought. It points the finger where you'd rather not have it pointed. But you did ask me. As for the rest . . . I'm as much in the dark as you."

Michael closed his eyes, then nodded, but his face showed the sudden bitterness, the despair he felt. When he opened his eyes again, Parker was looking down. "Thanks, Jack. You're right. It's not nice. But I feel better for knowing it. I . . . I feel as if I can get things straight in my mind now. Before, it was . . . confused. I felt I was losing my grip on things."

Parker smiled but didn't look up. "You won't do anything?"

"Like what? Throw punches?"

Parker met his eyes. "Who knows? You're not as helpless as you look."

"No," he answered, for the first time realizing what the operations meant. "No. Not helpless at all."

He would get better, stronger. He would spend every hour, every minute of his time getting better. And then, when he was ready . . . He closed his eyes, letting the tingling fade from his limbs and chest, calming himself. It had been a long day, a hard day.

"Michael?" Parker had felt the sudden tension in the fingers of the hand he held, then the slow relaxation of the muscles. He leaned forward, listening, then smiled, hearing the soft, regular pattern of his friend's breathing. Michael Lever was sleeping.

━━◆◆◆◆◆━━

TOLONEN STARED DOWN at the ruins of Nantes spaceport a moment longer, then turned to face Li Yuan's General, Rheinhardt. It was cramped in the cruiser's cockpit, with barely enough room for the pilot and the two big men, but no other craft had been available. All else had been destroyed.

"How did it happen?" Tolonen asked, indicating the gap in the smooth face of the City, the fallen stacks.

"We're not sure yet," Rheinhardt admitted, the somber expression on his face a perfect copy of the older man's. "There are three theories we're working on. The first is that subsidence, caused by water erosion, undermined the supports and weakened them."

"Is that likely?"

Rheinhardt shook his head. "Not really. The river's course has changed over the years, and it seems the water table has risen slightly in the last decade. Even so, most of the pillars are sunk into the rock. Besides, from what we can make out, most of them are still standing. The stacks simply broke away by the look of it."

"Or were torn away?"

"Maybe. That's another of the theories. That the sheer, unprecedented force of the storm—the tidal wave, particularly—simply ripped the stacks from the surrounding sections."

Tolonen nodded. "And the third?"

"One of our experts has come up with the idea that the constant vibration of the rockets taking off from the spaceport might have weakened the connections between the stacks over the years." Rheinhardt shrugged. "It seems highly unlikely, if you ask me, but we're following it up anyway."

Tolonen sighed deeply, looking out once more at the scene of devastation below. It was worse, far worse than he'd imagined it. The City was supposed to be safe. One hundred percent safe. For a century and more it had stood, undamaged by the elements, yet in the course of less than thirty seconds, three whole stacks had slid into the Clay, taking more than two hundred and eighty thousand people with them. If news of this got out there would be panic in the levels, rioting . . .

He shuddered. Rheinhardt had been right to call him in. Right to cordon off the surrounding areas and cut communications. But would it be enough? Could they really prevent word of this from getting out?

He leaned forward, tapping the pilot's shoulder. "All right. Take us back. I've seen enough."

Rheinhardt leaned close, lowering his voice. "Well, Knut? What should I do? Li Yuan has ordered me to destroy our friend Li Min and scour the Lowers of all Triad activity. And so I would gladly do. But that was before I knew of this." He took a breath. "This . . . well, it's the kind of thing that could set off the whole City, neh? Word of it must be quashed, and at once. But I've a problem. I haven't the manpower both to quash this and take on the Triads. You can see that, can't you, Knut?"

"I see it clear enough, Helmut. Besides, there'll be time enough to take on that scum, neh?"

"Then you'll speak to Li Yuan?"

Tolonen smiled grimly. "At once. In the meantime let's have the *T'ing Wei* earn their pay. Let's flood the airwaves with good news and rumors of spring. And for once let us pray that it's enough."

━━━━━

WONG YI-SUN lay there, wrapped in the ancient banner, like a wasp in a spider's web. Blood from a thousand hatchet cuts had darkened the fragile cloth, obscuring the original design, but the banner had once hung in Fat Wong's hall, in pride of place.

Lehmann stood over the body of his rival, looking down at the pale, birdlike face, and heaved a great sigh. He was close to exhaustion. For more than forty hours he had fought. Fought beyond the point of hope until, in the darkest hour, help had come. A hundred thousand *Hei*—GenSyn half-men used by Security as riot troops—sent in by Li Yuan to reinforce him. Turning the tide of battle in his favor. Giving him victory.

He shuddered, remembering the moment, then crouched, reaching out to touch the blood-encrusted silk. Peacock blue the banner had been, a great triangle of gold at its center. And in the blue had been embroidered a single bloodred pictogram.

Tian. Nan Jen. Tu. *Heaven. Man. Earth.*

It was *the* banner, brought from the Fu Chou monastery six centuries ago. Whoever held it led the great Council of the *Hung Mun*; was Head of the 489s, the "Big Boss" here in the lowers of City Europe.

Or so it had been. Until today.

Lehmann stood, then turned away, signaling to his men to take the body and burn it, banner and all. All that was ended now. Six centuries of tradition reduced to ash and dust. Now there was only he. All else had been destroyed.

He stretched, easing his tired muscles, considering what he had done. Two hundred thousand men were dead. Another eighty thousand—prisoners, taken in the early hours of the battle—would be dead within the hour. So he had ordered. And so it had to be, for he could not risk the slightest threat of opposition. Not yet. Not until he had rebuilt his organization and stamped his mark upon these levels.

He turned, looking about him, noting how his men looked at him: in awe, as if one of the ancient gods stood there among them. And inwardly he laughed. Right now he was triumphant, was king of these levels, the White T'ang, as they called him. But how long would that last? If Li Yuan took it in his mind to crush him; to turn his brutish *Hei* against their former allies . . .

For a moment his mind went numb. Tiredness, he told himself, but it was more than tiredness. It was like that moment on the slopes of the Otzalen Alps. That moment when he had looked down into the great crater where DeVore's fortress had been and seen only darkness. Then, too, he had felt like this, emptied of all thought, all enterprise.

He felt wasted, brittle-boned. A wraith. Victory, now that he had it, seemed a hollow thing. Hollow, because it had not been his. Because, at the final moment, he had depended on the favor of another.

"Yao Lu," he said, summoning one of his lieutenants.

The man hurried across and knelt, his head bowed low. "Master?"

"How much was in the chests you found?"

"More than two hundred million, Master," Yao answered, keeping his head lowered.

"And in the rest of the caches?"

"It is hard to say exactly, Master, but more than five hundred million, certainly."

Seven hundred million. It was a huge amount—much more than he'd expected. With such a sum at hand, what could he not do, given time? But that was it. The task of reconstruction was a lengthy one, a time-consuming one, and he had no time. Not if he wished to survive.

Just now one thing alone mattered. Placating Li Yuan.

"Yao Lu," Lehmann said finally, his decision made. "I want you to gather it all together and bring it here. Every last *fen* of it. And then I want you to contact the Major in charge of Li Yuan's *Hei* and beg an audience with him. It is time we paid the great T'ang his due. Time we paid tribute for the great service he has done us this day."

LI YUAN STOOD on the great viewing circle, looking down at the blue-white globe of Chung Kuo, one hand gently stroking his beardless chin as he thought things through. He had hoped to have a week up here—a week free of matters of State—but it was not to be. Tolonen was right. The severity of the damage to Nantes spaceport could not be overlooked. He had to deal with the matter urgently.

He shivered and turned away, looking about him at the room, remembering how often he had seen his father standing where he now stood. His father, deep in thought, one hand tugging gently at his plaited beard. One day Kuei Jen would stand here looking down, matters of State weighing heavily on his mind. But for now the child slept peacefully, unaware of the burden he would one day bear.

The thought made him smile, but the smile was tinged with a faint sadness. There were consolations, certainly, but sometimes the burden seemed too much to bear. Some days he felt like giving it all up, as his brother Han had once proposed, and handing it over to another. But that could not be. This was *his* charge, *his* duty.

What to do, though, about Nantes? That was the question. If he went down openly, Wang Sau-leyan was sure to hear of it, and that might prove disastrous. There was another option, however. He could leave his shuttle here and travel down on the service craft that was due to leave in two hours' time. That would get him to Nantes in plenty of time to deal with matters. Yes, and maybe he could persuade Wu Shih and Tsu Ma to meet him there. Secretly of course. Because if Wang *were* to hear of this, he might yet find a way to take advantage of the situation. And with the Triads still at war down there, it was important to settle things quickly, before the rumors began to spread and panic set in among the Lowers.

His decision made, Yuan climbed the steps quickly and went through, heading for the nursery.

Tseng-li was kneeling, his back to Li Yuan, when the T'ang came into the room. He was laughing, his laughter echoed back at him by the young child who clung to his outstretched arms. On the far side of the room the nursemaid, seeing Li Yuan, got up hastily, making to bow, but Li Yuan motioned to her, raising a finger to his lips and smiling. She straightened, but Tseng-li had seen the movement and half turned, realizing that someone had come into the room. Kuei Jen also turned, and, his smile widening, cried out to him.

"Papa!"

Laughing, Li Yuan came forward and bent down. Tseng-li leaned back, out of the way, as the little boy lifted his hands up to his father.

"They know their own," he said, getting up and giving a slight bow to Li Yuan.

"Some more than others," Li Yuan answered, looking from Kuei Jen to his secretary. "It is a sad thing that we who rule see so little of those who matter most to us." He looked back at his son, smiling broadly at him, then lifted him and hugged him tightly. "Like now. I have to go back down, Tseng-li, at once. Something has come up which I must attend to personally. I'll be gone two, maybe three days."

Tseng-li gave another bow. "Is there anything I should be doing while you are gone, Highness?"

"Nothing that cannot wait three days. My Ministers are capable men, after all."

Tseng-li laughed, amused by the irony in his cousin's voice.

"No, Tseng-li," Li Yuan continued. "Just take care of my son, my wives, while I am gone, neh?"

The fifteen-month-old Kuei Jen was making small burbling noises now and pressing against Li Yuan's shoulder, rubbing his small, dark head against the silk.

"He's tired," explained Tseng-li, dismissing the nursemaid with a gesture of his hand. "He has been up several times in the night."

"Then I'll hold him," said Li Yuan, with a small nod of finality. "It is rather pleasant, neh?"

"Just now," agreed Tseng-li, smiling. "But they grow so fast. My brother's children now . . ." He laughed, looking thoughtful. "They're too big to carry already. Besides, they get so independent."

Li Yuan nodded, watching his cousin carefully. Already Kuei Jen was settling against him, snuggling in against the warmth of his shoulder. "You miss your brothers, Tseng-li?"

"Sometimes."

Li Yuan sighed, smiling at the small, warm weight he carried, then looked back at Tseng-li. "A break would be good for you, neh? Maybe when I get back."

Tseng-li nodded, keeping his silence; but his eyes showed gratitude.

"Sometimes I think that family is all. The rest . . ." Yuan laughed softly, feeling the child stir gently against him with the movement. "Ill thoughts for a T'ang, perhaps, but true. Nor would I trust a man who felt otherwise."

Tseng-li, watching him, smiled and nodded. The child was asleep.

CHAPTER TWENTY-TWO

Circles of Dark

APTAIN HENSSA of the floating palace, Yangjing, moved across the room slowly, his legs drifting up as he turned and pulled himself along the guide rungs, then anchored himself beside the lieutenant at the screen.

"The codes check out?"

The lieutenant ran the signal again, then leaned back, letting his captain watch as the code broke down on the screen. Behind the sharp-etched lettering the image of the incoming craft was growing steadily larger, its complex computer-generated recognition pattern matching the programmed format perfectly.

There was total puzzlement on the captain's face. "Chi Hsing?" he said. "What would Chi Hsing want?"

The lieutenant stayed silent. This wasn't his decision. Orders or no orders, he wasn't going to shoot one of the Seven out of the skies. He had a family down below to think of.

"Send for verification."

"From whom?" the lieutenant asked, staring fixedly at the screen. He was conscious of the watching cameras, the tapes. No Board of Inquiry would find his actions reprehensible. He would act to the letter, or not at all.

For a full half minute the captain hesitated, while the craft drew slowly nearer. Then, abruptly, he leaned across and, steadying himself, tapped out a message on the touchpad. It was immediately coded and sent: *With respect, please advise purpose of visit.*

The lieutenant saw the worry in his captain's eyes, and, for once, felt some small sympathy for his normally overbearing superior. One did not ask a T'ang what his purpose was. Such a breach of etiquette might strip him of his rank.

For a time there was nothing. Then, as if there had been no query, the original request-for-docking signal came back. The craft was only ten minutes distant now and still closing. A decision would have to be made.

For the first time the captain looked down at his lieutenant and shook his head. "I don't like it." But he too was conscious, it seemed, of the cameras overhead and left it at that. Turning, he pushed off and drifted toward the far door. There, holding the top rung firmly, he twisted and looked back at the lieutenant. "Give them boarding clearance, but tell them there'll be a slight delay."

"And if they ask for a reason?"

The captain looked thoughtful a moment, then shrugged. "New security procedures, that's all." Then he turned and, pressing the hatch stud, slid through the irising circle into the corridor outside. The lieutenant watched him go, then turned to face the screen again, his fingers giving the clearance signal to the incoming ship.

———————

IT WAS CRAMPED in the shuttle. They sat in the forward compartment, six to a side, their helmets almost touching across the narrow space. Their suit systems kept them cool; even so, more than one of them had been sweating these past few minutes as the bulk of the floating palace grew larger on the screen above the hatch. They watched it in silence, knowing that these moments were the most vital of the whole mission. Here, as they approached, they were most vulnerable. One mistake and they would be so much iced debris, floating in the vacuum.

For a long time there was nothing. They could not hear the signal going out, nor did they know anything of the query sent back. Moment by moment the tension grew. Then, with a small click and a hum, the internal channel came on and the group leader's voice came across.

"We've got boarding permission. A small delay, it seems, then we're in. Good luck!"

There was a small buzz of talk, and a sense in them all of great relief. What lay ahead they had rehearsed to perfection. The worst of it was now behind them.

THE CAPTAIN had arranged the men in a semicircle about the boarding deck. They wore anchor shoes and full suits. Each held a small laser and a deflector shield. Beyond that he had said nothing to them. If he were right there would be time to give them simple orders. If wrong . . .

He smiled grimly, looking about him and listening to the sounds of the docking shuttle. If wrong he would need to trust to Li Yuan's understanding and compassion, for what he did now was an insult to Chi Hsing.

He shivered and stared straight ahead at the huge doors, waiting for them to open. His instincts told him this was wrong. Though the signals were correct, the situation felt wrong. Why should Chi Hsing visit now, and without warning? And why had he, Captain of the Watch, received no notice of the visit?

Against this strove another inner voice. Who else would use Chi Hsing's shuttle but the T'ang himself? Who use his codes? He was being ridiculous even to begin to think that something was amiss. And yet . . .

Perhaps this was why I was chosen. Perhaps they knew I would act this way. Whatever, he had gone too far now for half measures. He would see this through, whatever the personal cost. Whether his master understood or not, duty bade him take this action.

There was a sudden silence. The craft had docked. Then he heard a sharp hissing as the airlock filled. *Thirty seconds*, he thought, bracing himself, lifting his weapon and pointing it at the doors. He saw several of his men turn and look at him, then look back, not quite certain why they were there, or what was happening, but he kept silent a moment longer. *There'll be time*, he told himself. *Whoever it is, they'll not expect us here.*

The hissing stopped. There was a low groan, then, with the slightest hesitation, the doors began to slide back. Through the gap stepped three men, fully suited, the first in a suit of gold, trimmed with imperial yellow.

"Chi Hsing . . ." he began, lowering his gun and beginning to bow. All about him his soldiers were sinking to their knees, their heads lowered. But there was a movement behind the T'ang which made the captain look and hesitate, then raise his gun again. But he was too late. The air was crisscrossed with burning laser traces, and the screams of his men were deafening in his ears. He himself was shouting now, but his voice was lost in the general noise and confusion. The three men were firing at the kneeling soldiers, cutting them apart. Only he, miraculously, stood there in the midst of it all, untouched.

Trembling, he lifted the weapon and fired, watching as the gold-tinted visor split and then exploded.

It is not Chi Hsing, he told himself, as he held the beam on the falling figure. *It is not Chi Hsing*. But even as the lasers of the other men caught him, burning into his chest and arms and neck, he felt a great pang of sorrow. He had killed a T'ang, a Son of Heaven! And now his clan would be eradicated, the ghosts of his ancestors unappeased. His wife, his child . . .

He stumbled forward, then fell and lay still. One of the suited figures paused, looking down at him, then stepped over him and clumped on heavily toward the corridor. Behind him came others. Terrorists. *Yu*. The suited figure laughed triumphantly, then yelled instructions into his suit microphone.

They had done it! They were on board!

━━━━━━

OUT ON THE GREAT mid-ocean city of Sohm Abyss it was late morning. The restaurant was quiet, only a few people scattered about the tables. Kim was sitting in his usual corner, a half-filled *ch'a* bowl at his elbow, when Rebecca came into the room. Seeing him, she went across and sat, facing him.

He looked up, meeting her eyes, uncertain what to say. He had not seen her since the night of the party, but had kept to himself, working longer hours than usual and sleeping in the lab. For a day or two, he had even avoided coming here, lest she track him down. But he had known all along that he would eventually have to face her. To have it out with her.

"Hi," she said softly, offering a smile. "I wondered where you'd got to. I left messages on your comset. But maybe you didn't get them. I'm told you've been working hard."

He raised his eyebrows, as if he knew nothing about the messages, but it was untrue. He had seen them. More than a dozen in all, asking him to contact her and talk.

"I've been worried about you," she said, leaning toward him, the scent of jasmine wafting across to him. "I thought you might be angry with me about what happened. When I woke up that morning and you'd gone . . ."

He looked down. "I'm not angry with you."

That much was true. He wasn't angry with her, he was angry with himself, for having made such a fool of himself. And now he felt ashamed. Deeply, thoroughly ashamed. He had let himself down. Himself, and Jelka.

"Look, I'm sorry," he said. "I was drunk, I . . ."

She laughed softly, provocatively. "Not that drunk."

"That's not what I meant," he said, meeting her eyes again, his face deadly earnest. "I mean that it was wrong what we did. If I'd have been sober I would never have gone to your room."

"You mean you didn't enjoy what happened?" Her eyes were wide, staring into his. Reaching out, she touched his fingers, then closed her own about them. "Because I did. And I can't stop thinking about it. You and me, Kim, together in the darkness. It was wonderful. Didn't you think so? You and me, doing *that*." She shivered, squeezing his fingers tightly.

"It was wrong," he said again, steeling himself against her touch, the soft seductiveness of her words. "There's a girl . . ."

He saw the movement in her eyes. The surprise and then the calculation. "A girl? Someone you like, you mean?"

He nodded. "I made a promise."

"A promise?" She smiled, then frowned, the two expressions strangely coexistent in her face. "What kind of promise?"

"She's young, you see, and her father . . . well, her father is a powerful man. He doesn't want her to see me, so he's sent her away. To the Colonies. But I made her a promise. I . . ."

He stopped, realizing that he had said much more than he'd intended. But he wanted Rebecca to understand, to realize why that night with her had been so wrong.

Her fingers slowly loosened their pressure about his own. She withdrew her hands, then sat back, nodding to herself, a strange look on her face.

"So you fuck me and leave me, and that's it, huh?"

He shivered. "It wasn't like that. If I'd been sober . . ."

"If *you'd* been sober." She shook her head, her face suddenly hard, her eyes angry with him. "Don't you see it, Kim? Don't you understand things yet? Or is it only atoms and abstract forces that you comprehend? This girl . . . she won't wait for you. Not if her father's against you. They hate us, Kim. Don't you get that yet? On the face of it they may smile as they use us, but deeper down they hate us. Clayborn we are. Different from them. And they despise us for that."

"No," he said quietly, disturbed by the sudden change in her, the pent-up anger in her tiny frame. "Some of them, yes. But not all. This girl . . ."

She stood abruptly, staring down at him. "You still don't see it, do you? You and I, we're of a kind. We know how things are. How they really are. We know about the darkness down there. Know, because it's in us, every hour of every day. And we know what it's like to suffer, to be bought and sold and treated like mere things." She shuddered, staring down at him defiantly. "We're of a kind, Kim Ward. Don't you understand that yet? You *belong* with me. Wards, that's what we are. A pair. A matching pair."

He sat there, shaking his head, denying her, and yet a part of him saw the truth in what she was saying. He licked at his lips, then spoke, pained that it had come to this.

"What you say, Becky . . . it's true. We *are* alike. But that's all. And what we did . . ." he shivered, "it was a mistake. Can't you see it was a mistake?"

She stood there, staring at him; a long, angry stare that seemed to weigh him. Then, without another word, she turned and walked away, closing the door quietly, carefully behind her.

For a moment he sat there, staring at the door, conscious that it wasn't over, that he had not convinced her that it was over, then, turning his head, he realized that someone was standing there, not six paces from where he sat.

"Tuan Wen-ch'ang!"

The tall Hui bowed his head and smiled, showing his imperfect teeth. "Kim . . . May I sit with you?"

"Of course. Please . . ." Kim half stood, giving a tiny bow of greeting.

Tuan sat, setting his *chung* down in front of him, then looked across at Kim.

"You look disturbed, my friend. Is something troubling you?"

Kim looked down. If Tuan had come in while Rebecca was talking to him, he would have seen, maybe even overheard something of what had passed between them. Yet that was not what Tuan had meant. He was asking Kim if he wanted to talk about his troubles, to share them with him.

For the briefest moment Kim hesitated, wondering whether he should keep this to himself, but then, seeing the look of sympathy, of understanding in the tall Hui's face, he nodded and leaned toward him.

"It's like this . . ."

———————

"What's happening up there?"

Tseng-li stood at Li Yuan's desk, staring down at the screen set into the table's surface. He had been disturbed by the echoing metallic sound of the shuttle docking, and had come here quickly, not stopping to consult any of the others.

The lieutenant's face looked up at him, concerned. "I'm not sure, my Lord. Chi Hsing's shuttle has docked. About three minutes back. Captain Henssa went to greet him."

"Chi Hsing?" Tseng-li laughed, but his features formed an uncertain frown. "Are you certain?"

"The coded signals were current and correct. No one but Chi Hsing's personal Security could have known them, my Lord."

Tseng-li nodded, but he was thinking, *This is wrong. Li Yuan would have warned me. He would not have gone had he known Chi Hsing was coming.* For a moment he stood there, leaning forward as if in a trance, then, "Have they boarded already?"

The lieutenant looked away at another screen. "Yes, they're coming through even now. I . . ." His head jerked back, as if he had been punched, his cheeks visibly paler, his eyes wide. "*Aiya* . . . . . ."

The screen went black.

Tseng-li ran. Out down the slow curving corridor and on, into the second room on the left, nodding to the guard. There, he bent over the cot and unceremoniously lifted the sleeping infant from among its covers and ran on, out through the far door. People were stirring now, lifting their heads as he ran through their quarters, or coming out to call after him, but there was no time to stop and warn them. His duty now was to Kuei Jen alone. Already it might be too late.

At the hatch that led through into the kitchens, a guard raised his rifle and challenged him.

"Let me through!" he yelled, batting the rifle down. "Your prince's life depends on it!"

The guard watched him go through, his mouth open, then nodded and turned to defend the hatch, knowing now, if he'd not before, that something was badly wrong.

The kitchens were empty. Tseng-li ran through the long, echoing rooms, conscious of his own hoarse breathing, and of the half-dozing weight of the child against his chest. He was cradling Kuei Jen awkwardly, holding his tiny body firmly against him, afraid to drop or knock him.

On the far side of the kitchens he stopped, taking deep breaths, then listened. There were clear sounds of fighting now—explosions and distant shouting, then the harsh but muted sound of someone screaming. He thumbed the hatch's manual controls awkwardly and clambered through into a narrow, rounded corridor where he had to stoop and move more slowly. It all depended now on how quick the intruders were, how well they knew the layout of the palace. If they traveled straight up the hub they might have gotten there already, but he was gambling on them not doing that. The private quarters were at the front end of the palace, on the rim. If they were interested in the T'ang and his family they would go there first. Or so he hoped.

As he moved along this narrow tunnel all sound was masked from him. But at the end, he came out into the brightly lit well, and the noise came back. Voices. Uncultured, Mid-level voices. He swallowed, understanding at once. Terrorists!

It was hard to judge how far away the voices were. They could be down at the far end of the hub still, or they might be directly above him, at this end. If the latter, then he and Kuei Jen were dead.

He crossed the open space, then set the child down carefully in its blankets, praying that it would not wake and cry. He straightened up, breathing heavily, then opened one of the dozen or so lockers built into the wall and took out the infant-sized pressure suit. Quickly he fitted and sealed it, checking that the oxygen supply was working before fastening the helmet. Then, reaching up into another of the lockers, he took down his own suit and pulled it on.

He had wasted more than two minutes getting suited up. Now it was more important than ever to be quick.

Here, at the "lower" end of the palace, there was only the narrowest of connecting tubes from the rim to the hub. It was an emergency and maintenance run, with a single stretch of laddering up the inside of a plain metallic pipe. Clutching the child to him, he began to climb. It looked simple, but he was climbing away from the fast-rotating rim toward the hub. As he progressed along the rungs he would grow steadily more weightless. Carrying the child he would need to be careful. The last part of the climb would be awkward, difficult.

And maybe, just maybe, they would be waiting for him.

━━━━━

KIM WAS SITTING on the edge of the desk, going through the latest batch of results with Feng Wo-shen and another of his assistants, when the doors at the far end of the laboratory swung open violently.

"Becky . . ."

He stood, looking across at her. Little more than an hour had passed since he had last seen her, yet Rebecca looked quite awful. Her eyes were dark and puffy, her hair disheveled. She had torn her silks—ripped or cut them—and they hung raggedly from her, like the clothes of a low-level beggar. But these were as nothing compared to the strangeness of her stance, to the tense, animal poise of her, the fierce hostility in her eyes.

She stood there a moment, staring at him, then, slowly, very slowly, she began to come toward him, a strange awkwardness to her movements that he recognized at once. So Luke had been, before they'd come for him. And Will. And finally Deio. Each one in turn, like unstable formations of atoms, spinning violently out of shape.

She had regressed. Returned to what she'd been, down there in the darkness of the Clay. Or almost so, for there was still a spark of sanity in her eyes, the merest glint of light where once the bright fire of intellect had shone out.

Feng Wo-shen touched his arm. "Should I call Security?"

"No," Kim said, putting out a hand, as if to physically stop him. "No, Feng, I'll deal with this."

Slowly Feng backed away, drawing the assistant with him.

Rebecca had stopped, three paces from Kim, her body tensed, as if about to spring. Looking at her, he could almost see the darkness flowing from her. Darkness, like a great force of negativity, pouring from her eyes, her mouth, the corded muscles of her limbs. And yet there was still an element of control. Something still held her back— one tiny, quivering cord of reason held her.

Reason . . . or obsession.

She raised her chin slightly, as if sniffing the air, then lifted her arm, pointing at him.

"You were wrong, Kim Ward. You didn't understand."

Her hand was trembling, its frailty exaggerated by the movement, as if at any moment it would disintegrate. For a moment her mouth struggled to make shapes, as if some vital link between it and her inner self had been severed; then, freeing itself, it spoke.

"It should have been us. You and me. Together, like *Yin* and *Yang*, until the end of things." She shivered, an unnatural intensity making her tremble. "You're mine, Kim Ward, don't you understand that yet? Mine. It was *meant*."

She came closer, her eyes staring fiercely, defiantly into his. A muscle in her cheek was twitching now, jumping violently, as if something had got in behind the flesh.

"But you didn't want that, did you? You wanted something better than that, neh? Something *finer*." She laughed coldly, her face ugly, sneering now, her voice filled with a sudden venom. "You think you're something special, don't you? You think they really want you here. But it's not true. We're different from them. We're Clay, Kim. Clay. And they *never* let us forget it.

"Every smile they give us is a lie. Every word a deception. But you can't see that, can you? You're dazzled by the light of this place. So much so that you can't see the darkness underlying everything."

She tilted her head slowly, lifting it, looking back at him from a strange, unnatural angle. "Everything. Even your precious girl. But then, you wouldn't have heard, would you?"

He narrowed his eyes. "What do you mean?"

She smiled; a hideous, triumphant smile. "I've watched you . . . you know that? Followed you all these years. Kept tabs on what you've done, who you've met. That's how I knew."

The smile slowly faded. Beneath it lay a bleak, hard bitterness.

"It was Tolonen, wasn't it? Tolonen who sent her away. I checked, you see. I found things out."

He was silent, but her words made him afraid.

"Tolonen," she said again, her face hardening. "Jelka Tolonen. Your paragon of light. But do you know what she did? She nearly killed a man, that's what. A young cadet. Kicked him to death, almost."

He shook his head. "You're lying."

"Am I?" She gave a bitter laugh. "From what I've heard, your darling Jelka's a right little monster. Why, I've heard . . ."

The sound of the slap startled Kim. He was conscious of Rebecca stumbling back, of Feng's cry behind him, but before that there had been a moment of utter darkness. Of forgetting.

He gave a little shake of his head, as if coming to, then looked across at her again. Rebecca was standing there, one hand raised to her face, a startled, angry look in her eyes.

What had she said? What was it now?

He looked down at his hand. The palm stung, as if it had been sprayed with antiseptic. Then he looked back at her, at the red welt on her cheek. For a moment there was no connection, only a kind of numbness, a blackness where things ought to have been joined, and then he understood. He had struck her. Because of something she had said. Because . . .

She crouched, facing him, every cell, every atom of her being set against him now. In that brief moment of darkness something had changed in her. Whatever had been light in her was gone, extinguished by the blow. What confronted him now was more animal than human. Even so, the core of her obsession remained intact, undamaged. It was that which drove her now. That and nothing else.

Her voice too had changed; had shed the veneer, the polish it had had only moments before. It was harsh now and guttural, the words falling awkwardly from her lips, like shards of broken pottery.

"Yuu erhh mae-en," she said, one hand making a clawing motion at him. "Yuu aan mee, Kih-m. Turr-ge-thuur. Cle-ya. Wee urrh Cle-ya."

"No," he said, appalled by the dreadful sound that was coming from her. "No, Becky, please . . ." But it was too late. Snarling, she threw herself at him, teeth bared.

He beat her off, hurling her back against the desk, winding her momentarily, but she was at him again in an instant, her fingers clawing at his eyes.

"Becky!" He thrust her away a second time, barely aware of Feng moving around him and running for the door. "For the gods' sakes, Becky, no!"

But she was beyond words. With a savagery that frightened him, she leapt at him again, coiling her arms about him tightly, as if to drag him down into the depths she now inhabited. And this time he knew he would have to hurt her if he was to stop her.

Choking, he struck out at her blindly, hitting her in the face and neck and chest, surprising her with the viciousness of the blows, forcing her to loosen her hands from about his neck. As she staggered back, he brought his fists down hard, knocking her onto her knees. He was about to finish it, to strike her one last time, when there was a shout.

"*Ward! No!*"

Kim stopped, looking across. Administrator Schram was standing there on the far side of the lab, Feng Wo-shen and two armed guards just behind him.

"Come away, Ward. Now. We'll deal with this."

Kim looked down. Rebecca was kneeling just beneath him, her face tilted up toward him, but her eyes were blank now, unseeing. As he watched, a tremor seemed to go right through her, and then, slowly, her tiny frame slumped, collapsing in upon itself.

I've killed her, he thought, horrified. *Killed her . . .*

Schram was beside him now, taking control of things; ordering the guards to bind the unconscious girl and take her, then turning to point at Feng, instructing him to clear things up. But Kim was aware of none of it. He was back there, suddenly; back in Rehabilitation, kneeling beside the damaged cage, staring in at the lifeless bird, the vision so real that he felt he could almost reach out and touch it.

Again, he thought, letting a shivering breath escape him. *Events like ripples in the great ocean of Time, circles of darkness stretching out toward the distant shoreline of the future.*

He groaned, thinking of the friends he had lost. First Luke, then Will and Deio, and now Rebecca. Clay, they had been, each one of them, formed from the earth and molded by dark circumstance. But to what end? What point was there to all that death and suffering? What reason? So that *he* might go on? No. It made no sense. No sense at all.

"Ward!"

Schram was staring at him, concerned, and shaking him. "Snap out of it, Ward! It's over now. She's gone. We've taken her."

"Taken her?"

Kim turned, looking at Schram, seeing, behind the surface of the eyes, the savage delight the man took in this tragedy. For him this sad display had been a kind of triumph; proof positive that he was right— that Clay was Clay and could never be raised, never be made *truly* human. But Schram didn't understand. No, nor would he ever understand. He would have had to have been there, first in the darkness and afterward in the unit, with Luke and Will, Deio and Rebecca.

Kim sighed, realizing for the first time the depth of his loss. They had been something. Something bright and fine and wonderful. For a time they had promised everything. Like a beautiful, golden-eyed bird. A caged bird that had never flown.

"Come on now, back to work," Schram said, touching his arm, but Kim batted his hand away.

"Don't touch me," he said, glaring at the man. "Don't you *ever* touch me."

He saw the anger flare in the man's eyes and felt something harden deep within him in response. Slave or no slave, he would not suffer this kind of thing a moment longer. From here on he would fight it, wherever he came up against it, not just for himself, but for those who were no longer there to fight it. For the children of the dark he'd come to love . . . and had lost.

For Luke and Will and Deio, and, finally, for Rebecca.

"Call Campbell," he said, staring back at Schram defiantly. "Now! Tell him I want to speak to him. Tell him I want out of here."

THE EDGES OF THE HATCH were still hot from where they'd burned their way through. The *Yu* squeezed through delicately, then twisted and pushed as she'd been taught. The movement took her across the room, to where the lifeless body of the Security lieutenant rested in the chair, his arms floating out in front of him. Big globules of blood and visceral matter were drifting out from the shattered mess that had been his head. Unconcerned, the *Yu* swept it aside and pulled herself down beside the corpse.

A quick inspection showed that the man had had no chance to damage the desk. She turned and looked back at the hatch. One of her colleagues was looking through the jagged hole into the room.

"Well?" she said impatiently, using the narrow-band frequency that linked them all.

"All functional," the woman by the desk answered. "Vesa can put the power through again. I've got the tapes."

Leaning over the corpse, she took two small tapes from a pocket at the neck of her suit and slotted them into the surface of the desk. Power had been out only two and a half minutes, but it was time enough to sound warning bells down below on Chung Kuo. A squadron of fast and heavily armed fighters would be heading toward them already. The tapes might confuse them, maybe hold them a while, until things were more advanced.

Abruptly the power came on again. On one of the screens she saw two of her team, firing down a corridor, the bullets arcing with the Coriolis effect they had been warned about. On another screen she saw a figure in silks, floating motionless, facedown in the ornamental pool, a dark red stain spreading out from among the long black strands of its hair. A third screen showed two guards, waiting, their backs to a large, heavily ornamented door. They looked scared to death, but determined.

She watched a moment longer, fascinated, then looked away, busying herself, getting down to work.

───◆◆◆───

KRIZ STOOD on the viewing plate, looking down past her feet at the image of the world. Often, in the run-throughs, she had paused and, for the briefest moment, looked down. But this was different. This time it was for real. She could feel the long, cold drop beneath her. It was like standing with only a sheet of transparent ice between you and all that space. She shuddered and looked across the room toward the stairs, listening to the constant stream of messages in her ear.

It had gone well. Better than they'd hoped. Two minutes more and it would be all theirs.

"Kriz! Kriz! Are you there?"

It was Donna, her lieutenant. Right now she should be in Li Yuan's quarters.

"You've got him?"

"No! He's not here! We've missed him!"

Kriz frowned. It wasn't possible. His shuttle was still in the dock, and his schedule showed that he was here. "No," she said quickly. "Search everywhere. He has to be here!"

Donna came back to her at once. "And Kuei Jen too. He's not here either!"

"*What?*" Disturbed and angered, she hesitated, then rushed across the room and up the steps. "I'm coming through. Hold tight where you are." Then, changing frequencies, she spoke quickly to the three team members who had been left to hold the hub. "Anne, stay where you are. Vesa and Joan, move down the hub to the end. And be careful. There may be someone there."

She ran on, past fallen guards and through smoldering, damaged rooms, until she came to Li Yuan's private suite. Here, where they had expected the fighting to be hardest, things were untouched. That, more than anything, convinced her that Li Yuan had not been here.

"The wives?" she asked.

"Farther down," Donna answered, coming across. "We had to torch the rooms. The guards fought hard."

"And Kuei Jen?"

"He *was* here. The cot bedding was disturbed. His nurse knew nothing though. She was asleep. When she woke he was gone."

"Then he's still here." She smiled, reassured by the news. "Good. Then let's find the little bastard!"

———✦✦✦———

TSENG-LI SHIVERED. He could hear them coming, their heavy, weighted boots clanking with each step. "Another minute!" he hissed softly through his teeth. "Just give me another minute!"

Kuei Jen was already wedged inside the tiny craft they called "the coffin," attached by a web of cords in the niche where, normally, the engineer on duty would keep a spare air bottle. There was neither time nor room for finesse now, though, so it would have to do. And if they failed, well, it was better than dying here. And death grew more certain with every passing moment.

He was outside, in the cramped maintenance area beside the blister that held the small, beetlelike maintenance craft. For more than a minute now he had been working at the catch of the manual controls, trying to force it open with a wrench. But time was running out fast. Even if he managed to get it open and operate the override, there was no guarantee that he'd get back to the craft. He had visions of it drifting out slowly on its two-*li* tether, the outer hatch open to the vacuum. If Kuei Jen didn't freeze to death he would suffocate eventually. Unless Tseng-li could clamber back in somehow and close the outer hatch manually. And even then they had only twelve hours of air.

Things were bad. And getting worse by the second. He grunted and hit out at the heavy catch viciously, swearing beneath his breath. "Give, you bastard, *give!*" For a moment longer it held, then, with a hiss, it gave, the automatic controls springing the plate back so that it banged against his face plate.

"Well, sod you too!" he said, laughing, halfway between relief and sheer panic. Quickly he reached in and turned and pulled out the handle. At once he heard the dull concussion of the seals as they moved into place. The maintenance room was now an airlock, both of its access doors sealed off. It made him feel better, safer. It would take them minutes to cut through them. And in minutes . . .

He was about to turn away, when another of the controls caught his attention. A dial. It was calibrated finely, from o through to 2. At present it was set just over 1. A second set of figures gave rotational speed. He knew at once what it was. Smiling, he turned the dial slowly to the right. Then, with an abruptness that was almost vicious, he slammed the dial back to the left and left it there, turning to face the opening blister.

KRIZ WAS BY THE POOL when it struck. There had been a moment's sensation of heaviness, of pressure, then, slowly at first but with gathering speed, things began to happen. At first the feeling was quite pleasant, a kind of lightness that was as much of the spirit as of the body. Then, before she knew what had hit her, the huge sheet of water in front of her began to lift and break apart.

In her ear-mike there was a gabble of sudden panic. The palace was slowing down! Someone had stopped its spin!

"Anne!" she screamed, her feet coming away from the floor momentarily. "What the fuck are you doing?"

There was a moment's radio silence, then Anne's voice came through. "What's going on? Aiya! What's happening?"

Kriz understood at once. The override. Someone had got to the end of the hub before them. Even as she thought it, Vesa's voice came through loudly in her ear.

"It's sealed! Someone's sealed it off!"

"Use explosives!" Kriz yelled back. By now she was floating several feet from the floor. Huge lumps of water were drifting out and up, away from the pool. She could imagine the chaos elsewhere. "Once you're inside, there'll be a control panel. Try not to damage it. Reset the dial for one atmosphere."

She could feel herself shedding weight by the moment as the great palace slowed, its huge engines reversing its spin and bringing it to a complete halt. Soon it would be as weightless all around the rim as it was at the hub.

Suddenly it had all gone wrong. Badly wrong!

"Vesa, I . . ."

The ship shuddered. It was as if something had hit it. Something huge. Kriz felt herself thrown across the pool, big gouts of water colliding with her and turning her about. She was buffeted and slowed. Then, when she thought things had died down, there was a second, far bigger detonation, that seemed to pick her up and shake her about, then cast her down, like a huge hand pressing her firm against the bottom of the pool, flattening her.

———

FROM A HUNDRED *LI* out the first of the fighters saw it happen and caught it on camera. There was a flicker and a blurring of the starlight surrounding the tip of the hub. Slowly, almost gracefully, the spokes of the lower end fell away, severing the hub from the rim. Then, only moments later, the whole structure seemed to shudder and slowly buckle, a strange electric tracery surrounding the docking nodule at the top. The opposite end of the hub was swinging inward now, toward the rim, but even before it struck, the whole palace seemed to quiver, then shatter, like a fragile shape of glass.

For a moment the fighter's screen was incandescently bright. Then, very slowly, it faded to a flickering, ember-strewn black. There was a strong hiss of static on the audio band.

"What's happened?" said a voice, cutting through the distortion. "What in the gods' names is going on up there?"

"It's gone," said the pilot softly, disbelievingly. "Kuan Yin preserve us, it's gone!"

The Stone Within

"I SEE,'' said Tsu Ma, nodding gravely. He sat, all color drained from his face. "And has any wreckage been found yet?"

The man on the screen seemed to concentrate a moment, then nodded. He was wired to the console in front of him and was receiving reports by the moment. "Most of the wreckage appears to have stayed up there, but a lot of it has been falling. There have been reports of large chunks coming down into the sea off the Guinea coast."

Tsu Ma looked away a moment, then back at the screen, his whole face grown stiffer, a sudden anger making his eyes flare. "Who *did* this?"

There was no hesitation this time. "It was the *Yu*. Kiev had two minutes of taped material sent out from Yangjing before its systems cut out."

"*Yu* . . ." he said under his breath. Then, "How did they get on board?"

The Security man shook his head. "We don't know that yet, *Chieh Hsia*. Tracking reports certain . . . difficulties."

"Difficulties?" He was suspicious at once. "What kind of difficulties?"

"Well . . ." The man's hesitation showed his discomfort. He knew all the old adages about the bearers of ill news. "It seems we have half a day's tracking transmissions missing for that sector."

"Missing?" Tsu Ma laughed harshly. "That's impossible. There are backups to the backups, surely?"

The man bowed his head. "That is so, *Chieh Hsia*, but there is no stored record. Only a gap."

Tsu Ma was quiet, thinking, *Wang Sau-leyan. This was his doing.* But how prove it? How tie him to this foulness? Then, like a cold wave, dousing his anger, it struck him what this meant for Li Yuan: his whole family gone. Tsu Ma shivered and half turned, hearing the voices from the other room—hearing, at that very moment, as if in hideous mockery of events, Li Yuan's strong and vital laughter. *Laugh no more, Li Yuan, for your wives are dead, and your infant son.*

With difficulty he returned his attention to the matter in hand. "Put me through to Tracking. I want explanations."

There was a four-second delay, then a worried face replaced that of the Security man. "Gerhardt, *Chieh Hsia*. Head of Tracking, Northern Hemisphere."

Tsu Ma launched in at once. "What's happening, Gerhardt? I am told that you are missing half a day's transmissions. Is that possible?"

"No, *Chieh Hsia*."

"But true."

"Yes, *Chieh Hsia*."

"Then how do you explain it?"

Gerhardt swallowed, then spoke up. "It has been erased, *Chieh Hsia*. Someone here has removed it from the record."

"Someone?" Tsu Ma's voice was suddenly pitiless.

The official bowed his head submissively. "It is my responsibility, *Chieh Hsia*. I know my duty."

"Are you saying that *you* did it?"

Gerhardt hesitated, then shook his head.

Tsu Ma took a deep breath, then spoke again, his patience close to snapping. "This is no time for honor, man. I want to know who did it, and at whose instigation. And I want to know as soon as possible. Understand? We'll talk of duty then."

Gerhardt made to speak, then simply bowed. Tsu Ma cut the connection and sat there, staring blankly at the empty screen. Then, grunting, he stood up heavily and turned to face the doorway.

Wu Shih was standing there, looking in. Seeing the color of Tsu Ma's face, he took two steps into the room. "What in the gods' names is it?"

Tsu Ma licked at his dry lips, then, coming forward, took Wu Shih's arm and led him back through. There, on a couch on the left of the room, Li Yuan was sitting, a cup of dark wine in one hand. Tsu Ma looked to Wu Shih, then indicated that he should take a seat. Li Yuan, looking up, smiled, but his smile quickly faded.

"What has happened?"

"I have bad news," Tsu Ma answered him directly, knowing there was no way of softening what had to be said. "Yangjing is destroyed. There are no survivors."

Li Yuan opened his mouth, then looked down sharply. Carefully he put his wine cup down. Then, ashen-faced, his eyes avoiding theirs, he got up and left the room.

Wu Shih stared at Tsu Ma, his face a register of the horror he was feeling. "This is true?" he asked softly, then, shaking his head, he laughed bitterly. "Of course . . . You would not joke of such a thing." He took a breath, then, "*Kuan Yin!* How?"

Tsu Ma's voice trembled now. It had finally got to him. Seeing Li Yuan; having to tell him. "*Yu* terrorists. They got aboard somehow."

Wu Shih shook his head. "It is not possible."

"No?" Tsu Ma's voice was sharp. Too sharp. He waved a hand uncertainly at his fellow T'ang, then sat beside him. "I'm sorry . . . but yes, it is possible."

"Wang Sau-leyan . . ." Wu Shih said quietly, looking past Tsu Ma at the empty doorway.

"Yes," Tsu Ma answered him. "It could be no other. It has his mark."

"Then what?"

Tsu Ma laughed, the full horror of the irony striking him. "Then we must do as Li Yuan said. Nothing. Until we have conclusive proof."

Wu Shih got up angrily. "But that was before!"

Tsu Ma looked down at his hands. "Nothing has changed. Not even the fall of Yangjing could justify us acting without proof. Even Li Yuan would say as much."

Wu Shih snorted. "It fits you ill to be so reasonable with other's hurts. He has lost a son."

"And wives . . ." Tsu Ma added, remembering sharply his own part in affairs. "But we are T'ang as well as men. We must act by law, not instinct."

"What law does Wang Sau-leyan follow that he can butcher us and we do nothing?" Wu Shih strode across the room, then came back. "I cannot simply do nothing, Tsu Ma. I would choke on my own bile were I not to act."

Tsu Ma looked up at him, his eyes wet with tears. "You think I do not feel the same, Wu Shih? Gods, I would break him with these hands were it so simple. But we must be certain. We must act with justice. No man must fault us."

Wu Shih huffed again. "And if we find nothing?"

Tsu Ma was silent a long while. Then, meeting Wu Shih's eyes again, he smiled bleakly. "Then I shall kill him anyway."

———

WANG SAU-LEYAN sat up irritably and tore the black velvet covers from his eyes.

"Well? What is it?"

The servant kneeling in the open doorway lifted his head marginally. "It is Chi Hsing, *Chieh Hsia*. He begs an audience."

Wang glanced at the bedside timer and shook his head. Then, as if suddenly more awake, he got up quickly and wrapped his silks about him, then made for his study.

Chi Hsing's angry face filled the big screen above the desk. He barely waited for Wang to come into the room before he began.

"What is the meaning of this, Wang Sau-leyan? My shuttle! You have used *my* shuttle!"

Wang Sau-leyan frowned, confused, then came closer to the screen, raising a hand. "Hold on, cousin. I don't know what you mean. What about your shuttle? What has happened?"

Chi Hsing laughed cynically. "No games, *cousin*. This is serious. It could mean war."

Wang Sau-leyan's puzzlement was genuine, and Chi Hsing, seeing it, frowned and seemed to lean back away from the screen.

"You mean you do not know?"

Wang shook his head, feeling a sudden tightness in his stomach. "No . . . Something has happened, then?"

Chi Hsing took a breath, then, more calmly, answered him. "I had the news only minutes ago. Li Yuan is dead. With all his family. Yangjing has fallen. Blown from the skies."

Wang Sau-leyan felt a powerful surge of exultation pass through him, but kept his face a rigid mask. "Ah . . ." was all he said. But the news was like a sweet wind blowing after centuries of drought, sign of the refreshing rain to come.

Chi Hsing spoke again. "Then you knew nothing of this?"

Wang shook his head mutely. But now that he had heard, he knew. Mach! Mach had gone in early! "Who knows of this apart from you?"

"My private servants. A few of my Security staff."

"Then there is no problem. The shuttle will have been destroyed in the explosion. No one could trace it back to you, surely?"

Even as he said it, he knew the steps to be taken. Who to bribe, what records to destroy. There *would* be traces. The movements of the shuttle *would* be recorded. But action could be taken—if taken now—to erase such things. "There were no survivors?"

"None."

Again he fought to hide the intense pleasure he felt at the news. He took a breath, then nodded. "Leave it to me, Chi Hsing. I shall ensure that no trace remains."

"You swear you had no knowledge of this, Sau-leyan?"

Wang let his anger show. "Do not insult me, cousin. I knew nothing. And though this news pleases me, it brings me no pleasure to learn of your own fears. I feel it my duty to help you, cousin."

Chi Hsing was silent a moment, then gave the slightest of nods. "I do not like this, Sau-leyan. Nor do I share your pleasure at the news. This strikes to the heart of us all. I know your hatred for Li Yuan, but think. It might have been you or I. Whoever did this struck out at the Seven—at us—not only at Li Yuan."

Wang dropped his head, as if chastened. "I am sorry. You are right, Chi Hsing. But I'll not weep when I feel joy."

Chi Hsing stared at him a moment, then looked away, presenting

Wang Sau-leyan with a profile. "You realize the problems this will cause us?"

He did. And when Chi Hsing was gone from the screen, he sat there torn between anger and joy—joy at the news and anger at Mach's preempting the new proposals in the House. Mach's impatience would cause him problems—major problems. Still, if only each day would bring such problems! Quickly he tapped out a discreet code which, he knew, would worm its way to Mach, erasing all trace of its passage. It would ensure no contact between them in the delicate weeks to come.

It remained, then, only to deal with the matter of the shuttle. And that, like all else, he would do through certain men in Chi Hsing's own household. They knew not who they dealt with, only that such dealings made them rich. Let them attempt to cover his traces. And if they failed?

Wang Sau-leyan got up and walked back through to his dead father's bedroom, too excited now to sleep. If they failed to clear Chi Hsing's name it mattered little. The Seven would be Five. And with Li Yuan gone . . .

He laughed, then went briskly to the window and drew back the curtains. Outside it was dark, the moon low in the sky. It would be morning in two hours. He held his hands out before him, palms open, and looked down at them. Such smooth, white hands. For a long time he held them there, staring at them, then closed them slowly, smiling to himself.

Let them make their accusations. He, Wang Sau-leyan, would have clean hands.

He turned from the window, picturing himself there, in council, facing the angry faces of Tsu Ma and Wu Shih, his own anger tightly harnessed. "*You do me wrong*," he heard himself say. "*I knew nothing of this.*"

It was the truth. He laughed, delighted. Yes, for once it was almost the truth.

———————

LI YUAN LAY THERE in the darkened room, grieving, the hurt a vast weight, pressing down on his chest, crushing him; a dark and heavy millstone, beneath which he lay, helpless. To move was an effort, each hard-won breath a betrayal. They were dead.

In a moment of stillness, of unthinking nullity, someone crept into the room and knelt beside him. It was Tsu Ma. He felt the older man's hand at his neck, in the dark hair there; felt a wetness on his brow, then the softest pressure of his cheek against his own. Eyes closed, he held the other man tightly, letting the smothered grief escape. Then, when the pain of it seemed to have lessened, he felt Tsu Ma move back and release him. He sat, feeling hollow, staring sightlessly into the shadows.

"This much loss . . ."

Tsu Ma did not complete his words. Li Yuan turned his head slowly, facing him. There was such a pressure in his upper chest, such a need to say something, yet nothing came. He coughed, almost choking, then bent his head suddenly, succumbing to the sharpness of the feeling.

At the far end of the room the door slowly opened.

"*Chieh Hsia* . . . ?"

Tsu Ma turned his head, then stood and went across. "Yes," he said quietly. "What is it?"

There was a brief whispered exchange, then Tsu Ma came back. "Yuan . . . if you would go through and wash your face. General Rheinhardt is here. He has news."

Li Yuan stood slowly. In the light from the open door he could see Tsu Ma's face clearly; see the redness of the eyes, the wetness of his cheeks. "Rheinhardt?" he said hoarsely. "I thought no one knew . . ."

He frowned, and looked past Tsu Ma, toward the servant in the doorway. If Rheinhardt knew they were here, it meant their security was breached. Only Tseng-li had known.

Tsu Ma reached out and took his arm. "Freshen up, cousin. Then come to my study."

Li Yuan looked at him steadily, then shook his head. "No. I shall come as I am. Tears are no cause for shame."

They went through, servants and guards looking down, not daring to look. All knew how things stood. The rumor had gone out around the palace an hour back. Even so, they could not help but notice how Li Yuan bore himself. Such dignity in grief. Such strength.

In Tsu Ma's study, Wu Shih came to him and held him a moment before leaving. Then, with a nod to his private secretary, Tsu Ma also left the room. The secretary gave a deep bow, then went to the far door and opened it, letting Rheinhardt into the room. "I shall be here if you need me, *Chieh Hsia*," he said, bowing again, then left, closing the door behind him.

Li Yuan was alone in the room with his General.

"Who told you I was here, Helmut?"

"It was Tseng-li, *Chieh Hsia*."

Li Yuan was silent a moment, puzzled. Rheinhardt was unarmed, but he still suspected a trap—some kind of trickery. "When did he tell you this?"

"Less than an hour back, *Chieh Hsia*."

Li Yuan shivered. *Haven't you heard?* he almost said, then realized that Rheinhardt would have heard all, before even he had been told. He started forward. "What do you mean?"

"Just that I spoke to him, *Chieh Hsia*. He told me where you were. It was . . ." The General hesitated, venturing a smile. "It was a great relief to me, my Lord."

At once he understood. "You thought me dead?"

"The whole world thinks you dead."

"And Tseng-li?" Li Yuan took a step closer, his face caught between doubt and hope.

"He is alive, *Chieh Hsia*. As is Kuei Jen."

Li Yuan laughed, openly astonished. "Kuei Jen? Alive?"

"A scoutship picked them up. Their craft was damaged, but they were unharmed."

"Their ship?"

"A little maintenance craft. It survived the explosion. But they were lucky. It seemed like just another piece of debris. Only a visual contact saved them."

But Li Yuan was barely listening. He crossed the room quickly and stood over Tsu Ma's desk, studying the controls. Then, impatiently, he turned to Rheinhardt. "Where are they now? How can I contact them?"

The General came across and punched in the access code, then stepped back, away from the desk, leaving Li Yuan alone, looking down into the screen.

A soldier's face appeared and, with a quick bow, turned and called someone forward. It was clear that they had been waiting for this moment.

"Tseng-li!" said Li Yuan joyfully, as the familiar face came onto the screen. "How are you?"

Tseng-li bowed, smiling, his eyes wet. "We are alive, Highness."

"And my son? Where is my son?"

Another soldier brought Kuei Jen and handed him to Tseng-li, who turned back to face the screen, cradling the sleeping child. The movement disturbed Kuei Jen. He stretched and began to cry, one arm struggling against Tseng-li's neck briefly before he quieted and grew still again.

"Kuei!" Li Yuan called softly, tears of joy rolling down his cheeks. "My little Kuei . . ."

Tseng-li was silent a moment, strong emotions crossing and re-crossing his face. Regaining control, he spoke again.

"They were *Yu*, Highness. I heard them. But the craft . . ." He hesitated, then said it. "It was Chi Hsing's shuttle. His Security codes."

Li Yuan straightened up, a shudder passing through him. He had gone cold. "You are certain, Tseng-li?"

"Your guards were thorough, Highness, but they were betrayed."

Li Yuan moaned. His momentary relief at finding them alive had masked all else from him. Yet his wives were still dead, his palace destroyed. And now, he found, Chi Hsing had betrayed him.

"Not Wang Sau-leyan, then?" He said the words quietly, shivering, a sudden bitter hatred replacing the grief and happiness.

"I have no reason . . ." began Tseng-li, then stopped, seeing the look on Li Yuan's face. "Li Yuan, I . . ."

"Do your brothers know you live?" Li Yuan asked suddenly, changing the subject.

"They . . . No, they do not know yet, Highness."

"Then I will let them know myself. I would not have them grieve while you live."

Tseng-li opened his mouth, then bowed, understanding.

"And Tseng-li . . ."

He looked up again, meeting Li Yuan's eyes across the distance. "Yes, Highness?"

"I do not know how you managed it, but my debt to you is great. Whatever you want, you shall have it."

Tseng-li smiled bitterly. "There is but one thing I want now, cousin Yuan. I want him dead."

"Who? Chi Hsing?"

The bitter smile remained. "Not him. The other one . . ."

"Ah yes . . ." Li Yuan took a deep breath. "Yes. And I too."

⌄⌄⌄⌄⌄

TSU MA WAS WAITING for him in the anteroom. "Well?" he said, coming forward anxiously.

"Tseng-li lives," Li Yuan said, smiling at the news. "And my son, Kuei Jen."

There was a look of delight on Tsu Ma's face. He embraced Li Yuan tightly, then stepped back, a sharper expression on his face. "Then we know what happened!"

"Yes," said Li Yuan, looking down. "We were wrong, it seems."

"Wrong?"

"It was not our cousin Wang. Not directly, anyway. This was Chi Hsing."

"Chi Hsing?" Tsu Ma laughed, disbelievingly. "Why, he hasn't the guts!" Then, seeing how Li Yuan continued to stand there, the same expression on his face, Tsu Ma shook his head. "What proof is there?"

Li Yuan looked up. "They used his shuttle to board. His codes. What more do we need?"

Tsu Ma stared at him a moment longer, then nodded. "I'll call a Council, then . . ."

But Li Yuan reached out and took his arm. "No. Not this time. This time we do things my way."

⌄⌄⌄⌄⌄

CHI HSING WAS BOWED at Li Yuan's feet, one hand pressed to the cold tiled floor, the other clutching the hem of the young T'ang's robes. He was pleading now, almost in tears.

"What can I do to convince you, Yuan? I was betrayed . . ."

Wang Sau-leyan looked on from across the room, bitter and silent. He had been made to seem a fool. His own face had betrayed him. But surprise was not evidence and Chi Hsing had kept silent about their meetings. It did not matter what Li Yuan or the others thought privately. Before the world they needed proof, and they had none.

"You were betrayed?" Tsu Ma's voice was heavy with sarcasm. He made a sound of disgust and turned away, going across to where Wu Shih and Wei Chan Yin stood watching.

Li Yuan bent down and tugged the silk from Chi Hsing's hand. It was a savage, ugly gesture. Chi Hsing looked up at his fellow T'ang briefly, then lowered his head once more, humbling himself. All majesty had gone from him. He was a supplicant now, begging for his life. Li Yuan, on the other hand, seemed almost demonic in his power. His face was like a hawk's, pitiless, almost inhuman in its abstract cruelty. His eyes rested on Chi Hsing's topknot a moment, then he moved his head sharply and stared angrily across at Wang.

"And you swear Wang Sau-leyan knew nothing of this? You are certain of this, Chi Hsing?"

Wang made to speak, but Wu Shih barked at him. "Hold your tongue, Wang Sau-leyan! Chi Hsing must answer this!"

Incensed, he nevertheless did as he was told, glowering at Wu Shih. If the sight of Li Yuan's living face had been a shock, this now was almost more than he could bear. How dare they speak to him this way!

Chi Hsing shuddered, then shook his head. "Wang Sau-leyan knew nothing. I spoke to him, only moments after I had heard. I thought . . ."

"You thought what?" The cold anger in Li Yuan's voice was terrible to hear.

Chi Hsing took a breath, then spoke again, looking all the while at a spot just in front of Li Yuan's feet. "It is no secret that he hates you, Li Yuan. And so I thought—this is his work."

"And was it?"

"Take care," said Wang, taking a step forward. But he could see how things stood. All etiquette had been forgotten. Li Yuan, as ever, had ridden roughshod over tradition. These others were his dupes. His accomplices.

They were all awaiting Chi Hsing's response.

"He knew nothing. I swear it. His surprise was unfeigned. There is a tape of my call to him. I . . ."

"Enough!" Li Yuan said suddenly. He turned from Chi Hsing and came across, stopping in front of Wang Sau-leyan. Giving the slightest bow, he spoke again. "Chi Hsing, though disgraced, would hardly say such a thing lightly. And the tape—I am sure that it shows what he claims." He lifted his chin. "So, *cousin,* I must apologize for what I asked."

Wang Sau-leyan's face was red with anger now, his nostrils flared, his whole expression indignant, yet still he said nothing. Even in apologizing, Li Yuan had insulted him and made a mockery of tradition. And all the while his fellow T'ang had looked on, saying nothing.

Li Yuan turned away sharply, his back to Wang Sau-leyan, and looked across at Chi Hsing. "What, then, of you, Chi Hsing? What should we do?"

"This is a nonsense . . ." began Wang, but before he could say any more, Li Yuan had turned and placed one hand roughly, almost brutally over his mouth, pushing his head back. He spoke fiercely, as if to a vassal.

"Be quiet, Wang Sau-leyan! You have nothing to say here! Understand?"

Li Yuan removed his hand abruptly, glaring at Wang, then turned away again, leaving Wang to touch his bruised lip tenderly. There was murder in Li Yuan's almond eyes.

Li Yuan crossed the room again and stood over Chi Hsing. There was a look of disgust on his face now. "Speak up, Chi Hsing. What should we do with you?"

"Do?" Chi Hsing turned his head and looked past Li Yuan at the others, his eyes imploring them, but their faces were as hard as Li Yuan's. Seeing this, Chi Hsing dropped his head again, submissive. "There is no precedent," he said quietly.

"Nor for the destruction of a palace," said Wu Shih, but Li Yuan was uncompromising now.

"You have broken the most sacred trust, Chi Hsing—that which binds us who must rule Chung Kuo. For myself I would see you dead and your sons beside you in the ground. But this is not a personal thing. We must consider how best to act for those we represent."

Li Yuan paused and turned to face the others who stood apart from him. "We must decide now, and act at once. In this we must not be seen to be indecisive. There are those who would take advantage of our apparent disarray." He took a deep breath, then said it. "Chi Hsing must stand down."

"No! You cannot do this!" Wang Sau-leyan said, outraged. "There are but six of us here. We must wait for Hou Tung-po. A Council *must* be called."

Li Yuan tensed, but did not look at Wang Sau-leyan. When he spoke again his words were measured, and it was as if Wang had said nothing. "Chi Hsing must do this for us. He must appear before the world and confess what he has done. Then, before all, he will stand down. And his lands will be forfeit to the Seven. We shall rule the Australias as a colony, with a governor who will report directly to us in Council."

Both Chi Hsing and Wang Sau-leyan were silent. It was Wu Shih, the eldest of them, who spoke next. "So it must be. For the sake of us all. And you, Chi Hsing, must be a sleeping dragon. You will retire to your estate and take no more part in the doings of this world. Your wives, your sons, will live, but they will not inherit."

At this Wang Sau-leyan came forward and stood between Li Yuan and the others. "Again, this cannot be! This is a matter for Council!"

"Are you opposed to this?" Tsu Ma demanded angrily.

"There are forms . . ." Wang began, but Li Yuan interrupted him. "We shall vote on this. Right now."

Wang Sau-leyan faced him angrily. "No! This is not right! Hou Tung-po is not here. We cannot act like this!"

"*Right?*" Li Yuan sniffed. "You have not understood me yet, have you, cousin? My wives are dead, my palace blown out of the sky. And you talk of forms, tradition . . ." He laughed scathingly. "If you are so worried, let us meet form this way. Let us count cousin Hou as opposed to what we do. Would that be *fair*, Wang Sau-leyan? Would it be *right?*"

Wang bristled visibly. "And Chi Hsing?"

Li Yuan shook his head. "Chi Hsing has no say in this."

"No say?"

Li Yuan spoke angrily, each word clearly and separately enunciated. "It is as I said. He has no say."

Wang Sau-leyan stood there facing him a moment longer, then turned away sharply. "Do as you will, then. I'll have no part of this."

"Your hands are clean, eh, cousin?" It was Tsu Ma who taunted him. But it did not matter now. It would be as Li Yuan said.

"You will do this?" Li Yuan asked, looking down at Chi Hsing. "I have no choice?"

"No," corrected Li Yuan. "*We* have no choice. For myself, as I said, I would kill you now."

Chi Hsing hesitated, then bowed lower, placing his forehead to the ground miserably. "Then I shall do as you ask."

━━━━━

LI YUAN STOOD on the balcony outside his dead wives' rooms, a thick cloak draped about his shoulders. It was dark and chilly. Overhead a thin, ragged cloud blew fitfully across the sky. Through screens of leafy vine the light of the crescent moon cast a mottled silver over everything.

Kuei Jen was sleeping. Tseng-li had been sent home to his brothers. Below Li Yuan, in the palace grounds, a doubled guard patrolled silently. Only he, it seemed, was restless. He turned, sighing, and looked back into the empty, silent rooms, remembering.

How strange it was. Before, if he had been asked, he would have said that it was not love he felt for them, more a kind of warm familiarity, a feeling of physical comfort, and he might have smiled wistfully and shaken his head, as if puzzled by the question. But now he realized just how foolish he had been. How childish. Only now, through grief and loss of them, did he finally understand just how much they had meant to him.

Love. How clearly his father's words came back to him now. Love was the thing that failed. Love . . . a thing too insubstantial, too fragile to hold and keep, and yet, in the end, there was nothing stronger, nothing more real than love.

He shuddered, then stretched, feeling tired beyond words. In the greater world huge changes were taking place even at that moment. Under Wu Shih's direction, Chi Hsing was standing down and a Governor was being appointed to run the Australian continent. Yet those changes, great as they were, seemed as nothing compared to the changes in his heart. There was no measuring such changes. They blotted out the stars themselves, casting vast, dark shadows on the perceiving eye.

Yes, he thought, bowing his head. *Death not Love is master of this world.*

As he stood there, looking in at the empty rooms, small memories of them returned to him. Against the emptiness he saw his second wife, Lai Shi, turn and look across at him, laughing, that strange, flirtatious movement of her mouth, special to her alone, making him smile. Beyond her, the youngest, Fu Ti Chang, sat reading an old romance, her jet-black hair like a fine veil over the pallor of her face. As she turned to face him he caught his breath, finding the innocence of her dark eyes suddenly quite beautiful. And if he turned, he could see Mien Shan, there on the far side of the room, the great mirror behind her, smiling as she cradled her son and gently sang to him. How much he had liked that curious pursing of her lips when she sang. How much he missed it now.

The memories faded, vanished. *Empty rooms,* he thought. *That's all I have now. Empty rooms.*

He placed his hand against his neck, the warmth of his fingers strange against the night-chilled flesh. He pressed, then gently tugged at it, feeling the strength of muscle, the hardness of the bone beneath; all of it so tenuous, so transient. All of it dust before the wind. Perhaps, then, it was best to go as they had gone, in one brief and sudden burst of pain. Pain, and then . . . nothingness.

"Best . . ." he said softly, letting his hand fall away, and gritting his teeth against the sudden upsurge of feeling. Best? Who knew what was best? And yet he was charged to know—or, at least, to seem to know. It was what made his grief so different. So special. And yet it was only grief, for all that, no different from the grief of countless millions who had suffered since the dawn of Man.

But was grief all? Was there no more to it than this? Li Yuan drew the cloak tighter about his shoulders, then offered the words to the chill and silent air.

"Must it always be like this? *Must* the heart become a stone?"

He stood there for a long time after that, feeling a kind of disgust for what he was. Then, abruptly, he crossed the room and went through to where Kuei Jen was sleeping and woke his nurse, telling her to prepare the child to travel.

———————

FEI YEN MET HIM in the Great Room at Hei Shui. He had given her no notice of his coming and she had had no time to ready herself. She had thrown a pale blue gown about her and tied back her long, black hair, but her face was unmade, her nails unpainted. It was years since he had seen her look so natural. Hesitantly, her face showing deep puzzlement, she crossed the room to him, then knelt at his feet, her head bowed, awaiting his command.

"You've heard?" he asked her softly.

She gave the smallest nod, then was still.

"I . . ." he looked about him, conscious of the guards by the door, the nurse behind him, holding Kuei Jen. Abruptly, he turned and dismissed them. Then, bending down, he lifted her chin and made her look at him. "I have to talk to you. I . . ."

Her eyes, always the most beautiful thing about her, robbed him of words. For a moment he knelt there, close to her, conscious of her warm, sweet smell, of her nakedness beneath the gown, and wanted only to hold her; to close his eyes and hold on tight to her.

She moved back, away from him. "Why?"

Her eyes looked briefly at his hand where it yet hovered, awkward, between their faces, then met his own again, their intensity surprising him.

He drew his hand back, looking down. How explain what had made him come? It was more than sudden impulse, yet even he knew how unreasonable it seemed. This had ended years ago. And to come here now . . .

"What do you want, Li Yuan?"

Her voice was softer than before. He looked up at her, not knowing what to expect and found her watching him strangely, her eyes trying to fathom him.

"I thought . . ." she began, then fell silent. Her mouth had fallen open slightly, its wet softness there before him, as in his dreams.

"I've been thinking of you," he said. "Of us."

He saw the pain in her face and, for the first time, understood what she had suffered; saw the emptiness that no number of casual lovers could fill. Slowly, tenderly, he reached out and touched her cheek.

"Don't," she said, but the slight pressure of her cheek against his fingers gave the lie to the word.

He shivered. "They're dead."

Again there was a moment's pain in her face, awful to see. Then she nodded. "Did you love them?"

His fingers grew still. "I did not think so. But I must have. It . . . it hurts."

She bowed her head. There were tears in her eyes now. "Is that why you are here? Because of them?"

He took a long, deep breath. "I do not know."

For a moment he thought of telling her of that moment earlier— out in the dark, beneath the moon—when he had seen things clear, then shook his head.

"No," he said at last. "It isn't that. Or not just that. I . . . I missed you."

"You *missed* me?" she said, a trace of her former bitterness surfacing. She saw him wince and at once was contrite. "Li Yuan, I . . ." She dropped her head, swallowed. "I am sorry. It is hard. Harder than I can bear some days."

He gave a single nod. "I know."

He looked at her more carefully now and saw the faint crow's feet about her eyes, the lines at mouth and neck and remembered that she was eight years his elder. His dead brother's wife, and once his own. But she was still beautiful. Still the most beautiful woman he had ever seen. Again he wanted to kiss her and hold her, yet he felt constrained. Death came between them, darkening their understanding of how things were.

He stood, turning away from her. "I do not know what I want. I am confused. I thought . . . I thought that if I came here it would all come clear again. That maybe it would be as it was."

For the first time she laughed; a bitter, ugly sound. He turned, looking at her, and saw how all softness had gone from her face.

"Do you mean to be so cruel, Li Yuan, or is it still some sickly innocence that makes you so insensitive?"

"I didn't mean to . . ."

"You never mean to. You just do."

She sat back, glaring at him, all humility gone from her now; more, suddenly, the woman he had known and lived with. His equal. Ever his equal. "Are you such a fool that you cannot see it?"

He shook his head, but already he was beginning to understand.

"It cannot be as it was," she said, getting up slowly and coming across to where he stood. "There is more than death between us. More than other wives, other husbands. Time has changed us, Li Yuan. It has made you what you are, me what I am. Only the outward forms remain—time-ravaged things that look like we once were." She paused, looking up into his face. "We cannot go back, Li Yuan. Not ever."

He was silent, uncertain.

"Do you still love me?" she asked suddenly. Her face was fierce, uncompromising, but in her eyes he could see something else, deep down, hidden maybe even from herself. A fragility. A need. And for the first time he smiled; a tender, pitying smile.

"I have never stopped loving you."

Her whole face seemed to twitch and then reform, more ugly, more pained than before, but somehow also more beautiful. She had not expected this. Whatever she might have hoped for, his answer had surprised her.

She looked down, then turned away, all fierceness gone from her suddenly. Her chest rose and fell violently and her hands clutched at her waist as if to hold in all that she was feeling. But when she turned back there was anger in her face. "Then why? Why all of this if that was true?"

I don't know, he thought, and for the first time knew it was true. It could have been repaired. This, where they were now, was all his fault. Oh, she had been unfaithful, yes, but what was that? He had been hard on her—much too hard. Was it her fault if she had proved less than perfect? Had he loved only her perfection?

"I was young, Fei Yen. Maybe too young. I wronged you. I realize that now."

She made a small noise, then shook her head hesitantly. "What are you saying?" Her whole face was tensed against him, mistrustful now. She was afraid of what he was saying; fearful of being led by him and then discarded once again. These were old wounds, deep wounds. Why open them again unless to heal them?

"I am tired," he said finally. "And hurt. But that is not why I am here, Fei Yen. Nor do I wish to hurt you." He shook his head, genuinely pained. "That is the last thing I want, believe me."

Her voice was tiny now, tremulous. "So what then? What do you want?"

He looked at her; saw her again as he had once seen her, clearly, his vision purged of all hatred and jealousy. "I want you back. I want to try again."

She turned from him, hiding her face. "No, Yuan, that cannot be."

"Why?" He was astonished. Had he read her wrong? He had thought . . . "Fei Yen? What is it?"

She half turned to look at him, then turned and ran from the room. But in that momentary look he had seen. In some small way she was still in love with him. He took three steps toward the far door, then stopped, pain and confusion making his head whirl. *But if she loves me . . .*

For a moment longer he stood there, undecided, then he turned and went back out into the entrance hall. A guard came at his summons, then rushed off to bring the nurse and Kuei Jen. While he waited, Li Yuan went to the entrance arch and looked out down the steps toward the eastern slopes, remembering how he had once gone hunting there, in the woods, with his brother Han Ch'in.

The memory was ill—was like bile in his throat. He turned angrily and yelled, bidding the nurse to hurry. Then, with unconcealed bitterness, he pushed out through the doors and, ignoring the guards, ran across the grass toward his skimmer.

"Where to, *Chieh Hsia?*" his pilot asked, looking around at him, then back at the nurse hurrying across the grass, Kuei Jen bundled in her arms.

Home, he almost said, but even as he thought it he realized that there was nowhere now he could really call home. "Fukien," he said, finally. "Contact Tsu Ma. Tell him I have changed my mind. That I would like to stay with him awhile."

After Rain

At Heaven's border, the autumn clouds are thin
and driven from the west by a thousand winds.

The world is beautiful at dawn after rain,
and the rains won't hurt the farmers.

Border willows grow kingfisher green,
the hills grow red with mountain pears.

A Tartar lament rises from the tower.
A single wild goose sails into the void.

—Tu Fu, *After Rain,* eighth century A.D.

I T W A S L A T E . Kim stood to one side of the landing pad, the tall figure of Tuan Wen-ch'ang beside him, as the cruiser came in across the ocean from the northwest, its lights sweeping the dark waters. In one hand he held his pack—a lightweight holdall containing his notebooks, a portable comset, and a change of silks. In the other he clutched the envelope he had been given only twenty minutes back. Inside it were details of his new posting.

The craft lifted and circled to the north, hovering there half a *li* out while Security checked out its codes, the faint drone of its engines filling the still night air. Then, like a bee moving from flower to flower, it lifted up, over them, and settled on the pad with a gentle hiss of hydraulics.

Tuan looked down at Kim and smiled, indicating that he should go first. Kim returned his smile, pleased that Tuan had been posted with him, and turned, making his way across as the hatch irised open, the ramp unfolding onto the pad.

North America. That was where they were sending him this time. Back to the East Coast. Moreover, they wanted him to apply himself to something new—to genetics, the very field that Old Man Lever had tried so long and hard to win him to. He smiled at the irony, able, after all he'd been through, to see the funny side of that. More so because of the news that had come through only an hour past from Philadelphia.

Halfway up the ramp he stopped and turned, looking back, trying to fix this final image of Sohm Abyss in his mind. He had grown here. More here, perhaps, than anywhere else, for it was here that he had finally got back in touch with himself. Here where he had made himself whole. Or as whole as he could be without Jelka. The future now seemed far less threatening than it had been only weeks ago. His planned life with Jelka was no longer an unattainable vision but merely a promise delayed.

Tuan put a hand on his shoulder. "What are you thinking, Kim?"

"That I'll miss this place."

Tuan gave a surprised laugh. "Really? After all that happened?"

"Maybe because it happened. But it's not just that. I felt in touch with things here. Really in touch. Look at it, Tuan. You've the great ocean below and the sky above. It's magnificent, don't you think? And so open. So *connected*. Besides . . ."

Tuan raised an eyebrow, but Kim just smiled, letting it pass.

"I hear that our new boss is a good man."

Kim shrugged. "Curval's certainly the best in his field, if that's what you mean. From all accounts he's revolutionized genetics single-handedly these last twenty-five years. SimFic must have paid a fortune to wean him from ImmVac."

"As much as for you?"

Kim laughed. "You've seen my file, then, Tuan Wen-ch'ang?"

"No. But I've heard the talk . . ."

Kim looked away thoughtfully, then looked back at Tuan, smiling. "Whatever, it'll be interesting, neh?"

"And challenging . . ."

Yes, he thought, turning to go inside. Even so, he knew it was only a filling of time, a distraction, until she returned. Until he could see her blue eyes smiling back at him again.

◆◆◆◆◆

JELKA STOOD at the window of the Governor's apartment, looking out. Beyond the reinforced glass the surface of the moon was dark, the sun a pale and tiny circle low in the sky, glimpsed through a thick orange haze. To the east, along the shoreline of the great ethane lake, the spires of the refineries reached up into the darkness, their slender, needlelike forms lit by a thousand bright arc lamps. Beyond them the sprawl of Cassini Base, a city of four hundred and eighty thousand people, stretched to the foot of the ice escarpment; a towering wall of crystalline nitrogen. Clathrate, she had heard it called, and had noted the word in her diary. To tell Kim, when she saw him again.

She turned, accepting the glass that was offered her, and smiled. It was their last day on Saturn's largest moon. Tomorrow the *Meridian* sailed for Mars. So, tonight—if "night" was a term that made any sense in a place like this—the Governor had thrown a special reception, inviting the leading citizens from each of the nine colonies. They had been arriving here the last six days, all manner of strange craft cluttering the big hangar to the south of the town.

Jelka looked about her momentarily, taking it all in. They were a strange, austere people out here, sparsely fleshed and taut-muscled beneath the pressure suits they wore at all times. A tall, angular-looking race whose movements were slow, considered. A product of the harsh environment, she realized, and felt, once more, a kind of awe at it all. Over two million people lived out here in the Saturn system. Two million mouths that needed feeding. Two million pairs of lungs that needed air. Two million bodies needing water, warmth, and protection from the unforgiving elements.

One hundred and seventy-nine degrees below zero it was beside the great ethane lake. An unthinkably bitter cold that brought with it no end of technical problems for the men—and women—who worked Saturn's moons, mining and manufacturing, or harvesting the rich soup of complex hydrocarbons that lay within the great ethane lakes of this, Titan, the largest of the colonies.

She moved through the packed crowd, smiling, offering a word here and there, making her way across to the Governor, who stood with a small group of Security officers on the far side of the great circular room, beside the ancient orrery. She had met most of the people there on her travels about the colonies. Only tiny Mimas, closest to Saturn, had proved impossible to visit. Otherwise she had seen it all. And recorded it—for Kim.

"How are you, Jelka? Have you enjoyed yourself?"

She stopped to answer the query, smiling, remembering the man from Iapetus Colony.

"I'm fine, Wulf Thorsson," she said, clasping his hand momentarily. "And I have enjoyed myself greatly. I will be sad to go. But one day I will come back here, maybe."

The big man smiled broadly, placing both his hands over hers, as if to enclose them, or keep them warm. "With your husband, eh?"

"Maybe," she said thoughtfully, then, with a brief nod, moved on. Yes, they were good people out here. Reliable, trustworthy people. And so they had to be. If you couldn't trust your fellow man out here you were dead. Sooner or later.

She squeezed through between the last few people and came out beside the Governor. Helmut Read was an old friend of her father's; a big man, made from the same physical mold. The same mold, she realized, that Klaus Ebert and his son—her onetime fiancé—Hans Ebert had been cast from. The thought disturbed her briefly, then it passed. Like her father and Old Man Ebert, Read emanated an aura of certainty, of ageless, infinite capacity. There was no problem too great for him; no wrong that he could not somehow put right. So it was with her father, she realized. Even so, sometimes such men were wrong, however good their intentions.

Read turned and, seeing Jelka there, grinned broadly, welcoming her. "Come through, my love. Come and talk to us!" he said, taking her hands and drawing her close to hug her, then setting her there next to him, her hand clasped tightly in his.

He had taken her under his wing from the moment she had entered Saturn's system, three months back, and since then had gone to great trouble to show her everything he could. She could picture clearly the pride with which he had shown her the great hollowed shafts of the mining operation on Tethys, the enthusiasm with which he had talked of the expansion going on on tiny Phoebe, and of the plans to build a whole new city on the far side of Titan, where Huygens Base now stood. Things were happening out here, and far from being bored, she had found it all quite fascinating. But then, she had always felt that she was seeing it for two, and had tried to ask the questions Kim might ask.

And sometimes, just sometimes, the sheer beauty of it touched her.

As if, in this rawness, she had a glimpse of that same austere beauty that had once been Kalevala, the place from which her own people had come two thousand years ago, the land of lakes and rocks . . .

The Governor turned to her, squeezing her hand gently. "I am sorry you have to go tomorrow, Jelka," he said, looking at her sadly, as if she were his daughter. "I cannot express how much I have enjoyed having you here. Why, if I were twenty years younger . . ."

"And unmarried," added one of the officers, to general laughter.

"And unmarried," Read acknowledged, his smile broadening, "I would have found a way to keep you here."

"I shall leave with a sad heart," she said quite genuinely. "I had no idea what I would find out here, but I can see now why so many stay here. It is a beautiful place. Perhaps the most beautiful in the system."

"Then you do not mind the danger?" one of the officers asked, his slightly stilted accent typical of the Colonies.

"No," she answered, clear-eyed. "Indeed, that's part of its beauty, neh? That sense of living on the edge of things. These suits . . ." She tugged gently with her free hand at the strong but supple cloth beneath the rigid neck and smiled. "I've grown rather fond of mine. Why, I think I'll continue wearing one when I get back to Chung Kuo. Who knows, it might set a new fashion among the warm-worlders!"

There was delight at that, and laughter. Many times on her travels she had heard how soft they thought the "warm-worlders" of Chung Kuo; it being confided, at the same time, that they thought her different from the others who came out on the big tour ships like the *Meridian*. Totally different.

And so she was. Back there, close to the sun, she had felt cut off from her fellows; a stranger among "friends," always the outsider. But out here she felt strangely in her element and had found herself drawn—instinctively drawn—to these big, slow, fiercely independent people.

She smiled, looking about her at their finely sculpted faces. It took a special kind of person to come and live out here, two billion *li* from the sun; a special kind of mentality. The intense cold, the pressure, the fact that everything—food, water, air, *everything*—had to be manufactured: these factors had forged a whole new race. Or remade the old. She wasn't sure which.

For a moment she looked down, studying the ancient brass orrery nearby. Four tiny planets circled the sun closely—Mercury, Venus, Chung Kuo, and Mars. Beyond them, some way out, was Jupiter and then, the same distance out again, was Saturn, where she was now.

She had come a long way these past fifteen months. Was ten times farther from the sun than when she'd started. But her father had been wrong. She had not forgotten Kim. Not at all. In fact, the farther out she came, the more she thought of him; the more she tried to see things through his eyes and think of them as he might think of them. The films she took, the things she noted in her diary—all were for him. And if it took six years before she could see him again, nonetheless she would wait, holding herself prepared; saving herself for him. For the time would come. The time would surely come.

Three days ago his "letter" had arrived. At first she had set it aside, confused by the official-looking nature of the package, by the SimFic logo on the reverse. It was only some fifteen hours later, after a long and tiring tour of the Great Escarpment, that she returned and finally opened it.

It was the first time she had heard from him since that day when she had been hustled aboard the *Meridian* at Nanking spaceport. But not, it seemed, the first time he had written. From the things he said, it was clear he had written often to her. The thought of that angered her, even now. The thought that her father had been meddling again, keeping things from her, trying to run her life the way *he* wanted it and not as she would have it.

But now she knew. What her father had said, the last time she had spoken to him, had been a lie. Kim had not forgotten her. Far from it. And if her father thought she would change her mind, then he simply did not understand her. Not the way Kim understood her, anyway.

She looked up again, smiling at the thought. Yes, he alone, perhaps, understood her—perfectly, instinctively—and trusted her, the way these people out here trusted each other. In the face of everything.

Six years they would have to wait. Six years until she came of age. But she would wait. And in the meantime she would make her slow way back to him. Inward, ever inward toward the great sun of her being.

Knowing he would be waiting. Knowing he would be there, his dark eyes watching for her.

—————

MORE THAN A HUNDRED sedans filled the lawn before the Lever Mansion, their pole-men crouched quietly, waiting, while servants from the house went among them, offering bowls of noodles and tiny cups of rice wine.

Inside the house, the invited guests had gathered in the great library, talking in a hushed, slightly shocked tone. Only the day before, in the selfsame room, Old Man Lever had addressed them at a fund-raising meeting, his robust, no-nonsense manner inspiring many of them to believe he would be there a century from then, still urging them on. But now he was dead, and no end of rhetoric would bring him back. Not in this cycle of existence.

He lay now in a great casket at one end of the room, his gray hair combed neatly back, his massive chest unmoving beneath the pure white silks. For the first time in many years he seemed at peace, no longer striving for something that forever evaded him. No longer angry.

The guests had been arriving for the last four hours to pay their respects, coming from every corner of the great City. Last to arrive, tired by his journey from the clinic, was Lever's son, Michael.

For Michael, too, the news had come as a great shock. Like the rest, he had thought the Old Man would live forever. For an hour or two he had toyed with the idea of boycotting the funeral, of playing the part of the spurned son to the bitter end, but he had not felt right about that. No, for the truth was he still loved his father. The news of the old man's death had shaken him to the core. He had stood there, astonished; then later, alone with Mary, he had broken down, crying like a child while she held him. Now, solemn and dignified, he walked beside her through the door to his dead father's house, his bioprosthetics giving him an awkward, stilted gait.

"Steward Dann," he said, greeting his father's "Number One" in the great entrance hall. "I am most sorry that we have to meet again like this."

The Steward bowed his head low, clearly moved that Michael had come. "And I, Master Michael. I had hoped to welcome you back in happier circumstances."

Michael smiled tightly, then walked on, Mary silent at his side, as strong and supportive as ever.

At the entrance to the library he halted, turning to look at her, suddenly fearful. In answer she reached out, squeezing his arm gently, encouraging him to face what lay ahead.

He took a long, deep breath, then went on, the servants pushing the great doors open before him. Seeing him, the crowd within grew silent, all heads turning to watch as Michael crossed the room, making for his father's casket.

Looking down at the old man, Michael felt a wash of pain and longing so fierce, so intense, that it threatened to sweep him away. Then, with the faintest shudder, he bowed his head low and reached out to touch and briefly hold his father's hand.

So cold it was. So cold and hard.

He looked up, seeking Mary's eyes, for a brief moment a young boy again, fearful and bewildered; then, taking another long shuddering breath, he looked about him, smiling his thanks, his gratitude to all those friends of his father who had come to see him in this, his final moment on the Earth.

"Thank you," he said brokenly. "Thank you all. My father would have been touched. And I . . . I am greatly moved by your presence. He was a great man, my father. A great, great man."

Many looked down, moved by his tiny speech, but some stared at him openly, as if wondering what his game was; why he came now, the obedient son, when before he had denied his filial duty.

As he backed away from the casket, a faint murmur rose from all sides. Already that morning a rumor had gone about that Wu Shih would place a Steward in charge of the Company until a buyer could be found for ImmVac, either as a whole, or broken down into its composite parts. If the latter, many there hoped to benefit from Old Man Lever's death.

At the doorway, Michael looked back briefly, then walked on, willing himself forward, Mary half running to catch up with him. Out on the lawn he stopped, among the pole-men and runners who had stood and bowed before one of the Masters. Mary caught up with him there and held him to her tightly while he sobbed.

Finally, he pushed back, away from her. "All right," he said softly. "We're done here. Let's go."

"*Shih* Lever?"

They turned. It was Ainsworth, Old Man Lever's lawyer.

Michael looked down. "What is it? Is there something I have to sign?"

Ainsworth shook his head, then held something out to Michael. Michael took it and studied it a moment. It was the original of the Disinheritance Statement, the final page signed with an angry flourish by his father.

"I have one," Michael answered coldly, drawing himself up straight and holding out the document for Ainsworth to take back, something of his father in him at that moment.

"No. You misunderstand. He signed it, but he never registered it. He wouldn't let me. Which means that it's all yours, Michael. Imm-Vac and all the rest. Yours."

Michael Lever narrowed his eyes a moment, eyeing the man as if he saw him for what he was. Then, throwing the paper down, he turned and stomped away, Mary hurrying to keep up with him as he made his way between the rows of sedans and out toward the transit.

T HE TRANSCRIPTION of standard Mandarin into European alphabetical form was first achieved in the seventeenth century by the Italian Matteo Ricci, who founded and ran the first Jesuit Mission in China from 1583 until his death in 1610. Since then, several dozen attempts have been made to reduce the original Chinese sounds, represented by some tens of thousands of separate pictograms, into readily understandable phonetics for Western use. For a long time, however, three systems dominated—those used by the three major Western powers vying for influence in the corrupt and crumbling Chinese Empire of the nineteenth century: Great Britain, France, and Germany. These systems were the Wade-Giles (Great Britain and America—sometimes known as the Wade system), the École Française de l'Extrême Orient (France), and the Lessing (Germany).

Since 1958, however, the Chinese themselves have sought to create one single phonetic form, based on the German system, which they termed the *hanyu pinyin fang'an* ("Scheme for a Chinese Phonetic Alphabet"), known more commonly as *pinyin*; and in all foreign-language books published in China since January 1, 1979, *pinyin* has been used, as well as being taught now in schools along with the standard Chinese characters. For this work, however, I have chosen to use the older and, to my mind, far more elegant transcription system, the Wade-Giles (in modified form). For those now accustomed to the harder forms of *pinyin*, the following (courtesy of Edgar Snow's *The Other Side of the River*; Gollancz, 1961) may serve as a rough guide to pronunciation:

'*Chi* is pronounced as "Gee," but *Ch'i* sounds like "Chee." *Ch'in* is exactly our "chin."

Chu is roughly like "Jew," as in *Chu Teh* (Jew Duhr), but *Ch'u* equals "chew."

Tsung is "dzung"; *ts'ung* with the "ts" as in "Patsy."

Tai is our word sound "die"; *T'ai*—"tie."

Pai is "buy" and *P'ai* is "pie."

Kung is like "Gung" (a Din); *K'ung* with the "k" as in "kind."

J is the equivalent of r but slur it, as rrrun.

H before an s, as in *hsi*, is the equivalent of an aspirate but is often dropped, as in Sian for Hsian.

Vowels in Chinese are generally short or medium, not long and flat. Thus *Tang* sounds like "dong," never like our "tang." *T'ang* is "tong."

a as in father	ih—her
e—run	o—look
eh—hen	ou—go
i—see	u—soon

The effect of using the Wade-Giles system is, I hope, to render the softer, more poetic side of the original Mandarin, ill-served, I feel, by modern *pinyin*.

This usage, incidentally, accords with many of the major reference sources available in the West: the (planned) 16 volumes of Denis Twichett and Michael Loewe's *The Cambridge History of China*, Joseph Needham's mammoth multivolumed *Science and Civilization in China*, John Fairbank and Edwin Reischauer's *China, Tradition & Transformation*, Charles Hucker's *China's Imperial Past*, Jacques Gernet's *A History of Chinese Civilization*, C. P. Fitzgerald's *China: A Short Cultural History*, Laurence Sickman and Alexander Soper's *The Art and Architecture of China*, William Hinton's classic social studies, *Fanshen* and *Shenfan*, and Derk Bodde's *Essays on Chinese Civilization*.

The Luoshu diagram, mentioned in the Prologue, is a three by three number square

$$
\begin{array}{ccc}
4 & 9 & 2 \\
3 & 5 & 7 \\
8 & 1 & 6
\end{array}
$$

and was supposedly seen on the shell of a turtle emerging from the Luo River some two thousand years before Christ. As can be seen, all the numbers in any one row, column, or diagonal add up to fifteen. During the T'ang dynasty its "magical" properties were exported to the Muslim world, where they were used—as here—as a charm for easing childbirth.

Wu Shih's mention (in Chapter One) of "the three brothers of the Peach Garden" is a reference to Lo Kuan Chung's classic Chinese novel *San Kuo Yan Yi*, or *The Romance of the Three Kingdoms*, in which the three great heroes, Liu Pei, Chang Fei, and Kuan Yu, swear brotherhood.

The translation of Chu Yuan's *T'ien Wen*, or "Heavenly Questions," is by David Hawkes from *The Songs of the South: An Anthology of Ancient Chinese Poems*, published by Penguin Books, London, 1985.

The quotation from Jukka Tolonen is from a song on the album *Lambertland* by the Finnish band Tasavallan Presidentti, and the lyrics from the song "Last Quarters" are reprinted with the kind permission of Sonet Records.

The passage quoted from Book One [V] of Lao Tzu's *Tao Te Ching* is from the D. C. Lau translation, published by Penguin Books, London, 1963, and used with their kind permission.

The quotation from Rainer Maria Rilke's *Duino Elegies* is from the Hogarth Press fourth edition of 1968, translated by J. B. Leishman and Stephen Spender. Thanks to the estate of Rilke, St. John's College, Oxford, for permission. Those wishing a translation of the four lines used in Chapter Nineteen might refer back to the epigram used in Part Three of *The Middle Kingdom*.

The translation of Tu Fu's "After Rain" is by Sam Hamill from his wonderful anthology of Tu Fu's verse, *Facing the Snow: Visions of Tu*

Fu, published by White Pine Press, Fredonia, New York, and is reprinted here with their kind permission.

Once again, I find I have quoted extensively from Samuel B. Griffith's translation of Sun Tzu's *The Art of War*, published by Oxford University Press, 1963. I reprint the four passages used herein with their kind permission and only hope I have directed a few readers to this most excellent work.

Finally, for those of you unfamiliar with the pidgin Cornish used in Part Two of the book, here are translations of the relevant passages. First, the utterances of the Clay-men:

Avodya! Get back!

A-wartha! Up above!

An chy. Kerdhes! Tenna dhe an chy! The house. Go! Take the house!

Ena. . . . Ena ha ena! There. . . . There and there!

And Ben's whisperings:

Of ancow. I am death.

Gwelaf why gans ow onen lagas. I see you with my one eye.

Ow golow lagas dewana why! My bright eye pierces you!

Ow enawy a-vyn podretha agas eskern . . . My light will rot your bones.

Fyough, byghan gwas! Fyough! Flee, little men! Flee!

Furthermore, when the hologram of the Ox-faced angel says *Dyeskynna!* ("Come!"), there is a faint echo of The Revelation to John (6:1).

February 1992

A Glossary of Mandarin Terms

Most of the Mandarin terms used in the text are explained in context. However, as a few are used more naturally, I've considered it best to provide a brief explanation.

ai ya!—common exclamation of surprise or dismay.

ch'a—tea. It might be noted that *ch'a shu*, the Chinese art of tea, is an ancient forebear of the Japanese tea ceremony *chanoyu*.

chang shan—literally "long dress," which fastens to the right. Worn by both sexes. The women's version is a fitted, calf-length dress similar to the *chi pao*. A South China fashion, also known as a *cheung sam*.

chan shih—a fighter.

Ch'eng Ou Chou—City Europe.

ch'i—a Chinese foot; approximately 14.4 inches.

ch'i chu—spider.

chieh hsia—term meaning "Your Majesty," derived from the expression "below the steps." It was the formal way of addressing the Emperor, through his Ministers, who stood "below the steps."

chi pao—literally "banner gown"; a one-piece gown of Manchu origin, usually sleeveless, worn by women.

Chou—"state"; here the name for a card game based on the politics of the state of Chung Kuo.

chung—a lidded serving bowl for *ch'a*.

ch'un tzu—an ancient Chinest term from the Warring States period, describing a certain class of noblemen, controlled by a code of chivalry and morality known as the *li*, or rites. Here the term is roughly, and sometimes ironically, translated as "gentlemen." The *ch'un tzu* is as much an ideal state of behavior—as specified by Confucius in the *Analects*—as an actual class in Chung Kuo, though a degree of financial independence and a high standard of education are assumed prerequisites.

erhu—two-stringed bow with snakeskin-covered sound box.

fen—unit of money (a cent); one hundred *fen* make up a *yuan*.

han—term used by the Chinese to describe their own race, the "black-haired people," dating back to the Han Dynasty (210 B.C.–A.D. 220). It is estimated that some ninety-four percent of modern China's population are Han racially.

hei—literally "black"; the Chinese pictogram for this represents a man wearing war paint and tattoos. Here it refers to the genetically manufactured (GenSyn) half-men used as riot police to quell uprisings in the lower levels.

hsiao jen—"little man/men." In the *Analects*, Book XIV, Confucius writes: "The gentleman gets through to what is up above; the small man gets through to what is down below." This distinction between "gentlemen" (*ch'un tzu*) and "little men" (*hsiao jen*), false even in Confucius's time, is no less a matter of social perspective in Chung Kuo.

hsien—historically an administrative district of variable size. Here the term is used to denote a very specific administrative area: one of ten stacks—each stack composed of thirty decks. Each deck is a hexagonal living unit of ten levels, two *li*, or approximately one kilometer in diameter. A stack can be imagined as one honeycomb in the great hive of the City.

Hsien L'ing—"Chief Magistrate." In Chung Kuo, these officials are the T'ang's representatives and law enforcers for the individual *Hsien*, or Administrative Districts. In times of peace, each *Hsien* also elects a representative to the House at Weimar.

Hung Mao—literally "redheads," the name the Chinese gave to the Dutch (and later English) seafarers who attempted to trade with China in the seventeenth century. Because of the piratical nature of their endeavors (which often meant plundering Chinese shipping and ports) the name has connotations of piracy.

Hung Mun—the Secret Societies or, more specifically, the Triads.

hun tun—"the Chou believed that Heaven and Earth were once inextricably mixed together in a state of undifferentiated chaos, like a chicken's egg. *Hun Tun* they called that state" (from "Chen Yen," Chapter Six of *The White Mountain*). It is also the name of a meal of tiny saclike dumplings.

jou tung wu—literally "meat animal."

Kan pei!—"good health" or "cheers"; a drinking toast.

Ko Ming—"revolutionary." The *T'ien Ming* is the Mandate of Heaven, supposedly handed down from Shang Ti, the Supreme Ancestor, to his earthly counterpart, the Emperor (*Huang Ti*). This Mandate could be enjoyed only so long as the Emperor was worthy of it, and rebellion against a tyrant—who broke the Mandate through his lack of justice, benevolence, and sincerity—was deemed not criminal but a rightful expression of Heaven's anger.

k'ou t'ou—the fifth stage of respect, according to the "Book of Ceremonies," involves kneeling and striking the head against the floor. This ritual has become more commonly known in the West as *kowtow*.

Kuan hua—Mandarin, the language spoken in mainland China. Also known as *Kuo-yu* and *Pai hua*.

Kuan Yin—the goddess of mercy; originally the Buddhist male bodhisattva, Avalokitsevara (translated into Han as "He who listens to the sounds of the world," or "Kuan Yin"). The Han mistook the saint's well-developed breasts for a woman's and, since the ninth century, have worshiped Kuan Yin as such. Effigies of Kuan Yin usually show her as the Eastern Madonna, cradling a child in her arms. She is also sometimes seen as the wife of Kuan Kung, the Chinese God of War.

li—a Chinese "mile," approximating to half a kilometer or one third of a mile. Until 1949, when metric measures were adopted in China, the *li* could vary from place to place.

min—literally "the people"; used (as here, by the Minor Families) in a pejorative sense (i.e., as an equivalent to "plebeian").

Ming—the Dynasty that ruled China from 1368 to 1644. Literally, the name means "Bright" or "Clear" or "Brilliant." It carries connotations of cleansing.

niao—literally "bird"; but here, as often, it is used euphemistically, as a term for the penis, often as an expletive.

nu er—daughter.

nu shih—an unmarried woman; a term equating to "Miss."

pai nan jen—literally "white man."

pau—a simple long garment worn by men.

Ping Tiao—leveling. To bring down or make flat.

p'i p'a—a four-stringed lute used in traditional Chinese music.

san kuei chiu k'ou—the eighth and final stage of respect, according to the "Book of Ceremonies," involves kneeling three times, each time striking the forehead three times against the floor. This most elaborate form of ritual was reserved for Heaven and its son, the Emperor.

shan shui—the literal meaning is "mountains and water," but the term is normally associated with a style of landscape painting that depicts rugged mountain scenery with river valleys in the foreground. It is a highly popular form, first established in the T'ang Dynasty, back in the seventh to ninth centuries A.D.

shao lin—specially trained assassins; named after the monks of the *shao lin* monastery.

shih—"Master." Here used as a term of respect somewhat equivalent to our use of "Mister." The term was originally used for the lowest level of civil servants, to distinguish them socially from the run-of-the-mill "misters" (*hsian sheng*) below them and the gentlemen (*ch'un tzu*) above.

siang chi—Chinese chess.

tai—"pockets"; here used to denote Representatives bought by (and thus "in the pocket of") various power groupings (originally the Seven).

t'ai chi—the Original, or One, from which the duality of all things (*yin* and *yang*) developed, according to Chinese cosmology. We generally associate the *t'ai chi* with the Taoist symbol, that swirling circle of dark and light supposedly representing an egg (perhaps the *Hun Tun*), the yolk and the white differentiated.

T'ai Shan—the great sacred mountain of China, where emperors have traditionally made sacrifices to Heaven. T'ai Shan, in Shantung province, is the highest peak in China. "As safe as T'ai Shan" is a popular saying, denoting the ultimate in solidity and certainty.

Ta Ts'in—the Chinese name for the Roman Empire. They also knew Rome as *Li Chien* and as "the Land West of the Sea." The Romans themselves they termed the "Big *Ts'in*"—the *Ts'in* being the name the Chinese gave themselves during the Ts'in Dynasty (A.D. 265–316).

T'ing Wei—the Superintendency of Trials. See Book Three (*The White Mountain*), Part Two, for an instance of how this department of government functions.

ti tsu—a bamboo flute, used both as a solo instrument and as part of an ensemble.

tong—a gang. In China and Europe, these are usually smaller and thus subsidiary to the Triads, but in North America the term has generally taken the place of "Triad."

ts'un—a Chinese "inch" of approximately 1.44 Western inches. Ten *ts'un* form one *ch'i*.

wan wu—literally "the ten thousand things"; used generally to include everything in creation, or, as the Chinese say, "all things in Heaven and Earth."

wei chi—"the surrounding game," known more commonly in the West by its Japanese name of "Go." It is said that the game was invented by the legendary Chinese Emperor Yao in the year 2350 B.C. to train the mind of his son, Tan Chu, and teach him to think like an Emperor.

wen ming—a term used to denote Civilization, or written culture.

wuwei—nonaction; an old Taoist concept. It means keeping harmony with the flow of things—doing nothing to break the flow.

yamen—the official building in a Chinese community.

yang—the "male principle" of Chinese cosmology, which, with its complementary opposite, the female *yin*, forms the *t'ai chi*, derived from the Primeval One. From the union of *yin* and *yang* arise the "five elements" (water, fire, earth, metal, wood) from which the "ten thousand things" (the *wan wu*) are generated. *Yang* signifies Heaven and the South, the Sun and Warmth, Light, Vigor, Maleness, Penetration, odd numbers, and the Dragon. Mountains are *yang*.

yin—the "female principle" of Chinese cosmology (see *yang*). *Yin* signifies Earth and the North, the Moon and Cold, Darkness, Quiescence, Femaleness, Absorption, even numbers, and the Tiger. The *yin* lies in the shadow of the mountain.

yu—literally "fish" but because of its phonetic equivalence to the word for "abundance," the fish symbolizes wealth. Yet there is also a saying that when the fish swim upriver it is a portent of social unrest and rebellion.

yuan—the basic currency of Chung Kuo (and modern-day China). Colloquially (though not here) it can also be termed *kwai*—"piece" or "lump." One hundred *fen* (or cents) make up one *yuan*.

yueh ch'in—a Chinese dulcimer; one of the principal instruments of the Chinese orchestra.

Ywe Lung—literally, the "Moon Dragon," the wheel of seven dragons that is the symbol of the ruling Seven throughout *Chung Kuo*: "At its center the snouts of the regal beasts met, forming a roselike hub, huge rubies burning fiercely in each eye. Their lithe, powerful bodies curved outward like the spokes of a giant wheel while at the edge their tails were intertwined to form the rim" (from "The Moon Dragon," Chapter Four of *The Middle Kingdom*).

In Times to Come . . .

In BENEATH THE TREE OF HEAVEN, the fifth volume of the Chung Kuo saga, the pace of events quickens as the final years of the great Earth-spanning Empire of the Seven draw close.

The book opens with the courtroom drama of the GenSyn inheritance case—a case that takes the strangest of turns—after which, the action moves out to Mars, where, at a critical turning point in the Colony's history, Li Yuan's principle enemy, DeVore, attempts to kidnap Marshal Tolonen's daughter and make the red planet independent of the rule of the Seven. Circumstances seem in his favor, yet the actions of a lost race and one redeemed man—the traitor, Hans Ebert—result in unexpected developments, developments that strongly foreshadow events back on Chung Kuo.

For Kao Chen, disillusioned with his role as Major in Li Yuan's Security forces, these are trying times. Cut off from his wife by her mental illness and forced to serve a system he no longer believes in, Chen finds he must fashion a new life for himself . . . or go under. Yet he is not entirely alone. By chance he comes upon a young girl, Hannah, who, awakened to the ugliness and brutal unfairness of her world, wants to become its voice, its very conscience in the troubled years to come.

In North America, Michael Lever and his wife Emily Ascher find themselves the inheritors of a corrupt and decadent financial empire.

Encouraged by Emily, Michael presses for change, trying to create a more humane system, but in doing so he finds himself once more lined up against the entrenched forces of reaction—the Old Men he thought had died out with his father.

At Weimar, Lever's friend and ally, Kennedy, learns the bitter lesson that attaining power is sometimes far easier than exercising it. Frustrated by delays and compromises, he decides to take matters into his own hands and force the pace of change, even though to do so will bring him into direct conflict with the T'ang of North America, Wu Shih. And all the while the situation in North America is deteriorating. One single spark could set the great City alight, a spark that will eventually come from a wholly unlooked-for source.

For Ben Shepherd, the great artist of Chung Kuo, these are the years of his maturity. His first great work, *The Familiar*, is finally delivered to the world to great critical and popular success. But all is not well for Ben. His sister, Meg, has left him, and his monomaniacal drive to experience everything—and to record it for his art—leads him into further danger as he makes an expedition into the darkness of the Clay, that unlit wasteland beneath the City's floor.

Since the death of his wives, Li Yuan has become a recluse, shutting himself off even from his closest friends and ruling City Europe through his chancellor, Nan Ho. However, when his cousin, Wang Sau-leyan, T'ang of Africa, threatens him directly, he is forced to face events once more. Standing beneath the tree of heaven, at the graveside of his father and beloved elder brother, Li Yuan must decide the fate of his world. Should he try to make peace once more? Or should he fight a war, a war that is certain to destroy the very system of City and Seven that he has striven so long to preserve? In *Beneath the Tree of Heaven* the great world of Chung Kuo is brought to the edge of chaos. In fire and ice a new age is about to be born. . . .